Jeff Abbott is the internationally bestselling author of eleven novels, which are published in twenty languages. He is a three-time nominee for the Edgar Award. He lives in Austin with his family.

JEFF ABBOTT OMNIBUS

A Kiss Gone Bad

Black Jack Point

sphere

SPHERE

This omnibus edition first published in Great Britain in 2010 by Sphere

Previously published separately:
A Kiss Gone Bad first published in Great Britain in 2004 by Orion
Paperback edition published by Orion Books Ltd in 2005
Reissue by Sphere in 2007
Reprinted 2008, 2009
Copyright © Jeff Abbott 2004
Black Jack Point first published in Great Britain in 2004 by Orion
Paperback edition published by Orion Books Ltd in 2005
Reissue by Sphere in 2007
Reprinted 2009
Copyright © Jeff Abbott 2004

A CIP catalogue record for this book
is available from the British Library.

ISBN 978-0-7515-4436-7

Printed and bound in Great Britain by
Clays Ltd, St Ives plc

Sphere
An imprint of
Little, Brown Book Group
100 Victoria Embankment
London EC4Y 0DY

An Hachette UK Company
www.hachette.co.uk

www.littlebrown.co.uk

A KISS GONE BAD

In memory of Patti Stanfield
Who so loved the waters and a good laugh

Perhaps villages fill their own quotas
in mysterious ways,
so many mayors, so many idiots,
so many murderers, so many whores.

John D. MacDonald, *A Deadly Shade of Gold*

1

When the Blade (as he secretly called himself) felt blue, he liked to relax behind the old splintery cabin, where his three Darlings were buried, and feel the power of their vanished lives pulse through him. It was quiet in the shade of the laurel oaks, and on lonely evenings the Blade pretended that his Darlings lived with him, with their cries and pleadings and wet, fearful eyes. His kingdom was small, twenty feet by twenty feet, and he ruled over only three subjects. But he ruled over them completely, life and body and soul.

Today, with his portable tape recorder playing a worn Beach Boys cassette and the clear harmony of 'God Only Knows' drifting up into the oaks, he sat down between two of the unmarked graves: one of the mouthy carrot-topped girl from Louisiana who had fought so hard, the other the young woman from Brownsville who had cried the whole time and hardly deserved to be a Darling at all. He had selected a new Darling, a prime choice. But fear made his spit taste like smoke, because he had never wooed near Port Leo, much less wooed anyone . . . famous.

He had followed her for a daring ten minutes yesterday, sweat tickling his ribs, idling near her in the grocery store while she shopped with the big-shouldered boyfriend who had brought her to Port Leo. The Blade didn't like the boyfriend named Pete, not one bit, although he liked to think about all the mischief that Pete had been up to, starring in those nasty movies. The Blade had eavesdropped in the grocery, pretending to inspect the jug wines while the couple selected beer. She fancied

Mexican beer, one that folks drank with a lime slice crammed down the neck of the bottle, and he wished he knew its taste; but Mama didn't let him drink. The Blade hoped they would talk about sex, being their vocation, but Pete and his Darling talked about grilling shrimp, the rainy autumn, how irritating his Godzilla-bitch ex-wife was.

His Darling's voice sounded edgy, and impatient. *I'm tired of us sneaking around this town and you pissing off these dumbasses. Let's go to Houston to write your movie. I'm in big favor of Plan B.* The hint that his Darling was making a movie, here in Port Leo, tightened his throat with desire. The boyfriend muttered no. Then she'd said, *Jesus, let this crap with your brother go.*

The sweet agony of being close to her flamed into fear. He'd grabbed a gallon of cheap cabernet in terror and bolted for the checkout lines, crowded with new winter Texans. He'd fled to the cereal aisle and shoved the jug behind the Cheerios and waited until his Darling and her boyfriend left the store before venturing out.

They hadn't seen him, known him.

Pete was writing a movie? He didn't think that the films those two did involved screenwriting. Didn't they just point the camera, clamber on the bed, and do their artful moaning and thrusting with all the sincerity of professional wrestlers?

Last week he had driven into Corpus Christi when he learned that his soon-to-be Darling did movies, of an extremely dubious sort. He frequented adult bookstores, driving the two hours to San Antonio or the thirty-odd miles to Corpus Christi, avoiding the few establishments that were too close to Port Leo along the ribbon of Highway 35, never going to any single store too often, paying with bills worn thin from lying under Mama's mattress. He never asked the clerks for recommendations

– he didn't want to be remembered – and tried to fit in with the faceless men who wandered the too-brightly lit aisles of the porn stores. He was unremarkable: just another lonely guy with eyes only for the bosomy models on the video covers.

His research uncovered that she had acted in only a few movies; she had directed far more. He almost felt proud of her. On his last jaunt, off the sale table, he bought a video she had headlined five years ago, her last acting job. She went by the name Velvet Mojo, an appellation the Blade found tasteless. The tape was called *Going Postal*. He suspected the post office would receive a satirical treatment. Perhaps even a deliciously violent treatment. But the movie disappointed. No violence. And while his Darling was versed in erotic tricks involving stamps that made his tongue go dry, her friend Pete performed with her, which seemed . . . wrong. The Blade watched them couple again and again until the world's edges grew soft and his mind napped. He heard Mama cursing. When he awoke, he felt bleary and offended. She deserved rest with the pleasure of his company.

He could save her from this sordidness. He would.

That little shady spot under the old bent oaks, it would be perfect for her. But winning her would be tricky. Wooing other Darlings and avoiding suspicion had been easy. Louisiana and Brownsville and Laredo were far away. She was within a mile or so. And he would have to wait. He could not truly enjoy her now, but he could in a few days. His hunger sharpened, and he imagined her lips, speckled with her own blood, tasted of copper and strawberries.

The Blade stood with resolve. He would make her his. But first he would have to make sure that no one cared if she was gone.

2

The phone jarred The Honorable Whit Mosley awake at ten-thirty at night, out of a dream that melded campaign signs, incomprehensible legal mumbo jumbo, and his stepmother in a sheer nightgown. He cussed quietly and grabbed the receiver.

'This is Judge Mosley,' Whit croaked.

'This is Patrolman Bill Fox, Judge. Sorry to wake you, Y'Honor, but we got a dead body we need you to certify.'

Whit sat up in bed. 'Where?'

'At Golden Gulf Marina.'

Whit blinked and stretched. Golden Gulf was the rich-boy marina in Port Leo – no boats under fifty feet need apply. 'You got ID?'

'According to a driver's license his name is Peter James Hubble.'

Coldness settled in his stomach. *Oh, mother of God.*

Fox took his silence as an invitation for details. 'A girl showed up at ten, found the fellow dead, shot in the mouth.'

Well, this would make a splashy headline. All over the state of Texas.

'Okay, I'll be there in a few minutes.' Whit got up out of bed, a book tumbling to the floor. He'd fallen asleep trying to charge his way through the *Texas Civil Practice* text, the world's surest cure for insomnia.

'I'm wondering if this guy might be related to Senator Hubble,' Officer Fox mused.

No shit, Sherlock, Whit wanted to say, but Fox was a smiling, amiable man and he said nothing. Fox was also a voter, and Whit needed every vote he could muster.

4

'Pete's her son. He's been away for several years.' Whit managed to keep his voice neutral. 'If we're sure it's him, someone's got to call the senator.'

'Yes, sir. I'll talk to the chief about it.'

'Okay, thanks, Bill, I'll be there in a few.' He hung up.

Call the senator, hell. How about calling the dead guy's ex-wife? He picked the phone back up, started dialing Faith Hubble's number, and stopped. No point in freaking her out until he was sure it was Pete.

Please, God, don't let Faith have had anything to do with this.

Whit pulled on the wrinkled khaki shorts, a clean T-shirt, and the parrot-covered beach shirt he'd worn earlier in the day. He locked up the guest house behind him, hurried barefoot across the cement decking around the pool, and by the back door to the main house found a worn pair of Top-Siders in a pile of pool accessories. Through the windows Whit saw his father assembling a sandwich in the kitchen, no doubt needing nourishment for another bout of nuptial bliss. His father noticed him rooting for the shoes and opened the back door.

'Who called?' Babe Mosley asked. He wore a silk robe Hefner would have approved of.

'Dead body, Daddy,' Whit answered.

'Ah,' Babe said, watching Whit. 'You're not wearing that, are you?'

'Why?' Whit stuck his feet into the old boat shoes. A hole at the front of one showed a sliver of his toenail.

'Well, son, God Almighty, there might be some voters there. A crowd. You ought to look more judicial. Maybe a suit.'

'Daddy, I don't have time to change.' Whit kept his voice in check. Thirty-two and still his father lectured him. 'The corpse sure isn't gonna care what I'm wearing.' He pushed past his father and pulled a beaten navy

5

baseball cap that commemorated a Port Leo fishing tournament ('Pray for Marlins') off a hat tree on the kitchen wall.

'See, this hat's all civic. I'm set,' Whit said.

'Whit?' Irina called to him from his father's bedroom. He crossed the kitchen and glanced down the hall. She stood in the doorway, God help him, sporting a flouncy little peignoir that a hearty sneeze would send drifting. Living at home was a bad idea, and as soon as the election was over he was *so* out of here.

'Who rang, Whit?' Voice like warm caramel drizzled on skin.

'I got to go certify a dead body,' he answered, not looking at her.

'Tell him to put on a suit,' Babe hollered from the kitchen.

'A dead person? Who is it?' *Eet*, she said. Her Russian accent grew more feathery in sleepwear. For God's sakes, she came from a cold climate. Didn't she believe in flannel?

'I don't know,' he white-lied. If the son of the most powerful woman in the Texas Senate lay dead on a boat, Whit wasn't going to breathe one word before any official announcement.

His stepmother – twenty-five – gave him a smile that nipped the edges of his heart. 'Shall I make you some coffee to take with you? A sandwich?'

Yeah, if he was going to work a corpse with a bullet blasting open its head, he wanted a snack. But he smiled, grateful for the kindness.

'No, thanks. Be back in a bit.' Whit jingled his keys in his pocket.

'Be careful,' Irina called as he stepped out onto the grand front porch. Good advice. The previous three nights he'd dreamed of Irina in the most unmotherly

6

ways. Be careful, right. He might mumble *Irina* in his sleep, and Faith Hubble would justifiably castrate him with her bare nails.

The night sky glowed with far-off lightning. A freshly brewed storm hovered over the western Gulf of Mexico, scudding dark clouds over Port Leo. The October air blew heavy with the promise of rain.

Whit eased his Ford Explorer down the crushed-oyster-shell driveway. He sped down Evangeline Street, past the old Victorian homes, till he reached Main Street, then headed north, threading through downtown, toward the marina.

The Port Leo storefronts catering to the winter Texans and tourists stood dark. He sped past Port Leo Park and its attendant curves of grass and beach; past the dour, guano-grimed statue of St Leo the Great, the town's namesake because of his reputed ability to calm storms; past a line of trendy galleries selling the wares of the town's many artists. The large shrimpers' fleet docked at the downtown marina bobbed at rest. A couple of night-clubs, with cheesy names like Pirate's Cove and Fresh Chances (for what, Whit wondered – to catch syphilis?), remained open, strobe lights flashing against the windows, but few cars were parked in the lot.

A red Porsche 911, blaring K.C. and The Sunshine Band's 'Boogie Man,' bulleted past him. In his rearview mirror, Whit saw the wink of the roadster's solitary taillight as it braked to swerve onto a side street. *See you in traffic court soon, and I may double your fine for your music,* Whit thought.

Main Street merged into Old Bay Road, which snaked alongside St Leo Bay. A modest strip of grayish white beach, the color of dirty sugar, lay along the bay's rim, then there was the road, and then a line of rental cottages and retiree homes. Across the expanse of St Leo Bay the

7

jeweled lights of several pleasure boats cruised past. Whit lowered his window and breathed in the coastal perfume of dead fish, weathered wooden docks, and salt wind caught in high grass. A clump of signs along the road read ELECT BUDDY BEERE JUSTICE OF THE PEACE.

Campaigning sucked. Whit hated it. Election Day loomed just over two weeks away and Buddy, his esteemed opponent, had littered Port Leo with enough flyers and signs to endanger a forest. Whit had slapped several magnetic signs on his Explorer (Whit rechristened his car 'the Vote Mobile') and erected twenty small post signs at major intersections around the county. He had not made time to phone, knock on doors, and shake hands for votes, hating the idea of begging strangers to put him in a job. If Buddy Beere – who Whit considered to have an IQ lower than a swarm of gnats, even a big swarm – defeated him, Whit's local career options included scooping ice cream, working a fishing boat, or frothing lattes at Irina's.

He drove past a huge sign asking him to REELECT LUCINDA HUBBLE TEXAS SENATE. The pictured Lucinda waved with her trademark big red hair and her bright blue eyeglasses, simultaneously evoking a kindly aunt and a confident leader.

If this dead guy was Pete Hubble, *mess* wouldn't begin to describe it.

Whit wheeled into the crushed-oyster-shell parking lot of Golden Gulf Marina. The main building was a faded sea-green with white trim, now ablaze in the spinning red-and-blues of the police cars. This death had drawn an array of authorities: Port Leo police, Encina County sheriff's deputies, Texas Department of Parks and Wildlife cruisers, and the highway patrol. It looked like a law-and-order convention. The Hubble name must've gotten mentioned over the police bands and all came running for a quick peek.

Whit cursed under his breath.

A small crowd of marina residents had been ousted from their boats and milled in the lot, dressed in robes and shorts, watching the proceedings in the glow of the mercury lights.

Whit parked and grabbed a notebook full of JP forms, a pair of latex gloves, and a flashlight from the death-scene kit he kept in his car. Fox, the patrolman who had summoned him, stood watch by a swath of yellow police tape and nodded.

'Hey there, Judge Mosley.' Fox blinked at the tropical shirt and disheveled shorts. 'Come from a party?'

'No.' Whit grimaced. 'Down there?' At the farthest tip of the docks, an officer climbed off a hefty cruiser.

'Yes, sir. Damn nice boat.'

Whit ducked under the yellow police tape. *Maybe I should have worn the suit.*

3

Whit had served as justice of the peace for only six months, since the previous justice died in a car crash after several years in office. He'd accepted the appointment from the county commissioners, all cronies of his father's, because he needed Direction. Over the past five years since he'd shuffled back to Port Leo, his jobs shared only their brevity: photographing sports part-time for the paper, managing a defunct fifties-themed ice cream parlor with the ill-advised name of Shimmy Shimmy Shakes, and running a messenger service that never delivered profits.

His father measured success by oil leases, acreage, investment income, and wifely pulchritude, and believed in Direction (especially for English majors who had cost him fifty thousand dollars to educate at Tulane). Babe cajoled his buddies into appointing Whit to the remainder of the dead JP's term. Whit decided to give it a shot. *Judge* would make the most respectable addition to his crazy-quilt résumé.

Whit pored over justice court law but felt awkward and stupid every time he had to consult a book during a hearing, impatient litigants tapping their feet. He bought some dime-store eyeglasses to smarten his appearance and cut his blondish hair short but wore his beach-bum clothes (polos, shorts, and sandals) beneath the black sobriety of the robe. To Whit's surprise he liked the work: he adjudicated small claims and traffic court, which could be dishwater dull or raucously entertaining (depending on the cases), but he also issued arrest and search warrants, magistrated the arrested into jail, signed commitment orders for the insane, ordered autopsies, and conducted death and fire inquests.

With Encina County too small for a medical examiner of its own, Whit served as the first line of forensic defense. So far in his six months this unpleasant duty had reared itself four times: once with a car crash at the edge of the county, twice with drownings on St Leo Bay, and once for an elderly suicide who, his insides gnawed with pancreatic cancer, washed several fistfuls of Valium down with a fifth of vodka while listening to Hank Williams CDs.

Another death, and the whole county would be watching. All the attention could make or break his anemic campaign. *Great. Your lover's ex-husband is dead, and you get to rule on cause of death. Congratulations.*

Whit headed past the long line of docked boats on the T-head, most shrouded in bright blue coverings. Weekend boaters from Corpus Christi or Houston owned these craft. A few folks lived on their boats full-time, retirees or trust-fund babies. Whit ducked under another banner of crime-scene tape taped right at the boat's stern.

'Hello, Honorable.' Claudia Salazar, a Port Leo police detective, stood on the deck of *Real Shame*, watching him scale the ladder. A gust whipped her dark hair around her face, and she yanked it back over her ears. She looked decidedly more official than he did in her black slacks, white blouse, and a PLPD windbreaker.

'Hey,' Whit said. 'I heard this may be politically testy. No press yet?'

'We have a short grace period before they swarm, once it gets out that Senator Hubble's son is dead,' Claudia said. 'Get your quotes ready.'

'Has anyone called the senator?'

'Delford is,' she answered. Delford Spires was the longtime police chief in Port Leo. He had a full ruddy face and a natty mustache that made him look like a chunky catfish.

He followed Claudia across a pristine deck down to a living area and galley filled with clutter: a thick paperback propped open with a carton of Marlboros and an empty wineglass. On the floor a pizza box lay open with torn cheese and pepperoni glued inside. Two empty bottles of cheap cabernet stood on the coffee table. Each label had been peeled away from the bottles; little curls of paper dotted the floor. On one side of the den a series of windows faced the gunmetal waters of the bay. On each end, small stairs led to sleeping cabins. Claudia went to the aft stairs.

'Here's where he was found.' She stepped aside so Whit could enter the tiny stateroom.

The dead man lay naked on the bed, lying on his back, arms and legs spread, the sourness of death-released waste scenting the close air.

'I haven't seen him in fifteen years,' Whit said. 'But that's Pete Hubble.' He did not add that Pete Hubble had skinny-dipped with Whit's older brothers and once you saw Pete naked you were unlikely to confuse him with someone else. 'It might be best to get a formal ID from family or friends.'

Eddie Gardner, another police department investigator, stood in the corner of the bedroom, snapping photos. An evidence-collection kit lay open at his feet.

'You were supposed to wait for Judge Mosley to get here,' Claudia said.

'Sorry.' Gardner shrugged. 'Just taking some photos. I didn't disturb anything for the judge.' Gardner made *judge* sound like *dog turd*. He wore his thinning hair pulled in a short ponytail, aiming for and missing the surfer dude look. He was a recent hire from Houston and had tried too hard to go coastal with the flowered shirts and baggy shorts.

'Why don't you get started on searching and cataloging the rest of the boat?' Claudia suggested in a patient tone. Gardner went up the stairs with his smirk.

'Houston know-it-all,' Claudia muttered.

'Eddie's got to stop those public displays of affection for me,' Whit said. He pulled on latex gloves and switched on an overhead light. A bit of bedsheet was wrapped awkwardly around Pete's upper torso, a gun loosely gripped in his right hand, his mouth a gaping hole. His eyelids stood at half-mast, rimmed with blood.

'This just sucks,' Whit said.

'Did you know him well?' Claudia asked.

'He was friends with a couple of my older brothers. I knew his brother Corey better than him.'

Claudia cocked her head. 'Corey. He went missing, didn't he?'

'Yeah. About fifteen years ago.'

A hoarse voice called down to Claudia. 'I'll be back in a minute,' she said.

Whit probed – gingerly – Pete Hubble's throat for a pulse. Nothing, obviously. He poked the paling skin: cool but not cold, and rigor mortis had not yet begun.

The windows were shut in the cabin, but the boats at Golden Gulf were docked in neat succession. Surely someone would have heard the fatal shot. He raised the blinds on the windows. The two berths next to *Real Shame* were empty. On the other side was the open bay and the long pall of night.

Whit opened his notebook to a blank scene-of-death form. He heard more officers boarding the boat, into the galley and living area, Claudia greeting them, dividing responsibilities. Whit wrote: *Oct 12, 10:45 p.m. Peter James Hubble, male, age ~40, brown hair, brown eyes,*

13

six-six, around 220 pounds, nude except for gold chain with lion's head on it around neck, red-and-green dragon tattoo on right forearm, lying face up on bed, sheet wrapped partially around chest, 9mm Glock in right hand, bullet wound in mouth, blood spray on face.

Whit peered inside Pete's broken mouth, bringing his flashlight to bear on the damage. The tongue, the back teeth, the palate, the uvula, the smooth pink walls looked exploded. The back of the mouth was a gruesome tunnel boring to the brain. Pete had his lips wrapped neatly around the barrel when the gun went off.

'Ate the gun, didn't he?' Eddie Gardner asked conversationally. He had returned with his camera.

'Apparently.'

'Sheriff's deputies are helping Claudia, so you and I can get the body done.' He spooled film into the camera, still smirking. 'Love the shirt. Parrots are you.'

Whit ignored the jab, leaning close to the gun. 'Odd. The safety is on.'

'I pulled the gun out of his mouth so I could click on the safety. Standard procedure.' Gardner explained this in a tone usually reserved for addressing toddlers. 'Wouldn't expect you to know.'

Great. A Buddy Beere supporter. 'Did you take a picture first, with the gun in his mouth?'

'No. Forgot. Just trying to secure the scene, Judge.'

Whit wrote in his notebook: *Gardner didn't take requisite pictures, mention THAT in the inquest report.*

'So you knew this guy?' Gardner asked.

'Ages ago.'

'There's a whole bunch of adult movie videos in a cabinet by the television. And this guy's picture is on some of the covers.'

Whit stared at him. 'Please be kidding.'

Gardner grinned. 'Not kidding at all. You could hold a

14

blue film festival with all the porn up there.' He pointed at the dead man's prodigious organ. 'Jesus, a horse would be jealous. Makes sense he might make some money off of that.'

The son of a prominent state senator starring in porn films. The imagined headlines took a greasy turn in Whit's mind. He wondered if Faith knew.

He watched Eddie Gardner snap photos of seemingly every square inch of the bed, excepting the square inches that had landed Pete in movies.

'Eddie,' Whit said, 'please photograph the gun. I'm going to need those for the inquest.' Gardner took several shots of the pistol from different angles. Neither man spoke for a minute until Gardner finished the roll.

'You thinking suicide, Judge? Looks that way to me.'

'Why?' Whit asked.

'Big-built guy, no signs of struggle. It's hard to stick a gun in the mouth of a guy this big.'

At one corner of the bed stood a sleek video camera, mounted on a tripod, aimed at the bed. Gardner watched Whit examine the camera.

'Shit, maybe he was shooting a home movie with that little gal out there and things got rough,' Gardner said.

'Little gal?'

'Girl that found him. Looks like she's spent her last dime and got no place to go. Dirty, strung out.' Gardner laughed. 'She might have screamed bloody murder if she saw that dick coming at her.'

'Maybe,' Whit said. Gardner had all the appeal of head lice, but he had a point. Whit remembered a tidbit he'd read in a forensics book about bodily fluid residue. He carefully inspected the dead man's genitals with his latexed fingers; the massive penis appeared dry. There hadn't been immediate predeath sex, he bet, but the

15

medical examiner in Corpus Christi could properly make that determination.

Gardner watched him probe the organ. 'If it gets hard, yell.'

'Don't worry. I will.' Whit felt uneasy embarrassment again. No doubt Gardner would gossip back in the police station: *Jesus, Mosley felt up the dead guy's dick, can you believe it?*

Whit noticed a frame turned down on the bedside dresser, and he righted it. It was a photo of a young boy, on the verge of the teenage years, with a scattering of freckles and mischievous brown eyes. Hints of Pete Hubble lay in his face: the square jaw, the crinkled smile, the brown hair. Signs of Faith Hubble were the small ears, the slink of the raised eyebrow. It was an old photo of Sam Hubble, Pete and Faith's son. Sam was now fifteen, a bright kid Whit had always liked. He wondered how on earth the boy would take this news.

'The only suicide I've worked,' Whit said, 'the fellow turned every family picture to the wall before taking the big gulp.'

'Another vote for suicide.' Gardner loaded another roll of film. More flashes filled the room.

Still wearing his gloves, Whit flipped open the video camera's housing. No tape inside.

'Was there a videotape in here Claudia took?' he asked.

'Don't believe so.'

'Did you take it?'

Gardner frowned. 'Nope.'

Whit shut the case. Discarded clothing lay piled in the corner of the room. Still wearing the gloves, Whit picked through the mound. In the pile were faded men's jeans, a cowboy belt still threaded through the loops; a white T-shirt; and men's black briefs that must have clinched the family jewels in a vise grip. Nestled with the shirt were a pair of cotton women's panties, decorated with little intertwining violets. Whit hooked the panties with one gloved finger and raised them toward Gardner.

'Looky, looky, there must've been nookie.' Gardner glanced behind him to make sure Claudia Salazar hadn't returned to the room. 'Ought to check to see if the girl's got her delicates. I'll volunteer.'

'A hero in her darkest hour,' Whit said. 'What has the witness told you?'

'Her name's Heather Farrell. Got that scared-goat look of a runaway. We're running a check on her to see if she's got a record. She said she met Hubble on the beach over the course of the last week, and he asked her to come over tonight.'

Whit studied Pete Hubble's face. Little of the boy he had known remained in the dead man's looks. A memory bubbled up: Whit, barely twelve, hanging at the edges of one of Whit's brothers' birthday parties, full of raucous teenagers, and Pete sneaking Whit – youngest of the six Mosley boys – slugs of prime bourbon. He'd thrown up at the party's end, on the shoes of his oldest brother's date, and gotten the last whipping he'd ever received from his father. Pete. Mr Fun. At least before his brother vanished.

'I wonder how many fuck films he made,' Gardner said.

'Don't go broadcasting details of that career around town just yet.'

'Not a chance in hell that's gonna be kept quiet,' Gardner said. 'I guess all the pussy in the world can't make a boy happy. Think of all the women he must've had doing the movies.'

'Think of all the venereal disease.'

Gardner pondered this. 'Might suck the wind out of your sails.'

17

Whit opened the small closet that faced the bed. A small collection of men's clothes hung loosely on hangers: pants, sweatshirts, a stacked collection of baseball caps, captioned with ADULT ENTERTAINMENT AWARDS and HOT AND BOTHERED PRODUCTIONS and, oddly, UCLA FILM SCHOOL. On the opposite side of the closet blouses, women's T-shirts, sweatshirts, and jeans were neatly folded across hangers. Below was a box of loosely stuffed papers. On the floor a leather bustier, designed to rein in a majestic-size bosom, and a collection of hot-pink thong underwear lay in an untidy heap.

'A woman's been staying here.'

Eddie Gardner shrugged. 'Imagine. A guy who fucks for a living keeps a lady handy.'

Whit returned to the combined galley/sitting area. He heard Claudia and another officer detailing and bagging the evidence out on the deck, which was most in danger of being affected by the threatening weather.

Opposite the couch was a brand-new television, and videotapes were wedged into an open cabinet. Whit pulled up a tape from one stack. *Cleopatra's Love Slaves* featured an elfin-faced platinum blonde in a golden, vaguely Egyptian costume. She was about to lick a rubber asp caught in her cleavage. Behind her loomed an oiled, chesty fellow in a toga with a lusty stare: Pete. A list of performers covered the left side of the tape cover: Dixxie St Cupps and Rachel Pleasure and Love Ramsey. After several female names were listed 'Big Pete Majors' and another man; the casting wasn't split evenly by gender. But then, men generally weren't the main attractions. Velvet Mojo was credited as the producer and director.

Whit pawed through the rest of the cassettes: *Mixin' Vixens*, *More Lovin' Spoonfuls*, *Oral Arguments XI*. 'Big Pete Majors' was listed as a performer on every tape. Velvet Mojo was listed on all of them as producer and director, all under the Hot and Bothered label. Whit counted twelve tapes and noticed they were all done in the past year. Pete and his harem believed in hard work.

Whit sat in shock. He wondered if Pete's mother, the senator, knew of her son's career. Or Faith, who never mentioned her ex. Two extraordinarily bright, accomplished women – the shame would burn them both like acid. Personally. Politically.

He noticed books piled on the sofa. There were several books on screenwriting basics, dialogue, technique. Porn didn't require much in the way of story structure, Whit thought, but the books looked well worn.

The other collection of tapes – twice the size of the porn collection – was a world away from the adult tapes, and Whit recognized some titles only because he'd taken film appreciation years ago at Tulane for an easy A. *City Lights*, one of Charlie Chaplin's masterpieces. *The Battleship Potemkin*, a long-ago classic of Russian cinema. Abel Gance's *Napoleon*, D. W. Griffith's *Birth of a Nation*. *Gone With the Wind*. Films by Alfred Hitchcock, by John Ford, by Stanley Kubrick. And a bevy of obscure foreign cinema, films from Australia and Sweden and Italy that Whit had never heard of. Combine the two stacks and you would have the world's most bizarre film festival.

Whit peeked into the VCR and found a tape already in the drive. Still wearing his gloves, Whit powered up the television and the VCR.

4

The tape snapped into sudden focus. Pete Hubble walked along a curve of rural road, sauntering backward, talking into the handheld camera with the earnest patter of a tour guide. The time stamp in the corner of the screen indicated the footage had been shot ten days ago.

'Here's where my brother's car was discovered,' Pete said in his rumbling baritone. The camera panned over a clutch of small white frame houses with a private, ratchety pier jutting into the water. 'Before this was just beach and field, and kids parked here.'

'I'm sure you never did,' a woman's smoky voice commented, off-camera. She apparently was operating the camcorder.

Pete smiled. 'I was too shy.'

'You triumphed over your phobia.' A pause. 'Were the keys in his car?'

'No. Never found.'

'Any sign of foul play?'

'No. Mom made Corey work for the car. I couldn't believe he'd just abandon it.'

'They find *anything* in it?'

'A gas receipt, from Port Lavaca, was under the seat. So we know he or someone had been driving the car and had been up the coast.' Pete shaded his eyes against the sun. 'No prints in the car that weren't Corey's. Everyone thought at first that somebody kidnapped Corey. But never a note, never a call.'

'So start theorizing. Then we'll go slam some coffee.'

'Corey dumped his own car because it would have been traced too easily and he wanted to disappear,' Pete said.

'Why?'

'To make my mother suffer.' Pete shrugged into the camera lens. 'I don't know how to make that part work in the screenplay without Corey looking like a bastard.'

'Don't make him a saint if he wasn't one, Pete,' the woman said.

Pete shook his head and the tape fuzzed to blue, then resumed with Pete standing in front of a sign. JABEZ JONES MINISTRIES.

'Visual notebook, part two, still scouting locations for the shoot.' Pete pointed up at the sign. 'Here's where muscle-bound morons come to wrestle with their sins.'

'I remind you,' the woman's voice said, 'my daddy was a preacher. Be nice.'

'Jabez declined to be interviewed for my movie. It makes you wonder,' Pete said. 'I have a feeling he's just waiting to see the movie and sue big-time.'

'Let him sue your ass,' the woman counseled. 'Free publicity.'

Pete grinned. 'Like I'm gonna have to worry about publicity. I'm gonna be front page on every paper in the country.'

'Yeah. Right. Whatever,' the woman said. Annoyance dripped from her words, as though there was a secret she wasn't privy to and wanted to be.

The tape jumped again. Pete stood on a stretch of jumbled heavy granite blocks, a fishing jetty near Port Leo Park. The surf surged in and the waves slammed hard against the pink and gray stones, spraying droplets into the air. Wind whipped Pete's hair; the time stamp said this was filmed a week ago.

'Hand me the flowers,' Pete ordered. From out of the frame came a woman's hand, covered with jangling bracelets, offering a large bouquet of daisies and carnations, the kind found in the grocery checkout lines, wrapped in green paper. Pete tossed the bouquet into the waves; the flowers churned in the tide, bounced, vanished, churned again. The camera panned up to Pete's face.

'There's no grave for my brother, but we used to fish off this jetty. It's the best I can do.' He began to cry, softly.

A few moments of silence. 'I think I'm gonna bring Sam here,' Pete said, and the woman said, 'Oh, Jesus, you got to listen to reason,' and the film went black.

He looked over his shoulder, ejected the tape, and stuck in one of the adult offerings – *Johnny Ampleseed*. The new tape had only been rewound midway. It took less than twenty seconds watching Pete and two bleached blondes kneeling in an orchard to confirm Pete Hubble was indeed a celluloid sleaze. His timeless lines consisted of 'Oh, yeah,' 'Do it, baby,' and 'Now it's your turn.'

Whit felt sick. For Faith, for Lucinda, for Sam. Another part of him wondered: so what was living *that* life like?

Whit put the first tape back in the machine and powered off the television. Pete had been making a film project about his brother's disappearance. Going legit with a film career after working in porn, unless he had decided to inject adult themes into his family's tragedy. Whit thought probably not.

Whit went up to the deck. He spotted Claudia Salazar talking to a sheriff's deputy along the gangplank. Another deputy carefully packed a few bagged and tagged items into a large cardboard box. The ambulance had departed, replaced by a mortuary service hearse, ready to transport the body when Whit gave the go-ahead.

Whit waited for Claudia to head back to the boat. 'I'm pronouncing him dead as of 10:45 p.m.,' he said. 'I'm authorizing the autopsy and ordering an inquest. It's all right to transport the body now.' He scribbled details

22

on an authorization of autopsy form, signed it, then Claudia witnessed his signature. 'Is it you or Prince Charming that's in charge of the investigation?'

'Delford's given me the case. You thinking suicide?'

'Before we get to that question . . . he's a porn star.'

Claudia blinked, her face paling in the marina lights. 'Your shirt's funny, but you're not.'

He explained what he'd found, both the adult and legit tapes. Claudia rubbed her face. 'Holy holy God,' she mumbled.

'Back to your question,' Whit said. 'Suicide's certainly suggested. There's no sign of a note, but he turned down a picture of his son. I saw the same in a suicide down in Darius a few weeks back. But . . . considering this guy's livelihood, I'm wondering why that camera – with no tape – is pointed at the bed. And there's a pair of women's panties mixed in with his own clothes. Is our young witness missing any underwear?'

'Oddly enough, I haven't checked.'

'There's women's clothing in the closet, including some stuff you ain't gonna see the Junior League sporting during the Buccaneer Ball. If this girl isn't staying with him, it belongs to someone else.'

'You think . . . he was filming a movie and got snuffed?'

Whit shrugged. 'I really don't know.'

'This is turning nastier by the second.'

'Where is your witness?'

'Down at the station. Gardner and the deputies can finish the scene work, I'm going to question her and get a statement.' She jabbed a finger at him. 'Not a word, Whit, not a word to anyone.'

He jabbed a finger back at her but smiled. 'Gardner says this girl is a runaway. If you're not going to detain her I don't want her taking off before the inquest.'

Claudia nodded. 'I'll make sure she sticks close.'

'I wonder if the person taping Pete talking about his brother was our runaway.'

'Let's talk to her,' Claudia said. 'We'll compare her voice to the tape.'

They walked back to *Real Shame*. Claudia quickly inspected the tape collection and retrieved Pete's home-made tape, and they went back on the dock, toward the marina office. An angry voice boomed along the docks, and they saw a woman arguing with Patrolman Fox at the police tape boundary.

'Lady says she lives on the boat,' Fox called to Claudia. 'Her name's Velvet.'

'Velvet Mojo,' Whit whispered, 'is the director of Pete's movies.'

'Velvet Mojo sounds like a real bad wine,' Claudia said. 'It's okay,' she called back to Fox.

The woman was in her late twenties, with streaky blond hair combed back to her shoulders. She wore a dark long-sleeve T-shirt that read MEAN PEOPLE SUCK and baggy blue-jean shorts with scuffed sneakers.

'Velvet?' Claudia asked as they came to the tape.

The woman stared, and Whit saw fear in her eyes, fueled by the police, the crowd, the hearse.

'What's going on here? Is Pete in trouble?' the woman asked.

Whit immediately recognized the woman's voice from the videotape. Smoky, hinting of hazy bars and purred invitations.

'Maybe we could go inside and talk.' Claudia nodded toward the marina office.

Velvet shook her head. 'I want to know what's happened. Right freaking now.'

'And I want to tell you. But inside,' Claudia said.

'Jesus,' Velvet said, but she allowed herself to be led to

the marina office. The wind gusted against them once, smelling of rain.

Inside the office, Claudia gently steered Velvet to a couch and sat down with her. 'Velvet – pardon, but is that your real name?'

'Yeah, it's what I go by. But Mojo's made up,' Velvet said, as if that could be a revelation.

'So what's your real name?'

'Velvet Lynn Hollister.' Her gaze darted back and forth between Whit and Claudia.

'I'm Claudia Salazar with the Port Leo Police Department, and this is Judge Whit Mosley. He's our justice of the peace.'

'Is Pete in trouble? Did he—' She stopped.

'Pete has died,' Claudia said. 'He was found shot to death this evening. I'm terribly sorry.'

Velvet accepted this news without screams or tears. Her throat worked in the dim light of the office for a few moments. 'Dead? On the boat?' She held herself very still, hands fixed in her lap, eyes dry.

'Yes,' Whit said. 'He had been shot in the mouth. The gun was in his hand.'

They let Velvet digest that bit of news for a moment. She didn't move.

'Did he own a gun?' Claudia asked.

'No. He hated guns. Didn't want them around.'

Claudia glanced at Whit. 'Would one of his family perhaps have lent him a gun?'

'I avoided his family,' Velvet said. 'I wasn't up to their tight-assed snuff. His mother's an A-1 bitch and his ex-wife's her understudy. They didn't want us around.'

So Faith knew Pete was in town. Why didn't she tell me? Whit touched Velvet's shoulder; she didn't flinch away. 'Where would Pete have gotten the gun from?'

'The boat belongs to a friend of Pete's. He might have

25

gotten the gun from him. I don't know.' Velvet began to shiver.

'Who's this friend?' Claudia asked.

'A guy named Deloache. Junior Deloache. He lives in Houston, but he's got a weekend condo here.' Velvet grabbed Whit's arm. 'Did a doctor look at Pete? Are you sure he's dead?'

'I'm quite sure. I'm sorry.'

'Did you see any sign of depression in Mr Hubble?' Claudia asked.

'You think he killed himself?' Velvet sounded incredulous. 'No way. No way, no way, no way.' She stood, pacing away from the couch, shaking her head.

Claudia stood. 'I know this is hard . . .'

'You never knew him, Miss Thing, and you're gonna pretend to know him better than me? He . . . didn't . . . kill . . . himself.'

Whit asked the obvious question. 'How can you be so sure?'

Her glare would have savaged a tank. 'Because. He liked himself way too much. He wasn't depressed. If he's dead, someone killed him.'

'Fine,' Claudia said. 'Who would want him dead?'

Velvet's tongue dabbed her lips. 'Well, first of all, not me. I know how cops work and I didn't have any reason to want Pete dead.'

'What's your relationship with him?' Whit asked.

'We've been friends for a long time. We've worked together on a bunch of art films. Dozens of them.'

'So was he your boyfriend?' Claudia asked.

'Boyfriend. How milk-and-cookies. No.' Velvet frowned. 'Look, go talk to Jabez Jones. He used to be a famous wrestler, now he's a Jesus jumper on cable TV. You know him?'

'We know him,' Whit said.

Velvet nodded. 'Pete's working on a new film project and he wanted some cooperation from Jabez, but Jabez told us to fuck off. But yesterday, I came home from the grocery and Jabez is here and he and Pete are talking on the boat and I can tell Pete's upset – his face was lipstick-red, like his head was about to burst. Jabez was smirking like he'd just popped a good money shot.'

Her choice of metaphors, Whit decided, was clearly influenced by her career.

'We'll talk to Jabez,' Claudia said. 'Anyone else?'

Velvet pinched her lip between finger and thumb. 'His ex-wife, Faith Hubble. They'd been bickering over Pete getting to see his son . . . Faith didn't want Pete to have anything to do with Sam. Pete wanted joint custody, which I knew he wouldn't get, but he and Faith argued about Sam. A lot.'

Great, great, great. Whit cleared his throat.

'Where were you tonight, Velvet?' Claudia asked.

'Screw you,' Velvet said. 'There's no way you're gonna suspect a senator's flunky or a minister, right, so start barking up my ass.'

'I'm just asking where you were tonight, when you last saw him, what you last spoke about,' Claudia said easily. 'No one's barking up your ass, so just calm down and help us.'

Velvet shivered again and sat back on the couch. 'Pete had work to do on his screenplay.'

'About his brother?' Whit asked.

'Yeah,' Velvet said slowly. 'How did you know?'

'I saw the tape he had in the machine, scouting out locations, talking about his brother's car.'

'Pete wanted to be alone – he writes better – but didn't want to write down at the beach, which is where he usually goes. Said maybe I could go entertain myself. So I went and did some shopping, ate a burger down at a café by Port Leo Beach, and went to see a movie.' She stared at Claudia. 'I got my ticket stub, and the geek behind the snack counter flirted with me. Alibi enough for you?'

'I'd like to get a statement from you down at the station,' Claudia said evenly.

'Oh, shit, am I gonna need a lawyer?' Velvet grabbed Whit's arm. 'You're a judge, right? Do I need a lawyer?'

'You're not under arrest, ma'am,' Claudia said. 'If you want a lawyer, you can get one. We just want to get a statement from you.'

'Do you have someplace you can stay, Velvet?' Whit asked. 'Y'all's boat is a crime scene, and you can't stay there, at least for now.'

Velvet's shoulders sagged, the enormity of the situation settling upon her. 'You mean like friends? No, I don't have any friends here. I don't fit in with all you decent folk.'

Whit said, 'I'll be sure you have a place to stay.'

Claudia gave him a raised eyebrow that seemed to say, *Aren't you the little white knight?*

'Thanks, but I don't need your help.' Velvet stood. 'Can I see Pete? Maybe I should be the one to tell his mother.'

'The police chief will do that,' Claudia said. 'He's known Pete's mother for a long time. Let's get you down to the station, get your statement, and then we can go from there. Okay?'

Velvet crossed her arms. 'Take all the statements you need. Tell me how I can help. Because there is no freaking way that Pete killed himself. None.' Her mouth hardened. 'And if you people don't find who killed him, I'll make more trouble than you can imagine. I assume you both can spell lawsuit?'

5

The small crowd of marina dwellers was a mix of boat bums, Gulf wanderers, and snowbirds. They had little in common except a desire for quiet and the sun-driven crinkle around the flesh of their eyes. They'd been hurried off their boats and they stood clustered in the parking lot, bathed by the glow of the police lights. One could hear mutterings about life being too short and the wrong class of people booking at the Golden Gulf. An overeager Officer Fox had used the word *suicide* in an ill-advised sentence, and the rumor rippled through the small crowd.

The Blade listened to the murmured gossip. His heart jolted like he'd dosed himself with a tickly bit of electroshock. No one paid him much heed, only a couple of the boat bums saying hello. He kept his hands tucked inside his light windbreaker.

He watched a police officer forage in the trunk of a patrol car. The Blade wondered how the officer would react if he leaned close and whispered: *I have a passion I'd like to share with you. Come see my graves.* But he wouldn't. The city would decorate the officer. The news pretties would hail the cop as hero while labeling the Blade as crazy. The boat snobs right here would jockey for camera position and gasp, *Oh, yes, we're terribly shocked. He seemed like the nicest man.* And he probably wouldn't even get to tell his side of the story on TV.

Life was blatantly unfair unless you were willing to take it by the balls and squeeze hard. He watched as one older lady stopped and chatted with the whistling officer. He spoke and she hurried back to the crowd, where she whispered eagerly.

He stood and waited. The elderly lady panted with excitement, ferrying the sad news to each knot of people.

'It's the man who lived on *Real Shame* that's dead,' she said to the Blade and two other men. 'They think he might've shot himself. Isn't that terrible?'

Shot himself. Shot himself. What wonderful delicious morsels of words. If they were candy he would have eaten them and then licked his fingers.

He wanted to see his new Darling, to touch her, to feel the heavy weight of her hair, lick her skin, and exult in the warmth of her breath against his neck. She would need comfort, poor baby.

'I bet you that trashy girlfriend of his cheated on him and he killed himself.' The old woman lowered her voice. 'Wearing those thong swimsuits. A piece of trash.'

Like Pete Hubble hadn't been a piece of trash, too, thought the Blade. He wondered what interesting pops and creaks the old woman's jaw would make if he broke it.

'She probably won't stay in town,' the Blade heard himself say in his thin, wispy voice he so loathed. 'Not from here, is she?' *Stupid, dummy!* he berated himself. *Shut up, shut up!*

The old woman nodded at him. She had wrapped her fluffy hairdo in a protective cocoon of toilet paper, and the Blade thought she looked ridiculous. 'You're so right. Ought to go back to whatever cesspool she's from.'

He nodded politely. Yes, if everyone thought Velvet had left town, then wouldn't it all be easier for him? Perfect.

Three people emerged from the marina office. Lovely, one was his Darling. Why, she wore grief well, as cute as could be in her jean shorts. Pretty is as pretty does, Mama used to say. His mouth went dry with want. The three walked back to Pete's boat, went aboard, and came out

30

perhaps two minutes later. Velvet was sobbing. He could see her bent shoulders in the dim light of the marina.

A man walked with her, steering her toward the police cars.

Panic flamed in him. Oh, no. They were arresting her. That would not do at all, not at all . . .

But they – and now he could see in the dim light the other was a tall man, not a cop – went past the parked police cars, past the quiet ambulance. And he could hear his Darling sob, and – oh, this would *not* do – the man put his hand on her arm, tenderly. The Blade's heart boiled. The man opened the door of a Ford Explorer and she got in, the man helping her like they were on a date.

The man turned toward the crowd. The Blade, seeing his face, grimaced. Heat tickled the backs of his hands.

The Explorer pulled out into the street, and the small crowd of onlookers parted to make way for it. One of those magnetic signs was affixed to the door, white letters bold against a stylized red-and-blue background: KEEP WHIT MOSLEY JUSTICE OF THE PEACE. The Explorer passed within three feet of the Blade, and he saw his Darling's face, leaning against the passenger window. She had her fists pressed to her eyes. He heard the storm of her voice over the car's motor as it shot past.

The Blade hurried away. If they were arresting her, a cop would have taken her away. Not a judge. And she hadn't had a bag. She wasn't leaving town. That thought steadied him as he jumped into his beat-up Volkswagen. He didn't like her running around with that judge when she belonged to him.

That judge. That judge had seen her upset and wanted to help her . . . wanted to take her to his house and undress her and . . .

No. No. He knew he was letting his imagination run wild and imagination was his enemy until his Darling was

31

safely in his arms. Judge Mosley was part of law-and-order, after all, so he must be taking her to give a police statement. Or to fill out forms.

Yeah, you know what all those Mosley boys are like. You know.

The Blade revved his engine and headed toward town. He wanted her with him. Screw waiting. Maybe he could catch them before they got into Port Leo's downtown, on the dark bay highway. Flash his headlights, pull them over onto the shoulder or a dark parking lot. Get Mosley out of the car, gut him with one swift move, then cut his throat. He wondered if a judge's blood would reek of musty courtrooms and old thick books. Then he could whisk his Darling to his cabin and make her his, comfort her, take her away from the world's sadness.

He floored the accelerator.

6

'Do you think he suffered?' Velvet mopped her eyes.

'It was probably over in an instant.' Whit believed in mercy, and it was the likely truth.

She rolled down the window a couple of inches, and the cool of the wind slammed into her face. 'That little cop. Salazar. She any good?'

'She has an excellent reputation.'

'Here in Mayberry-by-the-fucking-Bay? How many murders do you have here a year? One?'

'None last year. I think one the year before that.'

Velvet wadded up her tissue. 'Oh, great, so she lives and breathes homicide. I feel so much better now.' She stared at him. 'So exactly what role do you play in this aside from chauffeur?'

'When there's a suspicious death, I examine the scene, meet with the people who knew the deceased, talk with the investigators, decide to order an autopsy or not, conduct the inquest, work with the ME in Nueces County if needed, rule on cause of death.'

Velvet's eyes widened. 'So never mind the cop. All you gotta do is rule it's murder and she *has* to investigate.'

'I have to make decisions based on the evidence. I got to be judicial,' he said.

She regarded his tropical shirt and ratty shorts. 'Yeah, when I picture judicial, I'm seeing you. What are you, twelve?'

He didn't know what to say to her; his inexperience gnawed at him. He cleared his throat. 'I promise you I'll be fair, and I'll listen to what you have to say about Pete's . . . state of mind.'

'When will the autopsy be done?'

'In the next couple of days. I'll get a verbal report from the ME first, but we won't have a complete report for a few weeks. And before you keep casting aspersions against me and Claudia, you ought to know that I grew up with Pete. I knew him and his brother.' *And I sleep with his ex-wife, so clearly I'm an interested party.*

'Pete never mentioned you.'

'He was more friends with my older brothers. But if someone killed Pete, we're not gonna let him or her get away with it.'

'I suppose it wouldn't be politically sound to let a Hubble be murdered and let the killer slip free,' she said bitterly. 'No, I guess you have to investigate to the balls when it's a state senator's son.'

'I know you're upset,' Whit said, 'and I'm real sorry for your loss, but is there some reason you're cranking on me?'

'I thought judges were all supposed to be big poker players. You don't got a poker face. I can tell by the way you look at me you think Pete and I are trash.'

'I don't have a negative opinion of you.' He paused. 'I want to help you.'

She unfolded and refolded her tissue. 'Who found the body?'

'A young woman. We think she's a runaway, although she's apparently a few days past eighteen, so I guess you turn into a vagrant then. Um, I saw a video camera set up in the bedroom.' She could draw her own conclusions, Whit supposed.

'That's not how you make a movie,' she snapped. 'You got at least two cameras, not just one, you got better lights than you'd have on that boat, you got a makeup girl. No way was Pete making a movie with that little-ass camera. He was professional.'

'But moving on to a new career?'

'Porn had worn him out. It's hard work, you know. He wanted to come home to research and write this script. And he wanted me to direct it once it was done.'

'So he gave you a chance to make a real movie?'

Her stare was acidic. 'Excuse me. Have you *seen* my movies? They *are* real movies, butthead. I'm the Spielberg of porn. I have plots and characterization and depth and everything.'

Whit suspected it was the everything part that raked in the profits. 'But this film about his brother had no adult-movie elements,' he said. 'Right?'

'Of course not. I wanted to try a different kind of project. You know, that's allowed if you're creative. Shakespeare wrote comedies and tragedies. It's only small minds that jam you into one freaking hole forever.' She turned back to the window. 'So where are you dumping me after I give this statement?'

'I suppose Pete's mother isn't an option,' Whit ventured.

'She'd cut my throat in my sleep and bathe in the blood.'

'You're sure you don't have any friends in town?' Whit asked.

'I don't want any friends here, thank you kindly.'

'Then I guess we'll get you to a motel. You got several choices: the Excellent, which isn't, the Port Leo Inn, the Gulf Breeze. A bunch of B and Bs. There's also a Best Western and a Marriott Suites, too.'

'I can't believe Pete is dead and I have to stay at a Best Western.' She managed a sniffle and a slight smile, friendlier than just a moment ago. 'Any room at your inn? I'm awful quiet and I don't take up much space.'

'You don't want to stay with me. I'm a dork who lives with his dad,' he said.

'But at the Best Western I'll be alone. I don't do alone real well. I need a Plan B.'

'I'm sorry.'

'You got a phone in here?'

'Yeah, a cell phone. Here.' Whit dug among the tapes and CDs in the storage unit between the seats and handed her the phone. He clicked on the interior light so she could see to dial. Another bit of brightness caught his eye. He glanced in the rearview mirror and saw a pair of headlights jouncing, rapidly gaining on them.

Velvet dialed and waited. 'Anson? Oh, good, you're in town. Huh? Oh, okay. This is Velvet. Let me talk to Junior.' A pause. 'Junior, listen. I got real bad news. Pete's dead.' A longer pause. 'I'm not kidding. He was shot. I'm okay. I'm holding up. I cried for a bit and now I am getting ready to cry some more. Then I'm gonna kick me some police ass if they keep saying he killed himself.'

Whit ran through his mental Rolodex of Port Leo, trying to place an Anson or a Junior. Velvet had mentioned a Junior Deloache as the boat's owner.

'I'm not leaving town till we know what happened. Judge Mosley says there's gonna be an inquest. What? I gotta go to the police station. Pete was on your boat and it's a crime scene and I'm booted. So I need a place to crash. Can I stay at your condo?' She listened and hung her head slightly. 'No, I don't know when you get your stupid boat back. Yeah. Yeah. Okay, sure, I understand. Sure. I'll just grab me a hotel room. Yeah, thanks for the generosity.' She clicked off the phone. 'Those bags.'

Whit glanced in the rearview mirror. The headlights behind grew larger.

'No luck?' he asked.

'I hate that greasy little Junior Deloache. He's this piggy-eyed stain, thinks he's a stud. Yeah, with a dick stretcher and a case of Viagra, maybe.' She shrugged. 'I

36

can't get into their condo. They're in Houston but are coming down tomorrow, so I guess I'll hotel it.'

'I thought you called a local number.'

'It's call-forwarding.' She blinked at the bright headlights that dazzled behind them. The lights began to flash from dim to bright and dim again. 'Somebody's in a tear-ass hurry.'

Whit glanced back in the mirror. 'He can go around me if he wants.' The car stayed uncomfortably close. Then the lights flashed, dim, bright, dim.

'He wants you to pull over.' Velvet handed Whit the phone in the headlights' glare.

'No, thanks.' Whit floored the accelerator. He pulled away from the car, and the pursuer dropped back dramatically to a more reasonable speed.

'Asshole,' Velvet commented. Whit checked the rearview mirror several seconds later and found the car was nearly gone.

'My office is right across from the police station,' Whit said. 'I can give you a ride to the hotel after you give your statement.'

Velvet misunderstood his charity. 'Look, I don't do thank-you fucks just because someone shows common human decency.'

'I can promise you I wasn't asking for one.'

'Why? You think I stink? Do you know how many guys have hit on me since I got here?'

'Probably lots,' Whit said.

Velvet hunkered down in her seat. 'Lots is half right,' she finally pronounced. 'Tons is closer.'

Whit turned onto Main Street and pulled up in front of the Encina County courthouse. It was a sprawling, grand oddity, shaped by the Moorish architecture popular on the coast a century ago, three stories of heavy Texas granite, designed to survive storm surge and hurricane.

37

The Port Leo Police Department stood across the street, a cracker-box of boring plain brick. They crossed the empty street together. The wind rustled in the drooping palms, and the clouds had dipped low, pregnant with rain.

'They aren't going to arrest me, are they?' Velvet asked suddenly, stopping halfway across the street.

'Did you kill him?' Whit asked.

'No. God, no.'

'Then don't worry. Tell them what they need to know. These are good people. They're not going to hang you out to dry. I promise you that.'

She crossed her arms, bowed her head, and the tears came in shudders, and she bleated Pete Hubble's name. Whit didn't dwell on niceties or politics. He took her into his arms and let her cry against his shoulder, like old friends consoling each other in the terrible reality of sudden grief. He couldn't stand there like a wooden post while a woman sobbed. She got his tropical-print shoulder wet and snotty, and when the shaking stopped Whit steered her into the brightly lit doorway of the police station.

7

The Blade watched his Darling and that goddamned good-for-nothing lecher of a judge embracing in the street. He tried to slow his breathing. He had drawn close to Whit Mosley's Explorer and retreated when his headlights, and the Explorer's interior lights, showed Velvet holding a cell phone. That wouldn't do to have them announce they were being chased or to have a stranger on a cellular connection overhear the Blade doing his best work. He followed them into Port Leo's town square and slowly parked, a block away in front of the black glass of the Gulfstream Bookstore, his head-lights cut.

Watching them touch – watching Whit Mosley touch a woman that belonged to *him* – sickened the Blade. He cupped the knife against the round fleshiness of his palm, feeling the bite of its edge. He took calming breaths and tried not to cry in frustration. Patience was beyond a virtue. It was the most basic rule of survival, and to bend patience meant mistakes. Mistakes were not affordable. He had read, in the literature of his own kind, of the most abominable errors: John Wayne Gacy inviting the police keeping him under surveillance to join him for breakfast right when the odd smell floated from the crawlway; Dennis Nilsen showing the first policeman who knocked on his door the grisly plastic bags in his London closet. The Blade decided long ago that he would not lie down and die. So he fell back, and he watched, and he turned on the tape player, and the reedy Beach Boys tape that had been the player's sole occupant for the last three years sputtered into life and the Boys, volume turned low, demanded he be true to his school. He prayed that his Darling would be true to him, singing along under his breath, taking the harmony line.

Mosley and Velvet went into the police station, and the Blade waited. A few minutes later, Mosley sauntered across the street to the courthouse.

You dirty little freak. You're nothing, not worthy to touch her, know her tears. I'm not the nothing. You're the nothing.

Mosley fiddled with the courthouse door and ducked inside the darkened building. A light flickered on a few minutes later in a first-floor office behind lowered blinds.

Perhaps Judge Mosley didn't lock up after himself.

He ran to the courthouse steps and tried the door: locked. Damn.

But no, he told himself. Not now. He shivered. One death by violence in Port Leo tonight was remarkable. Another the same night would bring the police out in droves. He walked away from the courthouse. Let Whit Mosley continue to breathe – for now – and let him rule that Pete Hubble died a suicide. He congratulated himself on his self-restraint.

The momentary pride evaporated when he saw the flyer hanging in the bookstore window. Only the dim shimmer from the streetlight illuminated the girl's face, printed on light blue paper taped to the inside of the window. The Blade blinked, his guts coiling like a frightened snake.

The eyes of his last Darling watched him from the flyer. She was smiling broadly. He had not seen her smile, from the time he had abducted her from a faraway parking lot to when he'd laid her in the shallow dirt behind his house.

HAVE YOU SEEN HER? the flyer asked, with MARCY ANN BALLEW written below the question. It gave the young woman's statistics of age, description, height, and weight, and when she was last seen: leaving work at the Memorial Oaks Nursing Home in Deshay, Louisiana, September 30. Her car had been recovered from a nearby Wal-Mart.

He read on, his throat feeling coated with sand. Her wallet had been found two miles outside Port Leo, along FM Road 1223, a week ago. Anyone with information as to her whereabouts was requested to call the Encina County Sheriff's Department or the Port Leo police. A reward was mentioned.

The Blade mentally replayed his time with his most troublesome Darling. When could her wallet have gotten out on the road? he wondered, and with a sick wrench he remembered. As he approached his enclave hidden away from the eyes of other men, she roused from the stupor he'd forced on her with the Valiums and she kicked open a window. He'd veered off the road, whirled to grab her, and belted her hard four times in the face, breaking her cheekbone and nose and knocking her unconscious. He was furious, having to hurt her before his fun; and the broken bones meant he'd never gotten to see her smile. He traced her smile on the paper with his finger: lovely. He missed her.

She must have thrown her wallet out the window before he punched her, trying to leave some clue of her passage. Now the police in Louisiana – and here – must know that she had come through off-the-path Port Leo, Texas.

He swallowed the swell of panic. The police would no doubt be questioning everyone who lived along FM 1223, between here to the county line. How hard would they look, and how hard would they look at him? Capture always lingered in the back of his mind, an unwelcome companion but one as steady as his shadow. Now it loomed as a distinct possibility, and he had not claimed his most precious Darling yet.

He could not take her now. The police would be watching her. But in a few days, especially if Pete was judged a suicide . . . then she would be ripe, a plum oozing with juice, to be plucked from the tree. Tonight was Monday. He could take her, he believed, by the end of the week. Friday or Saturday.

They could have a deliciously lost weekend together: movies if she were good, dinner, death. Then back to work on Monday.

The Blade began the somewhat arduous process of hatching a plan. What had he overheard Velvet call such contingencies in the grocery store? He remembered and smiled: Plan B.

8

The interview room at the Port Leo Police Department resembled a supply closet more than an interrogation facility. In one corner tottered a stack of old computer monitors. The department had upgraded their seven-year-old systems recently and no one wanted the old standbys. A box of shredded documents, ready to be re-cycled, was shoved against the wall. Two plastic con-tainers of office supplies filled another corner. An old wooden table occupied the center of the room, marred with circles from water cups and soda cans.

Heather Farrell, the young woman who'd found Pete's body, watched Claudia Salazar with mulish eyes. Police Chief Delford Spires sat next to Heather, quiet, letting Claudia take the lead in getting the statement. Claudia noticed, with affection, that there was a crumb of cake caught in his mustache, but she didn't want to point that out with the tape rolling. He had just returned from telling the senator her son was dead. She turned to the witness.

'Okay, Heather, this won't take long,' Claudia said. 'For the record, do you have some identification?'

Heather Farrell dug in her dirty jeans and produced a tattered driver's license, one that had expired. The birth date indicated that she was two weeks past eighteen. The address on the card indicated she was from Lubbock, in west Texas, far more than spitting distance from Port Leo. Claudia read the information off the driver's license into the tape, then handed the laminated card back to Heather, who proceeded to tidy her nails with the edge of the plastic.

'Your family still in Lubbock, Heather?' Claudia asked.

'Yeah.'

'Why did you leave Lubbock?'

'Dirt sucks,' Heather said.

'That's a good reason,' Claudia said pleasantly. 'Any others?'

'I'm an artist. Lots of artists here.' Heather shrugged. 'I thought for sure those galleries would want to give me a big-ass fancy show. Strange it hasn't happened yet.'

'You haven't updated your driver's license,' Spires said.

'Don't drive much these days.' Heather gave Delford a caustic look. 'Gunk's in your mustache, mister.'

Delford groomed out the offending morsel. 'Thank you, Heather.'

'Where are you living now, Heather?' Claudia asked.

The girl shrugged with a lazy roll of shoulders. A willfulness – either born of stupidity or of hard use – tugged her face into a constant, wary frown.

'Here and there. I camp out at the park down by Little Mischief Beach sometimes.'

'Do you have a permit to camp?' Claudia already suspected the answer.

Heather shifted in her seat. 'Darn, I lost it yesterday. I haven't found a friendly ranger to give me a new one.'

Claudia nodded toward the backpack in the corner. 'Those pretty much all your belongings?'

'Yep. Travel light. I don't believe in U-Hauls.'

'So you brought everything you had in the world along with you to meet this guy on the boat.'

'I guess,' Heather said with no energy in her voice.

'You moving in with him?'

'No. I just don't like leaving my stuff lying around.'

'Did he tell you his name?'

'Yeah. Pete Majors.' Heather took a swig of the tepid

44

cocoa Officer Fox had fetched for her. 'He said he was from Los Angeles.'

Majors, not Hubble. Big Pete Majors was his *nom de cinéma,* gleaned from the videotapes on the boat. Claudia saw a thin sheen of sweat on Delford's brow, despite the cool of the room.

'Did Mr Majors tell you why he was in Port Leo?' Claudia asked.

'He was writing a movie about his brother's death. But he was awful depressed about it. I think that's why he killed himself.'

'Where did you meet Mr Majors?' Claudia asked.

'At Little Mischief Beach,' Heather answered. Claudia jotted a note on the pad in front of her. Little Mischief was an aptly named, scrabbly beach north of Port Leo, a few miles from the Golden Gulf Marina, known as a kids' hangout, with a small park attached, dense with live oaks and red bays. A good necking spot, but there were better around the county.

Heather brushed fingers through her hair. 'The light's good at Little Mischief. I like to sketch the birds, the waves, the old folks walking on the shore.'

'Dopers love Little Mischief,' Delford interjected. 'Am I gonna find some weed in your knapsack, young lady?'

'No,' she said, rolling her eyes. 'I don't do drugs.'

Claudia steered them back on track. 'What was Pete doing down at Little Mischief?'

'He'd come down there with a notebook computer, to write or just chill out and throw pebbles in the surf.' She wiped a hand across her lips. 'Quiet but nice. He gave me money for food.'

Claudia made a note. 'This money he gave you. Any strings attached?'

A flash of resentment crossed Heather's face. 'Of course not. What do you take me for?'

More to the point was what Pete Hubble had taken Heather for. Claudia remained silent for a full thirty seconds, and Heather began to fidget. 'I'm not a whore, okay? He was just being nice.' She paused. 'Maybe he didn't need the money, since he was gonna kill himself.'

'So he gave you a loan. What happened next between you?' Claudia asked.

Heather Farrell finished her cocoa and began to tear the rim of the foam cup into strips. Specks of wet, powdery chocolate smeared onto her fingertips, but she didn't notice. 'Nothing happened. He seemed real sad. Lonely. Like he'd gotten bad news.'

'When did he invite you to his boat?' Claudia asked.

'He said he wanted to talk,' Heather said. 'He wasn't sure why he would go on living.'

'He barely knew you and yet he suggested to you he was suicidal?' Claudia said.

'Sometimes it's easier to talk with a stranger than a friend.'

'I suppose. What was this crushing sadness?'

'Pete said his brother . . . was the source of all the sadness in his life. I gathered his brother died young. And he made mention of some preacher that had screwed his brother over. Somebody Jones.' She glanced at Delford. 'He made it sound like maybe this preacher was responsible for his brother's death.'

Delford cut in. 'Pete tell you what proof he had?'

'No. But Pete bitched that he couldn't make a case stick.' She looked up from her lap, her eyes wide, like a child watching a parent for approval.

'You've got to be more specific,' Claudia said. 'What exactly did he say about this preacher and his brother?'

Heather scrunched her face. 'Christ, I didn't take a goddamned transcript, and he didn't make a ton of sense. I've told you what I know.'

46

Claudia let silence fill the room and began to tap her pen against the notepad. 'He ever suggest you come to his boat and take off your clothes for a movie?'

Heather gave a sharp bark of laughter. 'No! I'm not some street whore. I haven't had any problems with the police since I got here a month ago.'

'How'd you get over to the marina?'

'I hitched a ride into town from Little Mischief. I got to the marina a little after ten.' She tore a long strip of Styrofoam away from her cup and shredded it into confetti. 'So I go to his boat – he'd told me it's the big one at the very end of the dock – and I went aboard. I called for him, but there was no answer. The door was open. I went downstairs.' Her throat worked. 'And there was no one in the kitchen and the living room, so I knocked on the bedroom door.'

'It was closed?' Claudia asked.

'Yeah.' Heather dabbed at her lips with her tongue. 'I yelled out for Pete and pushed hard on the door. I saw him on the bed, right away, and the blood spotting his face.' She was quiet for a moment, a youngster staring at implacable death and realizing she would someday feel its grasp.

'I think I screamed. I think I would. I got off that boat like it was on fire. I screamed running down the docks, and people came.'

'See anyone suspicious around the boat? Or around the marina?' This from Delford.

'No.' Heather tented her cocoa-daubed hands. Claudia yanked a tissue from a box and offered it to Heather. The girl wiped her hands carefully and repeatedly. 'I was so worried about Pete, how depressed he was, I wouldn't have noticed anyone.'

Delford nodded solemnly.

Claudia thought: *You just don't strike me as the Girl Scout type, sweetie.*

'Do you have your panties on?' she asked Heather.

Heather's mouth twitched. 'Excuse me?'

'I'd like to know if you have on a pair of panties.'

'Why?'

'Just answer me, please.'

'Yeah, I got on panties. You think I'm running around without underwear on?'

'Show me, please. I need you to lower your pants enough where I can see you've got a pair on. Chief, would you step outside for a moment?' Delford blinked at this turn of questioning.

'He can stay. I don't care.' Heather stood and yanked down on her beltless jeans with a gentle tug. Claudia could see a slice of panties below the girl's waist, plain white, grimy.

'Thank you,' Claudia said.

Heather rearranged her jeans and sat. 'Let me guess. You found panties on the boat and wanted to be sure they weren't mine?' She was smarter than she acted. 'Those panties probably belonged to his lady friend.'

'You knew he had a girlfriend?' Delford asked.

'He mentioned a lady that lived with him on the boat once. But I got the impression he'd had his fill of her. He said she'd made a lot of money off of him, and he was tired of her.'

'We'll need you to stay in town, Heather, until our investigation is done.'

Her eyes widened. 'What, under house arrest?'

'No, but don't leave town.'

Heather leaned back in her chair. 'I think my statement is done, and I want one of them pro bono lawyers like on TV if you're going to ask me any more questions.'

'Two more simple questions,' Claudia said. 'Woman camping a lot, you carry a gun?'

Heather picked at the table with a dirty fingernail. 'No. I have some pepper spray, and I know how to kick a guy's balls all the way up to his throat.'

'You ever see this young woman around, maybe down at Little Mischief?' Claudia pulled a flyer from her notebook and pushed it toward Heather. Delford watched without expression.

'Marcy Ann Ballew,' Heather read. She scrutinized the photo, as if looking for some vestige of herself in the printed face. 'Sorry. Don't know her.'

'Where you staying tonight?' Delford asked.

Heather looked discomfited. 'Back at the park, I guess.'

'If you're still shook up, spending the night alone out in the dark's no fun.' Claudia softened her tone. 'You can crash here.'

'Oh, great, a jail cell,' Heather said. 'Thanks but no.'

'We'd leave the door open. You're not locked up. It's clean and warm.' Claudia ventured a grin. 'Real cute guy working the night shift.'

The face of Marcy Ann Ballew smiled up at both of them.

Heather shook her head. 'I am not staying in any jail cell.'

'Then let me call Social Services. They'll find a place for you.'

'You just want to keep a tab on me.'

'A tab to be sure you're okay,' Claudia said.

'I don't need a tab.' Heather stood. 'We done? I got to go.' As if she had errands to run, close to midnight.

Claudia clicked off the tape. 'I'll get this typed up and you can sign it.'

'Can I come back tomorrow and sign? I'm beat.'

'Sure,' Claudia said.

'Thanks for answering our questions.' Delford stood. 'And like Detective Salazar said, don't leave town, miss. There may be a death inquest and you may have to give testimony.'

'I'll stick like glue. Later.' She gathered up her knapsack and left without a backward glance.

Delford Spires shut the door. 'And they say charm school don't make a difference no more.'

'She seems awfully sure, on the basis of little detail and thin acquaintance with the man, that he committed suicide. Would a man really kill himself over something that happened to his brother long ago?'

'I worked the Corey Hubble case.' Delford sat back down. 'A heartbreaker. Here one day, gone the next, and never a sign of him again. I wonder what this connection is to a preacher. Corey sure wasn't religious – he was a little hell-raiser.'

Claudia told him about Pete's tape and the mention of Jabez Jones.

Delford clicked his tongue. 'Jabez Jones was just a kid then, too, and sure to God was never a suspect. Shit, there was never a sign of foul play in that case, period. Corey just ran off and landed himself into real hot water and never resurfaced.'

'Pete clearly thought otherwise,' Claudia said. 'I think I'll talk to Jabez Jones.' She watched Delford slump in his seat. She was fond of him, like one might be of an old-fashioned uncle.

'How are the Hubbles?' she asked.

'Devastated. I think they felt they'd just gotten Pete back in their lives. He's stayed his distance. Lucinda's a real strong woman, but this might undo her. They gave me preliminary statements.'

A twinge of irritation nipped at her. He'd assigned her

the case yet taken statements from the immediate family. Perhaps it had been best, she reasoned, giving him the benefit of a doubt, but she decided to explode the land mine.

'So do they know Pete was a porn star?' She explained the tapes.

'Holy hell, no. At least she didn't mention it to me. Why does a son hurt a mother so?'

'Maybe she hurt him. Parents can be rotten.'

Delford snorted. 'Lucinda gave Pete the world. It ain't her fault he didn't want it.' He sighed, a long, arduous wheeze, and stood. He regarded her with critical affection. 'You up for this big a case?'

'Of course.' She labeled the tape of Heather's statement and dropped it in an accordion folder.

'You okay about David?'

She closed the folder. 'I'm fine, Delford, really.'

'I noticed today that you weren't wearing your ring no more.'

Claudia's thumb rubbed along the bare ring finger. A band where the skin, shielded by metal that supposedly meant forever, stayed pale. 'Yeah, well, the divorce was final yesterday. I sent David back the ring.'

'I know it's a tough time, Claud, and maybe I ought to let Gardner handle this one.'

'There's no need,' Claudia said. 'Really, Delford, I appreciate the concern, but I'm fine and work is heaven for me right now.'

He coughed.

'I can smell the advice baking,' she said.

'I'd treat this like a suicide.'

'I don't think Whit and the ME have talked cause of death yet.'

Delford ran a finger along a curve of his mustache.

51

'Whit Mosley couldn't find his ass in the dark with three flashlights. After the election he'll probably be running a snow-cone stand.'

'No. He'll be a housepainter,' Claudia said.

'You ain't one bit funny,' Delford shot back. It was a Port Leo legend: fifteen years ago Whit and his five brothers had, in four masterful hours when Delford was away at a football game, painted Delford's house pink. Violent, electric, Pepto-Bismol pink. Delford, unwilling to be the butt of a joke, had viewed the Mosley boys like crazed terrorists, even after they repainted his house back to its original white. The rest of the town hid its laughter behind their hands and shook their heads in mock scorn at those wild Mosleys.

'You're still not over that prank,' Claudia said. 'That's why you don't like any Mosley.' She herself liked Whit Mosley fine. He'd palled around with her brother Jimmy as kids, fishing, gigging for frogs, swimming in the bay, and Whit never made her – the tagalong tomboy – feel unwelcome. He had kind eyes, gray as the bay when the clouds hung low. And he was easy to work with. The last JP, God rest her soul, puked at every single death scene and guilted Claudia into taking macramé and quilting classes with her. Whit kept his lunch and hobbies to himself.

'I don't like Mosley period. He's running the bench like a beach attraction,' Delford fretted. 'I'm just saying Pete smells like suicide to me.'

'Are you jumping or driving to that conclusion?'

'When I told Lucinda that Pete was dead, she asked straightaway if he'd killed himself. She told me in detail about the mental problems he's been suffering from over the past several years. It's in her statement.'

'She knew he was nuts but didn't know he was doing porn?' Claudia asked.

Delford frowned. 'Well, maybe she did know. But I wouldn't blame her for not mentioning it.'

'His friend Velvet insists he would never commit suicide.'

'Let's talk about Pete's friends. This boat he was staying on, *Real Shame*. It's registered in Houston. It's owned by a fellow named Tommy Deloache. In Houston, he's known as Tommy the Roach. Suspected drug ties, suspected money launderer.'

'And Pete hanging with criminals bolsters your suicide theory how?'

'From what Houston PD says, if the Deloaches wanted Pete dead, he'd be in the Gulf, sixty feet down wired to blocks. They tidy up after themselves. They don't leave bodies around to be autopsied.'

She stood. 'I'll keep you apprised of what I find.'

'Claud, don't get bent. I'm just asking you to be sensitive to a mother's grief. Remember Lucinda's got an election in less than a month, and this could derail it.'

'The senator wouldn't get more sympathy votes if he was murdered as opposed to suicide?' Claudia asked bluntly. 'Suicide sounds like maybe she was a bad mother.'

'Damn it, Claudia, you've never handled a death this high-profile. And my gut, which is both bigger and older than yours, tells me Pete killed himself. If you chase the wrong path and embarrass yourself, not to mention Senator Hubble, with all this unrelated garbage about porn and Corey Hubble and what not, that's going to be remembered.'

He shoved his chair hard against the table.

'Well, hell, Delford, if you don't have confidence in me, don't give me the case.'

'I'm just trying to help you. The case is yours. Just mind how you run it.'

She nodded, and he turned and left. Claudia stared at the door he slammed behind him.

9

'Why didn't you tell me Pete was back in town?' Whit asked.

He heard the sharp rasp of Faith Hubble's breath. 'Oh, Whit. God, babe, I didn't think it mattered. He said . . . he wasn't going to stay long. A couple of weeks, no more.'

'If I had an ex-wife, wouldn't you have wanted to know if she showed up in Port Leo?' he asked.

'We're not . . . dating, Whit. We're just . . . I mean . . . oh, God, I can't have this conversation now. Sam's out of his mind with grief, and Lucinda's a zombie.'

Whit hated having to press, but he did. 'Pete was writing a screenplay, Faith. I don't think he was just waltzing in and out of Port Leo on a quick jaunt.'

'Oh, God.' She couldn't hide the shock in her voice. 'Movie?'

'Did you know he was in the movie business, Faith?'

'I can't . . . discuss this right now. Sam's real upset. He needs me.'

'Fine. But I need to talk to you all tomorrow.'

'I want that. I want to see you.'

'Fine, I'll call you tomorrow. Please give my sympathies to the senator and Sam.'

'I will. And thank you, in advance, Whit, for your help. We appreciate it.'

They said their good-byes and hung up. Whit wondered exactly what kind of help he was supposed to provide, unasked.

Whit transferred his field notes to an inquest report and

assigned the death a case number. He had called the ME's office in Corpus Christi as soon as he got into his office to report Pete's death and the body's expected arrival at their facility. The on-call ME had phoned back and Whit gave her a brief summation of the case. He asked her to be sure and check the corpse for any signs of foul play, although from the body's condition suicide was indicated. He hung up and watched the clouds begin to pour a thin, steady rain on the sleeping town.

He gathered up a notebook from the JP Training Center that offered details on conducting a formal death inquest, locked up his office, and headed down the darkened hallways of the courthouse.

Grief, in whatever variety, reminded Whit of his mother. When he was two, she had packed up and walked away from her husband and six sons and vanished into the great blue of the world, and in odd moments he ached for her touch as he might ache for a missing limb. For the first time in weeks he wondered where his mother was, if she were dead or alive. He imagined her buried under an assumed name, or her unmourned bones bleached by the sun, a victim of terrible evil. But not always. He also imagined her munching a peanut butter sandwich, licking stray dabs of plum jelly from her fingers, watching *The Tonight Show*, curled on a bed with green sheets. Green had been her favorite color, she often wore a thin green ribbon in her blond hair, at least in pictures. He could not remember if he ever played with the ribbon.

He wondered if she ever thought of him. Perhaps five sons had seemed manageable and six was just one son too many.

His mother. Corey Hubble. Both gone into the maw of the world.

The difference between Whit and Pete, Whit mused,

was that Pete acted. Or at least attempted to peel back the layers of years toward truth and document what had happened to Corey.

Whit admired his guts.

So what had Pete found?

The police station's night dispatcher, a she-grizzly named Nelda, buzzed him into the building. Whit freeloaded a cup of high-voltage, road-tar coffee from her and collapsed on a rough old bench. Velvet was giving a statement to Claudia Salazar, he was told, and Nelda peered at him strangely when he said he'd wait.

Being a shoulder for Velvet was fine. A moron's level of political astuteness demanded that he do nothing more. But he knew she was alone, and he knew the shock of sudden, paralyzing loss. No harm in being friendly. Bitter pills were harder to swallow alone.

Delford Spires ambled toward him while he sipped his coffee.

'Hello, partner,' Delford said. 'You're not usually such a dedicated public servant.'

'Just waiting for Claudia to finish up with Velvet.'

'Claud can give the lady a ride to her hotel. Maybe you and I can chat for a second.'

Whit followed Delford to the station's back entrance, where the smokers were exiled under a metal canopy. The rain fell steadily and lightning webbed the sky over the Gulf.

Delford dug in his pocket for a pack of Marlboros and waited until he had one lit and two puffs down before he spoke. 'So you were gonna wait on Velvet?'

'I told her I'd give her a ride and talk to her about Pete.'

'A ride. I'll bet.' Delford blew out a calculated plume of smoke, edging Whit's face.

'I'm just being a nice guy.'

'You know what nice gets you with a loose woman?'

Delford rubbed the smooth dome of his balding head. 'A burning need for penicillin.'

Whit waited for the next nugget of wisdom to fall from Delford's lips.

Delford exhaled another stream of smoke. 'This is a hell of a mess, Whit. Hell of a mess.'

'Yes. I feel bad for Lucinda Hubble.' Whit tossed out a verbal card to see if Delford would trump.

Delford did. 'Oh, Lord, yes. I hated to be the bearer of bad news, but she had to know. Suicide is so goddamned selfish. And this so close to the election.'

Whit sipped his coffee, letting Delford believe silence signaled agreement, then said, 'We don't know that it's suicide, Delford.'

To their right, a blue-light bug zapper sounded a long, fuzzy trill as it dispatched some flying insect to creeper heaven. 'Of course not. But I been in law enforcement thirty years, partner, and you're wet behind both ears and balls. Pete Hubble clearly looks like a suicide to me. No sign of struggle, big old boy like him. He put that gun in his own mouth.'

Whit shrugged. 'I think I'll wait for the autopsy to make a ruling. But I sure don't see why he'd come home after all these years just to kill himself. Especially after he was starting a new film project.'

'I get it. You're just interested in the media circus, get your name in the paper for the voters to see. I think you owe some common sense and courtesy to Lucinda Hubble that this be handled quickly and quietly.'

'Since Dear Abby's not available,' Whit said, 'how does ramming a ruling through quickly get classified as common sense and courtesy?'

Delford stubbed out his smoke. 'It's called decency. Try to add it to your vocabulary, partner. Lucinda's done more for this county than most people have, and she's suffered a lot of tragedy in her life. So show her some compassion.'

'The woman has lost her son. I don't plan on being anything but compassionate. Especially if it turns out her son's been murdered.'

'And you wouldn't change your mind because she's a Democrat and you're a Republican?' Whit had had to make a party affiliation to get the appointment from the Republican-controlled county commissioners, but he felt lukewarm about allegiance to any political party.

'Party lines bore me, Delford.'

'I imagine. The only party line you're interested in is the one leading to the keg.'

Whit patted his pockets. 'I like that one. I better write it down and note the time and date you actually attempted a joke.'

'Listen, Whit.' Delford lowered his voice but kept his amiable smile firmly fixed. 'We all know you're sort of learning as you go, but you sure don't want the voters to realize that you're, shall we say, still climbing the learning curve.'

'For all your preaching about compassion,' Whit said, 'I haven't heard you show one bit of sympathy for Pete Hubble.'

'Lucinda doesn't deserve for that good-for-nothing son of hers to muddy her name from the grave. You're gonna be out there alone, Whit, looking like a fool when the police and the family – who know the truth – all say it's suicide and you're chasing shadows.'

'What is this, a good-old-boy plea to stay in step?' Whit said.

Delford shook his head. 'You must've sniffed some of that pink paint, son. I'm not pressuring you to do diddly. My judgment is based on years of police experience. This is your first big death case, Whit. You screw it up and it's real public, and it's right before the election.' He laughed and crushed his cigarette under his boot heel. 'And just a tip: voters don't vote for candidates who consort with porno queens.'

Delford went back into the police station. Whit watched the rain and finished his coffee. When he went back inside, Nelda told him Claudia and Velvet had left not three minutes before. He drove home, devoured a ham sandwich and a bag of corn chips while watching a *Monty Python* rerun on cable, and went to bed with his JP training materials. He read every detail on death inquest procedures.

He wondered how the voters would react if he and his brothers painted Delford's house again.

Reading the procedures, written in law's natively ornate style, made him drowse. His thoughts drifted to the last time he had been with Faith, making hurried love in a Laurel Point motel last week. She had seemed distracted, going through the motions of lovemaking without her usual ardor, kissing him as though she were tasting a sour peach. He had wondered if she was growing tired of him or preoccupied with Lucinda's reelection campaign. Now he wondered if it was because Pete had reentered her life.

He doused the lights. When he fell asleep he dreamed not of Faith or Irina or Velvet but of his mother, calling his name like a siren from the surf-churned rocks.

10

'That judge,' Velvet said to Claudia as they pulled into the Port Leo Best Western's half-full parking lot. 'Tell me about him.'

'What exactly do you want to know?'

'He said there might be an inquest. He gonna be fair?'

'Extremely fair,' Claudia said.

'He looks like a beach bum not tidied up all the way,' Velvet said. 'I directed a movie called *Here Comes the Judge*. I know, bad title, but schlock's part of the game. I worried that Flip Wilson's estate would sue. Did great on video. I had a guy who wore nothing under his judge's robes in one scene, and he did the court reporter and half the jury.'

'Wow, you really are a film visionary,' Claudia said, not wanting to hear a synopsis of adult movies. 'A real Scorsese.'

'Aren't you the meow kitty? I guess I shock you,' Velvet said.

'You're trying too hard to shock me.'

'And why would I do that?'

'If you don't think what you do is wrong, and you beat people over the head with it, they'll probably keep their opinions to themselves.'

'And what do you know about my profession? You know, most of the people in the adult film business are married. They work it just like a nine-to-fiver, then go home to their families.'

'I'm sure there are hired killers who have white picket fences. It doesn't make it respectable.' Claudia turned to her. 'I don't believe in exploiting people.'

'You ever use an informant in your line of work, Ms High-and-Mighty? Maybe someone who's fallen on hard times, gotten himself in a little lick of trouble, and wants to stay out of jail? And they can, if they give you names and numbers and know who's fencing what or where the marijuana's stashed?'

Claudia stopped the car in front of the lobby doors. Rain slid down the windshield, blurring the world. 'That's different. I'm enforcing the law.'

'You're taking advantage of their weakness to get what you want. Don't lecture me about using people, baby. I launch careers, I let lonely guys have some fun in the privacy of their own home, I show shy ladies how to make a man their love slave forever. It's a public service, if that resonates with you.'

'I have less than zero interest in debating you, Velvet. But I don't know of many women who could do what you do and not feel degraded. Tart it up however you like.'

Velvet regarded her with interest. 'I bet Whit wouldn't wear anything under his robe, if I asked him.'

Christ, lady, your old one's barely cold yet. David wasn't even dead, only her spanking-new ex, but she couldn't imagine touching another man right now. 'Ask him and see what happens.'

'Well, hello, raw nerve,' Velvet said. 'Didn't mean to trespass.'

'I'm not in the market, and I'm especially not in the market for Whit Mosley. I'm just being a realist. I know Whit. You're not his type, and you're involved in a case he's adjudicating.'

'Men are the simplest maps, honey, and no one can unfold one better than me. I just go for the thing pointing true north, and I learn all I need to know. Whit's no different.' She paused. 'He up for reelection, like Lucinda?'

'Yes.'

'I'm sure the Hubbles will be riding your ass like the Pony Express to run the investigation the way they want.'

'They don't have any influence over me,' Claudia said.

Velvet watched the rain splatter against the windshield. 'Whit defended you to me, said you were a good investigator. I just hope he's right. I'm sure in a little town sucking up to the right people makes all the difference in promotions.'

'You've suffered a really nasty shock tonight, and I'm real sorry about your friend. So I'm just going to ignore what you just said, because you don't know jackshit about me.'

'You're the one who got out the label maker, sweetie.' Velvet opened the car door and ran through the rain. Claudia, peeved, followed her.

They went inside the motel lobby and got Velvet checked in. Claudia asked, 'You're gonna be okay here alone?'

'I'd be better if there was a wet bar. I'll settle for a shower and a bed. Thanks for the ride.'

'We'll talk tomorrow,' Claudia said. 'I'll have a patrol officer bring you by some clothes and toiletries.' Let her see actual, respectable small-town nice. Maybe she would unleash a squad of church ladies on Velvet. No one could be nicer than church ladies on a mission.

'Thank you. Now go work hard and get the fucker who did this,' Velvet said. She turned off and went down the hall toward her room.

Claudia drove back to Golden Gulf Marina. The crowd had returned to their boats, although several craft showed lamps' glimmers from behind the curtains. People still awake, shocked at death's close amble, watching television or drinking decaf to lull themselves to sleep. In the gentle downpour she walked to *Real Shame*, watching the yellow crime scene ribbons flap in the breeze. She boarded and heard a low voice talking inside the cabin.

'Yeah, it's all taken care of. Not a problem.'

She opened the door and Eddie Gardner smiled, clicking off his cell phone.

'What's going on?' she asked.

'Not much, just finishing up.' He gestured to a stack of bagged items and rolls of film, neatly tagged. 'How did the statements go? You squeeze a confession?'

'Hardly. The girlfriend is sure he didn't off himself, and the young woman who found the body is sure he did. I'd like to send both to Credible Witness School.' Claudia thumbed through the stack of bagged items: bedding, individual items of clothing, including the pair of women's panties (Velvet had said forcefully that she owned no pair with violets on them), wineglass, wine bottles, the videotape that Whit had found.

'Find anything interesting?' she asked.

'Not counting the dirty movies, no. No contraband.'

She smiled. Gardner could be a toad but he wasn't a bad guy, just overimpressed with himself. Both the other single women at the police station pined to date him, although the attraction eluded Claudia. She ought to shove Velvet toward Gardner and away from a decent guy like Whit. She'd make Gardner's day.

'Delford – with all the tact of a fart in church – told me to treat this like a suicide.'

Gardner stopped piling the evidence into a case. 'It looks like one.'

'I know. But considering who this guy is, to automatically assume . . .'

'Well, Delford's a man of strong opinions, but he's solved practically every major case he's ever had. He knows police work.'

'He's old friends with Lucinda Hubble. She won't want her son's movie career brought to light, and I frankly don't blame her.'

Gardner shrugged again. 'Look, Claudia. Delford clearly has confidence in you. If he didn't trust you, you wouldn't be here.'

A sudden pang of embarrassment at having shown her doubt hit her. Gardner bent back to his work, not looking at her.

'I know. Thanks. Can I give you a hand with the evidence case?'

'Naw, I got it.' He hoisted a box to his shoulder. 'You coming?'

'In a minute. I want another look around.'

Gardner headed out the door, grunting as he carried the box. 'They've got Fox sitting out on the dock all night to watch the boat, make sure no one comes aboard.'

'Great. Thanks, Eddie,' she said.

In Pete's bedroom, Claudia carefully flicked on a light, using the edge of her hand. Black fingerprint dust marked the most obvious spots: the light switch, the door handle, the metal nightstand table, where Gardner and the deputies helping out from the sheriff's office had dusted and lifted prints. *Thank God David wasn't on duty*. She didn't want to see him up close and personal quite yet, and it would be impossible to avoid with her in the police department and him in the sheriff's office.

The body and the bedding were gone. She opened the closet door. She pulled some of the files out of the box. The minutiae of everyday life: phone bills, store receipts, credit card slips, bank records, all haphazardly clumped together. Pete wasn't rich, but he wasn't destitute. He had a balance slightly over ten thousand dollars in his Van Nuys, California, account according to his most recent statement, and he'd opened a new account last week at the Texas Coastal Bank, Port Leo branch, with an opening balance of four thousand. She jotted down the Van Nuys address; she wanted to check with the police there about both Pete and Velvet. It bothered her that he was staying on a boat with ties to a criminal family. Such affiliations did not appear overnight with a snap of the fingers.

She was searching the main cabin when Gardner came back aboard.

'Hey, Eddie, did you see a laptop computer?' she asked.

Gardner inspected a handwritten inventory pulled from his pocket. 'There was a small portable printer in the other room, but I didn't see a computer.'

'Help me look.'

Nothing turned up except some dust bunnies beneath a couch and a box of shotgun ammunition hidden in a back drawer.

'Two people have told us Pete had a laptop and now he doesn't,' Claudia said.

They searched again, behind furniture, in closets, in cabinets, for another half hour.

'I don't think it's here, Claudia.'

Claudia crossed her arms. 'So where the hell is it?'

11

Early Tuesday morning Whit awoke to his father prodding at him with a thick finger.

'Get up, little bit,' Babe Mosley rumbled, and Whit was lost in a childhood moment, his father between wives, Whit being ordered to rise before dawn and fix Daddy a coffee with bourbon. Breakfast at the Mosleys' had never been like in the cereal commercials.

Whit blinked at his father's frown. 'Shit. Did my alarm not go off?' Hopefully he was still dreaming, if he was going to suffer being referred to as 'little bit.'

'Why didn't you tell us last night?' Babe demanded. Despite his childish nickname he was a big barrel of a man, close to six-five and two hundred fifty pounds. He boasted a full head of grayish blond hair and clear blue eyes, but the cherubic face had softened like a souring cheese, moldered more by the dozen-plus years he'd spent drunk. The vodka aged him more than the weight of raising six boys and marrying four wives. Years of sobriety, combined with an addiction to various fitness programs, had restored his vitality, but no medicine had erased the drunkard's veins.

'My son's the goddamned judge – a job I got you, thank you kindly – and I have to hear that Pete Hubble is dead on the radio.'

Whit stumbled to the commode and luxuriated with a heavenly pee. Babe followed him to the doorway.

'Daddy, I can't talk about cases.' Whit flushed the toilet and started the shower.

'This is your golden opportunity, Whitman.'

Whit doffed his boxers and stepped into the hot spray. 'Say what?'

'Lucinda Hubble rules this county like Queen Bee Victoria. This story's gonna be huge. It's your chance to show the voters what you can do, boy.'

'I thought that's what I was doing for the past six months.' Whit squirted shampoo into his hand and soaped his hair.

'Yes, but this gets your name in the papers. Front page. You got to milk this, son. When you gonna do the inquest? You'll want to do a formal one, not just issue a cause of death. Make sure the Corpus paper's there. Get your photo taken a bunch, maybe at the crime scene. In your robe, and wear proper shoes for once. Issue press releases, all that.' Babe rubbed his hands together. 'That asswipe Buddy Beere must be shitting bricks with all this terrific publicity you're gonna get.'

'You get this morning's merit badge for good taste,' Whit said. 'A man is dead, you know.'

'I'm sorry for Pete and the Hubbles – you know that. What the hell was Pete doing back anyway? Where's he been?'

'Working for the CIA,' Whit answered above the roar of the shower, to give Babe a meaty morsel. 'Something about nuclear release codes in Ukraine. Perhaps we shouldn't tell Irina.'

'You're not amusing to your daddy.'

'Oddly enough, making you laugh about a death case wasn't on my to-do list today. I got breakfast at the Shell Inn with Patsy and Tim.'

Babe frowned. 'You tell Georgie to quit slinging mud all over town about poor helpless Irina.'

'News flash. You not only remarry again but you fund a competing café. Of course she's pissed at you.' Whit

68

rinsed shampoo from his head and soap from his body. Babe handed him a towel.

'Georgie'll forgive me – she always does. Women are far better at forgiving than men could ever be,' Babe said.

Whit thought of Faith Hubble and wondered if that was really true.

The Shell Inn was an establishment one might generously term a half-breed. The front of the restaurant offered serviceable meals, catering to the fishing crowd and the retirees who refused to slap down more than five bucks for a meat-and-two-vegetable plate. The back contained a funky, dark bar that boasted its own atmosphere – breezes of bourbon, mists of beer, warm fronts of tobacco smoke. For the old guard of Port Leo the Shell Inn, which had been in continuous business since 1907 except the five times it was nearly destroyed by hurricanes, was a basic requirement of life in town, up there with a newspaper and water service.

Georgie O'Connor Mosley perched by the cash register, sipping milky coffee and contemplating the *Corpus Christi Caller-Times* financial section. She had been Whit's first stepmother, his mother's oldest and dearest friend. Georgie and Babe had married more out of friendship and a mutual hope to provide six devastated boys a mother, but those reasons shriveled under the never-setting sun of reality. Georgie, relentlessly practical and blunt, and Babe, a roaring drunk still in love with an absent first wife, only lasted three stormy, legendary years. The six Mosley boys all loved Georgie without reserve. They knew the bullet she had taken for them. Babe had bought the Shell Inn for her the Christmas after their divorce, a parting gift, and Georgie kept the Mosley name to irritate him.

'Tell your daddy he should've listened to me about

69

those overseas stock funds,' Georgie said as Whit entered. 'I'm making a killing. I could buy and sell Babe's ass.'

'He's more conservative with his money,' Whit said.

'I would think anyone who imports firm young former Communist flesh into his bed would be receptive to new ideas.' Georgie kissed his cheek – she smelled of lip balm and oranges – and steered him to his corner table where Patsy Duchamp and Tim O'Leary sat.

'No coffee for Whit, Georgie, until he gives me a quote,' Patsy Duchamp said as Whit sat down. Patsy was the editor of the *Port Leo Mariner*, a biweekly paper, and like Whit she had trudged home carting an English degree from a prestigious college. Patsy's hair was as dark as a crow's feathers; she had sharp, penetrating eyes; and she rationed her smiles.

'No comment, Patsy,' Whit said as Georgie sloshed steaming coffee into Whit's cup.

'Quote, please.' Patsy's breakfast had already arrived, and she stirred a pat of butter into her grits.

'It looks like he died of a gunshot wound, but I'm not saying anything official until we get an autopsy report from Corpus.'

'I heard it looked self-inflicted,' Patsy said.

'I for sure have no comment now.'

'Then you'll call me the moment you know what the ME says, anyway. Or you better,' Patsy said. 'Pretty please.'

'When did you take a Pollyanna pill?' Pete Hubble's death might be the biggest story of the year, of the past five years, especially if it was murder, and Patsy lived for news to cover beyond city council and navigation district meetings, fishing tournaments, and high school football.

'You talk to the senator yet?' asked Tim O'Leary, the county attorney. Tim looked worn this morning.

'No. Late night?' Whit asked.

'Yeah.'

'Too much merlot or too much Graham Greene last night?' Whit asked. Tim only had two vices.

'It was an Australian cabernet, and too much Greene is impossible,' Tim said.

'You two aren't gonna start talking literature and ignore all this juicy news,' Patsy said. 'So let's talk Pete Hubble.'

'Actually, let's not,' Whit said. 'Let's talk about Corey Hubble.'

Patsy lowered her eggy fork. 'Oh, I smell me an on-going series of stories.'

'Patsy, if I farted, would it be off the record?' Whit asked.

Patsy looked stung. 'Fine, we're miles off the record.'

Whit glanced around. No one was seated close to their table, an orchestration of Georgie's. 'Tell me what you remember about Corey Hubble.'

'Annoying,' Tim said.

'A rotten little punk,' Patsy said.

'Never got over his daddy's death,' Tim agreed.

'Mad at the world,' Patsy added.

'Pissed at his own shadow,' Tim said.

'A pothead,' Patsy said. 'He hung around with dopers, you know.'

'I always thought he was gay. He hated sports.' Tim might relish his thick Tolstoys and full-bodied Syrahs, but he also worshiped football and fishing, preferences iron-cast in most male Coastal Bend genes.

'Not gay,' Patsy said. 'Corey dated my cousin Marian. In a way that should have gotten them on Jerry Springer. They beat each other up a couple of times. If memory serves, Marian told me Corey would diddle her for exactly one minute with a look of incredible gratitude on his face and then slap her around.' She lowered her voice.

71

'And I heard once he used to torture cats and Lucinda sent him to a therapist in Corpus, but that might have been political mudslinging. Cats are big with the retiree vote.'

'Do you remember anything about when Corey vanished?' Whit asked. His regular order of scrambled eggs, garlic cheese grits, bacon, and biscuits arrived, and Patsy and Tim waited until the waitress had refilled their coffee cups and retreated.

'People said he'd run away to embarrass his mother.' Tim gave a hangover frown to Whit's food. 'When he never came back, then I think everyone imagined he'd been murdered while hitchhiking or some other unpleasant end.'

Patsy nodded. 'It was common knowledge Corey resented Lucinda's career in politics. He'd already lost a father, and now here was his mother throwing herself into the most time-consuming career possible. Probably he got involved with the wrong people somewhere, South Padre or Galveston or Mexico, and ended up dead.'

Whit made a leap of faith that Patsy would stick to her word about being off the record. 'Do you remember Corey and Jabez Jones being particular friends?'

Tim faked puking. 'It annoys me no end that what Port Leo is going to be known for on television is an ex-wrestler who performs ab crunches while quoting Scripture.'

'You know, if my memory's not fading with age, Jabez was the last person to talk to Corey,' Patsy said. 'I covered it in the high school paper.'

'Could you do me a huge favor and dig up the clippings from when Corey vanished?' Whit asked.

'Nothing more you can say?' Patsy asked.

'No. Can I still have the clippings?'

'This is why God made little retired ladies bored

enough to do schlepp work at the *Mariner*. Sure, but what will you do for me?' Patsy asked.

'I'll call you as soon as I have prelim autopsy results,' Whit promised.

Patsy smiled. Like the Aztec goddesses, blood placated her.

Claudia had just finished showering after four hours of fidgety sleep when the knock came at her door. She pulled on her robe, wrapped her heavy black hair in a towel, and peered through the door's security hole.

David.

She had not seen him since he walked alongside her down the county courthouse hallway, saying quietly, *Listen, I'm sorry you did this, Claud. You know I still love you.* Her attorney had tucked a hand on her elbow and steered her away, past the flyers and the benches and the secretary puzzling over a soda choice at the Coke machine and out to the bright fall light, the morning haze burning to wisps over the bay. She had walked in married and walked out free and clear. She had gotten in her car, suddenly flustered and near weeping, and driven halfway across Port Leo toward the home they shared before she remembered she didn't live there anymore.

But she did still live in Port Leo, and both she and David were peace officers. Why not grab the inevitable by the throat and give it a good shake? She opened the door.

'Morning,' David Power said. He'd gotten his auburn hair cropped shorter than usual. He wore his Encina County deputy's uniform, and she noticed the creases were flattened. She had tended his uniform for him, since he'd burn his hand if he got within ten feet of an iron. Dark circles daubed the fleshiness beneath his eyes, and he'd missed a patch of reddish bristle on his jaw during his shave.

'Good morning. What's up?' *Keep it brief, keep it polite.*

'Just wanted to see if you were okay. I heard about the Hubble case.'

'Short on sleep, but fine.'

David shifted his beige Stetson from one hand to the other. 'You know, if y'all need help, the sheriff's department, we're glad to assist.'

'Thanks. It's under control.' She didn't say anything further, and he massaged the brim of his hat, drumming his fingertips against the band.

'Everything okay in your new place?' he asked.

'Yeah, sure.' She knew he wanted to be invited in, but she didn't want him in the little space she had staked out for her own. She drew the robe a little tighter around her front in atypical modesty.

His voice lowered. 'Jesus, Claud, I've seen your skin before. Remember Padre?'

They had honeymooned on South Padre, the mightiest and most beautiful of the long chain of Texas barrier islands, and unfortunately it had been the best time in the marriage, a week away from both their cloying families, a week away from car wrecks and burglaries and speeding tickets. David loved to invoke Padre, as if teeth-chilling margaritas, orange-bright sunsets, and spine-rattling sex could serve as the basis for the rest of their lives.

'David . . .'

His blue eyes narrowed and his fleshy mouth thinned. 'You're alone, right?'

'I told you there's no one.'

'Right. I never hit you. Took wonderful care of you. Never cheated on you. You just don't love me anymore. Same old, same old.'

'Are you coming to check up on me, spy on me, or belittle me?' She kept her voice neutral.

74

David Power's jaw worked. 'Check on you. Sorry. I crossed a line. It still hurts. It's gonna hurt for . . . an indeterminate period of time. I don't want to hurt you back, Claudia.'

'I'm sorry for your hurt. I am. But we've had this discussion a hundred times before, and there's no point in rehashing.'

Her phone rang and she said, 'Look, I've got to get going . . .' and he said, 'I need to ask you about something else . . .' so she shrugged and said, 'Wait a sec . . .' and hurried to the telephone.

'Hello?'

'Claudia Salazar?' A throaty woman's voice but brisk as a Marine.

'Yes, who's callling?'

'Hold please,' ordered Captain Brisk. Instead of Muzak there was a recorded, sleek baritone, with soft strains of 'America the Beautiful' playing in the background. The voice intoned: 'Proven leadership for the Texas Coastal Bend . . . Senator Lucinda Hubble. Democrat. Moderate. Protecting our children. Protecting our elderly. Protecting our precious coastal ecology and protecting our health care while protecting our economy.' Lots of protection. Claudia wondered if the faithful automatically wore condoms during rallies. 'A former nurse, Senator Hubble especially understands the needs and concerns of our retiree population. Vote November seventh to reelect Senator Lucinda Hub—'

The verbal pabulum broke off. 'Ms Salazar?' Not Miss Brisk, but instead a confident, bright voice.

'Yes, this is Detective Salazar.' Claudia had a sudden feeling she was going to need the title. She turned and saw David had stepped inside the apartment, shutting the door behind him, and he blanched as she used her maiden name. She had been Claudia Power for the twenty-two months of the marriage, but no more, and David in particular seemed to take her revived surname as a hard slap.

The voice on the phone honeyed slightly. 'Detective. Good morning. This is Faith Hubble. I'm Senator Hubble's chief of staff.'

'I'm sorry about your ex-husband, Ms Hubble.'

'Thank you. It's a terrible tragedy. My mother-in-law and my son are having a difficult time with Pete's death.'

And you're not? Claudia wondered. 'That's understandable.'

'I'd like to meet with you and find out where we are in the investigation.'

We, Claudia noticed, as though Faith Hubble were busily lifting prints and completing paperwork into the wee hours. 'We've collected a certain amount of evidence, but we don't as yet have autopsy results. I would like to talk with you and your family as soon as possible.'

'Talking with Lucinda – is that absolutely necessary? She's absolutely grief-stricken. And we already gave our statements to Delford Spires.'

'Yes, ma'am, and I'm sure this is a difficult time for you all but, yes, I do need to speak with her, as will Judge Mosley.'

'Perhaps you and I could meet first. To discuss how to deal with the media.'

Claudia watched David inspecting her bare apartment, his face emotionless. 'We already have policies in place, ma'am.'

'Yes, I'm sure you do, but this is far more high-profile than a drunken tourist drowning, and there's already been serious news leaks,' Faith said. 'Let's meet in an hour, shall we, at your office?'

'Fine.' Let them meet to discuss the press, but Claudia

76

would seize the opportunity for a frank discussion with the dead man's former wife.

'See you in an hour.' Faith Hubble hung up.

Claudia clicked off the phone. David stood at the apartment's large window, looking at the parking lot. 'You should have gotten a bay view, Claudia.'

'I've seen the bay every day of my life,' she said. She didn't want to mention she couldn't afford a bay view on her single-woman salary. 'Thanks for stopping by, but duty calls.'

'Speaking of duty . . . Poppy's birthday is this coming weekend, and I was hoping you could go to his party with me.' Poppy was David's grandfather, Patrick Power, closing in on ninety, now relegated to the care of a Port Leo nursing home but still the patriarch of the old-coast Irish clan. 'If you're not there, Poppy will wonder why.'

'Oh, David, that's not a good idea.'

'Um, well' – he gave her a half-apologetic smile – 'Poppy doesn't know about the divorce, Claud. He doesn't believe in divorce and we haven't wanted to upset him. His heart's weak, you know.'

Claudia believed Poppy's heart could serve as a rich source of granite. 'Tell him, David. I'm not going to play along in a charade.'

'Thanks a bunch, Claudia. Jesus. One favor. You know how Poppy loves you.'

'Yes, he's never missed a chance to pat my fanny.'

'You want to hurt me, fine, whatever. Just don't hurt my family.'

'I don't want to hurt anybody! I just want to have my own life!' Now she was yelling, doing exactly what she had promised herself not to do.

'This life is what you want?' David gestured at the drab apartment. She had hardly unpacked any belongings in the month she had been here. A few Salazar family

77

pictures stood on a dusty coffee table, dishes stacked in the sink, a futon unfolded in the den and sloppy with sheets. She'd let David keep most of the furniture just to spare herself the whining. 'You don't seem to be relishing your singleness.'

'I'm busy with work,' she said. 'Aren't you?' Anything to change the topic.

'Yeah. I'm working this missing-person case. Girl from Louisiana they think ended up here.'

'Marcy Ballew? You got that one?'

'Yeah.'

'I briefly met the girl's mother when she stopped by the station,' Claudia said. 'Terrible, not knowing what happened.'

David, that master of the wounded glance and gesture, took full advantage. 'Yeah. Not knowing what went wrong. I know exactly how the lady feels.'

12

Six berths down from *Real Shame*, where Pete Hubble breathed his last, was a fifty-three-foot workhorse Hatteras sports fishing boat christened *Don't Ask*. This was a craft used to take serious fishermen out into the deeper bowl of the Gulf, where the marlin and shark (hopefully) provided thrills at an exorbitant hourly rate. *Don't Ask* belonged to an oddball friend of Whit's, a man known to most people simply as Gooch. Gooch did not socialize overmuch. He was unfailingly polite and ethical in his dealings with other guides, the marina, and his clients, and admired for making small loans to guides who frequently needed a cash boost at the end of the month. Most of Port Leo was happy to give him his privacy, because Gooch was ugly and big and had a hard, no-tolerance light in his glare that explained his boat's name. Whit had only found him to be generous, loyal, and slightly east of sane.

For twenty minutes Whit had been mired in quicksand conversation with the marina manager, who could tell him nothing new about Pete and Velvet. The manager, who smelled slightly of soured baby formula and had an unnoticed glob of infant burp on his shoulder, explained that *Real Shame* had begun docking at Golden Gulf only five weeks ago and its bills were paid by check mailed from a company in Houston, TDD Holdings. The arrangement had been handled by an elderly man in a wheelchair who apparently worked for TDD, name of Anson Todd, and the manager had not seen Mr Todd again since the *Shame* docked. As for Pete and Velvet, they had not mingled much with the other marina residents, nor had they caused any trouble. Whit left the office, spotted Gooch on his boat, and headed down the T-head.

'An honest man would be at work by now,' Whit said as he came aboard.

'I chose to use this day for reflection and self-improvement.' Gooch grinned, showing slightly uneven teeth. 'I gave myself the day off. I figured you'd be back down here soon enough. You still holding the cops' dicks for them so they can pee straight?'

Kindness demanded one say Gooch was simply not handsome. His face was too gaunt for his body and married a too-prominent, bumpy nose with small, muddy brown eyes. He kept his sun-streaked hair cut short in a military burr. But he was powerfully built, stone-carved arms and legs, the kind of physique that encouraged burly bar patrons to keep observations about Gooch's unfortunate face private.

'Coffee, Y'Honor?' Gooch asked.

'Please, with milk and sugar.'

Gooch pointed toward the galley.

'You're the embodiment of the service economy, Gooch.' Whit fixed his own cup and went back up to the deck, where Gooch gobbled his way through a leviathan bowl of Cap'n Crunch.

'You want some?' he asked through a milk-dripping mouth.

'No, thanks.'

'Screw your stepmom yet?'

'My father and Irina are very happy, thanks for asking.'

'And you're very miserable,' Gooch said.

'You've got to make some more room on this wall for your diplomacy awards,' Whit said. 'I didn't see you docked here last night when duty called.'

'I spent the evening over in Port Aransas playing poker. I didn't sail home until this morning.'

'Were the gossips awake?' No hen yard could compare to marina liveaboards for rapid-fire rumormongering.

'All I've heard is that the guy on *Real Shame* shot himself in the mouth. Now it'd be a real shame indeed if that hot little number living with him on the boat really did it and got herself sent to girly prison, where she could never experience the joys of Gooch.'

'You've met Velvet?'

'Her name is Velvet?'

'Velvet Mojo.'

'Stripper or actress?'

'An adult-film director.'

Gooch set down his cereal bowl. 'No, we haven't met. Cute but rough. Like a mare that's been rode hard and put up wet, like my dad used to say.'

'Who would know about them here?'

Gooch shrugged. 'They kept to themselves. Not much for fishing and not much for boating. I saw them docking once. They needed about five people to help them dock properly.' He considered. 'Probably they talked with Ernesto.' Gooch went to his radio and spoke briefly. He left the radio on to hear the chatter of the working fishermen and guides across St Leo Bay and beyond. Whit could hear three or four male voices, joking, chattering, one complaining about a dearth of redfish, someone asking that a poker game be rescheduled for tomorrow, someone else hailing Captain Bill. 'Ernesto's the marina handyman. He sees the cops coming, he hides, so I bet no authority figure has taken a statement. He'll be down in a second. So spill details.'

Whit told Gooch, who he would trust with the launch keys for America's nuclear arsenal, what he knew thus far about Pete Hubble.

81

Gooch laughed. 'Lucinda Hubble walks around town like she's got a coal lump up her ass and none of us are good enough to sniff the diamond. Her boy's off making fuck films. I love it.'

'You've got to quit being overly sympathetic to people, Gooch.'

'I wonder if this Velvet was planning to ply her trade here.'

'Please don't tell me you want to audition.'

Gooch tapped his unshaven chin. 'It's an interesting moral dilemma. Most men pretend to have fantasies straight out of a porn movie, but how many would actually walk the walk and show their worth in front of rolling cameras?'

'Not me. I'm too shy.'

Gooch watched Ernesto Gomez hurry down the T-head. 'I, on the other hand, have a decided lack of inhibitions. I would be a natural, strutting among the starlets. But I wouldn't do a porn film either.'

'Why not?'

'Anytime you see a blue movie, remember this: those women were once somebody's baby girls. Do you think a single one of them thought in kindergarten: Gosh, when I grow up, please, God, please let me be smart and talented enough to be a porn star? No way. They're Barbie dolls who got bent along the way.'

Whit sipped his coffee. 'Pete Hubble was a kid once, too.'

'So he had some deep-seated shortcoming, and he was proving he was a so-called real man. Or maybe he wanted to piss off Mommy. Or maybe he wanted to just lose himself and forget some nasty shit. This concludes our Psych 101 lecture.' Gooch shrugged. 'I feel as sorry for him as I do for the women.'

'Even though he got to sleep with more women than you or I ever will? Combined?'

'So he screwed hundreds of women. You think he got to *sleep* with them? No, Whit. No real kissing, holding, enjoying each woman for her unique sparkle in her eyes, the taste of her skin, the shape of her lips when you bring her pleasure. No. It was assembly-line sex. No, thanks.'

Gooch stood and invited Ernesto Gomez in rapid-fire Spanish to come aboard. Ernesto was in his fifties, with a moon-wide face centered by a nervous smile. His left eye wandered slightly, and he kept that side of his face turned a bare angle away. In Spanish, Gooch offered him coffee and asked if they could converse in English as Whit's Spanish was execrable. Ernesto nodded and kept his tight grin locked in place.

'Judge Mosley grew up with the man who died,' Gooch added.

Ernesto frowned in sympathy. 'Very sad, yes.'

'Did you notice many visitors to his boat?' Whit asked.

Ernesto glanced at Gooch, who murmured in Spanish and nodded reassuringly.

'Pete had a few visits. A rich-looking lady. A teenage boy. The dirtbag.'

The rich-looking lady was probably either Lucinda or Faith. The boy was no doubt Pete's son Sam. 'The dirtbag?' Whit asked.

Ernesto's face wrinkled in distaste. '*Sí.* Bossy, no respect, young, too good for everyone else. Has Porsche but keep it dirty, don't take care of it.'

'You know this guy's name?' Gooch asked.

Ernesto shook his head. 'Sorry, Gooch. He come here once, twice a week, over the past month or so. Take the boat out for all the day, come back at night. Fishing I suppose. One time they argue, I'm fixing rot two boats down, I hear them. Laughing, yelling. Much drinking.'

'What did they argue about?'

Ernesto murmured to Gooch in a low torrent of

83

Spanish. Gooch patted him on the knee. Ernesto glanced back at Whit.

'Money,' the old man said. 'Money to be paid to Pete.'

'This man owed Pete money?'

Ernesto considered and scratched his lip. 'I think that how it was.'

'Yet you said they were partying together.'

'Not yesterday, not after arguing.'

'Can you tell me what they said?' Whit asked.

Ernesto grimaced. 'They talk too fast for my English. But dirtbag all red in the face. I hear them yelling, I come over to the boat, want to be sure all is okay. I see through the windows. Dirtbag took swing at Pete, but Pete, he strong and big. Dirtbag just heavy, has hands of man who never works. Pete pushed him down. Dirtbag left, very angry.'

Ernesto, pressed, gave a more detailed description of Dirtbag: heavyset, around five-ten, blondish, late twenties or early thirties, thinning hair, bright clothing, always loud.

'The teenage boy you saw – do you know a young man named Sam Hubble?'

'No. I saw the boy once, yesterday at lunch. I guess skipping school.'

'Any others you can remember?'

'Yeah, short guy last week. Handed me a piece of paper on his way to Pete's boat, blue and red and white, talked plenty. Smelled like mints, too much mints, you know?'

'That sounds like your esteemed opponent Buddy Beere,' Gooch said. 'Isn't he an unrepentant Altoid sucker?'

'This paper, what did it say?' Whit asked.

Ernesto waved hands. 'Wanting folks to vote. You see all those signs around now.'

'Campaign flyers from Buddy,' Gooch said. 'That savvy bastard, courting the illegal immigrant vote.'

'Did you hear anything last night?' Whit asked.

'No, nothing until the cops came. I was asleep.'

'You ever see any young women coming around to his boat?' Whit asked.

Ernesto nodded. 'Yeah, I forgot, with that preacher. The one on TV with the big muscles. He brought lady with him. But she big and scary, big muscles, like a man with titties.' Ernesto glanced back toward the marina office. 'Mike be mad I not working.'

'Don't worry about Mike,' Whit said. 'Have the police talked to you about this?'

Ernesto appeared stricken. 'No, please, mister, no *policia*. I don't know nothing about nothing.'

'It's okay. Don't worry,' Whit soothed. 'One other question. The woman named Velvet. You see her around much?'

Ernesto smiled. 'Velvet. Yes. She bakes good chocolate cookies. Every few days give some to me.'

Velvet baking cookies. Whit tried to summon the image and pictured a hausfrau in a leather apron and stiletto heels.

'You ever see her bake an éclair?' Gooch asked with a leer. Ernesto looked confused, so Whit asked: 'Did she and Pete get along okay?'

'Sure, yeah.'

'She mess around with any of the guys around the marina?' Gooch asked.

'No. She nice.' Ernesto put the bright smile back on. End of commentary.

'*Gracias*. I appreciate it, Ernesto.' Whit shook his hand. Ernesto hurried back toward the marina office.

'I'm guessing the rich lady was Lucinda,' Gooch said. 'Unless there's a bored matron around here in need of sexual servicing. Your stepmother, for instance.'

'Funny, with a hint of vicious.'

'You could outdo Pete Hubble on the annoying-your-relatives scale if you do your Oedipus impersonation, Whitman.'

'Jesus, Gooch, you're a crank. I'm finding a place to live right after the campaign . . .'

'Ah, yes. The campaign. Waging a fierce one, aren't you? I particularly enjoyed your interview on *Face the Nation*.'

'Are you done?'

'Whit, please campaign today. The thought of Buddy Beere at the bench makes me want to move to a judicially sound country. Like Cuba.'

Whit's cell phone buzzed. 'Hello?'

'Whit? It's Faith.' She sounded crisper this morning, less frayed with shock.

'How are you?'

'We're holding up. Lucinda finally slept last night; Sam slept with me. To just get his dad back and then . . . it's a hard thing for a kid.'

'I need to talk to y'all. For the inquest.'

'Would this afternoon work for you?'

'Yeah. How about four?'

'Fine.' Her voice lowered. 'I wish I could see you . . . just us. I could use a hug. Or something stronger.'

He didn't flirt back, watching a gull alight on the bow of *Real Shame*. 'How's Sam handling this?'

'My son is a tightly controlled mass of nerves. He's upset but he doesn't want to show that he is. His father did matter to him, even a lousy SOB like Pete.' Her tone turned bitter. 'A father always would.'

'What can I do to help?'

He meant to help Sam, but Faith took the inches and made them miles. 'Please just . . . hurry us through all this legal rigmarole. Don't drag it out with a public inquest hearing. Help me protect Lucinda and Sam from what is sure to be unpleasantness, Whit. You'll do that for me, won't you?' Her tone, usually cool, even in wriggles of heat, took on a slightly cajoling tone.

'I'll do what I can.'

The quiet stretched. But she finally said, 'I appreciate it. I'll see you at the house later.'

Whit clicked off his phone. Gooch studied a tidal chart and yawned.

'I must have a gift certificate for unwanted advice. Do this, do that. Rule it's suicide. Don't hold a formal inquest.'

Gooch raised a crooked brown eyebrow. 'Rule how you please, Judge, and screw 'em if they can't take a joke.'

13

Velvet came awake suddenly, in the bright haze from the motel windows. She rubbed her eyes and thought: *So now starts the rest of your life, babe. What are you going to do?*

Sleep remained impossible after that priss-assed cop dropped her off at the motel. She lay awake, listening to the hum of the air conditioner as it chilled the room, and the gentle bump of her heart as she hugged a goose-feather pillow close to her body.

Pete dead. And only yesterday he'd said to her: *I'm not gonna do another flick with you until all this with my brother is settled, understand? You can help me or you can fly your ass back to California, but I'm not leaving now.*

She'd pouted, furious. *Well, if you loved me you would.*

He'd set his lips tight and turned away from her. *I guess I don't love you, then, Velvet.*

And now, even though she was sure Pete hadn't meant it – the words could not be undone, loved away, erased, made into meaningless wisps.

Velvet thought about Lucinda Hubble and Faith Hubble, and a hot cinder formed in her heart. Hatred was too polite a word for what she felt. She thought of young Sam Hubble and her throat tightened, for Sam and Pete and what could never be. If God were merciful, Pete strutted in heaven now, and her own mother might be meeting him at the pearly gates, smiling at him with all the love she'd once lavished on Velvet, taking him by the hand, introducing him to the other souls flitting from cloud to cloud.

That image made her cry. *Like you believe in that shit anymore, girl.* Pete was probably frying in hell and scooting over in the bubbling oil to make room for her.

The cry did her good. Velvet dried her tears on the pillowcase. Enough weepiness, it was time for action. She needed a Plan B. The Hubbles clearly wielded influence here. The local powers-that-be, she suspected, would treat her as Pete's embarrassing girlfriend if it was suicide and a possible suspect if it was murder.

And she had zero intention of sitting like a lump and letting her ass be moved around the political chessboard.

She decided Claudia Salazar would be useless, but Whit Mosley wouldn't. She reviewed the mental picture she'd formed of him: nicely tall, trim, full blondish hair, tan but not from idling on a beach, face a little too boyish for his years, kindness in the smile. Smart but not snotty, a beach bum grown up, perhaps only recently. Average teeth, firm legs and butt, terrific hands – the checklist of how she typically evaluated the rookie male talent for her movies on initial meeting, before the pants dropped. She liked a man with strong hands. The hands were seen more in the movies than you would think – cupping breasts, running fingers through hair, holding faces for a kiss. And Whit might be putty to a woman with her talent and charms and persuasive skills.

At nine in the morning she called her production company's lawyers in Van Nuys and a few friends, ignoring the time difference between the Texas coast and California, breaking the sad news about Pete. She left a voice mail for the lawyers to find her some legal representation in Corpus Christi, a big-city attorney hardened enough to deal with pissing-mad senators and provincial police.

Then she took a bath, relaxing herself in the soapy hot water, and only when a stray thought crossed her mind did she sit upright in a panic.

What if whoever killed Pete thought she knew what Pete knew?

She didn't. He'd kept his research about Corey tight to his chest, just telling her all was going well. He had discussed none of the screenplay with her.

The killer might not believe that. She dried off, combed her hair, and sat naked as she leafed through the Coastal Bend yellow pages, researching pawnshops and gun dealers.

The images played across the television, the screen the only light in the cabin, and the Blade sat and watched as Big Pete Majors took Velvet Mojo from behind, both of them grunting like animals, she tilting her head to keep her wraparound sunglasses on during the pounding encounter. They moaned so much it sounded like they had intestinal disorders. Pete did not offer a range of theatrical nuance. He just knelt behind her, ramming with his hips while Velvet pleaded with him to go stronger and faster, more like a testy coach than a lover. Pete's face was as blank as the boys the Blade remembered from the mental home. He watched the tape twice before he finally fell asleep in his recliner.

He awoke in a sour mood because he had dreamed not of Velvet but of Whit Mosley, laughing at him. *You? She's gonna pick you over me? What reality does that happen in, fat ass?* The Blade had watched Whit in public and women smiled at him, whereas women suddenly recalled other appointments and hurried on their way when the Blade tried long conversations. Hating Whit was easy. The Blade imagined Whit dead, hollowed out, and himself stepping into Whit's skin, pulling the pallid skullless face over his own like a mask, fitting his fingers into Whit's fingers like gory gloves.

Why not kill Mosley as well as take Velvet? He considered. Dismemberment held a certain appeal, as did evisceration, although they certainly cut short the fun. He considered decapitation overrated; heads seemed mocking without bodies attached. The Blade had learned that truth the hard way.

He'd never wanted to kill a man particularly before, but it promised an interesting difference – like fries after a solid week of potato chips. He daydreamed about Whit dying from a slow, careful series of cuts, and a slow whisper filtered into his ears. He stared at the ceiling and its whirring fan. The fan, spinning, resembled a dark eye. Mama's eyes. He stared, barely breathing, only hearing Mama's voice telling him what he must do.

He awoke and knew he had slipped to that inky world that Mama had shaped. She used to say, with her sure smile, right before she warmed the wrench on the stove or clicked the clothespin shut on his little flick of a penis: *We're together forever, honeybunch, and don't you ever forget it.*

Thank God, he would think, that he had managed to become the hero of his own story. Mama had not won. He had. He would still.

His phone rang; he picked up and chatted through morning niceties, then listened.

'This young woman who found Pete's body,' the familiar voice murmured into his ear. 'Do me a favor. Give her some money. Get her out of town.'

'Sure,' said the Blade. 'I can do that for you.'

'Santa Fe is lovely this time of year, and I bet there's a nice, affordable youth hostel. Or perhaps Florida, if she's still set on a beach.' He listened to detailed instructions and hung up the phone.

His thumb began to itch for the keen sharpness of his knife. If Heather Farrell needed to leave town . . . well, many were the avenues. A hefty bribe paled compared to other options. He'd gotten away with this every time. (Well, except that one time, so very long ago.) Why not again? He was already in the mood.

He considered how best to approach the problem and how to avoid any messy ramifications. A lure, simple, would do. Nothing could interfere, after all, with his plan for Velvet. He ducked under the sagging bed he slept on and reached for his bowie knife. It was lovely, stout, and sharp enough to cut hopes and dreams. He rummaged in a box with MAMA'S STUFF written on the side in thick Magic Marker and found a worn sharpening stone. The Blade dragged the knife back and forth across the stone, a rhythmic caress that whispered: *Heath-er, Heath-er, Heath-er.*

The Blade flicked on his stereo. The Beach Boys sang in perfect harmony about their 409, and the knife moved to the beat.

14

Claudia wrote a terse report on the investigation's status and left it on Delford's empty desk. She grabbed a cup of thin coffee from the kitchen. When she got back to her desk, the dispatcher was buzzing her. She had a visitor in the lobby, Faith Hubble.

'I get the feeling,' the dispatcher whispered, 'she don't like waiting.'

The lobby was barely ten feet by ten feet, cramped with a chair, a side table of old magazines, and a rack of flyers on safety and community policing. The woman sat in the chair, pulling a loose string from the tattered upholstery and snapping it with her fingernail.

'Mrs Hubble? I'm Claudia Salazar.'

Faith stood and offered a hand. They shook hands quickly, and Faith followed Claudia back to her office.

From their phone conversation, Claudia had pictured a different woman. She'd imagined one of those no-nonsense Austin politicos, health-club firm and sorority-girl petite, blond-helmet hair, with a crisp suit and jump-when-I-say demeanor. Faith Hubble was a big-boned woman, approaching six feet tall, generously chested and thighed, with a creamy complexion and thick brown hair arranged in a hurried French braid. Pretty but loosely put together. Her Italian suit was tailored, black with a white silk blouse, but the jacket was already rumpled and a smear of jam soiled the cuff. Claudia imagined Faith more at home on a honky-tonk bar stool than a campaign trail.

'Have a seat, Mrs Hubble.'

'Thanks for seeing me on such short notice, hon. I

assume we're both pressed for time, so I won't dilly-dally with you – what's the status of the investigation?' Faith kept her eyes – bright hazel beauties – firmly fixed on Claudia's face, like a drill sergeant surveying a sweating recruit.

'Mostly we're waiting for lab reports.' Claudia was uneasy with the idea of snapping to and giving this woman a complete rundown, but she suspected Delford would provide the Hubbles all the information. There was little point in being evasive.

'And when will the lab geeks deliver?'

'Tomorrow. Or the next day.'

'Any way to rush them?' Faith asked. 'Obviously the family wants to know what happened as soon as possible.' Her voice was low and throaty, as though corroded by cigarettes or whiskey.

'Science can't be rushed. Certain tests take a certain amount of time.' Claudia paused. 'I'm sure you and the senator wouldn't want the tests to be inaccurate.'

'Honey, I'm dealing with a devastated mother and a heartbroken son. They need some sort of closure.'

No grief of your own? Claudia thought. Faith Hubble carried herself more like a woman inconvenienced than bereaved. *How would you feel now if David died, though?* A sense of loss would be inescapable. David had not been a bad husband, just not the right one for her. Their life had not been all misery. She hoped her heart would be big enough to mourn his passing.

Faith straightened her sleeve, noticed the jam, and muttered in anger. Her fingernails were painted cranberry red, and she clicked them together impatiently.

'I'm also dealing with a press corps with a decided lack of scandal or news in this campaign, and they're gonna be on Pete's death like dogs on ribs. They got deadlines and imaginations, hon, and they're gonna write. I'd like to be sure your department doesn't feed them newsy tidbits that are inappropriate.'

'We've told the press nothing but the bare essentials. That a man was found dead on a boat at the marina and we're investigating.'

'Pete's death was all over the radio this morning, Detective. They knew his name, that he was Lucinda's son.'

'I'm sure the press spoke to people at the marina. People could see which boat we swarmed over, I guess they knew his name. I'm afraid we can't stifle the public. Or Pete's friend Velvet.'

Faith rubbed her forehead. 'Do you know what it's like to have your life be tabloid fodder? It's like showering in a glass bathroom.' She shook her head. 'I know . . . that y'all know what Pete did for a living. Delford told us. And I can't let Aaron Crawford use this to defeat Lucinda. He could use Pete's suicide as an unfair disparagement on Lucinda's abilities as a mother.'

He was your husband. Father of your child. Do you even care one bit about him? Claudia wondered. 'Such a tactic might backfire. Voters might see it as a rotten attempt to gain from Mrs Hubble's personal loss.'

'Never overestimate the voters,' Faith said.

'No confidential information will leak from this department. I'll be sure all press inquiries are routed to me or Delford.'

'I'm thinking of my son. Not the political damage to Lucinda,' Faith said. 'Sam . . . doesn't know. You understand.'

'Sure.'

'And I would like to review any announcements that your department makes on the investigation.'

Claudia stiffened. 'That's not going to be possible.'

Faith set her chin in her palm and kept her tone

relaxed. 'Let me clarify, hon. I said review. Not approve or edit or block. If you're going to release damaging information about Pete, I'd like the opportunity to prepare a statement on the senator's behalf. Surely that's reasonable.'

Claudia suddenly felt dumb in the face of this woman's impenetrable confidence. 'We'll try not to blindside you.'

'Thank you, Detective. I sure do appreciate it.' Faith stood to go.

'I need you to answer a few questions first,' Claudia said pleasantly.

'Delford took our statements. Surely you've taken the time to review them.'

'It's best if I can hear it from you. Please.' Claudia gestured at the chair. Faith sat, folding her small Italian purse in her lap. It too was black. *All the trappings of widowhood without the teary inconvenience of grief.*

'Were you in regular contact with him?' Claudia asked.

'Not until he returned to Port Leo. Before that – perhaps a couple of times a year. Sam's birthday, if he remembered, and at Christmas. I imagine Christmas is his slow season.'

'With so little contact, you can't make a reasonable judgment as to whether he was suicidal, I suppose,' Claudia ventured. Faith had already mentioned suicide twice, as though it were a given.

Faith frowned. 'I think someone in porn has serious self-esteem issues. Don't you?'

'Perhaps. He didn't send you child support?'

Nails clicked. 'Why is that relevant, pray tell?'

'I'm trying to determine if his son was part of the reason to come home.'

'Making me and his mama squirm was the reason. We occupied seats of honor on his shit list, Detective. When Pete announced his intention to leave me and our infant

96

son and go to California for this folly of being in movies, I knew he'd fail. He had lofty goals but no real talent and the self-discipline of a drug addict. When I found out he'd ended up doing . . . adult films, I wanted to be sure he could never hurt Sam. Or Lucinda.' She rubbed her tired eyes. 'I'll give him a smidge of credit that he did send support for Sam every now and then, but he sent it to his mother. She would then turn the money over to me. I in turn would donate it to charity. Starving children in Ethiopia, monsoon relief in Bangladesh. Always a good cause far removed from us.'

'Why give away the money if it was intended for your son?'

'That money was earned on Pete's back. Or other body parts,' she said dismissively. 'I didn't want Pete's smut translating into food in my son's stomach.'

'When was the last time you spoke to Pete?'

Faith shifted in her seat. 'Yesterday morning. He phoned the house, wanting to talk to Sam.'

'How did he seem?'

'Depressed. Unhappy. If you had ended up like him – utterly failed, utterly cheapened – wouldn't you be depressed? He'd seen the lives that Sam and I have built. Sam and I have a good life. I think Pete regretted the choices he'd made. If our lives are the candy store, he definitely had his face pressed against the glass.'

'Do you know if he'd sought professional help?'

'Pete on a shrink's couch? Never. He thought couches were good for one thing and one thing only.'

'You didn't like the way he made his money or lived his life, but you didn't object to him seeing your son?'

Faith tented her fingers beneath her chin. Her hands were like ivory. 'No, I didn't like it. But Sam's like the rest of the Hubbles, he has a mind of his own. He wanted to see his father when his father came back, so I permitted

97

limited visits. Better that than Sam sneaking around to see Pete.'

'How would you characterize their relationship?'

'Relationship my ass.' Real anger tinged her voice. 'Sam spent most of his childhood wondering what was so wrong with him that his father shunned him – as though the child were the damaged goods, not the man. But when he got to know his father, Sam finally realized Pete counts as little more than a sperm donor.'

'You mentioned Pete was depressed when he called you. Can you be more specific?'

Faith fingered a wrinkle in her tailored slacks. 'He asked if he could speak to Sam. I told him Sam had already left for school. He begged me to let Sam know he'd called and I agreed. We said good-bye and hung up. That was the last time I spoke to him.'

'Do you know if Sam returned his father's call?'

'I gave him the message, but Sam didn't seem particularly interested in phoning his father back.'

'Let me get this straight, ma'am. He didn't mention to you, after y'all found out Pete was dead, whether or not he'd talked to his father that day?'

Faith shifted in her seat again. 'Sam probably talked to him, yes. I don't remember. It was a very long, upsetting evening.'

'How badly will it hurt his mother's campaign if voters learn Pete was a porn star?' Claudia asked.

Her throat worked. 'I have no idea.'

'Surely when he showed up, you had to calculate what the possible damage might be.'

'Lucinda has been an outstanding senator for the past sixteen years. She's easily won reelection and her approval ratings are high. There's no reason to think she wouldn't have the voters' support.'

'You sound like a press release given breath,' Claudia

said, and Faith stiffened. 'No one in her office was eager to advertise about Pete, were you?'

'I have no intention of being harangued by you.'

Claudia suspected the damage, from Faith and Lucinda's viewpoint, would be considered catastrophic. Nuclear. Career-ending.

'Do you know if he kept a gun?' Claudia asked.

'I have no idea.'

'Do you know if he was having financial problems of any sort?'

'No.'

'Do you know if he was involved with drugs, anything illicit?'

Faith's mouth tightened, as though a stench had drifted into the cramped room. 'If I'd suspected for a moment he was a drug user, I wouldn't let Sam within a mile of him.'

'Do you know if he was still involved in porn?'

'He told me he wanted to leave that business.' Faith rubbed her lip. Perhaps it was more politic, Claudia considered, for Faith to paint Pete as on the road to reforming. A bad guy who'd come home to Senator Mommy and seen the error of his ways before his unfortunate demise. 'If there is anything suspicious about Pete's death – if it's not suicide – then I suggest you take a long, hard look at that Velvet woman. She's entirely unstable.'

'How so?'

'How mentally stable could she be, sleeping with hundreds of men? It would warp a soul. Warp a heart.'

'Do you know she's done that? I thought she directed, not acted.'

'As if that matters.' Faith dismissed the difference with a flutter of fingers. 'You're a woman who works in a male-dominated profession, right, Detective?'

'Yes.'

'So do I. And a woman like Velvet is a traitor to all women. We fight and bust our butts to be considered equals, and she traps women as carnal playthings. Made-up dolls that exist only to pleasure men.' Faith leaned closer. 'She was obsessed with Pete. She didn't want him to come back to Texas, but she followed him. Pete might have been making the best effort to shed that world, and here she is, blocking his every move.' She leaned back. 'I think Pete probably killed himself. But if your tests argue otherwise, I think she killed him.'

'Funny. She says the same thing about you. At least that's what she told Judge Mosley.'

Faith's smile tensed, then relaxed. 'Thanks for letting me know, Detective. I'll sue the bitch for slander.'

Claudia had waited to see if Faith would broach the subject of custody. 'Speaking of legal proceedings . . . I understand Pete was considering fighting for custody of Sam.'

Faith blinked, then laughed. 'Surely you jest. He wouldn't have a prayer in family court.'

'He never mentioned a desire for custody of Sam?'

'No. Never. Not once. Who says so?'

'Velvet.'

'Consider the rather polluted source.'

Claudia shifted focus. 'Do you know anyone named Deloache?'

'No.'

'Did Pete ever talk about his brother Corey to you?'

A surprised blink. 'Corey? God, no. He's a forbidden subject.'

'With Pete? Or with the senator?'

'With Pete. It was too painful for him. They were real close.'

'He didn't tell you he was making a film about Corey?'

'No. He didn't – but Judge Mosley told me last night.

Pete never mentioned a movie to any of us. You can imagine how awful it would be for the senator, ripping open terrible old wounds.' She raised her palms up in mock surrender. 'Another perfect example of how unthinking Pete could be.'

'Pete had a laptop computer that's missing. Do you know where this laptop or a copy of his notes or script might be?'

'Good God, no,' Faith said. Claudia saw the faintest tremble of the woman's bottom lip. 'I assume . . . on the boat.'

'Did you ever visit him on the boat?'

'Yes. Once, when I went there with Sam. I wanted to be sure Pete was creating a suitable environment for visits. That whore Velvet wasn't around. That helped.'

'If you were on the boat, then I'll need to get your prints,' Claudia said sweetly. 'We want to identify everyone who's been aboard and see if there are prints not accounted for.'

'You must be joking.'

'I'm not. It's painless.'

Claudia took Faith's prints herself there in her office, quickly and efficiently. Faith spoke not a word during the procedure and wiped her hands clean with a cloth Claudia handed her.

'Senator Hubble and I will cooperate in every way,' Faith said. 'I just hope you'll cooperate as well and remember that the senator's done a great deal for this region.' She dropped the cloth back on Claudia's desk. 'Your family's been in Port Leo for many years, haven't they?' Her voice, asking, was shiny as a knife.

'Yeah.'

'Your dad's a shrimper?' Asking when it sounded like she already knew.

'Yeah.'

'That's a very honorable profession.' She gave Claudia a half smile, shaped like the cruel crescent Claudia remembered from high school: the popular girl grinning, closing in for the kill on some mouse of a geek. 'He ever have trouble holding on to his shrimping license?'

'No. Never. Not a bit of trouble.'

'That's good. You know, licenses are much harder to come by these days. The senator's trying to make sure we get the right balance between preventing overharvesting of the bays and protecting our economic interests.' Faith wadded up the ink-smeared cloth. 'I suppose some shrimpers will lose their livelihoods because their licenses will get bought out by the state. Or won't be available at all.'

Claudia said nothing.

'I certainly appreciate the information you gave me.' Faith's smile was as warm as summer honey. 'May I call you Claudia from now on?'

Claudia nodded. Faith Hubble shook hands and lumbered to her feet, tucking her too-little purse under her arm. Claudia walked her to the front door, Faith saying hello to every person they passed, and then headed back to her office alone, her stomach twisting.

She went to the quiet of the ladies' room and washed her face in icy water. She stared at her dripping face in the mirror. *Jesus Christ, Claudia, that mouthy bitch just threatened your father, didn't she?*

Maybe the woman was just making conversation. Or not. Maybe Faith Hubble was rattled after having to give her prints, feeling a little cornered.

She thought of her father, Cipriano, waving at her as his little shrimp boat chugged into St Leo Bay for a day's work, empty nets hanging behind him like ancient tattered flags, rope and nylon to cull a precarious living, him telling her to be a good girl.

One simple step would set her course aright. Take Delford's blunt but good advice and treat Hubble as a suicide. Pete Hubble was a moody loser, outcast from a respected family. He'd earned a debased living, and it wouldn't surprise her in the least if the toxicology tests revealed drugs in his system. He probably had killed himself and spared both his family and Velvet the shock of finding him by inviting Heather Farrell to the boat.

You're some cop. Quiver like a little kid and let those two tell you how to do your job. She fumed – she should have confronted Faith Hubble right then and there. She called Whit Mosley at the courthouse.

'Hey, Honorable, it's Claudia.'

'What's the matter? You sound deflated.'

'No, just tired.' Suddenly she didn't feel like embarrassing herself with private revelations to Whit. 'I wanted to update you on where we are.' She told him about her questioning of Velvet, the missing laptop, and her discussion with Faith, sticking to the facts. 'What do you think of suicide as an explanation?'

'Your boss came down hard on me last night to push for suicide,' Whit said. 'I didn't appreciate it.'

'He . . .' Claudia stopped herself. Delford Spires had been her ardent supporter, her mentor on the force. 'I know he's never been your favorite, but he is a smart man. I'm sure he meant well.'

Whit updated her about his discussion with Ernesto Gomez and the information he had gleaned. 'I'd like to know who this dirtbag is that Pete argued with on the boat. We should ask Velvet.'

'I'm going to have a background check made on Pete Hubble, see if he has a record in California. I'm going to check Velvet, too,' Claudia said. 'I'd like to visit Jabez Jones. His name keeps cropping up.'

'Take me with you, but I'm booked up until this evening with the joys of court,' Whit said.

Claudia said, 'I'll call and see when we can meet with him.'

'Fine. I'll call you as soon as I know details that are forensic and meaningful,' he said.

'Fine. Bye,' she said, still feeling peevish. She had a lot of phone calls to make, computer searches to do. She picked up the sheaf of pink messages left for her by the dispatcher. Two from Patsy Duchamp at the *Port Leo Mariner*, no doubt looking for a quote. One from her mother, no doubt to berate her for divorcing Deputy Wonderful. And one, surprisingly, from the Reverend Jabez Jones.

She reached for her phone.

15

Heather Farrell spent a damp night in a grove of bent live oaks near Little Mischief Beach, surrounded by bluestems that stood tall and thin and kept her hidden. Lying on her back, the limbs of the oaks were fingers of a gnarled claw pointing away from the bay, shaped by the ceaseless wind. At night the trees looked frightening, transplanted from the forest where Hansel and Gretel roamed. When she awoke she peeled a scrawny orange and ate, watching the few pleasure boats plying the waters on a brisk autumn morning. She got out her notebook and began to sketch the boats: the prows cutting the water, the foaming curl of wake left in their path, the hard angles of stern and bow and flying bridge.

She hummed as she drew.

She hoped Sam would come. His father was dead, and Heather knew propriety demanded Sam be at home. He was no doubt upset. But she hoped he might prefer the solace of the beach rather than his frostbitten mother and egocentric grandmother. He might prefer her.

Heather wished for a shower; she had settled for a quick sponge bath at the police station. She rubbed toothpaste on her teeth and gums with her finger and rinsed and spat with a gulp of water from her oversize water bottle she kept in her knapsack. She emerged from the oak motte and headed down to the shores of Little Mischief Beach, and found Sam there, watching the waves inch against the sand.

Heather came up behind him, wanting to touch the cool skin at the nape of his neck and feel his hair, the same color as his father's. Instead she gently touched his back.

Sam Hubble turned. The wind had reddened his smooth cheeks. Red lines webbed his eyes. A dribble of snot clung to one nostril.

'Hi you,' he said.

'Hi yourself.' She kissed him shyly on the cheek. She dug a tissue from her jeans pocket and dabbed his nose. 'It's okay. It's all okay.'

'We shouldn't be seen together,' he said softly. 'And one of my grandmother's jerks will probably be out looking for me. I'm supposed to be at home, inconsolable with grief.'

Heather loved that Sam used big words like *inconsolable* – he sounded so smart. Smart guys were sexier to her, but she didn't know many. She'd get him a little tattoo, maybe of heather in bloom, when they got to New Orleans, and then he'd just be to die for. 'So we sit tight?' she asked.

Sam shrugged and sniffed. 'Probably for the next week or so.'

'And then we can go? We can get out of here?'

'Yeah,' he said.

'But you'll be a runaway. No way is your grandmother going to let you go.'

'I got that covered. There won't be a stink – she and Mom won't come looking for me. That's a guarantee. They can tell people I've gone off to boarding school in Houston.' He wiped his nose with the back of his hand. 'If they don't let us go, then I start talking.'

Heather heard the resolve in his voice, but it didn't ease the churn in her guts. She leaned away from him and with her fingernail drew a heart in the soft sand. Their plan seemed utterly impossible, but she wanted in her heart to believe it would work. That they could be together, free of Pete and Lucinda and Faith. *Me, the smiley-girl optimist. There's a switch.*

'I want to believe this will work . . . that we'll be safe from them,' Heather said.

He didn't respond, staring out at the bullet-gray bay.

'Are you okay?' she asked.

Sam shrugged. 'He was a two-week dad. What's that, two weeks out of my whole life, Heather? Shit, I don't even want to figure out the percentage. I've been to summer camps that lasted longer.'

He fell silent. Heather ached to take his hand, but instead she kept her palm pressed against the damp cool of the sand.

He cried. Heavy, big tears for his father, and she hugged him close. He surrendered to hard, racking sobs, and Heather thought: *He couldn't cry like this in front of his mother or grandmother. Not allowed.*

'I'm sorry,' he gasped. He was fifteen, three years younger than her, and their being together was utterly insane. But the world was insane, so why couldn't they succeed? He leaned toward her as she wiped his cheek clean of tears and he kissed her, hard, and they leaned back in the sand, smearing the heart she had drawn.

Whit's day typified the joys of the justice court. He first magistrated into the county jail a sobbing carpenter from Darius, a small fishing community on Encina County's northern tip, who had blackened his wife's eye and broken her nose during a morning argument over burnt toast.

'Don't put me in jail, please,' the man pleaded. He was not much older than Whit, but he mewled and cried like an ashamed child. His wife's blood still splattered his T-shirt. 'I'm claustrophobic. I'll go apeshit, Judge. Please, please.'

'Listen, Mr Reynolds.' Whit wished he could refer to him in open court as *you sniveling little dick*. 'I don't want to hear one bit of whining, complaining, or bitching from you. Are you listening to me, sir?'

Big sniffle from the oversized baby. 'Yes, Judge, sure am.'

Whit informed the accused of the charges against him, his right to retain counsel, his right to remain silent, his right to request appointment of counsel if indigent – all the Miranda warnings the man had heard when he was arrested by the Encina sheriff's deputies. Big Baby blinked a lot, as though his brain were clogged, so Whit – carefully and calmly – walked him again, in plainest English possible, through his rights. It was his first arrest for family violence assault. Whit set bond at ten thousand dollars, the maximum.

'That's more money than Momma's got,' Big Baby wailed, forgetting Momma would have to pony up a percentage, not the whole amount.

'Such concern for a lady,' Whit said, 'is very touching. But wrong lady.' He stared at Big Baby. 'I'm also serving you with an Emergency Protective Order, Mr Reynolds, at your wife's application. That means, after you make bail, you can't go near her for sixty days.'

'But I love her,' Big Baby sniffed.

'Then you got sixty days to let your heart grow fonder. You go near her, you're gonna be right back in front of me and I will get medieval on your ass, Mr Reynolds.'

Big Baby was led out of the courtroom, bawling afresh, saying he sure hadn't meant to hurt his sweetie pie. Whit silently wished castration were back in judicial fashion. But he put his smile on and turned to the next case.

That morning, Pete Hubble tucked in the back of his mind, Whit signed arrest warrants for four hot-check writers (two of whom were sisters who had apparently gone on their overdrawn jaunt together, which made him a little sad); set a forty-thousand-dollar bond for a chronic burglar who had been captured driving away from his just-burgled ex-girlfriend's house with cash, electronic equipment, and all his sugar's lingerie; and heard guilty pleas from and sentenced six minty-breathed minors in possession of tobacco to twelve hours of community service each and a tobacco awareness class. Whit thought the class sounded worse than the public service, which usually consisted of tidying the beaches. The puffers' parents grimaced at him as though he were sentencing their little darlings to rock splitting, and he thought, *There's a dozen votes lost*. He saw Buddy Beere, his opponent, sitting in the back row of the courtroom, watching him with all the warmth of a spider approaching the squirming fly.

Grabbing a quick lunch at his desk, he ignored three phone messages from his father. He returned four phone messages from the newspapers in Corpus Christi and Houston, telling them that Pete Hubble had apparently died from a gunshot to the head and he was awaiting autopsy results before releasing cause of death. He'd never rated a phone call from the Houston paper before, and the rising prominence of the case made him nervous.

After lunch, Whit interviewed from the bench a Port Leo woman who had told her sisters and neighbors over the past week that President Kennedy was living in their attic, hiding from the Cuban missiles, and dallying with an aged Marilyn Monroe. The assassination in Dallas and suicide in Hollywood never happened and Kennedy, now with a shaved head and a beard, had been fishing along the bays of the Texas coast ever since with his blond companion. The woman claimed she employed them as a gardener and maid on occasion. For their protection and hers, she had taken to carting around a loaded pistol that was a family heirloom.

Whit nodded solemnly through her recitation of her

reality. She'd shaved her eyebrows and she often ran a finger along the hairless, ghostly arches, as though twisting the reels that played for her mind's eye.

The woman said, 'Mr President adores the water, but he just couldn't show his face on the East Coast again. And the rest of the Gulf Coast is closer to Cuba.' She lowered her voice. 'West Coast, too many cameras. And they shot Bobby there. That's why Jack stayed here. And that's why I keep the gun handy. Protection.'

'That's considerate of you,' Whit said. Her two sisters stood to one side, crying quietly. The woman smiled serenely as Whit signed the warrant to detain and transport her to a medical facility for a psychiatric review. Whit – as gentle as a summer breeze – explained to the woman that she would go to see some doctors at Port Leo Memorial. She smiled, determined to indulge him in this silliness. The constable led the woman and her sisters away. Traffic court didn't seem so bad then.

Court concluded, he walked down the private hall back to his small office, shrugged out of his robe (wearing a polo shirt, jeans, and Birkenstock sandals underneath), and hung it carefully on its hanger. He'd made three phone calls to the Nueces County medical examiner this afternoon, quick breaks between cases, and they hadn't cut into Pete yet. To make matters worse, a downtown drug deal had soured last night in Corpus Christi and three twenty-year-olds had shotgunned each other into oblivion. A woman had been found strangled over in Ingleside, and apparently Pete Hubble, senator's son, warranted no special rank to break ahead in the line of corpses. The deputy medical examiner, Liz Contreras, promised she would call him as soon as she had some details.

A musical, double-knuckled knock rapped at his door. 'Hey there, Whit!' Buddy Beere stuck his head in, with miles of smiles for his esteemed opponent.

'Hello, Buddy. How can I help you?'

You could vacate this office for me in a couple of weeks was the answer Whit imagined flitting across Buddy's mind, but instead Buddy offered Whit a friendly hand. 'I wanted to invite you. To a debate. Between you and me.'

Whit shook the proffered hand and Buddy sat down, uninvited. He reminded Whit of a teddy bear gone to seed. He was more stocky than pudgy, in his early forties, with brown hair straggling across his head. In campaigning he smiled a lot, as though grinning were as expected as breathing, crowing an ill-defined platform he termed 'real judicial fairness,' as though Whit managed the justice court with all the probity of a Salem witch trial.

'What exactly would we debate, Buddy?' Whit asked. 'Would you sign arrest warrants differently than me?' *Probably would. With a little happy face drawn next to his signature.*

Buddy shook his head. 'No. I mean on the critical issues facing voters. No offense, Whit, but your daddy, bless him, sort of waltzed you onto the bench and the voters don't know much about you.' As if that was Buddy's responsibility to fix, and as soon as he did Whit's unrobed ass would hit pavement. 'Other than your fondness for too-casual apparel.'

'Don't know me? I've lived here most of my life, and my family's been here since Texas was part of Mexico. What's to know?'

'Well, I was sitting in the back of the courtroom earlier. Observing. You sentenced those teenage smokers to community service. You could have given them a two-hundred-dollar fine.'

'Those kids are all from families living out at Port Leo Country Club, and community service will make a bigger impression than scribbling a check. They ought to get their hands slapped *and* a little dirty.'

'Well, we could debate the rightness of that real easy,' Buddy said with satisfaction.

Whit watched Buddy eyeing the black robe hanging in the corner. 'Buddy, don't you already have a good job down at the nursing home?'

'Sure do.' Buddy was an administrator at Port Leo's one nursing home, down in a crook of St Leo Bay.

'Well, then why do you want my job? It can't possibly pay you as well as the nursing home does.'

Buddy's florid mouth worked. 'I want to make a difference in people's lives.'

'Buddy, I frankly don't know what we would debate about. I sentence to community service – you'd do a fine. Big effing deal.'

Buddy's smile tightened at the brush with profanity. 'How about debating moral fiber?'

'Moral fiber? I'm opposed to it. Unless it fights colon cancer.'

'I've heard you've been keeping company with a woman of less-than-sterling repute.'

'Are we talking about Pete Hubble's friend?' *God, not Faith*, he thought.

'Yes.'

'Well, I heard,' Whit said, 'that you were keeping company with Pete and his friend Velvet as well.' A junior high refrain: *I heard she heard you said they said*.

Buddy's smile died a natural death. 'You better not be spying on me.'

'Is it true?'

'Why not just have me testify at the inquest?' Buddy asked, and Whit smelled a stinky political ploy.

'Buddy, I'm not subpoenaing you when we're running against each other.'

Buddy tugged at his lower lip, like a reluctant tattletale. 'Well . . . I was out campaigning and Pete stopped me.

He wanted to know how he could get close to his family again. He had been a disappointment to them and he wanted to make amends.'

'And what did you tell him?'

'To leave town. No one wanted him here at all.'

16

State Senator Lucinda Hubble kept a collection of heads on the top shelf in her study. Johnson, Nixon, Carter, Reagan, Bush, and Clinton represented the presidents; for the governors of Texas she had George W. Bush, Ann Richards, Mark White, Bill Clements, and Dolph Briscoe. All grinned like decapitated clowns, rubbery skin sagging without bones. Their false-lipped mouths gaped, caught between mirthful smile and slackened grimace. Lucinda also had one of herself, complete with trademark puffy red hair and big azure-framed eyeglasses.

Whit had arrived ten minutes ago, a little past four. The housekeeper, a dour Vietnamese sparrow of a woman, told him Faith was out, Lucinda was on the phone, and would he mind waiting in the senator's study? Anything to eat or drink? she offered. The kitchen and dining room tables creaked under the weight of the collected casseroles and salads and pies brought by neighbors and churchwomen and by the Democratic power elite. But only a few mourners stood gathered, nodding with awkward sympathy.

He wondered if the truth about Pete was leaking, like a slow hiss from a balloon. Faith had stood him up, perhaps off conducting damage control. What would people say to Lucinda? Sorry your son's dead or sorry he turned out so badly? The Democrats in the living room looked fretful. He followed the housekeeper and sat, studying the study.

Underneath the political gallery of plastic masks stood an old pinball machine themed BIG SPENDER, with a fat cat tossing bills to an admiring crowd of 1920s zoot suiters and flappers. Prominently behind her desk were her framed nursing certificates, yellowing with age. On the wall hung an array of photos: Lucinda Hubble with President Bush, with President Clinton, with Willie Nelson and Ann Richards, with a steady parade of Texas celebrities. In each picture Lucinda gave a thumbs-up, as though marking another successful conquest. Lucinda's office was almost too relaxed for a politician.

Warm, friendly. Where the senator could meet with the common folk, show she was just a good old gal.

There were no pictures of her sons. A couple of Faith and Sam, both formal portraits, the kind given as Christmas gifts in gold frames. Faith smiled, but only like she'd just passed a CPA exam. Sam looked like he'd wandered out of a National Honor Society meeting, serious and bespectacled and boring. The perfect political grandson. Certainly the two sons had been failures in that regard.

A small stereo sat in the corner, playing soft solo piano music. Whit wandered over to the stereo, picked up the CD's jewel box. Bach's *Goldberg Variations*, played by Glenn Gould.

'I find Bach a great comfort,' Lucinda Hubble said from the doorway. She looked sunken and diminished. She wore a faded olive-green cardigan and a pair of old khakis, as though she might be loafing in a library or tending winter pansies in her flowerbeds.

'Hello, Senator,' Whit said. 'I'm so very sorry about Pete.'

'Thank you, honey.' She cleared her throat and dabbed her eyes with a monogrammed handkerchief. 'These wells have just about run dry. I'm sorry to keep you waiting, but that was the governor and his wife on the phone.' She said this with only the slightest hint of superiority.

She came and stood by Whit, her fingers playing air

piano. 'Do you hear Gould? He hums and breathes along as he plays. All that careful structure Gould builds, note by note, each one a key brick in a musical house, each note, each rest, played to his own exactitude, but still he can't contain the passion he feels for the music.' She switched the music off.

'It's beautiful,' Whit said.

'Pete hated classical music,' she said. 'He hated anything touched by beauty.'

Lucinda Hubble gestured at the chair on the other side of the desk, and he sat. She eased herself down into a heavy leather armchair.

'Your daddy's already called, and he and Irina have brought us a lovely casserole. It's something Russian and quite unpronounceable, but I'm sure it's delicious. So thoughtful. You thank them again for me, honey.'

'Yes, ma'am, I will. And I won't keep you long now. I just need to ask you some questions so I can make a determination on cause of death.'

'Of course.' She placed her hands, palm down, on the expansive smooth teak of the desk.

He wondered if she knew about him and Faith. She had given no sign – no sly smile, no slight frown of disapproval.

He led with a suggestion for suicide. 'How would you describe Pete's state of mind in the past few weeks?'

'Depressed,' Lucinda said. 'He felt he had wasted his life because of the . . . particular career he had chosen.'

'You knew about the porn?'

Lucinda flinched at the word but nodded. 'I found out a couple of years ago. I called Pete at his home. He was apparently in the middle of shooting a film.' She crumpled the handkerchief. 'I could hear the women in the background. Laughing at me. Hollering about which one would get to appear in a scene with my son first.' She touched at her blue eyeglasses. 'Not what a mother ever wants to hear. I hung up. I told Faith. She already knew, she'd been shielding my so-delicate feelings. I was devastated, of course. I didn't speak to him again until he came back to town.'

'I think the press will find out,' Whit said quietly.

'Not from me, they won't. And if they find out from you or from Detective Salazar, or any member of either of your offices, I will hath more fury than hell,' Lucinda flared. 'I can't have Sam knowing about this. I just can't.'

Not to mention the voters. 'Do you think Velvet is going to stay quiet?'

'I can't control her.'

'Did Pete say why he was coming home?' Whit asked.

'He said he no longer wished to pursue his acting career.' Whit believed the words *adult films* or *dirty movies* or *skin flicks* were never going to pass her lips.

'How did he plan on supporting himself?'

'He didn't say. I assumed he had savings, or could find legitimate work. He does know – knew – film production. Perhaps at a television studio in Corpus Christi or with Jabez Jones's outfit.'

'How much contact did you have with Pete after he returned to Port Leo?'

'An hour, here and there,' Lucinda said. 'The chill had gone deep for years.' She sank slightly into the bulk of the cardigan. 'And selfishly, I did not want to be disappointed by him again. Pete thrives on disappointing others. I was happy to see him, but I wanted him to rehaul his life. I wasn't willing to get too close until I thought he was sincere.' Lucinda perceived the reaction in Whit's face. 'Perhaps I sound harsh, but mothers are mortal, too.'

'No, I know it must have been tough for you. He told you nothing of this Corey film he planned?'

'I didn't know one word until Faith told me this

morning. But I doubt Pete would have completed any real film. Bless his heart, he didn't have the talent. The drive.'

'I'm wondering why Pete chose Corey as a subject, after all these years.'

'Penance, I suppose. He blamed himself for what happened to Corey.'

'Why?'

'Aren't you the youngest of a whole passel of boys? Didn't your brothers take care of you?' She offered a wan smile.

'Yeah, when they weren't bossing me around or beating me up.'

Her smile faded. 'Corey disappeared on a weekend when I was out of town on business. He vanished while he was on Pete's watch, so to speak. Pete never forgave himself.' She shrugged. 'I think he's been killing himself, slowly, for a long time. When certain people do wrong, they turn away from the world. Isolate themselves, slip on the hair shirt and self-destruct. It's why he went into porn, and I think it eroded every bit of self-respect he had.' She looked at Whit hard. 'I've always believed you have to put your troubles behind you and soldier on.'

'Maybe he came across new information about Corey's disappearance. Like that Corey was still alive.' It was a balloon to float.

The silence hung for nearly ten seconds. 'I am certain Corey is dead.'

'Why?' Whit asked.

'Because Corey would have contacted us if he was alive. He wouldn't have let me suffer for all these years.'

'Why did Corey run away from home?'

'Don't resurrect the other worst day of my life.' For the first time she showed raw emotion, anger flaring her nostrils, her cheeks reddening.

Whit waited. Lucinda dragged her fingernails through her mop of red hair and gave a pained sigh.

'I will never be able to author a book on good mothering, Judge. Taxpayers are easier to corral than willful children. Corey got involved with drinkers. Dopeheads. All to punish me for the time I was spending in Austin and the higher standards of behavior I expected from my boys. After their daddy died I let them run wild, do what they wanted, but once I was elected, they had to toe the line. It was not too much to ask of them. Pete tried, at least, but Corey slipped the leash like a wild dog.'

'I know. I remember him, you know.'

'Yes. He would have been about your age, now, wouldn't he?' She pondered Whit's face wistfully.

'You don't think he's living happily on a commune in Montana or a farm in Virginia?'

'Does that really happen with most missing teenagers, Judge?' Lucinda asked with a touch of frost. 'I'd be overwhelmed to know Corey was in some idyllic retreat. Let me assure you the uncertainty of not knowing what happened to Corey is an ongoing thorn in my heart.'

'When was the last time you spoke to Pete, Senator?' Whit asked.

'A couple of days ago. I wanted him to come to dinner alone, but he wouldn't come without Velvet. He declined the invitation, told me he'd talk to me soon.'

'I'm curious. How had you and Faith explained Pete's absence to Sam?'

Lucinda smiled thinly. 'We told him Pete worked in industrial films – you know, training tapes, corporate tapes for business conventions. Sam accepted it. Pete never told him any different – it was part of the agreement for him to see Sam.'

'Did Pete ever talk about a change in the custodial arrangement?' Whit watched Lucinda's face turn pale.

'I don't understand.'

'Pete was contemplating suing for custody of Sam.'

The silence filled the study until Lucinda leaned forward and her chair squeaked. 'Judge, have you lost your mind? Be realistic. How on earth would Pete stand a chance in a custody hearing?'

'I don't know,' Whit said. 'You tell me.'

'He couldn't have been serious. No family court would give Sam to Pete.'

'Did he ever ask about joint custody, now that he was back?'

'That would be an issue between him and Faith,' she said sternly, and Whit thought, *Yeah, right, like you wouldn't be all in the middle of that.*

'Last point,' Whit said. 'The boat Pete was staying on, it's owned by a family suspected of being involved in a drug ring. Y'all know anything about them?'

He could almost hear a political future boiling away in the room.

'Most certainly not,' Lucinda managed to say. 'Pete's friends were his friends, and his associates have nothing to do with us. I would expect you would not leak that news to the press as well.' A vein throbbed in the hollow of her throat.

'So you didn't try to find out who was giving him room and board when he came back?'

'I don't like what you're implying, Judge.' For the first time he saw anger storm in her eyes, her jaw set, her mouth narrow.

'Sorry, but I find it hard to believe you just let him waltz back in the middle of an election and didn't research his friends, his benefactors, his purpose in being here.'

'I can't control what you believe. But I would be very careful as to what you imply to the world.' He saw her scrutinize him with new eyes. He was not being, he supposed, the easygoing Whit Mosley who liked to wander the beach and never put two shakes into a job.

'I'd like to speak to Sam.'

Her shoulders stiffened. 'Of course. Assuming that his mother or I am present. He is a minor, after all.'

'Of course. Thank you. You've been very helpful.'

'But' – she raised a finger – 'I ask that you not discuss this custody idiocy with Sam.'

'I can't promise that. I'm sorry. I need to talk to him about any subject relevant to his father's death.'

'I won't have you subjecting him to Velvet's foolish notions. I'm assuming she's the one claiming Pete wanted custody?'

'Yes.'

'A pathetic attempt to hurt us and I won't permit it.'

Whit kept his voice mild, out of respect for her loss. 'This is how it works. I interview him, and you or Faith can be there, and if there's nothing he can add, fine. Or I can call him as a witness at the inquest. Put him on the stand.'

Her fingertips worked along her palms, awkwardly kneading the flesh. 'Why don't you let me discuss it with his mother?'

'That would be fine.' Whit stood and offered his hand. She shook it, but the cozy neighborliness had evaporated.

He saw himself to the door, but before he left the Bach CD suddenly roared in the study, the icy cleanness of the notes as loud as hammers.

In the late afternoon the teenagers – aimless, tans not faded from summer gold – were out in meager force. Two girls sat cross-legged on an arc of crushed shells at one end of the beach. A boy waded in the gentle surf, black jeans neatly rolled up past thick calves, dragging a bamboo stick in the water, watching it cut a wake through the waves.

Claudia parked in the small, sand-smeared asphalt lot that fed off the old Bay Highway. From the lot she could see the whole, nearly straight line of the beach that terminated on the south with several acres of wind-bent oaks, and the private fishing pier on the north for Port Leo's nursing home. The pier, she remembered, didn't get much use, but two healthy-looking old ladies, their faces shadowed by big, neon-colored sun hats (one magenta, one turquoise), stood on the pier, trolling simple rigs with slack lines.

The elderly women reminded her of David, begging her to attend his Poppy's party. David was looping a hook back into her flesh, securing it into her jaw, making sure she could not dash from whatever shadow he might cast across the water of her life.

She saw Heather Farrell easing herself down the mangy slope of grass to the flat of the hard-packed beach, a notebook under her arm, a sandwich in her hand, the girl chewing and tossing a scrap of crust to a hovering gull. Other gulls swooped near, pleading with cries, waiting for the generosity to be extended. Heather popped another two morsels upwards and then ran, leaving the gulls to sort out the buffet. She sat, kicked off her shoes and ate, keeping her feet just beyond the encroaching tide.

Claudia sat down next to her.

'You wolfed that down,' Claudia said. 'You hungry? I'll buy you dinner.'

Heather dusted the crumbs from her fingers with a quick slap. She tucked a fleck of mayonnaise from the corner of her mouth onto her thumb, then wiped her thumb on her jeans. 'Do you always criticize other people's table manners?'

'We're not at a table.'

'Slap me. You really are a detective.' Heather watched the Gulf inch toward her feet, then retreat. She kept the notebook close to her, on the other side from Claudia.

'Brought this for you to sign.' Claudia produced a statement. 'Read it first and make sure it's correct.'

Heather scanned the document and signed her name at the bottom. 'There. Perfect. Satisfied?'

'You sleep okay last night?'

'Sure.'

'Amazingly unrattled by finding a dead body.'

Heather dragged a hand through her hair. 'What am I gonna do, run home to Lubbock?'

'I can help you find a real place to stay.'

'Aren't you out of your jurisdiction, officer?' Heather asked. No insolence laced her voice. 'Little Mischief's not in Port Leo proper.'

'The sheriff's department might consider you a vagrant, Heather. Camping out here.' She could call David, ask him to check on this beach later this evening.

Heather shrugged. 'I moved.'

'Where to?'

'A friend's house.' She wiggled toes at the froth of the surf as it kissed her heels. 'Since you're gonna ask me for all the details, her name's Judy Cameron. She lives on the west side of Port Leo. I'm crashing there. So you don't need to follow me around. I'm perfectly safe.'

'Judy have a phone number?'

'She didn't pay the bill and got disconnected, but her address is still in the phone book. 414 Paris Street. Beige brick house with a motorcycle out front.'

'Why don't I give you a ride back there now?'

'Why don't you quit hassling me?' Heather asked. 'Look, I'm all warm and gooey inside from your concern, but I'm fine. I'm a grown woman.'

'If there's anything you haven't told us about Pete's

123

death, you're going to be hip-deep in trouble. I won't be able to protect you then.'

'Shouldn't you have another cop here to play bad, if you're good?' Heather laughed. 'You ought to watch more TV and get your shtick down.'

'Why'd you buy Greyhound tickets this week? Two of them?' Claudia asked.

Heather turned her gaze back out across the bay to the hump of Santa Margarita Island. 'You're a busy bee.'

'It was easy to check.'

'Judy and I thought we'd go to see friends in Houston. That okay with the local Nazi regime?'

'I don't want you leaving town before this inquest.'

'You can't expect me to wait around forever.'

Claudia fished a card out of her pocket. 'In case Judy kicks you out.' She jotted numbers on the card and handed it to Heather. 'That's got my home and my office number. And my ex-husband's number – he's a deputy with the sheriff's department.'

'He cute?' Heather asked.

'Very,' Claudia said. 'Call. I'm around twenty-four/ seven.'

'I'll program you on my speed dial. Thanks.'

Claudia dusted the sand from her rump and walked away. When she reached her car, she watched Heather sitting, notebook open, sketching with a pencil, the sunset painting the low clouds orange and purple, the light beginning to fade.

Two pelicans glided across St Leo Bay with graceful swoops, the tips of their wings barely brushing the water. Claudia watched them fly, and then she drove back to town.

The two old women lumbered inside the nursing home, their cackles of laughter drifting down the beach to Heather. A Caspian tern, squeaking its nasally call, dove down into the darkening water, its bill bloodred but not from prey. The tern shot back into the sky, wet, dinnerless. Heather watched it. *You don't always get what you want, babycakes.* The tern tried again, farther out into the bay. Heather watched the surf-walking boy and the two chatting girls leave the beach. When she looked back out, the tern was gone. Shame. She opened to a blank page and began to sketch out the muscled wings, the probing beak, the egg-shaped head.

She stopped as the sun set behind her. She wished Sam were here, to drink red wine, cuddle up close to her, run his tongue along the backside of her ear. But he wasn't coming. No escape from the Hubble guardians. No escape at all –

A hand grabbed her shoulder.

17

Whit Mosley and Faith Hubble had first made love – an altogether too kind term, considering the bourbon and muscle cramps involved – in July. They met at a wind-down party after three days of ShellFest, Port Leo's annual salute to all things crustacean and culinary. Over ten thousand fairgoers, both locals and tourists, jammed the St Leo Bay area to guzzle beer, buy crafts, stomp to forgettable jazz and blues and country-western acts, and to deplete the shrimp and oyster populations through structured gluttony. Lucinda judged a shrimp recipe cook-off, glad-handed voters, and raced back to her Austin condo with Sam in tow to hear a classical piano concert at UT.

Faith didn't. She lingered in town, hanging out at the Shell Inn, drinking bourbon in a back booth with a clutch of old high school girlfriends. The women's group slowly merged with two more groups, which is what happens in a small bar where nearly everyone knows everyone else and has been drinking for three days. Tables were pushed together, drinks ordered again, and Faith sat next to Judge Whit Mosley. She vaguely remembered his brothers from her school days, knew he was the youngest of the wild and handsome pack of Mosley boys. Even though now a judge he dressed like a townie bum without two dimes, in his frayed, sun-faded orange polo shirt and weathered khaki shorts and Birkenstock sandals. But the legs leading to the sandals were nicely formed, and she liked his odd gray eyes and the direct and knowing way he smiled, not at all put off by her height or weight. She grinned at the quiet way he indulged the drunken boasts of his friends when the topic turned to fishing, not joining in but not deflating his buddies' hackneyed tales, and although his polo shirt was old and the neon orange a color out of style, the chest and arms beneath the fabric were tanned and firm.

He didn't look like any judge she ever knew.

She had been lonely for a long time, plowing all her time into Lucinda's career, and no one had given her jokes a sincere laugh in a long while. He offered her a ride home; she was drunk. She asked him to come inside and have a cup of coffee and a couple of aspirin to help sober themselves up (although she had watched him nurse a single Corona for two hours and knew the only drunk one was herself), and while they stood chatting in the kitchen and the coffee brewed, she surprised herself by reaching out for him and saying, 'Is that a gavel or you just happy to see me?' Her jokes got worse with more bourbon.

It wasn't a gavel and he amply liked her, too. They spent the next several hours in bed, half of the time sleeping, the other half making strenuous love. She was left gasping but energized, freeing some long-buried shadow of herself to face the world. She watched Whit nap and traced his lips with a fingernail while he softly snored. Since Pete had left her, the few men she'd allowed intimacy with her tended to be older and snagged in the intricate web of state politics. They talked of little else. Here was a man lying beside her who was younger with a flat stomach and long legs and probably not overly bright but he knew how to make her feel my-God shivery good. She brushed his light fuzz of whiskers grown in the course of the day, wondering how quickly he would bolt in the morning.

He didn't. He made love to her again, and she almost wept with pleasure and an odd relief. She didn't want a romance, but she did want him, warm and kissing her throat and giving his halfway smile as he filled her. They began to see each other discreetly. She didn't want Sam or Lucinda to know – he was the only private part of her life – and Whit didn't argue.

They saw each other perhaps twice a month. Faith and Whit learned about the constellation of small motels along the Coastal Bend, little way stations in Rockport and Aransas Pass and Laurel Point and Copano. They would meet, share a bottle of Shiner Bock while kissing and slowly unburdening each other of their clothes, soap their skin in the shower, make love on the bed, and then talk – about her work, about his struggle to learn enough law to be an effective JP, about books they'd both read. He was smarter than she thought. A love of reading was, other than sex, the only thing they had in common. All perfectly friendly.

But now he had failed her, and the memory of the taste of his skin soured in her mouth. Faith backed her BMW out of the Hubble driveway and gunned the engine toward Whit's house.

Faith rocketed over to the Mosleys', ready to carve Whit's guts into ribbons of flesh, but instead the storm turned to shower. She cried as soon as she saw him.

Babe and Irina were dining with friends in Rockport and would not be back for quite a while.

Faith and Whit sat in the cramped living room in the guest house, the Corpus Christi news turned on but muted. Pete's death – as the son of a prominent state senator, not as a porn star, which had not yet been mentioned by any news source – had been the second story, after the gunshot war that had slowed down the Nueces County coroner's office.

Faith's hard, heavy weeping slowly eased. Whit handed

her a wad of tissues to replace the ones she'd rendered sopping, and he poured them each a hefty glass of an inexpensive merlot. She gulped down a third of the glass in a long swallow.

'You don't think you can cry for someone you ceased to love a long while back.' Faith sniffed, tamped her nostrils with the tissues. 'I keep thinking of the boy I knew and married, not the sleaze he turned out to be . . . but he came home, and all I saw was the sleaze. Nothing more.' She drank again. 'This is good, Whit. Thanks. You know how he proposed to me? On Port Leo Beach, at midnight. The beach was closed, but we snuck in and sat on the sand and counted stars. He told me I had missed one, and then he dangled this beautiful diamond on a string before my eyes.' She studied the red depths of the wineglass. 'I loved him then – sure I did. But he married me only because his mother wanted it. I found out later she'd bought the ring for him and told him just how to propose. She knew what would light my fire.' She set the wineglass down, folded her fingers together in her lap. 'Whit, you've got to believe me . . . We didn't have anything to do with Pete's death. Nothing. And Lucinda, she shouldn't have come across so hard-assed with you.'

'Why didn't you tell me Pete was back in town?' Whit kept his voice gentle, quiet, and unaccusing.

'Because . . . God, we didn't want anyone to know he even existed anymore. But he cooperated with us. He kept a very low profile. I mean, I guess a couple of people commented to me he was back, but no production was made of it.' Her mouth twisted. 'Did you want to waste away our motel time chatting about my ex?'

'You didn't want people – or me – to know he was back because he had starred in blue movies?'

'Yes.' She took another bolstering slug of wine and shuddered.

'Not because he could derail Lucinda's campaign. And your career. Not because he was going to sue you for custody of Sam.'

'Look, as far as I'm concerned, Whit, this custody crap is a complete fiction Velvet dreamed up in her screwed-stupid little mind.'

'You asked me to help y'all get through this, to not make a big production of the inquest. But I'm not doing you any such favors until I know what's going on here.'

'I clearly don't mean diddly squat to you, do I?'

'This has nothing to do with us, Faith. But I don't believe a man who wants to get his child back just kills himself.'

'I don't suppose it's occurred to you the source of his depression was he knew he'd never, ever get Sam.'

'Yes, it occurred to me. It also occurred to me to wonder exactly why he'd even think he had a chance in court. Did he have something on you, Faith?'

'There's nothing that could trump porn!' she barked at him. 'For God's sakes!'

'There are worse crimes than dirty movies.'

'Not to a family court.' She stood. 'I came over here to talk, not to be grilled by you.'

'You came over to presume on our relationship,' Whit said. 'You're asking me to not make a public spectacle of the inquest for Sam's sake. But I'm asking you for an explanation of what was going on with Pete. This cuts both ways, sweetie.'

'I told you what I know.' She sat again.

'Perhaps I should excuse myself from the case.'

'No. Don't.' Panic flashed in her eyes. 'You do that, you'll have to explain why, and I don't want Sam to know about us.'

'Don't lock Sam in a glass bubble forever.'

'Look, it hasn't been easy for him . . . no father . . . his grandmother and I so busy. And now, with Pete dead, I can't rub salt in his wounds, please, Whit. Not now.' She covered her face with her hands.

'The boat Pete was staying on. It's owned by a family suspected of heavy drug activity up the coast.'

'Lucinda mentioned that.' She leaned back against the thick pillows of the couch and dropped her hands. 'Good God, he chose well, didn't he? One little explosive charge after another to sink his mother's ship.'

'He's the one who's dead, not Lucinda.' He sat next to her. 'Where were you last night?'

'Am I not supposed to be insulted at the question?'

'That's up to you, Faith.'

'I was at home last night, with Sam. I haven't spent enough time with him lately. We had dinner, watched TV, went to sleep early. It's all in my bland little police statement.'

'Okay,' he said. 'Thanks.'

She took his hand. 'I've been nothing but honest with you. I'm sure he killed himself, okay? All these other diversions – this Corey movie, this custody idea, him staying on a drug hound's boat – I'm begging, Whit. Keep it all out of the inquest, can't you? It has no place. If you don't you're letting a nobody like Pete win. Over me. Over us.'

'I can't promise that, Faith. I can't.'

She rose, her face contorting as though slapped. 'The problem with you, Whit, is that everyone has low expectations of you and you never fucking disappoint.'

A rap sounded at the door. Faith fell silent. Whit stood, wondering if she might go hide in the bathroom or closet, but she stayed put and he went to his door.

It was Claudia. 'Hi,' she said, and she glanced past his shoulder to see Faith Hubble standing by the couch, the empty wineglass on the coffee table, the half full one next to it.

'I'm sorry,' she said. 'I didn't realize you had company.'

'Come in,' Whit said. 'Mrs Hubble and I were just discussing her ex-husband. You want something to drink?'

'I'd love a Coke.' Claudia sat down while Whit busied himself dumping ice cubes in a glass and cracking open a liter bottle of cola. He brought Claudia her soda. The silence between the two women hung thick as fog on a cool winter morning.

Claudia broke the quiet. 'I'm glad you're here, Mrs Hubble. I just confirmed with Anders Sorenson that he was hired to represent Pete in suing for custody of your son. I thought you might be able to help us understand why.'

'As I was just telling the judge,' Faith said slowly, 'Pete's legal concerns were his own matter. He'd ignored Sam for most of fifteen years, and he was no parent. He had zero grounds for a serious bid for custody.'

'So why hire Sorenson?' Whit asked. Anders Sorenson was from an old Port Leo family, one of the best-regarded attorneys in the area, almost seventy, a scrappy, dapper little man feared in the courtroom.

'Because Sorenson's a big-money Republican who'd love to see Lucinda lose?' Faith flared. 'Shit, *I don't know what Pete was doing*. I can't repeat that too many more times without thinking the two of you are brain-damaged.'

Neither Whit nor Claudia spoke.

'I have to go, unless you have further questions,' Faith said. 'Sam is expecting me for dinner.'

'I would like to speak with Sam,' Whit said. 'Briefly.'

'Call me tomorrow and we'll set up a time.' She picked up her purse and didn't give Claudia another glance as she walked out the door. Whit followed her out of the guest house, past the pool. She didn't break stride and she didn't look back, and he didn't call out to her. He went back to the guest house.

Claudia stared at him. 'I heard her yelling at you before I knocked on the door.'

'I've known her for a while. She's upset.'

'And?'

'Her kid's the most important thing in the world to her,' Whit said. 'But she's right. Pete wouldn't have a prayer in family court.'

'Unless she's done something far worse than adult films,' Claudia said.

Whit sipped his wine.

'I thought you and I could talk to Jabez Jones together tomorrow morning,' she said. 'Your clerk said it'd work with your schedule.'

'That's fine,' he said.

She touched his arm. 'Anything else you want to tell me, Honorable?'

'No,' he said. 'Nothing else at all.'

18

Velvet eased the magazine out of her Sig Sauer 9mm automatic pistol. She tucked the Sig far down into her purse. Then she yanked it out of concealment, past tissues and car keys and compact. Four seconds. Too long, but stacking the gun atop her billfold and cosmetics made her nervous; she had no concealed weapons permit. She supposed she could always just fire through the thin leather of the purse.

Finding the gun had been easier than she imagined. She'd hired a cab to take her to Corpus Christi, rented a Chevy Caprice at the airport, and driven to a ragtag collection of pawnshops. She found that cash and a quick but ardent display of her professional skills spoke volumes to one particular dealer. She'd never seen a registration form.

She'd picked up a small tape recorder as well, the kind used by reporters. Voice-activated in case someone said something interesting she wanted to keep. This she stuck down in the depths of her purse.

Velvet practiced pulling the automatic from her purse for ten more minutes until the motion felt fluid and natural and the gun didn't feel so alien in her grip. If Junior Deloache became a problem, she thought, she'd have to fire without flinching. She imagined shooting him in the stomach – clearly the biggest target on him – and tried not to think about how much blood might explode from his guts.

Him or you. Just think of it as him or you if it comes to that. Junior was, she thought, most likely full of bluff, and he might even be useful to her.

Her fantasies shifted from gunning down a hot-breathed Junior Deloache to placing the cool barrel of the Sig against Faith Hubble's head and forcing that snide bitch to sing the truth. *Yes, I killed him, I killed him, please don't hurt me . . .*

A gentle knock rapped on the door. She went and peered through the peephole. Faith Hubble stared back at her through the security hole, arms crossed, frowning like she wanted to bite the world in half.

'Velvet? You there?' Faith called. She knocked again.

Velvet hurried back to her purse. She clicked on the recorder and found the ammunition in the bottom of the bag.

'You're stupider than I thought,' Gooch said.

Whit nursed his beer. He and Gooch sat in a deserted corner at Georgie's bar at the Shell Inn. Being a Tuesday night, the bar was mostly empty, only a few figures quaffing down liquid forgetfulness in the shallow light. The tarpons on the wall, mounted over draped netting, caught the glow of the television along their preserved curves. Georgie sat at the bar, smoking a cigarette and working the *New York Times* crossword puzzle with a bloodred pen.

He had just confessed to Gooch about his affair with Faith and was now receiving a quota of due lashings.

'What do you think Buddy Beere might make of this, Whitman?' Gooch rattled the ice in his near-empty glass of bourbon. 'He'll fry you into political hash.'

'Buddy doesn't have to know. And Pete's her *longtime* ex. I don't think there's a professional conflict in me handling the case.'

'Buddy will. And no secret in this county gets kept forever,' Gooch said. 'There's too many big mouths and prying eyes and booze.' He finished his drink with a toss and signaled to the vapid barkeep for a refill. She didn't see him, giggling with Eddie Gardner at the bar. Whit watched Gardner, who had pointedly ignored him. If Claudia was slaving over the Hubble case tonight, Gardner wasn't.

'I've discovered the silver lining. You blow the election, you can work for me,' Gooch mused. 'I'm thinking of buying a much bigger boat, you know, a serious party barge. If I do it, you can wriggle out from under Babe's wing and grab a real life.'

'Yeah. Scrubbing decks, gutting fish, keeping drunks from going overboard. And best of all, taking orders from you. My life's dream.'

'You ain't got room for snooty.' Gooch finally got the bartender's attention when she turned from laughing at a joke of Gardner's. She nodded and brought Gooch his drink. Whit watched the young woman hurry back to Gardner, intent on not leaving him shifted in neutral too long.

'Why do cute girls like a greaseball like Gardner?' Whit wondered.

Gooch shrugged. 'You ask this while diddling Faith Hubble.'

Whit considered. 'She's fun.'

'And willing. Is that all you require?'

'No.'

'What else? Breathing?' Gooch put a hand over his heart in mock horror. 'God help us, you're not in love with her, are you?'

'Of course not,' Whit said.

'So she's just someone you sleep with?'

'She's . . .' Whit stopped. *Lover* implied more emotional depth than either he or Faith had yet brought to the bed. *One-night stand* was logistically incorrect. *Sexual release* carried all the warmth of freezer burn.

136

He just liked her; he still liked her. 'We're in a shadowy area.'

His map of Faith's heart consisted of the roughest sketch. He knew Sam was her north star, her everything, with perhaps Lucinda and her political career a near second. But when they were together – from the first time – she had shown an openness toward him that he suspected few others saw. He didn't believe her capable of sticking a gun in a man's mouth and pulling the trigger.

He was pretty sure. Fairly sure.

He finished his beer. Crap. Not sure at all, even though he'd tasted her skin, felt the broad warmth of her back pressed up against his chest, explored the shape of her mouth, smelled chamomile in her hair, knew which ribs produced ticklish laughter. He didn't know the shape and size of her heart.

And Claudia. She'd greeted Faith with all the friendliness of a mongoose eyeing a swaying cobra. Claudia sure hadn't believed it was a simple interview. Miss By-the-Book would blow a mighty shrill whistle on him in two seconds flat if she smelled a conflict of interest. And he couldn't blame her.

Just then Whit noticed a chunky blond man lumber up from a darkened corner of the bar, wearing a gaudy-awful tropical shirt, and head out the door. He bumped into an older man entering the bar and said, 'Watch it, old fart.' The old man, already drunk, ignored him.

Whit said, 'Come on,' to Gooch, tossed dollars on the bar to settle the tab, and followed.

As they went out, the man clambered into a red Porsche. Grit and bird-guano splatters dusted the car. The Porsche jerked out of its slot and revved onto Main Street.

Whit ran to his Explorer, Gooch following.

'Explaining soon?' Gooch said.

'Heavy. Blond. Loud. He looks like the dirtbag Ernesto described. And he's driving a messy Porsche, just like Ernesto said.'

Whit tailed the filthy Porsche down Main Street, past the shopping district where seasonally challenged store owners had already hung Christmas decorations and dangled sprays of light in the palm and red bay trees. On his left was the bay, with rental condo developments lining the shore. Most had been built in the 1970s during a last-gasp oil boom and retained the unfortunate, granola-esque architecture of the time – boxy, with diagonally layered strips of wood for siding and balconies ringed with thick oak beams.

They drove past the Port Leo city limits for a half mile and the Porsche wheeled into a condo resort called Sea Haven. Its name was written in cursive rope for that authentic nautical air. Missing windows and sawhorses suggested renovations were under way.

The Porsche parked next to a flooring company's van, and the driver unfolded himself from the car. Big, with terminally moussed hair and pimp-bright clothes: a crimson tropical shirt adorned with purple parrots, bright yellow golfing pants, snow-white high-top sneakers. He straightened his britches with a decisive yank as he ambled toward the building.

Whit drove past, U-turned, and circled back. The man still stood in the yard, talking to an elderly man in a motorized wheelchair.

'Stop and talk to them or go on?' Gooch asked.

'Carpe diem and all that crap,' Whit said. 'Let's stop.'

The old man watched them park and raised a hand to silence the young man. Whit was suddenly conscious of the KEEP JUDGE MOSLEY megasize magnetic sign on the side of his Explorer. He and Gooch walked toward them. The steely scowl on the old man's face deepened.

'Hello,' Whit said. 'I'm Whit Mosley and I'm the justice of the peace here in Encina County.'

'I see.' The old man nodded toward the garishly patriotic vote-mobile, bright under the streetlights. 'I'm Anson Todd.'

Whit recognized the name from the marina manager; Todd was the man who'd made the docking arrangements for *Real Shame*. 'This is Leonard Guchinski,' Whit said.

'Charmed,' Gooch said.

Whit kept his eyes on the hefty guy. 'I understand you're acquainted with Pete Hubble.'

'Why do you ask or care?' the younger man challenged.

'Junior,' the older man said with a bored note of caution.

Ah, young Mr Deloache. 'I'll take that as a yes. I'm conducting the inquest into Pete's death and I'd like to talk to you about him.'

'We have nothing to say,' Junior said in a petulant voice. 'Nothing.'

'Come in for a minute,' the old man invited, as though he'd not heard Junior's pronouncement. His voice, scratchy, reminded Whit of a dusty, worn record. 'Junior, do me a favor. We're out of cereal and I'm not facing the morning without my raisin bran. Run down to the store.' He pivoted the wheelchair sharply and zoomed for the condo's lobby.

'Anson, we got cereal,' Junior called to the old man's back.

'Not the kind I like,' Anson said, not giving Junior another glance. 'Go.'

Junior, abandoned, stood slack-jawed and then loped to his Porsche and roared off. Whit and Gooch followed

Anson into the condo's lobby. Wood shavings, tattered wallpaper, and a half-dismantled reception desk, cluttered with a forest of empty soda cans, decorated the half-done vestibule. A couple of construction workers, begrimed with sawdust but getting excellent overtime, inspected unfurled blueprints with lukewarm interest.

'Late night to be working construction,' Gooch said.

'Late night to be bothering people,' Anson said.

They followed Anson into a cramped, rackety elevator. Anson punched eight, the top button.

'So you own this building?' Whit asked.

'No.' Anson declined further explanation. Anson Todd looked to be edging seventy. He wore a black turtleneck, gray sweatpants covering withered legs, and wire-rimmed glasses over cat-green eyes. An ugly, welted scar scored his temple, and his overlong gray hair was combed over to hide the mark.

'Let me guess. You work for Mr Deloache, Senior,' Whit said.

The elevator stopped, and Whit held the door for Anson to wheel himself out. Anson motored out of the elevator into a garishly appointed suite. It looked to Whit like an animal lover's apartment from hell: zebra prints on the wall, a leopard sofa, a tiger skin on the floor. The monotony of hides was broken by the neon-kissed furniture that had likely been purchased at the House of Lime. A thick-necked youth glanced up from the television; his overinflated physique made him look like he had been gulping steroids with his mother's milk.

'Hey,' the young man greeted Anson, a wary glance going to Gooch and Whit.

'Go watch TV in the master bedroom,' Anson ordered. 'Come if I call you.'

'Sure,' the monosyllabic hulk agreed. He lurched up

from the couch and stomped into another room, slamming the door behind him.

Anson Todd said, 'I love chaperoning the mentally deficient. Have a seat, Judge. Mr Guchinski.' He gestured toward an expansive leather sofa the color of a frozen margarita. Instead Whit wandered to the wall of windows that showed a panoramic view of St Leo Bay and the Gulf. To the north, the huge piers jutting out into the bay dazzled with light, and house lights along Santa Margarita Island glittered like a broken bracelet of diamonds.

'I see why you stay here instead of aboard *Real Shame*,' Whit said.

'Actually, the *Shame*'s not wheelchair-friendly. I stay off except for an infrequent fishing trip. Coffee? Beer?'

Gooch leaned against the window, thick arms linked behind his back. Whit eased onto the plush leather couch.

'No, thank you,' Whit said. 'We won't take up much of your time.'

'You won't need much, Judge. We don't know a thing about Pete's death. Yes, Mr Deloache Senior owns *Real Shame* and has for five years. But Pete was an acquaintance of Junior's. Mr Deloache never met him.'

'The gun that was found in Mr Hubble's hand wasn't registered.'

'If there was an unregistered gun aboard, then Mr Hubble or his lady friend brought it. Not ours.'

'She denies that.'

Anson smiled. 'Once she's over her grief, maybe her memory improves.'

Whit wondered if memory enhancements came in the form of fists or threats. 'I've spoken with witnesses who say Junior visited Pete pretty regularly at the marina. Argued with him about money. Behaved badly yesterday.'

'Define badly.'

'Tried to rough up Pete.'

'Junior? He's a teddy bear. He couldn't bruise fruit. Look, from where I sit, you got hearsay. You got anyone who's positively ID'd Junior as being there?'

'Don't,' Whit said. 'His father owns the boat.'

'Okay, yeah, but you got anyone who will ID Junior as being the argumentative type you're looking for?'

'Yes.'

'Really? 'Cause Junior wasn't here yesterday. Neither was I. We been in Houston the past few days, we just drove in this morning. Got a whole bunch of people who will confirm that.'

'Why are y'all down here? Because someone died on your property?'

'Junior's in charge of getting this resort project completed for his dad. You could call him a project manager. You should. He loves it.'

Whit raised an eyebrow. 'Let me guess. Junior manages the project and you manage Junior.'

Anson grinned. His teeth were yellowed from cigarette smoke.

'How well did you know Pete?' Whit asked.

'I met him just once. Let me tell you, Judge, I find porn boring. I find porn stars even more boring. Especially when they're male. Pete had all the brains of dandruff.'

'What about this money Pete and Junior supposedly bickered over?'

Anson cleared his throat. His voice took on a soft volume that had no softness in the tone. 'Look, Judge, I agreed to tell you what we know, not undergo interrogation. We knew the guy, we didn't have anything to do with his death, and Mr Deloache is gonna want his boat back pronto.'

'Mr Deloache is going to have to wait for the investigation to be over,' Whit answered pleasantly. 'Mr Deloache, both the senior and the junior, need to answer questions.'

'Let me ask you one. How many times was Pete shot?'

'Once.'

'Where?'

'The head.'

Anson crinkled his nose. 'Gee. Once in the head. Can I have suicide for four hundred dollars, Alex?'

'Or maybe it was an execution,' Whit said. 'Gangland style.'

'Gangland? Christ, I haven't heard that term since cable showed the James Cagney movie marathon.' Anson leaned back in his chair. 'Look, Judge, you want to explore slander, keep talking. We got a whole flock of lawyers up in Houston that wouldn't consider your ass a light hors d'oeuvre.'

'Yes, but my ass is planted up on the court bench, and from that vantage point I can call you and Junior as witnesses at the inquest. Mr Deloache, too.'

'I've told you we know nothing. And I got nothing to give you, Judge, except the pleasure of my company and a good cup of coffee.' He smiled. 'I bet you know the good fishing spots in St Leo Bay. We ought to get our lines tight some time.'

Whit imagined more of Anson's boating expeditions involved concrete mixes and pleas for mercy rather than suntan lotion and cheap bait. 'Thanks for your time. I'll see you in court.' He headed for the elevator, Gooch silently following, and pressed the button.

The fishing bonhomie vanished. 'It's not a good idea to waste Mr Deloache's time.'

'It's not a good idea to waste mine, either,' Whit said. The doors slid open, and Whit and Gooch stepped on the elevator. Anson Todd stared at them until the doors slid shut.

'You're such a bad ass,' Gooch said. 'I released a vast flood of urine into my pants, out of sheer terror.'

'You do smell funny,' Whit said. 'Watch me. I'll subpoena both of them so fast their beady little eyes'll pop.'

The elevator doors slid open with a creaky fanfare. Junior Deloache stood there with a box of raisin bran crushed under his arm and a six-pack of beer. He looked like a delivery boy gone to seed but a cold light of calculation touched his eyes.

'Hi, Junior,' Whit said. 'Could we talk for a second? Just outside?'

Junior shook his head. 'I gotta make sure Anson gets his Mr Plumb-r cereal.'

'I'd like to see what all you're doing with Sea Haven. I only have a couple of questions for you.'

Junior shrugged and Whit and Gooch followed him through the dismantled lobby to a large patio, aglow with fuzzy security lights, bare of furniture, with an emptied, cracked pool. A decaying cabana-cum-bar with a graying palm-thatched roof stood nearby, lopsided with neglect.

'Welcome to Groo-vin' Central,' Junior said. 'Once we get it cleaned up and lure all the young chickies here.'

Gooch said, 'Oh, yes, I just see chickies flocking here by the dozens.'

'You gonna have the money to finish?' Whit asked.

Junior gave him a scornful sideways glance. 'Why wouldn't I?'

'Didn't you owe Pete Hubble serious money?'

'Most certainly did not.'

'People at the marina heard the two of you bickering about money. Saw you shoving him around on your boat.'

Junior frowned, but Whit saw he had to think about it

first. 'Your sources are faulty, man. I didn't owe him money.'

Gooch asked, 'So what did Pete owe you?'

'And you would be who?' Junior asked. 'You the bailiff for the judge or something?'

'Gooch is just a friend along for the ride.' Whit wished Gooch would shut up.

'There was no owing of any sort, man. There's a real difference between friends goofing around and arguing. I just got a big voice.'

'When did you last see Pete?' Whit asked.

'A few days ago, last week. He and I took the boat out.'

'Do you want to talk about whatever this money issue was at an inquest hearing? Because I'll call you to testify if I think it's relevant. Or if you're not cooperating. I'm sure the police would be interested.'

Not testifying, Whit suspected, might be a family virtue long drummed into Junior, probably since he broke the legs of his first G.I. Joe in the nursery.

'I had no reason to want Pete dead. See, Pete promised me I could be in a movie.'

'The one he was making about his brother?'

'Tragedy is not my style. A, you know, different kind of movie.' Junior swiveled his hips with a not-so-subtle grind.

'I see. Pete was going to let you be in a groo-vin' movie,' Whit said in an understanding tone.

'Yeah, you're on board now. Fucking A.'

'Anson and your dad must've loved that idea.'

The smile faded.

'I got the impression whatever Anson said, you did.' Whit gently poked the box of raisin bran.

'Yeah, well, that's me being nice to an old fart. Anson's older'n hell, he already got one wheel in the grave.'

'So with Pete gone I guess your movie career is on hold.

Unless you can convince Velvet to cast you in her next opus.'

He grinned. 'That's no problem.'

'Why is that?'

Junior set the cereal and beer down, gently, stood, and rubbed his palms against each other, warming his fists for use. 'You know, you're grilling me like chicken, dude, and I don't got to give you the time of day.'

'Oh, yes, please let's get physical,' Gooch interrupted. 'I haven't had a workout today, and you got punching bag written all over your gut.'

Junior started a retort, then seemed to reconsider as he noted the size of Gooch's biceps. 'I sure as hell ain't gonna answer any more questions.'

'Fine. I'll see you in my courtroom.' Whit had found his weapon – Anson's and Junior's loathing of court – and wasn't about to surrender it.

A cold rage lit Junior's eyes. 'My daddy's attorneys will eat you alive.'

'What's with these attorneys and the food metaphors? Eat us alive and grilling you like chicken and consider Whit an appetizer? No wonder you're chunky,' Gooch said.

'Gooch. Don't,' Whit said. He shrugged at Junior. 'So start working your cell phone and get all of your daddy's attorneys down here. The bill the lawyers charge to your dad for all that travel time should be substantial.'

Junior considered this – calling his father to gather a bevy of lawyers in Port Leo – and suddenly cooperated. 'Look, Judge, you want to chase down the right fox, you need to look at the X-Bitch.'

'Who?'

'Pete's ex. He called her the X-Bitch, you know, like *The X-Files*? Freaking alien weirdo. She was about to drive him crazy.'

'How so?'

'Man, how didn't Faith? Over at his boat all the time, trying to sweeten him up. I caught Pete and Faith once, I swear, inches from fucking. Velvet would've had a coronary.'

'Velvet says Pete was just a friend.'

'Yeah, right, they're just friends after he's had his dick inside her a couple of hundred times. You know women don't think that way, not even porn stars.' Junior laughed, relaxing now that the topic was back on treasured ground. 'But the X-Bitch, hell, I think she kinda had a split personality going as far as Pete was concerned. She wanted him but she wanted him gone. She works for that old shit of a mother of his, and you know they were soiling their panties when he moved back. Jesus, he told me his mother offered him money to go away. He didn't want to do it and I'm all like, dude! Are you nuts? Take the money, ditch Port Lame here and go back to L.A., where life is real.' Junior shook his head. 'Shit, he should've taken that money. He really should've.'

Anson wheeled into view in the open doorway. 'Junior!' he bawled. 'Get in here.'

Junior picked up his groceries. 'I had every reason to want Pete alive, and his family sure as hell didn't. Later.' He turned and went back to Anson, walking past him without a word. Whit followed him back through the lobby. Anson wasn't in a mood to parry further.

'Good night, Judge,' he said with solemnity, and motored himself back into the elevator after Junior.

Whit and Gooch walked out of the lobby. Junior hardly appeared credible on paper, but his words gave Whit pause. If Velvet was right, and Pete was going to sue for custody, had Faith tried to disarm him with sex? And if Lucinda had truly offered her son cash to fade away . . . what had she done when he refused?

147

It suggested they knew damn well Pete might be suing for custody, and had more than a prayer of winning. But Junior would be hard to present as a credible witness.

'I must get the name of the reform school he attended,' Gooch said. 'I want to sponsor a scholarship.'

Whit walked past Junior's Porsche and noticed the rear left corner looked like it had suffered a minor accident. The left taillight was smashed. Whit remembered the one-eyed Porsche he'd passed last night heading away from the marina, trash disco blaring into the night – hours before Anson claimed they'd arrived in Port Leo.

The Blade was tired.

Midnight had come to Port Leo, his favorite time, and he stood beneath a canopy of live oaks and listened to the wind – the wind that had caressed, in its time, every inch of the world, every woman – whisper through the oak limbs.

It was a good day, he supposed. He knew where Velvet was, a toy just waiting to be opened. His plan for Heather Farrell had been put in motion. He could sleep and dream up a store of delights that, in the days ahead, he could make real.

Not every man, he knew, was so blessed and rich. He went into the garage to prepare his boat for its chores.

19

'Mom?'

Faith Hubble was jolted out of sleep. She had been dreaming: dreaming that Port Leo was gone, left far behind her on a boat arrowing deep into the bowl of the Gulf, and Pete stood to one side of her, Whit on the other. As the spray from the prow cooled her face against a blistering sun, the two of them seized her shoulders, upended her over the railing, and she plummeted toward a canyon of water, falling for miles. She had glanced up and Pete and Whit were gone, Lucinda and Sam standing in their places, watching her die.

She pulled her head from the pillow. Sweat touched her shoulders, her back, between her legs.

'Mom?' Sam said again. Purpling shadows marred the skin under his eyes. He looked as though he hadn't slept in a week. 'You okay?'

She smiled. She certainly was. 'Yes, honey, I'm fine.' She patted his hand. 'It's all gonna be okay. I promise you that.'

Velvet munched on a cold Pop-Tart and counted the money again, the bills new and stiff and feeling like revenge under her fingernails. She made the edges of the bills flush with a smack against the bedside table. As down payments went, it wasn't half bad. And since her production company wasn't being at all helpful on the legal front ('Sorry, Velvet. Don't know a lawyer in Texas and we just can't get involved' – the bastards), the money was more necessary than ever. Money from Faith to stab Faith, eventually. She liked the idea.

She finished her Pop-Tart then studied the pastry's box to see if the phrase was trademarked – not a bad name for a movie. Pop-Tarts. Could play up pop music, could play up oversweet breakfast treats. Damn. Trademarked. Oh, well. She folded the money – twenty thousand – into the bottom of her suitcase, hiding it inside a light wind-breaker.

She showered, considering her next move. Shooting Faith would have been a bad idea and she doubted that she could have pulled the trigger. But she had loaded the gun and stuck it in the bottom of her purse as Faith knocked on the door, just in case.

Just in case the crazy bitch tried to kill her.

But Faith had not had murder on her mind. *Listen, Velvet, you know and I know that Pete killed himself. You saying anything else is just a ploy for publicity.*

You mean a ploy for justice.

No. Publicity. I did a little checking, sweetie. Pete tried to kill himself four years ago, swallowing pills. I got the hospital records from Van Nuys. I'm giving them to the police and to Whit Mosley.

It doesn't mean anything.

You know what else I found out, sweetie? Your last five movies have bombed. You tried to get all artsy in-stead of just delivering the smut, and no one cares what you're doing now. You're broke, Velvet.

Get the hell out of here.

And Faith, instead of getting mad, gave her that super-ior little smirk. *So mature. Don't you know I can help you? Get you back on your feet so you can –* the smirk again – *get back off them right away. And you and I can both be happy.*

Velvet rinsed her hair clean of lather, turned off the shower, reached for a towel. She felt better than she had yesterday, when the knots and rocks in her gut shifted with every breath. She stepped out of the shower, wondering if Pete was looking down or up at her, and whether he hated her now.

Don't hate me, Pete. I promise you I'm not done with them yet, and Faith Hubble's going to fry, fry, fry. She would have to launder the money the Hubbles would be steering toward her, polish it with a veneer of respectability, before she called the papers in Dallas and Houston and Austin. It shouldn't, she figured, take very long.

She got dressed and checked the gun again, at the bottom of her purse. It fit in perfectly next to the hand-held tape recorder. Faith's voice on that tape – cajoling, begging, offering bribes for silence over Pete's still secret career – was better than any bullet. A bullet meant only a moment's suffering.

Suffering. She thought of Sam, Faith's pleas that he be protected from all the pain about Pete's career, and she remembered Sam and Pete sitting on the prow of *Real Shame*, Pete drinking a bottled beer, Sam sipping a Coke, awkwardly talking, settling finally on a discussion of baseball. Pete liked the Padres, Sam the Rangers, and she shamelessly eavesdropped, hearing them warm to each other, talking about trades and homers and a mutual loathing of the Yankees. Sam had finally laughed at one point. Warm tears had welled in her eyes and she thought, *Who the hell are you, June Cleaver?* Maybe she should say nothing forever, let Sam think his father just made industrial films. Pete wouldn't want Sam to be ashamed, to bear the brunt of his sins. Or she could take the money, throw it at Sam, say, *Here's what your mama wanted to pay me for silence, hon. Know who you're living with*.

She dug the creased business card out of her purse, smoothed it out, then dialed Whit's number.

At ten after nine Wednesday morning, Claudia drove past an elaborately painted sign that read JABEZ JONES MINISTRIES. Above the logo was a gold cross etched over a pair of gargantuan biceps.

'Did you know that Jesus did not work out on a regular basis?' Whit slurped a cup of hot coffee he'd snagged at Irina's café.

'Judas was flabby, too,' Claudia said. The road leading to the compound was surrounded by a dense growth of bent oaks and lined by hardy palm trees. They drove past another sign that read SALVATION AHEAD – FEEL THE BURN.

'So what happens if you go to hell? Don't you still feel the burn?' Claudia asked. She didn't feel the burn, but she felt the tension in the car. She and Whit hadn't talked since she'd seen Faith at Whit's place. Whit had seemed tired when she picked him up at the courthouse. He updated her about his talk with Junior Deloache and Anson Todd. Another angle for her to present to Delford, although she fretted her boss would welcome news of Pete's friendship with hoods no more than theories of murder. 'Do you think he's this corny on purpose?'

'Absolutely. It's sort of like asking if pro wrestlers consider themselves athletes,' Whit said. 'Do you remember Jabez Jones from school?'

'Vaguely. Geeky, glasses, the kind of preacher's kid you felt bad for because you just knew he never got to have one lick of fun,' Claudia said.

'I remember seeing him wrestling on TV. Joltin' Jabez Jones. I nearly didn't recognize him. Especially in gold tights.'

'God knows my father considers pro wrestling a religion.'

'God doesn't have much to do with his appeal,' Whit

said. 'He's just like those TV specials on pets that attack or cops' greatest chases or us all watching a president get caught with his pants down. Everything is entertainment now. He's just making lo-cal evangelism another genre.'

They turned into an asphalt parking lot. Jabez's compound was the original odd folly of a Fort Worth oil baron who had built a television studio outside Port Leo, part of an ill-conceived plan for a fishing network. The few shows he produced bombed and the compound stayed shuttered for a few years until Jabez Jones defected from the pro wrestling ring to start his church and show, *Holy Cross-Training*. It had found a shaky home on stations serving rural markets with low-powered religious programming.

The squat cabins were painted a glossy white. A game of women's volleyball, played in modest shorts and T-shirts adorned with gold crosses, was under way in a sand pit. A couple of men stood by, watching, attempting unsuccessfully to look pious while ogling the bouncing breasts.

'He's Hugh Hefner with a Bible,' Whit said.

Whit and Claudia were barely out of the car when the welcoming committee arrived. She was six feet tall, well muscled, and wore her platinum-blond hair closely cropped. She wore a tight white T-shirt with a gold cross emblazoned on the chest and cargo pants bulky enough to conceal an armory. Whit remembered what Ernesto had told him about one of Pete's visitors: *like a man with titties*. It was a crude, unkind, but effective description.

'Hi. I'm Judge Whit Mosley and this is Detective Claudia Salazar from the Port Leo police. We have an appointment with Jabez,' Whit said.

'Regarding?'

'He wanted to share some information with us regarding a case,' Claudia said.

'Follow me. But if he's not done with his taping, you'll just have to wait.'

Claudia and Whit followed the Amazon along a crushed-oyster-shell path that led down from the main complex toward a finger of the bay.

'I'm sorry, I didn't catch your name,' Whit said.

'Mary Magdalene.'

Whit shot Claudia a look. If Mary Magdalene was this tough, Whit thought, God only knew how butch Esther and Ruth were. Eve could probably kick major ass, too.

'This is an impressive setup.' Claudia gave Whit a frown that said, *Don't you dare laugh*.

Mary Magdalene nodded. 'Oh, yes, the Lord has smiled on Jabez.'

'He's smiling on that volleyball court,' Whit said.

'Jabez says exercise is a way of paying homage to what the Lord has created, in making man and woman. Building muscles is worship.' She flexed her own thickened arms.

'I've always believed our bodies are temples,' Whit offered. Mary Magdalene gave him a quick scrutiny, then apparently dismissed his temple as one devoted to a lesser god.

The volleyball bounced into the grass near them. One of the comely disciples chased it. She scooped the ball up, and Whit thought: *Do I know her?* But the young woman turned and sashayed back to the game.

'Jabez doesn't have much trouble getting a date, does he?' Whit observed in what he considered to be a completely friendly tone. Claudia withered him with a glare.

'Jabez doesn't *date*.' Mary Magdalene spat out the last word. 'He doesn't care a whit for the temptations of this physical world.' Her voice hardened. 'The temptations of the flesh are the seed of all evil.'

Whit surveyed the immaculately kept buildings, the

sand-rumped girls playing volleyball, the new Cadillac parked right by the administration building door with JABEZ on the plate. 'He's a real Francis of Assisi,' Whit said to Claudia, his voice lowered.

'Sissy?' Mary Magdalene had misheard.

'No, sassy,' Whit answered. 'He sasses that old devil, don't he?'

Mary Magdalene raised one platinum eyebrow. 'Jabez could kick the devil's ass, and don't you forget it.'

Whit and Claudia reflected on this platitude in silence. Claudia pinched Whit on the meaty part of his arm to ensure he wouldn't comment.

Mary Magdalene escorted them to a small stretch of beach full of cameras, portable sound booms, and spandex-clad missionaries. Sparkling white sand, cleaner-looking than the grayish beige grit on most Texas beaches, had been spread over the native soil.

Whit and Claudia stood back to watch the spectacle. Jabez Jones, well over six feet tall, two hundred thirty pounds of muscle with less body fat than a moth, lay on his side, scissoring his tree-trunk legs into the air, counting off reps while providing a little insight into the Book of Luke. Behind him two women (one svelte, one heavy for the dieting viewers to bond with) and a less beefy man mirrored his exercises, all beaming like angels.

'Now, hold the lift until the Scripture is done,' Jabez boomed. ' "I tell thee, thou shalt not depart thence till thou hast paid the very . . . last . . . mite." . . . There! Amen! Bless us all, did you feel the Holy Spirit invigorating your limbs? I know I did. I'm just coursing with the Holy Spirit right now. You keep doing those leg lifts and the devil himself won't be able to catch you. Now let's start our cool-down, and our Scripture for that is one of the more relaxing Psalms, a personal favorite of mine, number sixty-one.'

Whit resisted the urge to lead a cheer.

Cool-down completed, Jabez jumped to his feet, did a hand clap, reminded viewers about his 1-888 number and Web site to place requests with Jabez's Prayer Workout Chain or to order his fitness-theology tapes. 'Remember, your donations make all the difference in fighting flab . . . and sin! Praise God! Call now!'

God – who, in Whit's mind, represented the infinite beauty of the universe – as a weight-loss shuckster.

Finally a nasal-voiced director called, 'That's a wrap. Beautiful, Jabez.' Jabez gave a weary sigh and wiped the sand off his oiled legs. The crew began their cleanup.

'I'm curious, Mary Magdalene,' Whit said. 'Where does all the money come from to pay for this wonderful spread? Jabez's wrestling career must've been lucrative in that worldly goods way.'

'The Lord provides,' Mary Magdalene intoned.

'The Lord must provide on a real regular basis,' Whit said. Claudia shot him a look: *Quit antagonizing this woman.* Whit moved to the left a couple of feet to avoid another pinch.

Jabez Jones trotted over, smiling. 'Hello, Detective Salazar. Judge Mosley. Bless you.'

'Hello, Reverend.' Claudia nodded. 'We had an appointment?'

'Of course. Thank you for escorting them here, Mary. We can talk here along the beach, it's quiet and peaceful.' He gestured with his oak-tree arm down a stretch of beach away from the camera crew.

'Jabez?' Mary Magdalene clearly didn't want to leave his presence. 'I can stay—'

'Go. It's fine,' Jabez said.

'If you'll excuse me,' Mary Magdalene said, 'I have the Lord's work to do.' She uttered this with a mysterious air, as though this activity involved Navy SEALs, Russian microfilm, and Jimmy Hoffa.

They followed Jabez. The morning had turned shiny, the sky cloudless. A wheel of gulls cawed above their heads, swerved as one, and dived for food in the lapping surf. Shriveled husks of two dead Portuguese man-of-war jellyfish lay on the sand.

'Mary Magdalene seems real sweet,' Whit said.

'She's very devoted. I rescued Mary Magdalene from the streets of Houston. She was homeless, hopeless, strung out on dope, not strong. I made her strong,' Jabez said.

'You and Jesus,' Whit said.

'Absolutely,' Jabez agreed, as though he and the Lord made an awesome tag team. 'So, Whit. You're a JP now. How very . . . rewarding for you.'

'I like it,' Whit said.

'I surely hope you're reelected,' Jabez said. 'I mean, running that restaurant and that delivery service just didn't seem to be your calling.' The comment was topped with such a dollop of theocratic sugar that it might not be an insult. Jabez smiled in the light of his expensive muscles and his expensive compound and his expensive television crew.

'Gosh, Jabez, thanks. And I pray on a near-constant basis that you get picked up by a TV station that actually serves a metropolitan area.'

Jabez's smile never dimmed, but one of the balloon-shaped muscles in his arm tensed. The preacher turned to Claudia. 'I called because I thought I might be able to help you with your inquiries.'

'We understand you'd been to see Pete recently.'

'Yes. I offered him spiritual counsel. He and I have known each other for a long time. He was going through some difficult times.' He paused and dropped his little bomb. 'He wanted custody of his son.'

'That we knew,' Whit said.

Jabez crossed his bulky arms. Small gold crosses were tattooed on his knuckles. 'Oh. Well, perhaps I'm not being helpful. The Hubbles were, of course, opposed to him filing. Trying to settle with him. I guess you knew that as well.'

Whit and Claudia exchanged a quick glance. The Hubbles had consistently claimed no knowledge of Pete wanting custody. If Jabez was being truthful, then they were lying.

'What did he have on them that would have made them even negotiate with him? You only go out-of-court if you're not sure you can win, and Faith and Lucinda should have been as sure as saints,' Whit said. 'What leverage did Pete have?'

Jabez shook his head. 'Don't know . . . Your Honor. Pete kept that private.' But there was a flicker of an amused smile behind his solemnity, and Whit wondered.

'I understand you and he fought. Argued,' Whit said.

'Ah. Velvet?'

'Yes.'

'She misunderstood. Pete wanted me to be a character witness for him. I was willing, because I do think everyone can change, and Pete seemed sincere in wanting to improve his lot. But I told him he would need to accept God in his life, and he got mad at me then. There were no other arguments.'

'So did Pete discuss any other aspects of his life with you?' Claudia asked.

A pained look crossed Jabez's gladiator-handsome face. 'When I was in wrestling . . . well, some of my colleagues were attracted to women of dubious morality. Some of them worked in adult films, and I heard, through them, about Pete. I actually saw him at a dinner party a few years ago, hosted by a wrestling promoter. He looked terrible. He asked me not to tell anyone back here about his . . . career. I've kept my word. Gossip is the devil's venom poured in an ear. So do you suspect the Hubbles?'

So much for the evils of gossip, Whit thought.

'We have no suspects at the moment. We're not even sure it's a homicide,' Claudia said. 'Judge Mosley will be conducting the inquest in the next couple of days.'

'Would suicide surprise you?' Whit asked.

'I don't quite understand why he would come home and work on getting close to his son, then kill himself.'

Whit changed topics. 'Did he mention that he was working on a film?'

Jabez's mouth gave a cautious twitch. 'I prayed he would not resume his career.'

'No. A documentary about his brother Corey. He says on a tape we found that you refused to cooperate with him.'

The mouth twitched again and a muscle flexed under the cross-laden T-shirt. 'That's not so. I just couldn't be of much help to him. He had called me . . . when he came back to town. That's how we got to talking. He did ask me to tell him about the day Corey vanished.'

'And you said what?' Claudia asked.

Jabez paled under the store-bought tan. 'Well, I was one of the last to see Corey before he was reported missing. Pete asked me to restate what I remembered. I'm afraid I wasn't much help to him.' He stared out at the flat plane of the bay, stretching away like green glass.

'You and Corey strike me as unlikely friends,' Whit said.

Jabez shrugged. 'I wanted to help Corey. He was in trouble at school, at home, and sinking further. I thought I could help him reshape his life.'

'So he was like a project,' Whit said. 'You could get your Samaritan merit badge by turning him around.'

'That's a crude way to put it, but yes. If I didn't think God could turn around lives, I would never bother with a ministry.'

'And Corey was willing to be preached at?'

'You have an admirable ability for oversimplification, Whit,' Jabez said. 'It must serve you well in traffic court. No, he wasn't willing to be preached at. But he was willing to have a friend he could talk to, who didn't smoke dope, who didn't want to drag him down. I was a refuge.'

'You were a goody-goody. He was a punk. I'm frankly surprised Corey Hubble would give you the time of day,' Whit said.

'You just never know about people, do you?' Jabez said.

'So what happened the day Corey vanished?' Claudia interrupted.

'Corey had planned to spend the night with me. We were going to watch movies at my house. I'd gotten a tape of *Godspell*, thought he might like the music and it'd give me a way to witness to him. He called and canceled at the last minute, saying he was sick. I never heard from or saw him again.'

'Did Pete share any theories about Corey with you?' Claudia asked. 'Any information he had found about his brother?'

Jabez Jones considered for a moment, and the pause reminded Whit of a talented preacher waiting for the congregation to lean forward, eager for the next word. 'It makes no sense to me. Pete mentioned a possibility that Corey was still alive. And in some kind of trouble.'

20

'You know that motto, What Would Jesus Do? I look at Jabez and wonder, What Would Jesus Think?' Claudia said.

'He's lying,' Whit said.

'Prove it.'

'Oh, Christ, proof. My gut tells me. He's a publicity hound. If he can link himself to a high-profile death, he will.'

'Listen, Honorable, you can't prove he's lying any more than you could prove Faith Hubble has lied. Or anyone else,' she added quickly.

'You think Faith's lying?'

'Faith Hubble is running scared.'

'Don't pull a punch here.'

'She threatened my family, Whit. Very subtly. She implied my father might lose his shrimping license.'

'You must have misunderstood.'

'You don't misunderstand a threat to your father's livelihood. I felt like belting her in the face.' Claudia turned onto Highway 35 that threaded back to Port Leo. 'I sensed a weird vibe between you and Faith Hubble last night.'

'No. I've just known her for a long while. She's worried about her kid.'

'Don't let your friendship warp your judgment.'

'I'm going to get tired, very quickly, of you and Delford telling me how to do my job.'

'Don't get all huffy.'

Whit was silent for a moment. 'So say what you think, Claudia.'

'You have a political future at stake, Whit. I know you want to win the election, even if you act like campaigning is pimping. And I don't relish examining bodies with that grease-wad Buddy Beere. So all I'm saying is, you show the Hubbles a hint of favoritism, you're gonna get cooked. I don't believe for one second they can contain Velvet from leaking news of Pete's career. The news is going to hit big, and you better handle the inquest with every i dotted and t crossed.'

'As opposed to gunning for them. Like you,' Whit said dryly.

They passed the WELCOME TO PORT LEO – SWEET SPOT OF THE GULF sign, surrounded by smaller signs from city churches, the Chamber of Commerce, the Kiwanis and Rotary Club. 'As long as they don't gun for me. She guns for me, my family, I don't tolerate that.'

'I still think you're mistaken about Faith,' Whit said.

'I'm not getting into a fight with you, Honorable.' Claudia turned into the town square, parking in front of the police station. 'But why did Heather Farrell say Pete blamed Jabez for Corey's death? Jabez sure isn't going to tell us. How would Heather even know about a connection between Jabez and Pete?'

'Maybe she's got a different connection to Jabez. Other than Pete.'

Claudia shrugged. 'I'll track Ms Farrell down and ask her.'

Whit turned to her. 'Let's say Jabez is telling the truth. Pete thought Corey was alive . . . so where's Corey been all these years?'

Claudia's office was cramped. Delford sat in the creaky wooden chair next to her desk, eyes bleary red. Even his wax-perked mustache drooped, its tapered corners sagging. Whit slumped in the chair at Eddie Gardner's desk, his feet propped on a stack of papers.

Whit watched as Delford and Claudia brainstormed.

'The most obvious answer is usually the right one,' Delford said. 'Suicide.'

Claudia shook her head. 'Pete lived on a boat owned by established criminals. He wanted his wife's kid. He could derail his mother's political campaign. He was digging into a brother's disappearance that could have been murder and made accusations against a wanna-be television star. Are you and I looking at the same picture?'

'Yeah, well you can look at inkblots and come up with different interpretations, Claud,' Delford said. 'He was a pervert and he didn't have squat of a future. We've had more than one person say, and folks that knew him better than you and I, that he was depressed and maybe suicidal.'

'Your stubbornness,' Claudia groaned, 'is about to make me suicidal.'

'He tried to kill himself a few years ago. Faith Hubble got the police report from Van Nuys. He downed a bunch of pills and vodka.' Delford clicked his tongue. 'I'd have thought, Claud, you would have unearthed that little nugget.'

A slow creep of color bloomed along Claudia's cheeks. 'I'd like to see that report, if you don't mind.'

'Suicide once doesn't mean suicide again,' Whit said.

Delford growled low in his throat. 'No. Let's never grab hold of the obvious, shall we?'

Claudia turned referee. 'Let me tell you what else I've found before you two start debating. Pete's been arrested twice out in California: once for public intox, once for disturbing the peace and public nudity. Apparently while filming one of his little epics in the great outdoors. He didn't serve time. Both were over five years ago.' She flipped a page. 'Velvet has no record. She told me in her statement that Pete rented that laptop on a monthly basis from Baywater Computers. I called the store owner, and Pete hadn't returned the system. We still haven't located it. I'm going to get a diver down into the marina to look for it. Maybe it went overboard.'

Delford said nothing.

'Phone records I've got Fox checking out. Mostly calls back to California, although he has several calls to Missatuck, Texas, over the past week. Up in deep East Texas. Know it?'

'Never heard of it,' Delford said. 'So let's say it's murder, just to indulge you, Claudia. Who do you like?'

'Faith Hubble,' Claudia said instantly.

'Right. A respected leader and mother,' Delford said. 'Same for you, Whit?'

Whit felt like he was walking on quicksand in leaded boots. 'I don't know. Certainly Pete was a threat to the campaign. And Pete was serious about fighting for custody, although no one believes he had a prayer.'

'Given what we know,' Claudia interrupted. 'But it works if Faith's closet was dirtier than his.'

Delford snorted. 'That's hard to imagine.'

'Junior Deloache or someone working for him would be my guess,' Whit said. 'If you have a crime, look for criminals.'

'You're deep,' Delford said.

'Since you think I ignore the obvious, don't ignore the Deloaches,' Whit said carefully. 'I've got to go. Court and duty call.' He left.

Delford waited until Whit shut the door. 'Sloppy work, Claudia. Not learning about that suicide attempt. Doesn't make us look good.' His voice, usually a cajoling drawl, rang hard and steely.

'I'm sorry. I'll call the Van Nuys police right now and confirm.'

'See that you do,' Delford said. 'I got a meeting with the mayor. Let me know what you find out. And don't screw up again, Claud.' He slammed the door behind him.

Who the hell are you turning into, Delford? she wondered. She reached for the phone and asked Nelda to get her the Van Nuys, California, police department.

21

At lunchtime, Whit grabbed a booth in the back of Café Caspian, surveying the small crowd in his new stepmother's restaurant. Babe had cautioned Irina that the Coastal Bend population included many military retirees who might blanch at patronizing a Russian café. Whit privately thought most of the retired military males would rush (in well-organized step) to slurp Irina's coffee once they spotted her in her black miniskirt and white T-shirt.

Café Caspian was perhaps a quarter full, mostly retirees with a smattering of realtors, secretaries, and artists gossiping over Russian specialties like *piroshki* (meatfilled dumplings), *golubtsi* (cabbage rolls), *borscht* topped with sour cream, honey breads, and *blinis*. Whit wished he had invested in sour cream futures before Irina opened the café; he would have made a killing. She also served more mainstream foods, such as thick ham sandwiches; fish, shrimp, and oysters fresh from the bay; and what she called *bitokes à la Russe* – hamburgers dolled up with sour cream (of course), onion, and nutmeg. These had been an unexpected hit.

Tributes to both Irina's motherland and her adopted land decorated the walls: a beautiful color photograph of the Statue of Liberty; a portrait of Peter the Great. Reproductions of elegant Fabergé eggs and peasant Russian dolls lined a shelf; on another was a framed collection of miniature American and Texan flags. In the window hung several KEEP WHIT MOSLEY JUSTICE OF THE PEACE signs. Irina, the Soviet-born fiend for democracy.

Irina slid into the seat across from him, holding a steaming cup of tea and pushing her chestnut-brown hair back over her ears. Her face was elfin; he had always pictured Russian women as either kerchief-headed grannies, sun-and-nutrient-starved model waifs, or steroid-gulping swimmers. But Irina looked fresh and healthy, not tall but not frail, eyes of watery blue, and a generous mouth.

'Go campaign today.' She took her stepmother role seriously. 'Buddy Beere has a van covered with campaign signs patrolling Main Street.'

'He offered to debate me.'

'Of course you accepted.'

'No. I'm too busy doing the actual job. But I need two favors.'

'Tell me.'

'I need to borrow your computer.'

'Sure. You need the computer now?' she asked.

'I'd prefer to use it after hours, if you don't mind.'

'No problem.'

Why does a Russian accent nail you right in the crotch? Perhaps he had fixated on Natasha on the old *Bullwinkle* cartoons in a freaky erotic manner.

She jangled a set of keys from her pocket, pried a silver key off the ring, and slid it across the table. 'Extra key. Lock up when you're done. Second favor is?'

'I want you to befriend someone but you cannot gossip about it.'

'Who?'

'Her name is Velvet.'

'That sounds like a horse's name.'

'She's not. She's a friend of the man who died. She's a little unconventional, but she could use a friendly face. She's meeting me here for lunch. I'll introduce you.'

'You always find the strays that need help, yes?'

'Don't tell Dad. He'll just say that I'm not being focused on the campaign.'

Irina made a dismissive noise. 'Forget him. You know, I think I am the only one who knows the real you sometimes. Isn't that silly?' She leaned over and gave him an irreproachable peck on the cheek. 'You are a thoughtful boy, Whit.'

A boy, and he was older than she.

Velvet stepped inside the café. Whit waved her over, introduced Irina to her.

'You're Judge Mosley's stepmother?' Velvet, dressed modestly in tourist-trap Bermuda shorts and a pale yellow T-shirt, shook hands and sat, not taking her eyes off Irina. 'Maybe I should go recruit in Russia. I do training films. Corporate stuff.'

Irina smiled politely and excused herself. She returned with tall glasses of iced tea, took their order for salads and *bitokes*, and scurried to the kitchen.

'So now you're making training films?' Whit said.

'I cut a little deal with Faith Hubble. Mouth zippered shut for now. For Sam's sake. Pete wouldn't have wanted him hurt by, well, by the truth.'

'So you and Faith are bosom buddies?'

'I loathe that bitch with all my heart. But Sam's a good kid. I don't want him hurt. But I don't want them to just sweep Pete under a rug, either.'

'So how are you doing?'

She shrugged. 'I'm cried out. When do you have autopsy results?'

'Probably today. At the latest tomorrow.' He stirred his tea. 'Pete tried to kill himself once before. You neglected to mention that to us.'

'Oh, that. He took the wrong pills.'

'A dozen of them?'

'He took the pills because I didn't cast him in a quickie

168

movie I was making. We had a fight the week before, and I was fed up with him. Pete could be a prima donna. So he downed some tranqs and called me on his cell phone to drive him to the hospital. I didn't believe him, and by the time I got to his place he was tanked out. Otherwise I wouldn't have bothered with the hospital. I just would have made him puke. I've jammed fingers down throats before.'

'A lot of suicide among your co-workers, isn't there?'

Velvet shrugged. 'Shrinks kill themselves more than any other group. So don't be thinking my colleagues are all mental cases. We're not.'

'No, like me, you're all well-adjusted models of society.' He meant it lightly, as a joke on them both, but he'd punched a well-pummeled bruise.

'Yeah. Just like the well-adjusted models of society that buy all our movies.'

Their salads arrived, blanketed with blue-cheese dressing. Velvet waited until the server left before speaking.

'You probably don't know the names I've been called by your well-adjusted types when I've bothered to go on radio shows or done Web interviews. Whore. Slut. They cease to mean much after a while.' She offered a smile. 'I prefer to think of myself as a pleasure engineer.'

He laughed because he could tell she needed him to.

'At least this way I get to choose what I'm called, Whit. *Whore*'s a term coined by men to trample any woman with sexual vitality.' Velvet licked the blue cheese from her fork with a slow, baroque flourish of her tongue. Whit waited for the chain reaction of heart attacks to decimate the retired men in the restaurant, but no one keeled over.

'That makes you uncomfortable,' Velvet said. 'You're all squirmy boy now.'

'I am not.'

'What a squirmy man needs is a kiss gone bad,' Velvet said.

'A what?'

'In regular movies, ninety percent of the time, you get the kiss and that's it. Maybe they wriggle, real fakey, in bed. But it's antiseptic sexuality. In adult movies you get the kiss and two seconds later the cast is getting way down and dirty. I just call it a kiss gone bad. But it's really good. You know, you're my ideal audience. Single, a little bored, too respectable to ever solicit a prostitute but probably in need of sweet relief.'

'I'm not bored,' Whit said. He felt color creeping up past his collar.

'Have you ever seen one of my movies, Whit?'

'No.'

'Have you ever seen any porn movie? Be honest.'

'Yes,' he admitted. 'When one of my brothers got married, we had a bachelor party with an X-rated tape rolling on the VCR.'

'If you watched it, and it made your God-fearing little soldier stand at attention, honey, you can't look down your nose at me. I'm giving you and every other man what greases your wheels.' She lowered her voice even further. 'I bet my tapes are under more beds and hidden away in more closets here in your sweet little Gomerville than you would ever imagine.'

'What do you want me to say, Velvet? Good for you?'

'I just don't want you to act like what I do is so terribly wrong. I'm not filled with angst over what I do.'

'All this angst Pete supposedly felt about his brother's disappearance, is that really why he ended up in porn?'

'He did it because it's fun,' she said in a flat voice, fork poised above the messy salad.

'Fun. And that's why you did the movies, too?'

She began to eat her salad, not answering him, shoveling drenched chunks of lettuce in her mouth, staring at her plate. 'Drop the armchair psychology.'

'It's just that . . . you seem too smart for this.'

She glanced at him quickly. 'Oh, and so the blue movies are full of morons, huh? Judgie boy, I've worked with computer programmers, accountants, lawyers. People who want to make one flick, just for laughs, use a horny-corny name, get in, get out. You think they're better than me 'cause they do drive-by porn?'

'No,' Whit said. 'But I want to know why you and Pete did these movies.'

'Why? Want me to make you a star?' she asked.

'I'm quite sure I'd be a disappointment on film.'

'You got a good jawline. That's important. The camera likes you better.'

'So why? I just would like to know.'

'There's no soap opera answer. My folks didn't beat me, my dad didn't abuse me, none of that tabloid talk-show shit.' She set her fork down. 'I'm the worst-case scenario of a preacher's kid. My dad was a Methodist minister in Omaha. I wouldn't mind going back there one day, live life a little slower.'

'Your mom?'

'Died when I was four. Lupus.'

'I'm sorry.'

'I don't remember much about her, except she made the best lemon pie you ever ate. I'd sit on the kitchen floor while she baked, waiting to lick the spoon. And she liked gardenias. The house always smelled of them before she died.' She leaned back against the booth's seat. 'My dad married his church secretary just to give me a mama. She was a mean old cow who'd gone to the Hitler Secretarial School, and when I turned sixteen Dad was dying of cancer. He told me they'd slept together exactly one time. That was it. She cut him off right after because she had all the sensuality of a stale raisin. That's what's wrong with this world: there's not nearly enough love or happiness or orgasms.'

'About your mom . . . my mother took off when I was two. Never saw her again,' Whit said. 'And my dad was a drunk until I was seventeen.'

'Geez, you should've ended up on the other side of the camera with me,' Velvet said. 'Since nothing is our own fault and everything is the fault of our family's, right? Wrong. I don't blame my mom or my dad for any of my choices, Whit. I wanted to make a lot of money, I wanted to make movies, and I liked the sex.'

Whit pictured a little girl, sitting in a kitchen smelling of lemon peel and gardenias, the soft camouflage for a sickbed.

'I wanted to go to film school. Be the female Coppola. But that costs money, Whit, and I wasn't filling the bank waiting tables or mopping up spilled beer or tutoring kids in algebra. I met a guy. He said I could make a lot of fast cash, use a fake name, no one would ever know.' She paused. 'So I stayed in it. We build these little worlds for ourselves and then we never get to move out.'

'Meaning no one was gonna hire you for legit film work once you went down Porn Street?'

'The judge's robe does a nice job of covering your vicious streak.'

'It's vicious of me to point out the obvious?'

She said nothing.

'What you gonna do after Pete is buried?' Whit asked softly.

'Go back to California. Find the next guy who can supersize his boner when there's a camera three inches away and a crew of five standing around picking their noses.'

'Don't,' he said. 'Don't do that.'

She smiled but not the kind of smile that said aren't you sweet. 'Gee willikers, Whit, you gonna sweep me off my feet and save me from myself?'

'I just think you could . . . not do these movies anymore.'

'Why are you a judge?' she asked suddenly. 'You don't fit the type at all. Too free-spirited to be comfortable judging other people.'

'My dad got me the job,' he said, and she laughed.

'But you're sticking with it, right? You want to be elected. You're like a small-town Gerald Ford, wanting everyone to vote for you and really give you the job you got handed. Why?'

'I never wanted to be a politician. I hate that part of the job. But I think truth matters, even the little truths of small-claims and traffic court.'

'And death inquests.'

'Yes.'

'Bull,' she said. 'You like the power, Whit. I can see it in your eyes, that quick flash of *yes, I'm the judge, don't mess with me*. I like the power, too. When some lonely, horny guy slides one of my tapes into his machine, I have power over his pleasure. I can make him tingle all over or I can make him as limp as string. Never had much power as a kid, I bet.' She smiled, a cat warming up for a good purr. 'Littlest of six boys, you probably didn't get to pick when you took a pee. I'm not inclined to surrender my power any more than you are, Whit.'

Their *bitokes* arrived, and Irina plopped in the booth, chatting up Velvet, asking her if she'd walked through the shopping district and seen the Arts Center and the Maritime Museum. Velvet, steeped in sudden courtesy, spoke with complete assurance and sounded like an aspirant to the Junior League. Irina left them, patting Velvet on the hand, telling her how nice it was to meet her.

Velvet toyed with the prescription-pad-size dessert menu clamped above the salt and pepper. 'What if . . . you decide suicide, and more evidence comes later that says not suicide?'

'I can reopen the case, conduct a new inquest. But considering Pete tried to kill himself before, if the autopsy remotely suggests suicide . . .'

'I knew you'd cop out. You're not going to risk your own political neck to help me.'

'Give me something, then. Do you know anything he knew that could have gotten him killed? Anything specific?'

She shook her head. 'You don't think that's keeping me up at night? That maybe whoever shot him thinks I know what Pete knew? I don't. I don't.'

And he saw fear, a naked cancer, in her eyes.

It had been a bad afternoon for Claudia.

She got confirmation that Pete Hubble had once attempted – albeit clumsily – suicide. She hated that Faith Hubble was right. About anything.

There was a Judy Cameron in the Port Leo phone book, at the Paris Street address mentioned by Heather. Ms Cameron was a math teacher at Port Leo High School, but she had never heard of Heather Farrell and had no transients lounging at her house.

So Claudia gobbled a messy lunch of barbecue shrimp and coleslaw downtown, then headed for Little Mischief Beach. No Heather Farrell. The two scruffy girls on the beach she'd seen yesterday claimed not to know Heather or to have seen her.

She'd then stopped by the Hubbles, an exercise in futility. Lucinda, Faith, and Sam all stuck by their statements. Lucinda gave yes and no answers. Faith Hubble was polite but clearly irked at going through her statement again. Claudia remained friendly, crisp, and polite with them but feeling out of sorts and frustrated.

You don't like Faith Hubble, fine. Look at every suspect. Don't be blindsided, she told herself.

So she tromped back to the station to engage in a Deloache hunt. She spoke with the Houston and Galveston police departments and did simple queries against a statewide criminal database. Thomas Deloache Sr., age fifty, had a quilted history: twice dragged before a grand jury, but never indicted. He had started most likely as an enforcer for the Montoya crime ring and took over when Montoya and his son both died, ignobly, crushed by a beer-laden semitrailer on the Houston stretch of I-10. Thomas Deloache Sr. kept a low profile, but he was suspected of handling about five percent of the drugs funneled through the Houston-Galveston area.

Five percent was worth millions.

The successive generation of Deloaches offered mixed hope for a criminal dynasty. Two sons, Tommy Jr and Joe. Joe was the bright one, attended a Catholic prep school in Miami, went to college at Texas but didn't finish, opting to enter the family business early. Galveston police suspected him in two murders, but the lack of bodies and evidence stymied investigations. Junior marched to a different, perhaps palsied drummer. He had been arrested a few times on very minor charges, never anything worth more than a slap on the wrist. One hot check, swimming in very public Mecom Fountain in Houston when drunk, attending an illegal dogfight in Galveston. Barely finished high school, never attempted college. She went to go find her boss.

To her surprise Delford seemed more willing to listen to the potentials of a Junior Deloache being involved in Pete's death.

'Why would Junior Deloache be in Port Leo?' he asked.

'One of his dad's legit business concerns is a couple of small motels in Galveston. They're clean as a whistle, which is driving the Galveston cops nuts. Papa might be turning over that side of the business to Junior; it's less risky. He and his associate, a guy named Anson Todd, both told Judge Mosley they were renovating the old Sea Haven. And Judge Mosley thinks they've lied about their whereabouts the night Pete died.'

'I bet the Deloaches launder dirty money through the so-called legit businesses like these condos.' Delford tapped his finger against his lip. 'Do they know how the Deloaches run in the Houston drugs?'

'Probably different channels. Some from other parts of Texas, some up from Mexico, some in from the Gulf.'

'So why's he here? There wouldn't be near the market in Port Leo for drugs, unless shrimpers and retirees suddenly go coke-happy,' Delford said.

'But we've got navigable bays. Quiet beaches. Only a few hours from the south side of Houston, closer to Padre and all those tourists. And a lot fewer officers.'

Delford frowned. 'So Junior's here to smuggle drugs?'

'Junior may be exiled where he can do the least amount of damage. The Houston detectives told me he's famous for being an overgrown brat.'

'Even if Pete turns out to be a suicide we need to know about these people. Sit down for a minute.'

She sat, smelling a lecture in the air.

Delford flattened his palms on the table. 'Claudia, I have faith in you. But one area where you could stand definite improvement is in dealing with people.'

'Pardon?'

'Why are you grilling the Hubbles on their statements?'

'I didn't grill anybody. I hadn't even talked to them before today. I just wanted to review their statements with them, see if there was anything else they wanted to add.'

'There wasn't. I won't have the senator and her family treated like criminals.'

'I did no such thing.'

He rubbed his stubby-fingered hand across his eyes. He looked ten years older, she realized, than he had last week. There'd been a bad cancer scare with him last year, and a sudden tremble of worry took her. He was not a young man anymore.

'Are you okay?' she asked.

'Fine. Just tired.' He leaned back in his chair and a new

hardness tensed his jaw. 'I'm pulling you off as the lead investigator in the case.'

Her face felt frozen. 'Why?'

'Because one thing we're going to be in this department is professional, and you haven't been.'

'How?' *Don't get mad, stay calm*, she thought. A finger of sweat trickled down her back.

'You clearly don't like Faith Hubble, and it's coloring your view of this case. And given all the likely publicity, it's best Gardner takes the lead. You can still work on the case, just under his direction. I already sent him to Corpus this afternoon for the autopsy.'

Claudia heard her voice go ragged. 'This is unwarranted, Delford. You've never treated me this way before.'

'Defensive don't suit you. I've made my decision.'

She sat stunned.

Delford's phone buzzed. He scooped up the receiver and listened. 'Yeah, oh, yeah. I forgot. I'll send up Claudia.' He hung up and gestured toward the blue flyer on his wall of Marcy Kay Ballew. 'That missing girl's mother from Louisiana's here. Can you talk to her?'

'That was the sheriff's case.' David's case, to be exact.

'Technically, yes, but she's been wanting to know what we're doing in the city to help.' Delford shrugged. 'Maybe this'd be good for you to focus on now.'

'I'll talk with her.' Anything was preferable to sitting through an undeserved rebuke.

Not quite. 'By the way,' Delford said, 'your ex is with her.'

David sat, ramrod straight, his deputy's Stetson resting on his knee. His stare drifted to Claudia as Mrs Ballew talked; Claudia forced herself to concentrate on the woman's words.

'Marcy is a really good girl. The rose tattoo, that was simple foolishness. I'd already started saving for when she wanted to remove it. She is really quite sweet.' Mrs Ballew perched at her chair's edge.

'I'm sure she is,' Claudia said.

'And it would be easy for me to say I have no intention of being a pest, but I have every intention of being a pest.'

'You're certainly not a pest, and I want to assure you we're doing everything we can to search for your daughter here in the county.' David nodded at Claudia. 'Detective Salazar and I are used to working together, and I'm sure we can find your daughter.'

Gosh, you hardly ever spoke so gently to me. Claudia opened her copy of the Ballew file that David had brought; the same picture from the flyers was on top. A photo, probably taken at a chain department store, based on the cheesy fake background of an autumn-kissed farm and barn. Marcy had reddish hair, cropped short, slightly crooked teeth, thin lips, skin supple as a peach.

'No leads from the flyers yet, right?' Claudia asked David. He nodded and foisted his extrasympathetic gaze toward her.

Mrs Ballew swallowed. She was a spare, florid-cheeked woman, with a red frizz of hair and too-long nails painted a bright lavender. She wore khakis and a denim blouse, dressed for a day shopping at an outlet mall instead of beating the pavement for her missing child. 'Well, everyone back in Deshay said that Marcy ran off, you know, but I didn't believe it. Yeah, she had once before, but that was after a huge fight and she told me she was running off and I dared her to and she went to New Orleans for two nights and then ran out of money and came home, crying for her mama.' Mrs Ballew blinked, worn out by her monologue. 'Marcy don't have a boyfriend right now, so I don't think she took off with a boy.'

'And no one in your family, your circle of friends, knew Port Leo?' David asked. He kept glancing at Claudia and she thought, *Don't use this woman's grief just to get within two feet of me.*

'No, none.'

Claudia wondered if the Ballew girl had traipsed to the Coastal Bend for an unannounced vacation, lost her wallet, maybe turned to hitchhiking or hooked up with some of the party-minded sail bums that trolled from Galveston to South Padre Island. She hoped that was the answer.

'Will they drag the bay again?'

'Probably not, ma'am,' David said, 'unless we have new reason to.'

'Will they search again?'

'Until there's more evidence to point she actually stopped in the county, probably not,' Claudia said.

Mrs Ballew sagged.

'And you're absolutely sure that your daughter knew no one in Port Leo?' Claudia asked.

'She hung out with boys, sometimes, at the bars, and sometimes they weren't from Deshay. She never mentioned Port Leo to me.'

Claudia debated. No clues, no witnesses, no reason for the girl to be here. But she couldn't just turn this woman away. 'Tell me about Marcy.'

Mrs Ballew pointed toward the file. 'But you have the information . . .'

'I know. But it would be more helpful coming from you. You live in Deshay. How long have you been there?'

'Three years. We used to live in Shreveport. But in Deshay I got a job working for a cousin of mine at his shrimp restaurant, and he's promised to make me a full partner in a couple of years.'

Shrimping was big along the Louisiana coast, and it

was a lifeblood in Port Leo. Was that coincidence? But she'd consulted a map: Deshay was a fair ways north of the Louisiana coastline and huddled up close to the Texas border. 'Did Marcy work?'

'As little as possible,' Mrs Ballew said, as if by rote, and she burst into tears, long, heaving sobs that carried the force of long suppression. Claudia hurried around her desk and squatted next to Mrs Ballew, put an arm around her, and placed a tissue in the woman's hands. David fiddled with the brim of his Stetson, paling under his freckles.

'Sorry,' Mrs Ballew gasped as her crying subsided. 'I'm sorry. I'm sorry.'

'You're doing great,' Claudia assured her.

'I always said she didn't work hard enough, Jesus, and now I'm so afraid she's dead, and I make fun of her for being lazy. But that was the thorn between us, you know. Not a joke but the one thing I got mad at her for, the not working hard enough.' Mrs Ballew exhaled a long *who-oosh* and wiped her face and nose.

'Tell me about her job.' Claudia pulled her chair close to Mrs Ballew's.

'She worked as a nursing home aide in Deshay. She'd change the patients' beds, mop up the floor, spoon lunch into their mouths. It was either that or road crew for the parish, out in the heat and wet. But she liked the clients, especially the old ladies. She'd tell me when a new widower arrived and all those old women would just start a-prissing.' Mrs Ballew mopped at her eyes. 'Marcy said she could make their last days happy if she snuck Viagra into the food.'

'What's the name of the nursing home?'

'Memorial Oaks.'

Claudia wondered why it wasn't a crime to use the term *memorial* in a facility designed to house the still-living. 'Tell me about the day she went missing.'

'September thirtieth, she worked her regular shift, from noon to ten at night. Usually she came right home, showered to get the Lysol smell out of her hair, got ready if she was going barhopping. She didn't come home.'

'The staff at Memorial Oaks were the last to see her?'

'Yeah. Her supervisor said she left about ten after ten. She stayed to help with a patient who'd puked all over himself.' As Mrs Ballew's lip trembled, she wondered the inevitable: *If Marcy had been her usual lazy self and not stayed that extra ten minutes, would she have escaped the boogeyman?*

'And none of her things were missing?'

'No, all her stuff was at home. Her car was found about ten miles away, at a shopping center parking lot. But she hated that center. She never went there, so I don't know why she would go that night.'

Bad with a capital B. The girl was, in Claudia's opinion, an abductee and probably dead. But how and why would her ID surface in Port Leo, hundreds of miles away?

David cleared his throat importantly but said nothing.

Claudia glanced at the file. The wallet, when found on the road outside Port Leo, had had a credit card and thirty-three dollars in cash in it. The most likely scenario was that the Ballew girl had been killed close to Deshay, although the Louisiana police had not turned up a trace of her. Assuming she was dead, someone – either the killer or an associate – had come to Port Leo, where they chose to throw Marcy Ballew's wallet – still containing cash – onto the road.

'We traced the movements of the registered sex offenders in Encina County, seeing if any of them had gone to Louisiana recently, if any had a connection to Deshay. So far nothing,' David said.

The words *sex offender* made Mrs Ballew go white.

'Deshay is a long way for someone to go to commit a crime against a stranger,' Claudia said. 'There must be some other connection.'

'I can't think of one,' Mrs Ballew said mournfully. So for the next forty minutes Claudia worked through Marcy's life: old boyfriends, old high school friends, former co-workers, any hobbies or interests. David hardly asked a question.

Mrs Ballew enumerated her daughter's interests. 'She did like watching cable TV, the movies, and she liked wrestling on TV a lot, and figure skating, what with the fancy costumes.'

'Wrestling? She ever watch Joltin' Jabez Jones?' Claudia asked.

Mrs Ballew brightened. 'Oh, yeah, the guy who became the preacher? Sure, she watched his show. She was a big fan of his.'

23

The Honorable Whit Mosley curbed the impulse to put the small-claims hearings on a kitchen timer. Watching the Augustine brothers bicker was like rewinding a moment from his own rowdy family's past, where the six brothers routinely waged war over who scarfed down the nacho chips and who erased the Super Bowl tape and who spread lard across a brother's bedsheets.

The division between the Augustines – who seemed to be sharing IQ points – was a homemade barbecue grill. Each side had laid out the facts of their case in a style that would have won them admirers on the tabloid talk-show circuit.

'Let me get this straight,' Whit said. 'Tony, you built the grill using your own labor, correct?'

'Damn straight. Sir.' Tony Augustine nodded. He was a year older than Whit and had been a minor bully in junior high, and now realized he might pay for past transgressions. 'Sweat of my own brow, Judge.'

'But you used Cliff's materials, correct?'

'That's right, Your Honor,' said Cliff Augustine. He had never pushed anyone out of the lunch line and suspected he had the moral high ground. 'I spent all the money on the materials: the bricks, the racks, the wiring, all of it.'

'And, Tony, because there would be no grill without your high level of craftsmanship' – the sarcasm was not lost on Judge Mosley's clerk, the constable, the Augustines, or the few spectators waiting to argue their own cases – 'you now want it back.'

'Well, yeah.' Tony gulped. 'I mean, we were gonna

share it, but now our wives ain't getting along. It's a real sweet grill, makes the best ribs you've ever put in your mouth.' A hint of bribery honeyed Tony's voice. Whit believed a plate of the heavenly meats might anonymously arrive at his doorstep, if all went Tony's way.

'It's ridiculous that two grown brothers can't resolve this,' Whit said. 'You're wasting this court's time, boys. So call me Solomon. I'm ordering that the grill be divided equally. Right down the middle. You get the right half, Cliff, and you get the left half, Tony.'

'That'll destroy it!' Tony exploded.

'Are you nuts?' Cliff demanded.

'Watch it,' Constable Lloyd Brundrett, who served as bailiff in Whit's court, rumbled.

'Sorry, Your Honor,' Cliff said in sudden meekness. 'I'm sorry. I'm very sorry.'

'Or option B is you two resolve this peaceably right now,' Whit said. Neither Augustine spoke.

'Fine, that's my judgment. The sheriff's deputies will execute this order at their earliest . . .'

'Wait!' Cliff yelled. 'Please. Please, Judge. Wait. All right, Tony built it. He can have the grill. I don't want to see it ruined.'

Tony pumped his fist in the air in a redneck jig.

Whit rapped the gavel and pointed it at Tony. 'Stop that celebrating. Right. This. Minute.'

The hand dropped; the hips ceased their victory sway.

'Tony, if your brother is letting you have the grill, I strongly suggest you work out a plan to reimburse him for the cost of his materials, over time and either with cash or barter. Maybe you could feed him and his family some of that barbecue you bragged about. You need to be a good brother. Understood?'

Tony finally nodded, surprised and still pleased.

'Fine. Case dismissed.'

His clerk handed him the file for the next case. Neighbors bickering over ownership of a lawn mower. In the next hour he adjudicated four more cases. Patsy Duchamp slipped in and sat in the back row of the courtroom. When he completed the last case and the courtroom emptied, Patsy approached the bench and slid him a folder.

'The news clippings on Corey Hubble you wanted, Whit,' she said.

'Thanks. The margaritas are on me.'

'Sure could use a good quote for the Hubble story.'

'I'm sorry, Patsy, not yet. I should hear from the ME's office real soon.' He tucked the file under his arm and promised to call her as soon as there was news.

Whit ducked down the hall into his office, relieved to have the day's docket done. Five cases in justice court resolved in barely an hour. The voters could not say justice wasn't damned swift in Encina County. Maybe he ought to make that a mainstay of his campaign.

Whit opened his office door and found Sam Hubble sitting in front of his desk, head bowed, hands in lap.

The boy stood slowly. 'Hi, Judge Mosley. You got a minute?'

'Sure, Sam. How are you?'

'Holding up. I'm kind of freaked about my dad.'

'That's understandable.' Whit's tongue felt thick and oily. He sat behind his desk, smoothing the black robe. Trying not to let the thought *I've been screwing your mother* play across his face. 'I know this is a tough time for your whole family.'

Wow, what next can I pull out from the bag of clichéd platitudes?

'I wanted to talk to you about my father. Stuff . . . I couldn't say with Gram and Mom around. If you want,

186

we can call them after I've said what I got to say.' His tone was resolute. He looked like Pete: broad-shouldered, tall, lanky, with a shock of brown hair. He'd inherited Faith's eyes, hazel and direct, and a thin slice of a mouth that reminded Whit of Lucinda.

'Then let's talk.'

'I'm sorry for what I did,' Sam said, and Whit's stomach dropped. 'My dad killed himself. I know because . . . I found the body. First. Not that girl.'

Thin light slanted through the half-shut blinds, and in the bars of shadow Sam reminded Whit not of the other Hubbles, but of lost Corey, hunched, beaten down.

'I didn't want anyone to know,' Sam said. 'But I can't do this to Gram, let her think . . . maybe Dad was murdered.' He swallowed. 'I went back to the boat Monday night. To see my father.'

'Did he know you were coming?'

'No. I just wanted to talk with him. It felt weird sometimes, knowing he had been gone most of my life and yet he was now just a few miles away.'

'Did you get along with him?'

Sam shrugged. 'He wasn't as bad as I thought he would be. But he abandoned Mom and me. I wasn't ever going to forgive him. Yeah, I could get along with him okay, but forgive, never. I think he knew that.'

Sam pulled a folded paper from his pocket and laid it on Whit's desk. 'I went to go see him about eight-thirty. The boat was dead quiet. So I went aboard and I found him.' The boy's voice quavered. 'I freaked. I tried to wake him, but he was clearly dead. His skin . . . it was still warm.' He wiped at his mouth with the back of his hand. 'I, like, froze, I didn't know what to do. Then I saw the note. It was on the nightstand table.'

'So you weren't at home with your mom, like you said in your statement?'

'No. I snuck out; there's a trellis by my window. It's a quiet climb. Mom didn't know I was gone. I'm sorry I lied on the statement. I didn't know what to do.' Sam's voice broke. 'Because of what my father wrote.'

Whit took a tissue from a box and carefully unfolded the note. It was written in typeface, from a computer printer:

> *I came home thinking I could fix what was broke in me and I can't. Mama, I'm sorry for the pain I've caused you and what I did to Corey. I killed him. I didn't mean to, but I did. We argued over his drug use all those years ago, and I hit him and he fell and hit his neck funny against the stair banister. He was dead in less than a minute and I panicked. Before you came back to town I took his body out past Santa Margarita Island and weighed it down good and dumped it. I didn't know what else to do. I have tried to deaden the pain of this for years with all the wrong things in life and I just can't go on. This way is better. Sam and Faith, please forgive me. I love you both. Velvet – I don't have the words. Be good. Mama – good luck in the election and I hope me ending my pain doesn't mess up things for you. You haven't had an influence on me in years so no one should blame you. I am just really unhappy about the person I am. Sam this has nothing to do with you at all. You are aces and I love you. I am so so sorry and please forgive me. Pete.*

Whit set the letter down on his desk. A tremble of nausea touched his stomach.

'You're going to have to give the police a revised statement, Sam.'

'I know. But I came to you first . . . My mom said you decided whether or not it was suicide. Will you go with me to talk to the police?'

'Sure. But I'd like to know why you kept the note, why you didn't say anything right away. There was a marina full of people there you could have told.'

'I know. I just . . . I didn't want everyone to know he'd done what he said to his brother. I didn't – I was worried about Gram's election, what this would mean. My grandmother . . . she's gonna kill me for this. Not helping out right away. Telling a lie.'

'What happened after you found the' – Whit nearly said *body* and managed to edit midstream – 'after you found the note?'

'I stayed with him, for a few minutes.' Sam lowered his eyes. 'I know, it sounds weird, but I didn't want him to be alone. It seemed wrong to leave him. I thought of calling the police, but I thought maybe, what with Gram's election coming up, maybe I shouldn't be in the news. So I just left, left the boat and left the marina.' He wiped his dripping nose. 'Pretty shitty, huh? Am I in big trouble?'

'Let's call the police and call your mother.' Whit picked up the phone and dialed the station. Claudia wasn't in, but he was transferred to Delford.

Delford blew out a long sigh. 'Now, here I was telling y'all it was suicide, and Jesus if you and Claudia bickered with me the whole way.'

'Sam is here, but his mother needs to be present if he's going to give a statement.'

'Of course. I'll give Lucinda and Faith a call right now.'

'Thanks. We'll walk across the street in a minute,' Whit said and hung up.

'I'm sorry,' Sam said.

Whit placed the suicide note into a manila folder.

Outside the sky was a sweet blue smear and the Gulf wind whipped Whit's robe around his legs. Sam shaded his eyes against the unclouded sky.

Two questions occurred to Whit. 'Did you notice whether your dad's laptop was on the boat?'

Sam shook his head. 'I didn't notice a computer around.'

'And did your father ever discuss a new film project with you?'

Sam shook his head. 'He didn't talk about his work to me. Did you know he made movies for driver's ed?'

'Yeah,' Whit said, 'I knew.'

They crossed the street and went inside to the police station.

'Quite the development,' Whit said after Sam had gotten settled in the chief's office. The Hubble women had not yet arrived but were on their way over. He and Delford had retired to the kitchen.

Delford filled a coffee cup with a shaking hand. 'God. Relief. I'll sleep better tonight.'

Whit folded his arms. 'You'll have that note tested for Pete's fingerprints, right?'

'Showboating is over, Whit.'

'It's typed, not handwritten. And his computer is still missing. Am I supposed to believe he typed a suicide note, then tossed his laptop into the marina?'

Delford started to argue, then shrugged. 'Damn, you're difficult. Fine. I'll tell Gardner.'

'Why not Claudia?'

'The case is Gardner's now,' Delford said through tight lips. 'Not that there's much of a case now, partner.'

Delford was right. Whit left. He didn't want to see Faith right now. He walked to his car, shrugging out of his robe. He tossed it in the backseat and drove a half block to the ice cream store he once managed. He was halfway through a chocolate-almond double scoop when his pager beeped. The Nueces County medical examiner's office calling.

24

'This doesn't have to be awkward,' David said. He smoothed his damp hair with the flat of his palm.

Claudia's fingers tapped against the computer keyboard. 'Of course not. But it is.' She finished her report and saved copies to the hard drive and a diskette.

'I don't want to make you uncomfortable,' he said.

She popped the diskette from the computer. 'You're not.'

'So what's bothering you?' He palmed his hair again. 'When you get mad, you don't vent. You keep it all locked inside. But I know you're steamed.'

He's not your husband anymore, and you don't have to skirt an issue to keep the peace. 'I felt like you were using that interview with that poor woman as a reason to see me.'

He laughed. 'Well, don't we think well of ourselves?'

'Am I wrong?'

'I didn't steer her to you. She wanted to talk with PLPD, and Delford said you. But I'm not sorry to see you.'

'David, aren't you hurt? Doesn't it bother you I didn't want to be married to you anymore?'

'Did you want to hurt me?'

'Of course not.'

His mouth thinned. 'Sure. Yeah. It hurts bad. I miss you awful fierce when I get home and it's just me and the TV. But, like you said, we're still gonna run into each other.'

The casual sweetness of his tone prickled her skin. 'Well, I think it's just best we don't overdo our time together. The point of a divorce was to be apart.'

'Was it all bad? Did you just hate me, or what?' He blinked. 'I would really like to know. I want to fix . . . whatever's wrong with me.'

She touched the back of his hand. 'Oh, David. No, it wasn't all bad, and no, I don't hate you,' she said. 'I feel like we got married because everyone said we were such a cute couple. It's not enough. I know some woman's going to scoop you right up, because you're a great guy, and I'll still be a moping loner. But I wasn't right for you.'

He carefully put his hat back on his head. She saw wetness glimmer in his eyes – he had never cried in front of her – and he said, 'Okay, thanks. I really did just want to know.'

David bumped into a smiling Eddie Gardner as he left, the two men exchanged friendly hellos, and Eddie dumped a photocopied piece of paper on Claudia's desk.

'Suicide note. With prints from Hubble and his son,' he said. 'And it clears up the Corey Hubble case, too.'

Claudia read. 'My God. Are they going to look for Corey's body?'

Eddie shrugged. 'The Hubbles asked we not release the note to the press. I suppose the Coast Guard or maybe the parks department will look for remains, but that's gonna be a waste of time. Mosley's inquest is gonna be just a formality now.' He smiled and sat. 'Man, I love clearing cases.'

'Congratulations.' Claudia turned back to her paper work on two burglaries she had cleared on Friday, wishing she could slap the smirk off his gaunt, ten-dollar-tan face.

An hour later, Eddie left for drinks at the Shell Inn with most of the day shift. He invited her to go, but she declined with a polite smile.

'Hey, no hard feelings, right?'

'Of course not,' she said. He grinned, slapped an Astros

cap on his head, and sauntered out, whistling 'Cheeseburger in Paradise.'

She waited until he was gone for ten minutes and headed down the hall.

The old files of the Port Leo Police Department moldered in a locked back office. It was quiet now at six p.m. None of the other detectives were here, most of the clerks had headed out, and the patrol shift was out cruising Port Leo.

Unlocking the ink-black storeroom, she pulled on a chain to click on a naked lightbulb. The room smelled of old paper, damp brick, and, oddly, garlic. She went to a wall of cabinets. The files were organized by year, and then in turn by case number. Only a few major cases had not been cleared. She wondered what murderers still walked free, with the warm sun of Port Leo aglow on their faces, full of easy confidence that they would never pay.

Claudia pulled Corey Hubble's file. It was thinner than she expected. The disappearance of a state senator's son surely would mean a thick, bulging file. This file was starved for data.

She scribbled her name in the sign-out book along with the file number and returned to her office.

An old file was simply a snapshot of a tragedy. No papers in here could capture the boy that Corey Hubble had been: what was his favorite TV show, did he like chicken or beef wedged in his enchiladas, which local jetty did he think had the best fishing? All these fading papers represented was bureaucratic eulogy.

Delford Spires had been the detective on the case, one of his last before being promoted to police chief. She noted the year of Corey's disappearance and did some quick math: Delford had been with the Port Leo police for fifteen years at that point. She began to read.

Senator Hubble had reported Corey missing on July 21. She had gone to a Democratic women's group meeting in Houston, leaving sixteen-year-old Corey and twenty-one-year-old Pete at home. Pete and Faith were recently married, Faith finishing college at Texas A&M in College Station, a few hours distant. Faith had not been home that weekend. She had been at summer school, completing her degree.

Someone had typed out a rough chronology, based on Delford's interviews. Thursday, July 19, Lucinda had left for Houston. The boys spent time at their jobs: Pete working for a video store, Corey for a florist as a delivery boy. Friday, July 20, Corey planned to spend the night at a friend's house, the friend being Jabez Jones, the son of the minister at the God's Coast Evangelical Church.

Pete claimed that he had last seen his brother on Friday, shortly after lunch. Corey acted upset but would not discuss what the problem was. Claudia looked through the papers for Pete's statement and found the corroborating quote: *Corey came back from being at his job and he was furious. Pissed. Upset. I asked what about and he wouldn't tell me. But he said that he was going to go fix what was wrong. I asked him what he meant and he just said he'd teach her.* No hint that Pete might have beaten his brother to death at that point.

The chronology went on. Pete worked that afternoon at the video store, then went out for hamburgers and barhopping with three male friends. He got home shortly after midnight. Corey was not there, having planned an overnight stay with Jabez Jones. The next morning Pete worked all Saturday at the video store, starting at nine, and he did not get home until after five that afternoon. His brother was not at home, but Pete did not consider that unusual – his brother was often out. Pete fixed himself dinner and his mother arrived home unexpectedly, a day early from her conference. She wanted to know where Corey was, and when Pete didn't know, she started calling friends. They were unable to find him. She then reported him missing to the police at nine o'clock that night.

Claudia dug down for a statement from Jabez Jones. It was there, but added nothing to what Delford had already noted. Corey had called and canceled the sleep-over. And then apparently vanished.

The rest of the reports and interviews painted an increasingly grim picture. School counselors called Corey manipulative, unstable, and attributed his behavior to his father's painful cancer death five years earlier. The boy seemed to have few friends willing to talk to the police. One of Corey's teachers described him as 'talented but erratic' and mentioned he had gotten into trouble twice for fighting in school. The teacher said that *Corey has a somewhat twisted view of the world being in place to primarily serve his needs. His dad died, so the world owes him. Clearly this idea is not sustainable. With change in life being inevitable Corey will face some real challenges. I worry that he has a not well-developed regard for the rights of others to have lives separate from his.*

Another note in Delford's scribble: *Some rumors that he is sexually active but only when he can be rough with the girl. Cannot yet get anyone to confirm this. He might have left if he roughed up some girl but have not been able to find anyone who would admit to sleeping with him. Pete said Corey dated Marian Duchamp, will check.*

Whit had mentioned that Patsy Duchamp claimed her cousin had slept with Corey and gotten slapped around for the trouble. There'd also been the rumor of animal torture Whit had mentioned to her, but she found no notes regarding that subject.

Corey Hubble stood out in her own mind as a kid who lounged in the smoking area at the high school, always slightly apart, not quite fitting in with the roughnecks, not hanging in with the populars (where she remembered Pete dwelling in splendor), not clustering with the geeks for collective security. She remembered he had blue eyes, wide, sad-looking. Several pictures of Corey Hubble lay stashed in the file, a school photo where he glared dourly at the camera, and several family photos. In them, Lucinda and Pete always smiled, Corey always frowned. There was only one picture of him smiling, sitting with his wasting father in a lawn chair, touching his father's pasty arm. Mr Hubble smiled with the thin certainty of the dying.

She paged through the rest of the file. An immediate search of the county turned up nothing except the boy's car, parked in a grove of windswept oaks not far from Big Cat Beach, found the day after he was reported missing. A detailed report on the car and its condition indicated no sign of foul play. An interview with one of Corey's friends indicated the vintage Mustang was Corey's pride and joy. He couldn't imagine that Corey would leave it behind if he was cutting out from town. St Leo Bay, Aransas Bay, Copano Bay, and St Charles Bay were searched for his body; nothing. The investigation widened, to San Patricio and Matagorda counties, to Corpus Christi, to South Padre Island, to Houston, to Austin, all places a runaway teen might find attractive. Nothing. The task force disbanded five months after Corey Hubble vanished, although the file stayed open and assigned to one detective: Delford Spires.

Periodic updates followed: a possible sighting in Houston, one from Dallas, one from San Antonio. Nothing resulted in a real lead. He was banished to the limbo of milk-carton photos, pictured on direct mail pieces as a public service. Nothing.

There was little indication in the notes that the FBI or Texas Rangers had proffered much help, although with Lucinda being a state senator one would think every agency in the state would be hunting Corey Hubble. Apparently not, or they had no more success than Delford.

Not a single thing to suggest that Pete Hubble had done away with his brother in the heat of an argument. No physical evidence in the house. No physical evidence in the Hubbles' small fishing skiff. Nothing.

She stuffed the file in her heavy purse and headed out the door. On the way she talked to Nelda, the dispatcher and main Guardian of the Files. Being a Baptist, Nelda hadn't gone to happy hour with the others. 'Do you remember any citizens phoning or asking for information about this case recently? The Corey Hubble file?'

Nelda nodded. 'Yeah, a guy stopped by. Big guy, late thirties, tall, kind of muscled up some. I remember he wore a lion's-head chain around his neck, not so classy-looking. I told him to talk to Delford.'

Claudia thanked her. So Pete Hubble, murderer of his own brother, wanted to see the file on Corey.

Why would he need it if he already knew the truth?

25

'Don't ever send me a famous body again.' Dr Liz Contreras, deputy medical examiner for Nueces County, had a voice that reminded Whit of crumpled foil – raspy, bright, a little grating.

'You finally get some pressure to hurry Pete Hubble along?'

'I got a call from the governor's office. Some aide to an aide with a degree in snotitude. I explained to said flunky I don't have powers over time and space to hurry up blood tests.'

'Then let me be the first to thank you for your quick work.'

'Don't thank me too quick. You need to chew out your evidence people. I've already had a chat with your delightful Mr Gardner.' She cleared her throat. 'Hubble's hands weren't properly bagged. The GSR readings are not going to be particularly accurate.'

Whit had counted on the gunshot residue tests to help him determine if Pete had been holding the gun when it fired. A high level of residue implied suicide.

'How was the bagging screwed up?'

'The bag on the victim's right hand wasn't fastened properly, and the bag itself has defects – holes, as if torn by rough handling. Now, that said, I found gunshot residue on the right hand, but the amount could have come from Hubble pulling the trigger and then the residue getting worn off with crappy bagging, or because someone stuck the gun in Hubble's mouth and Hubble's hand went to the gun or was by his mouth or jaw. It's not definitive that he pulled the trigger or that he didn't.'

Crap. If Liz said outright suicide, his ruling became simple. 'So what can you tell me?'

'Time of death was between seven and nine o'clock. He'd eaten shortly before he died, most of a pepperoni-and-mushroom pizza, a number of tostada chips, and several glasses of red wine. Death was instantaneous. Bullet entry wound through the mouth – the angle is consistent with a gun placed in a mouth with little or no struggle. So he wasn't lurching or fighting when the gun fired. That could indicate self-inflicted.' She made a humming sound, and he pictured her scanning her report. 'The bullet didn't exit the skull. I've retrieved it and sent it to the crime lab here. Dried blood around the mouth, specks of blood on face and hands. The specks on his face are blowback – blood and tissue bursting forward from the bullet's pressure moving through the head.' She paused.

'What?'

'Well, this amount of blowback, we ought to have seen it on Hubble's right hand as well. There's very little there.'

'Would the bad bagging of the hands account for that?'

'Maybe. But I would still expect to see as much blow-back on his trigger hand as on his face. The amount of blowback on the gun itself is consistent with what I would expect with a self-inflicted shot. Hubble's prints are readable on the gun, according to the lab. They said there were a couple of partials but not readable enough for an ID.'

He thought of Eddie Gardner, easing the gun out of Pete's mouth and thumbing the safety.

'Could that have happened if an officer handled the gun improperly?' Whit asked.

'Possibly.'

'Did he have sex before he died?' Whit asked.

'No.'

'We did find a pair of panties by the bed, mixed in with his clothes.'

'Then have Gardner check those panties for seminal traces or pubics. We will comb the deceased down for hairs and fibers not his,' Contreras said.

'What's your considered opinion as to homicide versus suicide? A lot of folks are watching me on this one.'

Liz Contreras's voice softened. 'That he is lying in the bed, with this bullet angle, is a big suicide supporter. There's just no sign of struggle. The lack of blowback and gunpowder residue could be attributed to the poor handling. But I can't say with certainty. If there's much reason to believe he was depressed or suicidal, you'll probably be safe in ruling for suicide.' She paused. 'He'd had a lot to drink, too. His blood alcohol count was point two – that's a lot of hooch, might supercharge any depression. Toxicology on narcotics will take a while longer. I've sent fingernail scrapings, hairs from up and down, and the bullet to the crime lab, along with hand swabs. They can do a double check on my work there. That's about it.' She paused. 'If your inquest is showing he was suicidal, you're probably safe in ruling that way, Whit.'

'Thank you, Liz. If I decide to do a formal inquest, you'll come testify?'

'Sure,' Liz said. 'Especially if you'll treat me to one of those Russian hamburgers at your stepmom's place.'

He chatted with her for a minute more, hearing all about her young daughter's dominance of the Pee Wee soccer leagues in Corpus Christi, then clicked off.

He called Delford, left a message asking him to call, and then nearly dialed Patsy Duchamp at the *Mariner* to give a statement. But he felt tired, and oddly disappointed. There was no case here to be solved, really, after all. And Patsy didn't have a paper hitting the streets again until Saturday. He could talk to her in the morning.

He went home, ate a quiet dinner with Babe and Irina, and was getting into his car to go to Irina's café to borrow her computer when Velvet pulled up. He stood in the yard and waited for her to get out of the car.

'You got a minute for me?' she asked.

'Yeah. I have some news for you,' Whit said. 'We have a suicide note.' He explained to her Sam's revised account.

She leaned against her car. 'No way, Whit. I sure don't believe he killed himself, and I sure don't believe he killed his own brother.'

'The note said Corey's death was an accident.'

'I still don't believe it.' She stalked around the yard in a circle, burning nervous energy. 'I don't believe it.'

'Why? Why not?'

'Because he was a genuinely sweet guy. He was. I can look at him the same way I look at you and know you couldn't kill someone.'

'We never, ever know people exactly the way they are.'

Velvet shook her head. 'I want to see this note.'

'The police and the Hubbles haven't released it to the press yet.' He watched her fidget. 'I don't think I can get you a copy. I'm sorry, Velvet.'

'His damned family. They'll say Pete was a murderer and a suicide. I mean, why not kick him when he's dead?' She crossed her arms. 'Don't you have autopsy results yet, anything to contradict that stupid note?'

He wasn't about to disclose Liz Contreras's findings, not yet. 'Nothing yet.' He paused. 'Tell me about Junior Deloache.'

She crossed her arms. 'Junior? What's to tell?'

'I understand he wants to be in movies.'

To his surprise she laughed. 'Honey, I couldn't sell tickets to Junior. The biscuit, shall we say, lacks yeast.'

'He says Pete promised him.'

'Only if Junior bought his way in.'

'You mean, an actor pays you?'

'Not exactly. I've known investors who've wanted to come watch the shoots or take some photos of their own. Or screw a starlet, if she didn't mind. But never while the camera was rolling.'

Whit studied her. 'Pimping for investors. What does that have to do with love and happiness and all that stuff you whacked me with at lunch, pray tell? Doesn't that make you just a glorified madam?'

'Life is a tough business.'

'And you're running right back into the sleaze.'

'What am I supposed to do, Whit? Put down roots here in Pleasantville?'

'Why not make this film about Corey that you and Pete planned?'

She stared. 'Without Pete? I don't think so. Plus, the purse is empty. He hadn't gotten the financing.'

'Any excuse will do, right, as long as you can make more porno crap.'

'This crap is what I do, and I tend to be quite good at it.' She stepped closer to him. 'Would you like to experience how good? We could do a tape together, never release it in the U.S. Distribute it in Asia only. No one here would ever know.'

He didn't say anything for ten seconds, and she laughed. 'No smart answer? Whit, under all that assurance you're such a white-bread boy. If I took you on, you'd be toast.'

'And if I took you on, maybe I could help you get out of the pit you're in. Deep in your heart you know porn's wrong. You know. I can tell you do.'

'I don't. I'm not one bit debased. I'm superior to any man who pays money for my tapes. And the last thing I need or want is a white knight to bring me a new set of morals. Mine are just fine,' she said. 'I don't tell you what you do is wrong. Let me guess why you're still living at home at your advanced age. Your stepmother's charms?'

'No.'

'Whit, you're a sweet man. But you look at me like a street whore maybe your church could sponsor. I like my life as it is.'

'I like you, period, and I don't want to see you ruin your life.'

'It's mine to ruin, as you put it.'

'If I rule for suicide, what are you gonna do?' he asked.

'I don't know. Does that note mention his career?'

'Not directly.'

'If it wasn't for Sam . . . I'd blast Lucinda Hubble with Pete's career in every paper I could.'

'Why do you hate her so?'

'Because, Whit, she hated her own kids. Pete told me once his mother treated him and Corey like stagehands in her great play of life. Faith should have been Lucinda's kid. She seems to relish the role of Little Miss Macbeth. If Lucinda won't stand by Pete when he's dead, I ought to hit her exactly where it hurts. With the voters.'

'Vendettas don't get you far.'

'They get you far enough.' She got in her car.

Whit stood in the yard, in the twilight, and watched her go.

'Excitable thing, isn't she?' a voice called to him, coming across the yard. Whit turned and saw Buddy Beere, dressed in a suit the color of a stale brownie and thick-knotted polyester tie, clutching a sheaf of campaign flyers.

'Hi,' Whit said.

'Hi, Whit. Hope you don't mind me canvassing your neighborhood. Just out meeting the voters.'

'Well, I suppose if you haven't grown up and known most of the voters all your life, you need to campaign.' He felt extraordinarily peevish, and the sight of Buddy, in his lumpy suit and sweaty brow and dork's tie, only irritated him.

Buddy didn't rise to the bait. 'If it makes you feel better, two houses on the street already said they were voting for you.' Considering there were at least fifteen houses, Whit saw the jab.

'Thanks.'

'That was Pete Hubble's girlfriend, right?' Buddy asked. 'You still chasing her?'

'Part of the inquest is gathering information on the deceased. To do that you have to talk to the bereaved. You'll have to learn that if you win.' Suddenly he was tired of arguing and jousting with this little man so determined to take his job away.

'Good night, Buddy.'

Buddy rolled his remaining flyers into a cylinder. 'Whit? One question. Did you have to buy your robe, or did the county buy it for you? I just want to be sure I get the right size.'

26

Claudia called Whit on his cell phone before she collapsed in bed, giving him an update on what she'd found in the Corey Hubble case file. He told her about the autopsy results and the bad bagging.

'You'll really have to discuss this with Delford,' she said. 'Out of my hands now.'

'I'm sorry,' Whit said. 'Delford's being unfair.'

'Well, let Gardner handle it,' she said. 'Apparently the lesson learned here is that the Hubbles warrant special treatment.' She paused. 'Gardner did do the tests on the note. There were two sets of prints. Pete's and Sam's.'

'I guess that settles that,' Whit said.

Driving to the Café Caspian, Whit watched gleaming lights dot the harbor: fishing boats, pleasure boats, the restaurants by the piers that jutted into the bay. His cell phone buzzed as he pulled up in front of the darkened café.

'I understand you are Sam's confessor.' Faith sounded hoarse and worn. 'He says you were very good to him. Thank you, Whit.' Less frosty than when she'd stormed from the guest house.

'You're welcome. How are y'all doing?'

'Sam is still upset, and of course Lucinda is having to deal with Pete's confession.'

'You talk to me like you're talking to the press.'

'Do I? I guess so. I've got spin doctors from Austin coming out of my ass. Forgive me. Sam is devastated. Lucinda is in shock. If Pete had just told her then what happened with Corey . . . my God, how their lives would have been different. The suffering we would have been spared. Needless, so needless.' She paused. 'I'm sorry I've been so testy. Frankly I could use about seven hours in bed with you.'

'Faith . . . do you believe the note?'

A silence. 'Of course I do. I feel horrible for Pete now, imagining what he must have gone through. Why he decided to steep himself in what passed for pleasure. Why he couldn't tell me . . .' Her voice broke for a moment and then she laughed, one of those soft laughs, not funny, made at the sadness of the world. 'I always considered him a failure as a husband. I must have been an equal failure as a wife.'

'After Corey vanished, did Pete seem different? Troubled?'

He could hear Lucinda's voice in the background, apparently talking on another line, soft and mournful. 'Pete was never the same. But all I can worry about is Sam, okay?'

'I'm sorry, Faith.' Condolences never counted for much with him. They always seemed designed to coddle the giver in the face of mortality. But he tried. 'I'm so sorry.'

'At least it's over. Thank you, Whit. Bye.'

He unlocked the café doors and headed back to Irina's office. An untidy whirl of papers covered her desk. A calendar from the local branch of the Texas Coastal Bank was pinned to one wall. Framed on her desk was a selection of photos of family in faraway Russia. A dour mother, a sunny brother who needed orthodontic work and wore his hair in an unstylish chop. Irina rarely spoke of them, as though they were from a chapter of life best forgotten.

He powered up her iMac, accessed the Internet, and found himself on the Yahoo! Web portal. He began with a search for 'Big Pete Majors,' the film name Pete Hubble had used for his career.

A number of Web sites popped into view, along with brief descriptions. Most of the sites appeared to be on-line businesses selling pornographic videos. The site with the highest relevance in the search proclaimed itself as 'THE Big Pete Majors site for the Truly Devoted Fan.' Whit clicked on it.

The site belonged to a Truly Devoted Male Fan of Pete's. It offered reviews of Pete's cornucopia of movies, a message board where Pete's fans could post deep thoughts, and a gallery of downloadable pictures of Pete, both by himself and in action with his co-stars.

No banner proclaimed on the site's front page that Pete was gone. The copy below the BIG PETE MAJORS UN-OFFICIAL TEMPLE OF APPRECIATION read: *If you're a Big Pete Majors fan, you've come to the right place! This is a labor of love for me (I'm Kevin). ALL Pete's fans are welcome here str8, gay, bi, whatever! Enjoy!!!!!!!!*

str8? Whit studied the arcane code a moment before realizing it meant 'straight.'

Kevin certainly had scads of free time. Whit explored the message board: there were a few dozen messages, some months old. Several messages were titled PETE LEAVING PORN?

It was a hot rumor, and Pete's devotees promulgated reason after reason: AIDS, erectile dysfunction, drying out in Betty Ford, conversion to fundamentalism, an ongoing bicker with porn directors. The final message was posted by Kevin: *It is my privilege (as you know) to know Pete slightly, because he's appreciated my efforts on-line, and I just talked with him via phone and he said NO WAY is he cutting out from porn!!!! He said to tell you all he really appreciates our concern, but he is due back in L.A. in a few months. He is doing some so-called legit work (hush hush) back in Texas (where one MAY surmise that everything is indeed bigger!). Don't know if he'll still be exclusive with director Velvet Mojo, but some Pete is better than no Pete. So stop the rumors, he's not sick and he's not dead and he should be back in front of cameras soon.*

The message was dated last Monday, early afternoon. Hours before Pete died.

Whit found nothing of interest in the rest of the messages – mostly discussions of which films showed Big Pete Majors to advantage (films of particular merit were awarded a 'two dicks up' by one enterprising pair of critics), comments on his acting skills, discussions of which starlets he had the hottest sex scenes with. All from participants with odd code names such as *lovergrrl* and *madforpete* and *boyslut69*. Consumers of sex – as opposed to those actually having sex – needed reviews before plunking down their hard-earned money, Whit supposed.

He scooted back to the Temple of Appreciation's main Web page. He found a link to send E-mail to Web master Kevin. Whit clicked on the link and typed in: *Hi Kevin, I'd like to talk to you about your recent conversation with Pete. I know Pete here in Texas, and I'm afraid I have some unsettling news and would prefer to talk rather than E-mail you. Would you please call me – my phone will pay the bill if you call my cell phone. 361 555-6788. Thank you. Judge Whit Mosley, Justice of the Peace, Encina County, Texas.* He hoped his title might induce a more rapid response.

Curiosity got the better of Whit, and he clicked on the gallery's front link. The pictures were organized by action. Pete alone. Pete receiving oral sex. Pete masturbating. Pete doing it doggy style. Pete doing it with Asian girls. With black girls. With bottle blondes. With two girls at once. A wide menu, to appeal to the widest possible lack of taste.

Whit remembered the boy that Pete had been: fun, carefree, quick to tease, helping to toilet-paper the oaks in front of Delford's house, high-fiving the Mosleys after the infamous Pepto-pink paint incident with Delford's house. That boy was gone. Maybe all this sex, all this pleasure, was a dam against the grief over what he had done to his brother.

Whit returned to the search engine and typed a search on 'Velvet Mojo.' The list returned a number of sites selling videos and one site entirely devoted to Velvet herself.

This site proclaimed itself to be *VelvetRocks! the only site for America's preeminent female director of porn*. A picture of Velvet that was at least five years old, dressed in a leather biker garb with carefully moussed platinum hair. She sat astride a gleaming motorcycle. A sternness hardened her face instead of the wanton pucker of the rising starlet. The site included a listing of the movies she had directed (over sixty), links to purchase her videos, a listing of awards she had garnered from the adult film industry (seven), and a whole bevy of reviews by the pornorati, as Whit mentally termed the more slavish fans. She had performed on the other side of the camera at the beginning of her career for ten films, two of which were described on the site as 'classics.'

There were pictures from her appearances, available for download.

A guiltiness Whit hadn't known since he'd stolen peeks at his older brothers' carefully stashed *Playboy*s when he was young rumbled along his bones. He had never seen naked photos of a woman he knew socially. But curiosity won the advantage over refinement, and he clicked on a thumbnail-size photo.

What slowly filled the browser's screen was a color still from a movie that portrayed postal workers breeding at will. Velvet was in a badly buttoned clone of a mail deliverer's uniform, her breasts about to break out from the confines of the cloth. Her blond hair was combed huge, her lips painted crimson, her cheeks rouged. One hand crept down from the flat plane of her stomach to the too-tight serge of her uniform's skirt.

Whit swallowed. Velvet looked far prettier in person, in her sweats and jeans and her hair not a cumulus cloud. In the picture she was a Barbie doll maddened with lust. She didn't look like any real woman he knew. The true woman lay buried beneath the trying-too-hard stance and the stage paint. He selected a second picture for download. As the picture slowly built, Whit could see that Pete lay atop her, her oversize breasts jabbing into his over-pumped chest, both of them grinning with ecstasy so faked it looked like pain.

A kiss gone bad, she had called it.

He clicked off the downloading picture before the whole bonanza presented itself. He knew these people. He couldn't watch them this way.

On a whim, he did a Web search on Pete Hubble instead of Pete Majors. He slowly paged through the results. Zip that was relevant: only a cluster of genealogy sites that listed various Peter Hubbles from the past three hundred years in their databases. He did a similar search for Corey Hubble and got one result back other than the regular cluster of genealogy sites. The enthusiastic Kevin's Pete-tribute site. Odd.

He moved the mouse toward the link at the same time the office lights went black and a finger of God shrieked past his ear. The iMac's screen burst with a bright, blinding nova. Whit fell behind the desk, clutching his head.

'Hello, Judge,' a voice rumbled from the doorway. Low, throaty, a man's voice, hoarse, neutral of accent or drawl. 'Stay down on the floor and you won't be hurt.'

Whit stayed exactly where he was, his heart pounding hard against the thin carpet. The desk shielded him, but in the pitch-dark he couldn't see his assailant. A faint electric crackle served as the dying gasp of the ruined computer. Whit heard his own ragged breathing, far too loud.

'Listen, Your Honor,' the polite voice said. 'I could have blown your motherfucking head off now and I didn't. That's because I want you to listen. Are you listening?'

'Yes,' Whit croaked. He tried to think of any weapon there might be in the office: nothing.

'Good. You rule that Pete Hubble committed suicide. If you don't, you die. And so does your father. And so does his wife. And so do Claudia Salazar and Delford Spires. You will all be killed at the same time, by, uh, multiple operatives. Understand?'

Jesus, Whit thought, *Jesus Mary and Joseph*.

'And should you go to other authorities with this threat, not only will you be killed, but also your five brothers and their families. In Houston and in Atlanta and in Austin and in New York and in Miami. We know where all our little Mosleys flock. Do you understand?'

'Yes,' Whit answered. His voice sounded raw.

'Say it with conviction. I think judges need conviction.' A small, sickening laugh. 'Pick one of your brothers. I'll kill him to prove I mean business.'

Horror flooded Whit.

'Pick a brother,' the voice said genially, 'or I order them all killed.'

Whit gasped. 'Please don't. I'll do what you want.'

'Which one?' The voice oozed enjoyment. 'Teddy in

Houston? It'd make Father's Day rough for his three little delectable girls. Or Joe in Atlanta? That software company probably pays him big, his widow should live large on insurance. How about Mark in Austin, who so wants to be a writer? Isn't he your favorite brother? Let's spare the world another crappy poet.'

'Please don't hurt them. Please!'

'Pick one,' the shooter snapped.

'Me. I pick me!' he screamed. 'Just leave them alone!'

A slight laugh. 'Said with conviction. So how will you rule?'

'Suicide, suicide, suicide.'

'Fine. I'm generous tonight so all your brothers get to wake up tomorrow and fuck their wives and breathe the air.' A pause. 'Sorry about Irina's computer, but better it than the back of her head.' In the darkness he sensed the shooter leaning over the desk, toward him. To look up would mean death.

'Now here's what we're going to do, asshole. You're going to stay kissing the floor here for the next thirty minutes. Because a buddy of mine is watching this café, and if a light comes on, or you move, I come back and shoot you. Do you understand me?'

'Yes,' Whit answered. 'I completely understand.'

'Don't let me down, Judge.'

Whit heard the door shut. He heard only the harsh labor of his own breathing. He fingered his neck, face, and ear; there was no wound. He lay perfectly still on the floor.

The guy sounded like – what? A polite psychopath? A government agent? Or like a tough guy who'd seen a lot of bad movies. *Multiple operatives.* Who the hell was this?

You willing to take a chance? With your life and your family's?

213

He let the thirty minutes pass, not moving in the darkness. His cell phone rang, and rang, and rang, but he did not answer it.

27

From the bay Port Leo appeared as a luminous stitch against the black fabric of the night. The always open Port Leo State Pier glowed along its long thrust into St Leo Bay, and even from this distance Whit saw stick figures moving, eclipsing the lights, and he imagined he could see the lines the fishermen cast out into the bay, as thin as spider's silk. Whit sat in the bow of *Don't Ask* and sipped at a jelly jar full of bourbon.

He had left the café, hauling Irina's ruined computer after him and cleaning up the debris. He'd phoned Babe, said he wouldn't be home that night and that he'd dropped Irina's computer while moving it. He promised to replace the computer.

Babe sounded unconvinced. 'You're not with this girlfriend of Hubble's, are you? You better not be blowing this election thinking with your dick.'

'I'm not, and thanks for the vote of confidence. Be sure all your doors are locked, Daddy. And keep your gun at your bedside.'

'What? Christ, Whit, what is it? What's wrong?'

'Just do it,' Whit said. 'I got to go.'

Whit felt safe in one place, and that place was now settled in the calm of the bay, a big-ass moat between him and the world.

Gooch poured the right bourbon and was the consummate listener. When Whit finished, outlining the investigation, the attack, and the threats against him and his family, Gooch said, 'Of course we have to destroy these people.'

Whit said nothing.

'It's an insult to the rule of law. Even when the rule of law is The Not-Always-Respectable but Ever-Honorable Whit.' Gooch sipped his spring water and stared out over the empty dark of the water.

'I should warn Dad and Irina and my brothers.'

'If this jerk wanted them dead right now, he wouldn't have bothered telling you. Listen to me. Whoever did this is scum and he deserves a quick ending.'

Whit listened to the water slap against the sides of the *Don't Ask*. 'If they're following me, they might figure out that I've told you.'

'I'm hardly the authorities. I'm simply a grizzled fishing guide.' Gooch finished his drink. 'I'm curious as to who could field this army of darkness, devoted to nothing but eliminating a legion of Mosleys.'

'Junior Deloache.'

Gooch shrugged. 'Junior doesn't strike me as the forceful type on his own.'

'So he sends one of his goons in his place.'

'But this person knew details about you, your family. Junior is not oriented toward homework. Who else's cage have you and Claudia rattled?'

'Well, Delford took her off the case and she's steamed about it.'

'But Delford was threatened as well.'

Whit shrugged. 'Could be a cover so I don't suspect him. But there's a huge stretch between Delford yanking Claudia off this case and then Delford ordering me to be shot at and my whole family threatened. My God, I've known Delford Spires for years. No way.'

'What about our senator?'

'Not Lucinda's style. You may not like her, but she's not the kind to use thugs.'

'Lucinda Hubble is exactly the type to use hired muscle. I am not fooled like our fair electorate. I do not find her amusing or colorful or even particularly bright. There is something missing in that woman's eyes, some common trace of humanity. I don't doubt she lets Faith's hands get dirty while she keeps her own gloves white.'

'But this guy clearly didn't know about the suicide note Sam found. The note makes it much more likely I'll rule for suicide, even without a threat. If the shooter knew about that . . . why threaten me? I think it puts the Hubbles in the clear.'

'Indulge me, Whit. What if it was a Hubble? Say your fair Faith.'

'I'm indulging.' Whit kept his voice steady.

'At the least Lucinda is Pete's mother. There's a bond there that should survive just about anything, and you say she was clearly torn about him coming home. But Faith, this is nothing but nightmare for her. If Pete comes home and sours the election for his mother, Faith loses her job. Pete wants her kid and thought he had enough leverage against her that he hired a lawyer. If he did have dirt, it had to be radioactive for him to be considered the superior parent. She's down two strikes. And she's fiercely protective of Lucinda. Her I could see.'

Whit took a hard swallow of the bourbon, let it burn his throat. 'She'd be capable of killing Pete. I have no illusions there. But they consider the case closed now because of the note. She doesn't benefit from this threat against me.'

'Unless she doubts you buy the note and wants insurance.' Gooch showed compassion the only way he knew how, by shifting subjects. 'And Jabez Jones? His name keeps popping up here.'

'I think not,' Whit said.

'Why?'

'Gunplay doesn't seem his style.'

'There's a lot of testosterone in his ministry. You

know, the Bible is deplorably violent.' Gooch smiled. 'You're neglecting one other possibility.'

'Who?'

'Velvet.'

'You're joking.'

'Am not.'

'She's the one clamoring hardest for me to rule homicide. It makes no sense.'

'Look, Whit, she could be working a carefully constructed sham. She looks like Pete's advocate, but she retires from town quietly when you rule suicide. She nicely puts herself out of suspicion.'

'I just don't see her as a killer.'

'Christ, Whit, are you sleeping with her, too?'

'No.'

'You never know about people, Whit.'

The statement and Gooch's even tone made Whit stop. 'No, I suppose not.'

Another blanket of clouds unfurled over the western Gulf after the fall of evening; Whit longed to see the long swath of stars that scored the autumn sky over the coast. He heard a soft whispering, and he looked over the bow. Barely discernible in the darkness, several dark shapes surfaced into the gentle cups of waves, puffed misty air, then slowly submerged again. A small herd of porpoises, sleeping. He listened to them rise and fall in their total calm.

'So how are you going to rule?' Gooch finally asked.

Whit set down his drink. The shakiness had passed, but the liquor hadn't calmed him – just made him scared and drunk, all at once. 'Ruling for suicide makes everyone safe. For now. But what does that say about me? You think people here would vote for me or respect me if they knew I caved in to a threat?'

'I've known cowards, Whit. You ain't one.'

'I lay on that floor for the instructed thirty minutes. I didn't even answer my cell phone when it rang.'

'Not cowardice. Prudence. Learn the difference.' In the dark, Gooch cracked his knuckles. 'I still vote we find out who's behind this and destroy them.'

'And by destroy you mean call the papers and the cops and put them away forever.'

'I mean making sure they can never threaten anyone again. By means fair or foul.'

'I can't support anything illegal, for God's sakes. I'm a judge.'

'Whitman. Please. The court of Gooch is eminently fair. These people put themselves at risk when they threatened you. You would have been entirely within your rights if you'd had a gun and shot the bastard. Self-defense. Think of this as extended, ongoing self-defense.'

'No.'

'I remind you that you could have chosen to run to the police. You did not. You came to me. Do you expect me to sit with thumb in ass while my friend is threatened? You knew I would take action.'

'I just don't want anyone killed, Gooch, for God's sakes.'

'You sell me short every time, Whitman. I never said I would kill anyone.'

'You never said you wouldn't.'

'You can hardly open up a can of certified, high-octane whoop-ass on these people and then start setting boundaries.' Gooch stood and stretched. 'I'll sleep under the stars, even if they're playing hide-and-seek tonight.'

'I have my own ideas on how to move forward,' Whit said. 'But I want to think them through.'

'Then we'll talk in the morning.' Gooch pulled a sleeping bag from a kit on deck and unrolled it, stretched out his big body on it without getting inside. 'Good night, Your Honor.'

'Good night.' A pause. 'Thanks, Gooch. I mean, really, thanks.'

Gooch turned his face in the direction of the sleeping porpoises. 'You're welcome.'

Whit went below to the guest stateroom and climbed into a berth. The draining of adrenaline throughout his body hit him hard. His head dropped onto the pillow, and his last waking thought was he had come as close to death tonight as he ever had and did he even want this stupid justice of the peace job anymore?

Or did he even deserve the job?

The Honorable Whit Mosley fell asleep before he could decide.

Heather Farrell stood in the dark curve of Little Mischief Beach. She knew Sam hated surprises – he was such a careful thinker – but money was money and they could use another five thousand. New Orleans was expensive. Sam never worried two seconds over cash, but Heather had searched in trash bins for half-eaten sandwiches, burgers doubling as housefly helipads, and fries cold and clotted with grease. Only she had the money sense. No amount of money lasted forever, and five thousand bucks was worth waiting on the cold dark beach in the middle of the night.

Heather eased down on the sand, holding her flashlight. In the dark of the beach she would be hard to find. Just like she and Sam would be. Once they got to New Orleans, they could rent a cheap room near the Quarter under invented names and nab some weed and lay in bed and smoke, spend whole days making love, stopping only to wander among the tourists, devour crawfish and boudin, and drink icy Jax beer.

It was funny. She wouldn't have touched a younger guy back in Lubbock, but travel broadened a girl. Sam was different than the pimpled boys. Confident, and funny, and making love he did not act or feel like a kid but a full-grown man. Sweet and kind. And smart, he had it all worked out where his mother and grandmother would have to let him go and have his life. He had convinced Heather his outlandish plan would work just fine.

Shoes crunched against the crushed shells along the lip of the beach. Her thumb moved to the toggle on the flashlight. Hand over the money, she nearly growled, as a joke, like she was robbing the guy. But then she thought he might not appreciate humor. He didn't smile much.

Funny the way people were, the way you could never guess about them, what lay under a skin –

'Heather?' a voice called softly behind her. She wasn't afraid, she knew he was coming, and she stood and dusted damp sand off her jeans. She clicked on her flashlight, the cone of light illuminating her worn sneakers.

'Hey.' A soft hiss of a laugh. 'You can turn that off.'

'Let's get out of here. I could use some coffee.'

'No, this won't take long.'

'All right,' she said. 'Do you have the money?'

'Yes. Five thousand dollars, as we agreed, and you and Sam Hubble leave town.'

The guy was so stupid. He had no idea she and Sam were planning on leaving town anyway, and here he was bribing her to do exactly what she wanted.

'It's going to screw over his grandmother in the middle of this election,' Heather said in her tough-chick voice. 'You sure that's what you want?'

'I want,' the man said. 'I'll miss *you*, though.'

'And I'll miss you, too. You never looked down on me.'

'Of course not.' A pause, the only sound her breathing and the soft swish of the waves. 'I like you, Heather.'

A coyness tinged his voice, and she wondered if numerous unsavory strings were attached to this sum of money. On the road a car passed, loud jazz blasting from the windows, and the man held himself perfectly still until the car was gone.

'The police,' he said. 'They questioned you pretty thoroughly about finding Pete Hubble's body.'

'Yeah. But they didn't bug me too bad. I could handle them.'

'Did you really not see anything? Hear anything when you went on Pete's boat?'

Suddenly her stomach roiled and a prickle rose along her arms, her legs, the small of her back. She just wanted the money, and she wanted off this dark beach. A whirl of what was going to be – a narrow little room in New Orleans, street curbs reeking of beer, blowing sugar off a hot beignet onto Sam's face for fun, zydeco drifting from a hundred open bar doors, her pockets heavy with money, Sam's breath cool against her ear after loving – flashed through her mind. Her throat ached.

'There was nothing to hear. I mean, Pete was already dead. He killed himself.'

'Yes. But the police doubt you.'

She blinked. 'No, they don't.'

'They know you lied to them.'

'I didn't lie. He was dead when I got there.'

'And you saw nothing suspicious? Heard nothing suspicious?'

'Nothing to see, nothing to hear,' she said, more annoyed than afraid.

'Just between you and me, were you going to make a movie for him?' She heard a creeping breathlessness in his tone.

'What?' she said. 'No.'

'Too bad. I would've liked to have seen him fucking you.'

Heather blanched. 'Just give me my money.'

'Yes, Darling,' he said, and the knife swung up hard, burying itself in her stomach, deep. His hand slammed over her mouth. Heather's eyes widened in agony and disbelief, and blood bubbled out of her, from the wound and surging past her lips.

Sam, oh Jesus, Sam help me, and then she tried to scream for her mother and then the knife was gone and she didn't even feel the flick across her throat but she slid into a strange darkness quite different from night.

The Blade held her close against him, smelling peanut butter crackers on her breath, feeling her death shuddering through him, then ended the embrace. Heather Farrell fell bonelessly onto the sand. Blood soaked his clothes, but after all, that was very easily remedied.

He wiped the knife on Heather's jeans. He pulled a large folded square of plastic from the back of his pants. It was warm from resting against his butt, like the knife had been. Carefully he rolled the body onto the plastic sheet and wrapped her in the shower-curtain shroud. He carried her toward the far end of the beach.

The fishing skiff bobbed in the shallow waves. He dumped the body into the boat, grabbed a small shovel and a plastic bucket, and dug up the blood-sodden sand. He motored the skiff into deeper water and aimed the prow across the heart of St Leo Bay.

He trembled. He really had nothing against her, didn't really want her the way he desired his Darlings, but now it was done and a shaky rush of triumph dried his mouth. Again, he was okay. Again, no one had seen. Again. For all the times he felt dumb as a stump, lost among other people, this he could do and do it okay.

The Blade steered the skiff out into the night, deep into the bay. He spotted a rather grand fishing trawler anchored in the middle, halfway between Port Leo and Santa Margarita Island, but its lights were down and he gave it a wide berth. The clouds lay heavy and low over the sky, like a second shroud, blocking out the clear stars, and he moved unseen on the waters.

28

At nine Thursday morning Claudia, supercharged by a large chocolate croissant from an art district bakery and a double espresso stronger than Gulf crude, waited to interview Jabez Jones about the Marcy Ballew case. David stood in the small bare study, hands on trim hips, inspecting the photos of Jabez body-slamming a thick-barreled antagonist during his pro wrestling days. David's uniform needed pressing, and she wondered if he wore it as a silent you-fled-domestic-bliss rebuke.

'I'm pretty sure all this wrestling's faked,' David said.

Delford had called her last night, asking her to work with David, per his request.

Are you pissed at me or what? she had asked. *Why are you putting me through the wringer? First you cut me from the Hubble case. Now you're inflicting my ex on me.*

I'm just expecting you to work with the man. It's a whole hour out of your day, Claudia. Just do it.

She wondered if the pay was better in Rockport or Port Aransas than Port Leo.

Jabez Jones entered, filling khaki shorts and a crisp T-shirt that read BE STRONG – I SAMUEL 1:9. His thighs looked like wooden blocks and a light sheen of sweat coated his face. Morning workout or morning prayer? she wondered. He mopped at his face with a hand towel.

'Hello, Deputy Power.' He shook David's hand warmly and nodded toward Claudia. 'Detective Salazar, we're blessed again with your presence. Carrot juice? Smoothie? We probably even have coffee, although I'm not fond of polluting my temple with stimulants.'

His temple. But Jabez's expression remained perfectly serious.

'No, thanks,' Claudia said. David shook his head.

'Well, I could use a protein shake,' Jabez said. 'Why don't y'all come with me and we can talk in the kitchen?'

They followed him to a kitchen where a young woman sliced cantaloupe with the precision of a jeweler. She gave Jabez a come-hither grin, but her smile froze when she saw Claudia and David.

Claudia thought: *Where do I know you from?* The girl's slender, doe-eyed face looked vaguely familiar. She moved with a complete awareness of her small body, setting down the knife with a shrug of short-snug hip, turning from the counter and leaning against it slightly to bring her breasts to full tilt against her shirt.

'Good morning,' she said.

'Rachel, would you mind excusing us?' Jabez said.

'Just a moment.' Claudia sidestepped around Jabez. She held up the picture of Marcy Ballew. 'Have you seen this young woman?'

Rachel glanced at Jabez, who shrugged. She studied the flyer. Claudia remembered her then, the girl from the volleyball game when she and Whit had interviewed Jabez before.

'No. I've never seen her,' Rachel said.

'Thanks,' Claudia said. Jabez nodded, so Rachel left. Claudia noticed David watching her exit. It was probably inspiring to a newly single guy, and she thought, *Quit it, quit looking at her*.

Jabez startled her. 'May I see the picture of who you're looking for?'

'Yes.' She handed it to Jabez.

'Her name is Marcy. We think she was in this area recently,' David said.

Jabez handed Claudia back the photo after a blink's worth of looking. 'I don't know her.'

'Her mother told us that she was a big fan of your wrestling career and your new show,' Claudia said.

The Adam's apple rose slightly in his oak of a throat. 'A fan? Well, I'm sorry I don't know her, then, and sorry I can't be of further help to you.'

Claudia smiled. 'I don't know about Deputy Power, but I think I will take one of those shakes you offered, if you don't mind. I'm afraid I skipped breakfast. Then we can ask you a few other quick questions.'

Jabez's smile was as tight as his shirt. 'Certainly. Melon or strawberry? I load them with vitamin mix and wheat germ as well.'

It would nullify the chocolate and the espresso. 'I'll have whatever you're having.'

'Nothing for me, thanks,' David said. 'Fruit tears up my stomach real bad.'

Jabez turned to fix the beverages.

'Do you take in runaways here?' she asked.

Jabez pushed aside the cantaloupe that Rachel had been slicing and began to peel a banana. He peeled a second one and upended both in a blender. Then he began to wash and slice several strawberries. 'People come to our camp for succor, for comfort. I believe they are safer with us than on the road, don't you?'

'I don't know much about what all you do here.'

'We pray, we minister.' He dumped the cut berries in with the bananas, poured in some milk and ice, and thumbed on the blender. Claudia waited until the pureeing stopped.

'This girl's ID turned up alongside a road two miles outside Port Leo.'

'She didn't come here.' He sprinkled wheat germ and shaved carrots and some other powder Claudia hoped wasn't strychnine into frosted glasses and poured the blended froth over them. He rummaged in the industrial-size fridge and held up an egg to her with a raised eyebrow. She shook her head and he cracked the raw egg into his frosted glass. She heard David gulp. Jabez garnished her glass with a slice of cantaloupe and handed it to her.

'Thank you.' The drink tasted sweet on her tongue but had the texture of cement mix. Jabez gestured for them to follow him.

They went into an adjoining living room-cum-training center. If Jesus preached poverty, Jabez wasn't listening. A state-of-the-art Nautilus machine towered in the corner. Expensive contemporary furniture – Danish, and out of character with the Victorian exterior of the home – adorned the room. A wide-screen television dominated one corner. Photos of Jabez's glory days in the wrestling ring covered the wall. In one he held aloft a weighted championship belt and snarled at the screaming audience of modern-day gladiator junkies.

One small cross hung on the wall, fitted in between a pair of ringside wrestling photos. No pictures of Jesus the gentle shepherd.

'We'd like to show her picture to your followers,' David said.

'They don't follow me. They follow Jesus. *Followers* makes it sound like a cult.'

'Well,' David said pleasantly. 'No offense meant.'

'You start a new church, offer seekers new answers to old questions, find success with it, and then people question you.'

'You glorify the body, though,' Claudia said.

He flexed the muscles in one arm. 'We consider our bodies temples to the Lord, since we are sculpted in His image. Our own bodies are reflected in the Body of Christ

228

that the church forms.' He ran a hand over the muscle in his arm like it was sacred velvet, a priest admiring his vestments.

'You certainly have a lot of young women here,' she said.

'I'm sure there are many young women at your own church.'

Claudia smiled. 'But they don't live with Father O'Hearn or Father Aguilar.'

'I don't sleep with these young women, if that's what you're implying.'

'You just focus on having female disciples? That it?' David asked.

His gaze hardened. 'The way I bring God to them appeals to them, just as a prayer book appeals to an Episcopalian or bowing toward Mecca appeals to a Muslim.'

'You're sure the Ballew girl didn't make her way here?' David asked.

'I will happily swear on a stack of Bibles that I've never laid eyes on her face before.'

'You are the only connection we've yet found between this girl and Port Leo,' David said bluntly.

Jabez drained his shake in such a pronounced swallow it reminded Claudia of a python downing a rat. 'You have no cause to bother us.'

'This girl had no reason to be in Encina County that we know of except for you.' Claudia set down her drink on a glass-topped table. 'I'm sorry, but I feel like you're not being completely honest with us.'

'I've given you no reason for doubt.'

'I wonder,' she said, hoping to shake the tree. 'You have this missing girl who might have come here to see you. You're seen arguing with Pete Hubble on his boat, and he is now dead. I suppose it might be coincidence. I suppose it might not.'

David shot her a questioning look with the barest shrug of his shoulders.

Jabez crossed his buffed arms. 'I don't get easily intimidated. Jesus is on my side, in my heart, in my brain. I can withstand Satan. Comparatively, you're not that frightening.'

'Satan can't get a search warrant, Reverend. And Satan can't put every aspect of your operation under a microscope. How do you think your television flock would react to news of you being investigated?' Claudia asked.

'On what charge? I've cooperated fully.' He laughed. 'I might expect this of a provincial buffoon like Delford Spires, but I always marked you as fairer and more intelligent, Ms Salazar.'

Claudia shook her head. 'So why do I believe I'm going to have to lean on you very hard to get the truth?'

He smiled beatifically. 'Lean away. I have a great PR firm in Austin. They've already laid out a plan for any crisis. Arrest, investigation, scandal – not that it's likely.'

She let the silence hang. 'Fine. Anything else, Deputy Power?'

David shook his head, a numb look on his face.

'Loved the shake,' Claudia said.

'Go with God,' Jabez said. She wanted to slap the sure smirk off his face.

They got into David's cruiser and shut the doors. David didn't start the car.

'You know, Claud, I miss that little spark of tough you got,' he said.

'You said you wouldn't do this. Talk about us.'

'Sorry. I just admired the way you wouldn't let him walk all over you.'

A group of Jabez disciples jogged past the parking lot, legs lifting into perfect beat, mouths moving to a chant of prayer.

'I knew I should've joined a gym,' David said. 'I saw the lustful stare you gave those arms of his.'

'You saw nothing,' Claudia said. Great. David was teasing her now, bantering.

As David drove down the palm-lined road leading to the encampment and halfway down to the highway, the girl Rachel stepped out of the growth, waving her arms. David stopped the cruiser, and Claudia lowered her window.

'Cops, right? Can we talk a minute?' the girl asked. Her voice shook.

'Sure,' Claudia said.

'Not here. Someplace else.'

David let the girl into the back of the car. Rachel ducked in and pointed at a side road, curving off to the right. 'Pull in down there so no one sees us. He's gonna be looking for me soon enough.'

David obeyed. Claudia turned to Rachel. 'Do you know that girl in the picture?'

'No, never seen her. But I know Pete Hubble.'

'What?'

'Pete's a friend from California. I did a couple of movies with him this year, and he lent me some cash.' Claudia studied the young woman's face, and saw anew the vixen clinging to Pete on the cover of one of the tapes. *Cleopatra's Love Slaves.* Done up as a horny Queen of the Nile, pulling a rubber asp through her cleavage and kissing the snake's head. Hadn't one of the stars had the silly name of Rachel Pleasure? Different hair, but the same girl, the same wide blue eyes, the same elfin face.

Rachel hunkered down in the seat. 'Just listen, okay? If I'm gone long, Mary Magdalene will kick my ass. Bitch already hates me.'

'We're listening,' Claudia said.

'Pete wanted dirt on Jabez Jones, and he asked me to

help him, said he'd pay me what I make in a month's work doing flicks. I said sure. He flew me out here and I checked into the camp.' Her voice wavered. 'We don't get to watch television – except for Jabez's show – or listen to radio or read papers, but last night I was in Jabez's room and heard them say on the TV news Pete was dead.'

'He shot himself,' Claudia said.

'But Pete was supposed to get me out. They watch us like hawks.'

'Didn't Velvet know you were here?' Claudia asked.

Rachel shook her head. 'He didn't want Velvet to know about his business. Plus she doesn't like me too well. I'm a way better actress than she is.'

'Um, we'll get you out,' David said. 'You want to go now?'

'Look, if Jabez knows Pete planted me here, no way am I staying. But I don't have the evidence Pete wanted.'

'What were you looking for?' Claudia asked.

Rachel bit her lip. 'Pete thought Jabez knew who killed his brother, years ago. He thought maybe Jabez had made all his money by keeping his mouth shut or maybe was in on his brother's death. I couldn't find anything about that, though, but I did find something else. Dope.'

'Do tell,' David said.

'I made sure I got close to him once I got here.' Rachel peered out the back windshield, as though the hounds had been released. 'That's why Mary Magdalene hates my guts. I'm the new favorite.'

'He says he doesn't sleep with his . . . followers,' Claudia said.

'Right. He was screwing me last night while the news was on. I had to keep lying there while he huffed and puffed and watched himself in the damn mirror. I thought I was going to die when I heard them talk about Pete. He's rough about sex, too. Something's not right with him, let me tell you. He likes to snort a little coke, especially when he and I are about to get busy. He keeps it in his bedroom.'

David revved the engine. 'If we get you out right now, will he flush the cocaine?'

'I don't know. I'm due for phone duty for the prayer line in thirty minutes. They'll look for me.'

Claudia frowned. 'Can you sit it out so he doesn't suspect and let us get a search warrant?'

Rachel nodded. 'If you think it will help.' She got out of the car. 'But hurry. And you got to get me out of here when you get back.'

'We will, I promise,' Claudia said. 'I promise.'

David backed out onto the road, floored the accelerator, and peeled down the road toward the highway. 'Jesus, Claudia. Jesus, this is huge!' he roared. 'Holy hell!'

Claudia thought: *Oh, no way was Pete gonna kill himself with that girl stuck at the camp. No way now Whit can rule for suicide.*

29

Lying on the bunk in the thin morning light, Whit opened the file of clippings Patsy Duchamp had given him yesterday. He heard Gooch clopping about on the deck. They had already scarfed a quick breakfast of yesterday's doughnuts and were chugging back to shore, where Whit would begin his great judicial charade and try not to get himself or anyone else killed.

A note from Patsy was stuck on the thick file of clips: *Whit, sorry if it's overkill, but the lady who did this is a retired military librarian, and let's just say she is a COMPLETIST. Hope this is helpful. You owe me a pitcher of Shiner Bock. Patsy.*

Completist was right. The woman had found practically every mention of Corey Hubble. Whit skipped the first clippings, looking for the ones specifically related to Corey's disappearance.

The first articles were entirely straightforward, except for the inherent lurid appeal of headlines like SENATOR'S SON MISSING or HUBBLE SUSPECTED RUNAWAY, and it was same information Claudia had shared with him from the police report. The tone of the quotes – most of which were from Delford and only a couple from Lucinda – went from fear of Corey being a victim of foul play to a seeming certainty that he had run away. No indication Pete, or anyone else, was suspected of killing Corey. The story garnered fewer inches as time passed. No new developments emerged.

He set the clippings from, during, and after Corey's disappearance aside and went back through the rest. One was Lucinda's husband's obituary, with Corey simply listed as a survivor. Many were articles about Lucinda's original campaign for the Texas Senate, picturing her stumping for votes with her two sons. Pete beamed, happy and proud; Corey wore the smile his mother told him to.

In a photo showing his mother on election night, when she narrowly won, Corey smiled in stunned amazement, as though victory was an unexpected pleasure. A few more clippings offered coverage of legislation Lucinda Hubble sponsored. He had stopped to read one article, dated a month before Corey's disappearance, about Lucinda's fiery stand on nursing home reform when his gaze drifted to a picture on the far side of the page.

It was a common photo for the *Port Leo Mariner*: proud fisherman hoisting aloft a sizable catch. The paper actively courted show-offs to promote Port Leo as an angler's paradise. Four goofily grinning teenagers held high a trio of big bullet-shaped fish. The caption read: *Tight Lines for Teens – Corey Hubble and friends caught a trio of beautiful red boogers, 22", 25", and 26", while out on St Leo Bay on Nov 22. Not pictured are the many biggies that got away. The kids used dead shrimp. Pictured (l to r): Corey Hubble and Marian Duchamp of Port Leo, Thomas Deloache Jr and Eddie Gardner of Houston.*

Whit stared at the photo. He tucked the clippings back into the envelope. Then he went up on the deck to help Gooch dock at the Golden Gulf Marina.

After Gooch gave him sound advice on how to avoid assassination throughout the day ('watch your ass something constant and scream fire if attacked'), Whit headed for his car. The T-head – and the docked boats – smelled of sharp diesel fuel, brewing coffee, and the sugary-piss tang of spilled white Zinfandel. He watched terns arcing over the gently rocking boats, scouring for generous breakfast scraps. His cell phone chirped. 'Whit Mosley here.'

'Hi. My name is Kevin McKinnon. You had sent me an E-mail about Pete Hubble?' A low baritone, calm, an accountant's voice.

Kevin, creator of the on-line Temple of Appreciation Web site, dedicated to Pete.

'Yes, Kevin, hello, thank you for calling back.'

'Yeah, well, what did you want?'

No point in hemming and hawing. 'I'm sorry to be the bearer of bad news. Pete has passed away.'

Silence. 'You're not funny.'

'I'm afraid I'm quite serious. I'm the justice of the peace here in Port Leo, Texas, Pete's hometown. He died Monday night. I'm supervising the inquest into his death.'

More silence. 'Oh, Jesus, oh, God.' The pain in his voice, the raw loss, stopped Whit.

Whit waited a moment, letting the man regain composure. 'I saw a posting on your site that you had talked with him this week.'

'Yes. How did he die?'

Whit told him briefly, without mentioning the suicide note. Kevin's low baritone became a breathy, agonized mewl. 'If this is a joke, it's in really bad taste.'

Under other circumstances an amateur pornographer chiding him on taste might have been good for a laugh over drinks with Georgie and Gooch. Deep grief colored Kevin's voice, sounding as true as the grief of the Hubbles.

'I'm so terribly sorry. But it would be helpful if you could tell me what you talked about.'

'I want some confirmation of this, mister. You fax me a death certificate.'

'How about if you call me at my office at the Encina

County courthouse? I'll give you the switchboard number, you can talk to the operator and know you're really talking to a judge.'

The offer disarmed him. 'Oh, shit. This is real?'

'You talked to him in the hours before he died. Did he sound suicidal?'

'Hardly. He sounded elated. He'd gotten the funding for his movie. His regular movie.'

'Did he mention where this money was coming from?'

'No. I guess he couldn't get the producers who regularly funded his porn work to back this movie. He said he needed a half million and he'd gotten it.'

Whit kept his voice under control. 'He had landed a half-million dollars?'

Kevin coughed. 'Why would he kill himself if he had gotten the money? That makes no sense.'

'He didn't mention who his investor was?'

'I'm sure. I can't believe he's gone.'

Whit wondered: *What was Pete to you, for God's sakes, a picture on a computer? Or more?*

'Forgive me, Kevin, but can you tell me what your relationship was with Pete?'

'Just a friend. Yeah, I dug his movies, I dug watching him, he was hotter than hell, man. But he was straight as an arrow. There was nothing between us. He liked that I had done a Web site about him. He was cool, thought it helped sell more videos for him, and it didn't cost him a cent.'

'Did he ever mention his brother Corey to you?' Whit remembered that the one Internet search he'd done on Corey Hubble pointed him toward Kevin's site, oddly enough.

'Yeah, he told me the whole sad story once. I posted a page about his brother on the site a few months ago, you know, thinking to help. A picture of Corey, details about when he vanished, a number you could call if you had information. Pete's answering service.'

'Did he ever mention any of these names to you: Junior Deloache? Or Eddie Gardner? Or Jabez Jones?'

'No. Sorry,' Kevin said. 'Jesus, now I got to write an obituary. Where the hell do I start?'

'Kevin, thanks. If there's anything else you remember . . .'

'Yeah, wait. The money. He joked about it. I figured his financier had just given him a check, but he joked about how heavy the bag was. Maybe he got the money in cash.'

'Thank you, Kevin. Thanks so much.' Condolence seemed even more awkward now than it had with Faith, but he tried. 'Please know how sorry I am for you losing your friend.'

'Thanks. Thanks. I got to go.'

Kevin hung up. Whit hurried to his car, made sure no mobsters hunked behind his tires, and fired up the engine. The car didn't explode. The day was off to a positive start.

Why would anyone give a no-talent porn hack a half million in cash to make a movie? Another hack, Whit thought. Junior Deloache.

His phone buzzed again.

'Where the hell are you?' Claudia demanded. 'I need a search warrant and I need it fast.'

'You aren't going to get away with this,' Mary Magdalene screamed. Claudia ignored her and watched two county deputies search the back closet of Jabez's master suite.

'It would be helpful if you would just tell us where Jabez is,' David said. His eyes shone brightly in excitement.

Mary Magdalene flinched. 'He was called away on the Lord's business.'

One of David's fellow deputies came in the room, shook his head. 'No sign of Jones on the grounds. Car's gone.'

'So where is he, Mary?' Claudia asked.

'I don't know.'

'You're his right-hand woman and you don't know.' Claudia crossed her arms, suspecting that Jabez leaving Mary behind to feel the heat was an increasingly tender subject. 'So I guess he just figured you could take whatever rap was coming. That's really Christian of him. What a guy.'

Mary Magdalene trembled, but not from fear.

A deputy, a lanky young Vietnamese man, carried an old, worn maple box from the closet. Inside was a thick Bible. Inside the Bible, in neatly hollowed-out trenches of Scripture, lay three vials of white powder. David daubed a bit on his tongue, tasted, and nodded at Claudia. 'The pause that refreshes. Co-caine, boys and girls.'

Claudia turned to Mary Magdalene. 'Help us, Mary, or we can't help you when the judge starts throwing books your way. Where is Jabez?'

Mary Magdalene fell to one knee, her mouth twisting in silent prayer.

'Start searching the other barracks,' David ordered, 'and let's call the DEA in Corpus. And we need to get an APB out on Jones.'

'She knows where he is,' Claudia insisted, pointing at the prayerful Mary. 'She knows and she's—'

Mary Magdalene exploded from the floor and pile-drove into Claudia, sending them both sprawling out into the small hallway. Thick fingers with sharp nails, like pikes, dug into Claudia's windpipe, and a fist slammed against her left eye. Claudia rammed upward with her knee, finding the softness between Mary's legs, and she grabbed Mary's thumb and bent back hard. A scream, and then the hands were yanked away, the other officers pinning Mary on her stomach, cuffing her in an instant.

Claudia climbed to her feet, David helping her. Her shoulder ached and the skin around her eye was numbed. Mary screamed imprecations, not the sweet language of theology but the salty poetry from her days on the street.

'I'm fine,' Claudia said before David could start fawning over her hurts. She knelt by Mary. 'You just complicated your life about a hundred times. I'm starting to think you're not particularly bright. Here's a chance to get smart, Mary. Where is Jabez?'

' "His enemies shall lick the dust," ' she hollered, her face purpling in rage. 'You'll die just like the trash does!'

'Y'all the ones licking dust. Or snorting it,' David said.

'Die like the trash does?' Claudia asked. 'Or die like the trash did?'

Delford Spires shook his head. 'I hope everything's nice and clean about how y'all got that warrant and did that search.' He pointed at Claudia's eye. 'That's gonna go shiner.'

'It's not like I was having my photo done soon for employee of the month.'

Stiff silence.

'So that leaves us, Delford, with an awful interesting situation,' Claudia said. 'Pete Hubble placed this girl in Jabez's camp. I can't imagine he would go to all that trouble, then blithely kill himself.'

Delford sipped a cold coffee. 'I can't explain away a suicide note, Claudia. Especially one that has just Pete's and Sam's prints on it.' His tone was final, dismissive, and he fixed her with a glower designed to make her crumple. She fired a salvo back, tired and achy and sick of being railroaded.

'I assume you've spoken with Judge Mosley about the coroner's findings and the problems with the bagging of the hands.'

'Yes, I have,' Delford said.

Eddie Gardner reddened. 'Claudia, you saw the body with me,' Gardner said. 'I didn't screw up the bagging.'

'I didn't say you did,' she said evenly. 'I'm just telling you what the ME and Judge Mosley said.'

Delford tweezed a mustache end into sharp perfection. 'Eddie, review the chain of custody for the body. Make sure we can account for the bag damage. Probably the goddamned mortuary crew tore 'em.'

'Yes, sir,' Gardner said. 'One other thing on Hubble. Since we have a time of death, we can locate the boats that came in and out of Golden Gulf during the period, since *Real Shame* was at the end of the T-head. Claudia and I already have accounted for five of the six boats that departed and all the boats that arrived. No one saw anything helpful.'

'And this last boat?'

'A cruiser called *Miss Folly*. Owner lives up near New Orleans and treks all over the Gulf coast. He didn't file a float plan.' A float plan was the maritime equivalent of a flight plan, required of commercial vessels, optional for personal craft.

'Let's get that boat found,' Delford said to Eddie. 'I don't want the press suggesting we're not being thorough. Claudia, let's talk.'

After Gardner had shut the door behind him, Delford folded his hands on his desk. 'I noticed you checked out the Corey Hubble file. Find anything interesting?'

'No, not really.'

'You're still pissed about being pulled as the lead.'

'No, it's your decision.'

'Claud, come on. I know you too well. You're madder than a wet bee. But listen, I want Gardner handling this.'

'Like he did the bags?'

'I did bruise your ego. Well, now.' A crinkle – a near smile – crossed his face. 'Point taken. Hubble's just about over, soon as Whit gets off his ass and issues a damned ruling. Focus on the Ballew case.'

'It's really the sheriff's case, not ours,' Claudia said. 'Unless you're scheming with mine and David's parents to stick us back together.'

Delford laughed, the low tremble that she knew, and she felt a sudden warmth again toward him, this contrary, whim-ridden old fart who could either advance you fast in the department or mire you down forever. 'Your mama scares me, Claudia, and I would be reluctant to cross her. I just want you to provide the sheriff's office with support. Consider yourself loaned to them.'

And therefore out of your hair, Claudia thought.

'So you go put some ice on that eye. Or a nice steak,' Delford said.

Claudia went back to her office. A whirl of paperwork covered her desk: two new burglary reports to follow up on, a shoplifting case. Gardner came in a few minutes later, swigging a Dr Pepper. He shut the office door and leaned against it.

'Aren't you clever?' he said.

'Pardon me?'

'You screw up, so you start trying to make me look bad.'

'You're mistaken.'

'You're gunning for me, Claudia. Maybe you damaged those evidence bags without me seeing.'

'Oh, get over yourself.'

He shot an unexpected missile across her bow. 'You

242

think because you're Mexican and a woman you should get all the good cases.'

'Just because you're an idiot,' she said sweetly, 'doesn't mean you should get all the bad ones.'

Eddie Gardner leaned toward her and growled, 'I bet you scratch when you fuck.'

She stood. 'Get away from me, and don't you ever talk to me like that again.'

He stepped back, a wounded look on his face. 'I don't know what you're talking about, Detective Salazar.' He opened the door and left.

She sat, bile polluting the back of her throat, wondering why autocracy and viciousness had suddenly fouled this perfectly nice police department. Delford had turned tyrannical; Gardner, who she always suspected was a pig, had gone from mildly amusing to no-tolerance disgusting.

She went down to the kitchen to get a glass of ice water. She found Patrolman Fox snacking on a Butterfinger bar. Chocolate gummed the corners of his mouth.

'What's up, Bill?' she asked, and he swallowed his candy.

'Working hard for Eddie. I wore my fingers to the bone phoning on the Hubble case.'

'What's going on with that?' She dumped ice into a glass and filled it from the faucet.

Fox shrugged. 'I called all the numbers on Pete Hubble's phone records. He knew some strange people, let me tell you. Most of them seemed to be people that he knew through his, um, film work.' The milk-breathed Baptist boy could hardly say the word *pornography*. 'I made notes. I haven't typed them up yet.'

Claudia picked up his scrawled pieces of paper. In the last days of his life Pete had called a couple of porn directors and a screenwriter in legit film. He'd called his mother, several times, his ex-wife three times. There were a couple of calls to the Placid Harbor Nursing Home – the home David's grandfather lived at, down by Little Mischief Beach, and that reminded her that she wanted to have another talk with Heather Farrell. She wondered who Pete knew there. And still the number in far East Texas, in the little hamlet of Missatuck, the one she'd tried the morning after Pete's death, and Fox had similarly gotten no answer. The phone company said that the number belonged to one Kathy Breaux. Pete had called her four times in the three days before his death.

Claudia went back to her office and picked up the phone. She dialed the Missatuck number. It was now disconnected, and no new number listed.

30

The afternoon light slanted through the tilted blinds. Bars of light and dark lay against Whit's desk – for once, cleared of the usual fan of papers and the half-full coffee cup. Whit sat across from Claudia, still in his judge's robe, an askew collar of yellow tropical-print shirt peeking out from the sober black. He had finished with traffic court by two, and she'd given him a quick synopsis of the developments with Jabez Jones.

'I don't care much about that suicide note,' Claudia said. 'But there's no way I believe Pete put Rachel into Jabez's camp as a spy, then decided to kill himself.'

Whit loosened a stray thread from the throat of his robe. 'Did Rachel say she'd told Pete about the drugs she'd seen?'

'Actually, no, she hadn't talked to him since she arrived at the camp. It was too risky, they thought. So let's say Pete found out another way Jabez was dealing.'

'Dealing?' Whit said.

'He clearly had more than he could personally use. Gives Jabez a motive.'

'I suppose.' Whit shrugged.

Claudia cocked her head. 'You sound like you've graduated from the Delford Spires School of Low-Key Investigation.'

'So Delford's finally made it to your hallowed shit list?'

'I've made room for him. Gardner's king.' She told him about her confrontation with Eddie Gardner.

'Be careful of him. Very careful,' Whit said.

'He's a mouth. I can handle him.'

'Seriously, Claudia,' Whit said, and she saw he was

dead serious. The sharp-eyed glare on his face was the one he usually reserved for magistrating repeat offenders and irksome litigants. His mouth twitched slightly. 'He's trouble.'

'Why's he on your shit list, Honorable?'

'Just don't cross him, okay? Trust me.'

'What's going on?'

'Nothing. Tired. Inquest is tomorrow at one. I decided to call a full one in the courtroom instead of just issuing a ruling of death.'

She supposed the political capital of a high-profile death was too good for him to waste right before an election. 'Sure, fine. I've got my notes ready to testify.'

He dug into his desk drawer and handed her a phone number. 'This is a number Pete used in California with an answering service. It might be interesting to see who in Port Leo, or in Texas, called him.'

'Haven't you been the busy bee?' Claudia said. 'Thanks, I'll have Fox check this.'

'I've got to go. Promise me you'll be careful.'

'About what?'

'Just be careful, all right?'

'Sure.' She walked back across the street to the police station, wondering who had wedged the coal lump in Whit's ass.

Whit watched Claudia cross the street, a sudden whip of wind from the bay mussing her dark hair. She tucked the errant strands behind her ear and darted inside the police station.

He let the blinds fall. That morning he had called each of his five brothers. He heard updates on teething nieces and upcoming software releases and the casual cruelties of writer critique groups. But nothing of bullets, of shady characters lurking in darkened driveways, ready to make innocents pay for Whit being the wrong judge in the wrong place at the wrong time. He ended each conversation with a story about random violence he claimed to have seen on TV and begged them all to be extra careful.

He had trudged through the day's duties of signing warrants, a brief truancy court, and a long and maddening traffic court session. Tomorrow was the inquest; he didn't have much time. He picked up the phone.

'Velvet? It's Whit Mosley. I need a favor from you. Do you still have a key to *Real Shame*?'

'I do.' She sounded lazy, sleepy, as though just awakening for the day. If she was, he wondered what she'd been up to all night.

'I'd like to stop by and borrow it, if I may.'

'The cops have a key.'

'I'd like to borrow yours.'

She was silent for a moment. 'Well, yeah, that's okay.'

'I've got an errand to run first, but I'll be over in an hour or so.'

'I'll see you then, Judgie.'

He hung up, doffed the robe, and in his beachwear shirt and khaki shorts and sandals headed over to the trashy west end of Port Leo.

The Blade watched the little waves surge up Little Mischief Beach, the sand flat, wet, and clean. The damp, fine air – the ocean exhaling – smelled of salt and freshness. No sign on the beach Heather Farrell had ever been there, no blood on the sands, not a gap-toed footprint to mark her passage.

He turned away from the water and the little voice, tinged with his mother, that whispered and berated in the curvy hollow of his ear roared: *Do you think she only had the clothes on her worthless back?*

He stopped. He turned toward the beach. Past the gentle crescent of sand, into the parkland, was a motte of live oaks, ringed with high grass. Hadn't he watched her there once, stretching against the Tower-of-Pisa bent-trees, scratching her foot?

She had to have camped nearby.

He bolted along the stretch of sand, up through the bluestems and the grasses, panic drumming its rat-a-tat in his chest, Mama's voice laughing at him, hiding in the wind.

He searched for a half hour among the askew oaks and the tall grasses. He found only a narrow rectangle of crushed bluestems, where a woman's sleeping bag might have lain recently. A discarded peanut butter crackers wrapper fluttered, caught in the tall grass.

The trailer park was named Rainbow's End. The pot of gold, however, was nowhere in sight.

He knocked on the wrong door, and a sleepy elderly woman told him Marian Duchamp made her home in trailer number six. The woman pointed over to an immaculately maintained trailer, a veritable palace among the weed-choked lots.

Whit wondered why anyone would voluntarily live on the Texas coast in a mobile home. One hurricane – one mild tropical storm – roaring ashore could move the trailer half a county inland. In small fragments.

Whit knocked once on the door. Inside, an afternoon talk show's theme jazzily trilled. The door lurched open. A woman who should have looked younger than she did, wearing frayed cutoffs and a faded Corpus Christi Ice Rays T-shirt, tottered in the doorway.

'Marian Duchamp?'

'Maybe.' She blinked against the bright afternoon light.

'I'm Whit Mosley, the justice of the peace for Encina County. I'm conducting a death inquest, and I'd like to ask you a few questions.'

'Um, okay. Um, what about?' Lunch had apparently been of the liquid sort.

'Corey Hubble.'

She stared.

'A friend of yours who disappeared several years ago?' Whit prompted.

Marian Duchamp digested this request. She was clearly drunk. A wine bottle rested against her hip: French Beaujolais, surprisingly, not your typical trailer-park fare.

Georgie, the walking she-database, had provided him with the local lore on Marian: a good-looking tomboy and jock up until the last year of junior high, when her father drowned in a boating accident. The dead father had reached from the grave to drag his daughter down; Marian Duchamp had raced into a self-destructive spiral of drugs, booze, and petty theft. Dropout from school, lived on her mother's mercy, Georgie had said. Just a shame.

'Corey. Yes.' She spoke slowly.

'Can we talk about him?'

'Well, I'm drunk, but you know, I'm not out in public, Judge, so I don't think that I'm in the wrong this time.'

'I'm not here to arrest or bug you, okay? As long as you're not planning on driving anywhere today, are you?'

'Don't have a car, so I guess not.' She laughed, a rough, unpleasant guffaw, and the wine wafted on her breath. She contemplated him with a half smile. 'I remember you. One of the Mosley boys.'

'Yeah, the youngest.' At once he almost regretted his words. Forever the baby of a certain notorious family. But when five older brothers had already speeded and fished and slept and drunk a path through the town's consciousness, cutting your own distinctive way got progressively harder.

'Yeah, I knew your brother Mark,' she said. Her smile warmed, not quite sultry but at least friendlier. 'Come on in.'

A sober feminine hand clearly maintained this space: gold-trimmed family photos, a small milk bottle holding fresh carnations on the dinner table, a sofa with neatly arranged pillows, embroidered with platitudes like BLOOM WHERE YOU'RE PLANTED and PRINCESS OF QUITE A BIT. Dust would not dare show its unsightly face; the home appeared as pristine as a freshly tended hotel suite. A stand of wine bottles, emptied, stood along the breakfast bar. Whit read the labels: Cakebread, La Crema, Cuvaison. Not a dollar vintage in the bunch.

'You have a nice trailer,' Whit said.

'I found quality help,' Marian smirked. 'And you know, good help is really hard to find. I'm ever so lucky. Have a seat. You on duty? Do judges do duty? Want a glass of quality red?' Her gaze drifted across his throat, his chest.

'No, thank you.' He sat on the couch, and she tumbled into the recliner. He knew she'd once been attractive in a lanky way, but now her skin looked sallow, her belly was a little wine barrel, and patchy shadow, new applied over old, caked her eyelids.

'What's Mark doing these days?' she asked.

'He's living in Austin, still single, getting an MFA in creative writing at UT. He's finished a novel and is working on a collection of poems.'

'Well, la-di-da, fancy, fancy, fancy. Po-ems.' She paused. 'I know some words that rhyme.' She confessed this with a tinge of embarrassment, as though she had neglected a gift handed her by the gods.

Whit let silence sit between them for twenty seconds, and Marian fidgeted and half smiled at him. 'I understand you knew Corey Hubble when you were kids,' Whit said.

'Ancient history now, like Vietnam and the Renaissance.'

'His brother Pete died recently, and he was working on a film about Corey's disappearance. We're interested to know who he talked to about Corey.'

'We being who? The police?'

'We being me, really.' He suspected she had no liking for the police. 'The inquest determines if someone is responsible for the death of another. The voters are my boss. I work for the county.'

'You don't work for Delford Spires?'

'He wouldn't hire me to wipe his ass,' Whit said. Marian, the wild teen, would have no love for a longtime police chief. 'I'm not one of his favorite people.'

Marian abruptly got up from the recliner and refilled her glass with Beaujolais. Not the gentle arc of a pour – more of a rough slosh, spilling the wine. She licked wine from her hand, then drank half the glass down, then refilled again before she tottered back to the recliner.

'So this is upsetting to you, or you're just thirsty?' Whit said.

'There's nothing to tell about Corey Hubble.'

'Pete didn't think so.'

'Yeah, and now he's gonna be crammed in a coffin for eternity.' She shuddered. 'No, thanks.'

Whit was silent. Marian Duchamp, in this state, could hardly be considered a credible witness. At least in court. But instead he got up, found a glass, poured in a small trickle, and sat again.

'I remember Corey, you know,' he said. 'I knew him, but not well.'

Watching him sample the wine, she visibly relaxed. She traced the ring of the glass with a fingernail. 'He . . . was jealous of you,' she said with a soft laugh. 'Does that surprise you?'

'Sure does. I'm nothing special.'

'Well, you had a mess of brothers. You always had family around. Corey didn't have nobody after his daddy died. Pete was the pet, and his mama just wanted to go write laws and fuck around in Austin. Serving the people, my ass.'

'Didn't he have you as a friend?'

She laughed. 'Friend. There's a nice clean word. We fucked now and then.' She watched him for a reaction to her crudity.

'He ever hit now and then?'

She giggled. 'Hey, I hit him back. He was a mean little shit when he got crossed.'

'You ever hear of him roughing up other women?'

She tongued the rim of her glass. 'I was the only one stupid enough to date him.'

'So what do you think happened to him, Marian?'

'I really don't know.' She sipped some wine, not looking at him. 'Why should I tell you anything anyway?'

'Well, I need your help, and you're the only one who can help me. No one else will.'

'That's a lousy reason.'

'You mentioned Delford Spires before.'

She shrugged.

'You think Delford did a crappy job of investigating Corey's disappearance?'

She laughed, not a funny or kind laugh. 'That was the fox watching the freaking henhouse.'

'Why?'

'Corey hated Delford Spires's guts.'

'Didn't every teenager in town?' Whit cajoled, laughing, tasting a little more of his wine. 'I was in the terrorist crew that painted his house pink. You remember that?'

She brayed laughter, recognizing the widely loved – or at least widely discussed – prank played long ago on the police chief.

'So what was Corey's beef with Delford?'

'I think,' she said slowly, 'Corey took off because Delford caught wind of what he was planning.'

'Which was?'

'Well, Corey was probably kidding – you know loud-mouthed kids, but he told me he was gonna kill Delford Spires.' She held her wineglass very still, in both hands.

Whit kept equally still. 'How did he plan on doing this?'

She shrugged. 'He had his daddy's shotgun.'

Whit watched her; she stared at the hem of her cutoffs. 'Why do you think he told you this, Marian?'

'Just to impress me. He was ten pounds of shit in a Dixie cup.'

'Why did he want to shoot Delford?'

'I don't know. He never told me why . . . so I never took him seriously. I mean, look, he couldn't have been serious. Delford Spires is still alive.'

'But Corey probably isn't,' he said, and she burst into tears.

'You think Delford killed Corey?'

She cried, she shrugged. 'Shit. I shouldn't have said anything. Shit.'

Delford might be many things – political, pushy, too good-old-boy for a changing world, but Whit didn't believe Delford was a cold-blooded killer. Especially a killer of children.

'Why didn't you tell anyone this?'

'I did. Corey's mama. I was afraid to talk to the police – afraid of Delford, I mean. I didn't know what to think.

So I told the senator, I phoned her, and she thanked me and nothing ever came of it. You know, I figured Corey would come home and she didn't want him into trouble with Delford.'

Marian Duchamp got up with overdone precision, stumbled to the kitchen, and freshened her glass.

We build these little worlds for ourselves, Whit thought, remembering what Velvet had said, *and then we never get to move out.*

'Do you remember two friends of Corey's? From Houston. A boy named Eddie Gardner, another boy named Junior Deloache.'

'Think so. They summered down here sometimes and fished in the fall on weekends. Junior always had lots of cash and dope to share.' She remembered too late Whit was a judge and murmured, 'Well, I don't do anything illegal anymore, okay?'

'What about Eddie?'

'Just some lame-ass friend of Junior's.'

And now he was a detective on the Port Leo police force. A very recent hire.

'You seen either of them around lately?'

She shook her head. 'Not in years, not since Corey took off.'

The door to the trailer opened, and a tall, fiftyish woman peeked her head inside. Her hair was pulled tight into a proper gray bun, and she wore a cleaning smock, festooned with a brightly colored, grinning cartoon chicken waving a spatula. She carried a grocery sack.

'Oh, excuse me, hon. I didn't know you were entertaining.' The lady smiled with maternal grace at Whit, as though about to pat Whit's head and offer him a sugar cookie.

'Oh, come on in, Mama,' Marian said. 'This is Whit Mosley – he's a judge.'

Whit helped Mama Duchamp tote grocery sacks. One bag clinked, full of bottles of wine: merlot, chardonnay, pinot noir, all of it the better stuff. He put the bags on the kitchen counter without comment, and Mama Duchamp murmured that she'd just brought some refreshments for her sweet baby girl and oh, she'd tend to getting those bottles put up.

'Have some red, Mama,' Marian called.

'Perhaps later,' Mama Duchamp said.

'I was just going,' Whit said. He thanked Marian for her time. She blinked, as if confused as to why she'd been crying, why he was here. With her mother in the room Marian seemed sunnier, as though reassured, like a puppy, that the milk dish brimmed full.

Mama Duchamp stepped outside with him, shutting the door on Marian's hollered, slurred good-byes.

'I know you're a busy man, with a lot of doors to knock on,' Mama Duchamp said. 'Good luck in the election. I hope you win. I don't trust people named Buddy. It's like they want to be your friend before you even know them.'

'Thanks. But I actually wasn't here campaigning. I was asking Marian about Corey Hubble.'

He could smell the wry odor of throat lozenges on her breath. 'Why?'

'She says Corey was planning to commit a murder before he vanished.'

'Oh, my lands. Marian doesn't know what she says. She doesn't think.'

'It's hard to think when you're drinking all day.'

Mama Duchamp's smile twitched. 'She's nervous. It soothes her.'

'Do you do this all the time? Bring her what she needs to live?'

Her long, narrow hands smoothed the chicken apron.

255

'Marian doesn't fend well for herself. She messes up. It's just easier if I . . . arrange things for her.'

'My brothers and I used to do that for my father. He was a drunk.'

'Don't you presume to stand here and lecture me.'

'For God's sakes. Aren't you tired of helping her along?' Whit asked.

She brought a hand to her lipsticked mouth. 'Tired of it? My God, Marian could be lying out in an alley, scrounging on a beach, selling herself for loose change. This way . . . I can keep an eye on her.'

In a cage nicely gilded by the glint from wine bottles. 'I suppose it's one way to be sure the kids stay in touch.' He felt a sudden fury with this woman, letting her daughter drown by inches in scrubbed comfort. 'I'll bet her liver's like wet tissue paper. Do you see the yellow tint in her eyes? That's death creeping in. Jesus, Marian's about my age. She won't have long. Get her some help.'

'Get off our property. I'm certainly not going to vote for you now, and I doubt that any member of the Garden Club will either once I make a few phone calls.'

'I don't want your vote, Mrs Duchamp,' Whit said. Her face crimsoned, and she fled to the trailer. She shut the door quietly.

Whit roared out of the trailer park. His hands shook.

Get up, l'il bit, make me some bourb'coffee. Now. Move your ass. Babe's voice, slurring from the past. And Whit crawled from bed, being extra quiet, and made the coffee, poured in the extra big dollop of whiskey to ease Daddy's morning nerves. He was eight.

Whit pulled in at the next gas station and filled his tank.

Delford. Corey. What else to that story was there? Say Corey did come after Delford with a shotgun. If Delford killed Corey in self-defense, there was no reason to keep it secret. Marian's testimony about Corey's plans would have made a self-defense plea simple. If Delford or any of the authorities had heard of Corey's threats, Corey would have promptly been arrested, charged, and dealt with in the judicial system. That was Delford's way. He would never play judge and executioner. He had too much at stake to risk it over a punk kid like Corey Hubble.

But if Delford had killed Corey, then Delford could eliminate every iota of bothersome evidence. This theoretical killing might be impossible to prove.

He tried to imagine Corey stalking Delford, a grungy doper rich kid following around a respected officer. Corey would follow Delford, learn his routine, attempt to strike when Delford was most vulnerable – so when was that? What had the boy seen? What had he known? Why was he headed north?

He wondered where Delford was that fateful weekend.

Whit got out of his car, filled his tank, bought a fried apple pie and Dr Pepper at the convenience store, and ate a second lunch, all the while considering what would light the fuse of a pissy, self-centered fifteen-year-old.

He didn't think of it until he thought about his own childhood, his own missing parent and what actions lit his own slow rage.

Jealousy. Resentment. The hungry need for a parent, even one who shows no interest.

Whit got on his cell phone and called Georgie.

31

Thursday evening, as the sun began its dip below the horizon, Claudia drove down Highway 35, searching for Heather Farrell. No one at Little Mischief Beach had seen Heather, and Claudia suspected that she might have moved on. Whit's constable, Lloyd, had not been able to serve Heather the subpoena to appear in court tomorrow. Lloyd was cruising around the other local parks, hoping to spot her, and was concentrating on the northern half of the county. Claudia decided that Heather might have migrated south.

At least her need to find Heather had taken her away from David's gloating.

'Claudia, we just made our careers. Both of us,' he had exulted. The Jabez Jones case was the biggest of his rather staid term in the sheriff's department, and he could hardly contain his excitement.

'You need to find Jabez first,' she cautioned. 'I wouldn't be counting any promotions until then.'

'What do you think I should wear for *Entertainment Tonight*, if they want an interview?' David wondered. 'They cover wrestling stories, right?'

'Your uniform.' Claudia knew any answer was easier than an argument for sanity. 'But pressed, okay?'

She turned off the main highway, at an intersection marked by crumpled, wood-grayed county piers, a reminder of the last big hurricane three years ago. The money to repair them had gone instead to new piers in Port Leo and Laurel Point. The piers were abandoned now except for a flock of pelicans, preening on the rotting posts. She remembered walking along the short piers with

David, hand in hand, breathing the smell of buttery popcorn, of salt, of dead mullet, of bait souring in the air, of spilled chocolate ice cream melting between the boards. Her wedding ring had felt newly heavy, a sudden anchor with a chip of diamond.

There was a small park on the south side of St Leo Bay, and she drove slowly past it. A family of three was strolling along the beach. An elderly woman sketched in the fading light, perched atop a picnic table, squinting at the wind-whipped bay. Claudia stopped and gave a description of Heather to the family and the woman. No one had seen her.

Claudia got back in her unmarked Taurus and headed farther south, the road curving down toward the hamlets of Encina Pass and Copano. She saw a white BMW speeding toward her, the driver intent on a phone. The car bulleted past, and Claudia saw Faith Hubble at the wheel.

Claudia lacked both a radar gun and jurisdiction. She headed down toward Encina Pass, and three minutes later she spotted Whit Mosley, getting into his Ford Explorer, the campaign sign magnets peeled off the sides. In the parking lot of a little puck of a motel, a twenty-dollar-a-night joint that catered to poor hipsters, tourists on bony budgets, and cheating husbands from Corpus Christi.

It didn't cater to justices of the peace and senators' chiefs of staff.

She pulled in beside Whit just as he started his car. She saw him force the smile, the faked-pleased look that suggested *gosh, I'm glad to see you* when it really meant *oh, shit* to the nth degree.

And a deep-inside part of her, never touched by David, twisted.

Claudia got out of her car. Whit powered his window down.

'Hi,' she said. 'What are you doing all the way down here in the bumfuck part of the county?'

He didn't answer right away. 'Talking with a friend.'

'Faith Hubble, maybe?'

He didn't say anything. 'I saw her speeding down the road not three minutes ago. I couldn't imagine why she was gracing a remote part of the county with her divine presence. So what's going on, Honorable?'

'I wanted to ask her,' he said mildly, 'about a shotgun.'

'Shotgun?'

'Corey Hubble owned a shotgun. I asked what happened to it after he vanished.'

'And you had to discuss this with her in a backwater motel?' She remembered their faces when she'd arrived at Whit's door – the way they both focused on her, the way they didn't look at each other with her standing there, the wineglasses set close together on the coffee table.

Whit clicked off his engine. 'I can't discuss it.'

'Can't or won't?'

'Doesn't matter. Either way I'm not talking about it.'

Claudia swallowed, aware suddenly of a sheen of sweat on her palms, the back of her legs, her shoulders. 'If you're involved with her . . . you should recuse yourself from the inquest.'

'I disagree, Claudia. But I can't discuss this with you. You're going to have to trust me.'

'Whit, please . . .'

'I have to go now. I'll see you tomorrow.' And he powered up the window and drove out of the lot. She stood in the oily smear of his parking place, watching him go.

She got back in her Taurus, and looked for Heather Farrell for another hour without success before she headed home.

Whit lay on his back in his bed, watching the ceiling fan rotate above him.

Did you think you were James Bond? A romp in the hay would loosen her tongue – she'd talk about whatever she knew about the day Corey vanished? The meeting had been rushed, the lovemaking awkward. Her kisses wore on his lips like sandpaper, and she had pulled away, frowning, saying, *We doing this or not?* And so he had, but the sex felt more duty than pleasure, and her finishing gasps when she arched against him sounded forced. Perhaps Velvet should have taped them with all the sincerity they had shown.

Faith claimed to know nothing about Corey's disappearance, a shotgun, or a grudge against Delford Spires. The more he talked, the more hastily she rinsed and dressed, and when she left all she said was, 'Give me a lead time of a couple of minutes, okay? And you drive back via Old Bay Road, not the highway.' Then the door shut, with not a single kiss good-bye.

And Claudia. He wanted to tell her, confide in her, but if he did, she and his family were at enormous risk. What if the man in the dark had been Delford or Eddie Gardner? What if his brothers were being watched right now, as threatened? The risk was too much. He would go on with his plan, conduct the inquest tomorrow, rule, and then worry less about the peace in his job title and more about the justice.

Finally he slept, and he dreamed of himself and Claudia's brother Jimmy, boys gigging for frogs in the murky backwash creeks, Claudia tagging along, the serious pest.

32

At twenty till one Friday afternoon the Blade debated whether or not he should take a seat for the inquest. The hearing would start shortly, but he did not wish to be conspicuous by his presence. It was pleasant to sit in the cramped confines of the VW Beetle and watch the few television reporters strutting on the county courthouse lawn. All three of them, from the local Corpus affiliates, primped their doughnut-glaze hair. Again the sudden urge to simply get out of the car, walk over to them, and say, *Do I have a story for you – but you must call me the Blade,* washed over him, and he pumped up his Beach Boys tape, listening to them implore Rhonda for help, and the desire ebbed. To the Boys, Rhonda was a patron saint of love; perhaps he could find a Darling with the same name one day. Encina County was a Rhonda-rich environment. And perhaps one day he would walk up to a reporter and let his infamy begin. But not today.

If that scum-bucket judge did his job and ruled for suicide, then Velvet would have no reason to stay. Her time in Port Leo would end, and her sojourn with him could begin. He would treasure each second with her, each second an eternity to play again in his mind for the rest of his life. His mouth dried with want. Then it would end, as always, and he would be sad for a while, until the next craving rose like a lick of fire.

So don't do this. Don't do this anymore.

The voice in his ear was not Mama's, but a boy's voice perhaps like his own from long ago. *I'm sorry for what I do but it has to be done. I need it to be done.*

He pulled his bowie knife out of its sheath and slid it

beneath the driver's seat. He had cleaned and sharpened it again after its last use.

The Blade saw Velvet hop out of her rental car and hurry inside the courthouse. She was modestly dressed, in black jeans, a thin, dark sweater, a baseball cap, and the reporters took little notice of her, which pleased him. He switched the Boys off. He could wait for her here. He smiled. Soon his Darling would breathe his same air, know his wanting, share the beginning of a brief forever.

Whit's clerk was a chain-smoking widow named Edith Gregory. She was on the outer edge of her fifties, with a thin, sparrow's body, dieted by years of smoking. She stood in Whit's office as he pulled his judicial robe over an unusually somber blue button-down and khaki combo and eyed him critically.

'Them pants need pressing,' she said. 'You think that little Russian gal could learn an iron.' Edith was friends with Georgie. 'Those Communists probably all wore grocery bags.'

'I'm responsible for my own laundry, Edith.'

Edith worked her empty fingers as if she had a cigarette. 'We need to get responsible for keeping you in office. I got to work for Buddy Beere, they gonna have to give me a raise.'

Whit straightened his robe and gathered the papers of the inquest record. 'Okay, let's go.'

Edith stopped him and he glanced at her. An unexpected softness touched her blue eyes, and he thought: *If my mom was alive and here she'd be about your age.*

'You just got this hangdog look on your face that's got me worried,' Edith said. 'Just remember, you're a judge. Act like one. Make me proud.'

Six months and she doesn't give me a pep talk until now. 'Thanks.'

They walked out of his office and down the hall. He followed her into the small courtroom. Lloyd, the constable, bellowed, 'All rise!' and the packed courtroom stood in near unison. The Hubble contingent occupied the front row: Faith, Lucinda, a tired-looking Sam, the rest of the Democratic power base for Encina County; to their left, Claudia Salazar, watching him as though he were a leper trying to blow kisses, and Delford Spires and Eddie Gardner, a couple of patrol officers; his father and Irina. In the back sat a large bevy of the curious, Velvet squeezed among them, replete in cap and dark glasses. In the back corner, to his surprise, Junior Deloache lounged, wearing a Houston Astros baseball cap and a Houston Rockets T-shirt. Deloache stared at him, and he wondered if he ruled for homicide if Junior would just go outside, flip open a cell phone, and call in the death orders.

'The Honorable Whitman Mosley presiding!' Lloyd blared. Whit sat and the crowd settled into their seats, wood creaking as butts eased down. He opened his inquest file, carefully prepared by his clerk. He glanced at the court reporter, borrowed from the county court. He wanted a written transcript of the proceedings to file in the inquest report.

Take step one and don't get killed.

'Good morning, everyone. This is a tragic event, this loss of life, and it has received a lot of local publicity. But this is a courtroom, and outbursts will not be tolerated. Anyone who creates a disturbance will be held in contempt and removed from the courtroom by the constable. Is that understood?'

Silence from the gathered. Lucinda Hubble looked pained. Velvet looked tense. Junior Deloache pushed his Astros cap back farther on his head and scratched his forehead with a beefy finger.

'Let me explain, quickly, the point of a death inquest hearing. It is to determine whether or not anyone is responsible for the death of another,' Whit said. 'I will question the witnesses. There is no jury in this case, and no one stands presently accused of a crime.' He glanced at Lloyd. 'Constable Brundrett, please call the first witness.'

Lloyd said, 'I was unable to serve process on Heather Farrell, Your Honor. I have not been able to locate her. I believe she may have left the jurisdiction. She's a known transient, and she lied to the police regarding her whereabouts.'

'Did you find any trace of her, Constable?' He already knew the answer but wanted it in the record.

'Yes, sir. We found she had bought two tickets on Greyhound. Her reservation on the bus was for three days from now.'

'But she's already gone?'

'Apparently, Your Honor.'

'Thank you, Constable. Next witness?'

'Calling Detective Edward Gardner of the Port Leo Police Department.'

Gardner came to the stand. Whit swore him in. Gardner gave a precise, rapid account of last Monday night's events.

'Did you find a suicide note?' Whit asked.

'No, Y'Honor. The deceased's son brought one to our attention later.'

'Who covered the deceased's hands with protective bagging?'

Gardner stared at him. 'I did, Y'Honor.'

'I was told by the Nueces County medical examiner's office the hands were improperly bagged.'

Gardner turned his gaze out to the crowd. 'Yes, sir. I checked the chain of custody. At some point before delivery to the morgue the bag covering the right hand was damaged.'

'The end result being the medical examiner's office had difficulty getting an accurate gunpowder-residue reading on Mr Hubble's hands. I suggest, Detective, before you investigate another crime scene that you refresh yourself on appropriate forensic procedures.' Whit knew he sounded like a textbook, but he watched as the borrowed court reporter recorded every word.

Gardner's face soured with anger. 'Yes, sir,' was all he said, but he did not look at Whit; he stared out into the crowd, as though at attention. Whit dismissed him from the stand. Claudia looked ready to jump out of her seat, notes in hand, but Whit didn't call her as a witness.

Next Dr Elizabeth Contreras, deputy medical examiner for Nueces County, gave the same summation of autopsy findings she'd given to Whit, stressing that she could not make a definitive call as to whether the gunshot wound was self-inflicted. Whit asked her only a few questions and Liz kept her testimony concise.

'Was there any other indication of violence to Mr Hubble?' he asked. 'Had he been drugged or assaulted in another way?'

'He was intoxicated, and we're awaiting toxicology results, but no, there were no other signs of violence on him.'

Whit thanked Liz and she stepped down.

'I'm introducing into the inquest record,' Whit said, 'a suicide note found at the scene by the deceased's minor son.' Whit held up the note, properly bagged. The audience was silent; tears coursed down Lucinda's cheeks. 'In fact, I would like to read the note into the transcript of this hearing.'

Whit read the note aloud in a slow voice, the final pain of Pete Hubble and his confession for the death of his brother Corey. Lucinda sobbed, noisily, and Faith hugged her. Sam trembled, his eyes locked on Whit. Velvet made some protesting noise; the other attendees shushed her. She glared at Whit as he finished.

Whit let the silence hang before he picked up his gavel. 'This court rules that the deceased, Peter James Hubble, committed suicide by self-inflicted gunshot wound on last October 12. I am going to certify a copy of the inquest summary report for delivery to the district court. This court is adjourned.' Whit rapped his gavel. It was over quick, and he saw the disappointment in faces that the hearing had been peculiar and short.

Velvet didn't disappoint. 'Are you freaking kidding me? What is this crap? Do I even get a chance to talk?'

'Court is adjourned, ma'am,' Lloyd warned in an even tone. 'You got a complaint, take it outside.'

Velvet yelled, 'If I can't get justice here, I goddamn well will get it somewhere else. Fuck you, Mosley!'

Whit ignored her, gathering his papers. A low chorus of boos erupted around Velvet, and she pulled away from one older woman who tried to console her. She stormed out of the courtroom.

Whit whispered to Lloyd, 'Follow that woman, please. I want to know what she does.'

Lloyd navigated through the throng leaving the courtroom. Claudia pushed past and caught Whit's arm.

'I'd like a word with you, Your Honor. In private,' she said. Her voice was low, but her tone was white with rage.

'About what?'

'About why you didn't call me to testify in this hearing.'

Whit shrugged. 'I really didn't see the need.' He stepped down from the bench.

Claudia stared at him, incredulous. 'The need? Jesus,

Whit! You ignored Pete's connection to Jabez, his dealings with Deloache, the bad blood with the Hubbles, the custody battle that was brewing. Christ, what didn't you ignore?'

He walked out of the courtroom by the back entrance, and she followed him down the hallway. The departing crowd buzzed like angry bees. Whit imagined Senator Hubble holding tearful court before the television reporters.

Claudia shut the door behind them.

'I really don't want to tell you what I think of you right now,' she said.

'You can. I don't break easy.'

'You had acres of room for doubt, Whit. The fact he consorted with known criminals. The fact that everything about this movie project seems to have vanished. The fact he was taking on his mother and wife for custody of his son. The fact that he had a young woman actively digging dirt on Jabez Jones and finding it.'

'The fact that evidence was improperly handled by your department. Maybe you should just trust me on this, Claudia.'

'Trust you? Trust you when you won't tell me why you've suddenly dropped a hundred IQ points? Christ, Whit, you have a responsibility! Or is your responsibility to make Faith Hubble happy?'

'Now the police don't have to continue the investigation.' He didn't look at her, doffing his robe and sliding it onto a hanger.

'I guess not. Delford'll have hard nipples over this.'

'Thanks for the image,' he said. 'You know, if additional information came forward at a later date, I could reopen the inquest.'

'I suppose so. But will big Faithie let you?'

'That's enough,' he snapped in a hard voice. 'You

might consider keeping your venom to yourself until you know the whole story.'

She ground her teeth together. 'Fine, Your Honor.' She made the title slightly mocking in tone. 'So tell me.'

'I certainly left enough room in the inquest record for more information to be brought forward,' Whit said slowly. 'I didn't call Sam Hubble as a witness, didn't have Heather Farrell testify to what she found, didn't mention the connections between Jabez and Pete, between Deloache and Pete, and I emphasized the sloppy job that Gardner did. Like you said, acres of doubt.'

Claudia stared at him. 'What the hell are you cooking up, Honorable?'

'I'm going to leave town for a few days.'

'Why?'

'It's the smart thing for me to do.'

She was silent for several seconds. 'Jesus Christ, Whit. Have you been threatened?'

She surprised him. He liked Claudia, but she had struck him as the plodding sort of investigator who was dogged and determined but not particularly given to flights of imagination. She seemed more given to flights of impatience, irritability, and stubbornness.

He kept his face very still. 'Of course not.'

Delford Spires opened Whit's door, knocking at the same time, and bestowed a thin smile – the kind used at funerals when you see someone you haven't visited with in a while and you're glad to see them but sick over the reason.

'Whit. Claudia.' Delford nodded. 'You kept justice swift, Whit. I know this has been hard on everyone.'

'Another cleared case,' Claudia said.

Delford shook his head. 'You're taking this the wrong way, Claudia. I've known Lucinda a real long time and I knew Pete. Just like him to come home and mess this up for his mama. She gave her kids the world and look what

269

it got her.' He brushed his mustache with a nervous flicker of his fingers. 'Now I want you to focus on helping poor Mrs Ballew in finding her girl.'

'How about finding Heather Farrell?' Whit said.

Delford shrugged. 'She's a runaway.'

'Who bought two tickets on the bus, didn't use them, and now has vanished,' Whit reminded him. 'I wonder who that other ticket was for.'

Heather being gone was unexpected to him. She might have seen something and been silenced by the same people who had threatened him. A sharp, hot shame crawled through his body. Yeah, Heather might be sitting under a railroad crossing right now, picnicking on fried fish, or she might be facedown in the bluestems, two bullets in her head.

If so, he decided, they would not get away with it. Fuck the election. 'I would certainly feel better if y'all would find Heather.'

'Fine,' Delford said. 'We'll put a notice out on the wires for the nearby counties. Claudia, would you excuse the judge and me for a moment?'

Claudia stepped into the hallway and closed the door behind her with a final stabbing glance at Whit.

'You think you're big shit,' Delford said. 'Let me give you every assurance you're not.'

'Get out of my office.'

'I don't like you dressing down Gardner in open court. You talk to me and only me about problems with my officers. You made our whole department look bad.'

Whit opened his mouth, full of sharp responses. He remembered the bullet whizzing past his ear, Irina, Babe, his brothers, their wives, his beautiful nieces, his wriggly nephews. *Not yet*, he thought, *not yet but oh, if you threatened my family I'm so going to fry you*. He said: 'I'll keep that in mind.'

Delford put his Stetson back on his head, as carefully as hanging a picture. 'See that you do. At least while you get to wear that robe.' He smiled and left, shutting the door behind him.

Whit sat down at his desk and waited. Lloyd returned in a minute, face flushed from exertion.

'What happened? Did she leave?' Whit asked.

'Yeah. With that guy in the Astros cap.'

Junior. Velvet had left with Junior, of all people. *If I can't get justice here, I goddamn well will get it somewhere else.* He wondered what sort of justice Junior might offer.

'Did it look like he forced her to leave with him?'

'No. They talked outside for a few minutes. She was all in a tizzy and he calmed her down. Then they walked to his Porsche, talked some more, and she followed him in her car.'

'Thank you, Lloyd.' Lloyd left, and Whit stopped at Edith's desk.

'I'm taking some time off, Edith. Please clear my docket and reschedule my hearings. If Judge Ramirez can take them, that's fine with me. If not reschedule for late next week.'

Edith frowned at him. 'Well, that's damn short notice.'

'Sorry. I have to go.'

'Shouldn't you be campaigning?'

Whit shrugged. 'In an odd way, I am.'

He gave her the inquest papers, had her make a copy for him, and then had the originals prepared for filing with the district court. He ran a quick errand to the police station, then drove toward Golden Gulf Marina, Velvet's key to *Real Shame* in his pocket.

33

Claudia returned to her office; Gardner was talking low on the phone, serious and somber, just saying yes or no. She felt a mix of worry and anger toward Whit. He was in some kind of trouble, she was sure, but he wasn't about to let her help him. Men. Thought they could do everything themselves. Truth be told, he was probably bedding Faith Hubble and that ruling was just a pure favor to her, cleanly sweeping a doubt-riddled case under the rug.

Do you really think so little of him?

Gardner finished his conversation and left without a word. He had barely spoken to her after their exchange. A pink message slip lay on her desk, David pestering her about the party for his grandfather. Perhaps a party would do her good, even if it was full of David's relatives, who seemed to regard her as clinically insane for leaving their darling boy and even being held at a nursing home, the kind of place that inevitably depressed her.

She opened the Ballew file, desperate to take her mind off Whit and Eddie and Pete Hubble. Maybe a reread would prompt her mind to look at the Ballew problem in a new way.

Wait a second. Speaking of nursing homes, Marcy had worked at one. The Encina County deputies had called the home in Louisiana and garnered nothing useful from the staff regarding Marcy's disappearance. Inspiration struck. She and David had concentrated on the flimsy connections between Marcy's wrestling interest and Port Leo, but what if there was a professional connection? She phoned the director of Port Leo's home, Placid Harbor, a snip-voiced woman named Roselle Cross.

'Ms Cross, have you ever heard of a nursing home in Deshay, Louisiana, called Memorial Oaks?'

'No.'

Claudia drummed a pencil. 'Y'all ever have much contact with the staff at other nursing homes?'

'Well, the administrators do, if there's a transfer. Buddy Beere usually handles that.'

'I'd like to talk to him.'

'Sure. He's usually around.'

'Thanks.' Claudia gathered her notes and the Ballew file and headed for the door.

The boat still smelled of death.

Whit closed the door behind him. *Real Shame* had not had its windows opened to the air since Pete had been found, and the atmosphere felt as oppressive as a wool blanket in summer. The Deloaches would soon take back possession of their boat and scrub away all traces of unpleasantness. He suspected that *Real Shame* would sail within days, away from police scrutiny in Port Leo.

He went down to Pete's stateroom. The air still smelled, slightly, of human waste and blood. The mattress still lay bare. The closets were empty. The diver Claudia recruited had found no trace of Pete's laptop and no sign of discarded diskettes or papers.

Whit figured Pete had not destroyed his research as a sad pre-suicide gesture. He had either shipped it off to someone else for safekeeping or the killer had taken it or destroyed it. Unless Pete had hidden it – and the boat still seemed the most likely place. And where had the supposed half million in cash gone? If Whit had either of those, he might have enough information to protect himself and his family. Or enough to get them all killed.

He rooted around the boat for an hour, finding nothing. No more tapes of Pete exploring scenes for his Corey movie, no computer diskettes squirreled away in couch cushions, no notes outlining the past. He was pawing through the small cabinets in the head when a phone rang. Not his cell phone in his pocket.

Whit followed the ringing to a bedside table. In a drawer was another cell phone. Its readout announced CALLER ID BLOCKED. He clicked the phone on.

'Hello?' he said.

'Hello? Pete?' A woman's voice.

'Yes,' Whit said, simultaneously thinking, *What the hell are you doing, dumbass?*

'Why aren't you answering your other phone?'

'Lost it,' Whit improvised.

'Look, some cop in Port Leo's been calling here and leaving messages. I had to fucking disconnect my number. I want to know what's going on.'

'Nothing.' He made his voice tired, indistinct.

'I'm still waiting on my money, sweetness.'

'Your money . . . okay,' Whit said. 'Let's get that to you.'

Silence hung like a blade in the air. 'Who is this? Where's Pete?'

'He can't come to the phone right now . . .' Whit tried lamely. 'Who am I speaking with?'

She hung up.

Whit clicked through the menu options on the cell phone. There were no unheard or archived messages, no numbers listed for speed dialing, no numbers listed in his phone book, no numbers listed in his call log. Pete had covered his tracks. Whit cursed.

But it had sounded long-distance, and the woman's voice was a soft, throaty drawl, definitely Southern, not one of Pete's California starlets. And she was expecting money. He pulled out his own phone and called the police station. Claudia was out and he had no intention of talking to Gardner or Delford. But he got Nelda, the dispatcher, to go look in the Hubble file and tell him that the phone number in Missatuck, Texas, the one that Claudia had been unable to get an answer from, was registered to a Kathy Breaux. He tried the number: disconnected, and no new number given in its place. He could force the phone company to give him the number. But chatting on the phone would accomplish nothing.

It was gambling time.

Whit pocketed Pete's phone and left the boat, hurrying to his car. He headed home, a loose plan he'd formed earlier taking solid shape. He called Velvet's hotel room, got no answer, left a message for her to call him on his cell phone. He left a vague note for Babe and Irina, packed a bag, tossed it in the back of his Explorer, and headed out of town. He didn't notice the flooring company van following him from the marina, idling on the other end of Evangeline while he stopped at home, and he didn't notice the van and another car staying a good distance behind him when he roared north onto State Highway 35, aiming toward Houston and the East Texas piney woods beyond.

Claudia hated nursing homes because she suspected she'd slobber her last in one someday. Probably a well-meaning niece or nephew would shuttle her ass into a Medicare bed, tsk-tsking the whole time about poor old Aunt Claudia.

Placid Harbor wasn't bad as nursing home facilities went. The word *placid* suggested residents in a drug-induced fog. But the view across St Leo Bay and Little Mischief Park was postcard pretty, and many of the residents were mobile and articulate, and management kept it clean. Not so bad for an iceberg to die on.

Roselle Cross's office was modest, furnished with a

Victorian desk, memorabilia from local Port Leo girls' softball teams on the walls, and photos of cheery and plump Roselle hugging residents. The decor in the photos showed these lovefests happened during Thanksgiving, Chanukah, Christmas, St Patrick's Day. Every day a holiday at Placid Harbor.

Roselle returned to the office. 'Buddy called in sick today, but I checked our files. We haven't had any transfers from any homes in Louisiana.'

'Where have you had transfers from recently? Say in the past year?' Maybe she could delve further into the Ballew girl's employment history, see if there was another connection through another home.

Roselle Cross kept a patient, holiday-quality smile and vanished into the front office. She returned five minutes later, armed with documents. 'Well, in the past year we've had three from Corpus, two from San Antonio, one from Aransas Pass, one from Port Isabel, and one from Austin.'

'What about transfers out? People leaving Placid Harbor for someplace else?'

She scanned her papers. 'One to Brownsville, one to Laredo, two to Corpus.'

'When these people transfer, how do they get here?'

'Well, with the close-by cities, like Aransas Pass or Corpus, usually it's an ambulance service that moves them. Or family members. Depends on the client's condition.'

'And what about the more distant towns?'

'Again, the family often brings the client. Or, for a charge, we can take or fetch them ourselves, depending on the client's condition.'

'So who would do this?'

'Buddy or more likely someone working for him. And a nurse or nurse's aide, if needed.'

'And nothing on Deshay, Louisiana?'

'Absolutely not.'

'Okay, thanks.' She stood to go. 'I understand there's a party here this weekend for my ex-husband's grandfather. Mr Power?'

'Oh, yes. He's a delight.' Roselle Cross managed to say this without the barest hint of sarcasm. Claudia liked her better immediately.

Claudia paid a guilt trip to David's Poppy, ready to shrug off blistering blame for making David unhappy if David had gained a spine and told his grandfather about their divorce. But luckily, Poppy was asleep, snoring in his bed with wild abandon, his mouth slack, lips pale with age. His roommate, watching a Spanish-language soap opera, turned up the volume higher and told Claudia in strident Spanish, 'You live your life for all these years and then you got to worry about roommates. Roommates, like you're in college. And me with a Purple Heart.'

Velvet awoke slowly. Clambering toward wakefulness required enormous effort; her limbs weighed like stone. The darkness around her was oceans deep, so dark that it was not an absence of light but light's very opposite.

She breathed and fabric blocked her mouth and throat. Her tongue, dry as sand, wriggled against the plug and felt rough texture of cloth and masking tape.

She strained to move. Cords bound her wrists and ankles. In her confusion she remembered a silly flick she directed two years ago, *Fit to Be Tied*, and mostly, she and the cast laughed and giggled through the scene. They had found nothing enticing and erotic in bondage, lacking few restraints themselves. Pete starred in the movie and groggily she called for him, but the mouth plug turned her plea into an inarticulate moan.

She ached – her head, her jaw, her stomach – and she became aware that thick, dense silk covered her eyes. She could see no light creeping in around the blindfold's edges.

Fear rose in her, sudden and sour as bile. She wrenched hard against the cords. They did not slacken.

She tried to remember where she had been.

Junior Deloache's condo. After that numbnuts Whit ruled for suicide, Junior had invited her over for a drink. To calm down and think over the next move, he said. Like he was suddenly Pete's advocate, the jerk, talking about the army of lawyers his father could command. But she had not wanted to be alone. She would have preferred having a glass of wine with Claudia Salazar, trying to persuade her to keep the case open somehow. A female friend, a tart in arms, would have been nice to have. She wanted to slap Whit; he had said he was on her side and God he was a liar. Kangaroo fucking court is what it was. But Junior was there, being kind.

Kindness had always mattered.

She remembered, coming out of the fog, a scream forming in her throat.

They're at Junior's condo, drinking whiskey. Anson's not around, thank God. He gives her the shivers, creeping around in that wheelchair. Velvet gets quickly and angrily drunk. Junior paws her breasts and mutters about film speeds and money shots.

'Let's do a movie,' he says. 'Right now. C'mon.'

She shrugs off his hand and pours more bourbon, thinking he'll be too drunk to get hard and too little to notice and suddenly he belts her, harder than she's ever been hit before. She realizes she spoke her thought aloud. The world devolves into a spinning circle of stars, and she fights as Junior yanks down her jeans, rips her thong in half, pulls loose her sweater, snaps off her brassiere. The

Sig's still in her purse and she clambers toward it, but he punches her once, twice, and she's lying on the carpet, stunned, bleeding. Through the foggy haze of pain she sees Junior setting up a camera, aiming it toward her, then shucking his Houston sports team clothes.

'Gonna make a movie now, bitch,' he says. 'The working title is Fuck Velvet Hard. *Already planning the sequel. Gonna call it* Velvet Tells Me Where the Fucking Money Is.*'*

'Stop it. Stop, Junior, this isn't funny.'

He is erect and he jabs a button on the camcorder. 'I'm not gonna get screwed over anymore. I'm a businessman. I'm gonna get to be in a fuck film, and I'm gonna get my money back.'

She stumbles to her feet, intent on getting that gun and shooting him, where's her damned purse, but he hammers her again, his fist bouncing off the back of her head, and she falls to the floor. She pukes up the bourbon and . . .

Then what?

She breathed around the mouth plug. God, this wasn't the movie, was it? Her head ached.

'Junior?' she tried to say.

. . . she hears the doorbell ring. Not the condo elevator door creaking open, not Anson wheeling back, but the other entrance, the stairs, and she hears Junior cuss softly.

A chair creaked, next to her. A finger, callused, ran along her cheek.

'No, darling. Junior's not here.'

She held herself very still.

The voice was low, a man's, a little gravelly. 'Would you like the gag removed, darling?'

She nodded.

'You should understand – no one can hear you, but I won't tolerate you screaming. At least not for now.'

A metal point inched down her leg. It stopped at her knee and pressed, gently.

'Owww,' she groaned.

'If you scream, darling, we'll get right down to my fun. I'll dig open those tits and we'll see if they're real.'

Velvet held perfectly still, not even daring to breathe.

'Nod once if you understand.'

She nodded.

The knife point left her knee. Gently the hands caressed her face. She heard a lock snap – *Jesus, he has this thing locked on my face!* – and the mouth plug was pried loose from her lips. A finger, wrapped around a damp cloth, cleaned out her mouth, dribbled welcome water over her tongue. She resisted the urge to bite down and take the finger off.

'There you go, darling,' the man said.

She wetted her lips with her tongue. 'Who are you?'

'I'm your new lover.'

A sick chill goose-pimpled her skin. 'Will you take off the blindfold?'

'Not for a while. More fun this way.'

Fun. That word again. 'Where am I?'

'Heaven.'

'Where's Junior?'

'Hell. Where he belongs.'

She offered a fake, soft laugh. 'No, really.'

'Junior isn't going to bother you anymore. I took care of him for my sweet darling.'

'Why am I here?'

'I need you,' he said.

Her tongue felt dry as dirt again. 'Yeah, baby, I can sure understand that. We all need. Perfectly natural.' She used her film voice, coy, trying to keep from shaking. 'But I can't give you what you need all tied up, baby.'

'Quiet now,' he said, brushing her hair with his fingertips.

'I have a name, baby. Velvet.'

He hummed, low in his throat.

'You untie Velvet, hon, you let me go, I'll give you what you need.'

She felt a finger run along her naked breasts, her stomach, the cup of her navel. She suppressed a shudder.

'What's your name, honey?' she asked.

She heard the chair shift. She could smell his breath, reeking of garlic and fried shrimp. He nibbled her ear and ran his tongue along its edge.

'What's your name?' she tried again in a whisper, her voice cracking.

'My name is Corey,' he whispered back. 'Corey Hubble.'

Then he climbed on top of her. She began to scream.

34

Whit drove, following Highway 35 as it snaked up the slow curve of the Texas coast, merging into Highway 288 north of Freeport, then sliding onto Interstate 10's thick rope when he reached the sprawl of Houston. He crept through Houston's never-ending rush-hour traffic and headed up toward the deep pine forests and shallow bayous of far East Texas. He could take I-10 to Beaumont and then 87 North to 1416, a farm-to-market road to the little town of Missatuck, where he suspected Kathy Breaux was waiting for Pete and her unexplained money.

Whit reached Beaumont around eight Friday night. The towers of the refineries glowed like an alien metropolis. With his window cracked he could smell the sour egg odor of natural gas and chemical plants, overpowering the barest hint of pine.

Hungry, he parked in the oil-stained lot next to a cheap diner with a neon fork spearing the window. In the counter he ate a greasy hamburger topped with kill-your-neighbors-strength onions and gulped a jumbo glass of iced tea. As he ate, he studied again the clipping file that Patsy had sent. He reread each article and found himself going back to the first article outlining Corey's disappearance:

‘Corey is impulsive,’ Senator Hubble said in a brief statement to the press. ‘I don't think Corey wants to be spending much time in Austin. I have no reason to suspect that Corey has run afoul of someone. I hope that if he is reading this he realizes the joke is over and he should please call us soon.’

The accompanying photo showed a stolid yet pained Lucinda Hubble leaving the Port Leo police station, brave, head held high but wearing dark glasses. A clearly shocked Pete, young beyond his years, walked next to her, grimacing. Delford stood next to Lucinda, a Rock of Gibraltar.

Of course he had.

The phone call to Georgie Whit had placed yesterday was a simple question of whether there had ever been rumor of a relationship between Lucinda Hubble and Delford Spires. Georgie, the human archive of local lore and gossip, had said, 'Well, they've always been friends. I wondered if Delford wanted more at one point. But I guess any chance of romance fizzled after Corey vanished. Lucinda never let another man close to her.'

It was circumstantial, it was wispy hearsay, but it made Whit wonder. A boy who felt anger and unending grief over his father's death and acid resentment toward his mother would not welcome a new suitor. Whit had felt the same sting when Babe split with Georgie and began wooing local divorcées. He had cordially hated all his father's girlfriends. Childish, yes, but common. But he still could not envision Delford ruthlessly killing a teenage boy.

He gathered up his papers and walked out of the diner, heading across the dark plain of the parking lot.

'Hey, fucker,' a voice boomed, and a hand borrowed from Goliath grabbed Whit off his feet, dragged him several feet behind the building, and slammed him into the back brick wall of the diner. The back of his head hit hard and pinwheels filled his vision. Whit lashed out with a fist and grazed a temple. He blinked and cool fingers curled into his throat, making themselves at home, squeezing the life out of him. His head pounded back into the bricks.

'Hey, fucker,' the voice repeated. 'Gonna talk.' In the dim light Whit could see Mr Words was a young, rough kid with thick arms, big hair, and a pair of narrow-lensed sunglasses most commonly found on pimps. He'd seen the guy before. The muscled-up kid at Junior's condo. Out of the corner of his eye Whit saw more movement, heard the quiet creak of a wheelchair.

Oh, shit.

'I hate a goddamned thief worse than anything,' Anson Todd said in a hushed voice. 'And you an elected official. Goddamn, American democracy is going down the fucking toilet. You corrupt bastard.'

'Yeah,' Mr Words agreed.

'What—' Whit attempted to breathe, grabbing at Mr Words's hand, trying to pry the fingers from his throat.

'I want the money, Judge Smart-Ass,' Anson hissed. He wheeled close to Whit and with an arthritic fist punched Whit in the balls. Hard. Whit gagged. Amazing how slight a punch it takes to savage a pair of testicles. Mr Words slammed Whit to the oily pavement, yanked his arm straight, spread his fingers against the parking-lot grime.

The throat grip relaxed momentarily so Whit could breathe and speak. 'What money?'

Wrong answer. Fist squeezed, blood fled from his throat. The wheelchair – heavy itself and full of old man – rolled over his fingers, backed up, rolled forward again. Whit gritted his teeth, wondering if he would first hear or feel the bones break.

'Don't fuck with us, Judge,' Anson said. He steadied the chair, letting its full weight settle on Whit's knuckles.

'Did a cop once,' Mr Words said. 'Never a judge. Cool. Start with fingers.'

'I don't have your money.'

'Get him into the van,' Anson ordered. 'You can have

284

your fun with him there.' He hacked phlegm. 'And shit, it's time for my medicine.'

Mr Words jerked Whit to his feet, keeping an iron grip on his throat with both hands. Whit tried to wrench free, hoping for a weak spot to punch or kick, but Mr Words was four inches taller and fifty pounds heavier, all muscle. Whit smelled the pineapple reek of cheap cologne, the soft odor of trash from the diner's Dumpster, the goon's sweat.

Mr Words hurried Whit along toward a dark blue van parked at the far end of the lot with a flooring company name on the side, Anson's motorized chair purring behind them.

'Cooperate, get off light,' Mr Words murmured in a spate of eloquence. 'You don't, die in fucking Beaumont. Talk to us. Be cool.'

The half million. They think I have it.

As Mr Words dragged him along by his neck, Whit considered options. A kick to the nuts and about a dozen hard punches to the jaw were the ticket. Actually, a small nuclear device would be the ticket. But Whit couldn't budge an inch. All he could see was the smeary grease stains of the lot, a few flattened cigarette butts, and the dark shadow of the van, barely illuminated in the halo of light from a streetlamp at the corner.

Head held down and stumbling, Whit saw the damage before they did. All four of the van's tires lay flat. He made a noise, and Mr Words stopped and saw and said, 'Well, fuck.'

Whit, the baby of six dirty-wrestling brothers, just needed that second. He fought just the way he learned at his brothers' knees and elbows and fists. He smashed his heel down on Mr Words's arch, gouging the foot with the modest heel of his loafer. Mr Words yelled. Whit slammed a forearm against Words's right arm, then elbowed backward into the thick throat. Mr Words yelped. Whit spun free of his hold, then drove headfirst into the man's abdomen. Mr Words staggered back and Whit jabbed hard with two left uppercuts that sent the kid sprawling onto the asphalt.

'Eddie, get the fuck out here!' Anson screamed. Whit whirled, trying to get his breath back. His throat felt like it had been scalded, his fingers felt like rubber, either broken by Anson's wheel or Mr Words's jaw. *Eddie.* Shit.

New plan. Run. He bolted and Mr Words kicked out, catching both his feet on a muscled leg hard as fallen timber, and Whit slammed hard into the pavement. *Well, you tried.* Fingers closed around his throat again, yanking him to his feet.

Movement came from behind the van. 'Eddie's indisposed.' A familiar voice. Gooch, holding a sleek automatic pistol, neatly fitted with a silencer. The pistol was aimed at Anson. The grip on Whit's throat tightened.

'Let the judge go, son,' Gooch said. 'Or I shoot the old man. Then you.'

Mr Words moved Whit in front of him as a makeshift shield. 'Or maybe I just break his neck if you don't drop the gun.'

'I can shoot you first, son,' Gooch said conversationally. 'Or I can shoot Anson. You want to explain to Papa Deloache how you got Anson killed?'

'Let him go,' Anson said quietly.

Even when whipped, Mr Words made an excellent lapdog. He let go. Whit gulped a long sucking breath, one that scorched his throat but his lungs savored.

'Judge, come here by the van,' Gooch said. 'I don't want you to get blood splattered all over your nice clothes.'

'Dumbass,' Anson snarled. 'You fuck with us, you don't have any idea what you're buying.'

286

'Oh, I do.' Gooch smiled. 'But fuck with me and you buy a grave no one will ever find. Understood?'

Whit leaned against the van. 'He said Eddie . . .'

'Eddie Gardner's in there. He's catching some shut-eye right now.' Whit peered inside; Eddie Gardner lay propped in the back of the van, bleeding lightly from his nose and mouth, but breathing. Yellow rope wrapped around his arms and legs.

'You. Get in the van,' Gooch ordered Mr Words.

The young man stared stupidly.

'Clearly you're no Fulbright scholar,' Gooch said, 'but do what you're told and you'll be fine. You come out of that van before I say, I shoot him and then I shoot you. You understand?'

Mr Words glanced at Anson; the old man nodded. The boy climbed into the van next to the unconscious Eddie, and Gooch slammed the door. He then held up a clear plastic bag to Anson: three black pistols, .22s, a switchblade, a blackjack, and a cell phone lay inside. 'I don't think I missed any of your toys when I went through your van, Anson. If I did, and Muscles comes out shooting, you get a bullet in the brain.'

Whit thought, *No, Gooch, don't do this,* but he said nothing, still rubbing his aching throat.

'I'm old, do your worst,' Anson huffed. 'I probably get a fucking colostomy bag next year. You think I'm afraid of you?'

'I don't believe you want to die one second before you have to, and I really don't think you want to see Muscles die. Isn't he Deloache's nephew?'

In the dim light Anson's stare narrowed. 'Who are you?'

'Why are you following Judge Mosley?'

'Kiss my ass.'

Gooch brought the gun up. 'How hard are the cops going to look for your killer, Anson? I think not very.'

'He thinks I took Pete's half million,' Whit coughed. Feeling was slowly creeping its painful way back into his fingers and throat.

Gooch raised an eyebrow. 'Anson?'

'I don't feel good. I need my medicine.' Moments ago he had been all snarl; now he was all plead.

'I got a permanent cure here if you don't start talking,' Gooch said.

Anson shrugged with a baleful look at Whit. 'You're like me, aren't you?' he asked Gooch. 'Always cleaning up other people's shit. We ain't done anything wrong, we're the wronged ones.'

'Oh, I bet,' Gooch said.

'Junior gave Pete Hubble a half-mil cash of his dad's money for some adult film series, because Pete promised Junior a percentage of the sales, the starring role, and all the bimbos he could screw. Well, that ain't the movie that Pete was making. He was making some shit about his fucked-up brother. Junior found out and wanted his – our – money back and Pete balked, kept saying it'd be a much better investment than porn. But Junior hadn't told his dad about this unapproved investment. We got to get that money back.'

'And you couldn't find it on the boat, so you figured the judge had it?'

'We been keeping an eye on Pete's boat, saw the judge leave it and head the fuck out of town like his ass is on fire. I figured he had it, or knew where it was.'

'I don't have your money,' Whit said.

'Don't feel bad that it's lost,' Gooch said. 'He bought it with the veins and noses of kids.' Gooch pushed his gun into the old man's face. 'Did you shoot at Whit the other night? Threaten him about the Hubble inquest?'

288

Anson shook his head.

'I don't mean you personally, Anson,' Gooch said. 'I'm talking anyone you know.'

Anson shook his head again. 'I . . . maybe Junior got a guy to come up from Corpus, some local muscle. Just a theory.'

'How'd he know about Whit's family?' Gooch snarled, grabbing Anson's throat.

Anson coughed. 'Junior . . . drinks at the Shell Inn. The owner brags about her former stepsons. In excruciating detail. Again, just a theory.'

'Ah. Thank you,' Gooch said. He eased his grip.

'I don't suppose it had occurred to you that Pete might have spent the money,' Whit said. He was surprised at how calm his voice was.

Anson huffed. 'Not in a few days in Port Leo. It's still our money. He lied to us and we want it back. I figured either you or that Velvet bitch had it.'

'Where's Junior?' Whit asked, a sudden icicle forming in his heart.

'He said he was going to Houston, explaining all this to his dad.'

'Bull,' Gooch said. 'You know damn well where he is.'

Whit pulled out his cell phone and dialed Velvet's motel room. No answer. He left another message with the motel clerk to have Velvet call him as soon as she could.

'Maybe Junior's trying to rough Velvet up the same way you roughed up me?' Whit said.

'Shit. He's not gonna hurt her. He wants to be in her movies.' Anson shook his head. 'Fuck films. No values left anymore, the world is just going down the toilet. Why Hollywood don't make a nice musical is beyond me.'

'Lecture your Sunday school class about it,' Gooch said.

Whit played a card. 'You know, I just heard on the radio that they caught Jabez Jones and he's talking. He had to get his dope from somewhere, and he might be implicating Junior.'

Anson kept his face stone still. 'I don't know what you mean.'

Gooch laughed, very softly. 'Whit, go back to your car. I'll join you shortly.'

'What are you going to do with them?' Whit asked.

'Just go.' Gooch's voice sounded soft, lazy, as though nothing was on the agenda more compelling than a tall glass of lemonade.

'No. I'm calling the police.'

'We're not doing that,' Gooch said.

'I'm a magistrate, for God's sakes. I'm having them arrested. At the least for assaulting a public servant.'

Gooch glanced back at Anson. 'What if the next schmuck they come after doesn't have the luxury of me to save their ass, Whit?'

'If they're in jail they can't go after anyone.'

'I can't testify in court, Whit,' Gooch said mildly. 'It's not going to happen.'

'You're not going to kill them.'

'May I suggest,' Anson said quietly, 'a compromise?'

'No,' Gooch said. 'Shut up.'

'Do you think this is how I wanted to spend my fucking retirement?' Anson said to Whit. 'Picking up after drunken, little-dicked morons who think they're tough?'

'Better than retiring behind bars and being sold for cigarettes,' Whit said. 'You lose those dentures, you're gonna be real popular. What can you give us on Junior Deloache?'

Anson smiled and shook his head. 'I ain't giving you shit on Junior, Judge.'

'Fine. Then I won't call the police. This isn't my

290

jurisdiction anyway.' He knew he'd miscalculated in pulling the moral high ground attitude with Gooch. Anson saw Whit's worry as weakness. He walked away and thought: *Please, Gooch, don't kill them.*

'Wait a second,' Anson called, but Whit kept walking. There was only the silence of his footsteps; no sounds of shots, no sounds of screams, no sounds of life ending. The highway gave off a distant rumble of its uninterested traffic. He sat inside his Explorer and closed the door.

Whit waited. And waited. Thirty minutes later, Gooch sauntered from behind the diner with a slight smile on his face. He climbed in next to Whit.

'I'm afraid to ask,' Whit said.

'They're fine. They're in custody.'

'Whose custody and under what charges?'

'Assault.' Gooch shrugged. 'That kid and Eddie beat me up. Anson helped him, you know.' He paused. 'I think the Feds might be interested in them. Drug trafficking, money laundering, all that kind of stuff. Sheer nastiness.'

'I see. Thank you, Gooch. You want to tell me why you followed me to Beaumont?'

'Saving your ass isn't a good enough reason?'

'Please tell me you didn't kill those men.'

'They're in custody, I told you. Go outside and see if you want.'

Whit walked to the back of the diner. The van with its four flats was gone. He walked back to his car.

'That diner any good?' Gooch asked. 'I'm starved.'

35

After leaving the nursing home, Claudia returned to the station. There was a message from David: Jabez Jones remained at large. Of course, no one was looking for Marcy, what with a high-profile quarry like Jabez. Claudia started the tedium of phone work. Buddy Beere was home with a bad cold, but he did confirm the transfers that Roselle Cross had mentioned. He sounded horrible, stuffy and wheezing, and said that he did personally supervise a few of the transfers, when family couldn't be bothered. He couldn't remember ever having hired anyone from Deshay, Louisiana, or having heard of the nursing home there.

'I do remember having made personal trips to fetch clients over the past couple of years,' Buddy said. He stopped for three thunderous sneezes. 'But other Placid Harbor folks handled transfers, and I can check my files on Monday if you want to know who exactly did what. Or sooner, if this is an emergency.'

'That's okay. I hope you're feeling better soon.'

'I'm mainlining NyQuil. I hope that's not illegal,' he laughed.

'I won't report you,' she said.

'Detective? I know you're buddies with Whit Mosley, but if I win the election, I just want you to know I'll work hard. And I'll look forward to working with you.'

'Thanks, Buddy,' she said, feeling awkward. 'I appreciate that. I'm sure we'd work together just fine.'

'Okay. Let me know if I can be of further help.' She thanked him again and hung up.

So no connection there between Deshay and Port Leo.

She rubbed her temple with her pencil's eraser. But what if there were similar cases to Marcy's? Her disappearance might be part of a wider blanket. Maybe.

So she phoned the Department of Public Safety in Austin, where the state's 'missing persons clearinghouse' database was located, and she gave them a set of parameters to check – young women, last seen at places of work.

There did not seem to be a spate of women abducted from nursing homes. DPS faxed her a list of disappearances, and she studied the dates. Odd. She flipped back to her notes from Roselle Cross. A week after the transfer of a client from Port Leo to Laredo last November, a young woman, Angela Marie Norris, had gone missing from a Laredo Taco Bell restaurant after her shift ended. In May, three weeks after a patient moved from Placid Harbor to another facility in Brownsville, another young woman, Laura Janelle Palinski, disappeared from a pizzeria she worked at.

Claudia called DPS back, and they faxed her details, descriptions, and photos of both young women, and she sat studying the pictures. Both bore a passing resemblance to Marcy Ballew with dark hair, round faces, naive smiles, but then they were all of a common type. Nice girls working in low-wage jobs, saving for college maybe, or just trying to live from paycheck to paycheck.

The times when Buddy – or whoever had handled the transfer – had been in the two towns were close, but not the same. And Buddy had not been alone on the transfers, there had been a nurse-practitioner accompanying him. But then, the women hadn't vanished when Buddy had been in town. And Buddy had never supervised a transfer from Deshay, Louisiana.

It was just odd.

She called the police departments in Laredo and

Brownsville, got the names of the detectives in charge of the missing-women's cases, and left messages for them to call her back.

She then called Roselle Cross's office.

'I'd like to know if Buddy was at work on these days: November 10 of last year, May 3 and September 30 this year.' Those were the days Morris, Palinski, and Ballew had all dropped out of sight.

'Why?'

'I'm just trying to piece together a chronology of where he's been.'

'My word. Do you suspect him of something?' The woman sounded appalled.

'No. It's a way to simply get a clearer picture. I just talked with him, he's being entirely cooperative.'

'Well,' Roselle Cross said, 'I'll have to check Monday morning.'

'Mrs Cross,' Claudia said, 'it's getting late, it's Friday night, I'm sure you want to get home. So do I. You can go check this on a computer in about five seconds. I just need to know if he took vacation or sick time then.'

'One . . . moment!' Roselle Cross said with clear peevishness and put Claudia on hold.

A pang of hunger gnawed at Claudia's stomach. She dug down in her purse for a candy bar she usually had stashed away in the depths and her fingers found paper instead. She pulled out an envelope marked OPEN IN PRIVATE. God, probably a love letter from David he'd stashed in her purse. She tore it open. Out slipped a copy of a newspaper photo. A teenage Junior, Corey, Eddie Gardner, and a girl holding fat fish. Whit had attached a note: *Not sure if this means a single thing, but thought you should know. Also: I think Junior gave Pete a half million. Maybe Gardner got it back for his old fishing buddy, the tough way. And maybe Gardner ruined those evidence bags as a favor to Junior. Thought you should know. Watch your back. Will call you soon. Be careful. Whit.*

She could have strangled Whit.

Mrs Cross huffed back on the line. 'Buddy was here those days. No vacation time.'

'Thank you,' Claudia said. 'I appreciate your help.'

Mrs Cross hung up without further comment.

Claudia dialed Whit's cell phone and got a message saying the phone was out of the calling area. She left him voice mail. 'You better call me back as soon as humanly possible,' she said, leaving her home and office numbers. She tried Velvet again at her motel; still no answer. The woman might have decided to leave town once the inquest went against her, but according to the clerk she hadn't checked out of the room yet.

Claudia went to Delford's office. He sat at his desk, his service revolver unholstered, sitting next to an untidy hill of papers. He glanced up at her with a sharp look; she was clearly unwelcome.

'Late night?' she asked, trying to sound casual. The hard look in his eyes made her throat feel thick.

'I just got a complaining phone call about you from some woman over at the nursing home.'

'You have bigger problems than me,' she said. She placed the photo and Whit's Post-it note on his desk.

'Jesus Christ,' Delford finally said. Claudia sat across from him.

'I don't understand,' he finally said. 'You're saying that's Eddie Gardner?'

'I think it is.'

'He knows Deloache,' Delford said.

'Yes.'

'Have you talked to him about this?'

'No. He took off hours ago.' She paused. 'Did you get a copy of his service record from Houston?'

'Of course. Eddie was as clean as a whistle. References, the whole shebang.' Delford pointed at the picture. 'Shit, maybe this is just coincidence. Kids go fishing on the jetties, meet each other during a day, then never see each other again.'

'Eddie and Junior are both from Houston.'

'Them and four million other people. Lots of kids from Houston fish here. Not a crime.'

'No, that's not. Dealing drugs and covering up a murder sure are.'

'You're just full of serious accusations, aren't you, missy?' Delford squinted at her. 'I mean, what's with you lately? You question how I do things around here, you check out files you don't got any business worrying over, you screw up evidence bags and blame a colleague . . .'

'I don't even know you anymore,' Claudia said softly. 'Why the hell are you having these meltdowns? Tell me, Delford. I can help you . . .'

Delford's phone rang and he scooped it up. He listened and muttered 'Holy Jesus' three times. Then he hung up.

'We got us a dead one. Floater in the bay. A girl.' Delford gulped, clicked his service revolver back in his holster. 'She's not . . . whole. Some sick son of a bitch carved her up.'

Velvet came awake suddenly. She had finally managed to doze after a while – time was impossible to measure – after he had finished his assault. Now she felt a wet rag move along her skin, cleaning her legs and privates, cleaning where she had soiled the sheets, removing them and curling towels under her hips. A voice humming 'Surfin' Safari,' ignoring her shivers of rage and fear.

296

'Soup, darling?' Corey asked. She nodded, barely.

He spooned lukewarm chicken broth into her mouth. She swallowed it and made herself not cry. *Some goddamned last meal.* She heard the spoon click against an empty cup. He dabbed her mouth, replaced the gag, and refastened the lock with a dainty click.

'Sleep now,' he said, and she heard him leave the room. The door shut and then there were five or six snicks – with terror she realized they were dead bolts being thrown. She was locked in times six.

Tears would not come. She strained and pulled against the cords, but they were intractable.

Jesus Christ, I've been raped, she thought in disbelief, and her father's unbending Methodist voice, the pride of an Omaha pulpit, crowded into her head: *Are you surprised what you do it's an abomination and a shame and you get what you deserve . . .*

No. She shook her head against the imagined voice. Her father never said those words to her. He'd never lived to see her sink. She shuddered and the tears came in a hot flood. She cried silently, the tears sopping into the blindfold, a pool of snot forming at her nose that she blew out to clear her airways. She wished for a cloth so . . . he . . . it . . . would not see she had cried.

Screw a handkerchief. Wish for a gun, so you can blow the son of a bitch straight to hell.

She must not crumple. Someone would realize she was missing and gone, Whit and Claudia would look for her. Wouldn't they? Shit, maybe she wasn't even in Port Leo anymore. She had no idea how long she had been unconscious.

Think. Think.

He had said he was Corey Hubble.

Oh, God, Pete and that movie. Pete had been too tight-lipped about his research. Pete *had* found Corey but

Corey didn't want to be found. Corey might be a complete freaking nut, a drug runner, a smuggler. Clearly he didn't balk at kidnapping or rape. Maybe he hadn't balked at fratricide.

She had to get out. She could not simply lie here and wait to be killed.

First she needed to see where she was. She needed to slip free of the blindfold. The restraints on her legs gave way enough that she could push with her heels and bring up her knees slightly. She did so, pressing her head down against the sheets. She felt a knot in the blindfold's side where the fabric gathered, and she pulled herself down, mashing the pillow against the fabric. Then she raised herself up again, pushed back, and tried to drag the blindfold off. Again. Again. Slowly the knot yielded its position, rolling up her scalp.

After several minutes of steady pushing, all breathless work, she had shoved the fabric up enough – all she dared – where she could open one eye.

The room was dark; one small lamp in the corner, down by her feet, emitted a feeble glow. The lamp was kitschy, featuring dancing circus elephants cavorting in a circle, the kind of lamp you might find in a child's room.

With the one eye she saw that the room was windowless – or rather that neat planks of black-painted plywood covered where windows had once been. Dingy wallpaper hung on the walls, strips dangling. The paper showed cartooned cowboys riding on the range, lassoes a-whirling, wild ponies bucking in corrals, the antiseptic, 1950s version of the Wild West. A child's room, left to rot.

She turned her head to inspect the cords; thin yellow rope, like the kind she'd seen on boats at the marina, although some softer material cushioned the rope around her wrists and ankles.

The bed she was bound to was metal, an old twin-size

contraption. She remembered with a grimace that the springs were noisy.

But metal meant parts. Sharp edges that might cut rope.

Yeah, and I'm goddamned Houdini. She pulled again, trying to free one hand, liberate one foot. The tape covering the ropes gouged her flesh. No ease, no relief.

She wept again, hating the rubbery taste of the mouth plug.

So talk him into letting you go.

She stopped crying. She snuffled, not wanting to block her airway.

How was she supposed to work that bit of mojo?

She heard her own voice, bickering with Whit in his yard: *I'm superior to any man who pays money for my tapes.*

She knew Whit believed she demeaned herself with her work, but this, this was debasement beyond her dreams. But she knew: she *was* greater than the men who snuck into the adult bookstores under cover of night, quickly paid in cash to rent her movies, ordered them via Internet anonymity, plugged the tape in darkened dens, and watched the men and women she arranged act the charades of love.

She knew what would turn her audience on.

What turned on Corey, clearly, was control. Brutality. Hurting her was foreplay to him. Her death would be his climax.

So she needed to slow his madness, subtly wrest control away from him. Her attempts to get him to see her as a person had flopped. He would not call her by name but by his creepy term of endearment. So maybe the solution was in being what he wanted her to be: an object. A nonperson who only existed to satisfy his lust.

But an object who would kill him dead, dead, dead.

Velvet took a deep breath.

'Fuck you, Corey,' she whispered.

She would be ready.

36

The shrimper was a thin, grizzled Vietnamese man named Minh Nguyen, and he was unusually calm, considering the catch in his illegal nets – the partial remains of Heather Farrell. The corpse, gutted and slashed, had been collected for autopsy.

'I can tell you the cause of death. A freaking nutcase,' the mortuary service driver told Claudia as he and his partner loaded the body bag into the transport, in the bright gleam of the harbor's mercury lights. After one good look at Heather's sad remnants Claudia vomited, leaning against a pier piling and spewing into the greenish gray water. She had never seen such butchery.

You looked for her, you didn't find her. You should have made her stay in a cell, you failed that poor girl. Please let her not have suffered. Claudia staggered away from the pier's end, wiping her mouth, hoping the others wouldn't say a word to her. Two other cops had puked, but they were both rookies.

Mr Nguyen, the shrimper, smoked a bummed cigarette while he repeated the story to the four officers ringed around the table. He was unflappable and precise about his account, and Claudia wondered if he had seen far worse in his life. The man was in his fifties, certainly old enough to have witnessed the horrors of war in his native land. Besides Claudia and Delford there was an investigator from the Encina County Sheriff's Department and a ranger from Parks and Wildlife, both of whom would be interested in any possible crime committed on the waters of St Leo Bay.

Mr Nguyen was trawling on the edge of the bay when

his net tangled. Night shrimping was against the law, but no one was debating with him about this at this point. A heaviness caught in one of the sleds had kept the netted shrimp from tumbling free, and when he inspected it he had found the girl's body, her eyes staring up at him from beneath a mask of wriggling shrimp.

It was nearly midnight when Claudia went out for a breath of fresh air. From the police station stoop she could see the curving arc of Port Leo Beach Park aglow in the streetlights, the statue of stern Saint Leo watching over the bay. Autumn moonlight made the small waves gleam. She watched a family, tourists, amble from one of the restaurants down near the water's edge toward the Colonel James House Bed and Breakfast. They seemed uneager to surrender the day. One of the family was a teenage girl, and she shyly waved at Claudia, sitting on the steps. Claudia waved back.

Jesus, Heather was someone's daughter just like that girl. She had told Delford she would call the girl's family in Lubbock and she had, but there was only an answering machine. The parents, perhaps out late, dining, wining. Not looking for their daughter, no, sir. What did people do who had runaway children? Did their lives resume with faked normalcy? She would keep calling. She heard footsteps behind her and Delford appeared.

He still looked gaunt and pale. 'We're gonna find this fucker, Claudia. Jesus. You expect shit like this in Houston, not here.' He mopped his brow and she noticed the dark circles underneath his uniform's sleeves. He was sweating as though fevered. 'I thought you were taking care of this girl.'

Her throat worked. 'I . . . she didn't want help. She didn't want protection. I tried.'

'Christ,' he said. 'Christ. Try harder next time.'

Silence fell between them, the soft sound of the waves,

boats creaking in the harbor a block away. Claudia's heart hammered in her chest.

'Marcy Ballew,' Delford finally said. 'Maybe this is what happened to her?'

'I don't know,' Claudia said. She told him about her research. 'I'm still waiting to hear back from Laredo and Brownsville on their missing-persons cases.'

'We got a missing girl and we got a butchered girl. And the way Farrell was killed, Jesus. He took out her organs.'

'Let's not get ahead of ourselves,' she cautioned. 'Marcy Ballew could be sitting on a beach in California for all we know. And I think that this might have more to do with Pete Hubble's death. For God's sakes, once it gets out that the girl who found him is dead herself . . . it's an awful stretch for coincidence, Delford. Surely you see that.'

He blanched. 'She's a transient. They're always easy targets. Sure could be a coincidence.'

'Maybe she saw something she wasn't supposed to.'

'Pete Hubble committed suicide. There was nothing for her to see. Hell, she was prone to amble at night. She just might have walked herself into some new trouble.'

Claudia kept her voice low. 'I'm not going to argue with you, because it seems pointless. But this is not like you, Delford. Bullying me. Sticking your hand in the middle of investigations. Just wait until the press learns the girl who found Pete Hubble is gutted and sliced up in the bay. You tell people there's no connection, you're gonna be looking for a new job. Why are you fighting me every step of the way?' She felt sick, breathless.

Delford Spires sank onto the steps next to her. All the bluster from before was gone, and she saw his hands tremble as he slowly rubbed his jawline.

'Whit Mosley believes – and I'm not sure how, since I

can't get in touch with him – Pete Hubble got half a million in cash from Junior Deloache. The money's gone. There's no trace of it in Pete's account. Pete's dead. Now Heather's dead. I think this missing money is at the heart of this, Delford.'

He blinked at her. 'Jesus Christ, this'll kill Lucinda.'

Claudia cared very little for Lucinda Hubble's feelings at the moment. 'It's already killed Pete and Heather.'

'You think the mob cut up that little girl and dumped her?'

'Yes, I do. At least based on what I know now. We need to find Deloache.'

'Yes,' he agreed. 'I'll talk to him.'

'You talk to Eddie yet?'

'Eddie's not answering my calls,' Delford said. 'I'm gonna go over to his house and see what's up.' He turned and headed back toward the station.

Claudia went back inside to the interrogation room. A slip of paper from the girl's jeans was there, secure in an evidence bag. Claudia stared at the phone number that had been tucked in the girl's wallet. It was blurred from the water but still readable. Faith Hubble's home phone. Maybe Faith had offered to help the girl, given that she'd had the trauma of finding Pete's body. Right. Faith Hubble, good Samaritan.

She turned to the worn, grass-stained duffel. After Heather's body had been found, Patrolman Fox and another officer immediately combed her hangout, Little Mischief Beach, for information. A couple of girls puffing cigs on the beach, transients, knew Heather and when told of her fate, shattered into tears. One produced a duffel bag within ten minutes. They thought Heather had just blown town and you know, they could sure use her stuff if she didn't need it. They'd last seen her on Wednesday night.

Claudia sorted through the contents. A pair of jeans, crusty with sand. A pair of panties. She examined the manufacturer and the size: on both counts, the same as the panties found at Pete's death scene. Claudia let out a long breath. She'd had Heather show that she had underwear on, but she'd been given a bathroom break before and had her duffel with her. She could have changed into a pair of fresh panties before Claudia asked. Maybe she was messing around with Pete Hubble and suddenly had to get dressed in a hurry.

Yeah, if she killed Pete. Or if she was with Pete when he was killed.

She called the crime lab in Corpus and asked them to compare any pubic hairs found in the panties in Pete's case with Heather Farrell's pubic hairs, once they had processed her body. She had a sick feeling that there would be a match.

She pawed through the duffel bag. Two sweaters, threadbare, a couple of T-shirts with Port Leo themes, one for the Port Leo varsity swim team. A small stash of cash: thirty dollars. A couple of bus tickets to go as far as Houston, unused – the ones the constable had mentioned at the inquest. Who was going with her? A notebook, full of stiff but accurate pencil drawings of whooping cranes, Caspian terns, egrets, and roseate spoonbills. Boats, people walking on the beach. She hadn't been kidding about being an artist. With instruction she might have been quite good. Another page, full of hopeful scribbling. *Heather Hubble. Mrs Heather Hubble. Heather Farrell-Hubble. Heather and Sam*, the H and the S ornately drawn together to form a lopsided heart.

Holy God.

The drive to Lucinda Hubble's house took three minutes. Lights were on, both upstairs and downstairs, even at the late hour. Lucinda answered the door, in silk pajamas and robe. The skin under Lucinda's eyes was dark, like a pale bruise.

She tore open the door quickly after Claudia's knock, her eyes wide. Seeing Claudia seemed to make her breath freeze.

'Hello, Senator. I'm afraid I'm the bearer of bad news. Is Faith here?'

'Bad news,' she repeated dully. But she led Claudia into the main den, where Faith was speaking softly into a telephone. Faith clicked off the moment she saw Claudia, not even bothering with a good-bye.

'What's going on?' Faith asked without preamble.

'The young woman who found Pete's body, Heather Farrell, is dead. A shrimper's net caught her body out in the bay a couple of hours ago.'

'Oh, my God,' Lucinda said, paling. The women exchanged glances.

'Was it an accident?' Faith asked. 'Did she drown?'

'Hardly. Stabbed, disemboweled, throat slashed.'

Claudia let the silence hang. Lucinda sank into a chair.

'There are those who might be tempted to treat this as a coincidence – Heather finds Pete dead and ends up dead herself in a matter of days. I don't believe in coincidence. I don't care how Judge Mosley ruled.' She glared at Faith Hubble, then turned to Lucinda. 'I never thought your son committed suicide, Senator, and I think so even less now. You have anything you want to tell me?'

Lucinda folded her hands in her lap. 'I can think of nothing that could help you. I'm horrified beyond belief that such a crime could happen here.'

Faith said, 'Let's call Delford,' as though Claudia were not sitting there.

That boiled Claudia's blood. 'We have another young woman missing, and if Heather's death is not related to

Pete's, I think it's related to this other case. Have either of you heard of Marcy Ballew?'

Both women shook their heads.

'She vanished from Deshay, in western Louisiana. She worked at a nursing home there.'

Faith shook her head, but Lucinda's mouth worked and she made a noise in her throat.

'Senator?' Claudia asked.

'No, I'm sorry, I don't know her. Or of her.'

'In Heather's jeans we found a piece of paper that had your home phone number on it. Had either of you been in contact with her?'

Faith looked stunned. 'Lord, no.'

'I gave the girl that number,' Lucinda said quickly. Faith looked over at her, surprised.

'When did you see Heather Farrell?' Claudia asked.

Lucinda folded her hands in her lap. 'I ran into her. On the street on Wednesday, I think it was. I gave her our number in case she needed any help. You know, a place to stay, food, perhaps some clothes or money. I – felt sorry for her.'

How did you even know what she looked like? Claudia wondered, but she decided to play this out. She turned to Faith. 'Did Heather Farrell ever call you?'

'No,' Faith said. She glanced over at Lucinda, and some unspoken code seemed to hover in the air between them.

'I'd like to talk with Sam.'

'Why?' Faith asked.

Claudia decided to fish a little. 'Heather Farrell hung out a lot at Little Mischief Beach. If Sam hung out there, he might have seen who else was around Heather.'

'I don't think Sam knew the girl. I mean, I'm sure he would have mentioned it if he had,' Faith said.

Claudia watched her. 'I'm quite sure Sam knew her.

307

She left a notebook in her duffel with hearts drawn around their names. Along with two bus tickets to Houston.'

Both women stared.

'I think I should call Delford,' Lucinda finally said.

'Fine.' Claudia smiled. She played her trump cards. 'I suspect the FBI will be interested in talking to Sam even more than I am. If Farrell's death is related to Ballew's disappearance, and Ballew was kidnapped and brought across state lines, the FBI takes the case. Maybe even before the election.' She let the cold knife sink and twist. 'Should I have the agents call you, Faith, or you, Senator?'

'You despicable bitch,' Faith said under her breath.

'Faith!' Lucinda gasped.

Faith grasped the arms of her chair. 'She's enjoying this. She's wanted to turn the screws on us for a long time.'

'You don't matter one iota to me,' Claudia said evenly. 'But I'd like to talk to your son. Now, please.'

Faith closed her eyes and a shudder went through her body. 'You can't. We don't know where Sam is.'

A minute later Claudia called Delford at the police station.

'Sam Hubble is missing.' She told him what she had found in the Farrell girl's belongings. 'I just spoke with the senator and Faith. Sam is gone. No sign of him. He took his own car.'

Delford wheezed. 'Goddamn it, you had no right to go over there . . .'

'That suicide note can't be for real. Sam Hubble faked it.'

'You think . . . that boy killed his daddy and Heather Farrell?'

308

'I don't know, but we need to find him.' She paused. 'Did you find Eddie?'

'No. He's gone. His car, everything, his apartment's empty. I . . . sent Fox over to Junior Deloache's. I just got a call. They found Deloache there. Stabbed to death, stabbed like two dozen times. Jesus, what's happening?'

Claudia leaned against the kitchen counter, Lucinda and Faith watching her. Sam Hubble, Jabez Jones, and Eddie Gardner had all gone missing. Heather Farrell was dead and her story about Pete Hubble was a lie. Junior Deloache was dead. Welcome to chaos.

'What's happening is that Pete Hubble stirred up the wrong hornet's nest. He stirred up the past. People are dying because of what happened to Corey Hubble all those years ago.' She waited for him to react, to speak, and he said nothing. 'If there's anything else you can tell me you better tell me right now, Delford.'

His breathing grew harsh. 'You're goddamned leaping to conclusions. No reason to think that note's a fake. Boy might have just gone partying in Corpus. You're making all kinds of unsubstantiated claims, bothering Lucinda. I won't have it, I won't have it from an officer of mine.'

She started to speak again. 'Delford . . .'

'Shut up. You're fired, Claudia.'

37

Whit and Gooch barreled on deep into Friday night, north, heading for Missatuck, Texas. They had left Gooch's car parked in a brightly lit trucker's stop on the outskirts of Beaumont. The easternmost slice of Texas unfolded ahead of their headlights, an endless ribbon of road bordered by tall loblolly pines. The weather cleared, the cool night the luxuriant reward for a too-long, sweltering summer. Whit drove, and Gooch sat in the front seat, reading a battered Mickey Spillane paperback by penlight.

'I can't read in a car, it makes me sick,' Whit said. There had been little conversation between them since leaving Beaumont, although Whit's mind was full of questions over Gooch's ability to make felons disappear.

'I'm highlighting the appropriate tough guy phrases for you so you know what to say the next time you encounter an Anson type. You're a little too Larry McMurtry for that crowd.' Gooch glanced. 'Although you acquitted yourself well against that slab of a kid.'

'I feel like I broke every finger in my hands on his face.'

'If you did, you couldn't steer,' Gooch said matter-of-factly. 'Enough self-congratulations. What matters is that Junior thinks you've got his moolah.' He shut the Spillane. 'Moolah, there's a word that needs a renaissance.'

'Perhaps Pete hid the money somewhere before he died.'

'For what purpose? Stealing from mobsters, even the IQ-challenged contingent that Junior represents, is an extremely bad idea.' Gooch shrugged. 'We may be crediting Pete with greater brains than he deserves. He may have only had one large working organ. I think that Junior-boy had Pete killed.'

'So where is the money? I would think if Pete doesn't have it, Velvet might.'

'I'm sitting in slack-jawed amazement. You generally consider Velvet as some whore with the heart of gold, pardon the cliché.'

'If she had the half million, wouldn't she give it back to Junior, having seen what happened to Pete? And if she took it she'd be gone, and Junior and Anson would be off in hot pursuit.'

'We don't know Pete ever kept it on the boat, but they thought it was on the boat.'

'Where else might he hide it?'

'Gee, in a bank?' Gooch asked. 'Has anyone looked in the poor schmuck's accounts?'

'Yes. Claudia researched his bank accounts. It's not there.'

'So who could have taken it?'

'Velvet. Anyone who came on the boat . . . me, Claudia, Delford, Gardner, the other cops. Heather Farrell. Sam Hubble.'

'Who do you like?'

'I don't see either of the kids taking it. They were too rattled.'

'Didn't you say Delford Spires was blasting you and Claudia?'

'Yeah.'

'He's probably threatened by Claudia in that she has twice the IQ,' Gooch said. 'Unless . . . maybe the De-loaches already had a different purpose attached to the money.'

'As in?'

'Drug money. Money that's due to be freshly laundered

and shouldn't be given away. Or money to grease local palms, perhaps Delford's.'

Whit considered. 'Okay. Say Papa Deloache gives poor Junior an operation to run. Off the beaten track from main centers of illicit commerce, like Houston or Galveston. Port Leo would qualify. Not too far from Corpus Christi or San Antonio, only hours from major markets like Houston and Austin.'

'And not too far from South Padre, where your seasonal business is. Junior would mix well with the college students, the old frat party guy with a thick wad of cash.' Gooch stared out at the darkness, the outlines of the pines etched in black. 'Of course, the frat boys and sorority girls would be laughing at Junior behind their hands.'

'Are you ever going to tell me what happened back there in Beaumont?'

'Jesus, quit bitching. Not a hair on their sainted little asses was hurt.'

'You've got friends in the police department there?'

'I'm not on the witness stand in your courtroom, am I?' He fell silent; topic over. 'So what do you hope to learn from this mystery woman Pete had called so often?' Gooch asked.

'She clearly expected money when she called Pete. She clearly didn't know he was dead.'

Gooch cracked a window, and the thick, earthy smell of the pine forests, stirred with the odor of gasoline fumes, streamed into the Explorer. 'You want me to drive for a while? You tired?'

Whit nodded. They pulled over and Gooch took the wheel. Whit moved to the passenger seat, feeling too revved to relax. But as the nighttime road unwound, he slept.

*

Whit and Gooch crashed at a cheap motel off the highway around two a.m., rose at seven, and arrived in Missatuck, a town three miles off the main highway with one bumpy major street and two stoplights, around nine Saturday morning. Missatuck was little enough that asking for a local address at the small grocery got results.

Kathy Breaux lived at 302 Cotton Creek Road. The house was a brick duplex in a very modest neighborhood, the only kind Missatuck offered. Ill-kept flowerbeds dominated the yard, and a motley crew of lawn gnomes congregated in one untilled bed.

'Let's be careful,' Gooch warned. 'Anyone who collects lawn gnomes is not to be trifled with.'

Whit rang the bell. No answer. He rang again and knocked. No answer. The door to the other duplex creaked open, and a woman in purple jogging sweats, holding a purple mug of coffee, stepped out onto the concrete slab that served as a joint porch. She was tall and skinny, with raven-dark hair pulled into a sloppy ponytail and a bevy of unfortunate whiskers on her chin.

'Awful early to be pounding on a door,' the woman observed in a gravel-bruised voice.

'I'm sorry,' Whit said. 'I'm Judge Whit Mosley. I'm a justice of the peace in Encina County, down on the coast, and this is my associate—'

'Dr Guchinski,' Gooch interjected and Whit kept his neutral smile in place. *Doctor. God help us.*

'I'm looking for Kathy Breaux,' Whit said.

The woman sipped her coffee. 'What do you want with her?'

'A man committed suicide in my jurisdiction, and he had called the phone number at this address repeatedly,' Whit said. 'We're trying to establish the reason for the suicide, and we thought Ms Breaux might know his mental state.'

313

The woman blinked. 'Who is this man?'

'His name is Pete Hubble. Does that name ring a bell?'

'Well, do you have some identification?' she asked.

Whit produced a laminated card with his name and title issued by the Texas secretary of state. He didn't offer her one of his regular business cards to keep because what he didn't want was her phoning the Encina County authorities. Buddy Beere, if given half a chance, would make widespread hay about any wild-goose chases Whit pursued right before the election.

She studied the card, then handed it back to him. 'Kathy's at work, got a double shift. It's about ten, fifteen minutes away. I can give you the address.'

'Thanks,' Whit said.

The woman returned with hastily scribbled instructions. *Follow Highway 363 to the Louisiana border, where it becomes Louisiana FM 110, go straight until you get to Deshay. Memorial Oaks nursing home is on the left after the second light.*

Deshay, Louisiana. A nursing home. A tremble rose along Whit's spine.

'Thanks,' he said.

'She's not in no trouble, is she?'

'No, I don't think so,' Whit lied.

' 'Cause she's a pretty good renter,' the woman added, as though this were a treasured commodity in Missatuck.

'Promptness with rent is always to be admired,' Gooch said. 'Thanks again.'

The woman shut the door, and they went back to Whit's Explorer.

'A nursing home in Deshay,' Whit said. 'That's where that Ballew girl vanished from, the one whose wallet they found outside of town. Her face has been all over those blue flyers, Claudia mentioned the case to me. It can't be coincidence.'

They drove thirty miles over the speed limit, zooming into Louisiana.

Deshay was the kind of town repeated ten thousand times across America: an unhealthy selection of fast-food chains, a neon-lit doughnut shop, a pair of peeling strip centers, a furniture store with plastic-sheeted inventory overflowing into the parking lot, and five gas stations lining the main road. Memorial Oaks squatted on a corner. Bricks the color of creek dirt lined the concrete walkways and ill-clipped Japanese boxwoods stood beneath the windows. The home didn't look dirty or unhealthy, just glum, a sad coda for lives in their final movements.

'Despicable the way we treat the elderly in this country,' Gooch said. 'When I hit sixty I'm moving my ass to China, where the old are revered.'

'I hate nursing homes,' Whit said under his breath. 'They're like parking garages for people.'

'Would you rather die young? I could call Anson and see if he'll hook up with us again.'

When they asked at the information counter for Kathy Breaux, the dour receptionist nodded toward a hall that fed off from the central hub.

'She's down in the television room, probably doing a little feeding,' the woman said.

Gooch whispered to Whit as they walked: 'A feeding. How evocative. Is there a trough?'

The room was large but fusty, its cornerstone a sparkling new TV that dangled the joys of the outside world. A trashy morning talk show blared from the set, mothers having their mouthy, punk- and Goth-dressing daughters made over into pink-angora debutantes. Several patients watched with blank stares fixated on the lives on the television instead of anything else in the depressing room, blankets covering their laps. An array of shiny black dominoes lay spread out on a table, awaiting players. No nurse loomed to greet them. One patient, in her early eighties, glanced up at them as they came in and gave them an intelligent smile. She was reading *The Norton Anthology of English Literature, Volume 2*, her bony, mottled finger stuck in the mammoth book, the other hand holding a magnifying glass.

'Hello, ma'am,' Whit said. 'How are you today?'

'Lovely. How are y'all doing?'

'We're fine, ma'am,' Gooch said. 'We're looking for Kathy Breaux.'

The old woman puckered in distaste. 'Kathy is no doubt outside, sucking a cigarette down to the filter, as I would if she gave me half the chance. She ought to be back in a minute.'

'Which way, ma'am?' Whit asked.

The old woman nodded toward a door that opened into a hallway. Whit thanked her and moved toward the hallway.

'I'll stay here,' Gooch said, 'in case she comes back.' He leaned down toward the woman to see what she was reading. She flopped open her book for him.

'Robert Browning?' Whit heard Gooch say good-naturedly. 'You're not wasting your time on him, are you? He's a psychobabble bore.'

'Nonsense,' the old woman said. 'Now, when *I* taught Browning . . .'

At the end of the hall Whit found a bay of large windows that opened out onto a grove of mossy oaks. In the foyer formed by the windows, a bathrobe-clad crone hunched in a wheelchair while a spare, trim woman, dressed in the bright magenta scrubs of the nursing staff, mopped up around the chair.

'Bad bad girl,' the woman chirped in a singsong voice

reminiscent of a preschooler ditty. 'You keep your hands off your diapy-diap now so I don't have to clean up after you again.'

A half grunt, half wail was her answer from the poor old woman in the chair.

'Excuse me,' Whit said. 'Are you Kathy Breaux?'

She gave him a bright smile he suspected was reserved only for visitors. 'Yes?'

'I'm here to talk to you about Pete Hubble.'

The smile barely dimmed. 'Who?'

'The man who placed several phone calls to your house over the past week.'

The grin stayed as fixed as stone. 'I'm sorry, I didn't catch your name.'

'Judge Whit Mosley. I was a friend of Pete's. He's dead.'

Her grip whitened against the handle of the mop.

'I'm conducting the inquest into Pete's death and I'd like to talk to you about why Pete was calling you,' Whit said.

'You know, I would love to help you with whatever this is, but I can't talk now. I'm working.' She tucked a lock of hair behind her ear with a coy little flick of the wrist.

'Considering this is an investigation into a possible homicide, I'm sure the home's administrators would be glad to provide us with a private office and time alone.' Whit kept his tone friendly. He'd heard enough voice to know she was the woman who had called on the boat. 'He was shot. In the mouth.'

'Please,' she said, 'let me get her cleaned up and then I'll talk with you.' She turned and wheeled the woman around in the foyer, then said, 'Oh, why don't you just come with me while I get her settled and then we can talk?' A tenseness framed her face. 'Just come right along with me.'

Whit got the distinct feeling she didn't want him out of her sight. 'Actually I need to borrow a rest room.' He had noticed a men's room right off the foyer. He didn't wait for her permission, he turned and ducked into the bathroom. He washed his hands while counting to one hundred, and then came out. Kathy and her incontinent charge were gone. He hurried back to the main room; Gooch was still there, arguing the merits of Victorian poetry with his new friend. No Kathy. Whit wandered back down the hallway, peeking into the rooms. One room was tidy with its lack of occupants. Another held an ancient black woman, napping and snoring loudly.

The third room was occupied. Whit peered into the dimness. An emaciated figure lay in a bed, a rope of drool uncoiling from his slack mouth, his eyes at half-mast. His dark hair was cut in a crisp burr, and an ugly scar split the hairline. His skin was sun-starved, his cheeks sunken, but Whit could see the man was young. Too young.

'Oh, my Lord,' Whit said.

It was Corey Hubble.

38

Velvet was awake when he returned. Wriggling carefully, she had worked the blindfold back into place. She kept her head turned to the side to hide any lopsided silk.

'Did you miss me?' Corey asked.

'Why do you hate me so,' she said, 'to do this to me?'

'I don't hate you. Not at all. I love you.'

She wanted to scream, *This isn't love, you freaking nut bastard. Even as screwed up as I am I know this isn't love.* Instead she said, 'Are you doing this because you've seen my movies?'

A soft laugh. 'I've seen your movies. Am I better than Pete?'

She didn't answer.

He touched her cheek. Gently. 'Tell me.'

'Of course you are,' she lied. She heard shoes easing off feet and hitting the wooden floor, the soft rustle of clothing sliding down legs, a jingling of keys tossed to the floor.

'Don't,' Velvet said. 'Please don't.'

Silence again.

'Why not?' Corey finally said, sounding amused. 'Since I'm so much better.'

'Because,' she said, her voice calmed with a mighty effort, 'you don't have to. Not this way.'

'I need to.'

'Corey?'

Silence again, longer this time. She heard the even rasp of his breathing, near her ear.

'What?' he finally said.

'Corey. Please don't.' She put even more fear into her voice than she felt.

'No talking now.' He climbed upon her and forced himself on her again. She gritted her teeth, tried to summon memories from faraway sweetness. The tang of lemonade on a summer day, the soft pine-cologne smell of her father's camel-hair jacket, cinnamon and butter pooling on hot toast. Sitting in the quiet dark of her daddy's church on a Saturday afternoon, leaning back in a wooden pew while he practiced his sermon, pretending to snore if the sermon got a little dull, him never getting mad. Pete, bedecking her with roses on her birthday. But all the good failed her and she screamed and cried, muscles aching, body sore. She told herself, *It will be over soon, over soon, over soon.*

It was. He lay atop her when he was done, his skin sweaty and smelling of burgers, her skin clammy. His face was buried in her hair, and she felt him breathing in its scent. Lingering on her, like they were lovers. She so wanted her gun. She would fire a thousand bullets into his guts and brain and what odd lump passed for a heart.

'Why did you kill Pete?' she asked.

'Who says I did?' His voice was muffled in her hair.

'Did you kill him to get at me?'

No answer. His seed trickled out of her and she wanted to vomit.

'Tell me,' she said. 'Please.'

'I didn't kill him. I wanted to, but I didn't.'

'Liar.' She couldn't hide her contempt.

He sat up, going on his knees, straddling her, and slapped her hard. Once, twice, three times. Her ears rang. Blood leaked from her nose. He stopped; she felt his erection return, pressed into her breasts.

'I thought I was your darling,' she managed.

He made a guttural sound. She could feel his legs shivering against hers.

Velvet wet her lips, tasted her own blood. 'Pete loved you, Corey. He only wanted to help you.'

Another low laugh.

'Do you want me to love you, Corey? Maybe I could.' She heard him laugh but not move. 'I can't love you if I don't know you, though,' she said.

'You love Whit Mosley.' His voice grew distant. 'I saw you hug him.'

'I sure as hell don't love him. I hate his guts.'

'Don't hate his guts. I might bring them to you.'

Velvet's tongue felt stuck. She expected him to rape her again, but instead he clambered off the bed. She heard him gathering his clothes and then the door shutting behind him. In a minute or so the soft hiss of a shower began to run.

He was gone. And he had not shoved the gag back in her mouth. With its tiny lock. Its edged metal lock.

In the end, of course, she called David.

Claudia awoke early Saturday morning and lay on the futon for an hour, her body stiff against the flowered sheets. She had no job. She had rent, she had food to buy, she had a car payment, she would have no health insurance, she had less than two thousand dollars in her checking account and less in a savings account, she owed six hundred on a Visa card with seventeen percent interest. Twice she reached for the phone to call her mother, but even before she dialed her mother's voice rang in her ear like discordant chimes: *What's wrong with you? You give up a wonderful husband, now you lose your job? What, you want to shrimp with your father? There's a future. Why did we bother sending you to school?* She wasn't up for her mother's blunderbuss catechism.

Heather Farrell's face swam before her, dream-edged, and twice Claudia stumbled to the bathroom, surrendering to dry heaves of sick and shock.

So she finally called David, whispering to him about losing her job, about failing Heather. He came over at seven-thirty in the morning, arrived with a bag of breakfast groceries, drew a hot bath for her, made omelets while she bathed and dressed in old nubby pajamas soft as a kiss. She heard him in her kitchen, sliding drawers, chopping vegetables, pouring juice, sizzling butter.

That didn't take long, did it, Miss Tough? You're just gonna let him right back in, aren't you?

She popped open the drain, let the soapy water begin its downward swirl. *Yeah. Maybe I am.*

They ate their eggs and biscuits and juice, and Claudia, rather than talking, went under a wave of exhaustion. She fell asleep curled on the futon, David lying beside her, stroking her dark hair.

She awoke at 10 a.m. Her blinds were lowered, the room grayish dark. She stumbled to the kitchen. David sat drinking coffee, reading the Corpus Christi paper.

He lowered the paper. 'Hope I didn't overstay my welcome. I thought you might want to talk when you woke up.'

'Thanks. Thanks for the bath and breakfast and everything.'

'But I want to get something straight, okay?' New steel in his voice she hadn't heard before. 'I'm not trying to take advantage of the . . . emotional train wreck you've just gone through. I'm saying that out loud because I know how your mind works, Claud, and sooner or later you're gonna think I'm trying to tiptoe back in.'

'Oh, David, I don't think that,' she said, unsure of what she thought.

322

'Okay. I just don't want you to be alone if you don't want to be.'

She got herself a cup of hot coffee – he'd brewed hazelnut, her favorite – and added generous milk and sugar. He had his back to her, sitting at the kitchen table, and she watched the set of his shoulders, his burr of auburn hair, his wiry arms, the constellation of freckles on the back of his neck. She wanted to hold and kiss him and feel him against her, and she nearly dropped her mug.

Carefully she sipped the piping hot coffee, standing in the kitchen away from him. He turned around in his chair. 'You want to talk options? Delford can't just terminate you, Claudia.'

'He could and did.' She shrugged. 'It's a right-to-work state, he can fire me at will. I had to go back in, surrender my side arm, my badge. I didn't have a box to clean out my desk, I guess I have to do that Monday.'

'Are you going to appeal to the mayor?'

'I'll write him a letter,' she said. 'But I don't think I'm overflowing with options here.'

'Come work for the sheriff's department,' he said instantly and then stumbled. 'I mean, you're a good investigator. You could work for DPS, too, or Parks and Wildlife, maybe.'

'I'm sure something will come up. I can always shrimp with Papa. That should drive Mama into the crazy house a full ten years ahead of schedule.' She finished her coffee. 'So what about your big Jabez Jones case?'

He shrugged. 'He was spotted in New Mexico. I think he's probably heading back to California, where he's got a lot of friends. The DEA agent from Corpus told me they think Jabez's donation receipts don't match the figures in his books. He's gotten maybe thirty thou in donations and three million on his ledgers. Mary Magdalene still ain't talking. Sits in her cell like a freaking Amazon warrior, silent.'

'I thought maybe Junior Deloache was bringing drug money into Port Leo.'

David nodded. 'Probably. With Junior dead, and Jones running, I wouldn't be surprised if there was a connection. That three million, maybe it's Jabez laundering Junior's money.'

'I just wish Velvet would turn up,' Claudia said, thinking of Heather's water-paled face. 'Her car was at Junior's condo, her purse with a gun in it, but she wasn't.'

'You think she killed him?'

'No. I mean, I doubt it, but who knows. I don't know her.' She gave a thin, nervous laugh. 'I for sure thought I knew Delford, but he turned on me quicker than a rabid dog.'

David shook his head again. 'With all this insanity, I can't believe Delford fired you. He needs everyone he can get.'

'Does he? If the crime's this big, the DEA and FBI will take it over. Delford'll just wax his mustache and make press announcements.' She retrieved the coffeepot, freshened their mugs, came and sat next to him at the table.

'I don't get how the Ballew girl fits in,' David said. 'Comes from Louisiana to see Jones, gets involved in this money laundering, and ends up dead?'

Claudia explained what she had found about the nursing home connections. 'It's strange, and maybe I chased a shadow,' she said. 'But I found, well, not quite a pattern, but a couple of odd coincidences of timing.'

'Are all your notes at the station?'

'Yeah. But I can get you a copy. I mean, it's really your case.'

David phoned the station and got a clerk to make copies of Claudia's notes on Marcy Ballew.

'Ask them if I've gotten any messages from out-of-town police,' Claudia said.

He did. He paused, gestured at her for pencil and paper, which she handed to him. He jotted notes.

'Well, this is interesting. You got messages from investigators in Brownsville and Laredo.' Neither police department had made much progress on the Morris or the Palinski case. Both women seemed to have vanished into thin air: no witnesses, no evidence.

'Let's call them back,' she said.

He reached for her phone. 'Not on my unemployed dime,' she said. 'Let's go over to the sheriff's department.'

She dressed quickly and they drove over. David made the calls, asking the investigator on duty if there was a nursing home near either woman's workplace. The Laredo detective said yes, there was a nursing home right across from the Taco Bell that Angela Morris vanished from, Bellewood. It was the same one that Placid Harbor had handled a patient transfer from. Brownsville didn't know if there was a nursing home near the pizzeria; they'd find out and call or fax David back.

So David called the pizzeria to ask if St Mary's Nursing Home was close by. No, not at all, the pizzeria was at the northern edge of town on Highway 77. St Mary's was on the east side of Brownsville.

'But 77's the main highway,' Claudia said when David hung up. 'Anyone going to St Mary's might still pass that pizzeria. I'd just like to know more about these transfers, about how they work, the time involved.'

David set the phone down. 'You want to go talk to Buddy Beere with me?'

'I'm not a cop anymore,' she said. The truth of it still sounded alien to her ears.

'You are to me. C'mon, you've already talked to the

325

guy. Better than sitting around updating résumés and harboring grudges.'

Now she smiled at him. 'Sure. Let's go.'

The little lock lay in the no-man's-land between Velvet's torso and her elbow, and if she moved her arm slightly, the lock and its strap teased her skin. But she could not move it toward her hand.

She wept briefly in frustration and then she slept again. Sleep was the escape door. In sleep her father's arms enfolded her and he said, *I forgive you I forgive you and I love you no matter what.*

She woke at his touch. She wasn't sure if it was minutes later, hours, time ceased to hold meaning.

'Need to pee?' he asked abruptly.

'Yes, yes,' she said. She had peed in the night, like a baby, and the towels were sodden with the smell.

'I don't got no more sheets or towels to put under you right now,' he said.

Of course not. Who has time to do laundry when you're busy kidnapping and raping? she thought crazily.

She felt a bag – roomy, made of soft chamois, reeking of dust and fuel – go over her head. He loosened the cords at her feet first, rubbing her ankles for her.

'I'm taking you to the bathroom. Now, you try anything, I'll cut and gut you, you understand?' he muttered.

'Yes. I'll be good,' she answered in a timid murmur. *I'll kill you if you give me a moment's chance.*

He slipped her hands free from the shackles. She heard the toss of keys again on the floor. She slowly massaged her wrists.

'Do what I say.' He pulled her to her feet. Bolts of numbness shot up her legs. She nearly fell, every muscle screaming. He yanked her forward and the doorjamb brushed her shoulder, and seven steps down – she was counting – along carpet that felt frayed, he steered her to the right. Cold tile prickled her bare feet.

He pushed her down onto a cold toilet seat.

She urinated, emptying her aching bladder. He hummed along, a bouncy tune she recognized as 'I Get Around.'

I am so gonna kill you. 'I need to poop, too,' she said in a very quiet voice.

'I'm not leaving.'

She couldn't see him with the sack over her face. 'Corey, you're not gonna find watching me take a crap sexy. Please.'

'No.'

'Please, Corey, please!'

'No.' He sounded amused again. He wanted her to grovel, wanted her to beg, just so he could say no.

If he kills you now at least it's over. She had acted the queen bitch dominatrix in her movies, and now she called up that icy, imperial voice. 'Do you get off on bathroom functions, Corey? How sad. I thought you were a real man.'

A long silence and she thought: *Either I got you or you're about to strangle me here on a toilet.*

He said, 'I'm not some freak. I'm normal.'

His denial almost sent her into peals of hysterical laughter. She gripped the cool bowl of the toilet.

'I know, Corey,' she made herself say. 'You're normal. And a normal man lets a lady go to the potty in private.' She paused. 'You do that, and I'll show you fun in bed you've never, ever seen before.'

Long silence. She prayed a true prayer, for the first time in a dozen years. *Please, God, please help me now. Please.*

'All right,' he said. 'I'll wait outside. But don't try anything.'

'I won't.'

She heard him step out and the door gently close.

She yanked off the cloth hood and ripped the silk blindfold from her head. The bathroom was small, decorated in sea-foam green tile at least thirty years old. The shower was a stall, and the shower rod was bolted to the wall.

There was a small bolt on the door. If she locked it he would hear.

'Hurry up,' he called.

'I am!' she yelled, putting a teary tone in her voice. She groaned, as if troubled by a pained stomach. 'Just a second.' If he heard her rummaging he'd crash in. She almost wept in anger. Nothing, nothing to fight with.

She knelt, gingerly opening the cabinet under the sink. Cotton balls. Toilet paper. Disinfectant spray.

Yes.

He shoved the door open. She sprang to her feet and jetted disinfectant hard into his eyes. He shrieked and fell back.

'EEAGGGGH!' he screamed, clutching his face.

Velvet shoved past him and ran down the hallway. To her left the hall opened up into a den and she saw a front door. She threw herself at it.

Locked.

'YOU BITCH BITCH BITCH.' He staggered to his feet, clawing at his seared eyes.

Six locks on the door and three were dead bolts. These she clicked open and tried the door again. Still locked. The other locks required a key.

Where would he keep the goddamned keys? Fighting a surge of panic, Velvet scanned the den. Nothing on the table except a plate dirty with sandwich crumbs and a milk-smeared glass. Nothing on the small kitchen counter.

She had heard the jingle earlier when he tossed the keys on the bedroom floor.

She turned and he charged at her, his face set in fury, his eyes red slits.

She grabbed a lamp from a side table and swung hard. It nailed him on the shoulder. He went down, and Velvet raised the lamp to smash it on his head.

He seized her legs, trying to topple her, and she slammed the lamp's base against his neck, then against the back of his head.

Don't let him get you down. He wins if he gets you on the floor.

Teeth closed around her ankle, biting hard and deep, down to the bone.

She screamed and fell to the floor, kicking him. His teeth tore the flesh of her ankle.

She grabbed the fallen can of disinfectant and fogged him again, trying to loop the lamp's cord around his throat. He sobbed and lashed out with a punch that caught her hard in the windpipe. She gagged, gasping for breath. He swung the lamp hard, connecting against her skull, the lamp breaking, and she went down, eyeballs rolling up. Her final thought was, *Not like this, no*.

The Blade stood, then sank down again. His eyes burned like the bitch had poked hot matches into the irises. He crawled to the sink and splashed water repeatedly into his aching eyes. She hadn't gotten him so good with the last cloudy burst of disinfectant, but the first had been unadulterated hell, toxic waste hitting his eye tissue.

She might have blinded him. Maybe even caused permanent damage.

He puked into the sink. He rinsed his eyes for what felt like an eternity. The pain subsided down to a dull roar, enough to where he could read the instructions on the disinfectant. Call a physician. Not an option right now. God, he would make this bitch pay. He went back to the rinsing.

Thirty minutes later, his hands still shaking, he could see well enough to relock the dead bolts and to drag her back to the room. Her left ankle was a meaty mess and she wheezed, but she was still unconscious.

This is what being nice brought, he thought. But none of the others had fought him so hard, and when the pain faded, that fire of hers would make punishing and crushing her sweeter than killing Mama. Oh, the fun. He hardened at the images, even with the pain in his eyes and his head. He'd hold her eyes open and spray till the can was empty. He put on his knife sheath so she could see what waited for her after their chemical games.

He choked down a half-dozen aspirin and slung Velvet over his shoulder. He tossed her onto the bed and started to retie her to the posts.

A knock pounded on the front door.

39

'You're in a bad situation,' Whit said softly.

Kathy Breaux sat in one corner of Corey Hubble's room, watching Whit. Her soap-roughened hands lay in her lap, fingers laced together. Her fingernails were short and bitten, and she smelled of the antiseptic that wafted through the home like souring perfume. Hair dyed a slightly too-bright red, a starved look about her face and hips. Gooch had left them alone, to go perform an important errand at Whit's request.

Kathy said, 'I don't know what you mean.'

'There's several different ways this can play out,' Whit said. 'Pretty much all of them involve me calling the police. And me calling the FBI. What happens between now and then will make a big difference.'

'Look, I just work here, okay? I just do what I'm told.' She kept her voice hushed, accustomed to talking around the napping old. She glanced at Corey, propped up in the bed, eyes shut, breathing slowly, abandoned to a world of his own.

'Just following orders? That didn't work at Nuremberg, why do you think it's gonna work here?'

'What do you want?' she asked.

'I want to know how this man got here.'

Kathy swallowed. 'John's been here at least five years. I don't know much about what happened to him.'

'John?'

'John Taylor.'

'I think his name's Corey Hubble.'

'I said I don't know what you're talking about.'

'I want to see his files. Go get them and bring them back here.'

'I can't do that.'

'I can either tell these folks you attempted to extort money from Pete to reveal his brother's whereabouts, or I can tell them you discovered this man's real identity and sought to help his brother find him. Your choice.'

Kathy Breaux stood and said, 'I'll be right back, then.' She hurried out the door.

Whit got up and went to Corey's bedside. He took Corey's hand; it was limp and bony and pale. Someone had created a new identity for him. Someone had financed his care all these years. That narrowed the suspects considerably. He had trouble visualizing Junior filling out insurance forms for a guy he turned into a vegetable.

It had to be the Hubbles. He tried not to think of Faith's face on the pillow next to him, smiling, tracing his lip with her fingernail.

'Hey, Corey,' Whit said quietly. Corey gave no answer. A thin dribble of drool collected in the chapped corner of his mouth, and Whit wiped it away.

'I don't suppose you're gonna tell me what got you here,' Whit said.

Corey kept his silence. The vicious trench of scar on his head looked like a bullet wound, long healed. Corey had been shot. The bullet must have obliterated his mind but not his functions, trapping him in this limbo.

If someone had tried to kill him, why keep him alive? Attempted homicide made no sense. It must have been an accident. But then why the secrecy? Because the accident and its circumstances, if revealed, must threaten someone powerful.

He searched Corey's room: neatly folded sweats from Wal-Mart, white tube socks, vanilla-scented hand lotion, an uncracked Bible. In the back of the closet lay a plastic bag of new sweats, also bought at Wal-Mart, a sales slip still inside. Paid with cash, but bought twelve days ago. He figured that was a Monday, an exact week before Pete's death.

He had no idea about Lucinda's schedule, but it would be easy enough to find out if she was out campaigning and where she was. Or where Faith was. He pocketed the receipt from the clothes bag, careful not to get his own prints on it.

So what did he owe Faith? A consideration phone call? *Honey, I'm about to reveal to the press that your long-missing brother-in-law isn't so missing anymore. You want to tell me what you know before I call the cops?*

If he cared for her, he owed her this. Didn't he?

Corey lay in the bed like a broken dream.

Not yet, he couldn't call her. He would need more proof. Fingerprints. Dental records. The business of proving who lay in this bed meant more than simply picking up a phone and summoning the press. They wouldn't run a story without harder evidence, and he had none.

Gooch came back into the room. Whit tucked Corey's cool hand back under the sheets. Corey moaned, rasped, a shuddery breath.

'Any trouble?'

'Nope. The local drugstore sells them.' Gooch produced a cheap disposable camera from the bag and began to snap photos of Corey from various angles. Whit had thought it an appropriate precaution. He told Gooch what Kathy had said.

'So what are you thinking?' Gooch asked.

'I think Lucinda put him here.'

Gooch gave him a disbelieving squint. 'I don't like her, but if her child was hurt, she'd want him taken care of.'

'He *is* taken care of. And his brother tracked him down here – he at least was in contact with this nurse here – and dies.'

'You're suggesting Lucinda killed one son because he found out about her other son?'

'I don't know. And that missing girl, Marcy Ballew? She worked here, then she vanishes from Port Leo. She has to be connected to this somehow.'

'Consider this,' Gooch said. 'Kathy knows that John Taylor really is Corey Hubble, long-missing son of a prominent politician. Maybe she wants to sell that information to Pete. And maybe the Ballew girl was in on the scheme. She goes to Port Leo to deal with Pete, loses her wallet, and ends up missing or on the run.'

'If Pete thought Corey was in this town, why not just come here and get him and publicize the hell out of it? It doesn't make sense,' Whit said.

'Maybe he didn't know. She's calling him from little Missatuck, Texas. Corey's in Deshay, Louisiana. God only knows what story she told him.' Gooch finished his roll of film.

Whit ran a finger along the burr of hair and scar along Corey's scalp.

'So you think Lucinda shot her own kid and set him up here?' Gooch asked.

'No,' Whit said, 'I think Delford Spires shot him.'

'Why would Delford shoot a teenager?'

'Before he disappeared, Corey told Marian Duchamp that he was going to kill Delford Spires. I think Delford and Lucinda were involved – he is still extraordinarily protective of her – and Corey found out. That weekend he vanished, I think he headed north to Houston, to the conference his mother was attending. Suppose Delford's shacked up there with Lucinda. Corey finds them, there's a fight, the gun goes off. Corey's wounded.'

'They would rush him to a hospital,' Gooch said.

'You'd think. But maybe Delford's worried he'll lose his job. Maybe Lucinda's worried about the political ramifications of her lover shooting her son. Obviously they chose another route.'

'How would they have taken care of him, though, if he'd been shot?'

'She's an RN. I saw her diplomas in her office, it got mentioned a lot in the papers when she first ran for office and she was big on health care, nursing home reform.' He shook his head. 'I don't know, Gooch, but this *is* Corey, and he got here with a new identity.'

'So how would this Kathy have found out about Corey?' Gooch asked.

'A Web site about Pete Hubble included a picture of Corey and the number to Pete's answering service – sort of an on-line milk carton. Kathy might have seen that and realized she was sitting on a financial opportunity.'

A jowly man with reddened cheeks and wispy blond hair stormed into the room. He wore a short-sleeve button-down shirt crisp with starch. A succession of chins nearly hid his tie's knot.

'I'm Felix Duplessis, the chief administrator here. Who the hell are you people and why are you terrorizing my staff?' he demanded.

'We're not terrorizing anyone,' Whit said mildly. 'I'm Judge Whit Mosley, from Encina County, Texas, and this is my associate, Leonard Guchinski.'

'A judge?' Duplessis blinked. 'One of our nurses said you're bothering this patient.'

'Good,' Whit said. 'It's about time someone bothered about him.'

'I'm asking you to leave.'

'We're not going anywhere,' Whit said. 'This man has

335

been missing for sixteen years and he's just been found, and we're calling the police and the FBI.'

Duplessis gaped. Whit explained. At the mention of Marcy Ballew's name Duplessis grew gray-pale. A return to the main office of the nursing home showed Kathy Breaux was gone. Duplessis paged her over the intercom.

'What can you tell us about John Taylor?' Whit asked.

Duplessis shook his head as he dug through a file. 'Not much. He's our youngest patient by far. He's supposed to be transferred today. We just received a call this morning.'

Transferred. Someone wanted the evidence whisked away, dumped in a fresh bed. 'How is his care paid for?' Whit asked.

'A trust fund pays for what the government don't.' Duplessis pulled a thick file with TAYLOR, JOHN on the tab.

'Who administers this trust?'

'A woman named Laura Taylor. From Texas. Austin, I believe.'

Faith worked out of Austin as Lucinda's chief of staff. 'Does she ever visit?'

'Rarely. She was here, oh, a couple of weeks ago.'

'What does she look like?'

Duplessis shrugged. 'Big old girl type. Early forties, tall, heavyset, pretty hazel eyes. No nonsense.'

Pretty hazel eyes. Faith.

Whit flipped through the file. John Taylor, thirty-two years old, born in San Antonio, Texas, suffered severe head injuries in a car crash sixteen years ago and vegetative since the accident. He had been moved to Deshay six years ago from a home in Texarkana, where he had spent the past ten years. At the back of the file were the transfer papers from Texarkana, the signature at

336

the bottom a loopy scrawl with the name typed beneath: Buddy Beere.

'Oh, no,' Whit said. 'Oh, no.' He reached for the phone.

40

David knocked on the door again. Claudia stood at the porch's end, watching the oaken limbs sway in the wind.

Yeah, stay out of the way, because you're not even an officer anymore, just a tagalong. Give David a peck, send him on his way, get on your own feet, find yourself a job. Maybe out of Port Leo.

'Mr Beere?' David called through the shut door. 'Sheriff's department, open up, please.' He gave Claudia a half smile, warm, just happy she was there. She half smiled back.

They had driven out to Buddy Beere's address in David's cruiser, outside the Port Leo city limits, cutting through a grove of bent live oaks, and driven into a small clearing, studded with a few laurel oaks and a tidy cabin. A van was parked next to the cabin. Beside it was a shanty garage, tilting slightly with age. The cabin faced away from the road, faced away from the direction of town and bay, as though the little house had turned its back on the world.

'Anyone home?' David called. 'Mr Beere?'

They heard movement inside then, a scuffling sound, someone hurrying across a wood floor. Locks unlatched slowly – six of them – and the door creaked open an inch. A brown eye – oddly reddened and squinting – peered out at them.

'Mr Beere?' David said.

'Yes?'

'I'm Deputy Power with the Encina County Sheriff's Department. This is Claudia Salazar, you spoke with her on the phone yesterday.' Claudia nodded, not drawing closer. She wasn't here in any official capacity and didn't want to give the wrong impression to Buddy that she was still an investigator. One hint of that and Delford, in his current mania, would press charges against her.

The eye blinked. 'Hello. Yes. Sorry it took me a while to reach the door, I was in the bathroom.'

'Not out campaigning today?' Claudia asked in a little too-bright tone from her end of the porch.

'Oh, no, not today,' Buddy said.

'Over your cold yet?' Claudia asked.

'Mostly. Thank you.' The door did not open any farther. 'I don't want to give my cold to y'all.'

David cleared his throat. 'We don't mind. Your boss is helping us with some inquiries. We're reviewing when certain patients were transferred into your nursing home.'

Buddy opened the door a little wider, and over David's shoulder Claudia could see his whole face now, round, soft, some slight scarring from old acne, a puzzled look. He wore surgical scrub pants, the kind she'd seen at the nursing home, a thick T-shirt. He slid his hand up along the locks set into the door.

'Transfers? Gosh, all those records would be at Placid Harbor.' He opened the door a little more. He was stronger than he looked, stocky, arms and chest thicker than she would have guessed from the hunched way he bore himself about town.

'Okay, Mr Beere, would you mind stepping outside here for a moment?' David asked. 'So we can talk?'

'Sure. Let me get my sandals. There's splinters on that porch,' Buddy Beere said, reaching by the door. 'Just a second—'

David turned and took four steps toward Claudia, shrugging, a question forming on his lips: 'You wanna ask . . .' and then a blast of thunder exploded from the door. David fell, blood and flesh flying from his shoulder.

339

Buddy Beere stepped entirely out of the door, bringing the shotgun around and up. Claudia threw herself off the porch as the barrel roared again and little meteors screamed past her, heat cutting near her throat, her hair.

She had no weapon. She scrabbled to her feet and ran for David's cruiser. Another blast and the cruiser's windshield dissolved into pixie dust. She was a clear shot in his sights. She swerved left hard, running low, putting the corner of the shanty garage between her and him.

Another blast, into the cruiser's hood. He was laughing. No, giggling.

Mother of God, he's killed David.

Claudia hunkered down by a corner of the weathered garage, trying to guess which approach he might take. There was a rifle and radio in David's cruiser, but it was twenty feet away and she imagined Buddy Beere, the gun steady in his hands, watching for her to stick her head out as a sweet target.

The garage might offer a weapon, but once she went in, she would be pinned. The doors were antique, opening in the middle like a horse's stall. Unlocked and slightly agape. Running across Buddy's acreage offered little in the way of cover, beyond the motte of live oaks situated on the wrong side of the garage. To the other side seacoast bluestems grew thick but only thigh-high. Not enough. He could take a leisurely bead on her head and fire at will.

She heard the kick of his feet coming along the side of the garage, between her and the police cruiser. She made her choice.

She slipped inside the garage. It was neatly kept, small windows offering a hint of light. Tools were aligned along the back wall, a broom, a set of fishing tackle, an old sky-blue Volkswagen Beetle parked on the right side, cramped in the space. A trailer, carrying a small fishing skiff, was next to the Beetle. She hurried to the back of the garage, squeezing between car and boat. Her eyes ranged along the back wall of the garage: screwdrivers, wrenches, a pair of wicked-looking gardening shears.

'Claudia?' she heard Buddy's voice ask. He said it *Clau-di-a*, the honeyed singsong a child might use in playing hide-and-seek, hoping to lure a playmate into the open. She grabbed the gardening shears and hunkered down behind the skiff; it offered the most immediate cover. But it gave her the least room to run or fight. She crouched, the shears heavy in her hands.

Shot pummeled through the doors, just in case she'd been hiding there. Sunlight glowed through the frail, splintered wood. Silence followed, and she saw one of the doors creak open.

'You know,' Buddy said, almost conversationally to the empty air, 'John Wayne Gacy invited the surveillance cops to breakfast at his house. That's when they noticed the funny smell and found a basement full of dead boys. I always thought he should have killed the cops – how stupid just to cave. Dennis Nilsen pointed to where the chopped-up remains of his darlings were when the police came knocking. He should have at least killed those cops, gone out with a bang.'

Kneeling, breathing through an open mouth, she saw his feet paddle past the other side of the Beetle. 'Come out now,' he called. 'I don't want to shoot up my nice car and boat, and I'll make it quick.'

She didn't move.

'That other cop, he's messy but still breathing. Come out or maybe I go back up there and make sure he stops.'

She didn't move. He began to walk toward the back wall. A few more steps and he would be able to spot her. She braced herself.

As he turned, the barrel swiveling toward the ground,

she launched herself up, slamming her forearm against the blued bottom of the shotgun's barrel. It swept right, exploding, cannonading into the garage wall. She pistoned her legs, driving Buddy hard into the side wall of the garage. She dropped the shears, both hands grabbing hold of the shotgun, trying to wrest it away.

He slammed the shotgun barrel against her head, hard, twice, stars and sharp pain blurring her vision. Shoving up with her arms, she got the gun above her head and powered her knee square into his gut.

He squirmed back, gasping, still holding the gun, and she kicked, hammering him in the mouth. Teeth broke and lips opened under her boot's heel. Buddy staggered back, blood bursting from his torn mouth. She pulled hard on the shotgun. It discharged once more in the air, deafening in the small space of the garage.

With a scream he yanked the weapon free from her grasp and swung it at her head. She fell to her knees, ducking, taking the blow on her shoulder. He pulled the gun back to its firing stance, squeezed.

Nothing.

Empty, jammed, she thought. Buddy charged at her, raising the Model 870 like a club, and she plowed back into him, knocking him to the dirt floor. She scooped up the fallen shears and vaulted into the narrow skiff to clamber toward the garage doors. He rammed the side of the light boat with his body, and she fell from the prow, diving headfirst, scraping her back against the trailer hitch, hitting the hard-packed dirt. The shears were beneath her and she twisted, trying to free them from her own weight. She saw Buddy squeezing through the narrowed space between the tipped boat and the Volkswagen. He tried to vault it, land on top of her, but he tumbled headfirst as she scrabbled out from underneath the boat.

He grabbed her ankle.

Claudia screamed, trying to kick him again. He tugged her back toward him, the shears slipped from her grasp, and she saw him pull a long brightness from a shoulder sheath. Bowie knife.

He slammed the knife into her calf, and she screamed her throat raw in one second. She felt her own flesh tearing, the knife colder than ice. She kicked hard with the other leg, impacting collarbone, and pushed away, frantically grabbing for the shears. She smelled her own blood as her fingers closed around the shears' handle. Pain – beyond pain – raced along every nerve in her body.

He lifted the knife from her flesh.

'Quit fighting, quit fighting!' he yelled. He climbed on top of her and lifted the reddened knife. Claudia rammed the shears into his gut, hard, feeling Buddy Beere's innards part before the points. She surged to a sitting position as she pushed, felt the blades slide along rib bone, and the shears vanished into him, all the way to the hafts.

Her face was an inch from his. She felt the bowie tear into her shirt below her arm, the blade catch in the fabric, its edge whisper along her skin.

Buddy did not scream. He fell away from her, hands slapping the shears' smooth handles. Blood seeped from him and she crab-crawled backward, smelling his blood, her blood, kicking the dirt between them. Buddy lay on his side, blinking at her, mewling.

'No . . . Mama, help . . .' he wheezed.

'You fucking loser,' Claudia gasped. She hobbled to her feet. Agony lanced her leg, blood greased her skin. She staggered toward the cruiser and threw herself inside, glass from the broken windshield crunching under her. Buddy Beere still lay on his side, the shears protruding from his stomach, mouth a wet ruin from her kick, eyes dimming of life.

Claudia flicked at the radio. It still worked. 'Officer down . . . help me . . . this is Claudia Salazar . . . with David Power. Officer down . . . officer down . . . He's been shot, gunshot . . . I've been stabbed . . . suspect is Buddy Beere . . . I think I killed him . . . officer down . . . we're at Buddy Beere's house off FM 1223 . . . couple of miles past Port Leo on the right . . . 4704 FM 1223 . . . hurry, hurry.'

She clutched her leg. Movement at the edge of her vision. Through the shattered windshield she saw a woman, stumbling from the house, naked, bruised, her face a mass of blue.

The county dispatcher's voice blared on the radio, telling her to hold on, help was on the way.

'Velvet!' Claudia called. 'Velvet!'

Velvet limped toward the car but saw Buddy collapsed in the shadow of the garage. Claudia, clutching her leg, pulled herself out from the cruiser. Velvet stopped, stared at Claudia, then stared back at Buddy.

'Velvet, honey, it's okay . . .' Claudia gasped. 'It's gonna be okay.' God, she hoped. She wasn't sure she could stay conscious much longer. *And David, oh, babe . . .*

Velvet knelt by Buddy, yanked the shears out with a decisive pull, tore open the scrub pants, and began to perform crude surgery. In the distance sirens roared in their approach.

'Velvet! Stop! Stop!' Claudia called.

The blood flew upward with Velvet's blows, dotting her face, and soaked the ground.

'I need to talk to Claudia,' Whit said into the phone.

'She don't work here no more, Judge,' the weekend police department dispatcher, a lady named Trudy, told him. 'Delford fired her. She went and raised holy hell with the Hubbles, and he canned her.'

'Hell over what?'

'That girl they pulled out of the bay . . . the one that found Pete Hubble's body, apparently she had something going on with Sam Hubble and Sam's disappeared, although Delford don't want to put out an APB. I heard him and Claud arguing about it. Delford's furious with Claudia, I don't even dare say her name aloud when he's around.' She quickly told him about Junior Deloache, Heather Farrell, all the whirl of death since he left town.

'God Almighty.' Claudia fired. Heather and Junior dead. Sam missing. Jesus. His stomach tottered on the lip of a pit. 'I need Spires's home and pager numbers.'

Trudy gave him the numbers.

He dialed Delford's number. No answer. He tried the pager number, keyed in the nursing home's number, hoping for a quick response.

Think. Think.

Buddy Beere knew about Corey Hubble. Perhaps even assisted in the grand deception. Pete had found out where Corey was and Buddy silenced him. Perhaps silenced Marcy Ballew as well.

But how did Buddy learn that Pete had found Corey? Who knew what Pete knew? Not even Velvet, he'd kept even her in the dark. Not Kathy . . . killing Pete meant no money, and Whit didn't even know if she knew Buddy Beere.

'They authorized him to be moved,' Felix Duplessis said again, sitting in his chair, staring at Whit. His face sagged with the worn look of someone who suspects a good day will not come in the immediate future. 'The call came this morning. She insisted he be moved to a home up in Shreveport immediately.'

'She?' Gooch asked.

'John's trustee,' Duplessis said. 'Laura Taylor.'

'Let me have her number, please,' Whit said. Aside from the Austin number was a 361 area code: Texas Coastal Bend.

Duplessis clicked on his speakerphone, and Whit dialed. The phone chirped and a woman's voice answered.

'Hello?'

Duplessis said, 'Miz Taylor?'

A pause. 'Yes, this is she.' She sounded tired, anxious, and exactly like Faith Hubble. Whit leaned over the phone, still silent, his eyes closed.

'This is Felix Duplessis at Memorial Oaks in Deshay. How are you?'

'All right. Have you moved John yet?'

'There's been a delay here, ma'am.'

'He has to be moved immediately to the home in Shreveport. That's what we pay for. Immediately.'

'Well, yes, ma'am, but we've had a problem,' Duplessis said. 'There's a gentleman . . .'

Whit stood by the speakerphone and leaned down. 'Faith. It's Whit. I'm here. I found Corey.'

No answer from the other end of the line.

'Faith?' Whit tried again. 'Are you there?'

'I'm here,' she finally said.

'Why does Corey have to be moved so quickly?'

346

'I . . .'

And as soon as he asked the question, he saw his own logic misfire. Pete had died because he learned the secret. The secret the other Hubbles had cultivated and manufactured. But neither Faith nor Lucinda knew of his plans for the movie, that he was blood-hounding Corey's trail.

Pete would have had only one confidant, one person he needed to turn against the Hubbles.

'Is it Sam?' Whit asked. 'It is. Sam.'

'He's run off. He may be on his way there.' Her voice broke. 'Whit, don't let him do anything . . . stupid. Please.'

'He killed Pete,' Whit said. 'He killed his own father. Goddamn it, Faith. You knew?'

'If Sam is there . . . please don't hurt him. Don't hurt him!'

Whit turned to Felix Duplessis. 'We need to move Corey . . . I mean, John. Or get guards here, one of the two. Now.'

'Now, wait a second, we just got to get this sorted out . . .' Duplessis said, and through the blinds Whit saw a BMW slide crookedly into a parking space, bumping a van. A lanky figure loped toward the nursing home's front door.

'Faith, he's here,' Whit said. 'Sam's just pulled up. Do you know if he's armed?'

Gooch bolted from the room.

'Don't hurt him!' Faith screamed. 'Please!'

Whit ran out of the office. He spotted Gooch heading toward Corey's room, pushing the wheelchaired patients back into their rooms, telling the aides to get them out of the hallway. The aides, collecting the breakfast trays, began to argue with him.

'Call the police! Now!' Whit yelled back at Duplessis. His yell made the hallway go silent.

347

'Whit!' Faith screamed from the phone. 'Don't hurt him, he's my baby, don't . . .' and her voice vanished as Duplessis jabbed a button and dialed 911.

Whit reached the lobby just as Sam Hubble, wearing a denim jacket and dark glasses, left the information desk with a nod, heading toward the north ward of rooms.

'Sam!' Whit yelled.

Sam Hubble turned.

'You fucker.' Sam reached behind him, pulling a Ruger from its tucked spot in the back of his jeans, hidden by a baggy T-shirt. He pointed it at Whit's head, six feet away. The woman at the information desk screamed and ran down the other hallway.

'It's over, Sam,' Whit said, holding his palms up. 'It's over. I just talked with your mother. She wants to talk to you. Give me the gun and let's go to the office and talk with her.'

'You fuck my mother so you think you can tell me what to do?' Sam narrowed his eyes into a hateful stare. 'I don't think it works that way.'

He knew, oh, damn. He knew like Corey knew, years ago. 'I don't want you to get hurt. Your mother's on the phone, she wants to talk with you.'

'I hate you,' Sam said. 'Why did you have to come here, drag her into this?'

'It's over,' Whit repeated. 'The only person Pete would have trusted with the whole story of what he found was you. You're the only one he would have told, because he wanted you to be with him. He had dirt so bad on your mother and your grandmother that he actually might have won custody from them. So he told you what happened to your uncle Corey, but you decided to side with the home team. Your grandmother and your mother. You didn't want Pete ruining their lives, so you ended his.' He softened his tone. 'It's over, Sam. Put it down.'

'Shut your mouth.' Sam gestured with the Ruger. He glanced at the others in the lobby: a woman visiting a wheelchair-bound man, both cowering by a coffee table. 'I start shooting and maybe I don't start with you.'

'There's no point in hurting anyone else. The police are on their way. Give me the gun and let's go talk to your mom.'

'No.' Sam backed down the hall, keeping the gun leveled at Whit. Whit followed him, slowly.

'Pete told you what he thought you should know about your perfect family, all to convince you to be on his side.'

Sam hurried down the hallway, residents and aides and nurses scrambling and screaming, hurrying into rooms. At the end of the hall Whit saw Gooch move out from Corey's room, then duck back in.

'He was lying,' Sam managed. He bumped into a food tray trolley, shoved it over. Fish sticks and macaroni greased the floor. The gun shook in his hand. The boy began to cry.

Whit kept his voice even, his movement even with Sam's, close but not too close. 'Monday night he thinks he's spending it with you, he sends Velvet away. And maybe you call, tell him you need some time to think. He's alone. Your friend Heather goes to see him. You hide out on an empty boat nearby, maybe. Had she been befriending him for you, spying on him? They drink, she flirts. Maybe she sets up the camera for him. You sneak aboard. He strips and gets on the bed, maybe she strips, and you come into the room, shove the gun in his mouth, and fire. Or she does. Which was it?'

'Heather didn't do nothing,' Sam whispered. 'Stop saying that.'

'He's dead, your family's safe, and you found a bonus: a half million in cash. You've also got his computer and all his notes on Corey. Heather pretends to find the body, but when your father's other associations start producing questions, you produce a suicide note. And Pete conveniently confesses to his own brother's accidental death. Just so no one bothers to pick up looking for Corey.'

Sam stopped. They stood ten feet away from the end of the hall, near Corey's room. The screams had died down as the terrified clients took cover, except for one rasping old woman's voice calling from a nearby room, 'Nurse? Nurse?'

'I couldn't let him . . . couldn't let him do this to us.' Tears streamed from Sam's eyes.

'I know you were just trying to help your grandmother, Sam. Your mother's on the phone, down at the office, she wants to talk to you. Give me the gun and come with me. We know how all this happened. There's nothing to be gained from hurting Corey or anyone else.'

A shrill of sirens screamed in the parking lot. A hard light gleamed in the boy's eyes.

Sam muttered, 'Fuck you,' and Gooch launched himself from the door, pile-driving the boy down, smashing a fist against the boy's wrist. The pistol fell and Whit grabbed it.

Sam wriggled beneath Gooch, cursing, crying. Gooch yanked him to his feet, holding him with one massive arm.

'You okay?' he asked Whit.

Whit watched Sam's face. 'Yeah. Sam, Jesus, Jesus, Jesus.'

Officers charged into the hall, demanding all three of them lie facedown. Whit put the gun on the floor as ordered and put his face on the cool tile. Duplessis hurried among the police, explaining, telling them Gooch and Whit were okay.

As the Deshay officers pulled Sam down the hall, he sobbed, 'Let me call Heather. Please let me call Heather.'

Oh, God, he doesn't know.

Whit went to go deal with the police and to tell Faith her son was still alive.

Hours later, when evening began its soft slide into Deshay, Whit returned to Corey Hubble's room. Corey lay in the bed, eyelids like half-moons, moaning softly. A police guard at the door nodded Whit in.

Whit pulled up a chair next to the bed.

'Well. Hello. It's been a long while. I know you and I weren't close, but I also don't know . . . what you can hear, what you can understand. I'm gonna assume it's more than we think.' He touched the bone-thin arm under the sheet, remembering the smiling boy holding a proud string of redfish aloft. 'The fishing's been good this year, Corey, although I sure haven't had time to go. We don't have a prayer in football season this year. The coach doesn't know his butt from a hole in the ground, so we're all resigned to losing. We ought to do better in basketball next spring, one of the Lindstrom boys is six-seven. And would you believe I'm a judge? I know: a Mosley acting all respectable. But it may only be for a little while now.' He cleared his throat. 'I went to go see Marian Duchamp. She cares about you, you know, even if things weren't exactly running smooth between you . . .'

The talk went on for another hour before Corey dozed into sleep. Whit stayed by his bed, watching the ghost breathe.

42

The one true suicide note composed that October in Encina County read as follows:

I deeply regret the things I have done and left undone. I murmured that at church each Sunday for the past sixteen years and each time it felt like a bee's sting near my heart and God knew I was a rotten liar. If I make it to heaven I'll know He's forgiven me.

I take full responsibility for what happened to Corey Hubble and in turn what happened to Pete Hubble. I heard as a boy that love made you do great things, but I never figured good love would make you do evil. I write this not as explanation but as apology, and because regretfully Lucinda will not tell one moment's truth.

Lucinda and I became lovers before her husband died. His death from cancer was long and drawn-out, and the love between them faded long before he got sick. We were very careful and discreet, but Corey found out about us after Lucinda's election to the state senate. I don't know how, maybe he started following his mother and spotted us at one of the motels we used. He delivered flowers for spending money, so perhaps he saw us where we shouldn't be. While we were staying at a friend's house in Houston, Corey surprised us. He burst into the upstairs bedroom with a shotgun and we fought. I got the shotgun away from him, but then he grabbed for my service revolver and I grabbed it back and it fired twice, once hitting him in the head. He was hurt, but he didn't die. Lucinda's an RN. She stabilized him but refused to take him to a doctor because she was worried about the scandal. I began to cease to love her then. What kind of woman does that? A kiss can fool you. But I went along with her idea, scared shitless of losing my career, and we drove the boy to Texarkana, where she knew of a nursing home where she could cut a deal. She'd been doing legislation on nursing home reform, so she knew which homes were crooked and might cut her a deal and would benefit most from her protection. Lucinda greased some palms and he got care at the home. We thought he would quietly die but he didn't. We returned to Port Leo late that Saturday, me driving Corey's car, Lucinda driving mine. I took command of the investigation into Corey's disappearance, and I stamped out any evidence that could point to him having fallen victim to violence.

I am sorry to the people of Port Leo for betraying their trust, but I was young and foolish and scared. I have read a lot on head and brain injuries, and they are confounding, unpredictable things. Corey hovered over our lives, not alive and not dead. He haunts me even now.

The administrator at the home (Phil Farr) was a goddamned crook, and he'd done Medicare fraud before, creating clients that never existed. After we took Corey there Lucinda protected this home against agency investigations. Farr and this clerk made Corey into John Taylor. This clerk was a creepy little bastard who was suspected at one point of smothering a lady patient at the home, but nothing came of that. Now we know that clerk became Buddy Beere and followed Lucinda eventually to Port Leo, and now he has killed some poor young women. I take blame for that as well.

I thought Lucinda had killed Pete, or perhaps his ex-wife Faith. I did not want a murder investigation centering on the Hubbles. I behaved badly. I am sorry to the people I have hurt. I am not sorry to Lucinda Hubble, and the people of the Coastal Bend should not suffer her one moment longer.

I apologize to the people who have suffered so because of my mistakes, including Claudia Salazar, who I wrongfully terminated and should have her job back. Claudia, don't hate me. I always loved you more than a little. God forgive me my wrongs.

– Delford Morton Spires

He hanged himself with a stout length of rope. His service revolver lay on the floor below his feet, polished and oiled, next to his gleaming badge and his carefully folded uniform.

Claudia and Whit stood on the slope of land leading away from Buddy Beere's cabin, watching the work crew spear the ground with their shovels. The men dug slowly, carefully, methodically unearthing the land around Buddy's house, looking for the mortal remains of Marcy Ballew and the women from Brownsville and Laredo. Claudia stood on crutches, her leg heavily bandaged, her hair pulled up from her eyes. Whit leaned against an old laurel oak. He held blank autopsy orders, ready to fill out in case the searchers found human remains.

Whit watched her. Her face was emotionless. 'You sure you want to be here?'

'It's okay. You got to look the beast in the eye, Whit.'

'You gonna bring David here when's he released?' Whit asked. David was recuperating at a Corpus Christi hospital, having suffered severe bone and nerve damage in his back and chest from the shotgun blast. He was out of immediate danger, but the road to rehabilitation looked to be long and winding.

'If he wants to come,' she said, not looking at him.

'You haven't talked about David much.'

'David . . . needs me right now. Badly.'

Claudia said nothing for a long while, watching the dirt slowly pile.

A pair of FBI agents came out of the cabin, notepads open, arguing. Buddy's belongings had been boxed and catalogued and no doubt would be sent to Quantico for the criminal psychologists to purr over. All the evidence they would need to scribe their papers on Buddy Beere, add him to the literature of the compulsive killer. Patsy Duchamp, given a meaty story, had delineated most of the facts in the paper, and Whit had read the account with a greasy kink in his stomach: Buddy was born Darren Burdell in Milwaukee, with a hophead mother who disciplined her tot with blades and lit cigarettes. Little Darren killed his mother at age thirteen when she tried to castrate him. He decapitated her an hour after her death, which gave the social workers pause. He spent time at a juvenile home and mental ward, seemed to improve, worked odd jobs. Fell out of sight and headed south, apparently killing the occasional prostitute or runaway. One pundit quoted on television opined that Buddy preferred work at nursing homes since he would get to see people expire on a fairly regular basis. This might also explain his desire to be a rural JP. Serving as coroner, inspecting dead bodies, would have been delightfully stimulating for him. Credit-card receipts showed he had visited Deshay at least twice a year – perhaps treating Corey as a trophy, an example of his cleverness, paralleling the serial-killer fixation on visiting hidden remains of victims. A check of the human resources files at Placid Harbor showed that Buddy, armed with a master password, had altered the personnel records three times to indicate he was present at the nursing home when he was not. The dates were the dates when Marcy Ballew, Angela Norris, and Laura Palinski all vanished.

Claudia watched the federal agents walking around the cabin. 'I wonder why he didn't bury Heather if he buried the others,' she said in a dead voice.

Whit inched onto the thin ice. 'You couldn't have saved Heather, Claudia. You couldn't know she was in mortal danger. Neither did she.'

'I could have convinced her to stay in a safe place.'

'Stop it,' Whit said. 'She was a co-conspirator in murder. No way was she going to get close to you or let you help her. You saved Velvet and David and anyone else Buddy would have killed along the line. That has to be enough.'

'Delford could have told me.' She suddenly shivered. 'He could have turned himself in. He had years of outstanding service on his side. He could have cut a deal, testifying against Lucinda.'

'You want pearls with your hair shirt, Claudia?' Whit said. He put an arm around her, and she leaned against him, old friend to old friend.

They watched the work crew begin to dig on a fresh stretch of land, between the oaks. Fifteen minutes later the crew found bones. Claudia stayed in the shade of the trees while Whit completed the autopsy authorizations.

Four days later Whit came home to find Faith Hubble, out on bond, sitting on a deck chair by his father's pool, waiting for him. She wore jeans, a dark blouse, a ball cap, dark glasses. The uniform of the incognito.

'I assume I'm not in violation of some restraining order,' she said, not lowering the glasses. 'I'm behind on reading my mail.'

'You're not,' Whit said. 'But if my father spots you here I imagine he'll say you're trespassing.'

He couldn't see her eyes behind the sunglasses. 'I suppose you will say you were just doing your job,' she said. 'Destroying my son.'

'Me? Look in the mirror, Faith.'

He saw her hands tremble. 'My mother always said I had dreadful taste in men. I think you and Pete proved her point.'

'Go see your son at the jail, Faith. While you can. They don't arrange visits between prisons.'

'You're a cruel bastard.'

'I spent about five seconds feeling sorry for you,' Whit said. 'Lucinda dragged you into the cover-up, made you dirty your hands instead of her. But you did it, willingly, for years, Faith. If you hadn't, Sam never would have had a reason to kill his father.'

'You don't know thing one about my life . . . what my life has been like . . .'

'No, I don't. I can't comprehend it.' He felt a tremor of revulsion that he'd ever touched her.

She stood. 'We have very, very good lawyers. And I promise you, when justice is served and our names are cleared' – a straight reading from their press statement, he thought – 'you're done in this town. You won't be able to get a job scrubbing toilets.'

'Probably not,' he said. 'I have a feeling you'll have filled that position.'

Selected election results from the November 7 election:

Texas Senate, District 20, (Encina County tally only):
    Aaron Crawford (R): 11,587
    Lucinda Hubble (D)*: 939
     *Hubble formally withdrew from race 10/24

Justice of the Peace, Precinct One, Encina County:
   Buddy Beere (D)**: 12
   Whitman Mosley (R): 5,347
   **deceased but not removed from ballot

Whit could only suppose those twelve voices of democracy did not read the newspaper or voted strict party lines, death and felonies notwithstanding. Whit watched the results with a somber Irina and Babe, gave Patsy Duchamp a neutral comment for the paper, and went to bed.

You don't act like a judge and you end up getting elected, he thought before sleep claimed him. *Politics is just strange enough for you to stay.*

The Honorable Whit Mosley savored the beauty of the late January afternoon as the borrowed *Don't Ask* puttered out of St Leo Bay and beyond Escudo and Margarita Islands. Before him lay the wide-open Gulf of Mexico, the sea gunmetal gray, the waves whipped by just-right wind. January had been warmer than usual, the breezes sweet, the sunlight healing. Gorgeous, the fresh air like vitamins sucked straight into his lungs.

'You let me know if you get seasick,' Whit called to Velvet. She sat in a chair, face tilted toward the sun. She had returned from L.A. for Sam's trial, starting in two days, and had been quiet since Whit picked her up at the Corpus Christi airport. She had hugged him fiercely but said little, nodding when he suggested spending an evening out on the Gulf and out of the reach of the reporters.

'Just don't steer this leaking contraption like a drunk man.'

'Speaking of drunk,' Whit said, 'where are these legendary margaritas you promised?'

'I knew you'd put my ass to work.' Her first laugh.

He dropped anchor and followed her down into the spacious cabin. She was dressed in casual jeans and rugby shirt, her hair pulled back into a modest ponytail, and skin lightly touched with makeup. This was the Velvet, he thought, that might have been if the cameras never rolled. The Velvet that still might be.

'What can I do?' Whit asked.

'I don't trust you to mix the booze right, but you can juice me some limes while I work my tequila magic.' She inspected the bottles in Gooch's bar. 'I'm gonna kick Gooch's ass if there's no Grand Marnier in here.'

'I strongly suspect Gooch's boat is Grand Marnier-free.'

'Shows what you know.' She raised a half-empty bottle in victory from the cabinet. 'Just hiding back here, waiting for me.'

She began to rinse out a blender. He sliced the limes. They worked in amiable silence.

'I should hate Sam and oddly I just feel sorry for him,' Velvet said suddenly. 'He doesn't deserve it, but I do.'

Whit poured the lime juice into the cleaned blender she had set next to him. 'I thought I knew what family tragedy was. I didn't.'

Velvet poured liquor into the blender and turned it on. Whit moved behind her and hugged her, carefully. She leaned back against his shoulder. He felt the flutter of her sigh.

She finished the drinks and he tasted. 'God, that's good,' he said.

'A tart margarita is my specialty.' She blinked. 'That used to be a joke.'

He smiled. She didn't smile or laugh much; he couldn't blame her. They took the blender up to the deck. The two of them drank and played at fishing, caught nothing, and listened to a strange mix tape Gooch had made: Smashing

Pumpkins, Italian opera, Patsy Cline, Jimmy Buffett. Sad songs but somehow not so sad they hurt. They sang along with *Margaritaville*, and Velvet leaned back against Whit's chest.

The sun sank into the horizon. They cooked steaks, and Velvet blended another pitcher of margaritas. The night air was crisp but not damp, the breeze a constant caress. They talked as the moon rose, Velvet reminiscing about growing up in Omaha, Whit telling tall tales on his brothers, thinking, *This is it, this is life, this is fixing her*.

Sitting on the deck, Velvet and Whit watched the stars glimmer over the Gulf and finished the hearty dregs of margarita. Whit was drunk, pleasantly and amiably so, for the first time since coming back from Louisiana. Velvet leaned back against his chest, her hair scented with the tang of lime juice. The stars, away from the smears of light crowding the coast, were like virgin light glistening in their first night. Velvet started to count them.

'Each one's a wish you get to make,' she said.

Whit let her get to a hundred before he kissed the side of her throat.

'Don't,' she said.

He stopped. But she didn't pull away from his arms, his lap.

'I'm sorry,' he said. 'I thought . . .'

'I know, Whit. You want to make . . . what happened to me right. I love you for that. I'm not gonna let what that bastard did to me dictate the rest of my life.'

He was quiet, listening to the water lap against the hull. 'But you don't want me.'

She shook her head, turned to face him. She traced his jaw with her fingertip.

'I got a Plan B. I'm going back to Omaha when Sam's trial is done. No more movies for me.'

'I'm glad. Very glad. But . . .'

'And so, I'm kind of taking life slower. If you and me . . . well, it would just be for the short while before I left. I don't want that anymore, Whit.' She laughed softly. 'I went so long not saying no, and now I say no to a guy like you. I got no brains.'

He kissed her once, softly, letting the boat rock them like a cradle, and finally she fell asleep against his shoulder. She slept in his arms until the morning, and he watched over her, counting the stars for them both.

BLACK JACK
POINT

For Charles

PART ONE
The Devil's Eye

There comes a time in every rightly constructed boy's life that he has a raging desire to go somewhere and dig for hidden treasure.

— Mark Twain

1

In shimmering heat, Jimmy Bird smoked a cigarette and paced off a rectangle of dirt. About the size of a grave, a little wider, a little longer. Jimmy wasn't good at math – that algebra in high school where they mixed letters and numbers together had been his undoing – but he could eye a piece of ground and calculate how long it took to clear and dig to a certain depth. Ditches. Garden beds. Graves. The earth on Black Jack Point fed salt grass and waist-high bluestems and Jimmy pictured a hole six feet across, six feet down. He figured it would take him and his partners three hours of steady digging, being a little slower in the dark. Then an hour or so to sort through the loot, load the valuables on the truck, and good-bye poverty. In a few days he'd be poolside in the Caribbean, chatting up coffee-colored girls in bikinis, fishing in water bluer than blue, buying a boat and lazing on its warm deck and watching the world not go by.

But he felt uneasy even with millions in the dirt under his feet. *What if somebody sees us?* he'd asked this morning.

Then we take care of them, Jimmy, Alex had said.

What do you mean take care of them?

I mean just what you think. Alex said it with that odd half smile, caused by the little crescent-moon scar at the corner of his mouth. Like he was talking to a child.

I don't want none of that, Jimmy Bird said, and as soon as he said it he knew he'd made a big mistake. It showed a lack of drive, a complaint he'd heard about himself from his wife, his mama, his daddy, even his little girl.

Alex had kept smiling like he hadn't heard. That smile made Jimmy's bladder feel loose.

I mean we shouldn't leave a mess, Jimmy quickly amended. *That's all I meant.*

Alex smiled, patted Jimmy's back. *No messes. I promise.*

Jimmy Bird took a stake with a little flutter of fluorescent orange plastic ribbon topping it and drove it into the middle of the ground. Make it easier for them to see in the dark. He felt relief that old man Gilbert wasn't going to be up at his house tonight. He couldn't see the Gilbert place through the density of oaks, but that was for the best. No one to see them. No one to get hurt.

No messes. I promise.

Jimmy Bird didn't like those four words the more he considered them – maybe *he* had gotten demoted to *mess* – and he patted the pistol wedged in the back of his work pants for reassurance. Patted the gun three times and he realized it was just the bop-be-bop rhythm of his little girl patting the top of her teddy bear's head. He'd miss her most of all once he left the country. He'd send her some money later, anonymous like, for her schooling. She might get that math with the letters and numbers mixed together way better than he had.

By his reckoning he would go from ditchdigger to multimillionaire in about twelve hours. Jimmy Bird slung the metal detector back over his shoulder and moved through the heavy growth of twisted oaks.

They drove home early because the bedsprings squeaked.

Patch Gilbert was a romantic but a bed-and-breakfast full of artsy-fartsy bric-a-brac was not his idea of a love nest. But his lady friend, Thuy Linh Tran, had wanted to go to Port Aransas, even though it wasn't terribly far from Port Leo and could hardly count as a real getaway.

4

Thuy thought Port Aransas romantic because it was actually on an island; you rode a little ferry to get there, and you could watch the porpoises darting in the ferry's wake. They'd had a nice dinner and red vino at an Italian place, Patch had taken his pill to rev his engine, they'd snuggled into bed, and he didn't even have Thuy's modest gown off before they discovered the bedsprings on the genuine antique bed screamed like banshees every time they moved.

'We're not making love in this bed, Patch,' Thuy said.

'But I took a pill.' At seventy he felt no erection should be wasted.

'No.'

'It's Monday night. This place is mostly empty. Ain't nobody gonna hear us, angel.' He started nibbling on her ear.

'No.' She was sixty-nine and more stubborn than he was. So they had quarreled – the trip was her idea but it was for his birthday, and he wasn't happy with this squeaking turn of events – and in a fit, they got dressed and checked out and just drove back to Port Leo, to Patch's old house on Black Jack Point. The drive was mostly awkward silences. It was midnight and they were both in sour moods and Patch suddenly worried that Thuy needed a little courting. She wanted to go straight home when they got back to his house but he convinced her to come in and make up and drink a little wine.

She wasn't sleepy. Arguing had riled her up, made her more talkative; so he was hopeful she'd spend the night.

'How long's it been, baby, since you walked on a beach late at night?' Patch Gilbert poured Thuy another glass of pinot noir. 'Now that's romance, a beach real late at night.'

Thuy smiled. 'I ran across a beach at midnight, with three children in tow, hoping not to get shot and to find a

5

spot on the boat. When I left Vietnam, Patch. It wasn't romantic.' She leaned over and kissed him, a chaste little peck against his wine-wet mouth. 'I should go. I haven't been up this late in years.'

He felt their time slipping away. Her kiss gave him that shivery energy of being twenty-five. At least inside. 'Come down to the beach with me.'

'I thought you retired from sales.'

'Well, honey, if I have to *sell* you on the idea—'

'You didn't sneak another one of those pills, did you?'

'Don't need 'em.'

'Shameless.'

'We don't have time for shame. Listen, we'll just get the sand in between our toes.' His voice went husky and he took the wineglass from her hands. 'It feels good, the wet sand against your skin.'

'Patch.'

'Baby.' He kissed her gently, almost shyly. He felt the neediness in his own kiss, the hopeful wondering – not felt since high school, before the marines, before selling drilling equipment for so many years, before cancer took Martha and left him alone – if there was going to be any dessert on his plate. He loved Thuy but had never broken the habit of lovemaking as careful conquest.

'I'm too old for anyone to call baby,' Thuy said.

'Never too young,' Patch said. 'Let's go.' He took her hands in both of his and stood. Gentle insistence worked wonders. After a moment, she stood with him.

The night was clear but the moon was an ill-lit curve. Patch frowned, because he loved the moonlight on the bay, on the sands, on the high grasses. It silvered the world, made it lovely as a dream. Tonight was too dark. He and Thuy walked down the long path, a line of gravel threading through the salt grass, down to a small curve of beach. The blackjack oaks were gnarled and bent from the constant wind from St Leo Bay. He and Thuy slipped off their shoes – boots and socks for him, espadrilles for her – and they walked to the edge of the surf, the summer-warm water tickling their toes.

'The Milky Way.' Thuy pointed at the wash of stars. 'We call it *vãi ngan há*.'

'What do you call kissing?'

'*Hôn nhau.*' She ran a finger down his spine and he grinned at her. 'I counted those same stars as a little girl. I wanted to know exactly how many there were. I wanted them all. Like most children I was a little greedy.'

'I'm greedy for you,' Patch said.

They kissed, and she leaned into him, the surf wetting the cuffs on his jeans. He was sliding a worn hand under the silk of her blouse when he heard a motor rev steadily, then purr and die. He leaned back from her.

'Patch?'

'Listen.'

He heard it again, a truck motor, the engine rumbling, a door slamming, down the beach and over to the west, deep in the grasslands, in a thick growth of oaks, from the southern end of Black Jack Point.

'Goddamn it,' he said.

'What is it?'

'Kids joyriding on my land.' He walked up the beach, smacked sand off the bottom of his feet, hopped, pulled on socks, yanked on his cowboy boots.

'Let them be. Let's count the stars.'

'They're trespassing,' he said. 'Digging ruts in my land.'

'Maybe they're looking for a makeout spot.'

'Not here. This is *our* spot.'

'Just call the police,' she said.

'Naw. I'm gonna go talk to them. You go on back to the house.'

7

'No.' She slipped on her flats. 'I'll go with you.'

'Might be snakes out there.'

'I'm not afraid.' She took his hand. 'I'll show you how to lecture kids.'

They walked up the beach, into the grasslands, into the darkness.

2

As Stoney Vaughn wiped the smear of blood and brains from his hands, a sick fluttering twist in his guts announced: *You just screwed up your life for ever, buddy.* It was an unusual feeling. Failure. Shock. The loss of control that flooded his heart. He glanced up at Jimmy Bird, loading the newly boxed coins into the dark hollow of the storage unit. Intent on his work, Jimmy wasn't looking at him, or at Alex either. Alex was watching along the corridor of storage units, a gun in his hand, making sure that no one saw them. The only light was from the truck's headlights.

Stoney wadded up the hand wipe Alex had thought-fully offered, threw it on the floor, reconsidered the wisdom of that act, and tucked the bloody wipe into his backpack. Against the hard heavy lump of stone he kept wrapped inside. He had to be careful now. He swallowed the dryness in his throat, kept the shudder out of his voice. 'Alex. This changes everything.'

Alex Black didn't even glance his way. 'Not really. I planned for this.'

'How, exactly, did you do that?'

'We lay low for a while. We can't buy the land right away, obviously.'

'Obviously.'

'So we wait a bit. One of those nieces will be wanting to sell soon, and then you can unfold the wallet and play your little get-famous game.' Alex stepped back inside the storage unit, unclipped a flashlight from his belt, played it over the boxes. 'Which one's got the Eye?'

'There. Small box on the top,' Jimmy Bird said.

Stoney forgot to breathe. He felt the heavy weight of

the emerald in his knapsack, feeling bigger than a fist, bigger than a heart. Oh, Jesus, Alex would kill him. Alex pried open the box, played the light over the big fake green chunk of rock Stoney had slipped into the emerald's place. He'd been so careful, going through the loot, finding the stone first, replacing it with the fake before the others even spotted the emerald. He waited, watched Alex glance over the stone.

Then Alex shut the box.

'Gentlemen,' he said, his head down, his round wire-rim glasses catching the glow from his flashlight, 'here's the plan. We double lock the doors. Stoney, you got the key to one lock, I got the key to the other. Alibis, those are your own problem. But none of us knows the others, none of us ever heard the others' names.' He glanced over at Jimmy. 'You come with me. We'll clean up your truck, get rid of the evidence.'

'The bodies—' Stoney started.

'Aren't going to be found for a long time,' Alex said. 'If ever.'

'I knew him. The cops'll come talk to me,' Jimmy Bird said. His voice was hoarse, trembling.

'Maybe not.'

'I don't want to sit around. I want my cut now.'

Alex stared at him.

'I'm just asking for what's fair,' Jimmy Bird said.

'Sure. I understand. But first, man, we got to get your truck cleaned up. We'll give you your cut tomorrow, help you redeem it for cash, get you out of the country.'

'Thanks. I just want what's fair.'

'Fine.'

After the three men stepped out of the storage unit, Alex slid down the door, fastened a lock onto one side. Stoney, his hands steadier than he thought possible, fastened the other. *Click. Click.* Locked.

'Now,' Alex said. 'Mr Bird. Mr Vaughn. I know you'll both behave. Now that you're accessories.' He turned the flashlight's beam up into his boyish face.

'Don't threaten me, Alex,' Stoney said. 'You don't have a dig without me. You wouldn't have any of this without me.'

'That's right, Stone Man,' Alex said. 'I also killed two people for you tonight. So maybe you owe me more than I owe you right now.'

Stoney kept his mouth shut.

'Let's go, Jimmy. Stoney, we'll talk in a week. Not before. Calm down. I just made all your wishes come true.' Alex smiled, slapped him hard on the shoulder. 'Go home, sleep tight, don't let the bedbugs bite.'

Stoney forced a smile. He watched Alex and Jimmy Bird climb into the winch truck. Stoney got into his Porsche. He followed the truck out of the storage lot; it turned right, heading south back to Port Leo. Stoney turned left, heading up toward Copano Flats and the comfortable sprawl of his bayside mansion. He jabbed at the radio and head banger rock – *Nirvana, great,* he thought, *the voice of a dead guy* – turned up too loud, blasted the car.

He kept one hand on the steering wheel, the other hand in the knapsack where he'd placed the emerald. It felt hot in his hand, which was crazy; buried in the ground for nearly two hundred years, it should be cool.

You just stole a couple million dollars from a homicidal maniac, he thought.

Stoney Vaughn made it a half mile down the road before he had to pull over and throw up.

3

Four o'clock Tuesday afternoon, court done, justice dispensed, and the Honorable Whit Mosley wanted nothing more than to swim twenty hard minutes with his girlfriend in the warm Gulf off Port Leo Beach, eat a big steak at the Shell Inn, cuddle with Lucy on the couch, watch the Astros raise his hopes again, make love at the end of the game, right there on the couch like they'd done night before last while the postgame show droned. Lucy liked baseball as much as he did. But now Lucy was standing in his office door, frowning, not looking in the mood for a steak or a swim or a ninth-inning delight.

'I think Uncle Patch is missing,' Lucy said.

Whit shrugged out of his judge's robe, let the black silk fall to the floor, glad to be just in his regular Hawaiian shirt and old khakis and Birkenstocks again. The air conditioner in the courtroom sputtered with signs of age, and this July in Port Leo had been blister-hot, everyone in traffic court cranky, and his robe smelled a little stale. He'd have to wash it tonight. Judicial laundry. Not listed in the job description.

'He's not down here at the jail,' Whit said. 'No senior citizen discount.'

'Don't joke, Whit,' Lucy said. 'He's not at his house. His car is there – he's not.'

'I thought he and Thuy went to Port A.'

'I called the B and B I booked for them and they checked out last night. Didn't even stay a few hours.'

'Maybe they went to another hotel.'

'But his car is *here*, Whit.'

'What about his fishing boat?'

12

'Still here. His doors were unlocked. And there's wine-glasses out on the table. Two of them, one with wine still in it.'

'So they came home and didn't clean up. Maybe he's just out with Thuy in her car.'

'I called Thuy's daughter. They haven't spoken to her today either, which is unusual. They said she calls them every day. Whit, really, I'm worried. They're old.'

'They sure don't need chaperons.'

'You're not listening,' Lucy said. 'I have a bad vibe about this.' She fingered the little amber crystal around her throat. 'Something has happened to them. Call your friends at the sheriff's department, or help me go look for them.'

'The police won't do much of anything for twenty-four hours,' he said, not thinking, and she burst into tears.

He had never seen Lucy cry before. He took her in his arms, let her rest her face against his shoulder. 'Okay, Lucy, okay. I'll call the sheriff's office, all right? And we'll start making phone calls. We'll find them. But when Patch finds out you've made all this fuss, you got to take the blame for it.'

She sniffled. 'I will. Okay, thanks, baby. My aura's feeling calmer already.'

'Sure, Lucy.' He didn't pay much heed to her talk of auras and vibes, but it was part and parcel of Lucy and part of loving her. He kissed her forehead, wiped away her tears with the ball of his thumb.

He dialed the Encina County sheriff's office, figuring that within an hour or so Patch and Thuy would be found out fishing along a stretch of Black Jack Point, and all would be good and fine.

It didn't happen.

The sheriff's office, once called, found a broken window

at the back of Patch Gilbert's house. Lucy noticed certain items missing: a silver candelabra, a cookie jar in which Patch kept ample cash, a jewelry box that was a family heirloom. The search began.

Patch Gilbert owned over two hundred acres on Black Jack Point, and on late Wednesday morning, the searchers found the turned earth along the edge of his property. The disturbed soil was a hundred yards up from the beach, a rectangle of torn loam hidden among the thick fingers of the oaks, broken grasses draped over the ground like a shroud.

The deputies and volunteers started digging and Whit made Lucy wait up at Patch's house.

'Wait here with me,' she said. 'Please.' She was shaking, her freckled arms folded over each other, her hair a mess from having dragged her fingers through it nervously.

'I can't, sweetie. I got to be down there.' He was justice of the peace, and because Encina County didn't have its own medical examiner, he also served as coroner. If there were bodies he'd order the autopsies, rule on cause of death, conduct the inquest if it was needed. His chest felt sucked dry at the thought of Patch and Thuy murdered and buried. But he didn't like the vacant, broken look in Lucy's eyes.

He put an arm around her and turned to Deputy David Power. 'Maybe I should wait with Lucy.'

David made a dismissive noise. 'You're supposed to be down there,' he said, as though comforting relatives of the dead was second-class duty compared to forensic investigation.

'You don't need me until you find bodies,' he said, and he felt Lucy's skin prickle under his fingertips.

'Sure, Judge, whatever.' David Power turned and headed down toward the thick copse of oaks.

Lucy watched him leave. 'Well, he's an asshole. Lots of negativity.'

'He doesn't like me,' Whit said. 'I'm friends with his ex-wife.'

'Maybe you should go down there,' she said. 'I'll be okay.'

'I'll stay here as long as I can.'

He and Lucy sat in Patch's den, a dark room covered with thick brown paneling in turn covered with fishing trophies and a fake muscled marlin. He held her hand and watched *All My Children* to avoid thinking about what the shovels might be unearthing.

Lucy stared at the screen. 'I cooked dinner for the two of them last week. Meatloaf. I burned it a little 'cause we got to talking and I was drinking too much beer. It tasted like a shingle. They didn't complain, ate it with a smile.'

Whit squeezed her hand.

'I should call Suzanne,' she said. Her cousin, her only family other than Patch.

'Let's just wait and see.'

They watched a commercial offering tarot card readings for a call-per-minute charge while an energetic woman with a doubtful Caribbean accent proclaimed the future to amazed callers.

'That approach is so misleading,' Lucy said. 'Look at her. She's hardly listening to that caller – she's just slapping those cards down.' Her voice was flat as she pretended the searchers weren't tearing up her uncle's land.

'I'm sure your psychics do a better job, sweetie.' Lucy owned the Coastal Psychics Network, which, as she put it, served the needy and the bored across Texas.

'At two bucks ninety-nine a minute, that is robbery.' She fingered the amber crystal on her necklace. 'I at least run a clean ship. Maybe I ought to advertise more. I'm cheaper than Madam Not-Reading-the-Cards-Right.'

He hugged her a little closer, gave her a tissue for her nose. 'Need to tell you something about Patch.'

'What?'

'He was the one suggested I call you for a date.'

She laughed but it was half tears. 'Did he now?'

'Called me up after you were in my court. Said I had given you too heavy a sentence for those unpaid tickets.'

'Not unpaid. Ignored on principle.' Same argument she'd used in court. A little more effective with him now. Patch had settled her five hundred dollars' worth of fines. She'd done her community service, Whit checking on her a little more than needed.

'He said I ought to even it out by taking you to dinner.'

'Old men playing matchmaker is a bad idea.' Lucy wiped at her eyes. 'Because they won the war they think they know everything.'

A deputy – young, sunburned, blond buzz cut bright with sweat – appeared in the doorway. 'Judge Mosley? Could I speak with you?' His mouth barely moved as he spoke.

'Are they dead?' Lucy asked. 'Is it them?'

'Yes, ma'am. It looks like it's them. I'm real sorry.'

Lucy put her face in her palms. 'Well, shit. It *was* a bad vibe,' she finally said from between her hands.

4

Claudia Salazar let the sun warm her closed eyes. She had dozed on the pool lounge chair, the water evaporating off her skin, thinking, *I could get to like this*.

Claudia's past few days had been a bitch: finally closing out a series of burglaries on Port Leo's south side, aimed squarely at the tourist condos, by arresting a repeat offender who sadly had three kids and was bound back to jail; covering two extra late shifts for a patrol officer friend who was down with a bad summer cold, because the whole Port Leo police department was short-handed; and then the terrible Gilbert/Tran murders, which were beyond Port Leo's jurisdiction but the sheriff's office and the police department helped each other with high-profile cases. David Power, her ex-husband, had politely declined the police department's help and her thought had been: *Pride goeth before a fall*. It was the most biblical thing she had thought in years. She wondered, without ego, if he was too irritated with her to want the department's help.

She decided not to care. As of today, she was officially on vacation.

She opened her eyes, sat up on the lounge chair, watched Ben standing by a table between the pool and the French doors, fiddling with a stubborn cork on a wine bottle.

'What a rotten guest I am,' she said. 'I fell asleep.'

Ben Vaughn pried the cork out and grinned. 'You're exhausted. Don't worry about it.'

She smiled. If she'd gone swimming with David, drunk wine in the early afternoon, then dozed, he would have used it as a basis for analysis: *Did I bore you? What's wrong with me?* Ben just let her be, and she was grateful for that.

Claudia stood, feeling self-conscious in a new purple bikini a bit too adventurous for her, pulled a long T-shirt over her head, and smoothed it out along her hips. 'No more wine. Two glasses is my limit.'

'You're on vacation,' Ben said. 'I made lunch. Hope that's okay.'

'I'll find it in my heart to forgive you. So what can I do to help?'

'Just sit. You're my guest.' Ben disappeared back into the house.

The deck for the pool ran along the edge of St Leo Bay, and in the summer heat the bay water looked green as old glass, the waves like white lips rising to the surface for a kiss, then vanishing. She put on her sunglasses. Vacation. Well, a few days off and then back to the grind. But sitting on a multilevel deck, with a private dock, backed by the house that had to be approaching seven thousand square feet . . . well, it was better than eating takeout and watching old movies on video, which was how she'd spent her last vacation.

Ben returned, carrying a tray. Two huge shrimp salads, the shrimp firm and pink, perfect crescent-morsels, slices of avocado, a small crystal pitcher filled with a home-made dressing, rolls steaming. He set the lunch down in front of her.

'Where's the chocolate?'

'Ingrate.' He poured them each wine again, held his glass aloft in a toast. 'To a great vacation for you. And to old friends.'

'To old friends,' she said, clinking her glass against his. *Friends. Funny word,* she thought. *It could cover too much ground.* They'd been lovers long ago but she

18

couldn't look at him and think *ex-lover*. He was too different now from the shy, gangly boy she'd known.

'And we didn't even have to catch the shrimp,' Ben said.

'Sometimes I'm relieved by that. Other times I think it's a shame. My dad's the last Salazar who's still shrimping.' The smile dimmed slightly on Ben's face and she set down her fork. 'I'm sorry. I didn't mean to bring up an unpleasant memory . . .'

Ben smiled again. She liked his smile, warm and happy, with a front tooth slightly crooked. 'It's okay. My folks have been gone a long time, Claudia. I miss them but you keep going on.' His parents had been lost in a sudden storm on the bay's edge, their shrimp boat swamped. Ben had been sixteen at the time, his brother, Stoney, just starting college. 'I might have made a good shrimper.'

'You would have gotten bored.'

'But you're your own boss.' Ben took a small sip of white wine. 'Out on the water, out in the sun. Now Stoney, he would have sucked at shrimping.'

Claudia glanced around the deck, the private dock, the too-big-for-her-taste house. 'It wouldn't have paid the mortgage on this place.' She liked the pool, the lunch, being with Ben, but felt an awkward consciousness of being in his brother's house, as though she were trespassing. She had kept glancing at Ben, trim in his modest swimsuit, with his nice hands and his smile, and wanting to kiss him, but she wouldn't. Not here. If she kissed him she might not stop and his brother might walk in at any moment. 'What exactly does your brother do? You said investments?'

'I can never quite figure it out. He did venture capital work out in California for a while, got a little singed in the dot-com meltdown, decided he wanted to come home. He does a lot of consulting for financial services firms in Dallas and Houston. He's trying to get me into his business.' He shook his head. 'Stoney used to steal my allowance, set up a lemonade stand with our money, give me a cut. We'd make more than our allowances put together. I think he's still following that business model.'

'It seems to be working.'

'He has expensive hobbies. Cars. Boats. Treasure hunts.'

'Treasure hunts?'

'He's financed some treasure dives in the Florida Keys – you know, galleons that wrecked in shallow water, got buried by the sands on the bottom. Takes a team to recover them. It's his obsession. Crazy-ass way to risk your money. You got to make the big bucks to play that game.' His tone went wry.

'And you're not interested in the big bucks?'

Ben grinned again. 'Me in finance? I'd be doomed. The clients would be doomed.' He shook his head. 'I like teaching, but the pay sucks, and too many of the kids are unmotivated and the parents care even less. I'm starting to think you seriously got to have a call to teach, like being a priest.'

'Or a cop,' she said.

'Or a cop,' he agreed. 'You ever think of giving it up?'

'Last year, briefly. But no, not seriously.'

'Living here with my brother – well, Stoney's spoiled me.' Ben speared the last fat shrimp in his salad, pushed it through the little pool of dressing in his bowl. 'But I don't have a talent for making money.'

'Money's not everything.'

'It can sure buy a whole lot of it.'

'Still.'

'You're right. And God knows Stoney's not what you'd call happy. He's nervous. Jumpy. I don't want to think what he was like when he worked in a high-stress job.'

'Let's talk about something other than your brother,' Claudia said. The three glasses of wine and lazing in the summer sun made her suddenly feel a little playful. 'That was a delicious lunch. Thank you. I didn't know you could cook.'

'I knew you'd had a hard week,' Ben said. 'Least I could do. Citizens should support their officers in blue every way they can.'

A tease colored his tone and she skimmed her toetips along the muscle of his calf, just to flirt back a little. She stopped as the French doors opened. A man came out, tall and brown haired like Ben, but a little thicker in the shoulders and the stomach, dressed in a summer khaki business suit, but no tie, the shirt buttoned to the throat. His hair was gelled, combed to Ken-doll perfection, and he didn't smile until Ben turned toward him.

'Hi, bro,' Ben said. 'Come on out.'

'Don't want to interrupt,' the man said.

'It's your house,' Ben said. 'You can't interrupt. Claudia, this is my brother, Stoney. Stoney, Claudia Salazar.'

Stoney Vaughn offered Claudia a hand with nails manicured as smooth as pearl. His grip was firm but the flesh of his palm was soft. 'Claudia. I remember you from school. I was a few years ahead of you. Nice to see you again.' His gaze went quickly down her, to her breasts, her hips, back to her face, quicker than a blink but she saw it and was glad she had on the T-shirt.

'Hello,' she said. 'You have a lovely home.'

'It's comfortable.'

His modesty was so false she almost laughed. Instead she said, 'Will you join us?'

'I can't today. I've got to do some work up in my office. But you two enjoy yourselves.'

'Claudia's taking some time off from work,' Ben said. 'She's an investigator with the Port Leo police.'

Two beats of silence. 'Really. That must be fascinating work,' Stoney said.

'If you find burglaries riveting.'

'Claudia likes to fish,' Ben said. 'Maybe tomorrow morning we could take the *Jupiter* out into the Gulf, have some fun. Why don't you take the day off, come along? Bring one of your girlfriends. Who's on the A list this week?'

'None of them. I'm in the doghouse. I've been too busy to call. Work's just been a bitch lately. Y'all go, though.'

'No, do come,' Claudia said.

'Yeah,' Ben agreed.

'Sure,' Stoney said. 'That sounds great. Claudia, lovely to meet you. Enjoy the pool. Have fun.'

They shook hands and Claudia watched him hurry back in. She had the oddest feeling he wished her and Ben gone, out of his sight, out of his house.

5

Whit grabbed his forensics kit and followed the young deputy down past the manicured lawn, through the thick growths of wildflowers and the high grass. Ahead was the wide bowl of St Leo Bay; Black Jack Point occupied the northernmost stretch of the bay's reach, with Port Leo south and at the middle of the curve. The bay breeze shuffled the hot, sticky air, and on the wind Whit heard the murmuring voices of the deputies, of the Department of Public Safety crime scene crew. For a moment, the crowd out of sight, the voices sounded ghostly, even in the eye-aching sunlight. He remembered being here as a boy, Patch telling the local kids he let fish and swim off his little dock, *You know, Black Jack Point's haunted by old Black Jack himself, and by pirates and Indians and settlers that got scalped, got their throats cut. Be sure nothin' don't grab your foot while you're swimmin'. It won't let go. They like a young soul best. Taste goooood.* And the safe thrill of being scared and being fairly sure that Patch was joking. Mostly sure.

They hadn't moved the bodies. The hole was deep, nearly six feet, the soil threaded with torn grass. He knelt at its edge while the DPS crime scene tech snapped off photos. The group was silent now, the buzz of the mosquitoes the loudest sound.

Patch Gilbert lay on his back, arms spread, dirt still covering most of him, his mouth open wide and loam pooling between broken teeth. His face was ruined, beaten into pulp, a plane of graying hair askew on his scalp, little broken tiles of bone peeking through his forehead. Thuy Linh Tran lay atop one of Patch's arms,

23

as though he cradled her in a comforting hug. Dirt was scattered on her bloodshot irises. A bullet hole marred her forehead.

Whit slipped plastic bags over his shoes, carefully stepped down into the grave, touched Patch's throat, then Thuy's. He wrote down the time on his death scene form. For the record. Suddenly the promise of tears burned at the back of his eyes and he wanted to cry for this funny, good old man and this generous woman, but he didn't want to lose it. Not in front of this crowd. He felt David's stare against his back.

Whit stepped back out of the grave. He began his work of detailing the scene for the inquest report and the autopsy orders, keeping his eyes on the papers. It was easier that way.

David knelt down by Whit. 'I think the man got hit with a shovel. Hard. Repeatedly. Probably even after he was dead. Wonder why the killer shot her, though. Maybe broke the shovel on him, couldn't use it on her.'

'Patch would have fought hard,' Whit said.

'He's an old man,' David said.

With about ten times the heart and guts you'll ever have, Whit thought.

'Makes me think of a case I read,' David said. 'Up in Oklahoma, '65 or '66, old couple got killed while out walking, buried right off a hiking trail . . .'

Whit tuned him out. David loved to recite old police cases from true crime collections as though they held all the beauty of love sonnets. All the details and none of the context. Whit bit his lip. When David paused for breath, Whit asked one of the techs to take extra photos of their faces, of their wounds. The techs did, and measured the depth of the bodies, carefully clearing more dirt back from the corpses when one of them gave a little cry of shock.

'What is that?' The tech stepped back from where Thuy's feet still lay partly buried and Whit saw two curves of brownish skull exposed.

'Look here,' another tech said, clearing away dirt next to Patch's knee. A crooked brown bone of finger, bent as if to beckon. 'Old bone. Real old.'

'Don't touch it,' Whit said. 'Stop the digging.'

'Why?' David asked.

'There's other remains buried with them. I got to call the guy in San Marcos. This closes down everything.'

'We're not stopping. This is a serious crime scene—' David began.

'They talked about site analysis in JP training. You have to stop the dig.'

David took a breath of infinite patience. 'What guy in San Marcos?'

'Forensic anthropologist. I don't remember his name. But he's got to check out the site. They must've gotten buried in old unmarked graves.' Whit wiped the sweat from his brow. 'You can't move 'em until the FA's here with his team.'

'Judge Mosley's right, David,' one of the DPS techs said quietly. 'He's talking about Dr Parker. He can be here in forty minutes. DPS sticks him on a chopper and rushes him down here.'

'Fine,' David said. His lips went thin as wire. 'Get this guy here, then, quick.' He turned away from Whit to confer with the DPS team.

Whit took out the notepad he used at death scenes, jotted down descriptions of the bodies, talked in a low voice with the DPS photographer while she snapped footage, told her what angles would help him at inquest. He tried not to look at Patch and Thuy's broken faces.

Instead, he kept glancing at the old, worn bones.

*

The forensic anthropologist – a banty rooster of a man named Parker, a fortyish fellow with a shaved bald head and sporting a Yankees cap – arrived by DPS chopper within an hour, accompanied by a team of graduate students armed with dental picks, brushes, trowels, string and stakes.

Whit left them to their work, spoke words of comfort to Lucy and her cousin Suzanne and the Tran family, all waiting up at Patch's house. He came back down as the afternoon began to melt into night. The Port Leo fire department set up lights so the work could continue. Parker and David talked a lot, David losing patience and getting it back. The team sifted dirt from the site, carefully, and found more bone fragments, little pebbles of teeth. When Parker got up from his digging to gulp a cup of water, Whit cornered him at the jug on the back of a DPS truck.

'So what is this looking like, Dr Parker?'

'Off the record, Judge?'

'Yeah.'

'Because I don't like to commit before all the data's gathered.'

'So don't commit.'

'We haven't removed bones yet but there's at least two skeletons in there, more likely three. They're badly disarticulated – they're not laid out as if they were buried and then not disturbed again.'

'Why would the new bodies be on top of them?'

'I think these old bones were dug up, dumped back in the dirt, and your murder victims dumped on top of them. The whole site's a jumble. I mean, bones that look that old, you expect it. Ground settles over time, bodies sink. But these seem, well, shuffled.'

'Anything other than the bones?'

'Latches. Nails. Locks. A few slivers of wood.'

'Locks?'

'Locks.'

That was freaky, Whit thought. Why would you put a lock on a coffin? 'You said wood. From a casket?'

'Possibly.'

'Wouldn't a casket have kept the bones better organized?'

'Apparently not these.' Parker finished his water. 'Don't think they were buried in caskets. Coffins would have mostly rotted away by now, anyway.'

'These bones . . . how old are they?'

'The wetter the soil, the browner the bones get over time. These are pretty brown. We'll assemble the skeletons as much as we can tonight and tomorrow. We'll probably remove the bones in the next few hours, once we've cleaned away the dirt, gotten samples, sifted, photographed and mapped the site. If we can identify the make of the nails and latches, that can help us date the bones.'

'The family of the murder victims are friends of mine,' Whit said. 'We'd like to get Mr Gilbert's and Mrs Tran's bodies out of there as soon as possible.'

'We'll hurry,' Parker said, a softening in his tone for the first time. 'You'll need to transfer the old bones to my custody for examination, Judge.' Whit nodded and Parker headed back to the dig, flush with light from the fire trucks.

The diggers worked tenderly, quietly around Patch and Thuy, as though the couple slept and the techs were gentle spirits, come to grant them sweet dreams. Finally they were done. The bodies were lifted out slowly, placed on clean sheets. Whit filled out an authorization for autopsy, had David countersign it. He watched the bodies taken away by the mortuary service for autopsy in nearby Nueces County. The service people carried the bodies carefully on their stretchers. The forensic anthropologists continued their work around the old bones, industrious and steady as ants.

By midnight, Wednesday fading into Thursday, the FA team had put an astonishing assortment of bones – including three human skulls, brown as walnuts – into paper bags. Whit signed over the bones to Parker and the FA team headed to Corpus Christi to sleep and finish their work. Lucy slept upstairs. Whit had showered and lain with her until she dozed off, then come down to Patch Gilbert's empty den at two a.m., unable to sleep. He watched an old *Perry Mason* rerun. Perry's was a perfect world for you, one where justice ticked along sure as clockwork.

Whit let the TV mumble along and sat in front of the bay window. He cracked open the window so he could hear the murmur of St Leo Bay. The night was dark, the moon shy behind clouds, the fireflies glowing and vanishing like candlewick embers, just snuffed out between wet finger and thumb. The fire truck lights still blazed over the now-canopied site, an officer standing watch.

The old house was full of the old man, his laughter, his teasing. On a side table there was a bottle of Glenfiddich that Whit had seen Patch open only last week. He found two shot glasses and picked up the bottle. He poured the shots of fine Scotch, one for him, one for Patch.

He didn't touch either drink for a long moment, then downed both. The Scotch burned his throat a little, made his eyes water. Closest to tears he would get.

Patch. Thuy. Promise you. Whoever did this won't walk.

He went to bed, curling next to Lucy, shielding her from the night.

6

'Patch Gilbert wanted a hundred thousand dollars. Raised real quietly,' Gooch said. 'You know how I feel about publicity. I'm not talking to the police, but I'll tell you about the deal.'

Gooch opened a Shiner Bock. He and Whit watched the noontime sun play along the ripples in the Golden Gulf Marina. The summer live-aboards were gearing up for lunch, the inescapable Jimmy Buffett tunes drifting across the waters, lunchtime beers popping open, hung-over throats clearing and gearing up for another half day of lazy life.

'Am I supposed to be grateful?' Whit pulled a soda from the cooler. 'Goddamn it, Gooch, don't you do this to me.' Thursday morning court had been full – traffic and small claims – but Whit was distracted, bug-eyed from lack of sleep and anxious to hear back from Parker on the bones and the Nueces County ME's office on the autopsies.

'I don't know that I was the first or only person Patch approached.' Gooch leaned back in the lounge chair, took off his T-shirt in the bright sun, closed his eyes. His chest was big and broad, dark with tan but white where the scars lay. One, small and blossom-shaped, looked like a bullet wound, another like a healed slash across his abdomen, another like a long-ago stab in his shoulder. He never talked about the scars.

'Why would he ask you for a hundred thousand bucks?'

Gooch opened one eye to stare at Whit.

It was strange to have your closest friend stay an

enigma. Gooch could stare down hired killers, practice the intricacies of hand-to-hand combat, and make troublesome people disappear into federal custody. He was a fishing guide, captain of a premier boat named *Don't Ask,* and yet something far more. He was one of the ugliest men Whit had ever seen, with a face a mother might reluctantly love, but he had charisma that drew certain people like moths to a flame. Gooch had saved Whit's life several months ago, disposing of drug dealers with all the ease of a priest dealing with tardy schoolgirls. And Gooch had made it clear that explanations as to the *how* would not be forthcoming. Whit had sensed that Gooch waited then, to see if the friendship would survive, if Whit would respect his obsessive need for privacy. Whit was glad to be alive and pretended like nothing had happened.

'People consider me resourceful and discreet,' Gooch said.

'Ah,' Whit said. A heavy sailboat crawled into the marina; on it, three women in bikinis turned their faces and flat bellies toward the warm sun. Whit watched them lean against the rails in glorious idleness.

'So what level of detail you want?' Gooch asked.

'Go deep.'

'Fine. Patch was a steady client of mine. Took him and some of his old army friends fishing. He knows I know a lot of people. People with money. So he asked me if I knew of folks who might be interested in a very quiet, private investment. People who could part with a hundred thou and not blink.'

'Patch could have sold some of his land if he needed money.'

'Apparently not an option he considered,' Gooch said. 'I told him I would need to know more. He said he'd tell me more if I got an investor or two willing to talk to him.

I told him I couldn't waste the time of wealthy people, that I had to consider these folks were my clients and if this was some half-assed scheme it was going to make me look bad. Shit, maybe he was selling life-size Chia pets, you know?'

'He gave you no indication why he needed this money?'

'Just asked me to line up some multimillionaires. Which, frankly, represents a very narrow slice of my client pie.'

'And you think he approached other people?'

'He struck me as being in a hurry. I asked why he couldn't go to a bank; he said he wanted it quiet. But fast. I believe the term he used was "hot and big enough to blow this town off the map".'

'So he wanted no attention now, but whatever he was working on would create a great deal of attention later.'

Gooch sipped beer. 'So there's your anonymous tip. Was it good for you?'

'Maybe he was blowing smoke, Gooch. Maybe he owed someone a big chunk of money. Someone decided to collect.'

'Possibility,' Gooch said. 'You knew him better than I did. Was he a gambler?'

'No. He was always just the nice guy who'd let you swim and fish off his land. I've never heard of him having debt problems.'

'Blackmail?'

'Patch? He bragged about taking Viagra. He was incapable of being embarrassed.'

'An old man bragging about medicated hard-ons is one thing,' Gooch said. 'Maybe he had a deep dark secret that had finally grabbed him by the throat. Or someone close to him was in trouble and needed the money.'

'Not Lucy.'

Gooch clicked tongue against teeth, cleared his throat, watched a little red sailboat putter out into the bay.

'Don't start dumping on Lucy again,' Whit said.

'Lucy is lovely. Charming in a giddy, goofy sort of way. Impeccable ass.'

'But.'

'I'm not sure she can read a book, much less a mind on the other end of a phone.'

'Why can't you like my girlfriend?'

'I don't want to see you conned.'

'She's not a con artist.'

'Yes, telephone psychics are known for their high ethical standards.'

'You haven't really gotten to know her.'

'That's true. If you're happy, I'm happy. Fucking deliriously happy.'

Whit stood. 'I've got to get back to the courthouse. I'll let David know what you said.'

'But you'll keep my name out of it?'

'Yes. I'll try.'

'Patch wasn't a quitter,' Gooch said. 'I'd look hard to see if he found that money someplace else.'

'Found his wallet and her purse.' David sat in the one straight-back chair in Whit's small office. It was shortly after one o'clock on Thursday afternoon. 'Dumped in beneath the bodies. Cash and credit cards gone.'

'So this was a robbery gone wrong?'

'Burglary, Judge,' David said. 'You know the difference.'

Maybe it was a robbery turned burglary, or the other way around, but Whit decided to be rock-solid polite. Act like a judge for once. Let David be acid; acid was just asshole with a different final syllable. 'A burglary, then?'

'Yeah. Tran and Gilbert cut short their stay in Port A,

head home two days earlier than expected, catch a perp breaking into the house. Perp kills them both, buries them on a remote stretch of the Point where they're not likely to be found for a while.'

'The killer laid Patch's head open. There's no sign of that attack having taken place in the house,' Whit said.

'Then it didn't. Maybe they took the old folks from the house, hauled them down into the oaks, killed them there.'

'They. Sounds like more than one person. And for all this effort they got a little cash and silver? They don't bother with the electronics?'

'Look, Your Honor. You spend a little more time in this business, you'll see things usually aren't too complicated. Criminals are dumb as stumps. If they were smart they could go be investment bankers. Or judges.' A hint of amusement surfaced in his tone. 'Killer or killers got surprised, they kill the old folks, they take off.'

'Why bury the bodies? Why not just dump them in the bay?'

'They'd float up faster.'

'It's quicker to tie weights to someone's feet than to dig down deep enough to hit old graves,' Whit said. He started to mention the anonymous tip from Gooch, but David raised a hand.

'Listen, Judge. You pretty sure you gonna rule these deaths as homicides?'

'Of course, yes.'

'Then that's all you need to worry about, Your Honor. Anything beyond that, you're stepping on my toes. And my toes, they're real tender. They get hurt real easy. And my feet hurt, I'm in a bad mood. We're clear?'

'Yes,' Whit said. 'I'm going in to Corpus, to meet with the ME and with Parker and his people around four. They have to sign custody of the old bones back to me.

33

You want to go?' He'd mention the tip then, let David squirm the whole thirty miles into Corpus. Better than listening to talk radio.

'Sure. That's fine. I got a suspect to go question this afternoon.'

'You do? Who?'

'Pick me up around three. We'll head into Corpus.' David winked, put on his Stetson, stepped out of Whit's office, said a hearty hey to Edith Gregory, Whit's secretary, then headed out down the courthouse hallway with a strut. 'I'll tell you about my suspect then if the mood hits me.'

'Oh, you're gonna be in the mood,' said Whit.

Alex Black closed the door to his room at the Sandspot Motel and flicked on the light. With its freeze-your-ass air conditioner and an ongoing next-door groan-a-thon from a couple he dubbed the Honeymooners, this temporary home held few charms. He wanted to leave. He wanted to go to the storage unit and run his hands over the coins, feel the heft of the Devil's Eye, say a silent *fuck you* to every archaeologist and bureaucrat who had ever crossed his path. Instead he sat down and called his father on his cell phone.

'Bert Exton's room, please.' He waited for the hospice receptionist to connect him, endured bad muzak for a few moments.

'H'lo?' Tired, weak-sounding.

'Dad. How's today been?' Alex said.

'Only about a three. Yesterday was a nine. Felt great. You shoulda called yesterday.'

'Well, soon as I finish up this dig, Dad, I'm coming to Miami. See you for a spell.' *And get your poor ass out of that death trap, and we'll go to Costa Rica. Let you die peaceful under a beautiful sky. Maybe near some ruins, just for old times' sake,* Alex thought. 'How's that sound?'

'That'd be great.' Weak cough. 'You liking Michigan?'

'Sure.' What Dad didn't know couldn't hurt him. Dad thought he was on an Ojibwa artifacts dig. 'Good place to spend the summer.'

'Bureaucrats giving you hell?' A little rally in Bert's voice.

'No, sir. No one's giving me hell.'

'That's good. Proud of you, boy.'

What Dad didn't know. 'So tomorrow's gonna be, what, at least a six? You keeping a good attitude?'

'Screw optimism. Yeah. We'll aim for a six. You get here, maybe you sneak me in a six-pack, okay?'

'Sure, Dad.' He'd sneak in freaking Moët for the old guy. Alex said his good-byes, hung up. He had buyers lined up for the coins – dealing strictly in cash, no questions asked. And he could find a buyer – probably a Colombian trader – for the Devil's Eye, but a big emerald like that he'd have to move carefully. Even getting it appraised would draw unwanted attention. He could be in Miami in a week, any loose ends wrapped up.

Stoney was the one remaining problem.

He lay back down on the bed and began to imagine various deaths for Stoney Vaughn. Quick ones. You didn't want to spend any extra time with Stoney if you could help it.

7

In the clear sunshine of the Gulf of Mexico, the blood and gore painted sparkles across the green waves. Filmy scales glistened like jewel dust. Torn shrimp pinwheeled down from the surface, pink and brown and white, a kaleidoscope of flesh. Slivers of fish guts bobbed, the light shifting their colors from red to green to gray as they sank beneath the water.

'Beautiful,' Claudia said.

'Gross,' Ben Vaughn said. 'But I mean that in a real manly way.'

Thursday morning Claudia stood at the open back of *Jupiter*, a forty-eight-foot luxury craft, fishing rod in hand. She usually preferred fishing on the open deck of a boat, but *Jupiter* offered the cool shade of the cabin, a cushioned wicker chair, a glass of grapefruit juice at her elbow. She watched a heavy Gulf shrimper chug away from them, its wake now colored with the pool of chum Ben had poured overboard.

Ben hoisted himself up the ladder from the swim platform. He washed his hands of brownish film at the sink. 'You ready to fish the buffet?'

Claudia smiled. 'Am I ever.'

'Sort of glad my brother didn't tag along.' Ben sat down next to her, relaxed, grinning. 'I'm not sure what a third wheel is on a boat.'

'Sweet of him to let us use the boat.'

'Stoney's too busy to play with his toys. I'm glad I'm not. Summer vacation.' Ben leaned over and kissed her, easy. 'That's for luck.'

She cast her line into the spreading heart of gore,

nailing its center. He cast after her, his line hitting the edges of the chum smear.

'You don't need any coaching.'

'I just need someone to vouch for my unbelievable fish stories if I end up not catching a thing,' she said.

'We each caught a whale, right?' Ben sipped at his soda.

Claudia watched sleek figures dart and turn beneath the bloody cloud. Within seconds a thick-bodied yellowfin hit her line. She jerked once, setting the hook, and then let the monofilament line spin out as the yellowfin raced away, revving along for a hundred and fifty feet. The tug and play went on for ten minutes, and soon the strength at the other end of the line faded. Claudia reeled her prize in and carefully held the bullet-shaped yellowfin aloft for inspection.

'A real beauty. You're gonna outfish me, aren't you?'

'The day is young.' Claudia eased the heavy yellowfin into the customized live well in the salon's corner and cast her line out again.

But her luck didn't hold. Her next cast caught a fight-filled bonito that tired after ten minutes. As Claudia reeled the bonito toward the boat a dark shape flashed beneath the faded slick of chum and her line went slack.

Ben pointed into the murk. 'Shark. Grabbed your fish for lunch.'

Claudia watched a ten-foot silky rocket underneath the boat. Sharks. An odd tickle touched the base of her spine. 'I hope he enjoys the lunch I caught him.'

'Let's find less crowded waters.' Ben went up to the flying bridge and steered *Jupiter* away from the shrimpers' wakes, moving far out past a weather buoy marking seventy-five miles from the Texas coast. They spent the next hour or so hooking king mackerel and ling.

Ben pulled up a big ling, inspected it, let it go. The fish

hit the water and dove down into the hard blue dark. 'Best catches I've had lately. That kiss worked.'

'All mine do,' she said. 'So I got a question. Why'd you call me, Ben, after all these years?'

He cast his line again, let it settle. 'You aren't with David anymore.'

'It's funny. Now I actually never feel I was with him.'

'You didn't love him?'

'I did. But not the way you're supposed to.'

'There's a recipe?'

'There's a minimum requirement. He and I were comfortable together. But comfort wasn't quite enough.'

'Did you ever think of me when you were married?'

'Yes,' she said. 'A few times. But if you had shown up on my doorstep all you would have gotten was a friendly hug and a cup of coffee. I took my marriage seriously, Ben.'

'I'm sure you did.' Ben took her hand. 'I never told you this, but you were my first, Claudia.' He grinned. 'I had to get you out in the middle of the Gulf to confess that. No danger of anyone overhearing.'

'I suspected as much, if I remember.'

'Couldn't admit it to you. The guy can never be the virgin.'

She squeezed his hand. 'Well, I forgive you, Ben.'

He leaned over, kissed her, soft and gentle but not tentative. Not the lips of the boy she had kissed at seventeen, not the boy she had given her own virginity to, but a man surer and wiser with his touch. He broke the kiss first, kissed her closed eyelids.

'Now I'm really glad Stoney didn't come. Plus his girlfriends are all idiots.'

She wondered what it would be like to make love on the deck of the boat, out here in the middle of nowhere, the sun their only blanket.

'I'll fix us sandwiches, open a nice wine,' he said.

'You made lunch yesterday. I'll do it.'

'Naw. You're my guest. Just relax. I'll be back in a sec.'

Claudia nestled deeper in the lounge chair, letting the breeze of the Gulf hum over her. Really happy to be with Ben. And, she thought with a degree of rationality about love she rarely allowed, Ben Vaughn was a known quantity. The kind of guy her family would embrace even though they had adored David. Her mother, who considered being over twenty-five and single a sign of social leprosy, would surgically attach Claudia to Ben to bolster the chances of marriage.

But do you like Ben or just the idea of Ben? Are you just lonely and he's familiar, someone you know won't hurt you?

Ben brought homemade chicken salad sandwiches on thick sourdough bread, potato chips, and sliced fruit.

'You slaved over this,' she said.

'Yeah, opening containers. Stoney's housekeeper stocks the boat when we take it out. I was thinking maybe we could cruise over into Port Aransas later, eat at the Tarpon Inn if you like.' But Ben didn't give her a chance to answer the invitation, his gaze going past her, his eyes crinkling.

'That boat's in trouble,' he said.

Along the wave-broken cobalt of the waters Claudia spotted a Bertram sportfisher in the distance, a single man at the bow, waving a red blanket like a flag.

'Dumb ass,' Ben said. 'Seventy-five miles out and he doesn't bother with enough fuel.'

'Maybe that's not the problem.' Claudia waved back at the man. He was now hoisting a baseball cap, bright red.

'We'll see.' Ben hurried up to the flying bridge, tried to call the boat on standard Channel 16. No response. Ben

39

whipped the wheel about hard and closed the distance between *Jupiter* and the drifting boat. Claudia stood on the deck in front of the bridge as Ben steered toward the Bertram.

Within minutes they pulled close to the sportfisher; its name, *Miss Catherine*, was written in faded blue script on its stern, with *New Orleans LA* beneath in smaller letters. Claudia moved up to the bow, smoothing her wind-whipped hair.

The man standing at the bow of *Miss Catherine* was in his forties, a little heavy and rosy-cheeked, his skin tanned. He wore dark sunglasses and a baggy white T-shirt with a Tampa Bay Buccaneers logo on the front and faded orange shorts. He gave Claudia a sun-squinted smile full of straight teeth.

'Hello the boat,' Claudia called. 'You in trouble?'

'My alternator's busted. Lost power for the engines and the radio.'

'You're a ways from New Orleans,' Ben called.

'Oh, that's old. I live in Copano now,' the man said. 'This is what I get for hauling around my mother. She's down in the galley bitching a blue streak at me.' He shrugged, tossed the red blanket down. 'I'm Danny.'

'I suppose you need a tow?' Ben sounded polite but unenthusiastic. Copano was ten miles up coast from Port Leo and Claudia knew giving a tow would mean no candlelit dinner in Port Aransas.

'We'd be happy to take you in,' Claudia said.

'If I could just borrow your radio, I can summon my tow service.' Danny gave Claudia another apologetic smile. 'And maybe my mom can borrow your head.'

Ben came down from the flying bridge, squeezed along the narrowness between the rail and the cabin on the deck. 'Sure, not a problem.' He tossed one end of a docking rope to Danny. 'I'm Ben. This is Claudia.'

'Thank you so much. Y'all are lifesavers. You've got a beautiful boat.'

'Thanks,' Ben said. 'You fish today?'

'Some ling.' Danny shrugged toward the empty reel mount on his boat. 'Sharks nabbed the tuna I got.'

'Yeah, they'll rob you,' Claudia said.

Danny gave her an agreeing grin. He slid bumpers over the edge of his boat, finished fastening the rope tethering *Jupiter* to *Miss Catherine*, vaulted lightly over both railings, and pulled a Sig Sauer pistol from under his T-shirt, from the band of his baggy shorts.

The smile stayed in place, the gun aimed at Ben. 'Sharks sure do rob, don't they? Just be calm, and no one gets hurt.'

Ben paled under his sunburn and took two steps back. 'For God's sake, man, you want cash? I've got maybe a hundred in my wallet . . .'

'What I want,' Danny said, 'is for you to be cool and *hush*.' He blasted a sharp, two-fingered whistle and two men bolted out onto the deck of *Miss Catherine*, guns in hand, beading them on Claudia and Ben. Nylon stockings stretched over their faces, contorting their features into doughy lumps.

'Jesus,' Ben said.

'Let's just put those guns down,' Claudia said, stern.

Danny stared at her. 'Don't we have big balls for a—' he began and Ben charged. Ben barreled into Danny and the Sig barked, splinters erupting from *Jupiter*'s deck as the two men slammed into the railing.

The two other men from *Miss Catherine* jumped aboard *Jupiter*. Claudia swung at the first one, a thin rail of a guy, surprising him, her fist connecting with his cheek, knocking him down. But the other attacker, built big and brawny, hammered her on the jaw. She hit the deck, landing on her side, and the barrel of an automatic pistol gouged into her temple.

41

'Cool it,' the thin one – with what appeared to be electric-red hair underneath his nylon mask – screamed. 'Stay the fuck still or we see if your brains match your pretty little outfit.'

Ben was down, too, a gun pressed to the back of his head, eyes wide with shock.

Don't tell them I'm a cop, she mouthed, unsure if he could read her lips.

Ben barely nodded, the big bruiser frisking him with all the gentleness of a wrestler.

'I got some cash, just take it. Okay?' Ben's voice steadied. 'No need to get rough, okay? No need for trouble.'

Danny came and knelt by Claudia. 'You okay, miss?' In a gentle tone, like he cared.

'Yeah,' Claudia said.

The thin kid said, 'Love boat's over, babe.'

Danny leaned over Ben. 'Now where's our buddy Stoney?'

'What?' Ben said. 'He's at home.'

Danny stared down at him. He glanced at the bigger of the two thugs. 'Gar, go below. Find Stoney. Don't kill him.'

'He's not aboard. He canceled coming with us,' Claudia said.

The skinny redhead jabbed his gun barrel into the small of her neck. 'Don't contribute to class discussion unless you're called upon, sweetness.'

'Stoney's not here,' Ben said. 'We're not lying to you.'

Danny didn't look at him. They waited. Gar – the big guy – returned. 'No one else is aboard, man.'

'Well,' said Danny. 'Then I guess I better come up with a new plan, shouldn't I?' He leaned down close to Ben and Claudia. 'Let's start with your names, kids. Just who are you and why are you on Stoney Vaughn's boat?'

'I'm Stoney's brother, Ben. This is my friend Claudia.' Ben's voice remained steady.

'Ah. A brother. Fucking poetic justice.' Claudia saw Danny lean close to Ben's face, pivot the gun barrel against Ben's forehead. 'Stoney stole from me. Killed to do it. I want what's mine, and you're gonna help me.' He smiled at Ben, smiled at Claudia with a grin that said his mouth wasn't quite moored to the brain. 'A brother is something I can use.'

8

Thursday afternoon, Whit drove out to Black Jack Point. The police dig was done, but an officer remained parked near the tented site and another officer – looking bored out of her mind – sat in a patrol car up where the private road met the highway. Maybe to keep the curious or the indiscreet away. She waved Whit through.

The house reflected the Gilbert fortunes over the years. In the center was the old house, built in the 1820s, fashioned from sturdy oaks, its clear craftsmanship designed to defy the bay's cruel moments. Over the years prosperity dictated which additions had been made: a room on the east side; a new garage bright with white paint; a work shed, its foundation blanketed with a yellow explosion of wild lantana. Patch built the work shed himself, stone by quarried stone. Whit remembered helping him mix the mortar, the teenage boys who fished off the Point all helping out, a thank-you note to the man who'd let them use his land.

Lucy sat alone at the kitchen table, drinking a glass of iced tea. Funeral arrangement papers were spread in a fan before her. He saw Patch in her now: the same clear blue eyes, the determined jaw. But Lucy, for all her brass, had a delicacy in her mouth, her chin, her hands, and a gentleness – like Patch's – that was well concealed. She had not cried again since the bodies were found, showing the steel Whit knew was at her core.

'I don't want to shop for a casket again anytime soon,' she said.

'God forbid.'

She rattled the ice cubes in her tea. 'They won't be able

to fix his face right, will they? He's all broke, Whit. They broke him.'

He sat down next to her.

'Have they arrested someone?'

'No. But David says he has a suspect.' He took her hand. 'I don't know who.'

She drank her tea. 'The sheriff's office took Patch's answering machine, his computer yesterday. I wrote down his messages. I thought maybe there were more people I should call. But what do I say, Whit? He can't meet you for lunch – he's been murdered?'

Whit glanced at the messages: an exterminator was due to spray the house tomorrow – they'd need to cancel that; three notes to return phone calls from Suzanne; the Port Leo library calling about an overdue book. All the daily doodlings of a life moving steadily along its course when fate got mean and reared up and smacked his nose back into his brain.

Whit called the Port Leo library, asked about the overdue book. Lucy watched him with a frown.

'Whit, who cares about a book right now?' she said when he hung up.

'Was he a regular library user?'

'Lord, no. He didn't want to look at it unless it swam, batted baseballs, or might kiss him.' She sat back down next to him. 'What's this book he checked out?'

'*Jean Laffite, Pirate King.*'

Lucy shrugged. 'I never saw him reading anything but the newspaper and *Sports Illustrated*.' She paused. 'You haven't talked to Suzanne yet, have you?'

'No. I told her I'd visit her later, get a statement for the inquest.'

Lucy tore at her paper napkin under her tea glass. She ripped it into thin shreds. 'You said they've got a suspect.'

'You making a bet?'

45

'I'm an unforgivable bitch,' Lucy said. 'Yes.'

'Who, honey?'

'Suzanne's boyfriend, Roy Krantz. He and Patch didn't get along too well.'

'You never mentioned that.'

'They never saw each other more than once a month,' Lucy said. 'Fangs shouldn't be bared that often.'

'Lucy. This is serious. You point at him, it's going to be taken pretty seriously. At least by me and probably by David.'

Lucy's voice went small. 'You don't want to believe you know a person who could kill two people in cold blood.'

'But you think Roy could.'

'Bad vibes fairly explode from him,' Lucy said. 'And I know what you think of my vibes. But I'm even being logical. He was in prison once. For drugs. Not a fact Miss Suzanne advertises.'

'Drugs don't necessarily involve violent crime,' he said and she frowned. 'But why would Roy hurt Patch and Thuy?'

'Suzanne's in the will. She gets half of this land, the money in Patch's accounts. I'm sure it's a fair amount.'

'Can't she say the same about you?'

'But I don't have a bad relationship with money like Suzy Q does.' Lucy cleared her throat. 'Patch told me and I'm not supposed to know, but he wanted to be sure I didn't give her any money, not like I got more than two bucks anyway. Gambling problems.'

'How deep is she in?' he asked.

'Real deep. Patch said nearly a hundred thousand in debt, Whit.'

A hundred thousand. The lucky number.

Lucy kept on. 'Suzanne and Roy drive up to Bossier City or fly over to Biloxi every few weeks. Or gamble on the casino boats out of Rockport or Galveston. She's pissed away her money, and Patch wouldn't give her two cents to rub together. I told David Power this morning.'

'And how did David take your suggestion, Lucy?'

'He furrowed his brow. Very insightful aura. He's a deep thinker.'

'Maybe if he's thinking about wells and water, and even then I wouldn't be too sure.'

'I know that Suzanne won't be happy if she thinks I'm accusing her boyfriend.'

'Clearly.'

'But don't I have a responsibility, Whit?'

'Yes.'

Lucy took his hands in hers. 'I should have stayed here to house-sit for him. I've done that before. Roy – or anyone – wouldn't have tried to break in if I was here.'

'You don't know that, Lucy.'

'I'm playing the what ifs. It's the worst game in the world. It's like a terminal game. You second-guess yourself to death.' She wiped the back of her hand along her mouth. 'If you're gonna break up with me, this'd be a real bad time.'

'Why on earth do you think I'd break up with you?'

'I'm just saying,' Lucy said. 'Don't you break up with me for at least three months.'

'I don't want to break up with you.'

'Because you love me, right?' Lucy stared at him. 'I'm not trying to paint you into a corner, Whit. Trust me. I feel a love vibe from you but you're not saying it, and if you're feeling it, this'd be a real good time to let me know.'

'That I love you? Oh, Christ, Lucy, sure I love you.'

'You don't have a future in greeting cards.'

'I love you, Lucy. I'm not going anywhere.' There. Said. Not so hard once the words bit into the air.

'I love you, too, Whit. I do. I've never loved anyone like I love you. I want you to know that, and this is all going to be all right, isn't it?'

'Baby. Yes. It's okay.' He got up, kissed her. She kissed shy at first and then she kissed him hard, eagerly, her palms pressing against his back. The phone rang; she broke the kiss.

'Hell,' she said. She answered the phone. He could tell by her tone it was a relative or a family friend calling, distant somewhere, who had just heard. Lucy sank into a chair by the phone, started mumbling thanks, a brief explanation of the tragedy. Whit put her tea by her. She patted his hand in thanks, and he went into the study.

The Glenfiddich bottle he'd poured from last night was still there. He picked up the whiskey and noticed, for the first time, the tag entwined with a thin gold ribbon along the bottle's neck. Handwritten.

To celebrate days of old. Stoney.

Whit tucked the bottle back into the bar. Seeing Suzanne Gilbert wasn't going to be pleasant now, and he decided he might as well get it over with.

I love you, Lucy had said. He felt a little shiver of happiness, of nervousness, of new possibility opening before him.

Lucy stood in the doorway. Pale again, the flush from their kiss gone. 'The sheriff's office called while I was getting off the phone with one of Patch's army buddies. They want me to come in. For questioning.'

9

The kidnappers slipped over Claudia's eyes a blindfold, heavy chamois cloth, reeking of boat polish. Hands clamped on her arms and yanked her to her feet, steered her belowdecks. She heard Ben stumbling, gasping next to her.

The air in the cabin lay hot and still against her skin. Hands pushed her to the main salon's carpet. They tied Claudia's hands in front of her, the rope laced down to her feet and bound again. The knots were thick as doughnuts. She heard Ben's wet breathing, like that of a tired, heavy dog.

'You're going to be so busted,' Ben said.

'Doubtful,' Danny answered, a decided coldness in his voice that hadn't been there when he spoke to Claudia. She heard him pacing back and forth near their heads, perhaps inspecting them like prize tarpon.

'Where's the journal?' Danny asked. 'Where's the emerald?'

'I don't know what you're talking about,' Ben said.

'Let me cut the bitch,' Gar said, his mouth close to Claudia's ear. 'Maybe an inch at a time, start with the ring finger.'

'Why don't you just calm down?' Danny said, tension edging his voice. 'We're not at that stage quite yet. Search the boat.'

They ransacked *Jupiter*. Cabinets torn open, leather cushions ripped, mattresses gutted. This went on for at least a half hour, the boat searched from stem to stern.

Claudia pegged their positions from their voices. She had already labeled them: Danny, Redhead (a throaty, giggling tenor), and Gar (a low baritone.) She heard fabric rustle as one of the men dropped to his knees between her and Ben. Then fingertips, gentle, against her shoulder.

'The wrong place. The wrong time.' Danny touched her gently. 'I want to be a better person than that. Truly. I'm sorry for you, miss . . .'

'Leave her alone, asshole! You touch her I'll kill you!' Ben screamed.

'Shut up, brother. I'm not like some people I could name who slaughter the innocent. We are gentlemen here, aren't we?'

His partners made no answer. Lips smacked to her left, juicy-kissy, and the taste of copper tinged her mouth.

'Listen, we'll be expected back within a couple of hours,' Ben said. 'We go missing, my brother will have the coast guard looking for us. They'll hunt you down.'

'Texas is a long swim away. Let me tell you what you're going to do,' Redhead said. His voice held the hard brightness of a game show host. 'You're going to get onto the lovely, fancy onboard phone system here, call your brother. He wants to see you again, he's going to transfer five million dollars into a series of offshore numbered accounts. In the Cayman Islands. The Bahamas. Anguilla. When all that's done, we're going to let you and your girl go home to your families. Sound good?' He laughed.

'You're fucking nuts,' Ben said.

'Five million's not a lot to him,' Danny said. 'We could get greedy. Take all of it.'

'Kill you if we wanted,' Gar said.

'Don't be rude,' Danny said.

'Stoney doesn't have a liquid five million just hanging around. Hell, it's in stocks, funds, real estate.'

'It's happening, baby, *hap-pa-NING*!' The redhead, giddy with putting the screws to people.

50

'Ben,' Danny said. 'It's easy. I want three things from your brother. What he stole from me, which is a document, a journal. A valuable artifact connected to that journal, which is an emerald. And five million, to compensate me for killing my cousin, who was a nice guy. There. Isn't that simple?'

'You're fucking crazy. My brother doesn't have what you're looking for, and he wouldn't hurt your cousin or anybody else.'

'Isn't your brother a little interested in treasure hunting? Hasn't he filled a goddamn library full of books on it?'

'Just as a hobby. Jesus.'

'Hobby. It's gone past that. Time for Stoney to pay the piper. C'mon.' Claudia heard Ben yanked to his feet, his shoes scuffing the carpet near her knees. Wetness landed on the back of her neck. Ben's blood.

'Gar, put Claudia in the stateroom,' Danny ordered.

Hands hoisted Claudia up in the air, crushing against her breasts and her hips, hurried her like a battering ram down the small flight of stairs and through the stateroom's entrance, heaved her onto the torn mattress. She twisted as she fell, rolling, facing the ceiling.

'Give me a moment, Gar,' Danny said. The stateroom door closed. But she heard gentle breathing nearby, near her face.

'Claudia.' It was Danny. 'I am truly sorry.'

'You sound like a reasonable man,' Claudia lied. 'Stop this. Let us go. Please.'

'If you and Ben are innocent in all this, well, then I'm sorry. But how much do you know of Stoney Vaughn's life?'

'I don't understand.'

'Day-to-day living. Does Stoney help old ladies across the street or knock them out of his way? Pet dogs or kick them?'

51

'I really don't know him,' she said.

'Do you think Stoney could commit murder? Kill a man in cold blood?'

Her throat dried. 'He's a respected businessman . . .'

'Ah. His money makes him a saint?' A sarcasm she didn't like at all tightened his voice.

'No,' she said. 'Just as this mistake you're making doesn't make you a bad person, Danny. Please. Stop this.'

Long silence again, the only sound the slap of waves against the hull. 'What's done is done. Life doesn't offer erasers.'

'No. It offers choices. You can choose to let us go. Piracy is a federal offense.'

'*Piracy?*' Danny giggled, a short, sharp laugh. 'Tell me, do you think of us as *pirates*? Because I love it, Claudia. You've made my day.'

'Let us go, right now, and—'

The door opened again.

'She behaving?' Gar's voice, low. 'Or you just copping a feel?'

'Save your crudity for your friend,' Danny said.

'I want to have a private chat with her,' Gar said.

'Private about what?'

'Don't get your dick in a knot, man. I'm not gonna hurt her. Go on.'

Claudia stayed very still.

'You don't tell me what to do,' Danny said. 'You work for me.'

'You want to know where these goods are, right? I can get her to tell without hurting a hair on her head. If she knows. Just give me a minute. You need to go help with Ben talking to Stoney.'

The bedsprings creaked as Danny stood up. 'I'll be back later, Claudia. You'll be fine,' he said. And then she heard the door shut.

A thick fingertip cruised along her scalp, parting her hair. The fingernail, hard and uneven, gouged into the tender nape of her neck.

'You fought us,' Gar cooed. 'A little fishy like you. That pisses me off.'

'Sorry.'

Gar daubed his finger at the blood drop on her neck, smearing it along her flesh like finger paint. Slow. Gentle. Suddenly he tangled his fist in her hair, slamming her head hard against the bed's headboard. Her teeth knocked together, her jaw, already bruised, throbbed. She winced but didn't cry out.

'You don't mess with us, okay, fishy? You don't fight us. You don't talk unless you're talked to. Understand?'

'Yes,' Claudia said.

The end of the bed creaked under his weight. He took hold of her bare foot – she'd lost her sandals during the fight – and put a pincer grip on her little toe. 'I don't like your answers, I break it. Where'd you learn to fight?'

'A defense class at the community center,' Claudia lied. She suspected the correct answer – the Corpus Christi Police Academy – might land her over the railing with a bullet in her head.

Gar squeezed her toe. She held her breath. 'Where's your purse?'

Oh, God. Her police department ID. She didn't have her gun in her purse – she was on vacation and hadn't felt the need to carry today while fishing – but her badge and ID were in the purse, in a separate wallet from her driver's license, credit cards and cash.

'I don't know. Around. I don't think I've got five bucks in my wallet.'

She heard him stand and walk around the stateroom. She couldn't remember where she had put her purse.

When Ben had given her a tour of the boat, she'd set it down along the way. They were in the larger master stateroom. Outside it was a short hall leading to a small guest stateroom with bunk beds and a head, then the small stairs leading to the main salon. At the forward end of the *Jupiter*, more steps leading down to the small galley, then a stateroom, also with bunk beds, a head, and a separate shower. She figured the purse was either in this stateroom or in the salon where they kept Ben.

Drawers opened and closed; she heard an unzipping that filled her mouth with sour-tasting fear until she realized it was the zipper on her purse. Keys jingled – the keys ringed to her wallet.

Did he see the ID? He'd kill her if he knew she was a cop, she had no doubt.

A wallet snapped open. 'Claudia Marisol Salazar of 55 Mimosa Street, apartment 23, Port Leo, Texas,' Gar said. He'd found her driver's license. She waited for him to spot and open her police ID wallet, say, *Oh shit,* and close his fingers around her throat.

Instead Gar pressed his thick, wide hand into the small of her back. 'So this nice fancy boat, it stays at Stoney's house?'

'Yes.'

'Anyone else there besides Stoney? Staff for the rich man?'

'I think there's a housekeeper who comes when asked. No one living there but Stoney and Ben.'

He grabbed her little toe again, gave it a hard twist. 'Lying's gonna cost you.'

'I'm not lying,' she said. 'Look, piracy is a federal offense. Adding homicide to it isn't going to help you.'

He snapped the bone of her little toe and she screamed into the pillow.

'Did I fucking ask for a lecture from you?'

'I'm sorry,' she managed to say, the pain sharp as a blade.

He released the broken toe, tickled and kissed the bottom of her foot, took hold of the fourth toe. 'I tell my buddy maybe I like you real good, maybe I want to spend a little quality time with you, he'll stop laughing so much. He'll go green with envy. He gets real jealous if I take an interest in a pretty girl like you. He'll break every bone in your body, starting with the rest of your toes and then the fingers and working up to ribs, collarbone, major organs. And no one out here to hear you scream. So don't lecture me.'

Claudia bit the pillow. The stateroom door opened again.

Danny said, 'I told you to leave her alone.' Sounding a little uncertain, trying to be in command.

'I didn't do nothing,' Gar said.

'Her nose is bleeding. I won't tolerate you hurting her.'

'I got something for you to tolerate. She's his puss, man. She's no better than he is. Price of the choices you make.'

'Did he hurt you, Claudia?' Danny asked.

Claudia hesitated for a moment before choosing her answer. 'I tried to kick him and he dissuaded me.'

'You're not to hurt her,' Danny said, 'unless she tries to escape. And by escape, I don't mean she mouths off at you or you feel like dishing out fists. You understand?'

'I don't see no captain's hat on your head,' Gar said. His weight pressed against her ribs, his erection poking into her thigh.

'Be a good girl,' Gar whispered in her ear, 'and I'll keep myself on a leash. Be bad, and I'll play with you. For hours on end.' Gar made a wet kiss against her ear. Then he left the room and shut the door.

Silence. Danny must have walked out with him.

Claudia lay in blindfolded darkness, shivering. *They're not gonna let us go. They're not. Even if Stoney pays this ransom. They knew this is Stoney's boat. Knew he was supposed to be out on the water today. Didn't know he canceled. How?*

A journal. A jewel. Treasure hunters. Crazy, but she could not worry about that now. The only thing that mattered was getting help or getting the hell out of here.

So how are you going to get you and Ben out of this?

The kidnappers had the guns but they quarreled among themselves, improvising since Stoney wasn't here, no backup plan in place. So they were being stupid and she would be smart.

Claudia twisted around on the mattress and managed, by dragging her head down the bedding, to nudge the chamois-cloth blindfold a hairbreadth off her eyes. Again. Again. She could see below the blindfold's edge. The stateroom was dark. Thin light filtered in from the oblong portholes above the bed, cut into rods of black and white by half-opened shutters. On the walls were reproductions of old sailing maps and a framed set of antique coins. Next to the closet hung another yellowed print – a portrait of a man with flowing black locks, wearing a rakish hat and a blue nautical jacket, in an arrogant stance. The print was vaguely familiar, something she'd seen in a tourist bar in Port Leo, but she couldn't place it. She looked at the picture as a focus point, took calm, steadying breaths.

First get loose.

She rolled across the bed. Her hands were bound in front of her and by lying on the bed's very edge and inching forward, she was able to reach and slide open a side table drawer. No gun, no pocketknife, nothing inside but a weathered paperback and a self-winding watch. The bookshelf, a small one, didn't even hold a heavy bookend. A closet stood on the opposite wall but she remembered it only held clothes and hangers. She rolled up to kneel and look out the rectangular portholes above the bed; the stateroom was directly beneath the salon, where she and Ben had fished in luxury, and below the portholes was a small swim platform.

Smash the glass in the frames, cut the ropes? They'd hear her, and she wouldn't have time to free herself.

If she could ease out the porthole – no guarantee she'd fit – she could wriggle onto the swim platform. And then what? More than seventy-five miles out at sea, no way to call for help, roasting in the sun until they found her. Or she fell off and drowned. Bound foot and hand as she was, she could hardly wriggle up and across the main deck without them hearing her. Maybe she could ease into the water and slice her ropes on the propellers. *Yeah, just like a movie action hero.* One flick of the propeller switch and she'd shred like cabbage, assuming she didn't drown first. She remembered the silky sharks, plowing through the yellowfin school. She might be too big for the silkies but sharks didn't measure their meals. They just ate. They would still take her, make her a five-course meal, a leisurely limb at a time.

She listened. In the quiet roll of the waters she heard them threatening Ben, shoving him into a chair, Ben protesting. She lay very still, breathing through her mouth.

She heard a phone ring. Ring. Click on. 'Good afternoon, this is Stoney Vaughn.'

'Good afternoon, Stoney.' Danny's voice was creamy as butter. 'This is your friend Danny, from New Orleans.'

A pause, then Stoney, annoyed, 'I told you to quit calling me, you fucking nut.'

'We've got your brother and his girlfriend.'

Silence.

'You weren't on your little boat today. Were you too busy killing people, stealing, ruining lives?'

'Stoney,' Ben said. 'He says you took something of theirs?'

Silence again. 'They're lying. Is this some sort of sick joke?'

'The Devil's Eye, Stoney. Give it to me – along with the journal you stole and a big freaking wad of cash, just to make up for all the grief you've caused me – and we'll be even. And I'll let Ben and his friend go.'

Then Stoney's voice, not much more than a whisper, 'I don't know what the hell you're talking about . . .'

Claudia struggled to a kneeling position, fumbled for the handle, started cranking open the porthole. *See if you can slide through the porthole. Get up to the deck. Radio for help. Now, while they're occupied.*

Slowly, the pane of glass began to rise.

10

'So you haven't seen Jimmy since Monday?' David Power asked Linda Bird. He didn't like to sit during questionings; he liked to stand. Pace around the room a little like a lawyer. Because the interviewee was always nervous talking to the police, guaranteed nervous, even if they were as pure and innocent as a half dozen saints, and him standing made them a little smaller. That was the goal, make them feel small and they'd crack. The Encina County sheriff, Randy Hollis, sat across from Linda Bird, doodling interlocking circles on a legal pad.

Jimmy Bird's wife looked up at David. Her hair was cut in a style last fashionable ten years ago, frazzled from home dye jobs. A small patch of acne scars, badly camouflaged with makeup, dimpled her cheeks. 'Yes. I told you that already.'

She wasn't feeling small enough yet. He crossed his arms. 'No need to get upset, if you don't got anything to hide, Linda.'

'You either believe me or you don't,' Linda Bird said. 'If he's gonna keep asking me the same things again and again, like a fucking parrot, I'm getting me a lawyer, because then he's just trying to trick me.' She glared over at Sheriff Hollis.

'I'll call you a lawyer right now, Mrs Bird,' Sheriff Hollis said. He had a low, pleasant voice, the kind that made for good radio. 'But no one is accusing you of anything except being Jimmy's wife, and we just want to know where he might have gone to.'

'Jimmy mention any places he might like to go? Where's he got family?' David asked.

59

'All his family's either in the cemetery or Tivoli, and none of 'em like him.'

'Names of his family in Tivoli?'

She gave them, an aunt and two male cousins.

'Patch fired Jimmy, what, a year ago?'

'Right before Labor Day.'

'Why?'

'Jimmy got mad that Patch wanted him to work on a Saturday and called him a motherfucker under his voice. Patch heard him and fired him on the spot. Jimmy begged him for another chance, but Patch said he'd crossed a line and he wasn't getting even a toe back over it.' Linda Bird lit a cigarette without asking permission; David glanced at Sheriff Hollis, who let it slide.

'Did Jimmy hold a grudge?'

'He really wanted that job back – Patch was a good man, easy to work for most of the time, and doing odd jobs for him wasn't too much hard work – but Jimmy's pride got the best of him. He talked about screwing Patch over.'

'How?'

'Flattening a tire, sugaring his tank. Kid stuff.' She tapped ashes into a coffee cup. 'He sure as hell didn't mention murder. Jimmy don't even like to spank our four-year-old. I've never been afraid of him and if he could go off and kill two people just like that' – here she snapped her fingers – 'then I don't know him. And if he's gone dangerous, I want police protection for me and my little girl.'

A patrol officer stuck his head into the interrogation room. 'David? Your other appointment's here.' David nodded and the dispatcher shut the door.

'You got a suspect?' Linda asked.

'It's on another case,' David said.

'Aren't you the busy bee?'

'How's the marriage?' Sheriff Hollis set down his pen.

A pause. 'I filed for divorce last week. He knew it was coming.'

'So he might have reason to leave town.'

'He might. Although he'd hate to leave our girl, Britni. He does love her – I give him that, even if he don't got the sense God gave a goose.'

'Why'd you file?' David asked.

'Irreconcilable boredom.'

Randy Hollis leaned forward. 'If Jimmy calls you, Linda, what do you do?'

'Tell him to stay the hell away. If he's innocent in this, then he should come forward. If he's guilty, give up. For Britni's sake. Is this all?'

'Judge Mosley's conducting an inquest. He may call you for a statement.'

'He's okay,' she said with a contemptuous glance at David. 'A judge's robe ain't the same as a uniform, doesn't make a man turn mean.'

David felt his temper rise. 'You be clear on this, Linda. Your husband calls you, you don't offer him any help. You don't want to be an accessory. I don't want to be charging you. Putting your little girl through that grief.'

'Try it without proof,' she said. 'This ain't Red China.'

She wasn't going to get small, David saw, so he asked Linda Bird a few more questions he already knew the answers to and dismissed her. She left and David had his hand on the door when Sheriff Hollis said, 'David. About Lucy Gilbert.'

'What?'

'Are you just taking another statement or questioning her as a suspect?' Asked like he didn't know the answer, and David could tell he did.

'Questioning her.'

'Why?'

61

'She and Suzanne Gilbert are Patch Gilbert's only relatives. They stand to benefit from his death.'

'That aside, what you got on her?'

'She runs a disreputable business.'

'You talking about that psychic hotline thing?' Hollis
said. 'How's that disreputable? My mother calls it, says
the girls on the phones are real nice and insightful.'

'You like your mother pissing away her Social Security
on phone psychics?'

'She can piss her money how she pleases. I heard Lucy
Gilbert's dating Whit Mosley.'

'So?'

'His Honor's not a big friend of yours, is he?' Hollis
capped his pen, gave David an unexpected frown.

'We get along fine.'

'No, you don't. You've never gotten along with him.
Never made the effort, far as I can see.' Hollis stood,
wadded up his page of doodles. 'You got a reason to
suspect Lucy Gilbert, a solid lead, you go for it. You
questioning her because she's the girlfriend of a guy who's
a pain in your ass, forget it. I won't have an officer of mine
abusing his position.'

'I resent that. Deeply.'

'I wouldn't want you to resent it shallowly, David,'
Hollis said. 'We clear?'

'Crystal.' David kept his voice steady. 'I need clarifica-
tion on some items in her statement. That's all. In fact,
my friend Judge Mosley and I are supposed to drive in
together to Corpus for the autopsy results and to meet
with the forensic anth team.'

'Good. Keep playing nice.' Hollis left.

David Power unclenched his fingers. Odd. Hollis was a
Democrat; Whit Mosley had been elected on the Republican ticket, although Whit looked more like a guy who'd
gotten lost and had wandered into a Green Party meeting

62

and stayed for the fashions. Why would Hollis take Whit's side? But he saw it then: both of them from old Port Leo families, the old moneyed families of the coast that didn't include the Powers. Old family allegiances meant more than political party lines.

It wouldn't buy you an inch with him.

He stepped out into the hallway. Lucy Gilbert stood there, along with an older woman he presumed was her attorney. The lawyer gave David a predatory glare, like a barracuda who'd missed breakfast, lunch, and dinner.

No sign of Whit. It surprised him; he thought Whit would be here, steam pouring from his ears. Perhaps, David decided, that was best for the moment. But he turned his friendliest smile toward Lucy Gilbert. *You just make one teeny misstep, bitch, you had a thing to do with these murders, you're mine.*

'Miss Gilbert? Thanks for coming in. I just had a few questions on your statement you gave the police. If y'all will just step this way . . .'

Patch Gilbert's older niece, Suzanne, lived in a grand development called Castaway Key, a series of streets and private docks that few born and raised in Port Leo called home. Her house sat facing St Leo Bay, and in the summer afternoon the bay hummed with craft: sailboats slicing the waves; jet skis buzzing like maddened bees; a pleasure boat loaded with urban weekenders cutting near the shore, extra-bad eighties dance music drifting from its deck. Whit rolled up the window.

Castaway Key was not aptly named. Many houses went for a quarter million and higher. Whit supposed anyone dressed like Robinson Crusoe, ambling along Castaway Key's resort-named streets – such as Hilton Head Road or Cozumel Way – would be summarily brought to him on charges of vagrancy.

Suzanne Gilbert's house was white and modern, and it glittered with windows large enough to drive a car through. Delicate palms and sprawling bougainvillea filled the beds near the curved stone driveway. Brightly painted Mexican tiles spelled out the house number. Suzanne, an artist, seemed flush rather than starving. Or maybe Suzanne was house-poor, and this mansion was a symptom of her supposed financial woes.

His cell phone beeped as he parked. 'This is Judge Mosley.'

'Judge. Hi. This is Linda Bird. I'm Jimmy Bird's wife. I think you know who he is.'

'I know we want to talk to him, ma'am.'

'Well, I just talked with that prick David Power. I don't want to talk to him no more, and the sheriff said I might have to talk to you. So I'm talking because' – she paused – 'I find the deputy to be irritating.'

'Yes, ma'am.'

'New Orleans. I think if Jimmy has run off he's gone there. Couple of times last month I hear him, late at night on the phone, talking, saying, *Alex*. I thought it was some drunk friend of his. They love to get tight and phone each other. Like goddamned teenagers.'

'I see.'

'Then the phone bill comes. We don't know people in New Orleans but there's three calls there, late at night. I pay the bills, as I have the job. I ask him about who he's calling, he says it's a mistake. He's a bad liar. I can tell he's lying.' She paused. 'So then I think maybe Alex is a girl. In New Orleans. How he got a girlfriend in New Orleans is beyond me, but I'm telling you because I sure ain't telling David Power. You want the number he called?'

'Yes, ma'am, I do.' She gave it to him and he jotted it down.

'You tell David Power he better fucking treat me nicer next time he sees me, or I'm filing a complaint. I got a lawyer now, what with getting the divorce, and I am in a filing mood.'

'I sense your resolve, Mrs Bird. Thank you.'

'You set bond on my brother last year,' she said. 'An amount we could handle. We appreciated it. I'm voting for you next time.'

He thanked her, stared at the phone number, nearly laughed.

Suzanne Gilbert opened the front door as he headed up the stairs. She wore black jeans, a black T-shirt, black sandals. *Idiotic in this heat,* Whit thought. Artist mourning clothes. She was very fair, attractive, a good five or six years older than Lucy. Her cheekbones and chin and nose were all precise and perfect, as measured as an architect's drawing.

She greeted Whit with a brief hug, so quick he wondered why she'd bothered. Whit suspected that Suzanne wanted to pat his blondish hair flat or put him in a suit, tidy him up for Lucy. He saw her eyes take in his clothes with disapproval: the faded polo shirt, the rumpled khakis, the sandals.

'How are you holding up?' he asked.

'Barely am,' she said in a tone that meant anything but.

Whit followed her into a high-ceilinged foyer and then to a living room. The furniture was modern and expensive, imported teak, leather surfaces of tan and black, the carpet a creamy white, brave for a beachside house. Abstract art filled the walls, lined the bookshelves. But all painted with the same crude hand, no eye for detail or form. Savagely mixed, the colors selected to hurt the eye. Jackson Pollock without the restraint. Whit sensed a sudden meanness in the pictures. They were ugliness

65

disguising themselves as talent. He hated the pictures on first sight.

He followed her to an immaculate, steel-dominated kitchen. A man who looked like he might drag his knuckles when he walked stood by the granite kitchen counter, drinking a bottle of Dos Equis. Big, thick-necked, with a shaved-bald head and wearing a black T-shirt and faded denim overalls. A bracelet of intertwining tattoos whirled around one melon-shaped bicep.

'I don't think you've met my boyfriend, Roy Krantz. Hon, this is Whit Mosley. He's the coroner and the JP here and he's conducting the inquest into Uncle Patch's death.' No, he hadn't met Roy. The few parties and events where Lucy and Suzanne crossed paths, Roy was always at home or sleeping or working on a sculpture. Roy shunned limelight, it seemed to Whit. Perhaps he had trouble fitting through the front door.

Whit offered a hand; Roy shook it and didn't try to squeeze Whit's fingers into pulp.

The phone rang. 'Excuse me,' Suzanne said. 'News has spread, and people want to bring over casseroles and cakes. You know how it is when you have a death in the family. Everyone swarms over with comfort foods and you gain ten pounds.'

As though weight gain were her biggest worry. Whit thought she needed a cheeseburger. But he gave his solemn, conducting-the-inquest nod. 'Of course.' She left the kitchen, scooped up a phone in the living room, spoke in a low voice.

'You're Lucy's guy,' Roy Krantz said. His voice was low and flat and sounded like it had been honed in a prison yard.

'Yes.'

'How's she holding up?'

'She's talking to the police right now.'

66

Roy raised an eyebrow. 'And what's she saying?'

'Family secrets, probably.'

Roy made a noise of thick beer-swallow, kept staring at him.

Suzanne returned. 'Something to drink, Whit?' Her voice glimmered a little too cheery, a little too hostess-bright.

'No, thank you. May we talk now? Privately?'

'Sure.' Suzanne glanced at Roy, then led Whit down a hall thankfully empty of abstract art-pukings. Two doors opened off the hall: one to a concrete-floored room cluttered with small iron sculptures of gulls, palm trees, flamingos, and assorted equipment; the other to another studio, bright windows framing the view of the bay. A huge canvas leaned near one window, covered with a stained dropcloth. A worktable stood nearby, dotted with oil paint in blues, mustards, venomous greens, as though poison dripped on its surface. Finished paintings – more of the obnoxious scribblings that hung in the living room – decorated the walls.

In one corner a huge roll of paper lay unfurled, with smears of bright acrylic paint dried on the paper. Whit glanced at it, then glanced again. Two round magenta globes looked like they'd been pressed on the paper from small, pert breasts. A roll of lime paint looked like a hip; multiple handprints lay in blue and pink. Other blobs resembled kneeprints, footprints, and one squat figure eight looked like apple-green testicles. Suzanne wore a bent little smile on her architectural face.

'You're very prolific.' Whit nodded toward the calmer paintings on the wall. It was the only compliment he could think of.

'I get bored working on a painting too long, so I paint quickly. But they sell quickly, too.' An offhand shrug.

'They're very interesting.'

Interesting apparently didn't cut it; she frowned. She sat on a paint-splattered stool and he settled on its twin across from her.

'You're probably wondering why I don't paint the bay, with a wonderful view.' Suzanne crossed her legs, dangled a black sandal off one alabaster foot.

'No. But you want to tell me.'

She gave a solemn smile. '*Everyone* here paints the bay. Every stupid little dabbler who can barely hold a brush between their fingers. And the required frisky gulls, little boats, swaying palms. Tiresome.' She pointed at one small painting, framed in silver, a violent swirl of purple spirals, gray crosses, and white froth that looked like nothing more than idle slapping of paint by an angry child. 'That's the bay. My interpretation of it. No adorable dinghies, no fishing grannies, no endangered whooping cranes winging back to the refuge. The bay as it is. Hard. Cruel. Like life is.'

He didn't think she knew diddly about hard life in this grand house. Maybe he should have her call Linda Bird. 'I'd like to know about your relationship with Patch.'

'Are you asking as a judge or because Lucy's said an unkind word or two?'

Now that was interesting. 'As a judge.'

'I loved Patch. Who didn't?' She tucked her sandal back on her foot. 'Artists live up to our stereotype now and then, get moody and mean when the work sucks. Patch always pulled me out of the blues, gave me a slap on the fanny when I needed it.' She spoke with the air of the artist, playing out each nuance until it wasn't a nuance anymore. But he saw in the dusky light how brittle her eyes and mouth looked under the fresh make-up. She had cried and cried hard.

'Did he ever help you in other ways? Say financially?'

'You ask that like you know the answer already.'

Whit shrugged.

'You know, Lucy doesn't make it easy to love her sometimes, does she? She does have a mouth.' She lit a cigarette, a thin, ladylike coffin nail in a pink pack, then offered him one. He declined.

'She told you garbage about me with great reluctance, right? Much wringing of hands? She got a vibe, right?'

Whit said nothing.

'Lucy was born with a finger pointing at someone else. Artists see patterns, honey, and I've seen plenty of this one.'

'She said you asked Patch for a large loan.'

'I was a little short on cash between paintings and asked Patch for help. He said no, I said fine, we were fine. He's not a bank. I understood.'

'You asked for a hundred thousand?'

Her eyes went wide. 'Good Lord, no. I asked for ten thousand. I got it from a friend. It's being paid off, no problems.' She tapped ashes into a crystal ashtray on the worktable, her mouth thinned. 'A hundred thousand. She ought to use that imagination for noble causes.'

'She said it's what Patch told her.'

'She's dead wrong.'

'She and Patch seemed to have a good relationship.'

'Lucy likes people who have things and will give them to her. I'm not one of those people. Patch was. He doted on Lucy, just a bit too much.'

'Can you think of anyone who'd want Patch or Thuy dead?'

'He only dated widows, and he was successful at it. I could see he might make another man jealous. Thuy, Lord, no. Gentle and kind as a lamb. Retired teacher, loaded with patience. I adored her.'

'You and Roy were here in town on Monday night.'

'Yes. I already gave a statement to the police. We were

69

here, watched the news, turned in.' She paused, tilted her head, gave him a melty smile. 'We fucked. Twice. So we were awake until midnight or so. That's not in the police statement but I don't mind total honesty with you.' Her smile shifted; his skin prickled.

'In a bed or on the canvas?'

The smile widened. 'You have a good eye.'

Yeah, it's real tough to make out painted, squashed boobs. He saw the perfection of her face created a sense of emptiness – like a house with no curtains in the windows. 'Roy's what to you, social engineering?'

'Radio Lucy strikes again.' She shrugged. 'It was a minor drug conviction, ten years ago. He's clean.' She exhaled a cool little stream of smoke. 'He was here all Monday and Tuesday with me, okay? Working. He's an artist, too. His studio's across the hall. Sculptures in metal. Gulls, lighthouses, coastal art for the gift shop crowd. He's not an artist at my level but he has potential.'

Whit glanced at the body prints on the paper on the floor and thought he saw Roy's rather limited potential at work.

'It's a lot of land at stake. With Patch gone.'

She frowned, as though he had dragged a dirty finger across one of her artworks. 'Well, the Gilberts have owned most of Black Jack Point since before Texas was Texas. It totals about three hundred acres. Fifty acres is mine. Fifty is Lucy's. Uncle Patch owns another two hundred.' She shrugged again. 'I've no idea of the details of Uncle Patch's will. I would suppose Lucy and I inherit. But we never discussed it.'

'But if you needed ten thousand dollars, why not sell some of your land?'

'We've always had an unspoken agreement not to sell, except as a group. Patch wanted to hold on to the family land, even when solid offers came in. Lucy and I always deferred to him.'

'Have you gotten many offers on the land?' Considering the value of waterfront property in parts of Texas, Whit wondered if the land provided a hard motive.

'One, oh, a month ago. I got a phone call from a real estate investor in Corpus. I wasn't interested, but I did refer him to Patch because he was so persistent.'

'Who was that?'

'Stoney Vaughn. He's got a big-ass house up on Copano Flats. Tedious type. I met him once at a Port Leo Art Center function. And another offer, about a year ago, from a company in Houston. We just say no. We don't want to sell. I don't know if that will change now, with Patch gone.'

The bottle of Glenfiddich had been from a Stoney. Maybe interesting, maybe not.

He thought of the skeletons. 'Patch ever mention any archaeological value to the land?'

Suzanne didn't answer for a second and he wondered if she knew about the bones. David and the DPS team had kept it out of the papers thus far. But a freakish detail like that was hard to muzzle with so many people now involved. She stubbed out her cigarette, glanced up at him through the trail of smoke. 'An archaeologist wouldn't find anything except old dead Gilberts and their junk.'

'No earlier settlement on the land?'

'Indians must have passed through or hunted there, I guess. Black Jack Point's always been wild country, though. I don't think anyone else ever built there but us crazy Gilberts.' She lit another cigarette. 'Speaking of crazy Gilberts, what do you see in Lucy? Do you mind me asking? Yes, she's very pretty but she's very contrary and a bit too high-maintenance.'

'She drives me nuts. She makes me laugh. She makes me think. For me that's pretty good.'

'Laughing is good. Sexy.' Her voice went a little lower. 'I bet Roy's a real giggle factory.'

'He can be very sweet,' she said, letting her smile grow. 'But I do bore easily.'

'I'm allergic to paint,' he said. 'I'd like to talk to Roy now.'

Her smile – more carefully crafted than her paintings – went flat. 'Sure.'

They returned to the den. Roy lay sprawled on the couch, drinking a fresh bottle of Dos Equis, watching *Jeopardy!* He didn't look up at Whit.

'Roy, Whit needs to talk to you,' Suzanne said.

'I barely knew Patch. What is the Tower of Pisa?' he said to the television, playing Architecture for $200. He was right.

'It took a lot of strength to beat a man like Patch to death,' Whit said.

Roy Krantz didn't take his eyes off the screen. 'Probably not. What is photosynthesis? You dumb asses.'

Whit leaned down, grabbed the remote, cut off the television in the middle of Botany for $600. 'Pardon me. I'm speaking to you. As part of a death inquest. If you don't want to answer questions here, you do it in a courtroom.'

Roy stood. Whit was tall but this guy was an oak. 'I told you, I don't know shit. And I don't like to miss my program.'

'Roy.' Suzanne shook her head.

'I'm sorry, baby.' For the first time Whit saw tenderness in Roy's sun-hardened face. 'Sorry. Okay.' He crossed his arms. 'I never got to know him, Judge. He decided in the first ten seconds of our acquaintance I was trash. So we declined to occupy the same place at the same time.'

'Let's talk prison records.'

Roy walked into the kitchen, got another beer, offered a bottle to Whit. Whit shook his head. 'I ran some dope for a school buddy, I got caught, I cut a little deal, school buddy didn't. I did a short stint and I've been spotless. Now I got my life back together here with Suze, doing my art, and people just want to piss in my beer.'

'Y'all do much gambling?' Whit asked.

Roy glanced at Suzanne and she said, 'Lucy.' He glanced back at Whit with a smirk. 'Actually, we do, and we have the means to and we're not in over our heads. I don't suppose it's occurred to anyone that maybe Mrs Tran was the target, not Patch. You grilling her family like this?'

'I couldn't say.'

'You come after me just because I got a record, that's the easy thing to do. Just as easy to get yourself sued for false arrest. For reporters to get a call to say some poor ex-con who's become a model citizen is getting hassled. You can't fucking bully people, man.'

'I didn't realize you felt bullied by me,' Whit said. 'Please don't cry.'

Roy took a step forward. Suzanne put a hand on his thick forearm. 'Roy. Don't let him bait you.'

'I'm not baiting anyone,' Whit said. 'Thanks for your time. I can see myself out. I'll let you know if you're needed to testify at the inquest.'

Whit drove out of Castaway Key. He remembered the time the land had been developed, this thin sliver of near-island, when he was a teenager. Once this was rough country, not too different from the Gilbert land, thick with salt grass, jutting out into shallow water with a handpainted sign that read PLEASE DON'T PET THE RATTLERS. *And how much is this land worth now?* Whit wondered. *Millions. So how much is that family land*

73

really worth to Suzanne Gilbert? Or maybe to her way-smarter-than-he-looks boyfriend?

He didn't want to think about how much it might be worth to Lucy.

11

Claudia wriggled her head through the open porthole, attempted to snake her body through. She eased one shoulder out. She turned, trying to navigate her head and the other shoulder out, but the opening was too narrow and the ropes, tight already, chafed hard, gouged her legs. She was angry enough to cry hot tears, and she hated to cry.

The heavy blindfold slipped around her neck like a loose scarf. *Shit. No getting that back over my eyes. That's probably worth a whole foot of broken toes.*

She pulled herself back in. A knot of rope caught on the porthole crank. Not good, not good. She caught her breath, eased herself free, and fell back against the bed. She tried to maneuver the blindfold back into place but she couldn't; her hands couldn't push it up far enough to cover her eyes and all her wriggling had loosened the knot too much.

She heard Stoney's shocked drawl over the speakerphone. 'I'll give you the money. Okay? But these other items you're asking for, I don't have, please.'

Gar said, 'Number one,' and Ben screamed.

'That was finger number one,' Gar said. 'Broke it. A pinky. You keep arguing I'll cut it off.'

'I don't have what you want!' Stoney said.

'Let's accelerate. I vote to cut off the brother's dick,' Redhead said with a giggle. 'Where did I put those scissors . . . ?'

'No, leave him alone!' Stoney yelled.

'We will,' Danny said. Claudia could hear the distaste in his voice. 'If you play along. First the five million.'

'Oh, Christ, oh, Christ,' Stoney moaned.

'Got your pen ready, sunshine?' Redhead said. 'Put a half million in this account in Grand Cayman.' He read off an account number. 'That's at the Great Commerce Bank of Grand Cayman. Move that first, will you?'

Stoney made a noise of unhappy agreement.

'Don't whine,' Redhead said. 'Then another half million in this bank in Anguilla. Here's the account number . . .'

More accounts, more banks, the slow carving of Stoney's fortune. Claudia gritted her teeth.

'Now. The journal and the Devil's Eye,' Danny said. 'You're going to take them to Staples Mall in Corpus. Tomorrow at eight a.m., when the mall opens for the elderly mall walkers. Go to the carousel at the middle of the mall. Leave the journal and the emerald in a Sears bag, each wrapped in plain brown paper and covered with a couple of paperbacks. You'll put the bag underneath the gray horse with the white mane, the red saddle and the bright blue ribbons. If the police are there, or I don't like how anything looks, your brother and his girlfriend die and I report the murder you committed to the New Orleans police. We get to that point, I don't care what happens to me. But you, you're finished.'

There was a long silence. Stoney Vaughn finally said, 'I don't know how long this transfer will take. After it goes through the banks in Houston we may not have immediate confirmation, and I'm not at my office right now . . .'

'We check with Grand Cayman here shortly, and you better hope that money's streaming in,' Redhead said.

'We can't control how long the transfer takes once it leaves my bank. You know that,' Stoney said. 'Let's say I do what you want. How do I get my brother back?'

'We'll drop off Ben and Claudia in a safe place after

76

we've got the journal and the emerald,' Danny said. 'We'll call you, let you know where they're at.'

'That's not good enough,' Stoney said.

'Our beef's not with them. It's with you. We're not into killing innocent people. And don't call the police or the coast guard or the navy or anybody. We see choppers coming, we see boats coming looking for us, they're dead in two seconds.' Danny didn't seem to notice the contradiction in his words, which made Claudia cold all over.

'You fucker,' Stoney said.

'Yes, but I'm the fucker in charge,' Danny said.

'Okay. Okay. Please, I want to talk to my brother.'

'Here he is. You got five seconds.'

'Stoney?' Ben said. He didn't sound scared or hurt to Claudia, more mad.

'Yeah.'

'Do what they say.'

'How did they get you? I don't understand.'

'Boarded us. Please, Sto—'

'Five seconds up, no more talk,' Danny said. 'Start the money transfers. We'll be checking on you. I'm calling you back in fifteen minutes.'

'That's not enough—' Stoney started and then his voice was gone. Cut off.

'Progress,' said Redhead. 'But I'll just keep these scissors handy, okay, Ben?'

Claudia heard footfalls on the steps outside the master stateroom.

Oh, God, the porthole's still open. She hadn't shut it.

The stateroom door flew open, hard, slammed against the wall.

Gar, with the stocking off his head. A heavy round face, brown eyes, dirty-blond hair askew from the stocking, full mouth. He noticed her blindfold was off.

'Goddamn it.' He yanked the chamois cloth back over her eyes with angry roughness. 'That better not come off again, you understand? We'll play this little piggy if it does.' He grabbed at her foot, twanged her broken toe. A bolt of fire shot up her leg.

She kept her voice steady. 'I'm sorry. It slipped off while I was trying to get comfortable.'

'Comfort's not in your immediate future.' He leaned down close to her, licked her ear with a pizza-greasy tongue. 'I'm not like Danny Boy, who plays nice with you. I don't believe in being in the wrong place at the wrong time. I think fate brought us together so we could have us a little fun.'

He picked Claudia up, threw her over his shoulder, and carried her out the door.

Stoney Vaughn sat in dismal shock in his home office overlooking St Leo Bay, staring at the banks and account numbers Danny had given him.

He lit a cigarette, fired up his computer, and tried to order his thoughts.

Danny had his idiot brother and that girlfriend of his, somehow. On *his* boat. And that lunatic wanted the journal that had led Stoney and Alex to the treasure, and the Devil's Eye. And five million in pain money.

Fuck that.

He abandoned thinking *how did this happen*, because he quickly decided that was pointless. He started thinking of how the cards might play out.

Bad hand number one: He transferred the money, turned over the goods, got his brother back. Wouldn't work. No way he could surrender the Eye – even the fake one in the storage unit – without Alex going nuclear. No way they could let Danny walk free. That went for Ben and his girlfriend, too, especially because she was a cop and God only knew what Danny had told her. Alex wouldn't stand for it.

And if he even tried to cut a separate deal with Danny, Alex would kill him.

Bad hand number two: He transferred the money but didn't turn over the journal or the Eye. Fool Danny, make him think they'd give up the goods and let Alex eliminate Danny during or after the drop. But then he was out five million bucks, and he didn't have that much sitting around. He had maybe a million, and then he had clients who were generous but didn't know it. He sometimes borrowed money and moved it back in when he got new clients. Most of his clients – carefully selected – were elderly, rich from birth, and patient regarding small losses. This creative accounting had bought him the boat and helped with the house, but he couldn't swing five million, not all at once, moved overseas. No way to cover that up.

Bad hand number three: He picked up the phone and called the police, and Danny turned him in for murder. Hell. A murder he didn't do but Danny didn't know different. Too much death – the guy in New Orleans, the old couple in Port Leo. He wasn't a killer but he was an accessory. Prison. No more golf, no more deals, no more treasure hunts, no more luscious coastal social climbers in his bed. Or Alex would kill him to keep him quiet.

Ben's dead no matter what I do, he thought. *If Danny doesn't kill him, Alex will.*

He got up, paced in front of the plate glass. They would be calling back in fifteen minutes, and he had a decision to make.

Danny thought Stoney had stolen the journal from him, killed his cousin in Louisiana. That meant he didn't know about Alex. Didn't know Alex existed. But Alex couldn't do much about Danny while Danny sailed freely in the Gulf.

79

So he had to get Alex and Danny both there and let Alex solve it. But first he'd cover his ass.

Stoney accessed the Internet, opened up a connection to his network management software that monitored and controlled the investment counselors' activities in his Corpus Christi office. He typed an administrator's code, entered some commands, pressed OK. He'd had this as a time-buyer, a backup plan in case his clients – or the police – got too curious about his records.

Stoney dialed the phone; Alex answered on the first ring. 'We have a problem.'

'Yes, we sure do,' Alex said.

'I need you, um, at my house. Now?'

'That would be my pleasure.' Clicked off.

Stoney decided, a boulder in his throat, he didn't like the sound of that at all.

12

Whit had called the Tran family from his cell phone – reluctantly acknowledging that Roy had a point about Thuy being a possible target more than Patch – and Dat, Thuy's son, had suggested meeting him behind the family restaurant. The Tran family worked close to Old Leo Harbor, the older and smaller shrimping harbor. Whit waited on the dock, watching one shrimper hosing down his boat, a flock of hungry gulls swarming above the decks, inspecting it for morsels.

Cong Ly, the Trans' restaurant, was only a hundred feet from the harbor and hustling from the back of the restaurant was Dat Tran, irritated and looking sick and puffing away on a cigarette as though it were his only solace.

'You don't mind if I smoke while we talk?' Dat said, the cigarette merrily burning away.

'Of course not,' Whit said. 'Again, I'm sorry for your loss.' He had visited the Trans briefly the day after the bodies were found. Thuy's two daughters and son knew nothing, they said. This was beyond imagining for them. The talk had been quiet, factual and brief. 'I just came from Suzanne Gilbert's house.'

Dat answered this with a stream of smoke.

'You're having to work today?' Whit asked. Given the family tragedy, he thought the restaurant might be closed.

Dat licked his lower lip. 'Tourist season. We can't afford to close. Other families, they're running it for us. I'm just here for the dinner rush.'

'I wanted to ask you how your mother and Mr Gilbert met.'

'Introduced by my nephew Sam.'

'How?'

'Sam was working on an oral history of the county, prepping for his senior thesis. He's at Rice, double-majoring in history and economics. Wants an MBA. Never wants to see shrimp again.' Dat blew out smoke. 'You know what the kids are like these days. He interviewed Patch for this county history, said he was funny and charming. Invited him to Sunday lunch at the restaurant. Patch met Mother there. Called her, asked her out for coffee.' He frowned, and Whit wondered if Dat was gripped by that insidious illness of grief, the if onlies. If only Sam hadn't chosen that history topic . . . if only he hadn't called Patch Gilbert . . . if only his mother had said no to coffee. *It could drive you mad,* Whit thought.

'Did you approve of them dating?' he asked.

'Usually it's the other way around,' Dat said, his voice tense. 'The Anglo disapproves of the Vietnamese.'

'I'm not asking from a racial standpoint,' Whit said. 'I'm just asking what you thought of them seeing each other.'

Dat flicked his cigarette into the harbor. It fizzed for a moment, was gone. 'Patch was a nice man. But not a serious man. Everything a joke, everything a party. My mother was a teacher, very serious about life. She took his interest seriously. I expected her to be hurt by him.' He lit another cigarette, his hands shaking. 'You're dating his niece, right? So I heard.'

'Yes.'

'Maybe Patch's family didn't like him dating a Vietnamese.'

'They've said nothing but fond and respectful words about your mother.'

Dat glared at him through the veil of smoke. 'Of course. She's dead now. Being nice costs nothing.' He

82

stared out for a moment over the flat of the harbor. 'That investigator, Mr Power, he said maybe it was a racial killing.'

Whit chewed his lip. Of course David would like the racial angle. He was politically minded, hungry for the sheriff's office, and solving a racially motivated crime would stick him firmly on the white steed of morals and justice. But there was no reason yet to think that race played a role, and he felt annoyed with David, perhaps needlessly putting the Trans through this subtle mental torture. Their mother dead was horrible enough. Their mother dead simply because of the color of her skin and the shape of her eyes seemed far worse.

'I don't believe they were killed because they were dating.'

'I can. Why not? Most people are blind-stupid. No other reason yet. You give us another reason and I'll listen to it.' His faith in humanity seemed badly shaken, another by-product of violent death.

'Did your mom ever mention Patch needing money, Dat?' Whit asked. 'A large amount of money, raised quietly?'

Dat looked surprised. 'No. Never. My mother was a very discreet woman, Judge. If Patch needed money and told her, she never would have betrayed his confidence. Was he in some sort of trouble?'

'I don't know. Perhaps.'

'He wasn't good enough for her.' Dat's voice trailed off and for an instant the mask of polite calm fell and Whit saw the man's grief, naked and cruel in its intensity. 'Sorry. I know you like the Gilberts. But that family. Their charms escape me. My mother made a poor choice.'

There was nothing to say to that, but Whit tried.

'We're all so sorry for your loss. I know Lucy and Suzanne grieve for your mother, too.'

Dat thumbed his second cigarette into the water. 'That's just so enormously comforting to me.' He stared at Whit. 'Why does a woman nearly seventy need to date, huh? Why couldn't she just stay home and watch TV like other old ladies?'

'I suppose, having survived so much hardship,' Whit said carefully, 'she valued life. Each day of it.'

'Yeah, well, look where that got her. People said we were lucky to have survived the fall of Saigon, survived the boats, gotten to Texas. Lucky. Lucky. That's us.' He turned away from Whit, heading back to the restaurant, his luck all gone.

'This is the plan,' Whit said. 'Can you go to New Orleans, find this Alex that Jimmy Bird was calling?'

'I can leave tonight. Be back tomorrow or the next day,' Gooch said. He and Whit stood in the shade of the courthouse, Whit waiting for David to come out so they could go to Corpus Christi.

'I tried the number,' Whit said. 'It's a motel. Bayou Mee. I also gave the number to the sheriff's office. Hollis or David will probably call the motel but they're not going to send someone to check it out.'

'Ooh, let me,' Gooch said. He stretched, popped his knuckles. 'It's been a boring summer.'

'Because David is targeting Lucy, and I want to find out where Jimmy Bird is. He's a disgruntled employee of Patch's.'

'So this is actually more about protecting Lucy than about justice.'

'Don't go if you don't want,' Whit said.

'No need to snap,' Gooch said.

'Sorry, Gooch. Be careful.'

'I almost hope Jimmy Boy's hiding out there,' Gooch said. 'The flip side of hiding is that someone might find you and keep you where you're at.'

'You don't hurt him, Gooch.'

'I can't arrest him. Can't bring him home. I just dispense justice as I see fit?'

That was a scary thought. 'No. You make another anonymous tip,' Whit said. 'No vigilante shit, Gooch.'

'How'm I ever supposed to have interesting memoirs someday, you keep cramping my style?'

Gooch turned and left and a moment later David emerged from the courthouse. He straightened his Stetson, watched Gooch's retreating back.

'Your friend always looks guilty of something,' David said.

'So do you,' Whit said. They walked along the grass of the courthouse yard. Two news vans, from Corpus Christi affiliates, sat like squat little vultures on the opposite side of the square. Whit hardly gave them a glance, grateful that his ever-casual attire made him look more like a latecomer paying an overdue fine than the county's JP/coroner. David slowed, as though wanting to stop and linger and talk to them. Already baking in the heat were two competing journalists, electrifying their audiences with overwrought prose: *Port Leo remains rocked by the brutal double homicide . . . A tragic end for elderly lovers . . . leaves unanswered questions.* Horror neatly filed into worn phrases to boost ratings. Those reporters had never heard Patch's booming laugh, watched Thuy's delicate hands move while she told a story, smelled the soft jasmine of her perfume.

'Big story,' David said as he started the engine. 'What we do is going to be watched. Carefully.'

'You should bone up on your preening,' Whit said.

'You might want to get a white shirt and tie,' David

said. He pulled the car past the reporters, giving them a friendly little wave. Whit saw him wince as he powered up the window, favoring the shoulder that had been shot months ago, as he always did. Whit wondered if the shoulder still troubled him or if David used it as a merit badge.

'You're not going to ask me about how my questioning of your girlfriend went?' David asked as they headed out of Port Leo, along Highway 35.

'No,' Whit said. 'I'm not worried.'

'Did you know she inherits the whole shebang?' David changed lanes, whipped around a slow-moving pickup. He said it as easily as asking if Whit wanted the radio on.

Whit was silent a moment too long.

'All of Patch's money, land, all of it. He cut out his other niece. I just talked with his attorney in Corpus. Patch made the changes less than a month ago.'

'I don't think Lucy knows. She told me they'd each get half.'

'So she said. She looked like she pissed her pants when I told her,' David said. 'Man, I love driving. Even in this traffic. Wish I had a BMW, something sweet to point down the road. Lucy can afford one now. That estate, with the land, it's gonna be many pretty pennies.' He glanced over at Whit. 'Maybe she can spring for that shirt and tie, Your Honor.'

13

'All right, here's the skinny on your bones.' Dr Parker sat across from David and Whit in a borrowed office at the morgue, where the forensic anthropology team had set up temporary shop. 'When I'm looking at bones I can only tell you so much. I don't have a way, from visual inspection, to tell you this man died in 1800 or 1900 or what have you unless maybe it was in the past three years. And these boys been dead way longer than three years. You want more specific, you call UT and get in the long line for carbon-14 dating, but that's real expensive and you don't need it.'

He cleared his throat, moved aside a stack of photos from the dig. 'You got three skeletons at the site. Three skulls, three partial rib cages, six tibia, and an odd number of finger bones and teeth. All died of bullet wounds. Sam got shot between the eyes, Tom and Uriah got shot in the back of the head. The fracture patterns . . .'

'You name them?' David asked.

'Sure, I name 'em,' Parker said. 'Helps me to remember they were once breathing people, happy, sad, hauling all the same baggage we carry around right now. Rotate through the alphabet like hurricanes. Up to S now. Let's see.' He shuffled papers. 'Now I can look at the skeletal remains and tell quite a bit. But because the disarticulation was so severe, we're making some guesses here. Sam was male, five six, European ancestry, about twenty-two at his death, right-handed. Tom was male, five five, European ancestry, about twenty-eight at his death, left-handed. Uriah was male, five eight, European ancestry, about thirty at his death, right-handed. I could be off, in that we might have matched the wrong long bones to the wrong skulls. But, hell, you got to start somewhere.'

'So they weren't Karankawas or Comanches,' Whit said. His own voice sounded too quiet, still processing what David had told him about Lucy.

'No.' Parker opened another file. 'Now, these other relics: the nails, iron latches, and locks. I sent those to my friend Iris Dominguez over at A&M-Corpus. She has books to help identify historical implements. Lots of latches were distinctive, being handmade back then, used to mark the work of a craftsman. Dr Dominguez says two of the latches come from a Spanish furniture-builder, Olivarez in Barcelona, active from 1770 until the late 1820s. The latches date from a design made around 1818. Another latch comes from a New Orleans furniture-making concern, LaBorde, active from 1800 until the American Civil War. The nails and the locks don't offer so much, less room for distinction.'

'This Olivarez and LaBorde, they made coffins?' Whit said.

'Not to our knowledge. They made chests, containers, furniture.'

Chests, Whit thought.

'So some point after 1818 is a reasonable guess? If our three boys have been dead so long, no one should have known about them being there,' David said.

'Maybe not. We even found a smaller bone chip in the grass near the surface. The bones therefore have to have been dug up first, then dumped back into the hole, covered some, then your murder victims were dumped on top. It really is strange.'

'What if . . . Sam and Tom and Uriah had been buried with something else?' Whit said slowly. *The latches. The locks,* he thought.

Dr Parker was quiet for a moment. 'I don't know what you mean.'

'You said these latches and locks could have come from chests. What do buried chests suggest to you?'

David gave a short little laugh. 'What, buried treasure? That's ridiculous.'

'Dr Parker?' Whit asked. 'Is it?'

Parker gave a thin smile under his Yankees cap. 'I don't know if there's a historical basis for it. I'm an anthropologist, not an archaeologist.'

'Your Honor,' David said, with great patience in his tone. 'Don't go off on a wild-goose—'

'I'm just saying. How do you explain these relics? David, you grew up on the coast, too. You've heard the legends. Sunken treasures off the coasts from Spanish ships caught in storms. Or Jean Laffite. He pirated in the Gulf. Patch used to tell stories about him and buried treasure. That crazy old hermit, Black Jack, that lived out on the Point and claimed to be one of Laffite's men.' He thought then of the book Patch had borrowed from the library: *Jean Laffite, Pirate King*.

'But they're just stories,' David said. 'Nothing more. Maybe these guys got buried with their belongings. That seems far more reasonable to me.'

'They weren't pharaohs,' Whit said. 'If they were killed and robbed, the robbers would have taken the chests with them.'

David rubbed his face. 'These men could have been buried in the chests themselves. We didn't find anything that suggested buried treasure at the site. I mean, honestly, do you hear yourself?'

'I'll send you a complete report when I'm done,' Dr Parker said. He seemed eager to be away from this argument. 'What do you want done with the boys when I'm finished?'

'The county will bury them properly,' Whit said. 'You can send them all back to my office.'

David stood, shook hands with Parker. Parker clapped a hand on Whit's shoulder.

'Buried treasure,' Parker said. 'Wouldn't that be something?'

'Wouldn't it, though?' Whit said.

'I've got your autopsies.' Dr Elizabeth Contreras gestured them to seats across from her metal-topped desk. She looked tired as she tucked a lock of hair behind her ear.

'Thanks for the fast turnaround,' Whit said.

'Their times of death were between midnight and four a.m. on Tuesday morning. Mr Gilbert's wound patterns are consistent with your typical garden-use shovel.'

'I thought as much,' David said.

'His nose, both cheekbones, and his jaw had multiple breaks, his collarbone and skull badly fractured. He would have died quickly. There are a number of post-mortem injuries to the body, including four broken ribs and a hard, shovel-point blow to the forehead. The killer kept whaling on him after he was dead.'

'Did he suffer?' Whit asked.

'I think not. Did you know him?'

'Yes. He was a family friend. A good one.'

'I'm so sorry, Judge.'

'Thanks. Anything else of note with Mr Gilbert?'

'No – just that it was a very brutal attack. Mrs Tran was shot to death, a .45-caliber. I think they shot her because the shovel broke, so she probably died after Mr Gilbert. She has defensive wounds on her hands and arms. Splinters from the handle. DPS can probably identify the handle manufacturer from the wood traces, the resins.' She cleared her throat. 'DPS also did fingernail swipes on them both – you may bear fruit with Mrs Tran. More likely that she scratched or grabbed at the killers during the assault.'

'Killers? Plural?'

Liz Contreras steepled her fingers. 'It just seems more likely. Let's say Gilbert gets attacked first and it's a surprise. Whoever killed him either didn't have the gun or didn't have time to draw before deciding to attack Mr Gilbert. Mrs Tran's got bruising on her upper arms. Maybe one attacker held her while another attacker killed Mr Gilbert. Then, with the shovel broken and their composure regained, they shot her.'

'So they were digging, one might assume' – Whit gave David a stare – 'and Patch and Thuy surprised them?'

'Maybe the killers were camping?' Liz said. 'Camping illegally. Campers sometimes carry shovels.'

'No signs of a campsite, but there were heavy truck tracks,' Whit said. 'So let's say there's noise from the truck, and they don't hear Patch and Thuy approach until it's too late. The two of them were supposed to be over in Port Aransas.'

'But they weren't. So maybe the killers knew their plans, expected them to be gone,' Liz said.

Knew their plans. So who knew about them going to Port Aransas? Hell, Patch might have told any of a thousand people in town what his plans were. Not a shy man. Or maybe not. Assume not. So Whit knew. Lucy. Suzanne and therefore Roy. Thuy's family. 'If you're right, the killers wouldn't have been worried about making noise.'

'Noise?' Liz said. 'I mean, you're saying noise above and beyond a regular truck, right?'

'Maybe the truck was doing more than revving its engines. Maybe it was loading something,' Whit said.

'Loading what? Out in the middle of nowhere?' Liz asked.

'Judge,' David said.

Liz glanced at the two of them, gauging the tension. Whit stayed quiet. 'I won't ask. You've got my report. The families can have the bodies back tomorrow.'

They walked into the parking lot, got into David's police cruiser. David started the engine but didn't shift into drive. 'The treasure idea. It's interesting, but until I see something more it's not relevant.'

'You can't ignore those relics.'

'I'm more interested in modern-day motives.'

'The killers had shovels and trucks, David. Do you think they were digging for oil?'

'I'm not jumping to a whacked-out conclusion, Judge. The skeletons could be old Gilbert family members. That seems far more likely than buried treasure in my mind. Surely you see that.' David eased out into Corpus Christi traffic, headed for the Harbor Bridge. 'I mean, I understand this treasure idea's interesting to you because it takes Lucy out of the equation. She's got the prime motive for the murder. She benefits the most.' He clicked his tongue against his teeth.

'Lucy had nothing to do with this. She didn't even know about the will.'

'You one hundred percent sure she didn't?'

'I am.'

'Certainty's a nice thing. You don't see it often. You want to grab dinner?' The unexpected olive branch made Whit suspicious.

'Why?'

'Christ, that's nice. We work together. I'm making an effort here.'

'Make the effort by not accusing Lucy.'

'We'll talk about it. You eat barbecue?'

There was a nasty calculation, Whit thought, in the smile, and he wanted to know what was behind it. 'Sure I do. Let's go.'

14

Gar carried Claudia out onto *Jupiter*'s deck. She was still blindfolded, and the heat of the sun touched her face and legs. He lurched and for a freezing moment she thought he was throwing her overboard. But then he settled her feet on deck, held her by her shoulders, and she realized he'd crossed the railing to the *Miss Catherine. We haven't really moved,* Claudia realized. She wondered how cold a watery grave would feel, the sky forever denied, your flesh drifting off your bones over the weeks, your leg bones and hipbones and ribs settling into the ooze, like artifacts, for the slow dissolve into muck itself.

'Don't do this,' she said. 'Please.' She balled her hands into fists, but she knew with a sick sinking feeling he was much stronger than she was. She needed a weapon to even the odds.

'He's not going to hurt you.' Danny's voice came from behind her. 'I just want to talk to you a minute.'

So this wasn't about rape, at least for the next five minutes.

Gar steered her – walking made her broken toe throb even worse – into a galley that reeked of burned pizza, with a thin odor of rum and sweat souring the air. He steered Claudia into a vinyl booth and pushed her into the seat.

'Now, Claudia,' Danny said. 'We can talk for a few minutes. While we wait to be sure Stoney's cooperating.'

Breath tickled Claudia's ear. 'If this deal sours,' Gar whispered, 'I'm gonna have fun with you. Pour some Wesson oil between your legs and have us a little marathon.'

Her heart struck her ribs like a hammer hitting piano wire.

'Let her be,' Danny said. 'Go back to the other boat.'

'Behave,' Gar said, presumably to her. Claudia heard a door close, the smell of the rum moved closer, vinyl crackled as Danny slid into the booth's other side. She put her hands – still bound in front of her – on the table. The linoleum was sticky.

'Don't be afraid,' Danny said.

'Yeah, right.' Gar's threat wriggled in her ear like a worm.

'I don't think he'll rape you. He's all talk. Those two boys, well, they slept in the same stateroom last night and I heard groaning. Don't think they had upset stomachs.' The barest hint of moral outrage colored his voice.

'He broke my toe because he didn't like what I said. And frankly, you're not in control of him or what he does.'

'I am.'

'You're not,' she said. 'I can hear it in their voices. Those two freaks are just using you to get at this cash. You're too gentle. You don't have the stomach for this or what it might take. You're as dead as me and Ben if this doesn't work out.'

'I'm sorry you're in this mess, but you picked your friends badly. You thirsty, hon? Want some water?'

'Please.'

A tap gurgled. Then he pushed a glass into her hands. She drank. He moved against the vinyl, making it squeak, trying to get comfortable. 'Tell me what you know about Stoney.'

'Nothing. I know Ben. I barely knew Stoney in high school.'

'High school. Before he was a millionaire.'

'Yes.'

'He much different now?'

'He has more lunch money.'

A match scratched, she smelled the flash of fire. Cigarette paper crackled its whisper and silky smoke brushed her nostrils. 'So in high school did he run roughshod over people? Kill anyone who got in his way?'

'Talk is cheap,' she said. 'What proof do you have he killed anybody?'

'Because only he knew about the journal,' Danny said. 'I told him about it, he decided he wanted it, and he killed to get it.'

The journal. The emerald. She'd heard him refer to both before. But this was about more, about stealing millions of Stoney's cash. 'Forget that for a minute, since he says he doesn't have it. Y'all can't get away with stealing his money electronically. Transactions leave electronic trails. You'll get caught within days.' She leaned a little toward Danny and smelled rum. 'Having a little liquid courage?' she asked.

'You want some?'

'Sure. For medicinal purposes. I get seasick when I'm uncomfortable. These ropes really hurt and my foot's aching.' Let him think she was delicate and helpless.

A dribble of rum trickled into her glass. 'Where you work, Claudia?' Danny asked, as though he were a bartender making conversation.

'I'm a secretary,' she lied. 'I work for a justice of the peace in Port Leo. Judge Whit Mosley.'

'You didn't work today?'

Today was Thursday. She had taken Wednesday, today, and Friday off. She would not be missed at the police department until Monday. But the pirates didn't know that.

96

'I took off today,' she said. 'Just today because Fridays we have juvenile court. It's always a zoo.'

'Damned kids.' She heard the soft puff of his cigarette. 'How about I call this judge? Tell him y'all ran into motor trouble down near Padre. You'll be out another day. I'll say I'm the mechanic fixing it. I'm sure he'll understand.'

She prayed, silently, that if Danny made the call Whit would have the presence of mind not to blurt, *What the hell are you talking about? She doesn't work for me.* Maybe this wasn't a good idea. 'He won't accept a stranger calling and making excuses for me. I'd have to talk with him.'

'We'll discuss that with my colleagues.'

'Colleagues. That's generous.'

Ten seconds of silence. She couldn't see his face. Frown of anger, smile of indulgence, scowl of disbelief? Or maybe ready to stub that cigarette out on her forehead.

'They breaking a deal with you?' she asked. 'They care about the money, not about punishing Stoney or this emerald or whatever it is you care about.'

'Hush now.'

'Maybe I can help you.'

'Why would you help me, honey?'

'Because I want to live. I'll get you what you want, if you'll get us out of this alive.'

She heard only the hard rasp of his breathing.

'You're not like those guys, are you? You're a little older, a little wiser. They're in this for the money. You're in it because you want the money *and* you hate Stoney. That's a big *and*.'

Now the silence stretched for half a minute. She couldn't stand it, so her words came out in a flood.

97

'Look. All I know about Stoney is he's got a big-ass house full of security. And I can get you past that security. Ben showed me the codes for the house last night, 'cause I might do some house-sitting for him and his brother when they go out of town. But I'll only help you if you don't hurt me or Ben or Stoney.' She wished she could tear the blindfold off, see his reaction to this lie. How did the blind navigate the emotions of the world, gauge human reaction? She listened for the quickening of his breath, for nervous tapping fingers against the table, for uneasy shifts in posture. But there was only the silence.

Then he said, 'Do you know why Stoney Vaughn's boat is called the *Jupiter*?'

'Because he thinks he's a god?' She spiced a little bitterness into her tone, figuring she might as well play into his resentment of Stoney by faking anger.

She heard him tap ashes. She sensed him leaning his head close to hers, his breath smelling of garlic, rum, tobacco. 'What do you know about Jean Laffite?'

'Who?'

'Laffite. The pirate Laffite.'

The words were so unexpected she didn't answer for a moment. 'Well, uh, he was a famous pirate in the Gulf a long time ago. I guess the last of the great pirates. There's all sorts of legends that he buried a lot of gold along the coast.'

'Jean Laffite had a schooner in his fleet called *Jupiter*. Stoney named his boat after Laffite's. He even has that picture of Laffite in his stateroom. Not nearly as good as the paintings I have, but still an okay one.'

She remembered the print. Yes. Laffite the pirate, confident and cocky.

'And do you know why this boat is the *Miss Catherine*?'

'Tell me.'

'Laffite's great love was a woman named Catherine Villars. She was a New Orleans quadroon – part black, mostly white – a legendary beauty. Skin like yours, Claudia, perhaps a bit darker.' He ran a finger along her hand but it didn't scare her.

'So you and Stoney are pirate wannabes,' Claudia said. 'Rent an Errol Flynn movie and get it out of your system.' This talk of pirates made her nervous. Pirates cut throats. Pirates made victims walk planks. Pirates raped and killed.

'Do you know what happened to Jean Laffite?'

'I don't imagine he ended up in a rest home.'

'No one knows. Terrible and beautiful, the not knowing.' His voice took a strange tone, one of slow, sickened anger that goose pimpled her skin. 'Here's the basics. Laffite used Barataria Bay in Louisiana as a base. Made his fortune attacking Spanish shipping. He sold his booty – mostly slaves and luxury goods – in New Orleans. His pirating kept New Orleans fat and happy in black-market merchandise, except Laffite didn't pay taxes.'

'They had IRS agents then?'

'Laffite's the social god of New Orleans, but he's an outlaw to the American government. So during the War of 1812, the British navy makes Laffite an offer: help the English capture New Orleans, and they'll give him gold, land, a high commission in their navy. Think how different our history might have been if the British had taken Louisiana.'

'Yorkshire pudding with jambalaya.'

'But Laffite tricks the British. He warns the governor about the British plans. Know what the Americans did to repay him?'

'What?'

'The Americans attacked Laffite's base, burned his operations to the ground. All for warning them. There's a goddamned sweet thank-you note.'

'Well, that wasn't very nice,' Claudia said.

'But Laffite's a patriot. A man of honor.' The heat in his voice rose. 'When Andrew Jackson arrived to defend New Orleans, Laffite offered his pirates to help defend the city. Jackson badly needed experienced fighters and weapons. So Laffite armed New Orleans – he still had more guns than the government, even after they destroyed his camp. With Jackson's blessing, Laffite and his pirates took charge of key positions as the British attacked.'

'And Laffite helped win the day,' Claudia guessed.

'He fucking dominated the day for them,' Danny corrected, battle in his own voice. 'His cannons shredded an overwhelming British force. The pirates became national heroes. President Madison pardoned Laffite and his men of their past crimes.'

Maybe Laffite just didn't want to lose his market, Claudia thought, but instead she said, 'And they all retired to Club Med.'

'Well, he wasn't gonna take a nine-to-five job. Once a pirate, you know. Eventually he left New Orleans for Texas.'

'And ended up on Galveston Island.' This part of the history Claudia knew – standard lore of growing up on the Texas coast.

'Imagine. A thousand pirates on Galveston, working all the waters of the Gulf, bringing Laffite their booty, funneling the goods to Louisiana. But one of his ships attacked an American merchantman. Laffite hanged the captain responsible on a beach gallows so that the American navy, from their ships off Galveston, could see the body dangling – but the US government wasn't appeased. They ordered Laffite out of Texas, out of the Gulf.'

Laffite sounded like ninety-percent asshole to her, barely a hero, but Claudia sensed Jean Laffite burned as real as the sun for Danny.

'The man had saved New Orleans but they forgot about that. Typical American arrogance. But Laffite obeyed. In spring of 1820, he sailed away, leaving Galveston burning to the ground.' He stopped, as though picturing the scene, a fading shot of an old black-and-white movie in which the cutthroats were the gallant heroes.

'Then what?' Claudia asked, wanting to slap him, to shake him, to say, *This happened almost two hundred years ago. Why am I gonna get killed over this?*

'The stories vary. Some say he went to Yucatán and died of fever. Some say he went to Cuba and died in a sea battle. Some claim he tried to rescue Napoleon from St Helena. One man, a supposed descendant of Laffite's, claimed Laffite returned to America under an assumed name, and lived out his life in small-town Missouri.' This last option was pronounced with sarcasm dripping from every word. 'But no one knows. Of course, so many say that he buried a treasure, worth millions, somewhere in Texas or Louisiana.'

'Treasure,' she repeated, thinking of Ben talking yesterday at lunch about Stoney. *He's financed some treasure dives in the Florida Keys . . . Crazy-ass way to risk your money.*

'Imagine the scene, Claudia. The government Laffite served so well in a time of need has completely betrayed him. He left as he promised, but the American navy shadowed and harassed him all the way down the coast. He would have had reason to believe the navy might board or attack him at any time. Or the British or the

Spanish might attack him. Remember, he was being evicted, leaving his base, leaving nothing behind. Nothing.' A pause. 'His only option to keep his treasure from falling into others' hands would have been to bury it so he could return when the heat died down and retrieve it.'

'It seems risky,' she said.

'Laffite knew the shallows and reefs in getting through the barrier islands and the bays. The American navy couldn't follow him there.' Danny cleared his throat. 'The proof was in the journal – real, actual documentation – that Laffite buried a fortune near St Leo Bay. Before Stoney stole it from me. Like you said, you help me, maybe I help you?'

He's inviting you in. The trickle of sweat began between her breasts, down her ribs. It was the only chance she saw; Stoney knew who Danny was, which meant a trail could be followed back to Gar and Redhead. She and Ben were guaranteed dead, unless she could make herself valuable.

Make it good, girl. 'Tell me more about this journal. Maybe I can figure out where Stoney hid it. I'm pretty familiar with his house.'

'Looks like an old diary, brown, leather-bound, small pages. Written in the 1820s by Dr John Fanning. He was the ship's surgeon on the navy schooner *Lynx*. According to Fanning, *Lynx* detained Laffite after he left Galveston, boarded his ship outside St Leo Bay, searched it for traces of loot from a Spanish treasure ship, *Santa Barbara*, which had been lost barely a week before. *Lynx* escorted Laffite to Mexico, dumped him there penniless, pardoned his crew. One of Laffite's crew, a drunk, told Fanning Laffite went ashore with a few other men and buried a trove from *Santa Barbara* at Black Jack Point – but that only Laffite returned. Of course the historians have it wrong, the Fanning journal rewrites Laffite's history. And I had it. It was *mine*.'

Claudia bit her lip.

'If the journal's right, the treasure might be worth several million now, on today's market. The historical value alone would be astonishing. Actual, provable buried pirate treasure. Think what the museums would offer, Claudia. The Smithsonian, for instance. Millions. And there was supposedly a great emerald aboard *Santa Barbara* – a huge Colombian gem called the Devil's Eye. It would be of . . . particular value.'

'So you approached Stoney about helping you find this treasure? And Stoney stole this journal from you so he could locate this treasure himself?'

'Yes.' He sounded completely serious, for a moment completely sane. If you ignored the words.

'But Stoney has money. He doesn't need a bunch of old gold that might not even exist.'

'He has money that anyone else can have. But a treasure, that's one of a kind. His ego can't resist it. And I don't think it's buried anymore. I think he's got it.'

'You think he dug it up?'

'I don't think he's been waiting around with his thumb up his ass,' Danny said. 'He came to New Orleans, where I live, when I was out of town, and he took the journal. He killed my cousin, who was house-sitting for me. A bullet to the brain. A cowardly way to kill.'

'I'm sorry your cousin was killed,' she said. 'Truly. But what happens to me if I help you? If I can get you this journal? Or this treasure?'

'Well, Claudia, I'll let you go.' Easy, like he was suggesting they grab an ice cream cone down at the beach.

Right. But she pretended to believe him. 'What about Ben?'

'Oh, I'll let him go, too. I don't have a quarrel with either of you. I have a sense of honor.'

'Yes,' she snapped. 'Your sense of honor's why I'm tied up and blindfolded with a broken toe.'

A silent minute passed. Then there was a gentle downward tug on the chamois blindfold. It slipped down to her shoulders, like a scarf. The light in the cabin was dim, and she blinked, but now she saw Danny sitting across from her. His thick dark hair was shot with salt, combed back from his temples, his eyes an earthy brown but feverish and bloodshot, a drunkard's eyes. Crazy-man eyes.

In his hand – aimed at her heart – he held an automatic pistol.

'If we're gonna help each other, I gotta trust you, you gotta trust me, right?' he said.

'That's true. And I would like to trust you, which is hard for me if I think you're going to kill me or Ben or even Stoney. Even if he's a killer and a thief.'

'I'm not the monster Stoney is, Claudia. I won't kill him. I just don't want him to have the treasure. It's mine. It belongs to me, in every moral way.' Heat colored his voice, his hand slapped down on the tabletop, emphasizing the last three words. 'I'll let him live if I get the treasure. I swear on my family's name.'

Then that makes it all just fine, buddy. 'You don't know me. Why would you trust me?'

'I don't trust you. You don't trust me either, I know. But I don't want to have to kill you. I want the treasure, I want to be shed of these two assholes now, and I don't want to go to jail. You get me into Stoney's house, you live. It's your choice.'

She said nothing for a minute. The hunger in his eyes

made her skin crawl. *Fine. It's his weakness. Use it against him to save you and Ben.*

'So we got us a deal?' he asked.

Claudia nodded.

15

'I'm begging you not to hurt my brother,' Stoney Vaughn said over the speakerphone. 'Please. Let me explain.'

'We just called the banks. Ain't no money streaming in,' Redhead said. No giggle now. 'Where're those scissors?'

'Jesus, Stoney, please,' Ben yelled. 'Give them what they want.'

Stoney's throat cleared. 'I can't. The transfers couldn't go through. The computer systems at my investment firm are down. We got a virus. They aren't going to be up until tomorrow.'

A moment's silence. 'Stoney, Jesus . . .' Ben said, his voice barely above a whisper.

'A virus, you know. Like that Anna Kournikova picture that got e-mailed around. It wasn't a picture, it was a virus. Our servers are down.'

Gar sprung up from the couch, pacing, angry little hums coming from him. 'So move it via another bank.'

'I can't. This server's got to work first. My accounts are all locked and accessed through here. Please, you got to give me more time.'

'Wrong answer,' Redhead said.

Ben felt the tickle of scissors moving along his jaw, his throat, downward along his chest. 'Stoney, please, they're gonna kill us! Give them what they want.'

'Stoney,' Gar said quietly. 'You understand our position. It's not negotiable.'

'Let me talk to Danny,' Stoney said. 'Let me suggest an alternative.'

'He's not here right now,' Redhead said. 'You can talk to us. We're all partners.'

'Oh. Well. I don't have this journal or this emerald he's talking about, okay? That whole idea, that's just fucking crazy, man. I don't have it. I'll give you the money. But you got to give me time.' He paused. 'As a sign of good faith, I raise the pot.'

'We're listening,' Redhead said. The scissors stopped their wandering, poised above Ben's stomach.

'Get Danny to forget about this imaginary jewel he's asking for. Eliminate it as a condition. Let my brother and his friend go. I'll pay you an extra half million.'

'Wait a minute,' Redhead said. He jabbed the speaker-phone's mute button. 'What do you think?'

Ben heard Gar let out a long breath. 'I'll take a half mil in cash over bullshit. But he still ain't wired no money yet. So that could be a fucking lie, too.'

Redhead jabbed the button again. 'How do you get us the extra money?'

'Is Danny there?'

'No,' Redhead said.

'I've got a half mil in a separate account.' A pause. 'But you get rid of Danny. You can have the money. But not him.'

'We can't access the accounts without him,' Gar said.

'That's your problem. I'll send it when he's done and gone, you understand? And then the rest.'

'Stoney, what the hell are you doing?' Ben said. 'Holy shit—'

'I'm saving your ass,' Stoney said. 'Now just hush, Ben.'

'And you just take our word we've gotten rid of him?' Redhead said after a moment's hesitation.

'No. You bring him to me. At my dock at my house at Copano Flats. I'll give you the money as cash when you turn over his body and my brother. His girlfriend, whatever. She's a cop. Do whatever you think is best.'

'Fuck,' Gar said.

'Stoney, for God's sake!' Ben screamed.

'Shut up, Ben,' Stoney said.

'Leave Claudia alone. Don't you dare fucking hurt her,' Ben said in a low voice. 'Please . . .'

'You could have the place swarming with cops,' Gar said.

'But I won't,' Stoney said, 'because I've just asked you to kill Danny for me. I have no reason to invite the cops to our meeting. Take the money and forget you ever heard of Danny, okay?'

'We'll call you back in five,' Redhead said. 'Be there.' He clicked off the phone. 'Interesting turn of events.'

'She a cop?' Gar grabbed Ben's arms, brought him off the couch.

'Fuck you,' Ben said.

'I'll take that as a yes,' Gar said.

'This could be a delaying tactic. I don't buy that about the computers being down,' Redhead said.

'But he wants Danny dead,' Gar said. 'And we get a half million as a bonus for what we're gonna have to do anyway.'

'Play it this way. Get rid of the woman. Don't take the risk she's a cop,' Redhead said. His voice was cool and firm. 'I'll set up new overseas accounts for us. Then let Stoney hear Danny die. Strangle him, you're strong enough. Make Stoney move the money then. Then we just see about whether or not he gets his brother back. Little brother might be mad about girlfriend getting offed and might talk to cops. Huh? You gonna talk, little brother?'

Ben made no answer.

'I'll take care of the girlfriend,' Gar said. 'Have a little fun first, though. I always wanted to fuck a cop.'

'No, you're not,' Redhead said. His tone went peevish, hurt.

'Don't worry. You're my favorite. Stay here. Just watch him.'

Ben heard Gar move heavily up the steps. 'Claudia!' Ben yelled. 'Claudia, Christ, no!'

A gun barrel jabbed hard into his testicles. 'One more word,' Redhead said, 'and I shoot them off.'

'You—' Ben started but he didn't finish.

'There, Christ, you happy?' Stoney's hands shook as he set down the phone.

'Wasn't so hard, now, was it?' Alex sat on the corner of the desk. Pissed as hell when he got here, but then he'd calmed when Stoney explained. It made Stoney nervous.

'My brother—'

'We'll worry about him later. First we got to make sure Danny can't tell what all he knows. You see that now. He put two and two together, he can't live to testify.'

'You screwed up,' Stoney said. 'Goddamn it. You should have killed him.'

'Our paths didn't cross in New Orleans,' Alex said. 'Is that my fault?'

'But my brother . . .' Stoney's voice faded.

'Hey, man, you could have done what they said. Sent the money flying along the cables. You didn't. Don't lay this on me.' Alex stood, looked out over the bay. 'They ought to be here soon, assuming they call back and all's well.'

Stoney leaned over and vomited into a wastebasket.

'That's nasty. Yuck.' Alex handed Stoney a tissue. 'Now. Problem number two. The emerald that's in the storage unit's a fucking fake, Stoney. Can you explain that to me?'

*

'So we gonna kill them,' Danny whispered.

'No killing anybody,' Claudia said. 'Not if we don't have to.'

'If you're gonna chicken out if push comes to shove, I need to know right now.'

She raised one eyebrow. 'Don't worry about me.'

'Fine, then. I got a plan.'

'Let's hear it,' she said. He had loosened the rope on her wrists a little and her hands prickled with returning sensation.

'I got chloroform on the boat, thought we might need it to subdue Stoney,' he said. 'When one of 'em comes back over here, you distract him, mouth off to him, and I slap 'im with the chloroform cloth.'

'Maybe something simpler,' Claudia said. 'Maybe you putting your gun at the back of his head and making him drop his gun.'

'What if he don't surrender? What if he shoots you or me?'

'He's not likely to do that with a gun at the base of his skull. And if you're behind him he can't shoot you.'

'He might shoot you,' Danny said.

'Then you need to press that gun hard against him so he knows you mean business.'

'If I shoot one, the other will hear.'

'You got a fire extinguisher here in the galley?' she asked. Danny nodded toward the cabinet under the sink. 'You put the gun on him, get him to freeze, I'll belt him in the head with the extinguisher. Knock him out.'

'That means you got to be untied.'

'Yes.'

Danny chewed his lip. Now that she could see his face clearly, study it, she didn't like the flat shine in his eyes. Not clever but cagey.

'You begged me to trust you, you got to trust me,' Claudia said. 'I can't be much help to you tied up.'

'You punched me,' he said. 'You're the toughest little cookie in the jar. You might try to take the gun from me.'

'Well, I won't,' Claudia said. 'You can trust me. It's your call.'

He put his gun down and loosened the ropes from around her hands. She kept her hands very still. 'If I take the ropes off all the way he'll notice.'

'I'll tuck my hands under the table.'

'What about your blindfold?' he asked. 'He'll be suspicious if it's off you.'

'Leave it off,' she said. 'If we lose, he'll kill me anyway.'

Danny took his Sig and got up from the galley booth.

'Do you have any other guns?' Claudia asked.

'No,' Danny said. 'I'm for gun control, actually.'

'Then give me the gun.'

'You'll shoot me,' Danny said.

Yes, I will, she decided then. *But later and in the leg.* 'This is ridiculous. I'm not going to shoot you.'

He still seemed to think, working the inside of his cheek.

She played a cautious card. 'Yes, you're just like your hero, Laffite. Heart of a warrior. You can't make the simplest decision.'

His eyes narrowed. 'You don't understand. I'm this close . . . after what all I've lost . . . I can't lose the Devil's Eye. Or the journal. It's what I've lived for, honey.'

His stare and his sad confession made her queasy. 'You gonna trust me or Gar and the redhead more?'

'I got a plan. You get down in the stateroom, lay down on the bed like you're sleeping. He comes down there to check on you, he's got to go down those narrow stairs. I put the gun behind his ear then, make him drop his.'

'In a stateroom there's not much cover,' she said. 'You're nice and safe behind him and I'm not.'

'It's just a variant on your original idea.' He sounded peeved.

'With all due respect, I don't think you have the nerve for this.' She kept her voice calm. 'I was in the army right out of school. Give me the gun and let me handle him.'

'I'm not giving you the advantage, Claudia. If I were you I'd shoot me – maybe not kill me, because you seem like a real nice lady – then get on the radio and call for help.'

'Where's your radio?'

'Up on the bridge.'

'It doesn't make sense for me to shoot you and then try to call for help. Your buddies might spot me up on the deck and open fire.'

He didn't say anything, rubbing his thumb along the Sig's handle.

'But they won't think anything of you being up there, Danny. Can you go up there, call the coast guard on Channel 16?' Sixteen was the regular monitoring channel, on which boats hailed each other in short order before moving their communications to another channel. A lifeline connecting all sorts of boats on the water, Channel 16 was monitored by the coast guard. 'Call a Mayday, tell them it's a kidnapping situation, request help.'

'And then I get arrested. No way.'

'You're going to get caught anyway. My plan's the only safe way out for you. I promise.'

Danny stared at her. 'But Gar'll have *Jupiter*'s radio tuned to 16. They'll hear us. Or they'll see me using the radio and they'll go nuts.'

'Then call on 22A. That's the coasties' liaison channel. Go up there, crouch down low, and get us some help.'

He shook his head. 'If they see me, they'll kill me.'

'They're going to kill you anyway and you're a moron if you don't see that.'

He suddenly – but gently – pressed the barrel underneath her chin. 'Listen. You're not the boss here.'

'If you kill me, Stoney won't give you what you want.' She felt calmer than she could have imagined with a gun held to her head by a clearly unstable man. But his finger wasn't on the trigger. He was playing with her and the idea of death, and she stared back at him.

'Get down to the stateroom.' Danny pulled her to her feet, gave her a little push. 'Lay down like you're sleeping or crying. My plan'll work.'

She didn't argue. The stateroom on *Miss Catherine* was tiny, the bedspread worn, smelling of Cheetos and beer, like a cheap motel room. On a side table was a stack of books. All about Jean Laffite and early Texas history, little bits of neon-colored paper sticking out from the pages like bright plumage. Clothes lay in an untidy heap on the floor. Danny prodded her with the gun, grazing the back of her head, and she clambered onto the bed, her foot throbbing.

'At least untie me so I can fight him if I have to,' she said.

He hesitated.

'So am I help or just bait?' she snapped.

'I'm deciding,' he said.

'I thought you were a gentleman. You're just an asshole.'

'Shut up.'

'No,' she said. 'I won't. You want my help, you better start helping me. Untie me. Or you're going to have to

shoot me, because I'm not cooperating with you anymore.'

He made a sigh of exasperation. 'This is why they
didn't have women on ships of old.'

'You told me before I picked my friends badly. You
picked yours worse. You get to pick again, at least for
now.'

'Danny!' Gar's voice rumbled from the deck.

Danny shoved her onto the bed. 'Pretend. We don't got
time for your plan.' And he hurried back up the stairs.
She heard the galley door smack open, heard Gar demand
in a low voice, *Where's she at?*, heard Danny answer in a
mumble that Claudia was scared, downstairs, he'd let her
try to take a nap, keep her out of the way.

She tried to wriggle her hands free from the rest of the
rope. The rope gouged her skin. She heard Danny saying,
'I don't think so.'

Claudia yanked her right hand free. Screw being bait.
She jumped up from the bed, huddled in the closet. Wire
hangers jangled above her head, tangled in her hair. She
needed a weapon; she clawed the hangers free from her
head.

*The hanger. Make it into a loop of wire, a garrote, grab
him from behind, choke the air out of him.*

She grabbed one, twisted it hard, unraveling the spiral
of wire at the top. Another twist. Another. Heavy footsteps pounding on the stairs, Danny screaming to wait
a goddamned minute. Fists hitting flesh, hard, the un-
mistakable pop of knuckle against jaw.

Not enough time. She dropped the hanger, looped her
hand around the length of rope hanging down from her
wrist. Maybe not long enough. Nothing, she had nothing.

The stateroom door flew open, smacked against the
closet door. She saw Gar, shirtless, his back a scrimshaw
of gaudy tattoos, a mass of muscle moving underneath

the faded inks. 'You ready for—' He stopped for a second, seeing the empty bed. But she couldn't spring out at him, the open stateroom door jamming up against the closet door.

She was trapped.

Gar glanced around, saw the sliver of her in the closet, smiled with half his mouth. 'Hidin' don't help.'

Claudia took a step sideways in the closet. Nothing in here, nothing to help her. Her fear tasted like smoke in her mouth.

'Change of plan, Officer. But you'll like it.' Gar slid the closet door open, grabbed Claudia by the hair, yanked her out of the dark narrow space. Shoved her to the bed. His pale chest looked wide as a door, his arms like pile drivers. She wriggled away from him. 'You don't fight me, you make it nice, I'll protect you from my boy. He's not gonna be happy, you gettin' what he likes. Oh, no. He might cut your eyes out when we're done. So you be a good girl and fuck nice and I'll—'

Claudia punched him, hard, across the jaw. He blinked, frowned, and blood welled up in the corner of his mouth. He cussed and backhanded her, the knuckles of his hand like rocks against her jaw. Little black flowers blossomed in front of her; he held down her throat, pressed his weight into her legs.

'I'm gonna fuck all the fight out of you, honey.' He grabbed her head and started pulling her up from the bed when the shot rang and she heard a sound like a hard thump on a melon. Blood exploded from Gar's nose, his mouth, spraying Claudia. She screamed. He fell on her, and she kicked out from under him, wriggling along the headboard, tumbling to the floor off the bed.

Danny kept the gun pressed to the back of Gar's head. He stared at Claudia.

'Oh,' he said. 'Oh. That's done.' Then he grinned at

her, proud of himself, the dragon slayer. 'Are you all right?'

Her vocal cords turned to ice. 'You killed him.'

Danny pulled the gun away from the blasted back of Gar's head. 'Sure I did.' Danny seemed to not quite believe his new bad-ass status, staring at Gar, as though the big man's shoulders would suddenly hitch with breath.

She stood, her jaw aching, her foot hurting from the broken toe. 'The redhead will come. Or maybe he heard the shot.' *Oh, God, he'll kill Ben.*

Danny turned the gun toward her. 'You could at least thank me.'

'Thank you,' she said. 'Don't shoot me.'

He tilted his head at her and she didn't like the dead, flat look in his eyes. No shuddering shakes over having just killed a man. The fact was done, filed, out of mind.

'I won't leave Ben at his mercy,' she said. She moved toward the door; he followed her with the gun.

'Stop, Claudia.'

She stopped.

'What are you doing?' he asked.

'I'm going to radio for help.'

She expected him to argue with her, order her to stop, but there was only the silence of the waves brushing the hull of the boats. Then the rev of an engine. Not theirs. *Jupiter*'s.

'Oh, no,' Claudia said.

'Stay,' Danny said.

She heard *Jupiter*'s motor rev again, and *Miss Catherine* swayed.

'If we're still roped to them . . .' she started and he lowered the gun.

She ran up the stairs, through the galley, and peered through the galley door's window out onto the deck. *Jupiter* was free from them, the lines cut. Gunning away from them. She could see Redhead in the flying bridge, hunkered down low, steering.

'He's running, he's taking Ben,' she said.

Claudia turned to face Danny and the foam hit the side of her face hard, cold and sharp, and pain knocked her down with an iron slap. She moaned, then liquid dribbled onto her face, smelling of stale air and medicine, and she was gone.

16

Dinner was the 'Vengeance Is Ours' special: grilled hammerhead, with little plastic cups of melted butter for dipping, drippy corn on the cob, and French fries thick as a finger. Whit Mosley and David Power sat in the canopied shade of the oaks bending over Stubby's. The food was excellent but the locale was not gourmet; rather, Stubby's was a trailer, with a walk-up window and a barbecue in the back that offered up pork ribs and brisket, except this morning Stubby's son had snagged a hammerhead on the edge of St Leo Bay and the unlucky shark debuted on today's menu. The tables were old cable spools, upended, each one surrounded by stumps weathered smooth from the rubbing of a thousand butts. Clouds filled the evening sky and it was still too warm and sticky for comfortable outside eating, but David wanted Stubby's. Plus fewer people meant it was less likely they would be overheard.

David bit into his shark, which made Whit think it was truly a dog-eat-dog world.

'Let's get one thing clear. I'm not gunning for Lucy because you're involved with her. You could give me some credit. I can't not consider Lucy. You understand that.'

'But you do have this other suspect. Jimmy Bird.'

'How'd you know?'

'His wife hates your guts. She called me. I called Hollis about it. She got an idea that Jimmy ran off to New Orleans.' Let him talk to Sheriff Hollis about it, Whit decided.

'Well, why didn't you tell me?'

'You were too busy telling me about Lucy,' he said. 'And Mrs Bird asked me not to talk to you.'

'She's just a drunk.'

'I got an anonymous tip today.'

David lowered his corn, butter dripping from his mouth. 'Aren't you popular?'

'I heard Patch Gilbert asked around town about quietly raising a hundred thousand dollars.'

'For what?'

'That I don't know.'

'I assume the tip didn't come from a loan officer at a bank?'

'No. Hence the anonymous,' Whit said with a thin smile. 'But don't you think it would be wise to check Patch's finances? Maybe see if he owed debts, gambling, I don't know what, but this had to be big.'

'We're already on that,' David said. 'Jesus, a hundred thou.'

'According to Lucy, his other niece, Suzanne, asked for a loan in that amount. Suzanne denied it to me. Said she asked for ten thou, Patch said no, she got the money from a friend. Lucy claims she and her ex-con boyfriend have gambling problems.'

'Lucy's sure well-informed.'

'Patch had money,' Whit said, ignoring the jab. 'At least he was land-rich. I don't see why he would need to be trying to get a private loan.'

'You sure you don't know who this tip came from? Was this a phone call?'

'It's just anonymous, okay?' Whit said. He owed Gooch his life; if Gooch wanted anonymity, Whit gave it to him. The lie felt slick and unpleasant on his tongue but he didn't change his mind.

'You know who it is, don't you?' David wadded up the wax paper that had held his grilled shark. 'That's all right. I'm not going to bust your chops over it, Judge. I mean, you're an officer of the court. A public official. You sure don't owe anything to law and order, no, sir.'

'Treat it like any other tip.'

'You sure this didn't come from Lucy?'

'It wasn't Lucy.'

David mopped at his mouth with a napkin, picked shark from between his front teeth. 'Uh-huh.'

'It wasn't Lucy.'

'I mean, it's one family member pointing the finger at another, right, maybe just a little. A little?' David held up his forefinger and thumb a centimeter apart.

'I know you don't actually suspect Lucy,' Whit said and made his tone sure.

'Was she with you Monday night?'

'Yes.'

'What did y'all do Monday night?'

'You already questioned her.'

'I'm asking you, Your Honor.' Stress on the final two words. 'As an officer of the court.'

Whit tore a French fry in two. 'We had dinner at my place. Watched a movie.'

'What for dinner, what movie?'

Asshole, he thought. 'Gazpacho. Grilled trout. A salad. Some Australian white wine she brought. I cooked the fish. The movie was *Shakespeare in Love*. She rented it.'

'Didn't think you did. And she didn't spend the night?'

He could argue but decided not to. They had nothing to hide. 'We both had busy mornings scheduled. She went home about eleven.'

'And you?'

'I went to bed.'

'When did you see Lucy next, Judge?'

'When she showed up at the courthouse to tell me Patch was missing.'

'She's in big debt. That psychic network thing? Well, you got lots of kids calling it. Parents bitch, charges get cut. Or the folks that charge up on their credit cards, they default, don't pay. But that don't mean Lucy's staff, her expenses, get cut, too. She's gotten in deep financially. She tell you about getting sued by a couple of creditors in the past month?'

Whit was silent.

'I thought not,' David said after a moment. He licked butter and shark from his fingers.

'That is still a real long road from murdering people the way Patch and Thuy died.'

'I found your button, now, didn't I?' The smile was coldly amused. Miffed, Whit saw, over the tips, over Mrs Bird calling him, over the idea of Whit having an advantage.

'I suppose Claudia was the same button for you,' Whit said, knowing as soon as the words were fired they'd hit like bullets.

David didn't blink. 'I'm over Claudia. You can tell her that the next time you see her.'

'You want to make trouble for Lucy? Fine. But watch where you step. Be very careful, David, because you take a misstep, I'm going to be on your ass like white on rice. I think I'll have a talk with your boss about these skeletons, since you don't seem to think they matter very much.'

'I didn't say that.' David stood. 'I'm keeping every angle open. That's what an investigator does. But I'll give you a piece of advice, Judge. I don't think you can afford Lucy Gilbert. The press won't be kind, and they love a little funky twist like her maybe killing two old folks to get the money to salvage her psychic hotline business.'

'I think you love the funky little twist more than finding out the truth.'

'Whatever,' David said. 'But you keep telling me to lay off Lucy Gilbert, I'm telling the press. I got the perfect phrases already in mind. And you're gonna be in front of a judicial review board or facing a recall election in two seconds flat.'

'Don't threaten me.'

'Don't worry. If she did it, I won't ask you to sign her arrest warrant.'

After David dropped him off at the courthouse, Whit drove home, to the guest house behind his family's grand Victorian, to do chores on his computer and gather some clean clothes before heading back over to Patch's to stay the night with Lucy. His father, Babe, and his Russian mail-order stepmother, Irina, weren't at home and he felt a tickle of relief. He didn't feel like talking to anyone. In his small kitchen, Whit poured himself a glass of ice water, then flopped on the couch, wanting to get back to Lucy but grateful for the peaceful quiet of the moment. He propped his feet up on the table. He'd head over to Lucy's in a few, get to bed early if Lucy let him. To-morrow was Friday, the long, annoying haul of juvenile court, his least favorite judicial chore, and then he'd . . .

His bedroom door was shut.

He never left it shut; in the little house in the summer, the window units froze a closed room into a miniature Antarctica and left the other rooms sticky-warm. You had to be careful; sometimes the door, old and a little warped, closed on its own if he brushed past it the wrong way.

Whit went to the door and listened to the rattle and hum of the overtaxed window unit. He opened the door. His bedroom was as he'd left it when he'd last slept in it, the night Patch died: books stacked next to the bedside phone, bed made in haste, dirty clothes in a tidy pile, ready for his Saturday laundry duty, closet door shut. He went to the closet, opened it. Clothes hung in neat lines, a cavalcade of ugly-bright tropical print shirts. In the corner was his computer and a small desk he used for work at home, with a few file folders and the *Texas Civil Practice* books. Nothing gone.

But the room felt subtly shifted, as though every item was just a hair out of place. He went through his files, his drawers, glanced under the bed. Nothing was missing. But the files on his desk were in two stacks instead of one, the books on his desk were leaning, and he hated that.

The room had been searched. He felt the odd tingly linger of an intruder in his space.

He went back to his front door. The lock appeared whole and unscratched. He checked his spare key – still hidden under the porch's neglected potted fern. He inspected the windows. A back window wasn't locked and he couldn't remember when – if – he had unlocked it. He locked the window, went back to the den, refilled his water glass.

He tried calling Claudia Salazar at home, wanting a shoulder to bitch on about David Power. No answer. He tried Gooch's cell phone. No answer either; Gooch was still presumably en route to New Orleans.

So who was in your house?

He checked every room. Maybe he had bumped the door the last time he left and it had shut on its own. Maybe David talking to him about Lucy – about what he didn't know, her inheritance, her debts – made him paranoid. Christ, what else about her life didn't he know?

Maybe she was embarrassed. Maybe she was ashamed.

It was time to get David off Lucy, time to find evidence that would point elsewhere. David was competent but not imaginative. He might dismiss Patch wanting secret funding of a hundred thousand or the skeletons found with the bodies. They could be little fringe elements that had nothing to do with the heart of the case. And Gooch looking for this Alex in New Orleans might lead nowhere fast.

So what else did he have? The name on the bottle, the guy Suzanne mentioned as interested in buying Black Jack Point.

Whit took his drink and sat down at his computer. He logged onto the Internet, opened a search engine, and did a search for *Stoney Vaughn*.

Results were few – a couple of articles in the Corpus paper, an article in some highflier financial magazine Whit had never heard of. He'd risen fast in the investment world, the kind of quotable grandstander the press loved. Scrappy son of shrimpers killed when he was at the University of Texas – where he'd gone on a full scholarship. Economics and history degree, MBA from Stanford. Worked for a venture capital firm in Silicon Valley for a while, took a hit in the dot-com bust, came back to Texas, and apparently started phoning the Social Register to get clients. The newspaper article included a picture. Average-looking, confident, hair a shade too glossy, a hint of gut, cool, confident, the kind of young man the numerous wealthy old ladies of the coast liked to have handle their money.

Not much else. Another link on the *Corpus Christi Caller-Times* site when he'd opened his office, another when he'd built that monstrosity of a mansion out on the Copano Flats, a link to something called the Laffite League. He clicked on the link.

A simple Web site opened, with an old portrait of a rakish man who wore a broad mustache and looked every inch the gentleman robber. Underneath the portrait was the text:

The Laffite League explores and celebrates Jean Laffite, the great pirate of the Gulf, one of the most unusual and mysterious figures in American history. Membership is open to all at dues of $50/year. We have chapters in New Orleans, Galveston, and Corpus Christi with a total membership over 100. We are academics, historians, teachers, students, businesspeople, jet pilots, nurses, retirees – anyone interested in the days of old. We sponsor trips to Galveston, Grande Terre, and other sites to explore Laffite history and also offer a quarterly newsletter on all matters Laffite-related.

Below the statement were links to newsletter archives, an on-line forum for Laffite discussion, and sites for historical research. And below that, a list of officers of the League, with Stoney Vaughn as president of the Corpus Christi chapter. He searched through the rest of the site. No mention of Patch Gilbert.

A fan club for a dead pirate. An overdue book about Laffite. Skeletons. And Stoney Vaughn, giver of whiskey, buyer of land, whose name kept sidling into view.

Whit clicked back to the newsletter articles, wondering if there was much discussion about buried treasure. He found none – this was all straight, well-footnoted history. The articles ranged from detailed analyses of the Battle of New Orleans during the War of 1812, where Laffite played a key role, to speculation of Laffite's ultimate fate. Several of the articles were attributed to a writer named Jason Salinger, and the short bio at the end of each minutely researched piece indicated Jason was a freelance writer working in Port Leo, Texas.

He looked up Jason Salinger in the phone book. Not listed. He could track him down tomorrow.

He saw, through his window, his father moving in the

soft glow of the kitchen lights in the big house and headed up there.

'You want me to change the locks?' Babe Mosley said after Whit explained.

'Just as a precaution, Daddy.'

'Why on earth would anyone be breaking in and then not taking anything?' Babe sipped from a cup of decaf, still a big man at sixty, his face creased and handsome.

'I don't know. But I'd feel better if you changed the locks.'

'I'll call the locksmith tomorrow.' He lowered his cup. 'You staying out with Lucy again?'

'Yes.'

'Come stay here.'

'She wants to be at Patch's house, and I don't want her to be alone.'

'I wish y'all would just stay here,' Babe said. 'I'd sure sleep better.'

'We're fine.'

Halfway up toward Black Jack Point, he thought, *Why wait? See if Stoney Vaughn's at home tonight. Ask him about the Gilberts.*

He drove past the Point, toward Copano Flats, looking for a big-ass mansion.

17

Stoney had only managed to keep Alex from shooting him outright by saying, 'I don't know what you're talking about with the emerald, but these guys are going to be here soon and we got to deal with them first.'

'I looked at it. Closely. It's not real.' Alex's voice was low and precise and getting impatient. 'The Eye's looking a little bloodshot.'

'I didn't know you were an emerald expert.'

'Where is it?'

'You're not supposed to have a key for both locks. We agreed.'

'You fucking stole from me and you're going to chide me?' Alex, his tone disbelieving, shook his head, the gun in his hand pointing at the carpet for the moment.

'I didn't steal from you.' Stoney glanced back out at the bay. 'Oh, God, here they come.' But it wasn't *Jupiter*. It was a smaller fishing trawler, idling along the near edge of the bay.

'The Eye, please. I'm not helping you with Danny and his boys if you don't cough it up.'

'Listen, I took it to protect it.'

'Really. How's that?' Like he couldn't wait to hear the details.

'Danny. Look, he knows we've done the dig, he's in the area, he's seen the papers about Black Jack Point and the murders. He knows we've got the Eye. He might find out where we'd hidden it.' He took refuge in outrage. 'Listen. You had a key I didn't know about. We're even.'

'We are so fucking not even!' Alex's gun came up, centered on Stoney's chest.

'If anything happens to me,' Stoney said, 'there are tape recordings of our conversations over the past couple of months. About Patch Gilbert. About the Laffite treasure, the Devil's Eye, your little fuckup in New Orleans. Multiple copies, hidden in multiple places. In multiple forms. Tape. Sound file. A couple of ways you might never guess. But sure to be found if I go missing or die, Alex. I'm not Jimmy. I'm not dumb.'

'You're bluffing. You wouldn't take that chance of fucking yourself over.'

'I might. For insurance. I've always been overinsured.'

Alex put the gun down, turned, and walked out of the office.

'Where you going?' Stoney said. He followed Alex down into the big white living room, full of old nautical maps on the walls, thick leather-bound tomes of history. Alex knelt by the stone fireplace, opened a decorative cylinder of long matches next to the equally decorative stone fireplace. The match was about nine inches long; it could burn for a while and you wouldn't singe your fingertips. He took the cylinder back to where Stoney stood at the bottom of the steps, punched him hard in the mouth. Stoney's lip split. He fell back, a little dribble of blood and snot smearing on his chin.

'Uhhhng,' Stoney said.

Alex grabbed the front of his shirt, shoved him back onto the stairs.

'Insurance,' Alex said, 'can be fucking expensive.'

Stoney spat blood. 'I can't believe you hit me, you shit.' But a little quaver in his voice gave him away.

Alex slapped Stoney, lightly, almost playfully. 'You steal the Eye from me. You call me, tell me Danny's got your brother and wants to make a trade. For the Eye. So, what, we give them the fake Eye to save your brother? And I never know the real Eye's gone? It's sort of half clever.'

'Like you'd let me give Danny the Eye. I'm not that stupid. You never would.' He mopped at his nose. 'You heard Danny's friends on the phone.'

'I did. I'm not impressed. You could have friends I don't know about, Stoney. Playing a phone prank of sorts. All designed to fool me.' He grabbed Stoney by the throat. 'Where's the Eye?'

'I won't—'

Alex ran the match tip – unlit – underneath Stoney's eyebrows, along the rim of his ear. 'Does it tickle?'

'Oh, God, no,' Stoney said. 'Please.'

'I don't want to burn you.' Alex struck the match along the wall; it flamed into life. 'But I will. Start with this. Then I'll drag you down to your dock. Get some gasoline worked in good on you. Kick it up a notch.'

'Oh, Mary, mother of God, no,' Stoney sobbed.

'Where is it?'

Stoney watched the fire. 'The Eye's on the boat. My boat. That's where I hid it. Danny's got it. He don't even know it.'

'And they're coming here?'

'Yes. Please, you can get it then.'

Alex blew out the match.

It was now close to eight.

'I don't think the bad guys are showing up, Stoney.' Alex watched the empty dock from the kitchen's bay window. The stars had begun to glimmer in the dying summer twilight. 'I think we've been stood up.'

'Jesus. They said they would bring my brother . . . for the money after they killed Danny . . .'

'You don't look good, man.'

'Christ.' Stoney reached for the whiskey bottle, took a tiny sip. Alex watched. Tiny sips didn't hurt until you'd taken a hundred of them.

'I think, Stone Man, you need to prepare yourself for bad news. I think these guys killed your brother and this girl of his. That's why they're not showing up. Can't get the cash for a corpse.'

Stoney let out a blubbery sigh.

'Now. Danny. He's out there somewhere.'

Stoney looked up at him, his face as blank as a new blackboard.

'Let's say Danny's still alive. But he's lost his bargaining chips, 'cause maybe these fuckheads killed your brother and his girl. So he's got to go somewhere. He's gonna try to get at you again – he'd rather have the treasure than you in jail, if it's one or the other. He can hardly accuse you of murder if he's done the same now. So where would Danny go?'

'I don't know.'

'He's got friends around here. You know him, Stoney.'

'No . . . no one I can think of.'

'Other folks in the Laffite League?'

'Some in Corpus, maybe. He's not well-liked; people think he's nuts.'

'Ah. You start making some phone calls.'

The doorbell rang. Stoney froze by the phone.

'Not a word' – Alex pulled his gun from the back of his pants, pressed the barrel beneath Stoney's eye – 'or I will kill you and whoever's on the porch. You understand?'

'Not – not a word,' Stoney said in a broken voice.

Alex hurried to the front door, quietly. He peered through the peephole.

Some guy, blondish, tall, standing on the porch, looking around. His head a little rounder from the distortion of the glass. Wearing a bright orange tropical shirt.

Alex moved back from the peephole. The doorbell rang again, a knock followed.

Alex waited. He peeked through a living room window, barely edging back the closed curtain, and saw the guy in the driveway, talking on his cell phone. Then clicking off the phone.

A knock again on the door, doorbell ringing.

'Mr Vaughn? Whit Mosley. I'm the JP here. I can tell you're home. Would you please open up?'

Alex waited. A few more knocks. After about five minutes Whit Mosley climbed into a Ford Explorer and roared off. Stoney walked back into the foyer.

Alex put the gun on him. 'A JP's a judge, right? Why's he here?'

'Probably to tell me my brother's body has been found,' Stoney said. His voice sounded a lot more even.

'They'd call. And it wouldn't be a judge.'

'I don't know and I don't care,' Stoney said. 'Put that gun down. I can't talk to you with it in my face.'

'You're not in a position to make demands. You've lied to me. We agreed we'd rebury the treasure on the land you bought out at the Point. Discover it together as Laffite's treasure, make a mint, get famous,' Alex said.

'You don't give a shit about that, Alex,' Stoney said. 'Not about the fame. You just want the treasure. But we can both get what we want. We need to work together, stop fucking each other over. Between the murders and now Danny everything's gone south. I'm making a drink and we can talk.'

He turned and went back into the kitchen. Alex lowered the gun and followed him.

'Where's the courage coming from?' Alex asked. Stoney poured a thin film of bourbon into a glass, topped it off with ice water.

'From knowing I'm going to make a great deal with you.'

'So. Deal.' Alex never enjoyed killing but he thought he

would really like killing Stoney, even if it was one bullet and quick, like snapping your fingers.

'First we have to find Danny. And find my brother.'

'This whole kidnapping shtick's not a fake?'

'I swear, Alex, it isn't. You can't take the risk that it's not.' He gulped at his drink. 'Danny could screw us both over, end it for us easy. He's nuts. He's not going to behave like a normal human being.'

Alex took a deep breath. 'So we sit and wait?'

'I don't start calling around to Laffite Leaguers, showing an interest in him. They'd remember that later. So get patient. He's going to call. No way he's not going to see this through. We wait here, together. You can kill him when he shows up.'

'Me? Why not you? It's your fucking brother he took.'

'Because you're good at offense. I'm better at defense.' Stoney put down his drink. 'And here's how we both stay happy. I'm willing to give you three-quarters of the gold and silver. You can melt it down or sell the coins on the market. I keep the rest and the Eye. That I rebury on the land, dig back up, have my glory.'

'As the only discoverer of actual buried pirate treasure in history.'

'We're both happy and we don't commit mutually assured destruction trying to fuck the other over,' Stoney said.

Alex tented his cheek with his tongue. 'What about your brother and this cop girlfriend?'

'They'll have killed her. My brother, he can be reasoned with.'

'Your brother might talk,' Alex said.

'My brother will never have to work again if he doesn't want to,' Stoney said. 'You don't worry about him. Now. You can play tough, try to rough me up some more, and completely fuck yourself over. Or you can crash here with me and see if Danny shows up tonight, and then we're home free. What's it gonna be?'

Alex crossed his arms. 'I don't sleep on couches.'

18

Gooch thought the Bayou Mee was appropriately named, as the two girls near its parking lot might say, *Buy. You. Me.* The Tulane Avenue open-court motel was grimy, the dive more residence than family fun stopover. It was a few blocks from the New Orleans Criminal Courts Building and nearby were several bail bond businesses, and Gooch wondered if maybe the Bayou Mee catered to those recently released from jail. He'd seen two women go from the darkened parking lot to rooms with new friends and return in a half hour, but they weren't shimmying hot-panted rears on the street corner; rather, the two looked more like regular girls, T-shirts and denim shorts, just hanging out in the motel lot, gossiping, and maybe if you knew the password, you'd get a date. Gooch spotted one police cruiser go by, not even tap on its brakes. Late Thursday night, the girls not too busy yet.

He'd paid for his room and said, 'I'm looking for a friend of mine.'

'What's her name?'

'Alex.'

'Don't know an Alex.'

'You know a man named Alex?' Gooch laid a fifty on the desk. 'You know any Alex at all?'

'What's he look like?' The clerk was a bony kid, dirty-blond hair, sullen, his nose pierced with a thin hoop of gold. He scooped the bill into his jeans pocket.

'Alex was here about a month ago.'

'But what's he look like? Names don't matter much here.'

'He might have had some phone calls back to Texas on his bill. Does that ring a bell?'

'You a cop?'

'Do cops give money for answering questions?'

'Sure, sometimes.'

'I'm not a cop. Or a PI.'

'Alex don't ring a bell. Most of the guys here have classier names than Alex, like Bubba or Hoss. Or John.' He laughed.

'Thanks,' Gooch said. 'Think about it.'

He went back to his room, started watching the girls. A truck pulled in, the taller girl leaned down, chatted, laughed. The shorter girl walked over to a plastic crate two doors down from Gooch, sat, lit a cigarette.

Gooch opened the door, walked past her. She glanced at him, made a little frown. He fed coins into a decrepit Coke machine.

'It's broke,' she called to him. His coins rattled in the machine.

'Works good enough to take money,' he said. 'My friend told me this was a real nice place to stay, and here you can't even get a sody pop.' He glanced at her, grinned.

She grinned back. 'Who's your friend?' she asked.

'You know Alex?'

'I don't believe I've had the pleasure.' She flicked ash off her cigarette.

'How about a guy named Jimmy Bird?'

'Nope. You sure have a lot of friends,' she said.

'Don't you?'

'I've always been popular because I see the best in people.'

He stood near her. She glanced at his face, which wasn't ever going to make a girl smile. She looked at his worn jeans, his gray T-shirt, scuffed boots, trying to make if he was a cop.

'The Alex I'm looking for might be in Texas now.'

'Better than here.' She was looking down at the ashes at her feet, stubbing at them with her sandal.

'Any Alexes ever work here?'

'No,' she said.

'Alex might have stayed here a month ago, for at least two days, maybe more.'

'I said I don't know an Al—' But her voice broke off and she looked back up at him with fear and a bit of confusion, as though she'd just understood a joke. She stood.

'What's your name?' he asked.

'I got to go.'

'Alex isn't a friend.' He'd seen fear in her face now. 'But I want to find him. Or her.'

'Baby, I love chatting, but any more of my time, you pay.'

'How much for an hour of your time?'

'Seventy-five.'

'I just want to talk to you,' Gooch said.

'Costs the same.'

He nodded.

'We should go to my room. I got some Comfort there. I could use a drink.'

Her room was on the opposite side of the court, the window missing, plywood up in its place. She said her name was Helen and she made them both drinks, Sprite and Southern Comfort, in little plastic cups. She didn't have ice cubes and the Sprite was a little warm.

'You're quite the hostess,' Gooch said. He gave her the seventy-five bucks, all of it. She counted it and sat down.

'I said something that scared you,' he said.

'Alex I don't know. But I know an Albert Exley. That was the name he used here. I called him Al 'cause I don't like Albert as a name. That's close to Alex, isn't it? He was here about a month ago.'

'What's he look like?'

'Wiry. Way stronger than he looks. Wears glasses. Brown hair, about six one. I saw him come in here, I figured, all I need, another social worker trying to get me to work at Popeye's Chicken. Or a Jesus freak.' Helen sipped from her cup. Gooch thought she couldn't be more than twenty-five, already faded, her skin pale and her hair a dark lank. 'Yeah. He's a social worker like Hitler was.'

'What did he do?'

'You a cop?'

'No. I'm a concerned citizen.'

'Someone needs to concern Albert Exley's ass off the street.' She pointed at the plywood. 'He put me through that window.' She raised her arm and he could see a web of healing scar threaded along her skin. 'Tore up my arms, my back, bad. And I'm practically his girlfriend.'

'Explain.'

'He's here for four or five days. I can't figure him out, why a guy looks like a professor is here. He hires me a couple of times a day, like he's passing the time.' She shrugged. 'I kept feeling he wasn't just hanging out here, he was in New Orleans on important business of some sort. But I know better than to ask. Just keep my mouth shut. Well, open, but you know what I mean.' She laughed.

Gooch wanted to give her a Greyhound ticket, say, *Just go somewhere else and start over and don't do this anymore*. She'd look at him like he was one of the Jesus freaks.

'We're getting along fine. One day he's gone most of the day, most of the night. Comes back in a bad mood. I think, he's been nice, I'll see if I can relax him. This was his room then, not mine, so I do him how he likes and he gets in the shower. He says I can watch TV if I want, 'cause there's not a TV in my room, and he knows I'm not gonna bother his wallet. His cell phone rings when he shuts off the shower, and so I click it on, thinking I'll just hand it to Al, be cute, and a guy calling starts yelling, all panicked. I'm telling the guy to calm down and suddenly Albert yanks the phone out of my hand, listens, then throws me through the window. I'm lying there, naked, bleeding like nobody's business. He grabs his stuff, jumps in his car, he's gone.' She shook her head. 'Cops looked for him, but I guess not too hard. I don't pay taxes so I don't pay their salaries. Jerry, the owner, he makes me move into this room, says it was my fault the window got busted. Cheap asshole won't put in a new window yet, and it's too hot.' Helen looked ready to cry.

'I'll speak with Jerry. You'll have a new window,' Gooch said.

She stared up at him.

'The caller. What was he upset about?'

She shrugged. 'I wasn't sure. I had trouble remembering real clear after I went through the window. I lost too much blood. But when I think about it, I think he was saying something like, "You dumb fuck, you got the wrong guy."' She finished her drink. 'You don't want to mess with Albert. He's nuts. He'd kill a person over answering the phone.'

'When I find him,' Gooch said, 'I'll put him through a window for you.'

'That's sweet. But you better grab him from behind,' Helen said, and despite the sticky heat she gave a shiver. 'Don't let that man see you coming. You don't get no second chance with him.'

Whit left Copano Flats, driving through the soft, scrubby land, turning back onto the main highway as night took real hold, heading south again toward Black Jack Point. Stoney Vaughn was either shy or rude; Whit was sure someone was at home, the lights on in the house, the Porsche and the beige van in the driveway, just the sense he'd gotten of an eye behind the door. Maybe there'd been a girlfriend over. He'd try again in the morning.

He'd tried Gooch again while waiting to see if someone came to the door – no answer. *All problems for to-morrow,* he decided, too tired and jumpy to think. *Go to Lucy, have an honest talk about David's claims, go to sleep.*

When he walked into Patch's house, Lucy was sitting in a fat armchair, her knees pulled up to her chin. Suzanne Gilbert sat across from her, an empty wineglass at her elbow. Roy Krantz lounged on the couch.

'Hi,' Suzanne said.

'Hi, Judge,' Roy said. No warmth, not surprising.

'You took a while,' Lucy said.

'I'm sorry. I had court business . . . what's wrong?'

'What isn't?' Lucy mopped at her face with her sleeve. 'Suzanne and I are discussing the land. Selling it. I think it's a bit too early for that – Patch isn't even buried yet.'

Oh, God, he thought. *Lucy hasn't told them Patch cut out Suzanne.*

'Offers're gonna come in,' Roy said. 'We already got a call from a Houston developer.'

'Who are these vultures?' Lucy said. 'I hope they call me. I got a whistle right by the phone. They'll be deaf when they hang up.'

'They're not vultures,' Suzanne said. 'They're business people.'

'Me, too, but I don't trade before funerals,' Lucy said. 'It's tacky.'

'Tacky like exaggerating private loan amounts,' Suzanne said.

139

Lucy ran a palm along the chair arm and didn't look at Suzanne.

'I love you, Lucy, and this pains me,' Suzanne said.

'I love you, too,' Lucy said. 'But your vibe is all bent.'

'We better go,' Roy said. 'Lucy, nobody meant to upset you.' He stood. 'C'mon, Suzanne.'

Whit walked them out to their car.

'I forgive her,' Suzanne said. 'The innuendo. She wasn't thinking straight.'

'Sure,' Whit said.

'There's not going to be any more silly accusations, right?' Roy said. 'We've got it straight now.'

'That's between you and Lucy,' Whit said to Suzanne, ignoring Roy.

They left.

He went back inside, sat on the arm of Lucy's chair, slid his arm behind her thin shoulders. She leaned into him, turned her face up for a kiss. One. Then another.

'The glue is gone,' she said. 'With Patch gone Suzy Q and I are not quite so sweet to each other.'

'Did you argue with them?'

'No,' she said. 'But Suzanne feels betrayed. She doesn't understand why I mentioned her money troubles. But she didn't yell at me. I wish she would've thrown a vase at me.'

'This will get better with time, Lucy.' He sat on the ottoman at her feet, took both her hands in his. 'Is there anything you want to tell me?'

'I'm not up for another firing squad tonight,' Lucy said.

'I rode in to Corpus with David. For the autopsy reports.'

'Oh.' Her voice went small.

'He and I had a talk about you. Do you want to tell me anything?' Whit asked again, his voice soft.

'No. I'm too embarrassed.'

'About your debt? Or the lawsuits? Lucy, I'm not mad but I sure wish you had told me.'

She didn't move. 'Do you bring your hearings home, Whit?'

'Not unless they're funny.'

'Well, I keep my business separate from our time together, too. I knew I shouldn't have mentioned Suzanne's gambling. This is just bad karma piling up on me.'

'How bad is your debt, Lucy?'

'I'm okay. Business picked up last month.'

'How bad?'

'Fifty, sixty thousand. I can get a bridge loan. Phone entertainment is a growth industry.'

'Have you really been sued?'

'David Power needs a doughnut in that mouth,' she said. 'Yes. A woman whose old mother called all the time. She was nutty, but she had a nice aura and so the girls helped her. No one was trying to take advantage of her, but I had to settle out of court. It's fine.' She stared at him. 'I'm sorry I didn't tell you but, Whit, you're a politician.'

'Barely.'

'You're still an elected official. I didn't want you to be embarrassed, dump me.'

'Thanks for the vote of confidence,' he said. He kept her hands in his. 'David says you inherit everything.'

'That's what he says.' She shook her head.

'You don't know?'

'There's a message in there to call Patch's lawyer . . . but there's a ton of calls. I haven't called them back yet.'

'Apparently Suzanne gets nothing.'

'No. That can't be right.'

'Patch probably didn't want his money gambled away. And he loved you, Lucy.'

She made a noise in her throat, covered her face with her hands. 'That makes me look worse, though, to the police.'

'David's blowing smoke right now. You ever hear of a guy named Stoney Vaughn?'

She blinked. 'The rich guy with the big house up the bay. I don't know him, just heard of him.'

'Patch ever mention him?'

She blinked again. 'I don't think so. Whit?'

'What?'

'You believe me, don't you? I didn't know about the will. Patch never said.'

'I believe you, Lucy.'

She leaned into his arm and they stayed that way, silent, for several minutes, the ticking of the den clock and the soft hum of Lucy's breathing the only sounds. 'Could you make love to me?' she said in a quiet whisper. 'I'm a wreck and you're all that makes me feel good right now. If you don't mind making love to wrecks.'

He kissed her, slow, and she kissed him back, tentative at first, then harder, surer. They went up to the guest bedroom. Lucy stripped him first, opening his shirt, sliding off his pants, kissing his mouth, neck, shoulders, chest, pausing just long enough for him to ease her out of her T-shirt and shorts, her bra and little red panties. They slid onto the cool of the sheets and when he entered her she clung to him, fingers and mouth and nails and toes, with a fierceness that made his skin sing.

They rested in each other's arms for a while. Then she kissed him deeply, her fingertips exploring the length of him, seeing if he might stir again.

'Whit?'

'Yeah?' he said in a thick voice, lying against the sheets while she took his measure.

'How much is the estate? Do you know? If showing an

142

interest in the money doesn't make David Power indict me automatically.'

'I don't know, Lucy.'

'If it's enough, I think I'll shut down the Coastal Psychics Network,' she said. 'It's been nothing but a headache.'

'So what will you do?'

'This all day.' She straddled him and guided him into her. The second time was even better. They were less tense and they rode the wave together.

'Is that a job offer?' he said when he had his breath back, laughing, liking the feel of her warm breath against his chest.

'I'm so the boss of you already,' she said. 'Love you.'

'Love you.'

'I'm safe with you, aren't I?'

'Always, babe.'

Finally she slept. Whit stared at the ceiling, tired, spent, ashamed for the millisecond of doubt he'd allowed himself to feel. He drifted off into heavy sleep and it seemed two seconds later the phone rang.

Whit grabbed it, trying not to shift and wake Lucy. The digital clock on the bedside gleamed: 1:47.

'Hello?' Whit whispered.

'Judge Mosley?' David.

'Yeah?'

'We found Jimmy Bird. Dead.'

PART TWO
Here There Be Dragons

There are few things as powerful as treasure, once it fastens itself on the mind.

— Joseph Conrad

19

The raw smell arose near a thick growth of oaks. Whit stood upwind of the grove. It was two-thirty Friday morning. A couple of summer-house kids, looking for a less crowded makeout spot, had found the battered winch truck nestled at the edge of the live oaks, just beyond the western city limits of Port Leo, away from the busyness of the beaches and the harbor. Jimmy Bird's body lay curled on the seat, the bullet hole in his temple surrounded by a direct-contact, mottled bruise from the gun. The gun – a .45-caliber – lay on the truck floor, below Jimmy's dangling hand. The DPS crime-scene crew pulled the body from the truck after their initial photographing and scene work. Whit filled out an authorization of autopsy form.

David finally came up to Whit to countersign the authorization.

'I suppose this wraps things up, Judge.' David scribbled his name across the sheet below Whit's signature.

'Yeah,' Whit said.

'Get the doubt out of your voice. There's a note in Jimmy's shirt pocket. Reads: "I'm sorry for what I did Monday." Broken shovel in the back of the pickup. And these were in his pants pocket.' David pulled a plastic Baggie from a paper bag, laid it flat on his palm, turned his flashlight onto his hand. A half dozen coins, roughly cut, clearly old, a shield capping one, a man's head crowned with laurels decorating another, one silver, the rest gold.

'These look old,' Whit said. 'Holy shit. I was right.'

'Let's not jump to conclusions, Your Honor. Maybe

Patch had a coin collection – we don't know. Jimmy might have stolen these from the house.'

'Lucy never mentioned Patch collecting coins. Neither did he.'

'Found cash and Patch's credit cards in the glove compartment. He's got to be the guy who did the break-in. This doesn't have to be complicated.'

Whit leaned in, examined the coins through the plastic. 'There's a date: 1818 – see? This one's 1820. Good God.'

'Yeah. And I know where you're going, back to this buried-treasure horseshit.'

Whit lowered his voice to a whisper. 'David. Look. Don't think of this as buried treasure. See it from another angle. It's archaeology. If there were professors out on Black Jack Point doing a dig for artifacts, and they got killed and dumped there, you'd have to consider people stealing those artifacts as a possible motive. Right?'

David nodded.

'Well, maybe this was just a dig we didn't know about. That no one knew about.'

David didn't nod, just shook his head.

'So, David, maybe Jimmy had accomplices. And if these coins are part of a treasure, where's the rest of it?'

David spat into the grass.

'Why are you resistant to this?'

'I'm not about to go in front of the press, or let Sheriff Hollis go in front of the press, and say those people got murdered over buried treasure,' David said. 'Christ. If that wasn't the case, we'd be fucking laughed out of town. No way are we going public with this. Let's just be real quiet about it right now, see what else we learn.'

It was as much as Whit could hope for. 'But we'll find out how much these coins are worth, right?'

'Yes, obviously.'

'I suspect they may be worth quite a bit,' Whit said.

'Jimmy couldn't have been depressed over being broke. Maybe Dr Parker's colleague, the one who identified the other relics – her name was Dominguez, right? She might know about coins.'

'You let me worry about that. I want to confirm if Bird's tire tracks match the tracks we found on the Gilbert property, and I want to see if there's any extra fingerprints on that truck or gun. Let's go wake the widow, Judge.' He shook his head. 'Much as I don't like Linda Bird, I don't want to tell her that her husband's dead.'

When he got back to Patch's, Lucy was awake, curled on the couch in a robe, watching the bargains unfold on the Home Shopping Network. He told her what had happened.

'But I don't think Jimmy Bird killed them,' he said at the end.

She sat up. 'Christ, Whit. David Power's been breathing down my neck. He finds the killer, and now you're going to debate him? What the hell is it between you two?'

He told her about the coins in Jimmy's pocket. 'They look old, very rare. Gold and silver. Why would he have those?'

Lucy folded her hands in her lap and said after a moment, 'Patch had some old coins.'

'You never mentioned that.'

'Well, we don't usually discuss my uncle's heirlooms.'

'I didn't know he was a coin collector.'

'He wasn't. He got them from his dad, I think. I don't really remember. He said once they were valuable. He didn't keep them out in the change plate, Whit. He had them in a drawer in his study.'

'How would Jimmy know where they were?'

'I have no idea. Maybe he made Patch tell him where they were. Maybe he knew from when he worked here before. I don't know.' Her voice rose, got an edge.

'Okay, Lucy, okay. Did he have them insured?'

She stared. 'I don't fucking believe this, Whitman. You don't believe me.'

'I do.'

'I don't know if he had them insured. Jesus. That Jimmy. Goddamn him. Uncle Patch never should have hired him in the first place.' She got up, went into the kitchen. Whit followed her, watched her pour a glass of water, pick at a cookie from the many comfort plates on the kitchen table. 'He killed them, then I'm glad he's dead.'

'There's nothing more to be done tonight. Let's go back to bed.'

'Fine. Okay.' She gulped down her water.

In bed, he spooned next to her, his arm over her, listening to her breathe. He could hear she wasn't falling asleep.

'Whit?'

'Yeah?'

'I'm sorry I snapped at you. This has all been upsetting.'

'I'm sorry, too.'

'I thought finding out who did this to them would make me feel better.'

'Probably not right away, hon.'

'I just need you to not be trying to one-up David Power.'

'It's not about a competition. I'm trying to help you.'

'Do you think David sucks as an investigator?'

'No. I really don't. But I think he abuses his power. I think he's hurt about his life, he's mad at the world, and he's a spoiler. He knows how to push my buttons.'

'Only works if you allow them to be pushed.' She rose up on one elbow. 'You've got a confession from a dead guy with a motive. Please stop pushing. Please? I can't take it anymore. I want this over and done.'

'Okay.'

'I can tell when you're not sincere, and it has nothing to do with vibes. I'm serious, Whit. I want you to stop.'

'Okay.'

She settled back into his arms, he didn't give an answer, and finally he heard her sleep. Only then did he close his eyes and let himself drift away, and in his sleep his breathing matched hers.

Lucy decided to put in a day at work and Whit, not due at court for two hours, followed her into Port Leo. Early Friday morning was not phone-jamming rush hour at Coastal Psychics Network. The little office was squeezed in between a grimy doughnut shop and a grimier liquor store in an old strip shopping center that had never seen better days. Two bored college students sat on duty at the phones, a black woman reading a physics textbook, chewing on the end of her highlighter, and a white woman watching *Today*.

'Hi, y'all. Slow night?' Lucy asked as they walked in.

'Yeah.' The first woman looked up from her textbook. 'People just don't have problems like they used to.' She slipped a tarot card into her textbook, shut the book.

'It'll pick up,' the other psychic said. 'We're moving into the Bored Housewives hours.' There was an embarrassed silence. 'We're sorry about your uncle, Lucy.'

'Thanks, Amanda.'

'You don't want to talk,' Amanda said. 'It's okay. I sensed that in your aura. Let me know if you want a reading later.' She glanced at Whit. 'Oh, dear, isn't someone's aura a little thin today.'

The two phone psychics looked at him, looked at each other, then back at Whit. 'You're the disbelieving boyfriend,' Amanda said.

'In more ways than one,' Lucy said, but not sounding mad anymore.

'Man, ditch your negativity,' the black woman said. 'It's an anchor on your soul.'

'I think I like being weighed down,' Whit said.

'It's not insurmountable negativity,' Amanda said. 'You have a beautiful spirit. You just need a cleansing influence. Some healing crystal treatments should clear you up.'

People pay a buck twenty-nine a minute to hear this crap? he thought. But he smiled and gave the peace sign. The two psychics frowned.

'C'mon back to my office, Whit,' Lucy said. She hustled to the back, to a small office. She had a foil mobile hanging from the ceiling, an assortment of thick multicolored crystals and sculptures on a shelf above the desk, books on ESP, the tarot, and guerrilla marketing on a table. She shut the door. 'Baby, after everything else, I don't need you upsetting the employees.'

'They started it.'

'They did not. They read you like a book. These are very sensitive, sweet girls and there you stand, thinking how stupid all this is. They can tell, you know.'

'You didn't read my mind.'

'I know you think this is bullshit, but it isn't to me, to Amanda and Lachelle, to our customers. Okay?' She was being loud and for a minute he wondered if it was for the women's benefit.

'Okay.' He took her in his arms. 'I love you. Does my aura show that?'

'Yes, actually it does.' She kissed his cheek. 'I love you, too. Tons. Beyond tons.' She hugged him hard. 'This'll all be over soon, won't it?'

'Yes.'

'Can we go away then? For a week, just us? Maybe Mexico. Hawaii. Disney World. I don't care.'

'Sure, Lucy. You pick.'

'No,' she said. 'You pick, and then I'll read it in the cards. I'll prove this works.'

'Deal,' he said. He left, letting her think he was headed to court.

20

Jason Salinger, at first glance, reminded Whit of a lawn gnome. He was short, bearded, with apple cheeks and fat pink lips surrounded by a thick beard. He wore a T-shirt that read FOOTNOTE FETISH.

Jason said, 'Don't knock over any of my books.'

Easier said than done. Whit followed Jason into a dingy living room converted into a library. Books tottered against a computer desk. More books covered the sofa and lay scattered across the floor.

'You're a big reader, then?' Whit stepped over a smaller stack of books and took a seat on the corner of Jason's sofa.

Jason looked at Whit as though he were mentally damaged. 'Why, yes, I am.'

Any books on social skills? Whit nearly asked but instead he smiled.

'Excuse him. He's a bear in the morning,' Jason's wife said. Cute and plump, dressed in faded jeans and a blue T-shirt, she was as sweet as he was dour. 'Aren't you, sugar pop?'

Jason made a strangled noise of agreement.

'Would you like some coffee, Judge Mosley?'

'No, ma'am, thank you. I've already filled the tank for the day,' Whit said.

'I'll have a cup, please,' Jason said.

'You know what the doctor said about you and caffeine.' She patted Jason's shoulder, gave Whit a maternal wink, although he guessed she was six or seven years younger than he was. 'I'll let you boys talk.'

Then Whit noticed the headless pirate in the corner.

Not headless. But an old tailor's mannequin, just the body's form, with a fancy blue coat, a red sash under the jacket, grayish pants. A sword and a revolver – they looked genuine – hung off the mannequin.

Jason swiveled a chair away from his computer desk and sat facing Whit. The Salingers' house was in an older, slightly untidy section of Port Leo. The lawn looked untended, the furniture in the house fresh from the consignment store. But the books in Jason's work area were fat, expensive hardbacks, lots of them, and his computer system was a top-of-the-line model.

'What can I help you with, Judge?'

'I understand you've done a lot of research on Jean Laffite.'

'I do freelance magazine writing, substitute teaching, some book editing for a couple of very small presses.'

'But Laffite's your own particular interest.'

'Sure. Gonna go to grad school in another year or so, write the definitive book on Laffite one day. Probably get a doctorate with a focus on Gulf history. Be able to teach anywhere from Texas to Florida that way. I don't do cold winters well.'

'I'm interested in the Laffite League.'

'This has something to do with Patch Gilbert, right?'

'Why do you ask?'

'Well, he came to the last chapter meeting in Corpus in May. I figured he was interested in joining. Sorry to hear about him getting killed.'

'You knew Patch?'

'No. I just met him that one time at the meeting. He was a friendly guy, introduced himself to everyone. You don't forget a name like Patch.'

'Let's talk about the League first. What exactly is it?'

'I can slice the Laffite League into three groups for you. The vast majority are people with a strong interest in history, perfectly nice and respectable. Then there are those who are interested in the legends of buried treasure, although there's never been anything other than old rumor to say Laffite buried his gold instead of spending it. But those folks have seen the movies, like *The Buccaneer*, and they think Laffite is Yul Brynner as a romance-novel swashbuckler.' He swiveled on his chair. 'Then there are the very small but fascinating subset of wackos. A few have claimed to be Laffite descendants, and have forged journals and documents to sell to the gullible or to try to live off the name.'

'Dangerous wacko or amusing wacko?'

'Amusing. There's a guy who calls himself Danny Laffite – it's not his real name. Nutcase in Louisiana, says he's Laffite's great-great-great-great-grand whatever. But harmless. He tricked some guy in Houston into paying ten thousand for letters supposedly written by Laffite to Andrew Jackson. Fakes, obviously. He ended up giving the money back and avoided prosecution.'

'He's in the Laffite League?'

'Was. They revoked his membership. Forgers don't make for trustworthy historians.'

'What about all these legends of buried treasure?' Whit asked.

Jason shrugged. 'There's no evidence Laffite buried an ounce of gold along the coast, but the rumors persist. Treasure means glamour. Adventure. Instant wealth attained in an interesting way, as opposed to the boredom of work.'

'Romantic money.'

'Sure. We all read or saw *Treasure Island* as kids. We all want to be Jim Hawkins, outwitting Long John Silver and finding the gold,' Jason said. 'Long John Silver. The only fictional murderer I can think of with a fast-food chain named after him.'

'The truth is less romantic than the fiction,' Whit said.

Jason jerked his head toward the mannequin. 'Every year I dress up in that costume, pretend to be Laffite, go to the schools, and tell them the stories. The kids want to hear about Laffite being a movie-style pirate: storming ships, cutlass in hand, saving fair damsels on blood-soaked decks. That's all crap. Laffite dodged taxes, sent out other captains to capture ships, dealt more in slaves and cotton than in gold. Was careful not to attack American shipping because that meant trouble. So he preyed on everyone else. More administrator than swash-buckler. And cold-blooded. A few months before he left Galveston a hurricane devastated the island. Not enough food for the thousand people living there. Laffite's solution was simple: round up every black on Galveston, slave and free, and sell them in the underground Louisiana slave market. Even the free black women who were married to Laffite's men. All hauled onto ships, the wives screaming for their husbands to save them. Laffite shot anyone who resisted. Fewer people to feed, fresh money in the coffers to rebuild after the storm. Simple and brutal.'

'But you admire him.'

'I admire his decisiveness,' Jason Salinger said. 'We're a much less decisive world now. We analyze. We agonize. We second-guess. Laffite never had that luxury. Maybe one day I'll write a book for business managers: *Business by Laffite*. You know, you find different avenues to make your money these days as an academic. Got to go mainstream.'

'So where did Laffite keep all his money? There were no banks in Galveston then, and presumably a legitimate bank wouldn't touch him.'

'He probably laundered money and gold back into the banks in New Orleans. He had the best lawyers in New

157

Orleans working for him. And he and his brother, Pierre, filed bankruptcy, saying they had very little. But of course mobsters today have hidden under that same cloak.'

'But any accounts would have always been in danger from the US government? If they suspected an account was Laffite's, they'd've seized it, right?'

Jason frowned but nodded.

A large map of the Texas coast was pinned above the computer. Whit stood and studied it. 'Indulge me. Let's just say, over the years, Laffite amasses a tidy fortune in gold. At least enough to get him started over if he abandons Galveston or his New Orleans accounts get seized. Or maybe he makes a few big captures right before he's forced out of Galveston. He can't go into port in New Orleans – he'll be arrested as a pirate if he steps on US soil, right?'

'Yes,' Jason said. 'He'd have been arrested if he set foot in America. His forces had already annoyed the navy by attacking an American merchant ship, although he'd executed the captain responsible. What finally empowered the American government to kick him out of Galveston was the capture of one of his ships, *Le Brave*, during an attack on a Spanish ship. *Le Brave*'s captain had papers that outlined the division of booty, written in Laffite's hand, with his signature. It was the smoking gun the navy needed.'

'So Laffite's on the run. He's got no place to go. If he's transporting gold he stands to lose it if he's stopped or attacked, right?'

'He was given a document guaranteeing safe passage by the US Navy to leave the Gulf. They wouldn't have bothered him.'

'But that wouldn't protect him from the Spanish, right, or any other country whose ships he attacked?'

Jason frowned. 'No, it wouldn't. But pirates really

didn't bury treasure very often. That's way more *Treasure Island* than common practice. I mean, it's accepted that Captain Kidd buried a treasure up in New England. But it's never been found.'

'But maybe Laffite's got a better chance for long-term survival burying this treasure – just for a few weeks or months – than hauling it around a gulf sailed by navies who are pissed at him and risk losing everything. He's a man without a country. Put yourself in his shoes. Where would you bury it?'

Jason stared at him, as though wanting to ask a question, but didn't. He ran a finger along the curve of the coast on his wall map. 'Not Galveston or Bolivar. Far too risky to be caught by an American patrol making sure he didn't return to the area to set up shop again. Maybe further south or north.' His finger moved south along the map. 'Laffite had camps up and down the coast. For sure in Matagorda Bay and on St Joseph Island.'

'Did he have a camp on St Leo Bay?'

Jason glanced at him, then back at the map. 'Legend says that he did, but no trace has ever been found.'

'Maybe he wanted to erase the trace of himself here,' Whit said. 'If I had buried gold I wouldn't have my name right over it in big letters.'

'His camps weren't fancy. Just shelters if he or his men needed to get ashore, say in a storm, or to hide from other ships. Just four walls and a spare cannon, maybe.'

'And one assumes if he buried the treasure he would mark it or come back for it quickly, if he could.'

'Sure.'

'So what happened to Laffite after he left Galveston?'

'No one knows. There were a variety of reports. He might have died, might have gone to Cuba or to Mexico. Recently it's been theorized he died in South America, as a freedom fighter.' He smiled. 'People are always trying to redeem pirates. We like them too much to remember they're murdering thieves.'

'So – possibly – he could have been kept from retrieving a treasure. Killed. Or imprisoned.'

'Possibly. Sure. We don't know with complete certainty what happened to him.'

'Do the legends get specific about where this St Leo Bay camp might be?' Whit asked.

'Some say Copano Flats, some say Black Jack Point. Obviously old Black Jack believed Laffite had been there.'

'You know about him?'

'Just that he was a crazy old hermit, lived out on the Point from the Civil War until about 1890. I don't know if he was black or his name was Jack. I think the Point must've gotten its name from the blackjack oaks that grow there. And maybe the name stuck to him, too. He claimed he'd sailed with Laffite as a boy and Laffite was coming back to the Point, gonna kill everyone in Port Leo because they'd taken his gold. Loony. He sure thought there was a treasure – he dug up enough of the Point. I guess the Gilbert family – they've had that land for ever – tolerated him. Sad, though. A whole life dedicated to greed.'

'Wouldn't you say that was Laffite's life as well?'

'Yeah, you're right. Except for saving New Orleans, which was pretty cool.' Jason raised an eyebrow again. 'You going to tell me about why you're asking all these semiloaded questions?'

'I'm trying to get a feel for Patch's life in his final weeks. Everything we discuss, Jason, remains confidential. I'm conducting an official death inquest.'

'Man, you're covering your ass.'

Whit shook his head. 'We have no indication that Patch had found any antiquities or relics of any sort.' That was true – Patch hadn't. Maybe others had. 'I would hate for a bunch of rumors to get started. Have people stampeding around on that land like a bunch of Black Jacks when the Gilbert and Tran families are grieving.'

'Of course not,' Jason said. 'I don't get off on rumors. I'll keep my mouth shut. But if there's a story . . .'

'There's not. I asked about treasure pretty much out of curiosity. It's what people first think of with Laffite and I knew Patch had this new interest in him. Nothing more.' Jason didn't look convinced so Whit shifted gears again. 'You know Stoney Vaughn?'

'Sure. He's the president of the Corpus chapter of the Laffite League.'

'Friend of yours?'

'No. Cat litter has more brains than Stoney. He's all into the treasure hunter mystique. He's financed treasure dives in the Florida Keys, where a lot of the Spanish galleons wrecked over the years. Tried to finance a partnership to dive on galleon wrecks down off Padre, but the state blocked him. The Texas Historical Commission, they hate treasure hunters. Any treasure in state waters or buried on public land is theirs by law, and they make sure you don't dive without their approval.'

'He finances treasure hunts?' Whit kept his voice flat.

'Yeah, well, in Florida. Lot more wrecks there, in the shallows along the Keys. I think he might have been in the group that financed Barry Clifford diving on *Whydah*, up off Cape Cod. That's the only sunken pirate ship ever recovered. They got a shitload of gold, silver, and jewels off it. At least Stoney likes to talk big about it. He paid for a trip for about a dozen of the Leaguers last year to go to Yucatán, see the town where Laffite's brother died.'

'Were Stoney and Patch buddies?'

'Don't think they knew each other, but they probably met at the meeting,' Jason said. 'Okay, now you got me hooked. You ask about Laffite's treasure and then you ask about a guy who does treasure hunts.'

'If there's anything to say . . . I'll give you the exclusive story. But don't hold your breath. And if you say a thing too early, no story.'

Jason raised an eyebrow. 'Okay.'

'Are there any other . . . treasure-hunter types around here, or in the Laffite League?'

'Stoney did have a friend who came along on the Yucatán trip, a guy he knew from Florida. Allen Eck, I think his name was. Yeah. Looked like a professor. Comes across as very cool. But, Jesus, what an asshole. We were taking a tour of Merida, a small town down there. The tour guide was telling about Laffite history, but got a couple of really minor details wrong. I mean, most people would never know. Allen told him he was wrong, very quietly, and the guide firmly said, no, he was right. Maybe just thinking Allen's some dumb tourist. I'll never forget the look Allen gave him, just beyond cold, like this poor stupid guide wasn't worth a roach's ass. But he didn't say anything more. Next day, they find the tour guide in an alleyway. Both arms broken, face a solid bruise, nose broken. Guy wouldn't say who attacked him – either he didn't see or he was too scared.' Jason shook his head. 'I know it's crazy, but I kept thinking maybe Allen beat up that man.'

21

Stoney tossed all night, like he slept on rocks, lying on a blanket in front of the big French doors leading to the dock. He'd switched all the lights on along the dock, waiting. No boats came out of the night. Alex got comfortable at the dinner table, gun in front of him, reading a thick book on seventeenth-century Asian piracy he'd found on Stoney's shelves, making noises of agreement and disapproval as he scanned the pages.

Finally he'd fallen asleep. He awoke once to hear Alex talking quietly on a cell phone. He heard Alex say, 'Fine. I agree.' Then nothing more but the sound of Alex clicking off his phone. He played possum, felt Alex's gaze go along his back. Stoney didn't go to sleep again for a while, but the whiskey he'd drunk earlier caught up with him and he drifted off.

He awoke at seven, his tongue stuck to the roof of his mouth, his back a solid ache. Along the dock the lights still gleamed. No boat, no Danny, dead or alive. He got up, went into the kitchen. No Alex.

He should have felt relief. He knew Alex wanted to kill him last night. Wanted to burn his face. Instead he felt panic at Alex's absence. Where the hell was he? And if Danny or his gang showed up while Alex was gone . . .

He went to the phone. No messages. He called the satellite phone system on *Jupiter*. No answer. He turned on the television, watched the Friday morning local news. No reports of a millionaire's brother kidnapped at sea, nothing on a missing boat or Ben and Claudia's bodies washing ashore.

He heard the front door open, hurried to the foyer, saw Alex coming in, closing the door behind him.

'Where the hell have you been?'

'They show?'

'No. Where were you?'

'Attending to some business.' Alex dusted his hands. 'You can cook, right? Eggs. Bacon. Black coffee. I need some protein.'

'What business, Alex?'

Alex's mood seemed ominously good. He patted Stoney's cheek. 'They may not be coming. Danny and his friends must have lost their nerve. Or maybe Danny killed his buddies.'

'Or he killed Ben,' Stoney said. 'He's got nothing to bargain with, except an accusation against me that won't hold up.'

Alex went into the kitchen, washed his hands. 'This girlfriend of Ben's. The cop?'

'Yes.'

'Maybe she took them all out.'

'She's one person. And a woman.'

'A gun and the knowledge and will to use it are a great equalizer. Call your boat again.'

'I already tried. There wasn't an answer.'

'Danny Laffite, he has a boat? Presumably they had a boat to board *Jupiter* with.'

'Yes.'

'You remember the name?'

'*Miss Catherine*. After Catherine Villars.'

Alex rolled his eyes. 'Start hailing that boat on the radio. Maybe they're trying to figure out how to trick us. Maybe they're playing it safe. Maybe they didn't want to come in at night.' He gave a wicked smile. 'Maybe they found the Eye hidden on your boat and they've sailed off to China.' The smile – wry, like he didn't care – stayed in place. It made Stoney's stomach sink.

'I got an extra marine radio in my office, high-end, long-range.'

'Let's see if anyone wants to talk to us,' Alex said.

Claudia awoke slowly because waking meant pain. Hard, throbbing pain that pulsed in her head like a heartbeat, each *pu-pump* a double shot of eye-clenching agony. The pain roared hard enough for her first cogent thought to be: *Don't move, because your brains will leak out your ears.*

She opened her eyes. Coldness – from air-conditioning – prickled her skin. Morning light, soft in color but a slap against her eyes. A slow awareness of the rest of her body – not welcome, everything hurt – crept along her nerves. She was tied again, hands behind her this time, wrists raw, foot a dull ache. A coppery, sour taste made her want to spit out her tongue. Bed sheets – smelling unwashed and of suntan lotion – lay greasy against her skin.

Tied up and tucked into bed.

'Danny?' Claudia called weakly. 'Danny?'

The door cracked open, light hit her eyes like a fist.

'You're awake,' Danny said. 'You worried me. You wouldn't wake up before.'

'What . . . what happened? I hurt . . .'

'You'll be fine.' A pause. 'It's good you didn't die, because then how could you help me?'

He sat by her on the bed, put a moist cloth dispenser next to her head, plucked a cloth free, gently wiped her face and her hands. 'Moist towelettes help you stay clean. You should wash each day,' he said, as if by rote. It sounded like a rule mentioned in a hospital, a mantra of nurses.

His tone was a little different today. She didn't like it.

She stayed still while he wiped her face, cleaning her skin and hair of dried extinguisher foam and her own spittle and blood. He brought her a glass of cold water. The water tasted bitter, but her mouth craved the wetness. He held her head up gently and she gulped the glass dry.

'Good girl,' he said.

'Untie me.'

'No.'

'You . . . you hit me.' Her mouth tasted like it was crammed full of wool.

'Just a little love tap,' he said. 'You'll be okay.' His jaunty confidence made her skin crawl. He smiled, shook a finger in her face she wanted to bite to the bone. 'Remember, we're going to Stoney's house.'

'Ben . . .'

'I wouldn't worry about him anymore. They're gone.'

'Gone where?'

'Sailed off. I'm certainly not looking for them now. He must've heard the gunshot, decided to take off. Zack – the redhead – he's basically a coward without Gar around. Probably dump Ben in the Gulf, ditch the boat close to shore, find a rock to hide under. Less likely he'd go to Stoney's house, cut a separate deal. But you just never know about people, do you?'

'You're a smart guy, Danny,' she managed to say. 'But you know the police are looking for me and Ben by now. And I need medical attention.' She put the edge of a whine in her voice. 'Please, you hit me hard in the head. I'm sick.'

'How about some delicious Aspergum? I have regular and cherry flavors.'

'I might have a fractured skull, for God's sake.'

'You're blinking okay,' Danny said. He frowned. 'Gar called you *Officer*. Why?'

She stared at him. 'I've no idea.'

'I think you're a cop, Claudia.'

'You think a lot of things, Danny, more than most people.'

He laughed. 'I suppose I do.' He ran a thumb along her lip. 'I wish we could be friends. Don't have a lot of those.' He sounded regretful.

'We can be. Untie me.'

'No. You'll nap for a while. I put a little of my meds into your water. I don't need 'em no more. I'm feeling awesome. I want you calm till we get to Stoney's house. I didn't want to go at night. I want to see clear. And let's say he's gotten his brother back from Zack. The brother being there, he'll make Stoney trade for you. Stoney wouldn't give a shit about you on his own. If he hasn't gotten Ben back, then I tell him I've got Ben with you, down below. See?' He smiled at his own cleverness.

She closed her eyes.

'Because I'm gonna call him when we get in close to shore. Tell him he's got to meet us out on the dock with the Devil's Eye and the journal.'

Claudia was silent.

'Then I'm gonna shoot him from the boat, make his head go boom like a ol' melon. Like Gar's did. Then I'm getting my stuff, 'cause he'll have it there at his house. I figured his house is big, he'll want the treasure where he can see it, know it's okay,' Danny said with a smile. Touching his fingers to her throat, taking the measure of her breath, savoring the moment. Flush with success at having bested Gar. She saw suddenly that Danny probably hadn't had a lot of success in his life.

'If he doesn't have this emerald there, you're screwed.'

'Okay. I'll shoot after he gives it to me or tells me where it is.'

'The journal,' she said. 'Tell me again what it looks like, Danny. Maybe I saw it at Stoney's.'

Danny studied her for a moment, touched her jaw – which ached still – with tenderness. Then he went to the cabinet in the stateroom's corner, unlocked it with a key from around his neck. From a drawer he pulled a piece of paper, bleary with photocopy streaks. He held the paper above her face.

She wriggled into position where she could see the page, written in the flowing scrawl that passed for nineteenth-century penmanship. Sorting the words was a struggle:

In late May 1820 a small force led by the schooner Lynx chased Laffite's little fleet (being two schooners and a brigantine) down the Texas coast. Feeling ran high that Laffite might simply move south onto other Texas islands and re-establish his pirating base. Captain Madison was ordered to ignore the safe passage that Commodore Patterson issued to Laffite, which made me uneasy. Our word in the Navy should matter. But in Vera Cruz Madison received reports of a Spanish ship, the Santa Barbara, carrying a trove of gold and jewels. SB vanished in the Western gulf – in fair weather – in the weeks before Laffite abandoned his privateering, and I suspect the government thought him involved. I fear no one informed Mr Laffite of this change in the government's attitude.

We fired on Laffite's ships south of Matagorda Bay, but he turned into the maze of bays and shoals, guarded by the thin strips of barrier islands, and we could not give chase without running aground. We caught him coming out of St Leo Bay the next morning. There was scant loot on his ship, some silks, Madeira, a few handfuls of coins at most – little enough for the great pirate. His crude, stupid men were hungry, and beaten. There was no sign of the Spanish treasure. Offers of immunity from prosecution won the crew over. We escorted Laffite's ship to Vera Cruz; I do not know what happened to him afterwards. We were all sworn – and paid in bonus – not to discuss this operation since it had disregarded a legal safe passage, and the navy wanted no embarrassment. I left Lynx in New Orleans, and tragically Lynx and all her hands were soon lost in a storm, on a cruise to Jamaica to fight piracy in the Caribbean. So I alone remain to give witness, but I cannot bear to dishonor Captain Madison's memory by confessing what the Navy did in public. Here I can write my thoughts without fear. For those who recall Laffite's heroic service to New Orleans – and to America – during our late War with the British, it seems particularly scandalous and unfair to have broken a promise, even one made to a pirate.

Ample discussion followed that Laffite had buried his booty along the coastline where he had evaded the task force and one of the younger pirates spoke of a nighttime expedition at Widows' Point in St Leo Bay, where only Laffite, out of four men, returned. But this fellow Jack was both simple and a hopeless drunkard whose story changed with the level of rum in the bottle. I think that the idea makes an excellent story and my grandchildren enjoy it so at their bedtime. I record it here simply as a matter of interest.

'Who wrote this?' Claudia stared at Danny as he lowered the paper from her face.

'John B. Fanning, ship's surgeon aboard *Lynx*. He wrote this journal years later. I guess his descendants found it in a family trunk and they put it up on an on-line auction site, simply mentioning it talked about Laffite and navy operations in the 1820s. They had no idea of its value. So I bought it. Widows' Point, see. That's what they call Black Jack Point now.'

Black Jack Point. Where those two old people had been murdered. David's case.

He didn't say anything for a minute, not looking at her, putting the copy back into the cabinet, locking it up. 'You should understand why this is all mine. By inheritance. My last name is Laffite. Daniel Villars Laffite.'

Claudia watched him. Finally she said, 'You're descended from Jean Laffite?' She tried not to laugh.

'And Catherine Villars, his great love. So that money, that hidden gold, it's mine. Mine.' His voice fell to a whispering mumble. He was used, she saw, to talking to himself, telling himself what he wanted to hear. 'No. One. Else's. I got the best claim on it imaginable.'

She gathered herself, tried to stay calm. At first she thought his grudge against Stoney was a battle between one treasure hunter versus another. But this. Jesus.

'You don't believe me,' Danny said, a low rumble in his voice.

'Sure I do,' she said. 'Why wouldn't I?'

'People laugh at me. Not much longer though. Not much longer.' His voice rose, spittle flying from his lips, hitting her cheek.

She didn't move, didn't react, put a gentle, calm smile on her face. 'Danny, it was sweet of you to share your meds with me. Really. But maybe you should take them again. Just because you want to be at your best when—'

He leaned down and slapped her, hard. She stared past his shoulder. He rubbed her cheek, his fingertips smelling of the moist towelettes. 'No. No more of those. Keep me from being me.'

The radio beeped. She heard its call through a little speaker in the cabin. A hail for *Miss Catherine*. Maybe Stoney's voice? Hard to tell. Danny rushed out of the cabin without giving her another look. She heard his feet pound on the stairs.

She had to get loose, fight him, there had to be a way. The stateroom was dark now, with the door closed and the shades lowered, thin slices of light lying in lines on the bed, but she inched over. A bedside table stood on each side of the narrow bed. With her hands tied behind her, she pried open one drawer with her fingers, rolled around to see what was inside. A pair of reading glasses, stubby blue pencils, a notepad. She eased the drawer shut with her foot, wriggled to the other side of the bed, and slowly forced the other table drawer open. She rolled again. Inside lay a pack of gum. A ballpoint pen, missing its cap. A scattering of pennies, dimes, and quarters. A set of nail clippers.

Clippers.

She turned her back to the drawer, easing around, and carefully leaned backward, her fingers wiggling, trying to close around the little plastic case of the clippers. Her fingertips brushed the dimes, the foil of the gum pack. Her fingernails tapped the plastic . . . and she leaned back too far, her exhausted muscles in her back and arms cramping. She fell off the bed, the drawer smacking hard against her neck and shoulder. She hit the thin carpet hard, teeth jarring together, one of her fingers jamming and she cried out in pain.

She raised her feet, shut the drawer, her back straining, her muscles begging for mercy.

The door opened. He stood there, watching her, the Sig in hand and she wondered, *Who's steering this boat?* He gently put her back on the bed, pulled the sheets over her like he was tucking her in for sleep.

'What were you doing?'

'Trying to stretch a little. I'm cramping everywhere. Please untie me.'

'I just spoke with Stoney. He's agreed to the trade. He asked to speak to his brother but I said no. He thinks I got Ben.' He grinned. 'So this will be over soon.'

And he shut the door behind him.

Her hand hurt like the devil; her head felt like it was full of sand. Tears of frustration stung her eyes. She blinked them back.

Not much time. She rolled back toward the drawer.

22

Whit was going to be late for Friday morning juvenile court, but that hearing was his least favorite chore, lecturing kids who ought to know better while their impatient or embarrassed parents, arms crossed, stood there as the county doled out the discipline.

He pressed Stoney Vaughn's doorbell. The same cars – a Porsche and a beat-up van – were still parked in the oversize curve of the driveway.

He waited. No answer. He tried the doorbell again.

Still no answer. Whit walked around the front of the house, around a corner, across a lawn so manicured golf could have been played on it, and down to the sprawling home's back. A metal fence enclosed the back, fancy wrought-iron curlicues at the posts' tips, but the gate was unlocked. The back wasn't a yard so much as a multitiered deck. He climbed up wooden stairs. At the top he could see two more platforms below him, a nice long private dock with no boat in residence, lights still on like they'd been left on all night. A pool, set into the deck. Expensive patio furniture, a restaurant-style grill built into the brick.

The French doors opened behind him. A man – Whit knew he was Stoney Vaughn, recognized him from the pictures in the articles on the Internet – stepped outside. The guy looked like hell, rumpled clothes, unshaven, like he'd slept on the street. Lip split and puffy.

'Excuse me,' Stoney said. 'This is private property.'

'I know,' Whit said. 'But you didn't answer your door.'

'Yeah, I sure didn't, did I?'

'I'm Judge Whit Mosley. I'm the JP and county coroner. I'd like to talk to you about two recent homicides.'

'Call my office. Make an appointment.' Stoney shut his mouth, as though reconsidering this as an initial reaction.

'I'm here now. You don't appear to be busy.'

'I had a late night working,' Stoney said. 'Sorry to be gruff.' He shut the door behind him, came out onto the deck in full light, glancing toward the stretch of the bay. 'And I'm afraid I have a business appointment in Corpus that I need to get ready for. I don't know how I can help you.'

'You knew Patch Gilbert, though, didn't you?'

'The name's vaguely familiar . . .'

'You sent him a bottle of Glenfiddich after talking to him at a Laffite League meeting,' Whit said.

Stoney shut his mouth, smiled, wiped his eyes. 'Oh. Yeah. I do remember him. Charming guy.'

'Was. You probably heard he got killed Monday night. Along with his girlfriend.'

Stoney's eyes widened. 'You're kidding me. Mr Gilbert's dead?'

'You don't watch the news?'

A pause. 'Not lately. And I'm deep in putting together a new business deal, so I've been working twenty-four seven.'

'More financing for treasure hunts?' Whit gave a look of angelic purity.

Stoney stared again. 'Um, no, but you sure seem to know a lot about me, Mr Mosley.'

'Judge, please. I prefer the formal title.' Whit folded his arms across today's shirt, lime-green with waltzing, bug-eyed pineapples.

'Uh, sorry, Judge. I'm out of the treasure-hunt game. Too expensive a hobby. May I ask how you know about me?'

'I'm conducting the inquest into Mr Gilbert's death. I'm trying to get a picture of his life in the months before he died.'

'Well, I met him the one time. We chatted.' A pause. 'I was interested in his land, asked him about selling. He said no.'

'And the other Gilbert family members – you approached them?'

'Am I suspected of something here? Do I need a lawyer?'

'I don't know, do you?'

'Do you have some ID? Because you sure don't look like a judge.'

Whit handed him a laminated card, showed his driver's license. 'I don't have a lot of time either, Mr Vaughn. But your name cropped up more than once and I wanted to know your connection to Mr Gilbert.'

'Vague at best, Judge.' Now Stoney smiled. 'Yes, I think I met another Gilbert – Suzanne, right? – and asked her about her land. She also declined to sell.'

'Not everyone wants every inch of the coast developed.'

'True enough,' Stoney said. 'Is there anything else? I'm sorry I couldn't be of more help—'

'Yes. Where were you Monday night?'

Stoney's smile faded, came back on. 'Um, I was here at my house.'

'Anyone with you?'

'My brother, Ben, lives here with me.'

'I'd like to talk to him, if I may.'

'He's not in at the moment.'

'When do you expect him back?' Whit asked.

'You know, he's taken my boat out for some fishing and R and R, and I'm not sure when he's going to be back.' The smile again. 'I don't even have time to play with the toys, but my brother does.'

'Okay.' Whit glanced toward the French doors. He thought he'd seen someone behind the glass, but with the glare from the sun, maybe he was wrong. 'Please ask him to give me a call.'

'Is this really necessary, sir? Honestly, am I in some sort of trouble? I mean, the police haven't questioned me or contacted me.'

'Thanks for your time,' Whit said. 'Oh. Since you're a treasure buff, maybe you can help me.'

'Uh, sure.'

'You got any books on old coins?'

The cutting was going slowly . . . too slowly.

On Claudia's second try for the clippers, she'd managed to slide open the large file. She found after experimentation that she could hold the file in her right hand and saw at the knots binding her hands together. But the file was too dull, jabbing her wrist every third stroke, and the rope unyielding. Her hands and forearms cramped. She lay on her side, keeping the tedious cutting motion going, the ropes death-grip tight, no progress.

She stared at the ceiling, thirsty, hungry, trying to think straight.

Stoney hadn't – since yesterday – called the coast guard. Otherwise helicopters screaming out of Corpus Christi would have spotted *Miss Catherine* from the air, radioed her position and heading to cutters who would have intercepted Danny Laffite. She'd be off the boat by now, Danny in custody, wheeled in front of eager psychologists who could mine a dozen papers out of his obsessions.

Does a man like Stoney Vaughn – self-made, into millions – let a guy like Danny Laffite order him around? Did he tell Gar that you're a cop?

If police were with Stoney, helping him lure in Danny, they'd say, *Don't say anything about her, don't risk panicking him.*

Maybe it was a stupid mistake. Or maybe Stoney hoped Gar would kill you.

She had to get free. Because Danny was going to kill her if Stoney didn't have this emerald. And if there was one bit of truth to Danny's story, Stoney might not wish her well either. Claudia pulled herself along the bed, her feet and hands still bound. And the purr of the engines, the full throttle of *Miss Catherine* told her Danny had abandoned caution and now was in a tear-ass hurry to get to Stoney's bayside house.

Danny was up on deck, leaving her below, but that might not last long.

She hopped across the floor. The closet door was a slider, one pane covered with a mirror. On the closet floor she found a pair of flip-flops, oversize for her feet. She put them on. The toe Gar broke was purpled and sore and she was about to make it feel worse. With her shoulder, she inched the closet door shut. She eased herself onto the floor, feet toward the mirror.

Now. *Either he'll hear you and come down and shoot you or the engines and the wind will mask the noise.* Time to find out. She thought of her mother and her gentle nagging for a moment, her father, so proud of her as a police officer. Her sisters and brothers, all good people that she loved dearly. David on their wedding day, smiling hugely. Whit, crazy, sweet Whit in a loud shirt and windblown hair that he'd forget to smooth down after he put on the judge's robe. The odd little twist he always put in her heart while knowing he wasn't really the one for her. Ben. Poor Ben, smiling at her, the nice boy grown into a better man. Probably dead now, thanks to Danny.

She aimed her feet and kicked hard against the mirrored door. It shook, wobbled in its cheap frame.

The engines still thrummed and hummed.

The glass webbed on the third hard smack, cracks in the mirror distorting her reflection. Her foot throbbed. She kicked again. Again.

Two big slivers of mirror fell out of the frame, one a crescent, the other a triangle. She stopped, breathing, listening to the engines. The roar stayed steady.

Now. The trick is to not lose a finger. Or all five.

Claudia turned, wriggled her back up against the bed, grabbed a corner of the cheap bedspread. On it dolphins and mermaids cavorted in tacky glee. But the fabric was thick and she covered her fingers and her palms with it. She took a deep breath, eased back toward the splinters, tried to lift the crescent of mirror. Her covered fingers closed around it. No grip. It shifted and fell from her hands.

Try again. Don't rush. Sweat dribbled along her ribs.

The third try, she got ahold on the sliver. She steadied with her right hand and slowly, slowly, gripped it until she was sure it wouldn't cut through the bedspread to her flesh. She leaned to one side, stretching, turning a sharp edge toward the ropes. There. She moved the glass, felt it slice into the meat of the rope.

Not too fast, and don't dare slip, or you'll cut your wrists open. That would be hysterical, yes. Lie here on the floor, tied up, bleeding out into the dingy carpet while Danny sailed them home.

She made a little noise in her throat as the first loop in the knot broke under the mirror's edge.

Slowly. Find the rhythm, feel the rope against you so you don't cut yourself. She sliced deeper into the big knot fashioned around her hands, forcing herself not to rush.

The knot began to unravel. She steadied her hand. Now the remaining rope was a thick strand right around her wrists, covering the tender lace of veins. Careful.

The deck began to pitch. Danny was in a hard turn, a sudden turn. The crescent slipped in her grip, an edge bit into her skin. She let the fragment go, rolled away from the closet. The deck pitched again, crazily.

Why wouldn't he steer like a maniac? He is *a maniac.*

The deck settled, the engines resumed their hum. A little ooze of blood tickled her palm. She pulled on the ropes and her left hand – uncut – came free. She pulled her right hand around to her front, saw a cut in the fleshy part of her palm, blood welling, odd that it didn't hurt much. Then as feeling crept into her numb hands, it stung like the devil. She unraveled the rope off her hand, grabbed the bedspread, stanched the bleeding. Not bad but worse than it looked.

Claudia cut through the ropes on her feet.

She wobbled as she stood, sensation ebbing back into her feet, arms, hands and the small of her back. She ached everywhere. She bandaged her hand with a T-shirt she found in the bureau, tearing off a sleeve and wrapping the fabric around twice.

She tried the door. Locked. A deadbolt, locked from outside, above the knob. She cussed under her breath, glanced around for a way to smash the door. Although Danny would hear that and come running, gun in hand.

The porthole. Salt and oily stains grimed over the glass. It was secured with four twisting locks. She began to undo them.

So what do you do? Bail out over the side and hope someone picks you up? You don't even know where in the Gulf you are. Maybe the cops are there at Stoney's house. Waiting, and you're running away from a rescue.

But her gut said that wasn't the case. She couldn't be far from the bay; he couldn't have wandered or waited too far away.

She unscrewed the final lock, yanked the panel free from the porthole. Wind and cold spray hit her face. Salt stung her lips. She saw two sailboats in the far distance.

Go. Go.

She prayed Danny Laffite didn't see her launch herself into the water, didn't run over her and crush her or chop her into floating mincemeat with the prop. Or didn't stop to shoot her five times in the back as she tried to swim away. But he'd shoot her for sure, she thought, when he found her untied. Maybe she could take him, surprise him when he opened the door. But maybe not. Danny had the gun, his muscles weren't aching from having been tied for hours, and he had the strength of the crazy on his side. There were other boats on the water. Someone would see her, God, yes. And if she waited . . . she'd lost one chance before, aboard *Jupiter*. He could stop the boat at any time to come fetch her and she wouldn't be able to fight back. *Seize the moment,* she told herself.

She turned and dug through the closet. No life preserver jacket. Nothing flotational. And no flares. Nothing but musty clothing. She found a big pair of blue jeans and remembered a news story about a young American girl who survived hours in the sea after a ferry in the Philippines capsized and sank, by fashioning her blue jeans into a crude float. Fine. She pulled on the jeans over her shorts. She saw a bright red pillow on the bed, small. Easy to see. Claudia grabbed it, shoved it under her T-shirt.

Claudia pulled herself through the porthole. She threw herself into the deep green, pushing away from the boat with all the strength left in her legs.

She hit the water like a stone wall. Air smashed out of her lungs, water closed over her head like six feet of packed dirt. The roar of *Miss Catherine* slicing through the waves sounded above her, churning, like gods rolling dice.

She kicked down, down, down into the endless green. *Stay down. Don't let him have seen you. Please God, give me a chance.*

She felt the Gulf close its cold fist around her, and when she could no longer hold her breath, Claudia kicked hard again and broke the surface, a wave roiling into her chest, knocking her back down. She emerged; salt burning her hand, her face, her eyes. She coughed, keeping her head clear, turned toward the widening wake.

Miss Catherine roared away from her, Danny standing on the flying bridge, steering through the crests. Not stopping, not turning back. He hadn't seen her.

She shivered. A wave picked her up in its swell and settled her back down. Her arms and legs ached like they'd been braided on a rack. Sharp, stinging pain hit in the hollow of her hand, and the T-shirt bandage she'd fashioned turned pink in the water. She thought of the silky sharks from a lifetime ago yesterday, tearing through the chum. Drawn by the blood.

She tried to get her bearings from the sun, looked toward where she thought the shore would lie. *Second-guessing yourself already?* she thought. But she saw in the distance two sails unfurled, the dot of a cruiser cutting through the waves. *He's racing toward shore. You can't be that far out in the Gulf. You can't be. Right?*

Claudia pulled the bright red pillow from her shirt and began to wave it back and forth every ten seconds, facing the boats. Then she trod water. Wave. Tread. Repeat. Repeat. Repeat. Repeat.

The boats headed away from her. As Claudia began to swim, the fatal heaviness of exhaustion began its terrible creep.

23

'I don't like a judge sniffing around,' Alex said.

'He was harmless.' Stoney stood in front of the bay window.

'He's been here twice.'

'He's talking to everyone who knew Patch Gilbert. It's not an issue.'

'Not an issue.'

'Look, he hardly asked me anything except where I'd met Patch. That was it. Said nothing about a land buy, nothing about Laffite, nothing. Okay? And I had to get rid of him. We couldn't have him around when Danny sailed up, or have him coming in and seeing you, could we?'

'No.' Alex took his wire-rim glasses off, cleaned them on his shirt, put them back on. 'If Danny's killed your brother, how are you going to explain the motive?'

'My boat's gone. He was on the boat. I won't have known what happened. Danny's a freaking nutcase. He finally snapped. He had a grudge against me no one could explain. Why do I have to explain anything?'

'You're a cold bastard, Stoney. I have to say.'

'I didn't want my brother to get hurt.'

'You didn't lift a finger to help him,' Alex said. 'Family doesn't matter to you?'

'You kill people and you lecture me about family?'

'I didn't have a thing against Gilbert and Mrs Tran,' Alex said. 'Old, and they'd had good lives, probably. Jimmy was too dumb to live. I didn't want them messing up my life. But shit, man, I wouldn't kill *family*.'

'I didn't kill my brother.'

'Sure you did. You stole from me. You probably let your brother die instead of parting with one red cent. You're a real honey.' Alex unwrapped a stick of gum, offered the pack to Stoney, who shook his head. 'Here's what happens when Danny gets here. We meet him down on the dock.'

'If Ben and Claudia are still alive . . .'

'She's got to go, man. Sorry. The kidnappers and Danny are dead, too. Your brother . . . you think he can be trusted, then fine.'

'You kill his girlfriend, he's not going to be happy.'

'He'll be less happy dead.'

'Don't kill him, Alex. Please.' Stoney glanced out into the curve of the bay that fed the flats. 'A boat's coming. Not mine. A sportfisher.'

'Danny Boy,' Alex said. 'Let's go say hi.' He tucked his gun into the back of his pants, closed a light jacket of Stoney's above it.

'You're wearing a jacket in summer? That looks suspicious.'

'Would you like to go shoot him, Stoney?'

Stoney opened his mouth, closed it again. They headed down the deck stairs toward the dock.

The boat chugged along, kept correcting course, as though the pilot was a bit unsure of his bearings. The morning had turned windy, the bay degrading into white choppiness.

'Stand behind me,' Alex said. 'Just a little.'

'Are you going to shoot him right away?' Stoney whispered.

'No, I'm not,' Alex said. 'Just do what you're told.'

The Bertram, in need of paint, hovered in close to the dock. But it didn't dock, staying about ten feet away. Stoney saw Danny – hair blown wild by wind and speed, standing in the shadow of the flying bridge.

Alex raised both hands, palms out, showing they were empty.

The sportfisher cut its motors. 'Who're you?' Danny called.

'I'm here to facilitate the transfer,' Alex said.

'Stoney,' Danny said. 'This some thug you hide behind?'

'You mean like you're hiding behind my brother and his girlfriend?' Stoney said.

'Where's the journal and the Devil's Eye?' Danny asked.

'Inside the house. Where's my fucking boat?' Stoney said.

'You ask about your boat before your brother,' Danny said. 'Nice.'

'We want to see that Ben and Claudia are safe before the exchange,' Alex said. 'This is a business transaction.'

'It's not quite like going to the ATM,' Danny said. 'You show me the Eye and the journal. You toss them to me on the boat. I pull out a little further. I let Ben and Claudia swim into the dock.'

'No,' Alex said. 'You dock, and you show us that our friends are fine first.'

'My way or no way,' Danny said.

'Fine,' Alex said. 'Sail off into the sunset.'

Danny frowned. 'I'll call the cops, tell them what you did, Stoney. Here and in New Orleans.'

'Call them,' Alex said. 'You're a kidnapper. And you don't have any proof. The guy who killed your cousin in New Orleans is dead. His name is Jimmy Bird. He shot himself earlier this week. He used us, he used you. Stoney didn't hurt your cousin.'

Stoney couldn't even look at Alex.

Danny stared at Alex, shook his head. 'I don't believe you.'

'You got to work with me here, Danny, to get what you want. Otherwise you're going to lose.'

'Who the hell *are* you?'

'I'm your only hope for getting what you want,' Alex said. 'Now. Dock. Or we walk away and you have nothing. Dock and you can have the Eye. We keep the rest of the treasure. Deal?'

Stoney could see it play out on Danny's face. The wanting. The obsession. The need to win, be right, not be the laughingstock anymore. 'I'm supposed to check in with my associates on Stoney's boat in ten minutes. I don't, they kill Ben.'

'You don't have Ben with you?' Stoney said. His voice rose.

'He's safe. I got Claudia.'

'That's fine,' Alex said. 'See, we're willing to trust you. We don't want Ben or Claudia hurt. Jimmy Bird's the one who screwed you over. I can show it to you in the paper, Danny. We'll give you the Eye and trust you that you'll give us Ben.' He slowly pulled out of his jacket pocket the fake emerald Stoney had left in the storage unit, let it glitter in the light. 'See. Yours. Just give us Claudia and Ben.'

Danny chewed his lip for a moment, then turned the wheel slowly in toward the dock. Alex kept the fat emerald aloft, holding it in his fingertips.

Danny hovered into position, pulled up against the dock. Stoney tossed bumpers against the dock to protect the boat, tossed a line onto *Miss Catherine*'s deck. Stoney quickly fed the rope around and through the dock cleat. Danny kept his gun trained on Alex.

'We don't have a gun on you,' Alex said. 'Put that down. Or I drop the Eye in the drink.'

'Toss it up here,' Danny said.

Alex smiled – Stoney saw it, thought, *Oh no, you're*

not – tossed the fake Eye high, toward Danny's reaching hand.

Danny grabbed at the stone one-handed, his eyes widening, as Alex pulled his revolver from the back of his waist and fired once. Blood burst from Danny's shoulder, and he fell backward onto the deck, screaming.

Stoney climbed aboard, Alex following. Danny lay on his back, sobbing in pain. 'You shot me. Jesus.' He sounded shocked.

'Go see if your brother and his girlfriend are aboard or not,' Alex said. 'I'll stay here with Danny.' He knelt by Danny, steadied him by putting a hand on his chest. 'It's okay, man. Calm down.'

'Oh, please,' Danny said. 'Don't kill me.'

'I won't,' Alex said. He glanced up at Stoney. 'What the fuck are you waiting on?'

'The guys that were with him . . .' Stoney said. 'They might be below.'

'Are they, Danny?' Alex asked.

'No . . . no . . .' Danny moaned. 'They're gone.'

'Go ahead, Stoney. Do some constructive work,' Alex said. And he motioned with his gun.

Stoney swallowed and hurried belowdecks. He checked the galley, a small stateroom, an empty head.

'Ben buddy? Claudia?' Stoney called in a low voice at the stateroom. 'It's okay. It's over.'

He unlocked the door, pushed it open with his fingertips.

He saw the loops of cut rope, the broken mirror, the open porthole. Someone had been here, someone was gone now. He looked out the porthole to see if maybe Ben or Claudia was swimming away right now, but the water in the little cove was empty.

Stoney went back up to the deck. Blood still pulsed from Danny's shoulder, Alex kneeling by him.

'No one's there. Someone was tied up but they cut themselves loose and must've jumped ship.'

'Claudia,' Danny said. 'I had . . . Claudia. I didn't hurt her.'

'What did you tell her, Danny?' Alex asked.

Danny blinked. 'Tell her . . . nothing. She doesn't know anything.' He winced as he moved.

'Where's Ben?' Alex asked.

'Gar tried to rape Claudia. Asshole. I shot him, dumped his body overboard. Zack . . . took off with the other boat. With Ben aboard.'

'You know who he's talking about?' Alex asked.

'I don't know any Gar or Zack,' Stoney said.

'Okay,' Alex said. His voice went gentle. 'Danny, who else knows about the treasure?'

'No . . . one. I didn't tell. Just wanted what was mine.'

'That's why you didn't tell the cops who you thought murdered your cousin. You didn't want anything getting in the way of you getting the Eye. You were gonna dig up illegal, same as us.'

'Where is my brother, you asshole?' Stoney demanded.

'I don't know. After you wouldn't transfer the money, it all went south.' Danny closed his eyes, opened them. 'It hurts.'

'I know.'

'Please don't kill me,' Danny said.

'I promised I wouldn't,' Alex said. He stood, offered the gun to Stoney. 'You do it.'

'What?' Stoney said.

'Your turn. I've done all the risky work. You've stolen from me, lied to me. He's your problem.'

'Um, really, no, that's okay. You do it.' Stoney took a step back.

'If you don't shoot him, I'll shoot you.'

Stoney gulped. 'Then you won't get the Eye.'

'I don't think it's on your boat, buddy. I think that's a little lie you cooked up so I'd stick around to clean up your mess. You wouldn't let your brother take off on your boat if the Eye was on board. I know you.' He smiled. 'Last night I evened the playing field. Moved the rest of the treasure while you slept on your fat ass.'

Stoney stared. 'You couldn't have.'

'Oh, but I did,' Alex said. 'Shoot him.'

'Please, no,' Danny said. 'You can't. I'm a Laffite.'

'No, you're not,' Alex said.

'Fuck you, I am!' Danny screamed.

'I won't,' Stoney said.

Alex aimed. 'Kidneys or heart? Your choice, Stoney. I'd pick heart if I were you.'

'Yeah, shoot him,' Danny said. 'He's the asshole . . .'

Stoney took the gun from Alex – he thought it would be heavy, but it was light as air – and pointed it at Danny, who started to scream.

I can't, Stoney thought. Then the gun pulsed and the top of Danny's head blew off, sending a red spray across the deck.

Danny stared up at him, eyes full of dismay and surprise, drops of blood clouding the irises.

'There. Not so hard, was it?' Alex said, like he was giving back a test with a B plus when a failing grade had been expected.

Stoney thought, *Now shoot Alex. Do it. Just do it and all this is over.* But he thought of the rest of the treasure, the hundreds of silver and gold coins, and he handed the gun back to Alex without a word.

'Now. We got two problems. The girlfriend, maybe he killed her.'

'I don't think so. I think she got away.'

'So she's out in the bay. Creates new risk, man. Changes everything. We gotta hurry. I need your help.'

'I . . .' Stoney stared down at the body. 'I just killed a man.' He thought his knees would go weak, he'd vomit. Nothing. He waited for his hands to start shaking but now he felt pretty good. 'If Claudia knows what Danny knew . . .'

'If she's out drowning in the Gulf, she may not be a problem,' Alex said.

'My brother . . . maybe we should go look for him. Take Danny's boat and—'

'No. Not much we can do there. Ben's either dead by now or they'll contact us. We got to deal with the problem at hand. Help me below.'

In ten minutes it was done. The deck hosed, the bilges partially opened, the pumps undone, the engines going full steam, *Miss Catherine* headed back into the bay. She'd be sunk in a few minutes, into the deeper reach of the bay, but probably not entirely submerged. But a mess, without a body.

They wrapped Danny Laffite in double-thick garbage bags, like a giant plastic burrito. Alex taped the ends closed, neat as Christmas wrapping. They put him in the back of the van, locked up the house, climbed into the car.

'Stoney?' Alex said. 'Take a good look at Danny here. You try to fuck me over, you're burrito boy, the sequel.'

But I'm like you. I've killed a man now, Stoney thought, *and suddenly I'm not so scared of you. Because I have the Eye, the trump card, and maybe you're gonna be the next burrito.*

But he played safe. 'I understand you completely, Alex.'

'You got a good idea where to dump him?'

Stoney nodded. They both sat into the van and roared away from Copano Flats, down the dirt and oyster-shell road.

'Now,' Alex said. 'I got a new plan. Just in case this Claudia shows up.'

Miss Catherine, never a proud ship, sputtered and gushed down into the muddy bottom of St Leo Bay, in a fairly shallow twenty feet. Water poured in, flooding the belowdecks, covering the bed where Gar died, the shattered glass that Claudia used to cut herself free. *Miss Catherine* tilted hard to port as she sank and the back stateroom flooded entirely, including the armoire holding the photocopied excerpt of John Fanning's journal that Danny had showed to Claudia. The seawater covered the paper as the armoire canted over, smashed through the closet doors, and rested on its side. Little spot croakers and hardhead catfish swam down the stairs and through the portholes and began exploring this new world.

24

'Whit,' said Gooch. 'I'd like you to meet Helen Dupuy.' Gooch, back earlier than Whit thought he'd be, by one in the afternoon on Friday, stood in Whit's courtroom as the last juvenile case wrapped up and a boy, chronically truant, and his embarrassed-to-the-bone parents left.

Whit still was in his robe, sitting at the bench. Gooch had an arm around a young woman, a slight thing, hair a little too frizzed, a hard, worn look to her, but pretty if maybe she ate a little more, slept a little more. Wearing faded jeans and an old blue T-shirt with a little rip in the shoulder that needed mending.

'Hello, Helen,' Whit said. 'I'm Whit Mosley.' He shook her hand.

They were alone now in the courtroom, Gooch biting his lip, Helen looking like she didn't know why she was here.

'I brought Helen back with me from New Orleans,' Gooch said.

'I see.'

'We caught the first flight out this morning,' Gooch said.

'You must've,' Whit said. 'You didn't tarry long in New Orleans.'

'I felt we ought to be back here ASAP.' He glanced at Helen. 'Helen, I need to talk to His Honor private-like for a minute, if you don't mind.' He gave her some change. 'There's a Coke machine down the hallway – take a left. Get yourself something to drink and I'll be there in just a minute.'

'Nice to have met you, sir,' she said to Whit.

'You don't have to call me sir.'

'I know better than to mouth off at a judge.' Helen gave Gooch a smile, went out of the courtroom.

Whit waited until the door shut after her. 'Who is she, Gooch?'

'She's a whore,' Gooch said, 'but not a crack whore.'

'That's good,' Whit said. 'Why on earth did you bring this young woman back from New Orleans with you?'

'Albert Exley. Ring any bells?'

It did sound familiar. 'It sounds like Allen Eck.' Whit told Gooch about the crazy treasure hunter described by Jason Salinger of the Laffite League and that Jimmy Bird was dead.

'Albert Exley. Allen Eck. Alex,' Gooch said. 'His names seem to be shrinking.'

'So who's Albert Exley?'

'The name used by the man who paid cash and stayed at the motel Jimmy Bird called and nearly killed that nice girl that just left.' Gooch explained what Helen had told him. 'If he's the same guy that Stoney Vaughn took to Mexico, then Stoney knows Allen/Albert/Alex. Triple A . . .'

'Triple A?'

'I ain't calling him by all his aliases,' Gooch said. 'Triple A was in touch with Jimmy. And Jimmy used to work for Patch. There's your connection.'

'But no proof. Nothing to give to David. Albert Exley and Allen Eck could be two entirely different people.'

'I don't think so,' Gooch said. 'Names too similar. One guy. Triple A.'

'So why was he in New Orleans?'

'From that phone call Helen heard and got shoved through the glass for, I think he was there to kill someone. I'm gonna do some hunting today, get Helen to help me, see if who all in New Orleans went missing or turned up dead during the time he was there. She's a quick learner.'

'I'll bet.'

'Don't you be that way, Whitman.'

'Shouldn't you have stayed in New Orleans to do this?'

Gooch shook his head. 'Triple A is here, man. *Here*. If he's this guy that Jimmy was in contact with, and he's the same treasure hunter Stoney knew, he's either been here or he's still here. Most of what I was going to look for is in newspaper archives. I can do all that via the Internet.' He raised an eyebrow. 'I sure as hell wasn't leaving you alone here, sniffing around. This guy's a freak.'

'Why'd you bring Helen, Gooch?'

'I could use some help, and let's just say she's motivated to find this Alex. He hurt her pretty badly. And second, well, she needs a vacation. Whores don't get vacation time. Least not paid. And plus, she knows the guy. We don't have a picture. I thought maybe she could find an artist in town, describe this guy, get a sketch for us.'

'Like a police sketch? Artists don't do that generally, Gooch. It's very specialized work.'

'Whatever,' Gooch said. 'The key is finding this guy, Whit. If the three different guys are all one and the same . . . you got your man, I'm telling you.'

'Take her to see Jason Salinger,' Whit said. 'Let them compare notes. That should help us know if Triple A is one person or not. Maybe he has a photo from Mexico.'

'Then, maybe later,' Gooch said, 'I might take her to a movie. If we're not tracking down this fuck.'

'Gooch, you aren't sleeping with her, are you?'

'Yeah, we slept together last night. Didn't screw. Just slept.'

'Just slept.'

'Yeah. She snores a little. That doesn't bother me.'

*

'I think, in short, you're screwed,' Suzanne Gilbert said.

Whit had thought he was done with the juveniles, with teen court ended and Gooch gone, but Suzanne was waiting for him in his office, arms crossed, still wearing black shirt, black pants, despite the hazy heat that had broiled Port Leo. Pouting. Pissed as a spoiled teenager being told no.

'Don't you feel like a solar panel?' Whit said.

'Don't fuck with me,' she said. Her tone was still pleasant.

'I'm not. What's wrong?' He pulled the robe off, over his head. He hated wearing black, even in the air-conditioned comfort of the courthouse.

She watched him smooth out his lime shirt and hang up the robe.

'Shut the door. This conversation is private.'

He did, gave her an indulgent smile, thought, *You have about five seconds to turn nice.*

'Lucy. She is apparently the sole heir of Patch's estate.'

Legal news traveled fast. He wondered who told her. Maybe Lucy. Maybe the lawyers. Maybe David. 'So I've heard. I haven't seen a will, though.'

'And her lover is in charge of the inquest.'

'Lover. I don't know if I've ever been called that before. Don't most people say boyfriend?' He sat behind his desk.

'It's going to make a nasty headline in the paper,' Suzanne said. 'You should recuse yourself from the case.'

'Lucy is not officially under suspicion. And she's not a blood relative of mine or a relative by marriage. I don't have grounds to recuse myself.'

'Of course she's not a suspect. Not with you working hand in hand with the police.'

'David Power is not exactly president of my fan club,' Whit said. 'They don't listen to me as to who they suspect. They handle the evidence, they make the calls. Jimmy Bird is the guy they think did this, Suzanne, so why are you pitching a hissy fit?'

She was mad about all that land and money not coming to her, and whatever he said wasn't going to placate her.

'Jimmy Bird has a wife and family, and he just suddenly turns to burglary? I don't buy it,' Suzanne said. 'Lucy, somewhere, has her hand in this. That will's going to get a hard look, too. And for you abusing your position to protect her, I'll go to the papers—'

'You know, go and do what you please, Suzanne,' Whit said quietly. 'You're mad because Patch cut you out. You're a disgruntled relative. The papers will give you the tenth of an inch you deserve.'

'Your career as a judge will be over.'

'I've been threatened with that before,' Whit said. 'It'd work if I got found screwing a goat. And even then it's only a maybe. I screw up, the judicial board'll spank me and I'll take it. You and the papers can try what you please.' He smiled. And he meant it. Before being elected, he'd run an ice cream shop, taken pictures for the newspaper, run a messenger service. All were decidedly less stressful than sitting on the bench and taking crap from this no-talent whiner. 'Bet I'm more popular in town than you are.'

'Don't make that bet, Whit.' Her tone softened. 'We can deal, can't we? I won't make a scene in the papers. I won't take your career down, which you seem to think is invincible but isn't. But we need to reach an agreement.'

'On what?'

'Lucy can afford to be . . . generous to me. Share a little.'

Whit stared. 'You're unbelievable.'

'I'm very believable.'

'You'll make trouble and contest the will – unless

you're paid off?' He shook his head. 'Go paint your butt and roll yourself another bad mural.'

'She's not worth it, Whit. Not worth your career. She's a phone psychic, for God's sake. Do you think she's, at heart, anything more than a con artist?'

'Con artist. That's good coming from you. You're better at working the cocktail party crowd than you are the canvas. It's the only way to explain why anyone would buy your shit.'

She stood. 'My paintings hang in the houses of lots of really, really good lawyers around here, Whit. Tell Lucy I won't contest the will if you withdraw from the case and she's willing to share, oh, let's say thirty percent. I won't be greedy.'

'You sure as hell won't be, because you're not getting one red cent.'

'Now that's up to Lucy to decide,' Suzanne said. 'Isn't it?'

The people Claudia Salazar had known in her life hovered around her, as though they could step on the waves and not dampen their feet. Her *abuelitas*, one stern, the other smiling. Her parents, her mother chiding her as though the boat she leapt from was the same as a good man: *Why would you leave a perfectly good boat, silly girl?* David reaching a hand down toward her, then vanishing. Whit, with his bad-boy smile he didn't know he had. Ben, sweet, folding his arms around her, letting her rest her head against his shoulder. She knew she was hallucinating, hunger and exhaustion and the salt water she couldn't keep from her mouth in the rolling waves working their toll. Her skin felt like it might slide off her organs, her bones. She had wearied long ago of alternating between treading water, swimming, and waving the electric-red pillow, of riding the waves up and then down again into the swells. The jeans – tied into knots of air pockets – didn't float and she finally let them sink into the emptiness below her. If she thought too long about the water beneath her – its depths, with bull sharks and jellyfish and the dissolved bones of sailors lost long ago – her breath caught in panic. She forced herself to stare at the sky, the vastness above, more comforting than the vastness below. The clouds could not hurt you.

She had tried to swim toward the coast, maintaining a steady pace, but it seemed to grow no closer. She wondered if the distant smudge of coast really was coast, or maybe a trick of the light and the water put there to tease her.

She swam, waved the red pillow, swam some more. She thought she saw a sailboat briefly in the distance but it seemed to vanish in the haze.

You can quit now, a voice she didn't recognize piped up. *It's okay. Just stop. Give up. Sink.*

'Shut up,' she croaked through cracked lips.

No shame in lying down. The water is only cold for a while.

Some instinct made her stop for a moment in the chop, wave the little red pillow with leaden arms.

There are things worse than being dead. Better drown yourself before the sharks get ahold of you.

'I won't taste good,' Claudia said. She swam again toward the smudge she thought was coast and wondered about Danny. About Ben, if Ben were alive or dead. The sky had been empty of planes and choppers and a cold ripple of grief in her belly, and between her shoulder blades, said, *No one is looking for you. They don't know where to look.*

She figured it was now past noon, and she used the sun as a guide to find west, to swim toward land. She wondered if this was the last time she'd see the sun, felt the hollowing sting in her eyes of having looked at it too much in trying to check her bearings. Maybe the next time the sun rose she would be lost for ever under the waves. Bones never found, her flesh broken apart by the salt water, her atoms scattered by the tides over the next century or so. She'd get to Thailand, Australia, India, Sweden, all the places she'd dreamed of traveling, a little bit of her in the grains of sand, in the foaming curl of the surf. *Just let go. Let go. Let . . .*

'No!' Claudia screamed.

Between her and the ever-distant smudge was a dot, moving, with a crescent of sail. Getting bigger.

She screamed with all her might, rose up out of the water, waving the tattered, sodden red pillow. Waving, waving, waving and screaming her throat raw.

25

Lucy was getting ready to leave Patch's house, purse in hand, dressed in jeans, a plain white T-shirt, fat-lensed sunglasses, and a baseball cap. Whit pulled up, parked his Explorer to the side so she could move her Chevy out. She opened the car door, tossed in her purse, stood by the car, waiting.

'How was afternoon court?'

'Slow. Glad to finish a little early. Where you going?' he asked.

'A few errands,' she said. 'I haven't gotten a thing done since Patch died.'

'I can do that for you.'

She forced a smile. 'It's okay. I'd rather go myself. I need to stay busy.'

He told her about the conversation with Suzanne. Behind the sunglasses she gave no sign of emotion, but she crossed her arms, tapped her feet in anger.

'Well. What do you want to do?' she said.

'If I recuse myself, the press might make an issue of it. Think that you're more of a suspect than you are. But this is really your decision, Lucy. At least about the will.'

'Mine. You mean ours.' She gave him a smile, the thin kind that is barely meant. 'We're a team, aren't we?'

'Yes.'

'Then forget Suzanne. Spoiled little bitch. She crossed a line she's never going to be able to step back over.'

'Okay.'

She gave a sick little laugh. 'I have no family left, Whit. Patch and Suzanne were it, and now . . . I'm not going to be able to forgive her.'

'Never say never. She's upset. So are you.'

'She's greedy. I hate greed in people. It's corrosive. Did you know that most of the callers at the psychic hotline want to know if they're going to get rich? Or win the lottery?' She shook her head. 'They never ask if they're just going to be happy. Find love. That's not enough for people anymore.'

'Forget the errands. Let's go inside, just be alone.'

'No. It'll be good for me to get out. A little alone time.'

'Okay, Lucy. I'll cook us some dinner.'

'No need. The church ladies and Patch's friends brought a ton of food. Heat yourself up some dinner. There's salad, too. Open wine if you want. Don't wait on me. I may be out for a while.'

He watched her pull out of the driveway. *I have no family left,* she'd said. *I'll be your family, Lucy,* and he nearly laughed, the odd way love kept sneaking up on you.

The fishing cottage was small, on a couple of private acres on the south edge of Laurel Point, fifteen minutes away from Port Leo. It was owned by one of Stoney's widowed clients who lived in San Antonio and rarely bothered with fishing. She'd given him a key a few months ago, asked him to get the real estate appraised, and he'd made and kept a copy for himself.

It was empty, of course, neat as a pin, decorated badly with nautical motifs: starfish light-switch plates, a mobile of crustaceans, fake compasses mounted on the walls like clocks. But very comfortable, a television in the corner, old bourbons and whiskeys in the bar.

'What the fuck good is a compass mounted on the wall?' Alex said.

'It's decorative,' Stoney said.

'It must be nice to have a house you don't even need.'

'The old woman who owns it, her husband invented an important valve on oil pumps. She's so rich she doesn't have to wipe her own ass if she doesn't want to.'

Alex had inspected the cottage, took a deep breath, said, 'It'll do.' The cottage was isolated, quiet, not a place anyone would look for Stoney. Earlier, he'd outlined the plan.

'Sooner or later your brother and his girlfriend are going to be missed. People come looking for them, they want to talk to you. But you're gone. So's your boat. So you're presumed missing, too.'

'Like I've been kidnapped?' Stoney said slowly.

'Yeah. At least until we see what's happened. They turn up alive, your brother might not be real thrilled with you since you wouldn't pay and told them to kill his girlfriend.'

'I never said that—'

'Listen. But if the gang that kidnapped *them* had operatives that also kidnapped *you* . . .'

'To get the money they couldn't get before,' Stoney said. 'Yeah.' So he thought for a moment, told Alex about the cottage, and they'd headed over after burying Danny's body in a thick grove of oaks, twelve miles inland. It had been hot, even in the shade, and both men were grimy and sweaty.

Alex washed his face off in the cottage's sink. 'Now that I've done the thinking to save your ass, where's the Devil's Eye?'

'I told you. You can have the rest of the treasure, man. Take it and go with your share. You want to come back when I'm ready to stage the dig on the Gilbert land, help me fake it, that's cool, too. I trust you. And I'll pay you well.' Cool confidence in his voice now. He'd killed a man and his hands weren't shaking, his stomach wasn't in knots.

'No. You're telling me now.'

'Remember. Anything happens to me, your name surfaces. Immediately.'

'Why should I believe that?'

'I managed to take down my investment firm's computer by remote control, Alex. I kept a virus executable file I could run on the servers, one the servers weren't protected against, in case I needed to freeze up my computers, if the Feds wanted to look too close at my records. I don't keep real backups. It's all insurance. I'm just a big believer in it.'

'You are fucking pissing me off.'

'Tough,' Stoney said, feeling tough himself. 'I needed insurance you wouldn't off me like Jimmy Bird and I've been very careful about how I set it up. You want to leave with your share of the treasure? Go ahead. But the emerald, it's mine.'

Alex stared. Stoney made himself not blink, not move. He thought Alex might say, *Well, screw the Eye*, and just shoot him. Stoney wondered what it would feel like to have the bullet tear into your skin, explode through organs, come out the back. He'd lie there dead for God knows how long, until old Mrs Mayweather in San Antonio decided to go fishing again and showed up at the cottage.

Alex's frown tightened, like he wanted to shoot Stoney but decided not to. Instead of going for his gun, Alex tucked his hands into his pockets.

'I've got some business to attend to,' Alex said.

Stoney felt a little shock of pleased surprise; he thought Alex would stick to him like glue. He felt relief at the idea of being alone. Some business? He wondered what that was.

Alex said, 'You need to stay out of sight, keep the lights off, don't attract attention here. You've been kidnapped, remember.'

'Shit. That Whit Mosley saw me. He knows I wasn't kidnapped this morning.'

'If he's a problem,' Alex said, 'I'll handle him.'

'You can't go kill a judge . . .'

'Stoney. There's probably a good marathon on cable. Try the Cartoon Network. Knock yourself out.'

After Alex left, Stoney made a phone call, poured a shot of Jack Daniel's, downed it like medicine, lay on the froufrou pillows of the Mayweather couch, drowsily replaying in his mind killing Danny. It wasn't so bad. He hadn't liked Danny begging for his life; that bothered him, but what was done was done.

He decided he'd rather think about Danny than about Ben. They'd never been particularly close as brothers, especially since Stoney made his money. Not ones to sit and talk about life. He quit thinking about Ben, got comfortable, dozed.

The knock on the door woke him from his drowse, and for a second he thought, *Well, there's Ben, back from fishing.* No. He was in the cottage. Waiting for a friend. Stoney stood, opened the door.

'Come on in,' he said.

Lucy Gilbert stepped inside, glanced around. 'Are we alone?'

'Yeah,' Stoney said. And as soon as he said it she pulled a gun from her purse, a big old revolver that must've been her uncle's, but cleaned and oiled, and she aimed it squarely at his chest.

'You bastard,' Lucy said. 'You killed them.'

'What's this?' He tried to keep an easy tone in his voice. He hadn't expected sweet, ditzy Lucy to be armed.

'You killed Patch and Thuy.'

'No, I didn't,' he said. Wow, three times today he'd had a gun aimed at him and he nearly laughed, except

Lucy looked a little ragged, and the third time might not be the charm. She was far more likely to shoot him. 'I didn't kill anyone, Lucy. I called you because I wanted to be sure you were safe.'

'I'm supposed to fucking thank you? No one was supposed to get hurt. You were just supposed to dig up the stuff. I sell you my land, you rebury it, end of story.'

'I didn't kill them,' he said again, 'but if you want the guy who did, I can give him to you. But just you. Not the police, though, that'd be a mess for both of us.'

'I hate you,' Lucy said and the barrel, trained right on his chest, steadied. 'Do you know what you might cost me? What you've already taken from me?'

'If you feel so righteous, pick up the phone and call the police. I'll just sit on the couch while you explain to them how you knew who killed your uncle and his girlfriend and didn't lift a finger.' He went and sat, crossed his legs.

'Don't think I won't,' Lucy said.

'Phone's right there.'

He waited; she waited. She lowered the gun, just a bit, down toward his crotch. 'Tell me what happened.'

Stoney did, quietly, saying how Alex had freaked when Thuy and Patch surprised them as they were finishing the dig, killed them both.

'And who killed Jimmy Bird?'

'Far as I know, he's a suicide.' Stoney watched her lower the gun, the barrel pointing at the floor. 'I'm not asking any more questions about it. Neither should you.'

'This Alex,' she said, 'does he know about me?'

'He knows you're Patch's niece. He doesn't know we know each other.' He cleared his throat. 'I'm really sorry about your uncle and his friend, Lucy. Truly I am. No one was supposed to get hurt. If it's comforting, it was very, very quick. They might have been afraid for a moment but it was as painless as could be.'

'Painless my ass. He beat Patch's head in with a shovel.'

'I know. First blow killed the poor guy. Alex just wanted to be . . . sure.'

'That is not comforting to me in the least, Stoney,' she said. She sat across from him in the heavy armchair. Closed her eyes. 'I can't believe this has happened. This had a bad vibe from the beginning and I ignored it.' She opened her eyes. 'You've fucked up my aura, Stoney.'

'You still have the emerald?'

'Yes.'

'Where is it?'

'Safe.'

'Alex wants it. He's not going to give up. I told him one lie about where it was, but he didn't buy it.'

She gave a little shudder. 'Why did you get involved with this guy?'

'A truly legit contract archaeologist wouldn't have agreed to do the dig. Alex did. And he'll do the re-dig on your land, make all the records and processes look clean.' He paused. 'You know your boyfriend came to see me.'

'Oh, God.'

'He knew I'd met Patch those couple of times.'

'Oh, God.'

'I said Patch was just an acquaintance. He believed me.'

'I want you to stay away from Whit,' she said.

He got up, sat on the armchair's arm next to her, put his arm around her. She felt good. He liked Lucy, her pert little nose, blue eyes, little barely visible freckles on her cheeks. *Nice tits beneath the blouse,* he thought, wondering if maybe those little kissable freckles were down there, too. He'd thought about what it'd be like to bed her, if she ever got over that judge and gave him a real glance.

'It's gonna be okay,' he said, patting her. 'I sure don't have a thing against him.'

She stiffened under his hand. 'So now what?'

'Alex might be a problem. Not just for me. For you. Or for your boyfriend,' he said. He had to be careful, not panic her overmuch. She might crack and run to Whit or to the police, even if it cost her everything. He ran a thumb along her shoulder blade.

She shrugged his hand off.

'Sorry, just trying to be a help.' He leaned back. 'I know you're upset – you got every right.'

'I don't want you to ever touch me, Stoney. You understand?'

'Sure, Lucy.'

'I love Whit.'

'I know you do. I'm sorry. I'm just trying to be a friend.'

'You let Alex kill my uncle and Thuy and you want to be my friend?'

'I couldn't stop him,' he said and then he had an idea, not a bad one at all, to solve his problems. It might work. 'Lucy. That gun. You really know how to use it?'

She narrowed her gaze. 'Why?'

'Like I said, Alex might be a problem.'

'You said you need him for the fake dig.'

'Sure. But he's gotten real unpredictable. Maybe if he doesn't want to do the fake dig on your land, just wants to take off, well, he might decide to hurt me. Or you, if he finds out someone else has the Devil's Eye. And he knows Whit talked to me. He might hurt Whit. I don't know.'

She stared. 'You want me to shoot Alex.'

'I want us to be careful, sweetheart. We get through this, we both get what we want. You get your money, you get out of your debts, you get Whit.'

'I don't know I want to sell you my land anymore, Stoney. And I think I have Whit—'

'Until he finds out about what you've done. Then he'll be gone, Lucy.'

'I want out. This isn't what I signed on for, Stoney.'

'Can't, Lucy. Train left the station.' He went back to the couch, smiled at her, thinking, *And I will fucking touch you when I please when all this is done.* 'I'm not suggesting you kill Alex, Lucy. Clearly not. Just want you to be careful. I mean, he thinks Whit's a threat to him, he's going to come after him. We're kind of pretending that I've been kidnapped right now—'

'What?'

'Just calm down. I don't want to go into the why. But the last person who saw me was your boyfriend. Alex considers him a threat.'

Lucy stared at the gun in her lap.

'You know how to use it?' he asked again.

'Patch showed me,' she said. 'When I was a lot younger.'

'Alex is staying at a little motel on the outskirts of Port Leo. The Sandspot. You know it?'

'Yeah.'

'Room 133.'

She didn't say anything, looked down at her fingers closed around the gun.

'Well, now you know where he's at, sweetheart,' Stoney said. 'The rest is up to you.'

26

The little prostitute was sitting on the flying bridge of *Don't Ask*, munching an apple, apparently enjoying the late-afternoon breeze and the shade.

'Where's Gooch?' Whit called as he came aboard.

'He said he had to hunt down someone,' Helen Dupuy said.

Hunt down. Not a good sign. 'Who?'

'I don't know. He said he'd call in a bit. He said it was okay for me to be here.'

She had decided he was an enemy. He sat next to her, kicked his sandals off. 'I'm sure it is. You're his guest.'

She finished her apple, wiped her hands.

'Do you normally get on planes with men you barely know?'

'That's a really stupid question,' she said. She seemed a little less intimidated by him out of the robe. 'What do you think?'

'You're either very trusting or you're very naive or—'

'Or maybe I just want to help Gooch get the guy who hurt me.'

'Okay.'

'You think I'm not good enough to be his friend. I can tell he told you what I do. You changed the way you look at me.'

'Gooch has the widest range of friends of anyone I've ever known.'

'He's nice. Really nice.'

'When he wants to be. Don't get on his bad side.'

'I bet I seen more bad sides than you have.'

'So how long are you staying?'

'I don't know. I don't have to rush back.'

'You don't have a pimp?'

'I have a manager. Gooch explained to him I had a civic duty to come help.'

'Oh, Lord.'

'I'm not a streetwalker,' she said. She drank from a glass of water. 'I got a regular clientele. Blue-collar guys. Most of 'em aren't even married. They just can't afford to spend a ton of money buying drinks for stuck-up girls who won't give 'em none.'

'More civic duty.'

'You want my help or should I just leave now?'

'I want your help, Helen.'

'We talked with Jason Salinger. He didn't have a photo, but my description of Albert and his of Allen Eck are both pretty much dead-on, except for Albert having black hair and Allen having brown. Both of 'em got a little part-moon scar on the corner of their mouths.'

'How did you explain to Jason what you wanted to know?'

'Just told him I was your secretary and you needed some more questions answered.' And like she was his secretary, she handed him a file. 'Here. Gooch and I got on his laptop and went into the back issues site for the *Times-Picayune*. We looked up all the crime stories from between June first and June fourth. And a couple of days each way past that. Gooch said you'd be interested in the top story.'

As he started reading she gave him a summary. 'Some rich guy up off St Charles named Danny Mouton. But he goes by the name Danny Laffite, claims to be descended from Jean Laffite – got a history of mental problems, it says. Someone killed his cousin, who was staying at his house. Single shot through the forehead, close range. They don't say the caliber in the paper.'

Like Thuy Tran.

'Was this Danny Laffite a suspect?' Jason Salinger had mentioned Danny Laffite, too, the supposed forger kicked out of the Laffite League.

'Nope. Visiting relatives in South Carolina at the time. Place was vandalized pretty heavily, apparently a TV, a VCR missing. A burglar. But Danny Laffite seems to have dropped out of sight afterward.'

'No arrests made?' He scanned the rest of the article, and a brief follow-up that was more about the checkered career of Danny Laffite than about the poor cousin, whose name was Phillip Villars.

'No. We printed out all the stories about homicides – there's always more in the summer in New Orleans – but Gooch said he thought only this one mattered.' She sipped her water. 'Gooch says Alex – that's what I'm calling him now – is a treasure hunter, y'all think, and might have a connection to this Danny Laffite guy.'

'Possibly a loose one. They have a mutual acquaintance named Stoney Vaughn.'

'So that call Alex got, that he'd offed the wrong guy? Maybe Danny Laffite was supposed to get killed, not his cousin.'

'Would you hand me the phone, please?' Whit said.

He dialed 411, asked for a New Orleans listing for Daniel Mouton on First Street. A message said the phone had been disconnected. He clicked off.

A hazy shape was starting to form. But with Jimmy Bird dead by his own hand, would David or anyone else give a crap?

'I'm going below and taking a nap,' Helen said. 'I had a long night and a long day and I'm tired.'

'Helen, thank you.' He hesitated. 'I want you to know I don't have a thing in the world against you.'

Helen Dupuy stood. 'I'm real aware I'm not good

enough for Gooch. I know it. He doesn't. Maybe you could let me have a couple of nice days before he sees it and gives me a plane ticket home.' Then she went belowdecks.

Whit went back to his car and his cell phone rang in his pocket. He answered. Within a minute, he was roaring out of the marina parking lot, speeding toward the Port Leo hospital.

'Jesus, you look good,' Whit said, touching Claudia's hair. Lotion covered her skin, bandages wrapped her hands, an IV dripped into her arm. Her lips were swollen like jelly candies, her face blasted red with sunburn.

'You're the worst liar on the planet. I look like hell. I feel like I ran a marathon. On my knees.'

She had spent nearly eight hours in the Gulf, treading water, waving her, as she told him, 'goddamned red pillow', until a sailboat with a retired Michigan couple aboard spotted her and pulled her from the water. They'd hurried her into Port Aransas. Even before they reached Mustang Island, she was wrapped in heavy blankets and on the radio with the coast guard, telling them about the kidnapping, giving them details on *Jupiter* and *Miss Catherine*, and saying that Danny was headed to Stoney's house at Copano Flats, off the bay.

'Danny Laffite,' Whit said. 'Christ.'

'But his boat didn't make it. Apparently it sunk earlier in the day, a bit off the Flats. No sign of Danny. And no one is at Stoney's house. They've sent people looking for him.'

'I saw him today.' Whit let go of her hand, sat on the edge of her bed. When he'd arrived she'd scooted her hovering parents out and asked a worried David to give them a moment's privacy, which had been granted with a frown but not an argument. She'd been talking with the coast guard command, the sheriff's office, and the FBI had been summoned in from Houston.

'Why?' she asked.

He told her the complete story then, all of it, from the discovery of Patch's and Thuy's bodies, the links he kept finding between Stoney Vaughn and Patch, the connection to the Laffite League, Triple A and Helen Dupuy, the murder a month ago at Danny Laffite's house, the suicide of Jimmy Bird and the coins found in his pocket, his theory about a treasure dig.

She told him Danny's story. Whit sat.

'It's David's case,' he said. 'I wasn't sure there was enough evidence about these connections . . . but based on what you've said—'

'We need to find Stoney Vaughn. Find Ben.' She closed her eyes. 'Danny and his thugs were demanding ransom for us right after the kidnapping. At least as of this morning, Stoney thought Danny had his brother. Which suggests to me that Stoney paid no ransom or the redhead – Danny says his name is Zack – never picked up the ransom.'

David stuck his head back into the room. 'Pardon me, Whit, but we need to talk to her some more.'

'Actually,' Claudia said, 'we all need to talk.'

An hour later, Claudia said good-bye to Whit, gave a feeble wave.

David watched him go. 'I mean, you and him, you can just take the fucking case yourselves.'

'David, no one could know that it was a much more involved case than anyone—' she started, but he was mad, his skin flushed.

'Christ. You're both gonna make me look like an utter fool. All this other stuff, it still doesn't change the fact that Jimmy Bird killed himself, left a suicide note pretty much admitting he killed Gilbert and Tran. The FBI's handling the kidnapping. They'll take it from me quick, and if all this is mixed up together, the Feds'll take that case from me, too. What the hell am I supposed to do, Claudia?' He stared at her, wobbled on his feet. 'You could have been killed. Christ.'

'I'm okay. I'm okay, David.'

He sat down on the edge of the bed.

'Find Stoney. Find Ben. Stoney Vaughn seems to be the driving force behind all this mess. Y'all find him – he's the key to this whole case.'

He nodded. It was like they were still married, she thought. He knew what to do on a tough case but he had trouble delving to the heart of the matter, letting himself get distracted too easily. 'Stoney Vaughn. Yes, you're right.'

He went and poured them each a cup of ice water. He brought her hers; she wasn't so thirsty now, with the IV hydrating her, but she took a sip on her sore lips.

'I need some more information from you if we're to find your . . . boyfriend.' He said the last like he had a roach in his mouth.

'David,' she said gently, 'this clearly upsets you. Why don't you let me talk to another investigator?'

'It doesn't upset me.'

She let it be.

He sat on the edge of the bed, had a notebook out but didn't open it.

'What else did you want to know?'

'Um . . .'

'Because I'm exhausted, David. I'm really, really exhausted. I'd like to get some sleep.'

'Sure.' He stood. 'Sure. I'll be back soon. You rest.' And awkwardly, he leaned down and kissed her forehead, quickly, chastely.

She watched him step out of the room.

Tomorrow. Tomorrow she'd be out of the hospital. She'd check herself out, help in the search for Ben and Stoney. The FBI, she knew, would be poring over the Vaughn house, looking for *Jupiter* up and down the Texas coast.

Maybe Ben still breathed. She'd find him if he did. And if he didn't, she'd find the bastards who'd killed him.

She fell asleep.

27

The elderly couple had lived near Encina Pass for nearly seventy years, close to the bay, in an old, small house made of heavy cypress. When the knock came on the door both were nearly asleep, having dozed off during a particularly boring cable movie. The old woman nearly jumped out of her skin with fright, touched the rollers in her hair in case one had worked loose. The old man rose from his recliner and answered the door.

The young man standing on the front stoop was sopping wet, with a heavy bruise marring his nose and cheekbones, like he'd been in a crash, smelling of the bay, shivering in the night heat, a broken pair of handcuffs dangling from his wrist. One finger was purpled, clearly broken.

'Could you – could you please call the police?' the young man stammered. 'My name is Ben Vaughn and I was kidnapped by some crazy people. I think they killed my girlfriend.'

Alex Black returned to his motel room Friday night, tired, frazzled, in need of a shower. He stood in the shower's hot spray for nearly twenty minutes until the water began to cool. He scrubbed soap hard into his skin and scalp until his body tingled. Then he toweled off with a vengeance, put on shorts and a T-shirt.

His cell phone rang. He picked it up, glanced at the readout. His father, calling from south Florida. At least it wasn't that dumb shit Stoney, him he couldn't deal with any more tonight.

'Hello?'

'Hey, son, how are you?' Big Bert's voice was dry with cancer, but optimistic, like always.

'You chasing the ladies tonight? Taking a breather to call me?' It was an old game between them, pretending an active romantic life was barreling ahead at full steam. Suddenly Alex's throat felt thick.

'I chase 'em but they run faster'n me these days.' A pause. 'Sure would like to see you soon.'

'Probably another few days,' he said. 'I'll be there soon.'

'Dig keeping you busy?'

'Client's a big pain, but it's okay.'

A dry click in his father's throat. 'Find anything interesting?'

'Well, not as interesting as gold,' Alex said, trying to cheer the old man up.

'What you getting?' Big Bert asked.

'Pottery shards, bones, arrowheads.'

'Not much junk to keep you from your old man.'

Alex didn't like his tone. Not telling something, skirting an issue. 'You feeling okay?'

His father gave a soft burp and Alex figured one of Big Bert's friends had sneaked him beer into the hospice again. 'Don't you get thrown out of All Saints, having a party.'

'That was from a Pepsi, thank you kindly.'

'I'm glad you're feeling okay,' Alex said.

'I never said I was.'

'Well. Okay. I got to go, Dad. I got an early, early morning.'

'Yeah. You got pottery shards calling your name.'

'Okay then. I'm gonna be there soon. Promise.'

'Don't take too long.'

Christ, what did that mean? 'Dad. Are you worse?'

'I just want to see you soon. Good-bye, son. I love you.'

'Yeah, back at you.' He did not want to think of his father wasting away in a hospice bed, the cancer he'd ignored for too long seeping through his body like rot. Big Bert belonged on a boat, diving for galleon treasure, hauling up lost Spanish coins. But always just to have Florida bureaucrats snatch them out of his hands. Bureaucrats had ruined him slowly with promises while breaking him on the rack of their antiquity laws. *Here, go get yourself an ice cream,* Big Bert would say to Alex as a little boy, handing him a piece of eight from 1690 or a doubloon from 1712. *Knock yourself out with a double scoop.* Funny, yes, but then the state government would take most of the gold, the IRS would sniff around Big Bert's boat, squatters would try to maneuver their boats over his dive spots, the treasure would be nibbled away by a thousand grasping hands more clever than good-natured Big Bert's.

His way was better, Alex knew, but he didn't want to discuss it with Big Bert. Let his father think he still scrabbled through the loam for pottery and beads and crap. He'd sell much of the treasure quick. He'd go to that hospice – such a nice crisp word for a death place – grab Big Bert, fly off to Costa Rica. Let him die in blue splendor under a bright, forgiving sun. Die happy.

Every day you waste with Stoney is a day you don't have with your dad. Tomorrow he'd get it sorted out. Find the Eye, eliminate Stoney. Screw Stoney's threats of posthumous exposure. He was tired of this game. He needed his money, he needed it now. He'd made new identities before, he could do it again. No one in Costa Rica would give a crap about him. And he could stay there for ever.

Alex clicked on the television, waited for the ten o'clock news out of Corpus Christi. First story was a dramatic hostage standoff at a church in Dallas, two people killed. Then the news was all Port Leo: a boat wreck in St Leo Bay, a Port Leo police officer rescued from out in the Gulf, Ben Vaughn's face on the screen as a kidnapping victim. Then Stoney's face, also described as possibly missing. At the least the authorities wanted to ensure he was well, considering his brother had been kidnapped.

Shit. Claudia Salazar was alive. But there were no other details offered, no mention of a connection to the deaths at Black Jack Point. At the end of the newscast the pearl-toothed anchor broke in to say that Ben Vaughn had been found in Encina Pass, alive and well, no details yet on his missing brother, financier Stoney Vaughn.

He picked up his cell phone, called Stoney at the fishing cottage.

'Your brother's alive,' Alex said. 'Congratulations.'

'I just saw on the news.' Stoney's voice sounded a little funny. Like he was surprised to hear from him. 'Where you at?'

He suddenly didn't like the question. 'Just around. Keeping a close eye on you.'

'So how long do I need to lay low? I can't stay holed up here for ever.'

'I suppose that depends on what your brother says,' Alex said. 'He accuses you of anything, you're fucked.'

'Ben would never do that to me.'

'You just fucked him over royally, Stoney. You might have lost that old brotherly love.'

'Ben's not like that.'

'You mean he's a better person than you,' Alex said. 'I think you want to stay there a couple more days, Stoney. Let them get good and worried about you. Maybe we'll make a fake ransom demand to your brother, just for show. Then you can crop up, no worse for wear.' *Yeah, right, dream on.* 'I'll call you tomorrow. Stay low.'

'I will.'

Alex got up, packed his bag. He liked knowing where Stoney was but didn't like Stoney knowing where he was. He checked out of the Sandspot, drove across town to a smaller motel, the Surfside – did every coastal hotel have to have an S in the title? – checked in, got settled.

On the way over Alex didn't notice the little Chevy, gold and violet and amber crystals dangling from the rearview mirror, following him.

28

Whit awoke early Saturday morning, Lucy shaking his shoulder. She still hadn't been home when he returned from the hospital, but he was exhausted. So he ate a sandwich, curled in under the sheets, felt her arrive next to him and spoon into him, felt her kiss on the back of his neck, and fell back asleep.

'Phone call,' she whispered into his ear. He hadn't even heard the phone ring. 'Guy sounds like he's squeezing coal into diamonds using his ass.'

Whit picked up the phone, listened, said, 'Uh-huh' and 'Okay' a couple of times, hung up, rolled under the covers.

'Who was that?'

'The FBI.'

'The FBI?' Lucy's voice rose an octave.

'Hoover doesn't run it anymore. You don't have to be afraid.' He wriggled his face deeper into the pillow. 'They want to talk to me about Stoney Vaughn. I guess I really was one of the last to see him before he vanished, or took off, or whatever.' He told her a highly abbreviated – and edited – version of Claudia's kidnapping. He sighed as she ran her hand along his back.

'What do they think happened to this guy?'

'I don't know. Maybe the kidnappers that took his brother went after him.' He didn't want to talk about Danny Laffite or Gooch's trip or any of the rest of it with her. Lucy couldn't keep her mouth shut, he thought, and all of it might upset her needlessly.

'So was this Stoney guy involved in Patch's murder or what, Whit?' She was whispering into his ear, running a

221

hand along the flat of his belly. 'I thought it was Jimmy Bird.'

'Stoney knew your uncle. That was the only reason I went to see him. His brother's kidnapping, it may have nothing to do with your uncle's death.'

She ran fingernails along his ribs; he loved that. He wriggled and smiled. 'No time, babe. I got to get showered for the Feds.'

'Okay,' she said.

He opened an eye, looked at her. 'You okay?'

'Yes, I'm fine. Tired.'

'Your errands took a long time.'

'No, I got back and you were gone. So I ate a quick dinner and then went back over to my apartment, to get some fresh clothes.'

'Okay.' He got up from the bed, started up the shower.

'Whit?' Lucy stood in the doorway, in a T-shirt and thin little white panties.

'Yeah, babe?'

'You're doing an inquest, what, next week?'

'Tuesday.'

'Why, if it was Jimmy Bird? He's dead.'

'It's just a formality, I guess. And maybe by Tuesday we'll know more. But I don't think he acted alone. That might be where David and I differ.'

'David's the cop, though, hon.'

'That he is.' Whit shucked his boxers, stepped into the hot spray. 'An inquest is just a format for determining if one person caused the death of the other. If I put it on Jimmy, it still doesn't explain the why of what happened.'

She kept standing in the bathroom, watching him shower.

'You find any insurance on those coins?' he asked.

'I haven't had time to look,' she said, and as he shampooed, he heard a brief flash of anger in her voice.

'Maybe they weren't Patch's. I really don't know. Could I look at the coins?'

'I'll see what I can arrange. I didn't mean to piss you off.'

'Conflict is bad for your aura, Whit. You're basically a peaceable guy. I get a bad vibe from you as long as this investigation is going on.'

Whit rinsed his hair.

'You're not saying anything smart back to me,' Lucy said.

'You said conflict was bad for me, baby.'

'I know you don't believe in my psychic powers. That's okay. You're scientific in nature and we don't have the imaging technologies to show auras like I wish we did. You could get it done like getting a CAT scan.'

'Lucy, if you say you're psychic, I believe you. Because I love you. End of story.'

She said nothing and he finished washing and when he turned off the water she was standing there, sobbing quietly.

'Baby,' he said.

'I'm such a big fucking fake. I don't see auras. I don't see the future. I get hunches, like any other person, and that's it.'

'Well, I never get a hunch, so you're ahead of me.'

'But I'm a fake. How can you love a fake? I don't say it's the Intuitive Hunch Hotline.' She pulled toilet paper off the roll, dabbed her eyes, blew her nose.

'Lucy.' Whit wrapped a towel around his waist. 'You're not a fake. You're like, well, a counselor without a license. Like I'm a judge without a law degree.'

'You were elected. You don't need one.'

'People elect to call you, get a little tarot, get a little advice.' He pulled her close, gave her a warm peck on the mouth.

'I want to get out of the hotline business,' she said. 'I want to make you proud.'

'I'm proud of you,' he said. 'Love you just as you are.'

'You're not proud of me, Whit,' she said.

'I am.'

'No.'

'Trust me, I am,' he said, toweling off, rummaging in the little duffel bag he'd brought. He found boxers, stepped into them, found a shirt, electric-yellow with sashaying whore-red crabs dancing across it. Pulled on khakis and stepped into his sandals.

'Don't wear that to meet the FBI,' she said. 'Wear a suit.'

'You're putting me in a crabby mood,' he said with a smile.

'Whit. Don't joke. I'm serious. I don't want to be an embarrassment to you.'

'Is this about Suzanne?'

'No. Me.'

'Whatever you want to do, I'll support. You want to keep the psychic hotline? Great. You don't want to do it anymore? Great. But you could never be an embarrassment to me.' He waved the shirt in front of her, slipped it on, began to button it. 'Way more likely I'll embarrass you.'

'I think you're wrong,' Lucy said quietly.

They kept him waiting twenty minutes, and as far as he could see – from the chair in Stoney Vaughn's expansive living room – the two federal agents were just sitting and talking, drinking Stoney Vaughn's coffee and not offering him a cup, making incessant short calls on their cell phones. He wondered – no, he knew. David had already talked to these men, painted an unkind picture of Whit, and that was why he was thumb-twiddling.

When one started a refill Whit got up and stood in the kitchen. 'Excuse me. Saturday may be your day to suck down hazelnut, but I have work to do. Either y'all talk to me now or make an appointment with my office.'

They both looked at him like he had a big streak of piss down his pants but one smiled and the other one pulled out a chair at Stoney Vaughn's kitchen table. Whit thought maybe Lucy was right that he should have worn the suit, and that made him even madder. But he sat.

They both had G names: Grimes and Gordell. Whit immediately dubbed them the G Men. Grimes was muscular and spare, all throat and shoulders and arm muscles with skin the color of teak. Gordell was chunkier, not fat, wide-set and blocky. Grimes had a Southern drawl; Gordell spoke with the nasal clip of New England. The G Men wore suits, nice, summer-weight blends, still far too hot for the Texas coast in July. Whit's shirt seemed to irritate Agent Gordell like a thumbtack in his seat; he kept glancing at it in disbelief.

'Judge Mosley,' Grimes said in his slow, friendly cadence, 'you visited Mr Vaughn yesterday?'

They always had to waste time asking what they already knew. 'Yes. In conducting an inquest into a double homicide this past week I found that there was a slight connection between Stoney Vaughn and one of the victims. I wanted to ask Mr Vaughn about it, so I came out here yesterday morning about eight-thirty. Mr Vaughn looked like shit warmed over, like he'd slept in his clothes, and I could smell whiskey on him. His lip looked split.'

'Like maybe he'd had a stressful evening?'

'He certainly didn't mention his brother and Claudia had been kidnapped. He knew, didn't he?'

'We're not at liberty to discuss that. Judge.' Grimes added the title with an embarrassed smile, like it was an afterthought. Like they even knew for sure.

'Claudia Salazar's an old friend of mine. We work homicides together. I wouldn't take it well if Stoney knew she was in danger and didn't help her.'

The G Men smiled politely. What he took well mattered not a bit.

'But there had already been a suspect identified in this double homicide, right?' Gordell said. 'A suicide.'

'As coroner, I haven't officially ruled that death a suicide yet,' Whit said.

'And you just decided, what, the sheriff's office was wrong and you'd keep pressing other angles?' Gordell said. 'A little presumptuous, wouldn't you say?'

David must have poured on the charm. 'I don't believe I have to justify my actions to you, sir,' Whit said politely.

'Excuse me?' Gordell said. Grimes glanced up from jotting on a legal pad, his face blank.

'Excuse me . . . Your Honor,' Whit corrected. He smiled.

'Your Honor,' Gordell amended. He didn't look repentant for one second. 'No offense meant.'

'Meant. Taken. Whatever,' Whit said. 'If I feel additional information is warranted for an inquest, I go get that information.'

'You're not a lawyer, are you? I mean, you're not one of those judges that's required to be formally trained in the law,' Gordell said with polite snideness.

'No, I'm not a lawyer. I'm an elected official.'

An unpleasant light glinted in the back of Gordell's eyes. 'I'm sure the voters might take offense at you not cooperating with the FBI.'

'How have I not cooperated?'

'Cocky. You don't see that much in politicians,' Gordell said.

'Jim,' Grimes said, a little weary.

'You didn't answer my question,' Whit said.

'Let's not get into a turf war, Judge Mosley. You'll lose and lose badly. We ask the questions. You answer them.'

Whit counted to ten. 'It's good I came here yesterday, as I can tell you Stoney Vaughn was alive and well then. If he's been kidnapped since then, or he's run off, at least I've narrowed the time frame considerably for you.'

'Thank you,' Grimes said.

'What I'd like to know is why,' Whit said.

'Why what?' Gordell said.

'Why were Ben and Claudia kidnapped?'

'Mr Vaughn is a wealthy man.'

'Mr Stoney Vaughn is. Mr Ben Vaughn isn't.'

'They thought Stoney was aboard.'

'Why did they think that? They knew his schedule?'

'We don't know yet, Judge.' Grimes cleared his throat. 'Quite possible the perps had been watching the house, waiting for his boat to go out. Maybe they just assumed his boat's out, he's out on it.'

'So. Stoney Vaughn has a vague connection to my murder case, and he gets smack-dab in the middle of a kidnapping. Now he's gone. It just doesn't seem coincidence to me.'

'You're the one on this buried treasure kick, right?' Gordell said.

'I prefer to think of it as archaeological relics,' Whit said. 'This whacked-out supposed treasure hunter, Albert Exley or Allen Eck or Alex, I want y'all to find out who this guy is.'

Grimes's lips tightened. 'We're appreciative of the information you gave Officer Salazar and to the other local authorities. But please understand, these various threads that may tie to a case, those are for us to sort out and prioritize, Your Honor.'

'Let me tell you why this matters. This Alex, this

certifiable nutcase, was in New Orleans when Danny Laffite's cousin got murdered. He put a poor woman through a window because she might have heard someone telling him he "got" the wrong guy. I think Danny Laffite had been in touch with Stoney Vaughn in the weeks before, trying to cut a deal to finance a dig for this treasure. But Stoney got greedy and sent Alex to steal Danny's evidence about the treasure and kill him. Only Alex killed the wrong person at Danny's house. Danny must have phoned Stoney after the New Orleans break-in, and Stoney freaked at the thought Danny was still alive.' He stopped, looked at the two agents. 'So if I were you, I'd be looking really hard at Stoney Vaughn's phone records. See if he called the Bayou Mee Motel in New Orleans. See if he had incoming calls from New Orleans or from South Carolina, where Danny Laffite was when his cousin got killed.'

'We've heard this is your style,' Gordell said. 'Not sticking to your judicial duties.' But Grimes was looking at him, head tilted slightly, with interest.

'You shouldn't listen to rumors,' Whit said. 'Has there been a ransom demand made for Stoney?'

'Thank you for coming by, Judge Mosley.' Gordell stood, didn't offer a hand to shake.

'I'm thinking Stoney didn't want to pay five million. Did he not have it? Maybe y'all are checking his finances, finding some holes . . . I could see him taking off.'

'Judge—' Grimes blinked at him, like he couldn't believe the words.

'I wouldn't buy a single share of a penny stock from that guy. And he had someone in the house here with him, I'm pretty sure.'

'Did you see someone?' Gordell asked.

'No. But I felt watched. Stoney didn't want me in the house. I asked him to lend me a book and he said no, he

228

didn't have one, looked back three times at the windows in a twenty-second period.'

'But you didn't see anyone.'

'No, I didn't. But there was a beige van here that's not here anymore. A Chrysler, I think. I didn't notice the license plates.' And that made him feel stupid, that if he'd been so suspicious he should have made a note of it. 'I don't think Stoney Vaughn has acted alone in this, and I think this Alex guy may be helping him. We have a description of him. We want people to be looking for him, too.'

'That's fine,' Grimes said. 'Give us the info, we'll see if there's anything to it.'

'Thank you, Judge,' Gordell said. 'We'll call you if—'

'Since I've answered your questions while you've looked at me like I was a urine sample,' Whit said, 'maybe you'll defrost slightly and help me. I'd like to speak with Ben Vaughn, and I'm guessing he's under your protection at the moment.'

'Speak with him why?'

'For the inquest into the Gilbert/Tran murders.'

'He's recuperating. Probably not up to questioning,' Gordell said. He stood, signaling the interview was complete. 'And we have certainly not treated you like a urine sample, sir.' He gave Grimes a glance: *This is a judge*?

'I just need five minutes with him.'

'We'll ask him for you,' Grimes said after a moment's hesitation.

'Thank you,' Whit said and stood.

'Judge Mosley,' Gordell said, 'I understand you're a big fish in a little pond here. But we think for a second you're interfering or fucking around with us, you'll be the small-town magistrate in front of a federal magistrate. You understand me, sir?'

'I understand you, sir,' Whit said. 'And if you don't

take me seriously and follow up on this Alex guy, I'm going to call every television station in Corpus Christi, Houston, and San Antonio and tell them that the FBI is purposely ignoring findings presented by the Encina County coroner. Me.' Whit smiled. 'It may only be news for a few minutes. But it'll be news.'

Gordell's mouth worked like he had a bee lodged in his gums.

29

Claudia saw Ben Saturday morning, after the FBI and the police had questioned him further. A guard stood outside his door, watching the nurses. She came into his room and he opened his eyes. He looked pale, a thick bruise on his face, his dark hair little-boy tousled on the pillow.

'Thank God,' Ben said and she came to the bed, crawled in next to him, hugged him. He hugged back, winced a little.

'Are you hurt? They said you were okay . . .'

'The ribs, a little, but not bad.' His voice was throaty. 'Face hurts. Jesus, I'm glad you're okay. Gar said he was going to—'

'He didn't. Danny shot him.'

'That's what your ex told me.'

'You spoke with David?' She sat up.

'Yeah,' Ben said. 'I mean, he questioned me last night. For about an hour, around three in the morning or so, once they really couldn't find Stoney anywhere.'

'Please be kidding. He didn't.'

'Sure. Claudia, it's fine. If it helps them find my brother.'

'Did David behave?'

'Perfect gentleman.'

'That's somehow worse.' She touched his chest. 'Tell me what happened. Everything.'

'Gar . . . was furious about not getting the money. He said he was going to rape you. The other guy—'

'His name is Zack,' she said.

'Zack, then. He freaked. I wanted to reason with him, tell him to call Gar off, but he belted me across the face with his gun.' He touched at the livid bruise on his battered nose, his cheek. 'When I woke up he had me tied and handcuffed in the forward cabin's head.'

'Where did he take you?'

'I think in circles. He didn't know much about boats, sweetie,' Ben said. 'Then he panicked, tried to call Danny on his boat, didn't get an answer.'

'Danny never mentioned that. He told me Zack would probably kill you.'

'The dumb shit probably couldn't operate the radio right. Asking on the wrong channels. But he did figure out the phone. I heard him make a call, asking someone to come and get him, he was stuck out on the Gulf in a big fucking boat he couldn't drive with a hostage. Crying about his boyfriend, cussing Stoney for not being on the boat and it all going down wrong. You would've thought his car had broken down and he was calling roadside assistance.'

'But Zack left Gar. He cut the lines.'

'I don't think so, Claudia. From what I heard, I think Gar cut those. To keep his boyfriend from interfering with him going after you.'

Claudia let out a long breath. 'So someone came and rescued him?'

'Not exactly. He told me he'd gotten the boat in close to shore and he didn't know how to drop the anchor but he was gonna swim in. Said all this to me through the closed door of the head. I kept thinking, he's gonna open it up, shoot me. Then he says he doesn't want to face a murder charge. Says he'll let me be if I just say Gar and Danny were behind it all, maybe do him a favor, not mention him. I'm saying, sure, not a problem. Thinking he's just going to shoot me when it comes time for him to leave. But then he was gone. I didn't hear another boat draw close, and I started hoping, he didn't set the anchor, we might be drifting into the Intracoastal. I was hoping to be a threat to navigation. Jesus, it'd mean people found me.'

'How'd you get out of the handcuffs?'

'I found a little wrench under the sink. Had to pull it to me with my toes. Stoney probably left it there the last time he fixed a faucet. He never puts up his crap. So I used it to hammer the lock, finally broke it, and while I'm trying, *Jupiter* went aground. I'm sweating bullets. I'm thinking, God, am I sinking? I smash the cuffs, get out, see that I've run aground on a little oyster-shell beach, on a little strip of island not far off the Intracoastal. I could see a freighter in the distance, heading down toward Corpus. Zack tore all the wires out of the satellite phone and the radio. I was so ready to be off that boat, thinking maybe you could still be rescued. I just got into the water and swam. Halfway to shore I'm thinking, maybe I could have stayed on the boat, set off a flare. I was just mental. Reached Encina Pass.' He squeezed her. 'Claudia. I thought for sure . . .'

'I know.' She kissed him then, and he was gentle, like he couldn't quite believe she was there.

He let the kiss linger and then said, 'My brother.'

'They'll find him.' She sat up. 'I want to talk to you about your brother.'

'Zack. Or his friends. They must have gone after Stoney for the money.'

'Your brother knew we had been kidnapped, Ben. He didn't call the police. He didn't tell anyone.'

'They said they would kill us, Claudia.'

'Did he or did he not refuse to pay ransom?'

Ben's mouth worked. 'My brother wouldn't do that to us.'

'Danny said the next morning that Stoney had agreed to a trade, thinking you were with Danny and me. So I'm ssuming he hadn't paid a ransom the day before.'

233

'Stoney said his computer systems were down, he couldn't do the transfer. Claudia, my brother's not some cold-blooded monster. You can't believe this of him.'

'I know you love your brother, Ben . . .'

'You heard him, didn't you? You heard him repeat back the account numbers for the transfer, Claud. But he didn't have this imaginary emerald that Danny wanted. Danny was fucking nuts, you know that.'

'Yes,' she said softly. 'But your brother didn't call the police. At any point.'

'The kidnappers took him before he could.'

'A judge – my friend Whit Mosley – saw him Friday morning at his house. Looking like hell. What if there's no virus, Ben? He didn't want to move the five million . . .'

'No. He couldn't move the money. He must've been waiting to hear from the kidnappers again. Zack's friends grabbed him. It's the best explanation. You don't believe what Danny said, do you?'

'I honestly don't know what to think about Stoney.'

'My brother—' Ben's voice broke.

'If I'm wrong, I'm sorry. I hope to God I'm wrong.'

'Stoney loves me.'

She said nothing.

'He was afraid they would hurt us if he called the police.' Trying to convince himself, convince her.

'Ben, Gar knew I was a cop. He called me *Officer*.'

Ben stared down at the sheets covering his lap.

'Did you tell them I was a cop?'

'No.'

'Did your brother?'

'I don't want to talk about this anymore, please. My brother isn't a bad guy, Claudia. We don't know the truth yet.' He moved slightly away from her on the bed.

He was too deep in denial. 'I care about you,' she said

'I don't want you hurt.' He didn't look at her and she felt the little gap grow. 'Ben . . .'

He let go of her hand; she took his hand in answer, squeezed hard.

'Don't say these things about my brother.'

'Okay,' she said. 'You need your rest.' She kissed his forehead. 'I'm going to go for a while so you can sleep, all right? You need sleep.'

Ben said nothing and she went to the door.

'Claudia?' Ben's voice, small, low.

'Yeah?'

'If he didn't refuse to pay the ransom . . . they came and took him, didn't they? They just don't give up on five million, not when there's another option to get it.'

'I hope not, Ben.'

'I mean, did he not think we were worth five million? He could have made it back in a few years, the way he worked, the deals he cut. God, I'm his brother.'

'Maybe they took him, Ben.' Odd, her tone of hoping that a guy got kidnapped, that it could be a remotely positive thing.

'But if he can't get to his money,' Ben said, 'won't they kill him?'

Ben was staying at the hospital, at least through the day. Claudia, tired but hating the sterile walls and wanting her own bed, checked herself out around noon. Her mother, Tina, accompanied her home, fussing the whole way, fluffing pillows, fixing a pan of chicken enchiladas and a plate of chocolate chip cookies that Claudia uncharacteristically had no appetite for. Claudia went to go lie down on her bed, trying not to think about how Stoney could betray Ben so completely. She was still exhausted and she catnapped, loving the feel of her own pillows, sheets, the solidity of the bed. She didn't like thinking about the water, with nothing but the depths beneath her feet.

A knock on the door woke her; Tina entered with a thick envelope. 'Something from work. The officer said you asked for it. Sweetie, I don't want you working, tiring yourself out.'

'That's okay, Mama.' Claudia sat up. 'Put it on the bed. I'll look at it in a minute.'

Her mother did, doused the lights again.

Claudia waited. Mama was exhausted, worn out from staying up most of the night fretting over her. Fifteen minutes later she glanced into the small den. Tina Salazar lay on the couch, snoring softly. Claudia covered her with a light blanket, went back to her room, and opened the file. She'd asked the Port Leo PD to get her what they could find from the New Orleans PD on Danny Laffite and his suspected associates in the kidnapping. She began to read.

Alex had stayed away from Stoney for the morning, sleeping a little later in his new, no-better motel room, dreaming of his dad, the two of them diving for treasure in the shallow waters off the Keys. He hadn't slept well; someone had knocked on his door at some point near midnight, waking him instantly, and he'd crept to the door with his gun in hand, finally peering through the peephole. No one there. He could hear teenagers laughing down the hall – probably just kids. But it unsettled his sleep and he didn't go back for a while, wondering how to best get his sick father to Costa Rica without attracting too much attention.

He got up, showered, dressed, turned on the local Saturday morning TV news. All Stoney – the missing financier. Nothing on Danny Laffite, though, nothing or the murders at Black Jack Point. But still. He needed to get moving. And he needed to take some precautions.

He drove the van over to the big grocery near the Port Leo harbor. It was a chain superstore, an H-E-B, the megachain in Texas, and the store was pink. Coral pink, the whole building, like all they sold was Pepto-Bismol. He slipped on sunglasses and a Marlins cap and went inside – it was busy, full of retirees and young babies, families, Mexicans, Vietnamese, Anglos, sunburned Yankees asking where the juice was in their nasal whines. He bought some doughnuts, a coffee, a small milk, and a box of hair coloring. Time for a change. Go punkish blond, cut the hair short, dump the van at the Corpus airport. The cashier looked a little funny at him, a guy buying blond hair coloring, but bagged it up with the food and took his money.

Alex was halfway across the parking lot when he saw Helen Dupuy.

She was walking toward the store just out of a truck – an old beat-up red truck, walking with a monster of a guy. Big-built, freak-ugly face, military burr of dark hair. And he thought she might have seen him, just two rows over, if she hadn't been looking up all goggle-eyed at this freak.

Can't be Helen, he thought, and he took a hard left, heading away from his car, asking himself what the hell he was doing, stepping behind an SUV, peering at her. Maybe not Helen. It couldn't be her. The two of them walked into the grocery, now forty feet ahead of him, and he turned and followed them, thinking, *No way it's her, no way.*

He kept his sunglasses and his cap on as he entered the store, scanned the register lines, the crowd of shoppers going their separate ways into the aisles. Didn't see them. He looked to his left, over at the bakery section clogged with morning pastry buyers and saw them, the guy pulling Helen through the maze of carts and screaming kids and tables of pies and doughnuts. He followed, hanging back, trying to keep at an angle where the woman couldn't see him. It was Helen, Jesus. She was wearing a halter, a plain blue one, not slutty – it was a hot morning. Above the top of the halter on her back was a discolored hatch of lines, the scars he must've put on her skin when he flung her through the glass window.

Big Ugly and Helen stopped, a round-faced man greeting Big Ugly with a call of 'Gooch!' Big Ugly starting to chat, introducing Helen to the old man. Now ten feet away, Helen's back still to him, Alex stood at the corner of the aisle where the bakery fed into the beer-and-wine section, trying to hear.

The old man must've been part deaf or just one of those old guys who likes to talk loud. Alex heard him say: 'You take me out next week. I got two buddies from Dallas want to come down and get tight lines. You open on Wednesday morning?'

'Might be busy, let me check.' Big Ugly had a low rumble of a voice.

Two kids arguing over a chocolate doughnut passed, their mother chiding them, and he missed what was said but then Big Ugly – Gooch? – said, 'I got a hot spot for red drum, over on the south side of the bay. I'll take you there, but you got to keep it secret, Fred.'

Fred roared. 'Yeah, I'm your man for keeping secret fishing spots. I call you tomorrow, we set it up? And think about where maybe we land some big tarpon?'

'Fine,' Big Ugly said.

A fishing guide, Alex thought. He heard the conversation end, held his breath, glued to the floor, waiting for Helen and this Gooch to turn into the beer-and-wine section and see him. Ten seconds. He risked a glance around the corner

They had moved past the baked goods, Helen holding a big bag of bagels, moving off into the milk and dairy, sticking close to Gooch, turning to smile up at him. He knew the line of her jaw, the slant of her smile. Her.

What to do? Suddenly the huge grocery store felt cramped as a cell. He moved past the registers, out into the lot. He hurried back to his car, scrambled inside.

How? Think it through. Someone made a connection to Helen Dupuy and brought her to Port Leo, how, who . . . Jimmy Bird. Jimmy had called him twice at that motel when he was in New Orleans, in his room, nervous about the several nights they planned to spend on Patch's land, searching with the metal detectors to find the buried cache. Giving him the motel number in New Orleans was a mistake. Jimmy dead, his phone records must have been searched for some reason. Found the calls to his room at the Bayou Mee. Why would a fishing guide bring Helen to Port Leo?

He fumbled for his cell phone, dialed Stoney at the fishing cottage. 'There's a whore I met in New Orleans here. At the freaking grocery, Stoney.'

'So?'

'So I met her when I was taking care of Danny, you dumb shit. She knows what I look like.'

'Get rid of her.'

'She's got a six-six musclebound bodyguard with her. I think he's a local fishing guide.'

'You must've made a mistake.'

'She blew me nine times in four days,' Alex said. 'I know what she looks like, man.'

'What exactly do you want me to do about it, Alex?'

'Don't take that tone with me, asshole.'

'I got my own problems. They have got my picture all over the news this morning. Christ, what Ben must think of me.'

239

'Like you care.'

'He's my brother.'

'But he was too heavy, wasn't he, Stoney?'

'You're not funny,' Stoney said.

'If I were your brother I'd shoot you in the knees for what you did,' Alex said. 'I'm coming over there. I got a couple things I need to do, but I'll be there soon.'

He hung up, weighed the options. Run. The mess had gotten deeper; it was now time to get the hell out of the entire situation. He thought about following this Gooch and Helen – and risk she'd see him? She might be even more dangerous than Stoney. No, it was too much right now; he needed to act but go on the defensive. He waited, saw them return to the truck, holding cups of coffee and a small plastic bag. They pulled out of the lot, drove down the street past the harbor to the curve of Port Leo Beach. He followed, four cars behind. Big Ugly's truck turned in, parked. Alex drove by, did a U-turn, drove by again. Big Ugly and Helen walked to one of the picnic tables near the beach, sat down, pulled bagels out of the bag, a little plastic knife, cream cheese. A breakfast picnic by the bay.

He couldn't get closer without parking near them, and he couldn't risk it. He turned and drove off from the park, scared now for the first time and feeling mad. Stupid Stoney. Stupid Jimmy Bird. Alex went back to the motel, scarfed down his breakfast without tasting it. He went through the Encina County phone book, going through the yellow pages for the fishing guides. Most had pictures of sun-squinting men smiling next to gargantuan fish. No picture of Big Ugly. But one ad, small in the corner, was for Don't Ask Fishing Services, just listed a phone number, and in little quotes below read: *Go with Gooch*. Alex dialed the number. A machine answered, 'You've reached Leonard Guchinski and Don't Ask Fishing. I'm probably booked, but leave a message and I'll give you a call back.' Alex hung up.

Leonard Guchinski. Now he had a name.

Alex applied the blond hair coloring, forcing himself to be consistent and careful, and while he waited twenty minutes to shower it off before finishing the treatment, he checked and rechecked the clips in his gun. He suspected he would need several. It was just shaping up to be that kind of day.

'I got some business to tend to today,' Gooch said. 'Whit's arranged for you to meet a guy who does criminal sketches. Describe Alex to him. He's driving in from Corpus. Then the folks on the boat next to us, they invited you to sail with them while I'm gone.' He slathered cream cheese on his bagel. 'They're friends of Whit's, too.'

'Business. About Alex?'

'Maybe,' Gooch said.

'Do you know where Alex is?'

'Nope.'

'But you know something, Gooch.' She frowned.

It was a little crazy. This girl could read him easier than most people, whom he presented the blank page to, and he'd only known her a couple of days. 'I just think you'll have fun with Duff and Trudy on their boat for a few hours.'

'Duff? Trudy?'

'Don't hold their names against them. They're bankers. They got to have names like that. FDIC requirement.'

'Did Whit tell them what I am?'

'What are you, Helen?'

'I'm a . . .' She stopped, as though the word had gotten harder to say.

'See. It's a blank. Fill it in with what you like.'

'Do you not want to have sex with me because you think you're gonna fix me?'

'I haven't known you long enough to have sex with you,' he said.

She shook her head. 'You're a strange man, Gooch.'

'You're not the first to notice.'

30

This fake kidnapping isn't going to work, Stoney thought.

He had hardly slept, and he picked up the phone once, to call home, to talk to Ben. But then he thought the phones might be tapped. And maybe Ben was at the hospital.

Facing the walls of the cottage, he wondered if prison would be so very different. He thought of his friends, the little social-climbing debs he got to bed, his house. He was a deal maker – it was how he made his money – and the long night made him think that perhaps he should cut a deal. The odds were shifting. Lucy was unstable. Alex was cracking. And if there was a woman in town who knew Alex from the time in New Orleans, well. He thought Alex was jumping at shadows.

He tried to construct a series of lies that would cover his ass more thoroughly, but could stitch nothing credible together that left him clean enough. He picked up the phone to call the police; no, he couldn't do it. Not the police, they weren't deal makers. A lawyer, yes. A lawyer to negotiate the deal. A high-powered lawyer.

He paced back and forth, trying to work up the courage. The worst was Danny. If he could convince people Alex had killed Danny, well, then . . . but the thought of not having the gold, the Eye, made his chest hurt. Take it for the value, maybe, just leave the country and—

The knock at the door made him jump. Alex. The door had no peephole, and the small windows meant you couldn't easily peek out of the curtains without giving yourself away.

So Stoney Vaughn opened the door. Not Alex. A big, ugly hulk of a guy stood there and he belted Stoney hard in the chest, landing him on his back on the floor. Breathing was a memory. He stared up at the ugly guy.

'Mr Vaughn? How you doing? No, don't get up. Don't talk.' The man closed the door behind him. 'Catch your breath. You gonna puke? That's a nice rug. Let me find a bucket. No? You okay?'

He picked Stoney up by the neck, like a schoolboy hauled by the scruff to the principal's office, dumped him on the couch, pulled a wicked, fat black foreign gun out of the back of his pants and let Stoney see it.

'Puh . . . puh . . .'

'Please? I admire politeness. Are you asking me to please not shoot you?'

Stoney managed a nod.

'I won't. At least not yet. Not for the next two minutes. But we're gonna talk – you understand me?' The ugly man leaned down close. 'My name's Gooch. I think you're trying to fuck around with friends of mine. You see this gun? That kills you in a second. Easy. You see this fist?' Gooch held up a big, thick-fingered, closed hand that looked more like an oversize hammer than a fist. 'That kills you slow. It takes its time. After about, oh, twenty or thirty punches, when the bones are all broken up and starting to stick out the skin, and I'm still pounding on you and my knuckles get abraded and I get in a fucking foul mood.' Gooch smiled. 'You don't want the old fist of death, do you?'

Stoney shook his head, got the force of his breath back with a shudder. 'How . . . how . . .'

'Did I find you? That's what I want to talk about. You and Lucy Gilbert.'

Stoney's mouth moved.

'And why you're holed up in a cottage when lots and lots of folks are missing you right now.'

'I . . . I didn't do anything wrong,' he managed.

'Who knows you're here?'

'Lucy . . . that's all.'

'How about a guy who likes first names beginning with A?'

'What?'

'Alex. Albert. Allen. What's his name this week? Asshole?'

'I don't know what you're talking about—'

Gooch cocked the gun, jammed it into Stoney's temple. 'This is a Soviet-made Shootyadickov-69. Very sensitive. It misfires a lot.' He pressed it harder, as if trying to reach Stoney's brains. 'Are you willing to put that much trust in Soviet engineering?'

'Alex! His name is Alex Black. Oh Christ.' Stoney's eyes bugged.

'Is the treasure here?'

'No.'

'Where is it?'

'I . . . I don't know. Alex has it.'

'Where's Alex?'

'He moves around a lot,' Stoney said. 'I don't know where he is.'

'I don't believe you, Stoney. The Shootyadickov doesn't believe you.'

'I don't have it – please, mister.'

Gooch studied him, seemed to think about it. He dragged Stoney over to the phone, placed a call, waited, hung up, called another number, waited, said, 'It's Gooch, call me,' hung up. He pushed Stoney back to the couch.

'C'mon, we're leaving.'

'You . . . can't kidnap me . . .'

'Don't whine. You're already kidnapped, right?'

Gooch hauled up Stoney, pushed him through the door. He pulled him away from the cottage, into a dense grove of twisted live oaks beyond the thick grasses above the beach. A beaten red pickup, a big Ford, was parked there.

'This is how it is,' Gooch said. 'I have absolutely no compunction about shooting you. You bug me, I'm firing. You're going to sit on the floor, hands where I can see them. You behave, you're going to be fine. I'm kind of the opinion you're not the big bad shark in the sea, is that right?'

'Alex . . . Alex is bad,' Stoney said. 'He'll fucking kill you.' He wanted to say, *Yeah, well, I killed a man*, but suddenly saw it wouldn't intimidate this guy. Wouldn't make him blink.

Gooch shoved him into the truck, revved the engine, tore out of the grove of oaks onto the road. He was a quarter mile from the highway when a beige van turned in hard, headed toward them.

'What does Alex drive?' Gooch asked Stoney, still crouched on the floor.

'Beige van,' Stoney said.

'Hello there,' Gooch said. He leaned out the window, opened fire. Gravel and crushed shell exploded from the road near the tires, sparks flew from the end of the van.

'Jesus!' Stoney yelled.

Gooch floored the truck and despite its beaten appearance the engine roared into sweet, precise power. The road was rough – part of the rustic charm – and Gooch left the highway, tearing through a grassy field, taking a hard right, careening down a rocky swath of weed and stone and roaring out onto a thin strip of beach itself.

'Did you know it's legal to drive on the beach in Texas?' Gooch said. 'Fascinating. Against the law most places.'

'Yes,' Stoney managed. He wondered if he could grab the steering wheel, wrench it, stop this guy long enough for Alex to shoot him.

Gooch gave him a long glance. 'I can smell stupid thoughts, man. Don't do it. I'll kill you.'

Stoney stayed put, his face buried in the worn upholstery of the truck, feeling it rumble off the beach, back onto grassland, then back onto the smooth road.

The van couldn't navigate down the long spill of rock to the sandy wet of the beach, and Alex drove back to the road, the van heaving like a horse, and peeled back toward the main highway – his only hope of cutting the guy off.

Gooch in that same red truck, leaving Stoney's hideaway, shooting at him, the gun in the hand rock-steady. He worked his own gun out, kept it in his left hand, steered right-handed.

The van rumbled onto the main highway, narrowly missing a Mercedes with an older couple. The driver laid on the horn. The woman lifted a manicured middle finger in salute and Alex nearly shot it off. Instead he swerved around them, bolted south to where the beach came closer to the main road. He kept glancing at the rearview mirror, thinking the red truck might burst from the trees or from another feeder road.

He drove all the way down to where a curve of beach came close to the road – no sign of the truck. He patrolled up and down the stretch of highway for a half hour but the only red truck he saw was new and had two women in it, pulling a horse trailer.

Finally he returned to the fishing cottage. Front door closed but unlocked. No sign of Stoney. No sign of a struggle.

So – Stoney had been kidnapped for real? Maybe

Gooch was a partner Danny Laffite had that no one knew about. Or maybe Stoney had switched sides, decided to get out from under Alex's thumb, gotten himself a new partner to take care of Alex. He swore. Screw worrying about getting the emerald, he should have killed Stoney the moment he figured out Stoney betrayed him. He felt the sting of his own greed.

Where the hell do I start looking for them?

He tried to calm his thoughts. Say Stoney decided to bolt, decided to hire muscle to cut out Alex. He'd have to call. Did Stoney have a cell with him? Alex went to the cordless phone in the cottage. There was a redial button. He pressed it. An answering machine clicked on, a low, comfortable drawl: 'Hi, you've reached the office of Justice of the Peace Whitman Mosley. Office hours are nine a.m. . . .'

Alex clicked off. Whit Mosley. That young judge in the loud shirt who came looking for Stoney to ask about the murdered old people.

So what the hell did a gun-happy Gooch have to do with a judge? He paced the floor for a minute. Maybe Stoney cracked. Decided to cut a deal and called the judge.

No. Police cars and sirens and Miranda rights would have been involved. Judges didn't hire mercenaries to kidnap people.

But maybe it was even worse . . . maybe they knew about the emerald, the treasure. Maybe the judge and Gooch were just chasing it for themselves. Alex could see it: Stoney, babbling that he knew where a fat emerald was and knew a guy who'd hid millions in rare coins and could they help him cut a deal? Maybe a cop or a judge would think, *Well, I'd like me some of that.* Even assuming Stoney hadn't cracked, Gooch had already found Stoney here at the cottage. They must know enough. And nothing on the news yet about the treasure. No one else knew.

But they had Stoney, who had the Eye, and could completely ruin Alex.

PART THREE
The Edge of the World

'For thirty years,' he said, 'I've sailed the seas and seen good and bad, better and worse, fair weather and foul, provisions running out, knives going, and what not. Well, now I tell you, I never seen good come o' goodness yet. Him as strikes first is my fancy; dead men don't bite; them's my views – amen, so be it.'

— the life philosophy of Israel Hands, pirate, in Robert Louis Stevenson's *Treasure Island*

31

The lunchtime heat wasn't unbearable, the breeze a cool comfort. Whit met Dr Parker and a bookish, attractive woman on the waterfront dock of a small restaurant near the Port Leo harbor for Saturday lunch. Dr Parker introduced the woman as Dr Iris Dominguez with Texas A&M Corpus Christi. Pronounced her name the Spanish way, *Ee-res*.

'The bones from the dig are in Iris's car trunk,' Dr Parker said. 'I can sign custody of them back over to you after lunch if you like.'

Whit saw the waitress approaching for the drink order keep her smile frozen in place at the mention of bones.

'He's really not a maniac,' Whit told her.

'The day is young,' Iris Dominguez said. She had a beautiful voice, soft but forceful, and a cool, unfussy elegance. Whit liked her immediately. They ordered hamburgers and onion rings, Parker asking for a Salty Dog, Iris and Whit ordering beers.

'So you want to know about the coins and you're bribing us with lunch.' Parker scooped a tortilla chip with salsa and popped it into his mouth.

'Yes, sir.'

'Why not just ask the sheriff's office?'

'I could. But I'm not popular with law enforcement right now. I just insulted the FBI.'

Iris Dominguez raised an eyebrow.

Parker laughed. 'And why did you think that was productive?'

'I'll see if it gets the results I want,' Whit said. 'Plus, I wanted to thank you and Dr Dominguez for your help.'

He smiled at Iris. 'You identified the relics. That was extremely helpful to me.'

'You're welcome. You've made my weekend interesting.'

The waitress arrived with their drinks; Parker licked the salt from the glass rim, sucked down half the grapefruit juice and vodka in a hard swallow.

Dr Dominguez waited until the waitress had departed. 'Okay. What do you know about coins?'

'They don't stay in my pocket long enough,' Whit said.

'Let me give you a quick primer. These kinds of coins weren't treated like how we treat quarters and pennies and dimes. They were created to make it easy to move massive amounts of wealth from Mexico to Spain. They might be struck in Mexico, shipped, and then immediately melted down in Europe.' She sipped at her beer. 'These are called milled bust coins, the last produced Spanish colonial coins. The gold coins come in denominations of eight, four, two and one escudo. The silvers are reales. Obviously the gold coins are worth more.' She dug in her purse, pulled out a file of photos. 'I took some pictures of the coins, nice big blowups so I can show you why these coins are particularly unusual.' She spread the photos out, one group to one side, the other by Parker's dwindling cocktail.

'These all have a typical reverse side,' she said. 'See the pillars and shield? Typical of many Spanish colonial coins. And these have double rosettes under the pillars. Very unusual.' She pulled the other section of photos into the center of the table. 'The obverse sides of the coins often have either a monarch's shield – like British paper money having the queen on it – or a design of the emperor's head, which you can see these have. Most of these are Ferdinand VII. Don't you think he had a weak chin?' She pointed with a pencil tip.

'Yes,' Whit said.

Iris flipped the picture back over to the pillars, to the letters encircling the design. 'You see the *Mo*? That means Monteblanco. Next, that's the denomination – this is an eight escudo; and next are the initials of the assayer. Here that's ET, Esteban Torres, the official of the Monteblanco mint. The other side has a date . . . Here, this coin was minted in 1819. Monteblanco was at that time the newest Mexican mint. Just opened. Freshly minted, you could say.'

'Iris doesn't get out enough,' Parker said. 'Does it show?'

'I think you're brilliant,' Whit said.

She smiled and Parker said, 'Hey.'

Just friends, Whit thought, *right.*

Iris tapped the photos with her fingernail. 'So I dove into the historical archives, called a professor friend of mine in Mexico City to run some local checks down there for me. A large cache of the original silver and gold coins minted at Monteblanco – with this unusual double-rosette design – was being shipped to Spain right after being minted, aboard a schooner called *Santa Barbara*. But according to the records, *Santa Barbara* was lost at sea in March of 1820, somewhere south of Cuba.'

'I see,' Whit said again. 1820. Jean Laffite's time. His heart neared his throat. This would make Jason Salinger's day.

'But the records of the time indicate that the weather was fair throughout that time in the Caribbean. So *Santa Barbara* probably didn't fall victim to a Gulf storm.'

Whit cleared his throat. 'I will embarrass myself a little now. But what if the coins were buried, as part of a treasure?'

'Yeah, I didn't tell Iris that part,' Parker said. 'I didn't want to influence her data.'

'You couldn't have,' Iris said dryly. 'You're talking about the locks. The latches I identified. They're from the same period as the coins. You think the coins were originally buried with those relics and skeletons?'

Whit lowered his voice, leaned forward. 'Yes, I do. I think Jean Laffite took *Santa Barbara* as his last prize, and he had no time to take and bank it under a false name in New Orleans. He was forced out of Galveston in the spring of 1820. Navies from Britain, Spain, and the US would have been hunting him in the Gulf. He had no base to hide, nowhere to run.'

'So you think he buried the *Santa Barbara* stash, hoping to reestablish later,' Iris said.

'He just never got reestablished,' Whit said. 'Is this too big of a jump?'

Iris Dominguez sipped at her beer. 'The coins have to have been somewhere for the past one hundred eighty years. They're worn but not from human handling.'

He thought of Lucy, her claim the coins were Patch's. 'You don't think they've been in a collection all these years?'

'No, Judge, considering what else you've discovered, I don't think so.' She closed her eyes. 'Oh my God, the historical significance. Enormous. An actual buried pirate treasure.'

Whit's throat felt dry. 'More valuable than the monetary significance?'

'I don't know. I'll see if I can locate a copy of the manifest from *Santa Barbara* from the archives. See how much gold and silver it carried – but even manifests didn't always represent an accurate count. There was a lot of corruption, theft in the financial system then. Sometimes up to forty percent of the treasure on a ship wouldn't even be on the manifest, to minimize taxes. And the Monteblanco mint was destroyed in a peasant uprising in 1822. Coins from Monteblanco are exceedingly rare.'

'It could be quite large, then.'

'It could be millions, Whit. The accounts of *Santa Barbara* I found also mentioned that the ship carried a noted Colombian emerald. No emeralds in Mexico – it's not a gem-rich geography – but lots of incredible emeralds out of Colombia. This one was particularly noteworthy. The Catholic priests nicknamed it the Devil's Eye.'

'Oh, Lord,' Whit said. He thought of Claudia's story of Danny Laffite's demands. 'The archives in Mexico. Do they have any information on this emerald they could send to me?'

'I'll ask,' Dr Dominguez said.

'Judge, what is it? What's wrong?' Dr Parker asked.

'You don't happen to know the value of the emerald, do you?'

'I should imagine it to be worth a few million. And of course, if it's become Laffite's treasure, and it's provable, then the value probably triples,' Dr Dominguez said.

'Iris,' Whit said, 'can you help me find out how someone might try to sell this Devil's Eye? Or these coins?'

'Sure.' She shook her head in pleased amazement. 'Actual pirate treasure.'

'Actual pirates,' Parker said. 'Can I keep those bones for a while? They just got way more interesting to me. They must have been the unlucky bastards who helped Laffite bury the treasure, then got killed for their trouble. Dead men tell no tales and so on.'

'So you're the famous Whit.' Ben Vaughn sat on the edge of the hospital bed, dressed in loose khakis and a T-shirt.

'I didn't know I was famous.'

'To Claudia and the FBI. Claudia thinks the world of you.' He didn't say what the FBI thought.

'I think a lot of her, too,' Whit said, and it didn't quite come out right and Ben glanced up toward him. 'Thanks for agreeing to see me.'

'What did you want to talk about?'

Whit sat on the edge of the room's institutional recliner. 'Your brother. I saw him.'

'So I heard.' Ben sat up. 'The FBI told me.'

'Where's he at, Ben?'

'I think the same gang that was after us took him. He was the initial target.'

'So Danny Laffite kidnapped your brother and sank his own boat?'

'I don't know.'

'Maybe Stoney hid so this same gang couldn't find him.'

'Maybe.' Ben sounded less sure.

'But he . . . what, leaves you and Claudia to die? Not very brotherly.'

Ben said nothing. The bruise on his cheek had gotten nastier with the passing hours, turning black and lemon-yellow. 'I told Claudia he wouldn't abandon us.'

'He just didn't want to tell the police.'

'He didn't want to endanger our lives.'

Whit sat next to him. 'I have five older brothers. Two of them I'm extremely close to. Two I'm not so close to but I love them very much. One I practically hate but I still love him at the same time. He's a prime-grade asshole but he's still, and always will be, my brother. He matters to me.'

Ben said nothing.

'You're not helping him, Ben. If you know where he might be, tell us. We all need some answers from him.'

'Listen, Stoney was in a panic. For all the swagger, he's not good with situations he's not firmly in control of or can't get control of.'

'All his brokerage firm's computer systems were down.'

'Well, see . . .'

'But Stoney took them down, Ben. He sabotaged his own network from his home PC. I just saw the computer forensics report; the Corpus police sent copies to the sheriff's office here. He broke the systems so he couldn't transfer the ransom funds.'

Ben stared at his bare feet. 'That still doesn't mean he hasn't been kidnapped.'

'Your brother financed treasure dives in Florida. I'd like to know more about those.'

'And you're here exactly in what capacity?' Ben said.

'Tuesday I'm conducting a formal inquest – a hearing – into the murders of Patch Gilbert and Thuy Tran. You heard about that?'

'Yeah.'

'The guy who's the number one suspect and who apparently killed himself had some rather rare and valuable gold coins in his pocket. They've been identified as being from the same time period as Jean Laffite's pirating.' Ben's eyes widened. 'I don't think Danny Laffite sounds quite so crazy now, do you?'

'Listen, Danny Laffite was a nutcase. Ask any of Stoney's friends who are in this Laffite League. Stoney was the big fish in that pond, lot of money, well-known, popular. He was the leader and that's who a loser like Danny gloms on to. I think, if there's any truth to this, Danny Laffite had some delusion about Stoney knowing where this treasure was and thinking Stoney wouldn't tell him.' He stood, a little shaky. Whit steadied him.

'I'm fine.' Ben flinched slightly at Whit's touch on his elbow.

'Sorry. I know you've been through an ordeal. I—'

'I know my brother a lot better than you do, Judge. You're Claudia's friend, and I know you both mean well.

But you're wrong. My brother wouldn't risk my life like you say.' He walked into the bathroom, splashed cold water on his face.

'Did you ever hear Danny or Gar or Zack mention a guy named Alex?'

'No.'

'How about Albert Exley?'

'No.'

'Allen Eck?'

'No.' Ben dried his face. 'I think, y'all find out who the other two kidnappers are, you're not going to find they got any kind of treasure or archaeological connection. They didn't give a shit about what Danny raved about. They used him, thought he was nuts. He had the boat and he'd given them a good target in my brother. They just wanted cash, pure and simple, and they thought they had a low-risk way to get it.' He paused. 'Maybe Danny Laffite killed those people on the Point, with the dead guy you mentioned. What a freak.'

'Your brother's lucky. Having a defender like you.'

Whit wondered just what Ben knew, how far he would go to protect his brother.

Ben tilted his head. 'Thank you.'

'I'll let you rest,' Whit said.

'Judge?'

'Yeah?'

'You and Claudia. Was there ever anything there?'

The question surprised Whit. 'No. We're just friends.'

'Good,' Ben said.

32

Claudia thought a good police file on a major case should contain not only the pertinent data, but read like a well-crafted short story or novel. The motivations, the fears, the human failings should all be subtly suggested between the lines of forensic data and witness statements. David thought her attitude nuts when they were married, told her if she wanted that from a file she needed to take a creative writing course.

The New Orleans police made a guess that the redhead called Zack was one Zachary James Simard, so the investigators thoughtfully sent his record along. The photo was indeed Zack, sallow face, pouty lips, calculating glare. Degree in finance from LSU, from a family from Lake Charles. Suspected of handling money and accounts for a drug-and-prostitution-fueled crime ring based in New Orleans that stretched eastward to Pensacola and over to Beaumont. Five years ago he'd done two years in a state pen in Louisiana on a marijuana-possession charge. He'd stayed clean since, or at least clean enough to avoid charges thus far and therefore avoid the pressure to testify, to make a deal with the Feds. He had dropped out of sight two weeks ago.

Gar Johnson, aka Gary Paul Jackson, born Gerald Paul Jones. Suspected of being a hired gun; suspected in a slaying in Biloxi and a double homicide in New Orleans. The victims were all drug dealers who, the police suspected, skimmed profits. The pair in New Orleans had been a young married couple, both mediocre jazz pianists tapping a living out of the second-tier club scene, dealing coke to the well-heeled on the side. Every finger on the couple's hands had been broken before they were shot; both the man and the woman had been raped and then their bodies dumped in a ditch in Algiers, a tough neighborhood. Claudia's stomach roiled.

Gar had served two stretches, one for armed robbery, and he'd been at Angola prison during Zack Simard's time there. They had been released within a month of each other and both headed for New Orleans. Maybe they'd been sweeties in prison.

She turned the page.

Daniel Villars Mouton. From an old-money family, he was the last of the Moutons, living in a grand house in the Garden District. But Danny had a record. Petty theft, shoplifting history books from a bookstore. Then the charge of forgery she knew about that had been dropped. A brief stint in a pricey mental clinic in Metairie, apparently checked in and then checked out by his only cousin. The Villars middle name was real, a family name handed down with pride, and Danny's reading about the great love of Laffite's life apparently fueled the delusion he was descended from the pirate. One diagnosis of schizophrenia, another diagnosis of bipolar disorder. A charge of marijuana possession that had been plea-bargained into nothing. Maybe the drug connection was how he'd met Gar and Zack.

Beneath these papers were notes and reports compiled from the investigation into the murder of Danny's cousin. Less than a month ago the man had died in a burglary gone wrong. A back window had been forced. Phillip Villars, age fifty and a widowed antiques dealer in the French Quarter, staying at his cousin Daniel's house during the remodeling of his own home, had apparently surprised an intruder and been killed with a single gunshot to the forehead. Left dead in a downstairs hallway. His cousin, Daniel Villars Mouton, found the body later that evening after returning from a trip and phoned police. Danny was questioned extensively, given his background, but he had an ironclad alibi – visiting friends in Charleston, South Carolina, for the past week, every hour accounted for – and neighbors and friends said for all his eccentricities Danny got along well with his cousin, the last two members of a faded family. Note on the file that the New Orleans police had no further leads. Just a report that Danny Mouton quickly dropped out of sight after his cousin's funeral.

He'd gone into hiding, she thought. Running and hiding from Stoney, maybe.

Not everything Danny had said was a lie. She covered her face, thought of his odd mix of earnestness, gallantry – he had saved her life when he could have let Gar rape and murder her – and absolute craziness. There might have been a decent person in there, someone who wanted to accomplish much, derailed by psychosis and drugs. A wasted life. She closed the folder.

Fingers tapped at the bedroom door; Claudia's mother stuck her head in. 'David's here,' she said. 'Brought brownies. Your favorite.' Tina retained a great fondness for David.

'Thanks.' Claudia followed her mother into her little living room. David stood there, in full-dress uniform, sweaty patches under his arms, his Stetson in his big freckled hands. Tina Salazar disappeared into the kitchen with the brownies, where she could still hear but pretend not to.

'I just wanted to see if you were okay,' David said.

'You phoned this morning, David. I'm still the same.'

'But still. You had such a horrible ordeal, hon.'

Hon. Like they were still married, still tethered to each other. He hadn't wanted the divorce. At times she had wondered if parting was the right thing, if perhaps she had sold him short. Maddening one minute, sweet the next, and she finally tired of the inconsistencies.

'They're still searching the bay for Danny Laffite's body,' David said. 'Assuming he's dead in the first place or that he drowned when his boat sank. But nothing.'

'Have they raised Danny's boat yet?'

'Probably tomorrow. Where do you think he is?'

'I don't think Danny would give up,' she said. 'It's entirely possible he killed Stoney Vaughn. He might have killed him, dumped the body somewhere. But he thinks this jewel and gold are in Port Leo, he won't be leaving.' She turned back to David. 'I absolutely don't see him sinking his boat for any reason, though. I guess I think he's dead.' She wondered for a moment, *And if he's not, you think maybe he might try to find you?* 'Maybe he grabbed Stoney, the boat wrecked, and their bodies are in the bay.'

'Maybe,' David said, glancing at Tina.

'I'm going for a walk,' Tina Salazar announced. 'Just down to the store for some milk to go with the brownies.' She kissed Claudia's cheek, patted David's shoulder, scurried out of the apartment.

'She wants us to be alone,' David said.

'I think you might be overanalyzing,' she said, although she knew he was right.

'Can I ask you how long you've been seeing Ben Vaughn?'

She owed him no answers but since he was involved in the case there was no point in arguing. She wished, though, he'd sent another investigator to talk to her. Of course, he wouldn't. 'Not long. A couple of weeks. Very casually.'

'Is he nice to you?'

'Very nice and pleasant. Did you expect he would be an asshole?'

'His brother sounds like a prime one.'

'I only met Stoney once,' she said, 'except for maybe back in high school.'

'I think Stoney Vaughn got scared and he ran to protect his money, and now he can't surface. I also think your boyfriend's protecting him. If he blocks this investigation in any way, he's going to be in serious trouble.'

'Wouldn't that just be perfect? How disappointing for you it wouldn't be your case.'

'Stoney Vaughn's house is in county jurisdiction. Just might be mine.' He sat down in the reading chair next to the sofa.

'So what does that mean, David? You're going to make trouble for Ben?'

'You could help us, Claudia. Find the brother. Get Ben to talk.'

She said nothing.

'Oh, gee, would that ruin your shiny new relationship if you helped us out?'

'Don't be this way.'

'I really hope you're not protecting Ben yourself, Claud. Know anything about your boyfriend's brother you're not sharing? Places he might go, resources he might have?'

'Absolutely not.' She stood. 'I told you, the FBI, everything Danny Laffite told me.'

'And that's being followed up on,' David said. 'Especially whatever grudge Danny had against Stoney Vaughn. Danny Laffite did have a cousin murdered in New Orleans last month. He was telling you the truth. We're determining if Stoney Vaughn was in New Orleans those days.'

Oh, don't let this be true, she thought. *It will kill Ben.*

'If your boyfriend' – the term said like he had mud in

265

his mouth – 'knew anything about his brother committing a murder, he's an accessory.'

'You're correct,' she said quietly. 'But if you start an unfounded witch-hunt against Ben, I'm going to have your badge for it. Promise you, David.'

'Whoa. Passion. Haven't seen that from you in a while.'

'Don't bait me. I won't bite.'

He hesitated. 'The last thing in the world I want is to see you hurt.'

'Unless you can do the hurting.'

'I'm going to tell you something no one knows. It's not to make you mad or to try to win sympathy or to gain advantage.' He crossed his arms. 'I still love you.'

Claudia said nothing.

'So I don't want you hurt. By anyone, including me.' He stood. 'I get around you, my mouth starts running because I'm mad still. I'm trying my best not to be. Enjoy the brownies. I'll call you if we hear anything about Vaughn or Danny Laffite.'

'All right.' She didn't know what else to say.

She watched from the window as David went down the stairs, putting his Stetson back on, heading to his sheriff's department cruiser. She watched him pull out of the parking lot. She picked up the phone, wanting to hear Ben's voice, but knowing he needed his rest.

Instead, she went back to the bedroom and opened the file from New Orleans.

Phillip Villars, the wrong place, the wrong time. Single bullet in the middle of the forehead. Thuy Tran died in a similar way.

If Stoney had been involved, where was this journal now, the one Phillip Villars had been killed for? If Danny was right, Stoney had it. Or knew where it was.

She had access to the house, to Ben, that might help her. And she could do it to protect Ben.

Yes, do that. Find the evidence against his brother and Ben may hate you.

Her mother came back with the milk, and out of duty Claudia ate two brownies.

'Nice of David to bring these,' Tina said.

'Yes,' Claudia said. 'He says he still loves me.'

Tina stopped a brownie halfway to her mouth.

'He's full of crap,' Claudia said. She told her what David said.

'David's all angry and hopeful at the same time,' Tina said. 'Maybe he loves you. But he wants you to squirm a bit, sweetie, feel as torn as he does. And if he can get you to sabotage your relationship with Ben, better for him, he thinks.'

'You're not taking his side?' This was a change.

'Today I'm taking your side,' Tina said, rolling her eyes. 'Enjoy the moment.'

'But David's right,' she said. 'I could get to Ben faster than anyone else could, if he's holding back.'

'You cops. You can never let anything be.' Tina ate her brownie.

Claudia kissed her mother's cheek. 'I think I'll go by the hospital, see Ben.'

But she didn't. Instead, Claudia drove to Copano Flats, toward the big Vaughn house.

33

'I don't think Lucy's very interesting as a suspect anymore,' David said. He'd run into Whit at the Coke machine in the courthouse hallway, Whit in the office to use the faster Internet connection than what he had at home, David doing whatever he did on a Saturday he had duty.

'You got a new mouse to play with?' Whit could guess where this was going.

'Jimmy Bird killed those old folks. No question. His tire tracks match the tracks found on the Gilbert land, same gun killed him as killed Mrs Tran. I just made your inquest real easy.'

'Thank you.'

'Now. What's interesting to me is your theory about how maybe Stoney Vaughn had a connection to old Jimmy.'

Whit fed quarters into the machine, selected root beer, waited for the can to drop. 'Or, wow, even better if Ben Vaughn did. Now wouldn't that get your nipples hard?'

'Be grateful for small mercies. I'm leaving your girlfriend alone.' He handed Whit the Saturday edition of the *Port Leo Mariner*, the semiweekly local paper. 'Nasty letter to the editor in there about you. You pissed off the other half of the Gilbert family. Bring that back when you're done, would you? I got a new puppy I'm training.'

Whit didn't open the paper, wouldn't give David the satisfaction.

David got a Coke from the machine. 'Given what's in that paper, you might have a crowd at your inquest. With a recall petition.'

'David, may I give you a friendly word of advice?'

'What?'

'You're never getting her back,' Whit said. 'Ever. And I don't think it'd make you happy anyway. So you might as well get over being mad at Claudia and all her friends you have to work with. You ever want to be sheriff? It's never going to happen, as long as you keep pissing on people.' He turned and walked off. 'I'll bring your paper back when I'm done.'

Whit took the paper back to his office, shut the door. He'd been searching for information on the Devil's Eye emerald and *Santa Barbara* on the Internet, impatient to wait on what Iris Dominguez and her colleagues might find. He'd found one site devoted to famous lost jewels that included a description of the Devil's Eye. There was no photo, of course, and the actual existence of the Eye was questioned by the article. The emerald's supposed weight – estimated by modern standards to be just shy of two kilograms – was listed, its story told as part of the billions in mineral and gemological wealth mined from the New World and dispatched to fill the Spanish treasury. Estimated value of the Devil's Eye – named by a disapproving priest of the viceroy who claimed the weak-willed stared at it, as though hypnotized – ranged from a million to four million US dollars. Having been lost for so long, its legend and value had grown.

His phone rang. 'Whit Mosley.'

'It's Iris. Listen, I talked with the gemologists in Mexico. You asked how you might sell an emerald like the Devil's Eye.'

'Not in a pawnshop, right?'

'Don't joke. My friends say there is an underground market for emeralds, and it's controlled by emerald traders in Colombia. You know Colombia suffers much violence and corruption. Prominent emerald traders there have been accused of sponsoring right-wing paramilitary groups. These are dangerous men.'

'And these men would be the buyers for the Devil's Eye?'

'If one wished to get the maximum amount of profit, yes. For a stone like the Devil's Eye, there'd be much competition.'

'So our seller has to have the balls to deal with rich Colombian extremists. How reassuring.'

'I thought you should know. I'll let you know what else I learn, as soon as I hear anything.'

He thanked her, hung up the phone. His stomach felt a little unsettled. He'd tried to imagine disposing of a treasure – how exactly would you go about doing this? The coins could be melted down or sold in small batches to collectors. But the emerald, if it was as grand as he thought it must be . . . Colombian right-wingers. How many guns, bombs, bribes could the Devil's Eye buy? That the case could move into international crime rings and violent politics made his throat go dry. He thought, *I bet Triple A and Stoney are gone. They got that emerald and took off to Bogotá and we'll never get them.*

He opened the newspaper to the letters to the editor. Suzanne Gilbert was a better painter than writer. But the letter still stung. The rant was adverb heavy. Accused Judge Mosley of malfeasance in ignoring the beneficiary of Patch Gilbert's death and asked for an investigation into Judge Mosley's inquest and finances, perhaps suggesting a bribe had been paid. He glanced at his phone: the message light blinked, no doubt the outraged voters of Encina County calling for his head. Maybe. He clicked the phone on: one hang-up, four messages from voters asking for an explanation about Suzanne's letter, not angry, but now curious.

His cell phone beeped and he answered it, hoping it wasn't another voter wanting a one-on-one explanation.

'You're not going to be happy with me,' Gooch said.

'I'm afraid to ask.'

'Could you get me a legal definition of kidnapping? Because I don't think I technically kidnapped Stoney Vaughn. I prefer to think of it as protective custody.'

Whit's mouth opened, then closed. 'You asshole.'

'That other guy, Triple A – although since I shot at him, I'm thinking we're on a first-name basis – this Alex guy, he drives a beige Chrysler van, by the way. I think he might have meant harm to poor Stoney here. I found Stoney at a fishing cottage in Laurel Point. We've moved on.'

'How did you know Stoney was at this fishing cottage?'

'That will upset you.'

'Like I'm not already upset.'

'I followed Lucy.'

'I absolutely do not understand.'

'I. Followed. Lucy.'

Whit's stomach lurched. 'Why, Gooch?'

'I've never trusted her. Sorry.'

'Where are you?'

'If I tell, you're in trouble with the law, and I think I should keep you free and clear.'

'I'm already an accessory to kidnapping if I don't report you.'

'Stoney went with me willingly. He's sure willing now. Aren't you, Stoney? Hey, Stoney!' Calling to him, loud, an echo in the room. 'Yeah, he's nodding big-time. He's a happy guy.'

'Gooch. Where are you?'

'See, you can't always take the direct approach, Judge. Stoney and I are going to have an extensive chat here shortly. We're going to find out who exactly Alex is, what he knows, where he's at, and then how Lucy's involved in all this. Find out what he knows about poor Patch and Thuy. It's gonna be fun and educational.'

'Gooch, don't—'

'Then I'll call you and fill you in. I won't say it's me. Then you do what you think best. Consider it an extended anonymous tip.'

'Gooch, you asshole, don't do this—'

'Helen's out boating with Duff and Trudy Smith, so she should be out of harm's way. Take care of her, okay? She's a good kid. She can stay on my boat long as she wants. 'Bye, Whitman. Don't turn your back on Lucy.' He hung up.

Whit dialed Gooch's cell phone. No answer. He called the marina where Gooch docked *Don't Ask*. The marina master said yeah, Gooch's boat was there, just fine – did he want to leave a message?

At least Gooch wasn't out on the water, conducting a floating inquisition.

He cursed Gooch. He cursed Stoney Vaughn. No idea where they could be . . . but there had been that brief echo when Gooch called to Stoney. So a big space. Covered roof. A big space but private so Gooch could have his extended, perhaps violent chat with Stoney.

Now where might that be?

Could be the old high school gym, awaiting a teardown in a month or so. There was a soundstage at an old television studio, now empty and for sale, on the edge of town. Possibly. Or . . . there was a marina on the north edge of the county, past the Flats, abandoned since being the part of the docks burned a year ago – but the big metal covering and high roof of the old marina were still there. No one used it, and Gooch had talked about buying it from the uninterested, unmotivated owners in Houston.

Whit grabbed his car keys. He had to stop this, reason with Gooch. The thought was nearly alien.

The FBI had the Vaughn house, but the agents knew who Claudia was and let her in.

'I'm getting the house ready for Ben to come home from the hospital,' she said and the two agents nodded and went back to their phones and laptops.

She searched carefully and as inconspicuously as she could, ignoring the nagging feeling that said she had no right to do this. First Stoney's bedroom. She found nothing of interest except a wad of a thousand dollars in cash, tucked in the back of the underwear drawer. She left the cash alone. The bathroom produced nothing but a daunting cache of toilet paper, fourteen different scents of high-dollar cologne, a nearly empty box of condoms, and expired cold medications.

She went to the top of the staircase and glanced downstairs; she could hear the drift of the agents' voices from the kitchen, talking on their phones, discussing the co-ordinated search for Stoney Vaughn. There had been a sighting in San Antonio, a couple of hours away, of a man who looked like Stoney. The most promising lead thus far.

She went to the study at the end of the hallway. Books lined the shelves. Stoney had not struck her as a book person, and many of the books looked too pristine to have been read – lots of recent hardcover bestsellers, crime fiction, investing, and finance. Biographies of business leaders. But one whole wall on the history of piracy, on archaeology and nautical salvage, on Jean Laffite and Texas history.

She browsed through them but decided as a hiding place it was too obvious. He wouldn't hide the journal here. Maybe a safe-deposit box – see if the FBI had access to that. Or Ben, if he could be convinced.

There was a PC on Stoney's desk, shoved to one side. The desk was in disarray – she suspected the FBI had sat down and copied the hard disk to see if there were any clues as to who had Stoney or where he might have gone. Easier than going through the rigmarole of getting actual custody of the hard drive.

Claudia sat down, powered up the PC, and opened Stoney's e-mail application.

'What are you doing?' Ben said from the doorway.

'What are you doing out of the hospital?' she said.

'I couldn't stay there. Not with my brother missing. I checked myself out. I'm okay.' He leaned against the doorway. 'What are you doing on Stoney's computer?'

She took her hands off the keyboard.

'Sending an e-mail,' she said coolly, with a smile. 'Is that okay?' She had wanted to see if there had been an e-mail from Danny Laffite, or other Laffite Leaguers, or Patch Gilbert or anyone connected to the case. Maybe Stoney made on-line reservations to go somewhere, maybe his browser had a history suggesting travel sites he'd visited.

'Sending an e-mail from here?'

'I just remembered something from when I was on Danny's boat,' she said. 'It's better to get it down in writing than give a statement.' She stood, turning off the system as if sending the e-mail was no big deal.

'Claudia. You were spying.'

'No. It's not my case. I don't have a warrant. I really was just logging on.' *Okay, the first lie to him. How does it taste in your mouth?*

He turned and walked away. She followed him to his bedroom, watched him lie down on the bed, put his arm over his eyes.

'I'm sorry, Ben.'

'It's in your nature to pry.'

'*Pry* is an ugly word. I'm trying to help you and I'm trying to find your brother.'

'Please don't get involved in this.'

'You know where he's at.'

'Not with certainty,' he said in a low voice. 'You think they've bugged my room?'

'Of course not, Ben.'

'So I'm supposed to tell you and betray my brother?'

'He betrayed you.'

'Innocent till proven guilty.'

'The authorities find that Stoney's involved in any crime, and they think you're protecting him, they're going to come after you whole-hog. Your life could be ruined, babe.'

He closed his eyes, opened them. 'If I think I know where he's at . . . and I tell you, you'll tell them.'

She made the decision. 'No. I won't.'

'Right, Claudia. You're a cop. You have to.'

'Why's he hiding?'

'I think he's ashamed of not paying. Maybe he doesn't have the five million to pay. So he's humiliated and he ran.'

'Then he didn't commit a crime. So this is a private matter between the two of you. I'll take you to him, Ben, if you know where he's at. You can work it out. Then he can come forward.'

'Would you let a guy who wouldn't pay his brother's ransom handle your finances, Claudia? That's what he's afraid of. The public response. His clients will dump him. He'll be ruined. He'll lose this house, everything.'

'It's not the public's business.'

'He sabotaged his own computer systems to keep his money safe,' Ben said. 'It'll get out. He'll be ruined because he panicked.'

'Ben, finding him is the only way to help him. He can't hide for ever. Where do you think he is?'

'Let me sleep on it,' he said. 'I'll give him another day.'

'So you've given up this he-was-kidnapped thing.'

'We would have heard a ransom demand by now,' Ben said. 'Don't you think?'

34

'As a kidnapper goes, you're okay,' Stoney said. 'Jesus, at least the food's tasty.' He had his nerve back once he saw that Gooch wasn't going to take a pair of pliers or a blowtorch to his feet or his balls. Right now they were eating Chinese takeout, sitting at a metal desk in the back of the warehouse.

After they had driven out of Port Leo, the truck ambling along, Stoney still crouched on the floorboards, Gooch had said, 'Your choices are two. You either help me, or you end up dead in the Gulf.'

'Tough call. I'll help you,' Stoney said from the floorboard of the car.

'I expect complete honesty. I don't get it, you're dead. You understand?'

'Yes.'

'First chance for honesty. Did you kill Patch Gilbert and Thuy Tran?'

'No. I didn't.' Thank God, he could say that and be honest.

'Do you know who did?'

'Yeah. Alex.' A pause. 'No one could have stopped him.'

'A person of conscience would have stopped him, but we won't judge you on your obvious deficiencies,' Gooch said.

'You're right. I didn't. But it wasn't planned. They weren't supposed to be there.' *Give a little ground,* he thought. Dealing with Gooch was a negotiation, not so different from the deals he'd cut when he worked in venture capital. He thought suddenly that, yes, he could handle this.

'How comforting. How deep in is Lucy Gilbert?'

'She knew we were getting the treasure off Patch's land because he refused to sell to me. I offered him too much for his land; he checked on me, found out I was into treasure hunting and he started wondering if maybe there was something valuable hidden on his land, what with me offering a price I thought he'd never say no to. He made the connection about Laffite, although he didn't have any proof. It just dug his heels in that he wouldn't sell. We'd used metal detectors to find the cache on his land. But there was no dealing with him, so I found out Lucy Gilbert needed money, approached her. She was going to sell her acreage to us and let us rebury it on her land.'

'Alex wanted to rebury it?'

'Not anymore. Maybe he never did. He gets a cut. I get the rest.'

'You,' said Gooch, 'are a fucking piece of work, man.'

'It seemed like a good idea at the time. Everyone would have been happy, no one hurt.'

'Yeah, if Patch got his hundred thou together and conducted a legitimate dig, you or Alex would have had to kill him anyway, right?'

'No,' Stoney said quietly. 'No.'

'Jimmy Bird?'

'He helped us. Alex shut him up.' He prayed Gooch wouldn't ask if he'd killed Danny Laffite. Maybe he would just assume Alex did.

'You need a new hobby,' Gooch said. 'Where's a place you and me can go and not be bothered?'

'What, I get to pick my place of execution?'

'I'm not killing you. I want a place where you and I can go and call Alex, set up a negotiation with him so I can kill him.'

'You're going to kill him?'

278

'The chances are fairly good,' Gooch said. 'I don't like him.'

'Why don't you just call the police?'

'They like courtrooms. Those take time. I'm taking a simple, blunt approach to a complicated situation. It's a public service.'

Stoney took a deep breath. Maybe this would work. Get Gooch to lure in Alex someplace private. Gooch could kill Alex. Then he could cut a deal with Gooch. Or maybe get rid of Gooch. He was afraid of Gooch but there was a bit too much cockiness in the big guy, and maybe he underestimated Stoney.

He thought of blowing off Danny's head and his confidence returned.

'You afraid of this Alex?' Gooch asked.

Stoney was silent.

'You say he's got the treasure.'

'He says he does. Or he's lied and it's still in the storage unit over in Laurel Point. But knowing Alex, he's definitely moved it. So he and I are at a stalemate.'

'Where's the Devil's Eye?'

Stoney took a deep breath. Now he needed to lie; he was going to lie because that emerald wasn't up for negotiation; it was his. 'I hid it on my property. Buried it deep in a flower bed, where the earth was already turned. It's safe. Alex wants it bad.'

'We'll use that as our bait then.'

'If you want a good place to talk to him,' Stoney said, 'I got one. I own a couple of warehouses down at the port in Corpus Christi. It's quiet down there. Alex could meet us there.'

'Stoney?'

'Yeah?'

'No tricks. It's a death sentence.'

'So what happens to me after you kill Alex?'

'How much are you worth, Stoney?' Gooch said.

Finally. Money. The universal language. Gooch could be bought; this was a sudden, warm comfort. 'About two million, I guess.'

'I can think of any number of local charities who need about a two-million-dollar donation.'

His gut tightened. 'That's extortion.'

'Fund-raising. You can rebuild your fortune. But you let people die. There's a price to pay for that. You can pick: prison, poverty, or pine.'

'Pine?'

'As in box, buddy.'

'I would pick poverty, then,' Stoney said carefully.

And so they had crossed the high Harbor Bridge in Corpus, the port to their right, the retired aircraft carrier USS *Lexington* docked to their left, grabbed takeout Chinese in downtown Corpus. The warehouse, in the heart of the port of Corpus Christi, was quiet on a Saturday, the streets deserted, the businesses mostly closed. Stoney unlocked the door with an electronic code. The warehouse was big but cluttered, a maze of tall boxes and crates and wrapped pallets. And now they sat, finishing the Chinese at a metal desk.

'What do you keep here?' Gooch asked around a mouthful of garlic chicken.

'One of my companies buys up furniture and equipment from failed businesses, sells it at discount.' Stoney shoveled in moo shu pork; he wasn't sure when he'd get to eat again.

'You're just a full-time vulture, aren't you?'

'I am sorry about your friends. I am.'

'Don't worry. You will be.'

Stoney ignored him. Eating the last of his moo shu, he searched his memory for any weapons that might be in the warehouse. He couldn't remember whether the old foreman kept a gun in the desk. He slid the metal drawer open a bit; the drawer was loose, came out too quick. No gun, just pencils and Post it notes and a thin little flask of Crown Royal. He pushed the drawer back but it didn't quite want to go.

That drawer would come right out in your hands, Stoney thought. *Heavy. Metal. What do you know?* He nudged the drawer back into place.

Gooch stood a ways off, talking on a cell phone, calling to Stoney if he were happy. *Yeah, I'm delirious with joy,* he wanted to answer but he played along, said he was happy, nodded. The room echoed slightly with their voices.

Gooch said, 'Let's discuss how we get your friend Alex.'

A freaking useless wild-goose chase, Alex thought.

He had been following the Honorable Whit Mosley from the courthouse square. Alex earlier ditched the beige van in the Port Leo Wal-Mart parking lot, and walked along the rows of cars until he saw keys dangling in a Ford Taurus, windows slightly lowered to dissipate the midday heat. A bumper sticker announced CARPENTERS HAVE BETTER WOOD. He drove the Taurus to a quiet apartment complex, quickly but calmly switched license plates with a lonely little red Hyundai at the back of the lot, tore off the offending bumper sticker, and drove to a Dairy Queen for a soda and a burger. There he found Whit's address in a local phone book and headed straight for the big Victorian house, thinking, *I'll just take him here. His buddy took Stoney. I'll take him.*

The woman who answered the door was blond and pretty in a melt-your-knees way and Alex thought, *Or I'll just take you, honey.*

'Hi, I'm looking for Judge Mosley.'

'His place is out back. The guest house,' the woman said. She looked to be a little younger than Whit, blue eyes wide enough to drown in, and her noticeable accent sounded funny. Russian, maybe. 'But he's not here right now. I'm his stepmother, Irina. May I help you?'

Stepmother? Jesus. He wished his dad had bothered to remarry. 'Well, um, ma'am, I had information for him on a case. It's kind of private.'

'Ah. He was here but went to the courthouse. His office is on the first floor. If the building's not open you could knock on his window. Fifth window on the left from the entrance. If he's not there he's probably with his girl-friend.'

'Thank you, ma'am.' Alex let Irina Mosley live and headed for the courthouse. He waited for forty minutes, running the AC in the Taurus until he saw Whit Mosley come out of the courthouse, run – in this heat, running – to a white Ford Explorer and get in and roar off. He pulled out after him, staying two cars back, blending in with the busy summer weekend traffic.

The judge had driven past the old marina, an old, for-sale television studio, the high school auditorium. Like he was checking out real estate to buy. Following him was becoming more difficult if not impossible. He was look-ing for something and he wasn't getting out of his car where Alex could grab him and run. He was hanging so far back he was not always keeping Whit Mosley in sight, worried he would be noticed, and finally the judge turned around and drove through Port Leo and north toward Black Jack Point. Alex followed.

Next to him on the car seat, his cell phone rang. Alex kept his eye on Whit's car. 'Hello?'

'Hello, asshole,' Gooch said. 'Want to deal?'

35

'We need to talk,' Whit said. Lucy lay across Patch's fat leather couch, a cool cloth on her forehead, a bottle of aspirin and an opened can of ginger ale on the floor.

'Okay.' She didn't open her eyes.

'About you and Stoney Vaughn.'

She didn't open her eyes, but she folded her hands across her stomach.

'Lucy, Jesus, look at me.'

She opened her eyes, turned her head.

'You know him.' He kept his voice steady.

'Yeah.'

'You knew Stoney was hiding at a fishing cottage.'

A long silence. 'Did he turn himself in?'

'No. Gooch has him.'

Now she sat up. 'Has him?'

'Stashed somewhere,' he said. 'Gooch grabbed him. He's using him to get at the guy who killed Patch and Thuy. Gooch found him by following you.'

'Shit,' Lucy said.

'This Alex guy. Do you know him, know his real name?' She hesitated and Whit said quietly, 'Answer me, Lucy, right now.' *Christ, who are you?* he thought.

She raised her chin. 'Don't speak to me that way.'

'You knew who killed Patch. And you said nothing.'

'No, baby, I didn't know. Not when it happened. I found out later.'

'You sure know how to keep a secret,' he said. 'That's a new one.'

'I did it to protect you,' she said. Now she tossed the washcloth on the floor.

'Protect me. You're one great shield, Lucy. You've just destroyed my career. Everything your cousin said about me in the paper today is going to be considered holy writ. You lied to me, to the police.' Whit stopped, sat down. 'Forget being a judge. I could care less. You've destroyed *us*. We're done. That's a thousand times worse.'

She reached for him; he moved away from her, as though her touch might scald. 'I said nothing because I didn't know for sure. And I knew if I came forward I'd lose you.'

'You've lost me. Jesus, you thought I'd stay with you?'

'So much for true love.' Her jaw quivered but her eyes were dry. 'I love you, Whit. That's why I did this. Stoney came to me when Patch wouldn't sell the land to him. Said he'd buy my land. I didn't even know about the treasure he wanted to move. But before the dig, he told me. Wanted me to be sure Patch was out of town. I was scared he'd do something to me if I said anything.'

'Right.'

'I gave Thuy and Patch that trip to Port Aransas to get them gone. Baby, I didn't know he'd changed his will. I swear. I swear, Whitman.'

'This isn't a courtroom.'

'Yes, it is. It's the court of Whit and you're judge, jury, and executioner.'

'Who killed them?'

She swallowed. 'Stoney says Alex.'

'Jimmy Bird?'

'Alex, probably.'

'The coins in Jimmy's pocket?'

'They're not Patch's. I guess they're from the dig. I guess Jimmy swiped them and Alex didn't know it.'

'Where is Alex?'

'Stoney . . . he told me where he was hiding. I went to the cottage with Patch's gun. Ready to kill him for what he'd done. But I couldn't just shoot him, not even him, in cold blood. He asked me to shoot Alex. Alex knows about you, was there when you came to Stoney's house. I followed Alex to the Surfside Motel. He's staying there, at least he was.' She stared at him. 'I thought of killing him. Make it look like a random shooting. I even knocked on his door in the night, just shoot him and run. Nothing to connect me with him. Because he might hurt you. But I chickened out. I'm . . . scared.'

He saw she was: rough, tough Lucy, breaking under the weight. He wanted to hold her, wanted to scream at her. His chest felt like it might explode. 'Where is this gun?'

'In my purse.'

He went to the purse, pulled out the gun with a tissue, checked the bullets, put on the safety, stuck it into the back of his pants.

'You running around with a gun.' He shook his head. 'Is there anything else I should know, Lucy?'

'I love you.'

He covered his eyes with his hands.

'I love you, too. I did . . . why did you do this?'

'I thought I was doing the right thing.'

'For you. Screw Patch. Screw Thuy.'

'If I turned on Stoney, I was afraid of what would happen to you.' She crossed her arms. 'Tell me something, Whit, you being all high and mighty. You say Gooch grabbed Stoney. Have you called the police?'

'No. I have reason to think Stoney went voluntarily with him.'

'Reason to think.' Her voice went low, angry. 'Bullshit. Stoney wouldn't. Don't tell me that lunatic Gooch gets a free pass and I don't?'

'This isn't a double standard.'

'The hell it's not. You lecture me, you tell me that

we're done, that loving each other doesn't make a fucking difference, but Gooch commits a kidnapping and you don't turn his ass in?'

'Fine. I'll call the police right now.' He picked up the phone. 'I'll tell them about you, too. This'll make David Power's day for the next year. Then I'll resign and—'

She grabbed the phone from his hand. 'Listen. I did this because I needed to make a lot of money, fast. I got debts, Whit, a lot of them. I didn't want you to know—'

'Just like David said.'

'I didn't want to beg for help, but I didn't know all this would happen. I swear. Please.' She put the phone back in its cradle; he let her. 'Okay. Stoney might have gone with Gooch voluntarily. Stoney's scared shitless of Alex. I don't want Gooch in trouble just because you're mad at me.'

'Mad at you. The understatement of the year. Mad doesn't quite cover what I feel.'

She swallowed, reached for him again. He stepped away and a hard, hurt light came into her eyes.

'Where is this treasure, Lucy?'

'Stoney had it, but he said Alex took it from him. Most of it is coins.'

'Most of it?'

'There's a big emerald—'

'The Devil's Eye.'

She took a deep breath. 'I'll make a deal with you—'

'No deals.'

'Let me finish my sentence, please.' She sat down. 'Let's say Gooch goes after Alex. But Gooch doesn't win. Maybe Alex comes after you or me. I don't know if he knows about me or not.'

'I'm thinking he doesn't. Otherwise you would be dead.'

'Okay,' she said, a little shudder in her voice. 'So Alex

doesn't know about me. I know where he's at. We just call the police with an anonymous tip about Alex. Just say he killed Patch and Thuy and Jimmy. Give them the room number.'

'And what, hope he's got evidence hanging around?'

'Maybe he does. Maybe he can be tied back to the crime scenes. But it takes him out. Stoney won't say anything if Gooch has saved him from Alex. Then we're home free.'

'Home free. What about Patch and Thuy?'

'Alex killed them,' she said. 'He's the one who pays.'

'It works until Alex points at Stoney, and Stoney points at you,' Whit said. 'I don't care about free and clear. And pardon me if I don't believe Stoney Vaughn. He could have killed them – you see that?'

'He's not lying.'

'Because why, Lucy? You sense his aura?' His voice rose.

'That's exactly why I wanted to sell the land,' she said. 'Because you sneer at me. You think running a psychic hotline is tacky, borderline dishonest. Even when I'm just trying to help people. I'm never quite good enough for you, am I?'

'I loved you like no one else, Lucy, and it still wasn't enough for you. Your self-esteem problem is in your head, not mine.'

Lucy opened and closed her mouth. She went and sat on the couch. 'So go. Turn me in. I don't care.'

He resisted the urge to hold her, to make her care again. His throat ached, his hands trembled. It couldn't be over but it was. *If you love her, truly, you forgive her, right?* He steadied his voice. 'Right now we need to find Stoney and Gooch.'

'What about turning me in? Isn't that at the top of your to-do list?'

'I'm giving you a chance to cooperate, Lucy. Where is this cottage Stoney hid out at?'

'Why?'

'Because I want to see it. I want to see if there's a sign of struggle. If Gooch really kidnapped him, then my path is clear. Will you show me?'

'Yes,' she said, and he saw the hope flash in her eyes.

It had taken guts to hang up, but Alex did it as soon as he heard Guchinski's voice and figured out who other than Stoney would be calling him. Let Gooch wait.

He stayed in his car, parked a bit down the highway from the turnoff to Black Jack Point. The phone rang again. Alex clicked it on.

'Do you want to deal or not, asshole?' Gooch again.

'I'm busy at the moment. Give me a number to call you back on.'

'Don't think so.'

'Then you call me back in ten minutes, Mr Guchinski.' And clicked off. Let him sweat that Alex knew his name.

But deal? How the hell was he supposed to deal? The only leverage he had left was the treasure and maybe Gooch didn't care about that. What the hell did Gooch want? The treasure? In exchange for Stoney? Fat chance.

Just go. Go get the stash, rent a truck, get the hell away from the coast, feel out your buyers, get the money, go get your dad. Go to that big blue sky in Costa Rica, sit on the beach, pretend he's not dying for a while. Forget the emerald.

But no emerald – the biggest prize, the one worth millions in one fell swoop after he made carefully placed calls to Bogotá – and all these loose ends. Helen. Guchinski. That judge. And Stoney, insufferable Stoney, getting the better of him. Claudia. Ben. And he'd spend the rest of his life looking over his shoulder? No way. He rubbed his face and when he brought his hands down headlights flashed in his mirror, a car turning and heading south. Whit Mosley's Explorer.

If you don't have leverage, grab it and take it. Alex shifted into gear and tore out after them.

The cottage was dark, no lights spilling along the beach or along the small private road. The sun retreated below the horizon. Whit kept his headlights pointed at the cottage's small door. It was closed.

'Not hanging off its hinges,' Lucy said. 'That's a good sign.'

Whit said nothing.

'So I'm getting the silent treatment?'

'No. I just have nothing to say. Stay here.' He got out of the car, she followed. He tried the door. It opened. He flicked on the lights.

The room was a mess.

'Not good,' she said.

'No. It's not from a fight. It's been searched. Or robbed.'

'Isn't this trespassing? Oops, you broke a law.'

'Lucy, shut up.'

'Do you think I don't have guilt that's eating me alive? But I didn't kill them. I tried to protect them.'

'I'm not blaming you for their deaths. Although it seems to me you could have warned Patch about them stealing the treasure off his land.'

She shook her head. 'I hope to God you're never afraid.'

'Danny Laffite. Is he dead? Did Stoney or this Alex kill him?'

'I have no idea.'

'He blamed Stoney for a murder and for stealing an antique journal from him. Do you know where that's at?'

289

'No.'

'I just can't figure . . . Stoney didn't know his brother and Claudia were going to be kidnapped. And that he would need to go hide himself. That old journal's the key to everything, if he wanted to rebury the treasure, right? It validates that Jean Laffite was involved, makes the treasure more valuable for Stoney's purposes.'

'Yeah.'

'So he has to pick a place to hide. Quickly. Why not where he had already hidden what was of great value to him? Alex doesn't give a crap about the journal. Stoney has access and no one would suspect him putting it here. His house, yeah, maybe a safe-deposit box. But not a client's house. Maybe the journal is what someone was looking for.' Alex? Maybe, to close a loose end. Gooch? No. Or Danny Laffite? How?

'Or maybe Alex was looking for the Eye. That's what Alex wants.' She straightened a couch cushion. 'It's not here, though. I hid it well, Whit. You'd be proud of me.'

He turned to stare at her. 'You have the emerald?'

'Stoney gave it to me for safekeeping.' Her tone went defiant.

'Tell me where it is.'

'No,' she said. 'It was on Patch's private property. They stole it. Now it's mine again. According to his will it and the rest of the treasure should have been mine all along. Stoney was never quite smart enough to look at it from that angle.' She gave him a smile, but not a warm one. 'So the Eye's my property and I don't have to tell you a goddamned thing about it.'

'I swear I don't know you.' He shook his head.

'But you don't want to know me, Whit. We're finished. You don't love me, so why shouldn't I say whatever crosses my mind? Do you want to look for this journal or do you want to call the police and turn in Gooch?'

'Let's look for the journal.'

'You and your double standard.'

He didn't argue with her and they began to comb through the house. The cottage was small but elaborate and Whit went upstairs to look through the two bedrooms. They were small but had been searched thoroughly and he decided this was pointless. If anything was to have been found, it had been taken already.

He had just opened a closet door when he heard Lucy cry out, 'No—'

'Lucy?' he called.

No answer for a moment, then a crash and she screamed, 'Whit!' Another crash. Silence.

Whit moved quietly, down the stairs, pulling Patch's old gun he'd taken from Lucy's purse, cocking it, stopping just above the corner where the stairs met the kitchen.

'Judge Mosley?' A man's voice called. Gentle, calm. 'You need to step down with your hands up.'

'I'm armed,' Whit called. 'And if you hurt her, I'll kill you.'

The answer was a single shot.

Whit froze.

'She's unconscious,' the voice called, 'so she didn't feel that. But I just shot off a couple of fingers on her left hand. You have five seconds to come out. Moving the gun to her forehead now—'

'No!' Whit stepped out of the stairwell, hands up, gun held between forefinger and thumb.

A man knelt by Lucy, a 9mm Glock in his hand, aimed squarely at Whit. He was rangy, tall, hair dyed cheap blond, round wire-rim glasses. He looked like a professor turned punk rocker.

'Drop it,' the man said.

Whit did.

'On your knees, hands on your head.'

Whit obeyed. He could see Lucy's hand . . . all five fingers, there, not shot.

'I lied,' Alex Black said. 'I really hate messes.'

36

Ben had kicked the FBI out. Or rather, Claudia thought, he had asked them to leave. He politely told them that he appreciated their help, he felt safe with Claudia around – she blushed at that – but he wanted to be alone and have some time to recover. And there was no proof, after all, that Stoney had committed a crime or actually become the victim of a crime. The phones were tapped in case Stoney or Danny Laffite or the boogeyman called.

The agents gave him thin smiles in answer, but they left, and from the window Claudia watched their cars cut through the Flats. After Agents Grimes and Gordell left, the house seemed too quiet. Ghost empty. She wondered if David might drive by on the pretense of checking on Ben. But the road stayed empty.

Ben clicked on the stereo. Soft Vivaldi filled the room, a whisper of violins and flutes. She stood by the fireplace, studying a nautical map, drawn in an ancient's hand, that hung above the mantel.

He came up behind her, put his hands on her shoulders. 'I'm glad you're here, Claudia. I'd be nuts in this house alone.'

'I like this old map,' she said.

'It's a reproduction, although if Stoney has too much to drink he tells people it's an original. Long ago a big chunk of the world was unknown. See, there's Europe, badly drawn – they didn't see the known world like it really was. You leave it, you reach the middle' – he pointed at a giant serpent in the waves, its head thrown back and tongue extending like fire – 'they say, "Here there be dragons." If that doesn't scare you off, go all the way and you sail past the edge of the world. Lost for ever. The point of no return.'

'I think this map is more accurate than a real map.'

He kissed her neck. 'Would you like some wine? Or some beer? You want me to fix you a michelada?'

'A michelada sounds good.'

He went into the kitchen, filled two tall glasses with ice, a dash of Tabasco and Worcestershire, a sprinkle of pepper, and a dollop of lime juice. Then he poured a cold Dos Equis lager in each glass. The beer darkened to the color of maple. He brought a glass to her and they sat down on the Mexican tile floor, watching the sunlight die over the bay. They sat side by side, their shoulders barely touching. Claudia sipped. The michelada tasted like a perfect steak, but cold and smooth.

'When will they bring *Jupiter* back?' she asked. The FBI had it, treating it as a crime scene.

'God only knows. I don't care. Not sure I ever want to set foot aboard that boat again. I suppose if something's happened to Stoney the boat is mine.'

She said nothing; he seemed mildly surprised at the thought.

'You hungry? I can grill up some amberjack,' he said.

They finished their micheladas and then he cooked them dinner, pouring cold sauvignon blanc and fixing salad, fish scented with herbs, risotto, sliced kiwis, deftly moving from pan to pan. She could see he was making a strenuous effort to shove the darkness of the past few days behind them. They ate, her appetite suddenly ravenous. She drank two fat glasses of the New Zealand white and mellowness tiptoed over her.

He was opening a fresh bottle when she began to shake, standing by the counter. She set the wineglass down, suddenly afraid it would break between her fingers. She felt cold as ice.

'Hey. Hey now.' Ben took her in his arms, held her close. Her breathing grew ragged.

'Something's wrong,' she said. 'De – de – delayed shock. I don't know.'

He steered her toward the couch, sat with her, warmed her with his arms. He said nothing, kissed her jaw, her throat, gently. She held him tight.

'It's okay, 'sokay.' A few moments later, the shivers subsided.

'Well, what was that?' she said, embarrassed. 'Aren't I the big baby?'

'You know how much braver you are than I am?' he said. He tipped her jaw, looked into her eyes. 'I cried. Locked up on that boat. Afraid of what they'd done to you. Afraid of what he was going to do to me.'

She took his face in between her palms and she kissed him. First on his giant bruise, gentle as a feather, then on his lips. He kissed back, a little tentative, like she might still be shaky. She wasn't. After five long kisses Ben eased open the buttons on her blouse, touched the lacy edge of her bra, nuzzled the top of her breasts.

'Let's make love,' he whispered.

He took her hands, led her upstairs to his bedroom. She undressed him; he undressed her, from head to feet, kissing the wrap that bound her broken toe, the bandages on her hands. She kissed the horrid bruise on his face again, the broken finger.

He kissed her in her middle and they moved the sheets into a slow tangle, Claudia finally surrounding him with her heat.

'Our first time in what, thirteen years?' she whispered.

'Lucky thirteen.' He laughed. He was confident with her, more sure of his touch; she was more relaxed.

'Worth waiting for,' she said, eager for the touch of his skin against hers.

'I always cared for you, Claudia. Always,' he said, closing his lips over her throat, his hands cupping her breasts. She felt the life in his mouth, his hands, and suddenly life seemed far sweeter than she had known, thinking of lying on that boat, bobbing in the waves, the sun a glaring, remorseless eye.

'Now,' she gasped. 'Now.'

Afterward, his breath warmed the back of her neck, and she fell asleep.

She didn't hear him rise from the bed.

'Doesn't hurt too bad, does it?' Alex leaned down, patted Whit on the cheek. He'd taken four steps toward Whit after Whit laid down the gun, smashed the butt of his Glock twice across Whit's face, knocking him nearly cold, opening his cheek. Whit sat, half-propped against the refrigerator, blood splattered all over his dancing pineapples shirt.

Lucy was still out, breathing shallowly, a trickle of blood oozing from her hairline and meandering down her forehead.

Alex Black squatted down in front of Whit, the gun aimed at Whit's stomach. 'Your friend Guchinski,' he said. 'Where's he at?'

'I don't know.' Whit's face felt broken. The cheekbone might be fractured. God, it hurt. His voice sounded thick and dopey.

Alex cocked the gun, aimed it at Lucy's head. 'Try again.'

'It's the truth. Please don't hurt her. I don't know where he is right now.'

'So what's his angle?'

'I don't know.'

'Bullshit, Your Honor. Can I call you that? Your Honor. I feel so privileged.'

'I didn't know he was grabbing Stoney. I didn't know he even knew where Stoney was.'

'How'd he find out the Stone Man was here?'

Whit paused. No way he'd point to Lucy. 'He must have followed you out here.'

'No, I don't think so,' Alex said. He closed his hand – fingers hard from digging, Whit thought; they felt like steel springs – around Whit's windpipe. Alex wormed the gun in between Whit's legs, pressed the barrel against his testicles. Whit quit breathing.

'Here's my theory, Your Honor. Stoney wanted to get rid of me. He got himself a new partner. He gave the Devil's Eye to new partner, who has a guard dog mentality. I think new partner was Guchinski, and he's cutting you in, too.'

Whit risked a very small, shallow breath. The barrel didn't ease its pressure.

'Now Guchinski has gotten Stoney hidden away and is calling my ass up, wanting to deal. But I smell a trap. What do you smell?'

'Gooch doesn't have the Eye.'

'Who does?'

'Stoney. You think he's gonna trust anyone with a multimillion-dollar emerald?' Whit breathed again, cleared his throat. *God, let this lie work.* 'I can't believe you fell for what he said. Giving it to someone else.'

'So you've chatted with Stoney.'

'Just that once. When you were hiding in the house.'

Alex smashed his fist across Whit's face. Whit tried hard not to cry out, to groan.

'I wasn't hiding.' Alex shook his head, ran his tongue along the little scar at his mouth's corner, gave a little annoyed laugh. 'I give you this, Judge: you got balls. Big ones. I pull the trigger here, there's gonna be, what, sixty percent of your balls left?'

'If you kill me or Lucy, you don't get the Eye,' Whit said. 'Gooch has Stoney under his thumb, and he'll never give it to you. Gooch'll hunt your ass down and kill you. An inch at a time.'

Alex picked up a cell phone from the kitchen counter. He keyed in a number, dialed. 'Mr Guchinski, you answering Stoney's phone now?'

Whit could not hear Gooch's reply. Alex stood, let the gun slide along Whit's bruised face, took a step back. On the floor Lucy stirred, moaned Whit's name.

'No. You listen. I got my own trump cards, fuckhead.' He held the phone close to Whit's mouth. 'Speak to him. Say hello. Say more than hello and I kill the woman.'

'Hello,' Whit said.

Alex yanked the phone back. 'I got the judge's woman, too. So you got Stoney, man. I don't care. Get rid of him now – he's nothing but trouble.' A pause. 'You want these two, you're gonna give me the Eye.' He glanced at Whit.

Shit, Whit thought. *He believed me. Or I just confirmed what he already thought, that Stoney has the Eye.*

Alex listened, winked at Whit. 'Give me directions,' he said. 'Okay. We'll meet there. In an hour or so.' Pause. 'We make the trade then.' He clicked off. 'People are fucking predictable.'

'What?' Whit asked.

Alex stared at Whit. 'Tell me, how come a judge is friends with a crook like Gooch?'

'We have a lot in common.'

'Yeah,' Alex said. 'Lots of judges in Florida are crooked, too. Trust me.' Whit saw a shift in his face, amusement hardening into contempt. He cocked the gun, kept it aimed at Whit, and stood over Lucy. She was trying to surface back to consciousness. The amber necklace around her throat was broken, the jewel loose on the floor. He wanted to reach over, fix it for her, hold her, tell her it was okay.

Her eyes fluttered open, looking at him but not quite registering him. Whit could see two little trails of blood from her hairline where Alex had pistol-whipped her, her right ear bloodied.

'I don't think she's in any condition to travel, do you?' Alex said with a crooked smile.

'What?' Whit said again. *Okay, I can be the hostage—*

'We don't need her.' The grin widened, the gun moved to Lucy.

'No, please—' Whit yelled.

'Devotion. That's nice,' Alex said. Then he fired three times.

37

Claudia awoke in complete darkness. The night sur-rounding her felt as solid as glass, and panic tightened her stomach, thrummed between her shoulder blades. She felt tied. Danny. Danny still had her, Gar waiting nearby, the tattooed arms ready to force the life out of her, hungry to force himself inside her. She sat up in bed, blinking, easing out of the snarl of sheets.

No Danny. No Gar.

No Ben in bed.

She glanced at the digital clock. Ten forty-six p.m. She'd drunk too much, the michelada and the wine too early in the evening; she wasn't used to it. She had a little head-ache, not bad. She got up, went to the bedroom balcony that faced onto the bay. The heavy curtains were pulled closed and she parted them an inch. St Leo Bay lay calm in the night, the moon a wafer in the wash of the Milky Way.

She closed the curtains, found her clothes on the floor. She stepped into panties, pulled her khaki slacks up over her legs. She groped for her bra and blouse and put them on.

She started down the stairs, toward the spill of light in the kitchen, heard Ben say, 'All right, I'll be there.' When she entered the kitchen he was standing by the granite-top counter, a cell phone in his hand. He set it down on the counter.

'Ben?'

'That was my brother, babe. He's alive.'

'Thank God,' she said. 'Where is he?'

'In Corpus Christi. He wants me to come see him. Right now.'

'He decided to come out from under his rock?'

He didn't react to her sarcasm. 'He's ashamed. Embarrassed that he panicked. But he's alive.' He took Claudia into his arms. 'He's at a warehouse he owns down by the port. You know a guy named Leonard Guchinski?'

'Yeah. He's nuts. How the hell is he involved?'

'Stoney's with this Guchinski guy, and I'm not quite sure why.'

'So what are you going to do, Ben?'

'I should call the police,' Ben said in a tone that said he actually didn't want to do that. 'Let them know he at least is all right.'

'You want to wait until you talk to him?'

'I kind of think I should.' He tucked the cell phone into his front pants pocket. 'You want to go with me?'

'Maybe this should be a private meeting,' Claudia said.

'I'd like it a lot if you came. He owes you an apology and an explanation. Maybe you can help us figure out how to deal with the authorities, help him avoid embarrassment. He's probably going to need a lawyer, too.'

'He's going to need a PR firm,' Claudia said. She wasn't worried about Stoney's embarrassment. 'Let me run upstairs, get my purse, and we'll go.'

The trunk was dark, so dark that when Whit shut his eyes he could not tell the world had gone darker. The rattle and bump of the Taurus shook him back to full consciousness as they sped down the highway.

I'm going to kill you, he thought.

If he simply lay here, prone with grief, Alex won. He had no doubt Alex's goal was to kill him, Gooch, Stoney, whoever got in his way. A clean sweep. If he thought too much about Lucy a sickening paralysis crept into him.

He had hardly moved since Alex punched him again for good measure and dumped him into the trunk. He felt in his pocket for his cell phone. Gone. He groped in the dark, trying to find anything that could be used as a weapon. Alex had been at Stoney's when Whit stopped by, but this car hadn't been. So either a rental or maybe stolen. Maybe Alex hadn't paid enough attention to what was in here if it was stolen, and the trunk seemed cluttered with junk.

His fingers found the rim of the spare. Soft material that felt like silk, maybe some clothes destined for the dry cleaner's. A small wrench, probably left out for the lugs of the spare. A book, a wilting paperback. A cool plane of metal, with three hinges on the side.

Tool box.

Whit slowly turned the toolbox around, found its opening. Closed, but not locked. He managed to open it, heard the clatter of metal tools as the car hit a bump in the highway. Waited for the car to slow, pull over to the side. If he made too much noise – if Alex thought he were anything but grief-stricken and broken now – Alex would kill him.

Taking his time, forcing himself to be calm, Whit let his fingers explore the tools. A tape measure. A hammer, which would be great to swing at Alex's face. A Baggie, with what felt like an assortment of screws, nails, and lug nuts inside. A small ball of twine. Pliers. His fingers found a bar in the space above the tools. A handle. The tool box had a lift-out tray, with another compartment beneath.

He eased the top compartment out. His fingers fumbled inside the deeper well of the box. More Baggies with nails or hooks. Screwdrivers with hard plastic handles, two or three. A ball peen hammer, the better to break Alex's teeth with if he got a chance. Masking tape, a roll thinned from use. Electrical wire. He pricked his finger on a long V of sharp metal, with wicked little teeth on each side, a carved wooden handle. He gently explored the tool with his fingertips. A wallboard saw, the kind used to slice through Sheetrock, to make cutouts for light switches and electrical outlets. But with that nice pointed blade for plunge cuts into walls.

All it takes is one mistake, Whit thought, *and, you murdering bastard, you just made it.*

'You're gonna sit here real quiet,' Gooch said. 'You mess this up so that Whit or Lucy gets hurt, you're the mess.'

'And I thought we'd gotten to be friends,' Stoney said.

'Yeah, I'm going to be godfather to your kids.'

'So what, I sit here and you negotiate with Alex?'

'No. You sit here and I get rid of him if I have to,' Gooch said. 'Then I give you to the judge and he figures out what to do with you.'

Talking to him like he was a kid. 'Be nice, Gooch. Or I'll press charges and you'll go to prison.'

'Are you quite so eager to get more in the public eye that way, Stoney? Sit your ass down,' Gooch said, and Stoney said nothing. He eased down into the chair behind the desk and Gooch turned to douse out the lights.

Now, Stoney thought. He grabbed the handle of the desk drawer, gave it a heavy yank.

The drawer slid out, fast, and Stoney swung it as he bolted around the desk, connecting with Gooch's skull as he turned. Gooch went down. Stoney brought the drawer down again.

Gooch's eyes went white. 'Fuuu—'

Stoney took the heavy end of the drawer and smacked it down hard on Gooch's head again, twice. Gooch sprawled across the concrete floor.

My God, that was fast, Stoney thought. He picked up the gun, groped Gooch's thick neck for a pulse. After a moment he found it. But Gooch seemed to be out cold. Stoney considered whether or not to shoot him. Easier than shooting Danny. At least he wasn't looking at him with a wet face and a horrible, blubbering pleading look. He pressed the gun against the back of Gooch's head.

But then headlights gleamed against the shuttered warehouse windows, a car turning in, and Stoney Vaughn threw a tarp over Gooch, took the gun, doused the last light, and stepped back into the shadows, into the maze of unopened crates and equipment in the clutter.

Stoney knelt down by a section of crates in the back. He checked Gooch's gun by flashlight, a full clip. He sat back, raised the flashlight, its little circle of light spilling along the crates five feet in front of him.

He froze. 'That bastard,' he whispered.

38

Whit felt the car come to a stop, heard the engine turn off. He had reloaded the toolbox, closed it, tucked the wallboard saw into the waist of his khakis, tightened his belt. He hoped he could pull the blade out fast without slicing himself open. He closed his eyes, thought of Lucy.

Her asking, *I'm safe with you, aren't I?* And him saying, *Always, babe.* Jesus, she'd wanted reassurance – she'd wanted to know he loved her no matter what.

He was crouched, shoulders against the trunk's lid.

C'mon, c'mon, he thought. *I want you.*

The driver's door slammed; he heard footsteps against concrete.

'Judge?' Alex's voice called, low, quiet. Even gentle.

'Yes?'

'I want you to lay facedown, hands laced on your head. You yell for help, you kick the trunk or me, you fart too loud, I empty this clip into you. You understand me?'

'Yeah,' Whit said. He lay down as Alex ordered, the little wicked saw sharp against his hip.

A key slid into the lock, the trunk door opened. The muzzle of a gun pressed into the back of Whit's neck.

'Up. Slowly. Not a sound.'

'You'll be in hell in less than ten minutes,' Whit said. 'You don't have a prayer against Gooch.' He got up, felt the saw hold in its place against his leg.

'You got in over your head, Your Honor. I don't hold greed against you. But you took on too much.'

He didn't want Gooch to kill Alex. He wanted to do it himself.

He stepped out of the trunk, the gun still firmly at the

back of his head, and the two men walked to the warehouse door. An electronic keypad was by the door and Alex entered in a code. The electronic locks on the door clicked open.

'You first, Judge,' Alex said.

Whit stepped inside the darkness.

'Guchinski?' Alex called. 'Put the lights on. Now. Or the judge dies.'

'Chill, Alex. It's all right.' Stoney Vaughn, a little rasp of voice in the blackness.

'Where's your new buddy?' Alex called.

'Barely breathing on the concrete floor. I bashed his head in.'

Alex waited. 'I don't believe you.'

'Come in and see.' Stoney's voice shook.

Fear? Anger? Whit wondered.

'What are you pissed about? Jesus, he kidnaps you. I try to save you—' Alex said.

'You're quite the hero,' Stoney said from the dark. 'You coming in or not?'

'Do you have the Eye, Stoney?' Alex said.

'Right here in my pocket.'

'Okay, we're cool, right? I'm coming in now.' And Alex did, pushing Whit along in front of him, not closing the door after him in case he had to barrel out fast. No light on in the warehouse, just the smell of dust and machinery, and oddly enough, the reek of greasy Chinese food.

'Alex,' Stoney's voice called. 'Shut the door.'

'Turn on the lights. What's with this fucking darkness act?' Alex's hands fumbled for the switches, couldn't find them.

The lights clanged on, Stoney standing ten feet away, a gleaming pistol in his hand.

'Nice gun,' Alex said.

'It's a Shootyadickov,' Stoney said. 'I got it from Gooch. Hello, Judge. Sorry about this. Jesus, Alex, you beat the crap out of him.'

Whit's heart sank. The wallboard saw was a stupid, stupid idea. Gooch down. Him stuck between these two assholes, each with a gun. He kept his hands down by his untucked shirt. 'He shot Lucy,' he said.

Stoney's lips – clenched together in a tough-guy sneer – parted. 'What?'

'She's dead,' Alex said. 'I didn't want to bring them both.'

'That . . . wasn't necessary. I . . .' Stoney said.

'You what?' Alex said. 'You need her land to rebury the gold so you can discover it and, what, get your picture on the fucking cover of *National Geographic*? Man, give it up.'

'I liked Lucy,' Stoney said.

'Yeah, she seemed real nice. A shame. I hate what I have to do sometimes. Where's the Eye?'

Whit kept waiting for Alex to say, *Well, Gooch is out of the game – don't need you* and shoot him dead. But instead Alex kept Whit in front of him, still a shield.

'Don't worry about the Eye,' Stoney said. 'I promised you could keep most of the coins. I'd get thirty percent and the Eye. That's more than fair. Let's just settle our accounts now, Alex.'

'I can get the coins for you tomorrow. Jesus, I kind of had my hands full tonight.'

'You'll get them tonight.' Stoney's face reddened.

'I can't,' Alex said.

'Sure you can. They're just about thirty feet away, in crates over there,' Stoney said. 'What I want to know, Alex buddy, is how the hell you got the treasure into my own warehouse.'

'Don't know what you mean.'

'The coins. They are all over there in that corner, crated, just as we left them in the storage unit,' Stoney said.

The silence hung in the air. *Now*, Whit thought.

'Alex,' Whit said. 'Stoney doesn't have the Eye. He's lying. He said it was in his pocket. Make him show the Eye to you.'

'Stoney. That's not a bad idea. I've missed seeing the Eye over the past couple of days,' Alex said. 'But slowly.'

'I was not speaking literally when I said it was in my pocket,' Stoney said.

'That means he lied,' Whit said. 'You were right. He gave it to Gooch. But now he's betrayed Gooch. You think he's gonna play clean with you?'

Alex took a step toward Stoney, keeping Whit close in front. Whit took a step forward in response, moaned, as though the pain of the beating had caught up with him. He closed his hand over his shirttail and around the handle of the wallboard saw.

'I didn't give it to Gooch,' Stoney said. 'He kidnapped me, Alex.'

'You seem to have suffered mightily.'

'We have to stick together,' Stoney said.

'Do we?' Alex said.

Late-night traffic was light heading into Corpus Christi. Claudia drove, finished a cup of hot coffee, the warm effect of the wine fading. Ben said he was too nervous to drive so they took her pickup truck.

'I think I would feel better if he'd actually apologized,' Ben said. 'On the phone. He sounded so cryptic.'

'Give it time. Maybe he thinks he didn't do a thing wrong.'

'How could that thought even live in his brain?'

'You've gotten angrier during the drive,' she said.

'Knowing he's okay, I'm finally feeling mad. I don't let myself get mad enough.'

'Not me,' said Claudia. 'I'm sort of comfortable with getting pissed off. You're way too even-keeled.'

The port area was aglow with lights as they reached the Harbor Bridge, arching two hundred thirty-five feet above where the Nueces and Corpus Christi bays joined. Claudia saw the blue lights centered on the USS *Lexington*, retired in the calm of Corpus Christi Bay, the Texas State Aquarium, the soft glow of downtown ahead of her. She barreled onto the Harbor Bridge, the traffic in front of her thin.

Ben squirmed in his seat, as though trying to get comfortable, and suddenly she felt rather than saw the gun hovering close to her head.

'What—'

'It'll help if you're even-keeled right now. I'm sorry.'

Her breath caught and Ben said, 'Just keep driving, okay? You're losing speed. Pick it up.'

'Tell me what the fuck you're doing or I'm going to drive the car off the bridge,' she said.

'No, you won't,' he said. 'I know you.' His voice quiet now, bled of the earlier anger.

'Ben . . . this isn't the way to help your brother.'

'He can rot in hell for all I care,' Ben said. 'He would have gotten us both killed. You think I give a shit about him now?' His tone softened. 'You, I'm sorry about. I couldn't help myself. Never quite got over you. If we hadn't been kidnapped . . . if you hadn't learned about all this . . . I wish you weren't a cop.' The lights of the bridge flashed by them. His voice toughened. 'Take the port exit. Then a hard right, then two more lefts until we get where we're going.'

Hadn't learned about all this . . . 'Are you saying you know where this treasure is?'

'Just be quiet. Talking is only going to make it worse.'

'What, you're going to kill your brother? And me?'

'I'm not going to kill Stoney,' Ben said. 'Even now, I'm not sure I could. My partner will take care of that.'

'Partner,' she said. 'Ben, no. Please. Don't do this.'

'Take the exit,' he said. 'Or I'll shoot you, and I'll shoot whoever's in the first car that stops.'

The bridge began its downward slope, toward Corpus Christi Beach and the port, and Claudia took the Port Street exit. It was a very short exit, forcing a hard right turn, and she thought of letting the car just go straight, crash, although she couldn't risk the life of anyone else who might stop to help.

'I really respect that you're not crying right now. Or calling me names.'

'I'm waiting for an explanation, Ben. Money? Jealousy of your brother?'

'Money. You know what it's like to be ten times smarter than Stoney and not have a hundredth of what he does?' He sighed. 'I wish you could come with me. But that's not possible. Turn left here. Then the next left.' She turned onto a side street dominated by one large warehouse, the lot by it empty except for a battered red pickup – she recognized it as Gooch's – and a nondescript Ford Taurus. She parked on the other side of the truck, away from the Taurus.

'Turn off your headlights.'

Claudia thumbed the switch and the little lot went dark.

'Now what?' she said. Her own service revolver was in the compartment between them. She couldn't possibly reach it without him blowing her head off. He opened the compartment, fished out her gun, put it in his lap.

'You know,' Ben said, 'I'm grateful we made love. Truly. We're going inside.'

'So no one will hear you kill me?'

He started to reply, but gunshots sounded inside the warehouse, three of them in rapid fire. 'Shit.'

The gun wavered for a second and Claudia flung open the door, threw herself out onto the asphalt, the driver's-side window exploding above her. She crabbed under the car as Ben scrambled out of the truck.

39

As Alex fired, his arm outstretched past Whit, Whit slammed hard into his arm, pinning him into the wall and trying to pull the gun from his hand. He got his fingers around the grip, gouged Alex's wrists but Alex grabbed the back of his head, smashed it hard into the concrete wall.

Whit went down thinking, *Stupid, stupid.*

Alex pressed down on him, knee in his back, and Whit saw Stoney lying on the floor, bone and blood and shredded jaw showing.

'That was fucking stupid,' Alex said. 'You missing your girl? You want to see her?'

'I know where Gooch hid the Eye, dumb shit. Shoot me and you'll never get it.'

'Bullshit,' he screamed. 'You would have told me to save Lucy.'

'I didn't think you'd really shoot her.' His right hand closed over his shirttail and the hidden saw's handle. But he couldn't pull it free, not with Alex's weight on him. 'Let me up and I'll tell you.'

'You'll tell me now.' Alex grabbed Whit's left hand, flattened it on the concrete. Jammed the hot barrel of the gun against the back of Whit's hand.

'I'll show you,' Whit said.

'Show.' Alex froze. 'It's here?'

'Let me up and I'll show it to you. Don't shoot off my hand.' Whit let out a scream, a sob. 'Just don't shoot off my hand, man, please. I'll show you. Please?' He began to mumble and cry.

Alex hesitated for two seconds. 'Okay.' He eased up

into a squat by Whit. 'Get up, you pussy.' His voice was thick with contempt.

Whit got to both knees, holding his side, lips quivering, fresh blood smearing his broken cheek. Then, slowly, to his feet, his hand under the tail of his shirt, like his side ached.

'Please . . . please . . .' Whit said, unsteady on his feet, like standing was an ordeal. 'Please, I'll show you . . .'

And then in one swift motion he slashed out at Alex with the little wicked blade.

Claudia had counted on Ben running around the car to finish her, hoping he'd think she'd try to put distance between her and his gun. So instead she rolled under the car. She heard his feet pound around the truck's back, trying to get a sight on her, seeing if she was hit or running. She saw his feet – tennis shoes bright white in the dark – she let him race past her, peering into the dark of the lot and the loading docks, listening for her running feet and looking for her moving shadow. She rolled out from under the truck as he started to curse, the broken glass crunching under her shoulders. Ben turned and she barreled toward him in a flying tackle. His gun blazed and she felt the devilish whisper of a bullet sear past her head. She slammed hard into him, smashing her forearm into his throat, driving her knee into his groin.

He went down heavy, his head cracking against the pavement. She piled on top of him, one hand yanking his hair back and the other hunting his eyes. He screamed and elbowed her hard, shoved her down onto her back.

It was dark, a dim gleam of lights from the warehouse and the port blocks away, and she saw faint shine on a gun's barrel – he'd had both guns; he must've dropped one when she kicked his feet out from him. The shine was a half foot from her hand and she seized the gun, prayed the safety was off, swung it toward his face and fired.

Missed.

He stumbled to his feet, turning and running for the warehouse. 'Freeze! Ben!' He didn't freeze and she fired twice in the dark. She heard the wet-meat sound of a bullet striking him, heard him sprawl along the steps leading to the warehouse.

She ran to where Ben lay. In the thin light from the shuttered windows she saw the wound in the lower part of his back, blood a black spurt. He breathed in sharp hitches, groaning.

'Holy God,' Claudia breathed. 'Holy God.'

Gunshots inside, and she'd just shot a man. Gooch in there, maybe in trouble. She ran back to her truck, fumbled for the cell phone.

Missed, Whit thought in that split second.

The blade missed and Alex would shoot him before he could stab again. But then Alex's eyes went wide, shocked, his hand went to his throat and the blood fountained. Alex trying to scream and nothing coming but blood.

Alex's eyes flashed with rage and fear and horror and he brought the gun back up toward Whit but then he dropped it, the other hand going to his throat to stem the flood. He fell to his knees. Whit grabbed the gun, stood there.

'How does it feel?' Whit said, his voice breaking. 'How does it—'

And he saw Alex's lips forming the word *please*.

The organic coppery smell of rupture filled the air, overpowered the scent of gunfire.

'Gooch?' Claudia's voice called.

Whit saw her coming through the still-open front door,

her service pistol out, in a firing stance. He tried to speak, as silent as Alex.

Claudia ran to him, seeing Alex bleed out his life, toppling to the floor, grabbing at Whit's shoes. She gasped at the sight of Stoney's body.

Whit didn't let go of the saw; its handle felt burned to his hand.

Claudia tore Alex's shirt off him, pushing the fabric around his throat, trying to stanch the flow of blood, apply useless pressure, telling him help was on the way.

Whit said, without looking at her, 'Gooch is here. Help him.'

'Whit . . .' Claudia started.

Whit set Alex's gun on a table. He dropped the saw on the floor.

'Let him die, Claudia. Just let him die.'

Alex paled, stared up at him, then through him.

'I'm going to find Gooch.' Whit's voice didn't sound quite right.

'Jesus, Whit,' Claudia said. 'Jesus.'

40

Claudia went with Whit to the Coastal Psychics Network on Sunday afternoon, not having slept that night. He had a spare key Lucy had given him two weeks ago and he opened the doors. The business was closed, the psychics mourning at home.

'I didn't think straight. Didn't think about where she'd hide it,' he said.

'We don't have to do this now, Whit,' Claudia said.

'She loved this place. And I don't want it here,' Whit said. 'If I'm right. Her office is this way.'

Jean Laffite's treasure was finally confirmed to consist of twenty thousand dollars' worth of gold bars, ten thousand in silver bars, and a cache of rare 1820-minted Monteblanco coins worth, in numismatic and historical value, five million dollars. Scattered among the coins and bars in the crates used by Alex and Stoney were fragments of bone and soil from the Gilbert dig site, including a finger bone. The Corpus Christi police kept the treasure in the warehouse under heavy guard while they processed the shooting scene and called the Texas Historical Commission. But the Devil's Eye was yet to be found.

In her office, Whit glanced at the small foil mobile, the scattered books on ESP and phone marketing, still with their little neon Post-its as bookmarks, worn from her thumbing. On the mantel above her desk were the crystals, amber and yellow and clear and green and red. Arranged just so for the healing powers they emitted. He didn't feel healed.

'There,' he said.

'Oh, Whit,' Claudia said. 'I don't think so. These are too small.'

'No. Look,' he said. He inspected several, then ran his finger along the largest green one. It was the muddy green of a riverbed. He scraped paint off the stone with a thumbnail and the soft green glow came through, the color of time. The seductive green of envy.

'Jesus. It's really sort of ugly.' He handed it to her. 'Iris Dominguez can tell us if this is it. Or a gemologist. Right now I don't know where else to look. Hiding it here is classic Lucy. Plain sight. She—' He stopped.

'Whit . . .'

'I never want to see it again, okay, Claudia?'

'Okay,' she said. 'Listen. I'm worried about you. We need to talk.'

He stared at her. 'The way you shot your boyfriend. I meant to say that was well done, what with it being so dark.'

A day later four gemologists said the Devil's Eye was worthless: the right size, but not the valuable emerald. A nicely done copy, not worth millions, not worth anything at all. At some time – either by a thief in Mexico before *Santa Barbara* sailed or by Jean Laffite or by Stoney – the Eye was replaced with a worthless hunk of green crystal.

Claudia stopped by his house and told Whit about the report. He was silent. She wondered if he had slept.

'Whit?' she said after the silence grew too long.

Finally he said, 'People will keep looking for it, won't they?'

'I suppose they will, after all the news coverage. Dig up Stoney Vaughn's yard, or the rest of Black Jack Point. David's mentioned they've already chased some folks off Stoney's land. Thinking he hid some of the treasure there.'

317

He turned away from her.

'Whit?'

'I figured out the person who snooped through my house was Lucy. She knew where my key was, under the fern on the porch. I guess she wanted to know if I had notes on the murders, if there was any way she could be implicated. Or if Stoney was implicated. Whatever might lead back to her.'

'Maybe Lucy came here, waited for you to come home, wanted to tell you the whole truth. Then she lost her nerve, left.'

'It's nice to think that,' he said, 'isn't it?'

When Claudia got home David was waiting there in shorts and a T-shirt. He sat on the stairs leading to her apartment with a cold twelve-pack of Shiner Bock.

'What's this?' she said.

'I think we should get drunk,' David said. 'I'm more likely to apologize when I'm drunk.'

'That's a good reason.'

'Someone finally put you through more hell than I did,' David said. 'Jesus, that sucks. I'm sorry, Claudia.'

She let him in and they drank the beer, her sitting on the couch, him on the floor. She drank the first one fast, too fast, and made herself promise to take longer for the second.

'So Ben was in it with Alex Black from the beginning?'

'I wasn't the only seduction in Ben's life,' Claudia said.

David raised an eyebrow.

'Ben got seduced himself. Living with a wealthy brother who was living on the edge of the law in more ways than one and wasn't paying a price for it. Of course Ben is not talking and he's using Stoney's money to hire some fancy defense lawyer from Houston.' She sipped her beer. 'I won't get a chance to say this on the stand at Ben's trial unless we find evidence, but I think Ben found out about Stoney's plan to steal treasure from Patch Gilbert's land and fake an archaeological dig on Lucy's land. And if he'd gotten to know Alex Black through Stoney, he would have seen that Alex was more interested in the treasure's financial value than in the fame of discovery. Ben didn't have Stoney's blind spot for glory. So he must have cut a separate deal with Alex. They would have grabbed the treasure and then Alex would have eliminated Stoney. But then they didn't plan on Patch and Thuy Tran showing up and having a double murder complicate their whole deal. And they sure didn't count on Danny Laffite coming after them with a gang and a vengeance.'

She finished her beer. David handed her another. 'You know what pisses me off?' she asked.

'What, honey?'

'That fucker,' she said. 'He abandoned me with Danny and Gar, maybe he even cut a deal with Zack Simard to get him to leave us behind on the other boat. He knew Gar would kill me, kill Danny. I'm sure he killed Zack Simard at some point, dumped the body, ran the boat aground. He looked like the poor little victim. The whole time he was in with Alex Black. I'm pretty sure Stoney never called Ben that night, apologizing and asking him to come to the warehouse. That was Alex and Ben's plan: get rid of Stoney, get rid of me since I was pushing on Ben to help the cops, leave the country with the treasure.'

'He should have stuck with teaching.'

'Ben molding young minds – I may puke.' She downed more beer, wiped her mouth with the back of her hand. 'I don't think it would surprise me if he and Alex had planned on getting rid of each other, in the end. Greedy bastards.'

'Claudia, it's not your fault.' David rested his chin on his knees, gave her a sad smile.

'What?'

'I know you. You're pissed at yourself for not having seen through this guy. Listen, his own brother didn't see through him.'

'I'm smarter than Stoney Vaughn ever was, please.' She shook her head. 'I think my career at the PD just flat-lined. Jesus, he's ruined a couple of major league pleasant high school memories for me.'

'Memories?'

'He was my first, David, back when we were in high school.'

He opened another beer. 'You mean I wasn't?'

'I never told you you were. You were my second.'

'Well,' said David, 'you weren't my first either.'

'I think I'll wear a red dress to Ben's trial,' she said, a little drunk. 'That asshole.'

'I'm sorry,' David said. 'For you. For Whit.'

'You can't stand him.'

'I'm gonna try to stand him, Claud.'

She smiled for the first time. 'Now you're drunk.'

They drank too much, both of them, and they ended up kissing but she wasn't drunk enough to sleep with him. She wouldn't let him drive, so David slept on her couch and at one point in the night, dehydrated and hungover, she got up for water and she watched him sleep and to her surprise a little part of her missed him.

Then she went back to bed, hoping it was just the beer.

41

Lucy was buried next to Patch, in Port Leo's big, grand Catholic cemetery. Afterward, Whit felt as hollow as though his bones had been plucked from beneath his skin. He took a month off from court, got a retired county judge to fill in for him. He did not have to rule on Lucy's cause of death or see the autopsy papers. He let Gooch take him out on the waters each day after the funeral, the summer roaring into its hottest days, sat and stared at the flat of the bay, watching the waves live and die in their brief existence.

The third week Gooch invited Claudia and she sat with Whit on the stern of the boat, in chairs designed for deep-sea fishing. Gooch stood on the flying bridge, steering out into the Gulf. Helen Dupuy had gotten work in Port Leo, cleaning at a bed-and-breakfast, and could not join them. Whit drank a Coke, not talking much, only saying how the Astros were bound to disappoint again this summer.

'Lucy enjoyed baseball, didn't she?' Claudia said.

Whit didn't look at her. 'Yeah.'

She touched his hand. 'I didn't love Ben – I hadn't quite gotten past the infatuation point. We hadn't been together very long. But you loved Lucy.'

'Yes, Dr Claudia, I did.' Sounding a little irritated with her now.

'But you haven't grieved for her.'

'Of course I have.'

'Tell me, did killing Alex make you feel better, Whit?'

He stared at her, turned away. 'This is going to be a damn long day fishing.'

'It was self-defense. But you killed him. You even told me to let him die. Not that anything could have saved him then.' Her words – unsaid in the long quiet of the past weeks – came in a rush.

'Claudia, let it go.'

'Are you worried you're like him in some way? He killed Lucy, you killed him – you think you're on his level?'

'No,' he said after a pause. 'I don't feel anything about killing him yet. That bothers me.' He looked away. 'But Lucy. I . . . yelled at her. I ended it with her. I said terrible things to her.'

'You had every right to be mad at her, at what she'd done. You can be mad at someone you love.'

'That only works if you get to say you're sorry, Claud.'

'She knows, Whit. She knows.' She laced her fingers with his.

Gooch stopped the boat, dropped anchor, called down that it was time to fish.

'Let's go swimming first,' she said.

'You want to get in the water? After you nearly died out here?'

'Not the water's fault. What am I supposed to do, avoid the Gulf for the rest of my life?' Claudia stood, took off her T-shirt, dropped her shorts. She had a swimsuit underneath, a navy two-piece, not cut too brief.

'Is that a police-issue bikini?' Gooch called.

She shot him the finger, dove over the edge. She surfaced. 'Come on, it feels great,' she called to Whit, who stood at the rail.

He didn't move.

'Whit, come on.'

Whit shucked off his shirt, cannonballed over the railing like he thought he'd better before he changed his mind. Broke to the surface, let the gentle wave swell pick him up, settle him back down. Claudia kicked away from him, giving him space.

'It feels okay,' he said.

She watched him dive down, surface, again and again, swimming through the waves, and if there were any tears on his face she could not tell.

They swam, they fished, Gooch saying no more than two sentences about what a good job his Washington lawyer had done in keeping his record clean. They talked instead of baseball, of books, of perhaps a trip to Austin for a long weekend to hear Lyle Lovett play. The day was warm and sleepy, the water fine and greenish-blue, the sky smooth as pearl. On the way back in through the bay Whit watched Claudia doze in her chair and he wanted to reach out and touch her hand and say, *I know how bad Ben hurt you. I know, and still you worry about me and I can't believe how you care. But I'll be okay. Given time, I'll be okay. I will choose to be okay.*

But Whit didn't say any of these things. He just closed his eyes and let the sun warm him. Knowing that here, with these two people sacred to him on this boat, he had a wealth to outshine rare gold or the most precious gem. More than he could ever need.

Notes and Acknowledgments

The lore about Jean Laffite – and his buried treasures – is rich along the coasts of Texas and Louisiana. For this novel, I have drawn on sources both historical and legendary. Laffite, the great hero of the Battle of New Orleans and privateer, left New Orleans to continue his pirating operations on Galveston Island. Laffite was ordered out of Galveston in 1820 (also often cited as 1821) by the United States Navy. He burned Galveston to the ground, most of his pirates dispersed, and Laffite sailed off into the Gulf; after that point, history blurs the line between fact and romanticized fiction. Did he die of fever in the Yucatán? Or did he die in a sea battle or in a Cuban prison after committing more piracy in the Caribbean? Did he die in a battle off the coast of Cartagena, Colombia? Did he retire to South America and a generally peaceful old age? As of this writing, we do not know with absolute certainty.

I have drawn on legends local to Aransas and Matagorda bays in Texas: that Laffite buried a large treasure there after abandoning Galveston, since he was facing pressure from both the American and British navies and did not want to be captured with his remaining booty aboard his vessel. But my 'end history' for Laffite is entirely of my own imagining, although Dr John Fanning and *Lynx* were real. And since Port Leo, Black Jack Point, St Leo Bay, and Encina County are fictional places, Laffite's presence there is of course fictional. The supposed descendants of Jean Laffite and Catherine Villars – did she exist or not? – who are described herein are entirely fictional. There was no Monteblanco mint in Colonial Mexico.

In researching and writing this book, I am indebted to the following:

- My wife and children, for their extraordinary support and patience;
- Genny Ostertag and Peter Ginsberg, for insight and support in finding the heart of the book;
- Joe Stanfield, for coastal hospitality and unfailing generosity;
- Sue Hastings Taylor, author and preeminent historian of Aransas County, who shared lore about Laffite in the Texas Coastal Bend and took me to probable treasure dump sites in the maze of offshore islands and inlets;
- The Honorable Nancy Pomykal, Justice of the Peace, Calhoun County, TX, and the Honorable Patrick Daly, Justice of the Peace, Aransas County, TX;
- Sheriff Mark Gilliam of Aransas County and Rockport, Texas, Police Chief Tim Jayroe, for answering questions with great courtesy, patience, and humor;
- Mark and Pam Kohler. Mark is a friend since early childhood and an extraordinarily gifted painter, and both he and Pam provided information on art;
- Mindy Reed, for research assistance;
- Dr David Glassman, forensic anthropologist at Southwest Texas State University, who kindly walked me through the burial and recovery scenario;
- Casey Edward Green and the staff of the Historical Center at Rosenberg Library in Galveston, for access to their famous Laffite archive and assisting me in my research;
- Robert C. Vogel, Jean C. Epperson, Reginald Wilson, and Jeff Modzeleski, Laffite scholars extraordinaire, who answered questions on Laffite's history and related subjects with patience, good humor, and thoughtfulness;

- Patricia Mercado-Allinger, state archaeologist, Texas Historical Commission;
- Malcolm Shuman, fellow author and contract archaeologist, for sharing his thoughts on his everyday working world;
- David Lambert, for investments information;
- John Bauer, attorney, for information on probate law and proceedings;
- Scott Curren, who provided access to his sportfishing boat, the model for the *Miss Catherine;*
- Horace Green, who provided information on metal detecting;
- The Laffite Society, Galveston, Texas, for warmly welcoming me and then not stringing me up for playing goombah with their favorite historical persona. Needless to say, the Laffite Society consists of people far more polite, intelligent, friendly, and charming than certain members of the Laffite League, which is an entirely fictitious invention. The Laffite Society can be found at www.thelaffitesociety.com.

Of course, any errors are my responsibility, not theirs.